AQUAMAN

AQUAMAN

AQUAMAN

AQUAMAN

THE LEGEND OF
AQUAMAN

AQUAMAN
Who destroys the Sea King
The Ocean Master or Black Manta?
AQUAMAN
FIND THE FRIENDLY PARADEMON!
AQUAMAN
SWORD OF ATLANTIS
KURT BUSIEK
BUTCH GUICE
AQUAMAN
YOU!
YOU DIP THIS TO HER!
AND NOW YOU DIE!!
JUSTICE LEAGUE
JOHNS
LEE
WILLIAMS
THE NEW 52!
the SLEEP-WALKER from the SEA!
JLA
OUR WORLDS AT WAR
UNITED THEY FALL
THE LEGEND OF AQUAMAN
JUSTICE LEAGUE of AMERICA
STARRO THE CONQUEROR!
AQUAMAN
UNDERWORLD
REBIRTH
AQUAMAN
DC UNIVERSE
REBIRTH
AQUAMAN
GENESIS
AQUAMAN
AQUAMAN
JABBERJAW
CAPTAIN CAVEMAN
the BRAVE and the BOLD
BATMAN
AQUAMAN
AQUAMAN
THE NEW 52!
YEAR ONE
AQUAMAN
AQUAMAN
TIME AND TIDE
1st ISSUE
FLASH
AQUAMAN

IN THE SHADOWY DEPTHS OF ATLANTIS, HIS LIFE WILL CHANGE FOREVER!
AQUAMAN
DC UNIVERSE REBIRTH
GENESIS
THE BRAVE and the BOLD
BATMAN
AQUAMAN
THE SLEEP WALKER from the SEA!
AQUAMAN STANDS ALONE!
HE'S THE DEADLIEST MAN ALIVE—
DEADMAN LIVES AGAIN!
METAMORPHO
SUPER FRIENDS
Adventure COMICS
URBAN RENEWAL!
UNDERWORLD
The OCEAN MASTER!

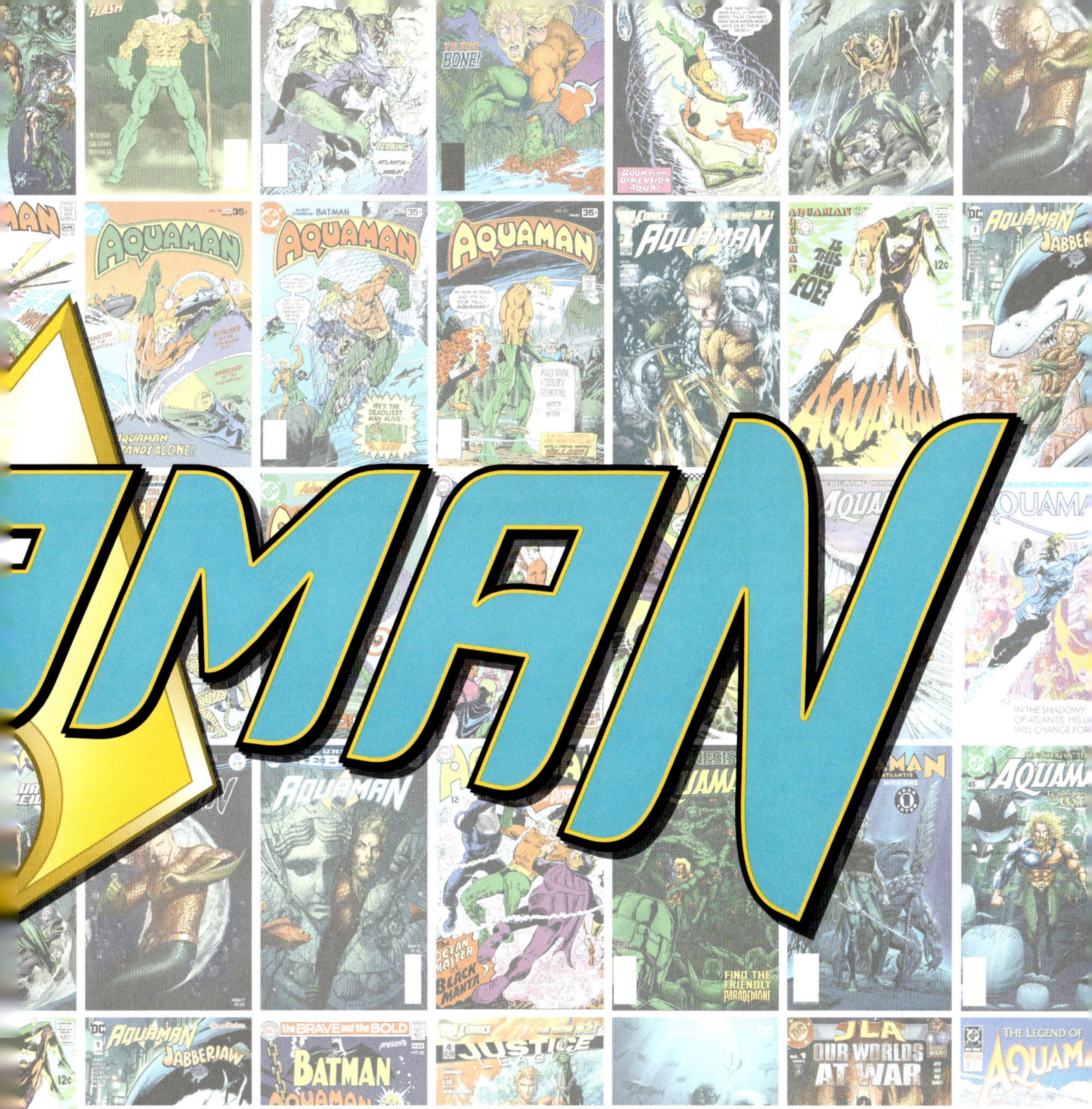

80 YEARS *of*

THE KING OF THE SEVEN SEAS

the DELUXE EDITION

JIM LEE, SCOTT WILLIAMS, *and* **ALEX SINCLAIR**
collection cover artists

AQUAMAN created by **PAUL NORRIS**

SUPERMAN created by
JERRY SIEGEL and **JOE SHUSTER**
By special arrangement with the Jerry Siegel family

WHITNEY ELLSWORTH
MORT WEISINGER
JACK SCHIFF
LEN WEIN
GEORGE KASHDAN
JOE ORLANDO
DICK GIORDANO
PAUL LEVITZ
NEAL POZNER
MARK WAID
KEVIN DOOLEY
EDDIE BERGANZA
JOAN HILTY
PATRICK McCALLUM
ANDY KHOURI — EDITORS – ORIGINAL SERIES
ROBERT GREENBERGER
DANA KURTIN
RACHEL GLUCKSTERN
HARVEY RICHARDS — ASSOCIATE EDITORS – ORIGINAL SERIES
TOM PALMER JR.
SEAN MACKIEWICZ — ASSISTANT EDITORS – ORIGINAL SERIES
REZA LOKMAN — EDITOR – COLLECTED EDITION
STEVE COOK — DESIGN DIRECTOR – BOOKS
DAMIAN RYLAND — PUBLICATION DESIGN
TOM VALENTE — PUBLICATION PRODUCTION

MARIE JAVINS — EDITOR-IN-CHIEF, DC COMICS

ANNE DePIES — SENIOR VP – GENERAL MANAGER
JIM LEE — PUBLISHER & CHIEF CREATIVE OFFICER
DON FALLETTI — VP – MANUFACTURING OPERATIONS & WORKFLOW MANAGEMENT
LAWRENCE GANEM — VP – TALENT SERVICES
ALISON GILL — SENIOR VP – MANUFACTURING & OPERATIONS
JEFFREY KAUFMAN — VP – EDITORIAL STRATEGY & PROGRAMMING
NICK J. NAPOLITANO — VP – MANUFACTURING ADMINISTRATION & DESIGN
NANCY SPEARS — VP – REVENUE

AQUAMAN: 80 YEARS OF THE KING OF THE SEVEN SEASTHE DELUXE EDITION

PEFC Certified
This product is from sustainably managed forests and controlled sources
PEFC
PEFC/01-31-106
www.pefc.org

DC Comics, 4000 Warner Blvd. Bldg. 700, 2nd Floor Burbank, CA 91522
Printed by Transcontinental Interglobe, Beauceville, QC, Canada. 1/6/23. First Printing.
ISBN: 978-1-77951-019-8

Library of Congress Cataloging-in-Publication Data is available.

TABLE of CONTENTS

THE EARLY YEARS 7
by Mark Waid

("THE SUBMARINE STRIKES")* 9
More Fun Comics #73, November 1941
Writer: Mort Weisinger
Artist: Paul Norris

"AQUAMAN GOES TO COLLEGE" 17
Adventure Comics #120, September 1947
Writer: Joe Samachson
Artist: Louis Cazeneuve

"THE UNDERSEA LOST WORLD!" 24
Adventure Comics #137, February 1949
Writer: Otto Binder
Artist: John Daly

"AQUAMAN JOINS THE NAVY!" 30
Adventure Comics #232, January 1957
Writer: Unknown
Artist: Ramona Fradon

"AQUAMAN MEETS AQUAGIRL!" 36
Adventure Comics #266, November 1959
Writer: Robert Bernstein
Artist: Ramona Fradon

"THE KID FROM ATLANTIS!" 43
Adventure Comics #269, February 1960
Writer: Robert Bernstein
Artist: Ramona Fradon

KING OF ATLANTIS 50
by Paul Kupperberg

"THE DOOM FROM DIMENSION AQUA, CHAPTER I" 52
Aquaman #11, September-October 1963
Writer: Jack Miller
Artist: Nick Cardy
Cover by Nick Cardy

"BETWEEN TWO DOOMS!" 78
Aquaman #35, September-October 1967
Writer: Bob Haney
Artist: Nick Cardy
Cover by Nick Cardy

"THE EXPLANATION!" 102
Aquaman #46, July-August 1969
Writer: Steve Skeates
Penciller: Jim Aparo
Inker: Frank Giacoia
Cover by Nick Cardy

"A QUIET DAY IN ATLANTIS" 126
Adventure Comics #437, January-February 1975
Writer: Paul Levitz
Artist: Mike Grell
Colorist: John Albano
Letterer: Milt Snapinn

"AND THE WALLS CAME TUMBLIN' DOWN" ..133
Aquaman #62, June-July 1978
Writer: Paul Kupperberg
Penciller: Don Newton
Inker: Bob McLeod
Colorist: Adrienne Roy
Letterer: Shelly Leferman
Cover by Jim Aparo

"SCAVENGER HUNT!" 151
Adventure Comics #475, September 1980
Writer: J.M. DeMatteis
Artist: Dick Giordano
Colorist: Adrienne Roy
Letterer: John Costanza
Cover by Brian Bolland

THE RULER OF THE DEEP GAINS DEPTH 161
by Robert Greenberger

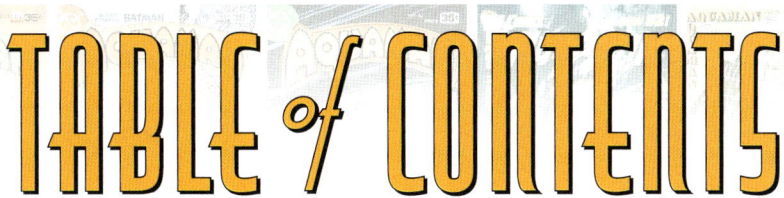

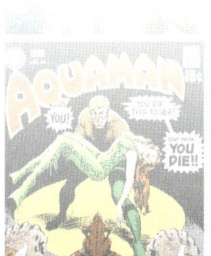

("THE RISE AND FALL, AND RISE AND FALL OF ATLANTIS")* 163
Aquaman #1, February 1986
Writer: Neal Pozner
Penciller: Craig Hamilton
Inker: Steve Montano
Colorist: Joe Orlando
Letterer: Bob Lappan
Cover by Craig Hamilton

"THE LEGEND OF AQUAMAN" 189
The Legend of Aquaman Special #1, May 1989
Writers: Keith Giffen and Robert Loren Fleming
Pencillers: Curt Swan and Keith Giffen (breakdowns)
Inker: Eric Shanower
Colorist: Tom McCraw
Letterer: Agustin Más
Cover by Curt Swan and Eric Shanower

"A CRASH OF SYMBOLS" 234
Aquaman #0, October 1994
Writer: Peter David
Penciller: Martin Egeland
Inkers: Brad Vancata and Howard M. Shun
Colorist: Tom McCraw
Letterer: Dan Nakrosis
Cover by Martin Egeland and Brad Vancata

"ONE DEMON LIFE" 257
Aquaman #37, October 1997
Writer: Peter David
Penciller: Jim Calafiore
Inker: Peter Palmiotti
Colorist: Tom McCraw
Letterer: Albert DeGuzman
Cover by Jim Calafiore and Mark McKenna

"A DATE WHICH WILL LIVE IN INFAMY" 281
JLA: Our Worlds at War #1, September 2001
Writer: Jeph Loeb
Penciller: Ron Garney
Inker: Mark Morales
Colorists: Richard & Tanya Horie
Letterer: Richard Starkings
Cover by Jae Lee

THE NEXT EIGHT DECADES 325
by Paul Levitz

"AMERICAN TIDAL, PART 3" 327
Aquaman #17, June 2004
Writer: Will Pfeifer
Penciller: Patrick Gleason
Inkers: Christian Alamy
Colorist: Nathan Eyring
Letterer: Rob Leigh
Cover by Alan Davis and Mark Farmer

"FIVE OF A KIND, PART 4: ROGUE ELEMENTS" 351
Outsiders: Five of a Kind—Metamorpho/Aquaman #1, October 2007
Writers: G. Willow Wilson and Tony Bedard
Artist/Colorist: Joshua Middleton
Letterer: John J. Hill
Cover by Joshua Middleton

"THE TRENCH, PART ONE" 377
Aquaman #1, November 2011
Writer: Geoff Johns
Penciller: Ivan Reis
Inkers: Joe Prado
Colorist: Rod Reis
Letterer: Nick J. Napolitano
Cover by Ivan Reis and Joe Prado

"UNDERWORLD" 401
Aquaman #25, August 2017
Writer: Dan Abnett
Artist/Colorist: Stjepan Šejić
Letterer: Steve Wands
Cover by Stjepan Šejić

COVER HIGHLIGHTS 431

BIOGRAPHIES 436

**Stories in parentheses were originally untitled.*

AQUAMAN
GENESIS
AQUAMAN
AQUAMAN
AQUAMAN
AQUAMAN
YOU!
YOU DIE!!

THE EARLY YEARS

by **MARK WAID**

He couldn't control sea life.

He could live out of water indefinitely.

He wasn't a prince or a king.

He wasn't even from Atlantis.

But he was Aquaman.

In *More Fun Comics* #73 (November 1941), writer Mort Weisinger and artist Paul Norris introduced to the world an aquatic champion substantially different from the one we know today. We were told that this stranger's late father, an anonymous, widowed scientist, had years ago discovered an abandoned underwater city he believed to be the ruins of sunken Atlantis. Studying its scientific journals, he was able to imbue his young son—also unnamed—with the ability to "live and thrive under the water." As Golden Age origins go, Aquaman's wasn't terribly elaborate (taking up all of three panels), but something about the hero struck a chord with the readership even as so many of his *More Fun* contemporaries—Johnny Quick, Dr. Fate, the Spectre, and others—gradually faded from view. Aquaman never achieved star status in his early years, not once appearing on a single comics cover, but he was popular enough to join a very exclusive club: he, Superman, Batman, and Wonder Woman were the only DC superheroes whose stories were published continuously from the 1940s all the way through the 1970s.

The first addition to the Sea King's cast, in his second adventure, was his sole recurring foe: Black Jack, a pirate who crossed paths with Aquaman no fewer than 20 times throughout the 1940s before vanishing abruptly, last seen in early 1950. In Aquaman's third outing, we saw his "Aquacave" for the first time, and in *More Fun* #84, he finally got a supporting cast member (of sorts): Ark, the faithful sea lion. (Though he wasn't yet "talking" to fish telepathically, he clearly considered all denizens of the deep to be his friends.)

Exploits of this World War II era very often pitted Aquaman against Nazi and Japanese soldiers, which kept every story from being about lawless divers plundering sunken ships or down-and-out seafaring surface dwellers who needed a helping hand. (Unsurprisingly, there wasn't a lot of crime underwater.) Proving that his early continuity was as fluid as the oceans in which he swam, in *More Fun* #87, Aquaman discovered Atlantis a *second* time—with no mention of his earlier connection to the mythical city—and never revisited.

In 1946, Aquaman moved from *More Fun* to *Adventure Comics*, his regular berth for the next 15 years. With no more Nazis to punch, his tales became a little tamer as he faced low-stakes smugglers and swindlers and protected imperiled sea explorers. During the *Adventure* era, Aquaman accumulated two new friends. The first—Phineas Pike, the Sea Sleuth, a clumsy, wannabe Sherlock Holmes (*Adventure* #140)—disappeared after a handful of unremarkable appearances, but longtime Aquaman fans know the other one well: Aquaman's faithful and beloved companion, Tusky the walrus (*Adventure* #108). And how did Tusky communicate with the Sea King? In *Adventure* #109, we saw our first real reference to Aquaman's telepathic command over aquatic life.

In 1951, Aquaman's evolution took a mighty step forward. Up until then, his adventures had been predominantly drawn, after Norris, by journeymen Louis Cazeneuve and then John Daly, artists whose work was adequate but not terribly refined. But with *Adventure* #167, the feature was taken over by artist Ramona Fradon, and the

difference was night and day. Fradon's work was infinitely more polished and more exciting than that of her predecessors. Fradon saw Aquaman through the 1950s and on into the 1960s, defining his look so thoroughly that, without question, she remains to this day "the" Aquaman artist for many fans.

As the 1950s progressed, Aquaman gradually took on more of the characteristics we now associate with him. In *Adventure* #212, his yellow gloves began giving way to his trademark green ones; in issue #229, another fan favorite, Topo the octopus, joined the cast; and #230 was the (surprisingly late) first indication that Aquaman couldn't live out of the water indefinitely, with the hard-and-fast one-hour time limit being codified in #262. But it was *Adventure* #260 that became the ultimate turning point for the strip, creating real, ongoing continuity for the first time.

"How Aquaman Got His Powers," written by Robert Bernstein, revealed Aquaman's origin, and this new one bore no resemblance to what had come before. For the first time, we learned that Aquaman was Arthur Curry, son of an Atlantean exile named Atlanna and an American lighthouse keeper named Tom Curry. Equally as significant, the story established Atlantis as a regular locale in the mythos, a magnificent domed city that Aquaman wistfully longed to visit but feared he could not because of his mother's expatriate status.

Nonetheless, Atlantis remained a presence. In *Adventure* #266, Aquaman met another exile, and in #269, a third—a boy he named Aqualad and raised as his own.

At last, the solitary Sea King had someone with whom to share his adventures—the scope and breadth of which were about to explode. And now these adventures are yours to share, too.

***Mark Waid**, a* New York Times *bestselling author, bought his first DC comic at age four and never stopped. After serving the company as an associate editor in the late 1980s, he went on to pursue a full-time career as a comics writer and has, in the 30-plus years since, published nearly 2,000 stories. Among them are his collaboration with artist Alex Ross,* Kingdom Come, *one of the all-time highest-selling American graphic novels, and long runs on* Flash, Justice League, *and many other superhero and humor titles. Currently, he serves as publisher for Humanoids U.S. He lives in Santa Monica but never goes to the beach because his Irish skin would burst into flame.*

SO YOU WEREN'T REALLY CONSIDERING LERON'S ULTIMATUM, WERE YOU, AQUAMAN?
NO, MERA... JUST STALLING FOR TIME -- TO GIVE MY FINNY FRIENDS THE CHANCE TO ARRIVE IN LARGE NUMBERS!

AQUAMAN
MANY HAVE HEARD THE LEGEND OF AQUAMAN, BUT WHO WILL BELIEVE SO STRANGE A TALE? MOST AMAZING OF ALL THE SECRETS OF THE SEA IS THE STORY OF AQUAMAN, WHO, LIKE A WATER-GOD OF OLD, DWELLS IN THE DIM UNKNOWN DEPTHS OF THE OCEAN, LEAPING FORTH TO DO BATTLE WITH THE EVILS AND INJUSTICES OF THE WORLD WE KNOW.......
A
AN UNARMED SHIP SPEEDS OVER THE HIGH SEAS ON ITS ERRAND OF MERCY—AND SUDDENLY FALLS VICTIM TO THE TORPEDO OF A RUTHLESS SUBMARINE-RAIDER!
WE'RE SINKING FAST! LOWER THE LIFEBOATS—WOMEN AND CHILDREN FIRST!
1.

THE KILLER-CRAFT COMES TO THE SURFACE, LIKE A VULTURE SCOUTING HIS PREY.
LOOK! THE LAST BOAT LEAVES— THE CAPTAIN TAKES CHARGE.
RIGHT, LIEUTENANT, AND HE SEES US. LISTEN, HE'S GOING TO HAIL US!
U-112
YOU'VE FIRED ON A DEFENSELESS SHIP, YOU COWARDS! A SHIP CARRYING REFUGEES AND HOSPITAL WORKERS!
REFUGEES—HOSPITAL WORKERS! THEY MUST NOT LIVE TO TELL THE PAPERS THIS STORY! SINK THAT LIFEBOAT!
AT ONCE, SIR! FIRE!
U-112
BUT AT THE VERY INSTANT THE GUN BELCHES FORTH ITS SHELL—
A HAND—FROM OUT OF THE SEA!
—A SUDDEN FORCE WHIPS THE BOAT FORWARD, ESCAPING THE INTENDED DOOM BY SCANT INCHES!
THE BOAT SAVED, THE STRANGE SWIMMER DIVES TOWARD THE SUBMARINE.
WHAT? A SINGLE MAN HANDLE THIS BOAT LIKE THAT? IMPOSSIBLE!
BUT I SAW HIM! THERE HE GOES NOW!
2.

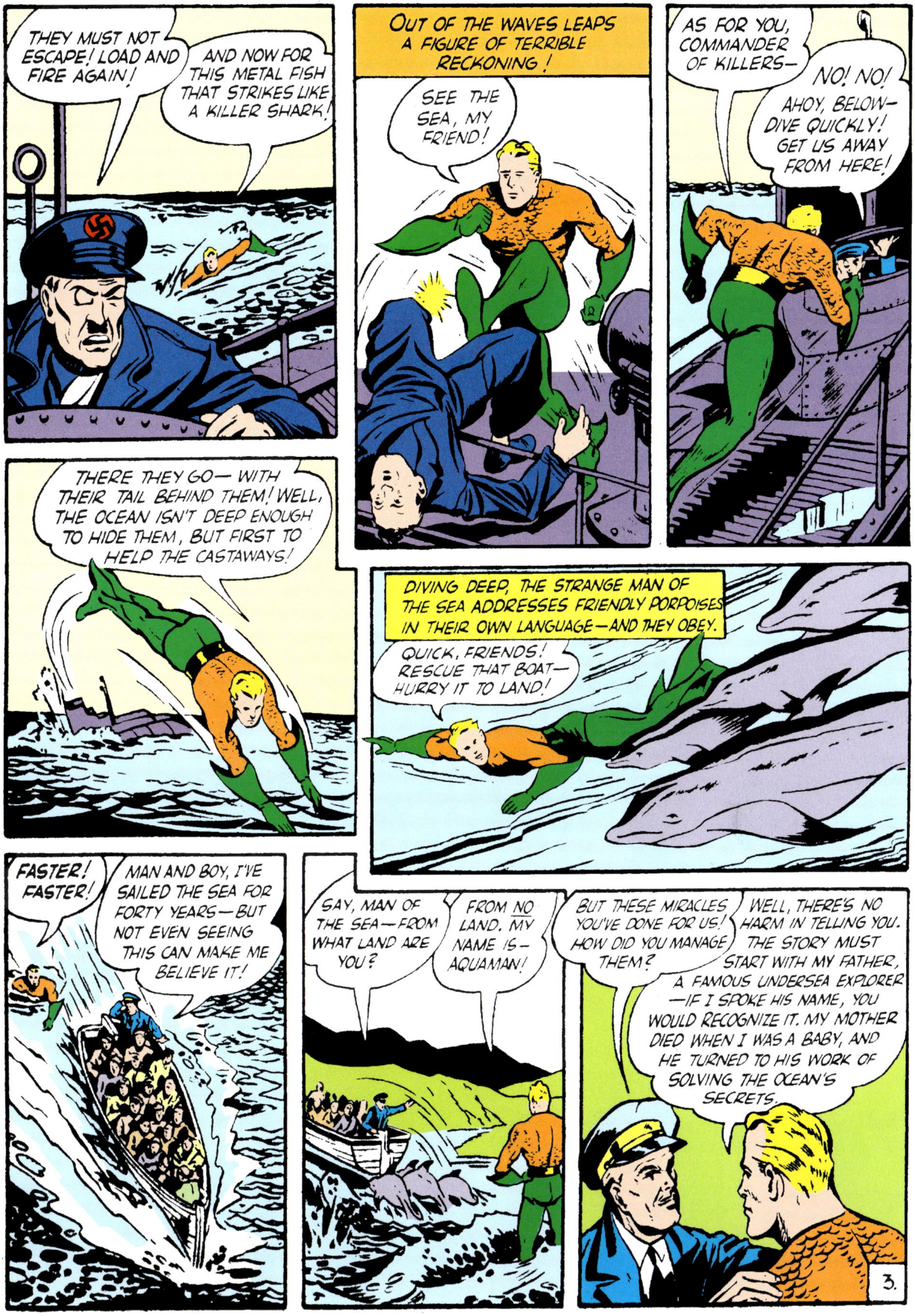
THEY MUST NOT ESCAPE! LOAD AND FIRE AGAIN!
AND NOW FOR THIS METAL FISH THAT STRIKES LIKE A KILLER SHARK!
OUT OF THE WAVES LEAPS A FIGURE OF TERRIBLE RECKONING!
SEE THE SEA, MY FRIEND!
AS FOR YOU, COMMANDER OF KILLERS—
NO! NO! AHOY, BELOW-DIVE QUICKLY! GET US AWAY FROM HERE!
THERE THEY GO—WITH THEIR TAIL BEHIND THEM! WELL, THE OCEAN ISN'T DEEP ENOUGH TO HIDE THEM, BUT FIRST TO HELP THE CASTAWAYS!
DIVING DEEP, THE STRANGE MAN OF THE SEA ADDRESSES FRIENDLY PORPOISES IN THEIR OWN LANGUAGE—AND THEY OBEY.
QUICK, FRIENDS! RESCUE THAT BOAT-HURRY IT TO LAND!
FASTER! FASTER!
MAN AND BOY, I'VE SAILED THE SEA FOR FORTY YEARS—BUT NOT EVEN SEEING THIS CAN MAKE ME BELIEVE IT!
SAY, MAN OF THE SEA—FROM WHAT LAND ARE YOU?
FROM NO LAND. MY NAME IS—AQUAMAN!
BUT THESE MIRACLES YOU'VE DONE FOR US! HOW DID YOU MANAGE THEM?
WELL, THERE'S NO HARM IN TELLING YOU. THE STORY MUST START WITH MY FATHER, A FAMOUS UNDERSEA EXPLORER—IF I SPOKE HIS NAME, YOU WOULD RECOGNIZE IT. MY MOTHER DIED WHEN I WAS A BABY, AND HE TURNED TO HIS WORK OF SOLVING THE OCEAN'S SECRETS.
3.

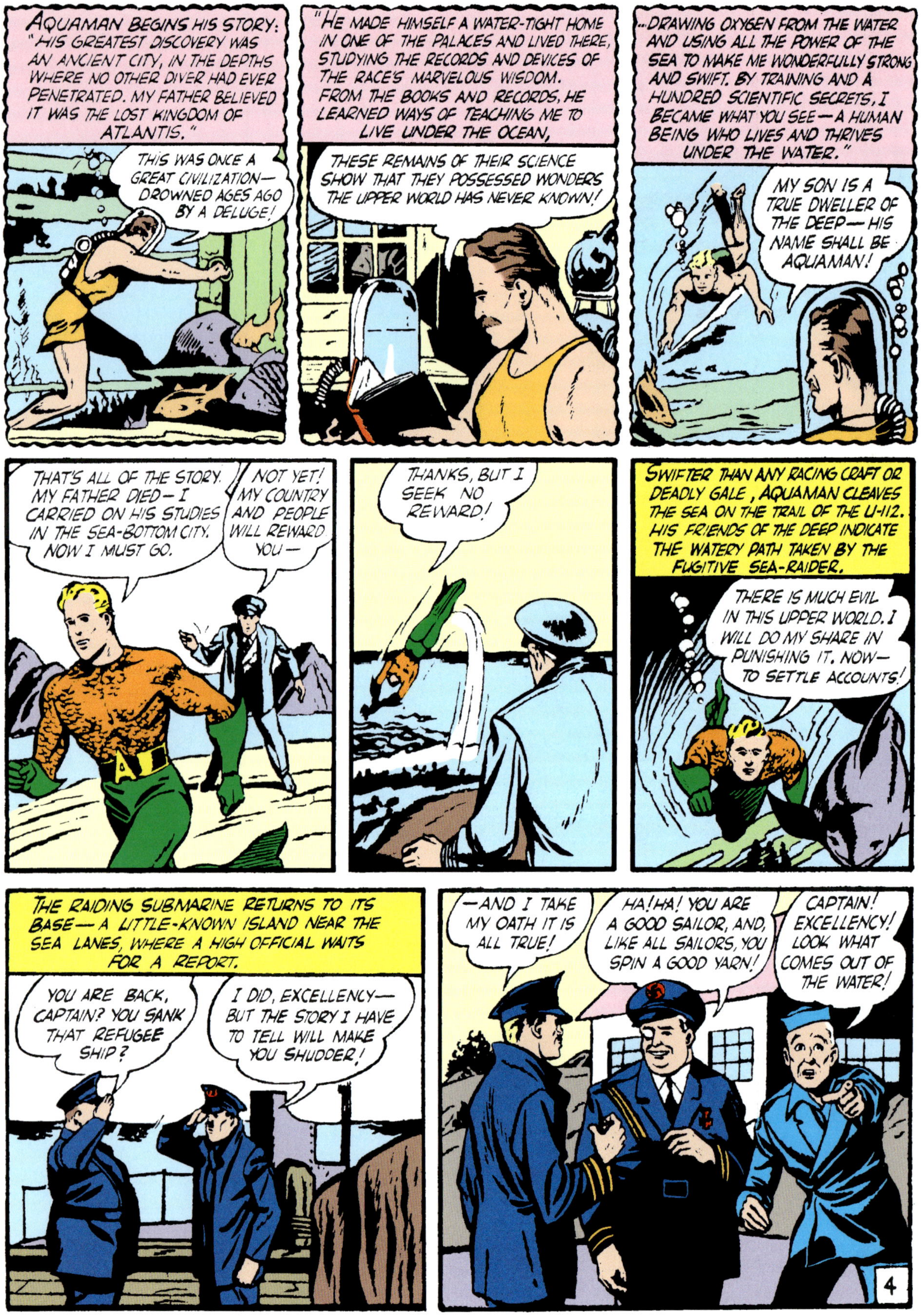
AQUAMAN BEGINS HIS STORY: "HIS GREATEST DISCOVERY WAS AN ANCIENT CITY, IN THE DEPTHS WHERE NO OTHER DIVER HAD EVER PENETRATED. MY FATHER BELIEVED IT WAS THE LOST KINGDOM OF ATLANTIS."
THIS WAS ONCE A GREAT CIVILIZATION— DROWNED AGES AGO BY A DELUGE!
"HE MADE HIMSELF A WATER-TIGHT HOME IN ONE OF THE PALACES AND LIVED THERE, STUDYING THE RECORDS AND DEVICES OF THE RACE'S MARVELOUS WISDOM. FROM THE BOOKS AND RECORDS, HE LEARNED WAYS OF TEACHING ME TO LIVE UNDER THE OCEAN,
THESE REMAINS OF THEIR SCIENCE SHOW THAT THEY POSSESSED WONDERS THE UPPER WORLD HAS NEVER KNOWN!
...DRAWING OXYGEN FROM THE WATER AND USING ALL THE POWER OF THE SEA TO MAKE ME WONDERFULLY STRONG AND SWIFT. BY TRAINING AND A HUNDRED SCIENTIFIC SECRETS, I BECAME WHAT YOU SEE— A HUMAN BEING WHO LIVES AND THRIVES UNDER THE WATER."
MY SON IS A TRUE DWELLER OF THE DEEP— HIS NAME SHALL BE AQUAMAN!
THAT'S ALL OF THE STORY. MY FATHER DIED— I CARRIED ON HIS STUDIES IN THE SEA-BOTTOM CITY. NOW I MUST GO.
NOT YET! MY COUNTRY AND PEOPLE WILL REWARD YOU—
THANKS, BUT I SEEK NO REWARD!
SWIFTER THAN ANY RACING CRAFT OR DEADLY GALE, AQUAMAN CLEAVES THE SEA ON THE TRAIL OF THE U-112. HIS FRIENDS OF THE DEEP INDICATE THE WATERY PATH TAKEN BY THE FUGITIVE SEA-RAIDER.
THERE IS MUCH EVIL IN THIS UPPER WORLD. I WILL DO MY SHARE IN PUNISHING IT. NOW— TO SETTLE ACCOUNTS!
THE RAIDING SUBMARINE RETURNS TO ITS BASE— A LITTLE-KNOWN ISLAND NEAR THE SEA LANES, WHERE A HIGH OFFICIAL WAITS FOR A REPORT.
YOU ARE BACK, CAPTAIN? YOU SANK THAT REFUGEE SHIP?
I DID, EXCELLENCY— BUT THE STORY I HAVE TO TELL WILL MAKE YOU SHUDDER!
—AND I TAKE MY OATH IT IS ALL TRUE!
HA! HA! YOU ARE A GOOD SAILOR, AND, LIKE ALL SAILORS, YOU SPIN A GOOD YARN!
CAPTAIN! EXCELLENCY! LOOK WHAT COMES OUT OF THE WATER!
4

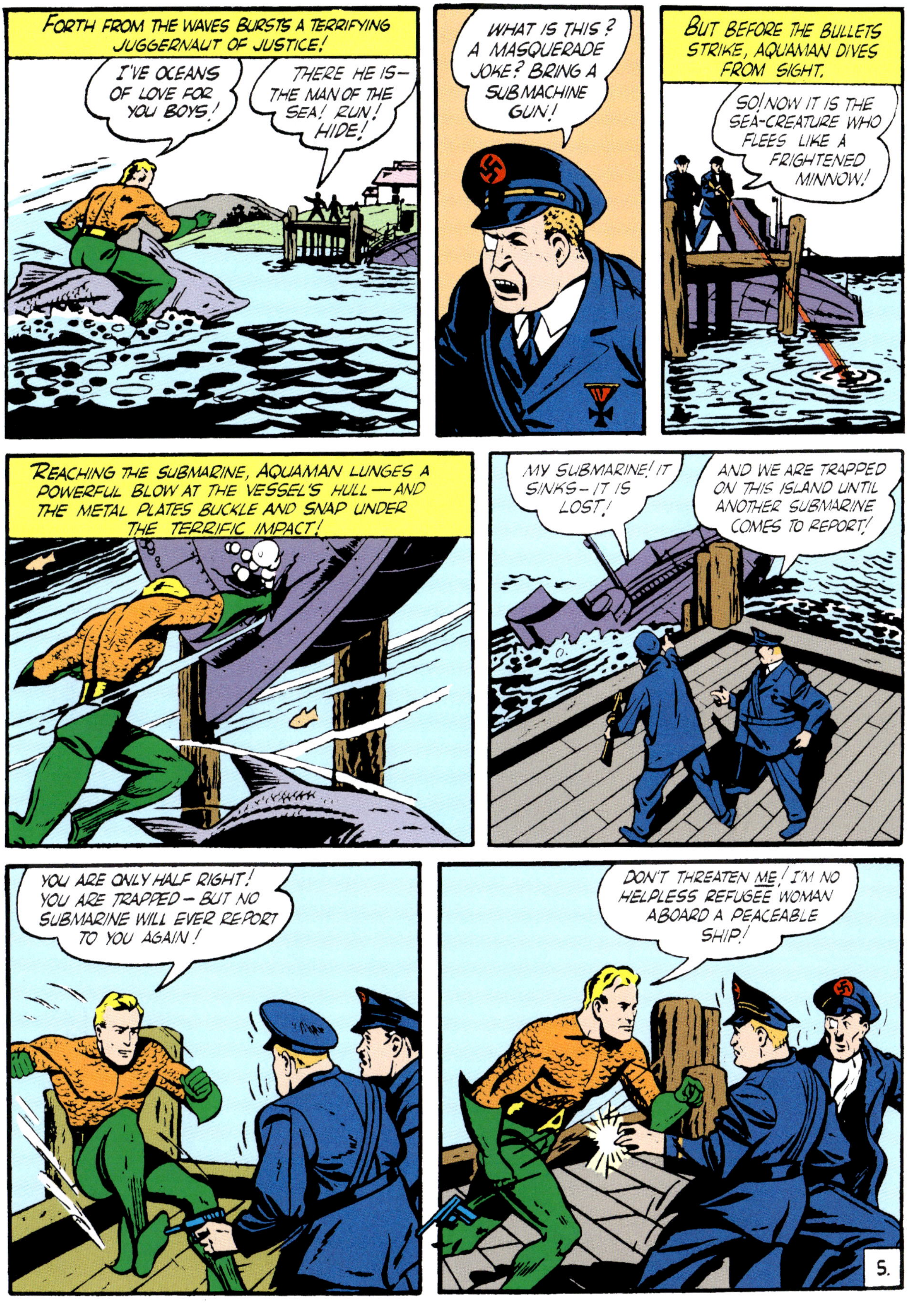
FORTH FROM THE WAVES BURSTS A TERRIFYING JUGGERNAUT OF JUSTICE!
I'VE OCEANS OF LOVE FOR YOU BOYS!
THERE HE IS— THE MAN OF THE SEA! RUN! HIDE!
WHAT IS THIS? A MASQUERADE JOKE? BRING A SUBMACHINE GUN!
BUT BEFORE THE BULLETS STRIKE, AQUAMAN DIVES FROM SIGHT.
SO! NOW IT IS THE SEA-CREATURE WHO FLEES LIKE A FRIGHTENED MINNOW!
REACHING THE SUBMARINE, AQUAMAN LUNGES A POWERFUL BLOW AT THE VESSEL'S HULL— AND THE METAL PLATES BUCKLE AND SNAP UNDER THE TERRIFIC IMPACT!
MY SUBMARINE! IT SINKS— IT IS LOST!
AND WE ARE TRAPPED ON THIS ISLAND UNTIL ANOTHER SUBMARINE COMES TO REPORT!
YOU ARE ONLY HALF RIGHT! YOU ARE TRAPPED— BUT NO SUBMARINE WILL EVER REPORT TO YOU AGAIN!
DON'T THREATEN ME! I'M NO HELPLESS REFUGEE WOMAN ABOARD A PEACEABLE SHIP!
5.

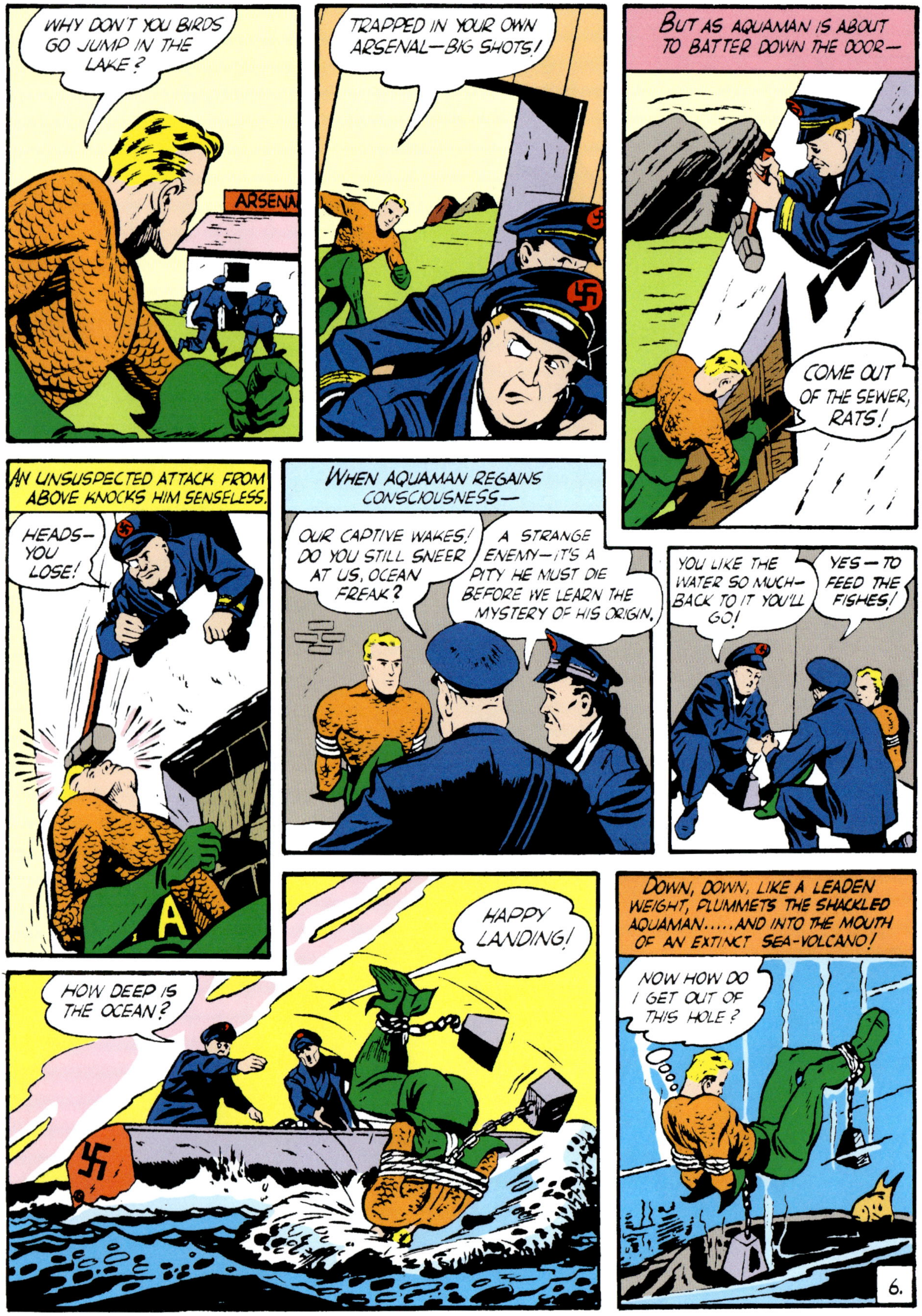
WHY DON'T YOU BIRDS GO JUMP IN THE LAKE?
ARSENA
TRAPPED IN YOUR OWN ARSENAL—BIG SHOTS!
BUT AS AQUAMAN IS ABOUT TO BATTER DOWN THE DOOR—
COME OUT OF THE SEWER, RATS!
AN UNSUSPECTED ATTACK FROM ABOVE KNOCKS HIM SENSELESS.
HEADS—YOU LOSE!
WHEN AQUAMAN REGAINS CONSCIOUSNESS—
OUR CAPTIVE WAKES! DO YOU STILL SNEER AT US, OCEAN FREAK?
A STRANGE ENEMY—IT'S A PITY HE MUST DIE BEFORE WE LEARN THE MYSTERY OF HIS ORIGIN.
YOU LIKE THE WATER SO MUCH-BACK TO IT YOU'LL GO!
YES—TO FEED THE FISHES!
HAPPY LANDING!
HOW DEEP IS THE OCEAN?
DOWN, DOWN, LIKE A LEADEN WEIGHT, PLUMMETS THE SHACKLED AQUAMAN.....AND INTO THE MOUTH OF AN EXTINCT SEA-VOLCANO!
NOW HOW DO I GET OUT OF THIS HOLE?
6.

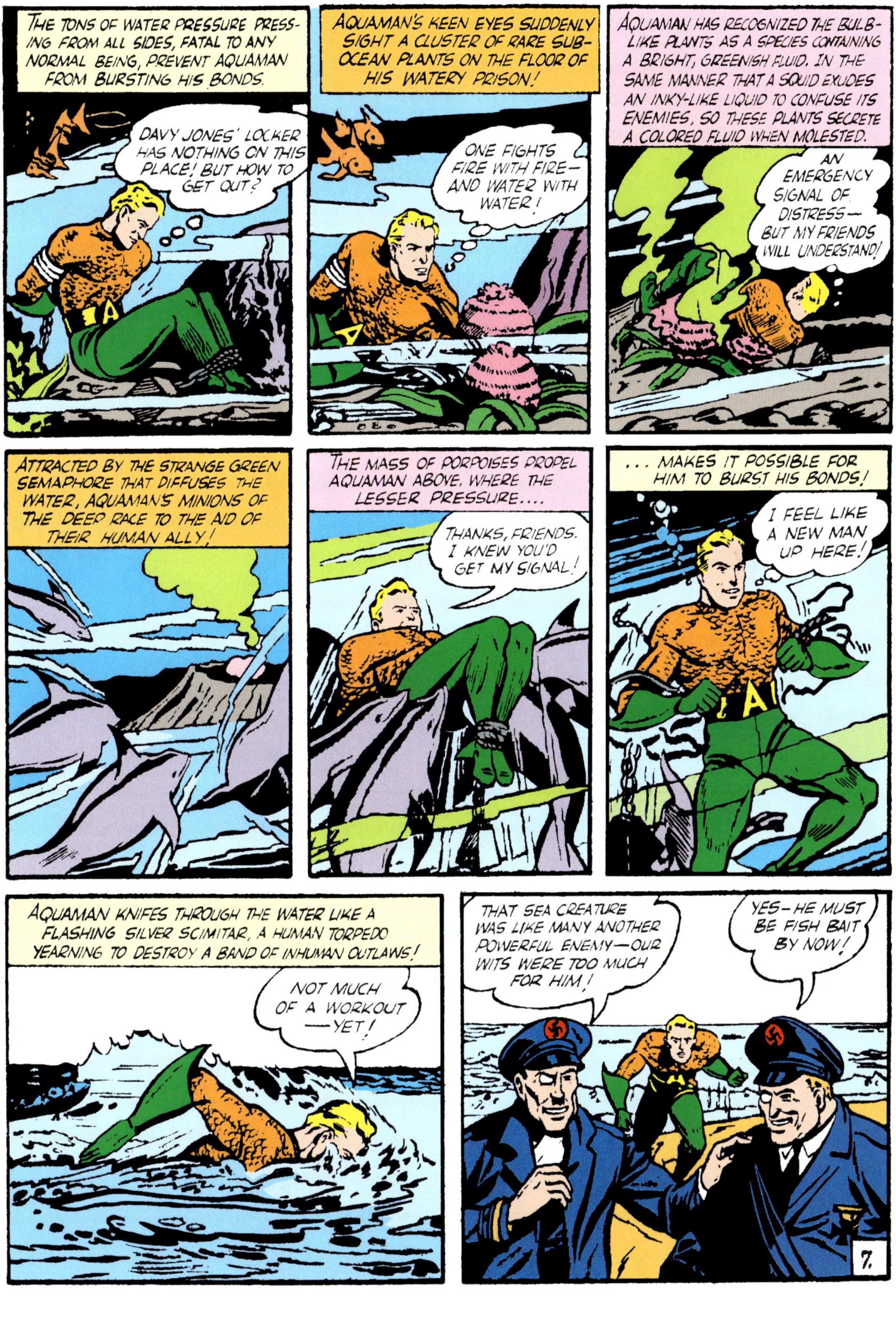
THE TONS OF WATER PRESSURE PRESSING FROM ALL SIDES, FATAL TO ANY NORMAL BEING, PREVENT AQUAMAN FROM BURSTING HIS BONDS.
DAVY JONES' LOCKER HAS NOTHING ON THIS PLACE! BUT HOW TO GET OUT?
AQUAMAN'S KEEN EYES SUDDENLY SIGHT A CLUSTER OF RARE SUB-OCEAN PLANTS ON THE FLOOR OF HIS WATERY PRISON!
ONE FIGHTS FIRE WITH FIRE—AND WATER WITH WATER!
AQUAMAN HAS RECOGNIZED THE BULB-LIKE PLANTS AS A SPECIES CONTAINING A BRIGHT, GREENISH FLUID. IN THE SAME MANNER THAT A SQUID EXUDES AN INKY-LIKE LIQUID TO CONFUSE ITS ENEMIES, SO THESE PLANTS SECRETE A COLORED FLUID WHEN MOLESTED.
AN EMERGENCY SIGNAL OF DISTRESS—BUT MY FRIENDS WILL UNDERSTAND!
ATTRACTED BY THE STRANGE GREEN SEMAPHORE THAT DIFFUSES THE WATER, AQUAMAN'S MINIONS OF THE DEEP RACE TO THE AID OF THEIR HUMAN ALLY!
THE MASS OF PORPOISES PROPEL AQUAMAN ABOVE, WHERE THE LESSER PRESSURE....
THANKS, FRIENDS. I KNEW YOU'D GET MY SIGNAL!
... MAKES IT POSSIBLE FOR HIM TO BURST HIS BONDS!
I FEEL LIKE A NEW MAN UP HERE!
AQUAMAN KNIFES THROUGH THE WATER LIKE A FLASHING SILVER SCIMITAR, A HUMAN TORPEDO YEARNING TO DESTROY A BAND OF INHUMAN OUTLAWS!
NOT MUCH OF A WORKOUT—YET!
THAT SEA CREATURE WAS LIKE MANY ANOTHER POWERFUL ENEMY—OUR WITS WERE TOO MUCH FOR HIM!
YES—HE MUST BE FISH BAIT BY NOW!
7.

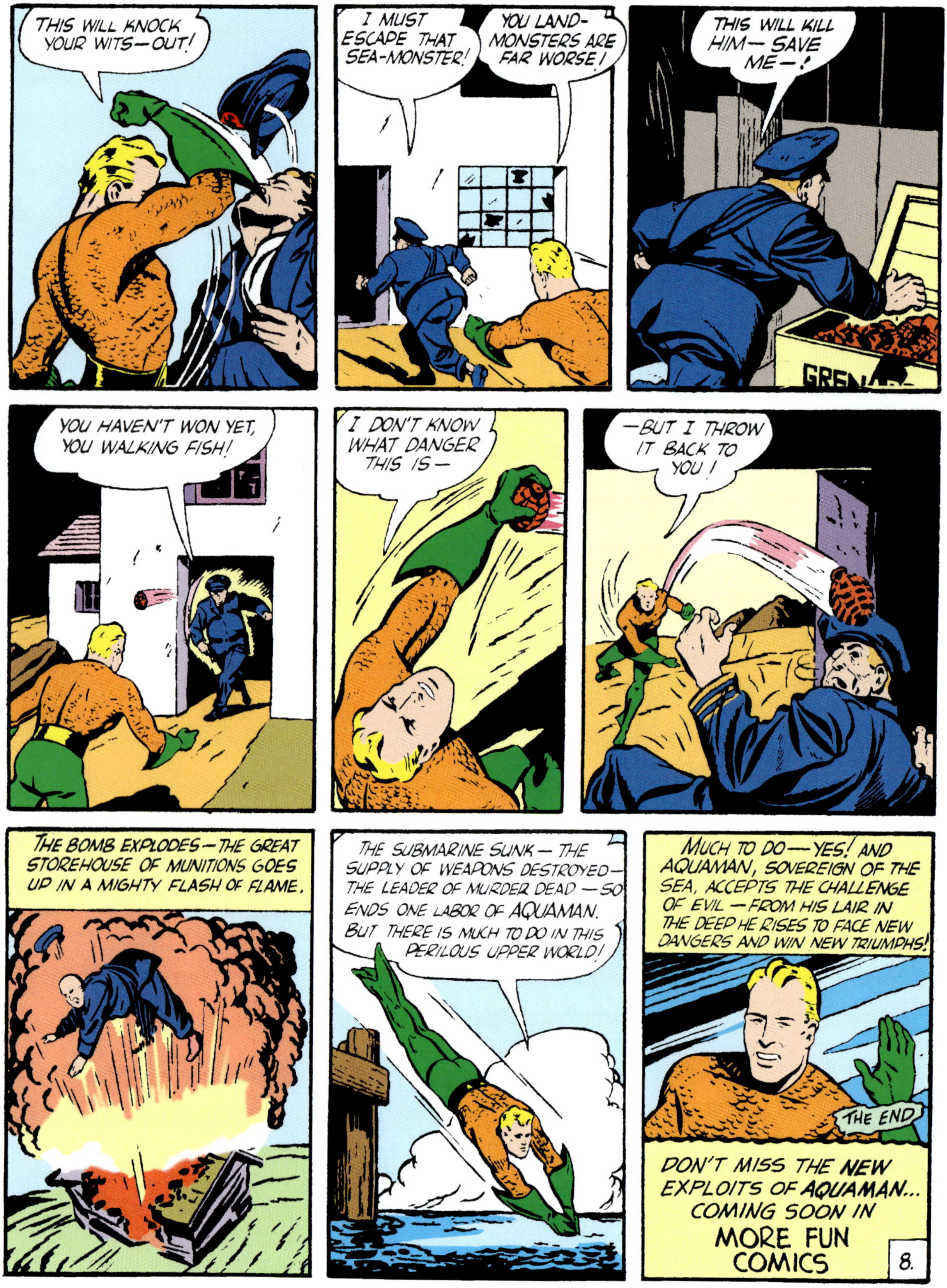
THIS WILL KNOCK YOUR WITS—OUT!
I MUST ESCAPE THAT SEA-MONSTER!
YOU LAND-MONSTERS ARE FAR WORSE!
THIS WILL KILL HIM—SAVE ME—!
YOU HAVEN'T WON YET, YOU WALKING FISH!
I DON'T KNOW WHAT DANGER THIS IS—
—BUT I THROW IT BACK TO YOU!
THE BOMB EXPLODES—THE GREAT STOREHOUSE OF MUNITIONS GOES UP IN A MIGHTY FLASH OF FLAME.
THE SUBMARINE SUNK—THE SUPPLY OF WEAPONS DESTROYED—THE LEADER OF MURDER DEAD—SO ENDS ONE LABOR OF AQUAMAN. BUT THERE IS MUCH TO DO IN THIS PERILOUS UPPER WORLD!
MUCH TO DO—YES! AND AQUAMAN, SOVEREIGN OF THE SEA, ACCEPTS THE CHALLENGE OF EVIL—FROM HIS LAIR IN THE DEEP HE RISES TO FACE NEW DANGERS AND WIN NEW TRIUMPHS!
THE END
DON'T MISS THE NEW EXPLOITS OF AQUAMAN... COMING SOON IN MORE FUN COMICS
8.

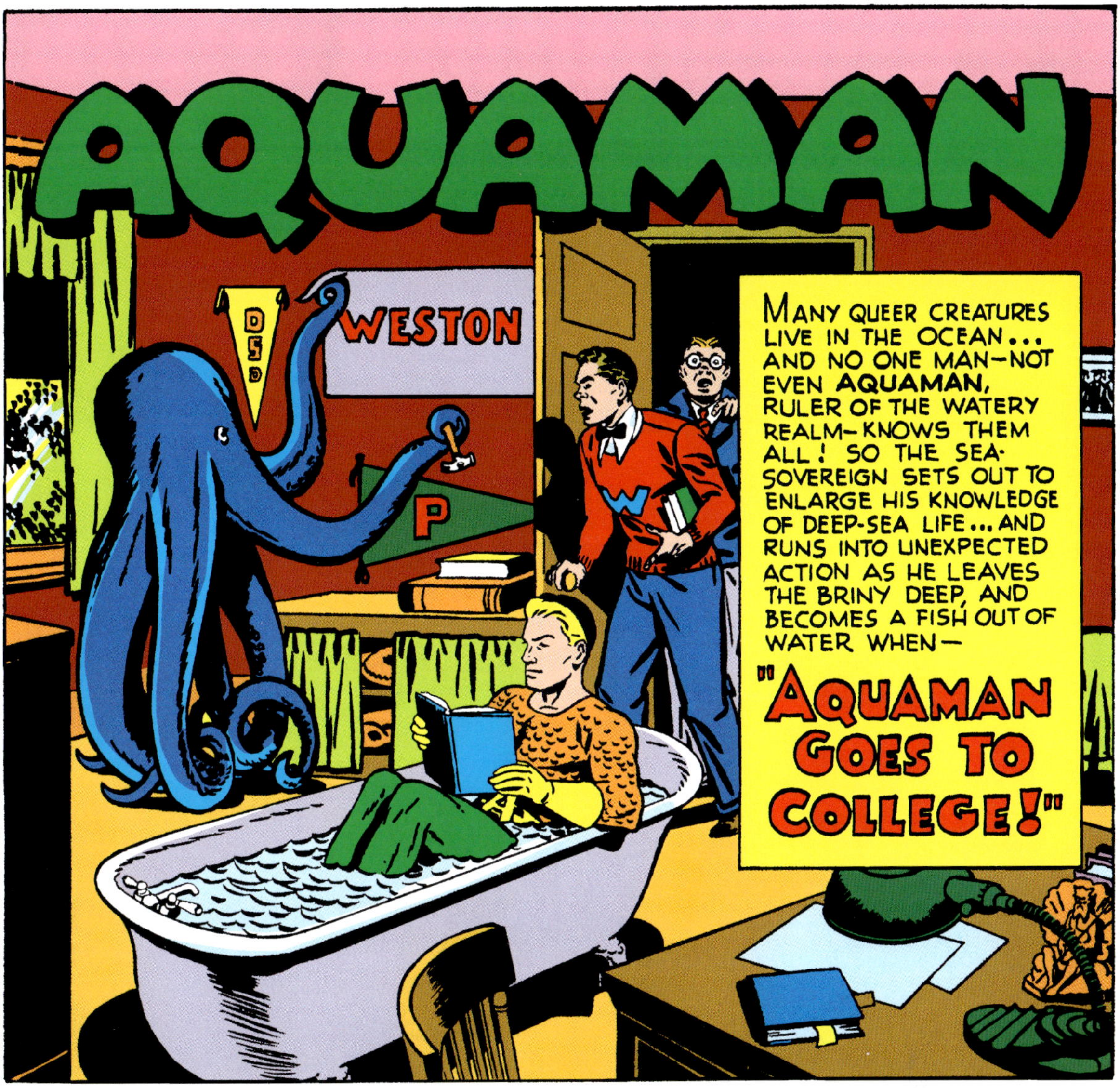
AQUAMAN
WESTON
DSD
P
W
MANY QUEER CREATURES LIVE IN THE OCEAN... AND NO ONE MAN—NOT EVEN AQUAMAN, RULER OF THE WATERY REALM—KNOWS THEM ALL! SO THE SEA-SOVEREIGN SETS OUT TO ENLARGE HIS KNOWLEDGE OF DEEP-SEA LIFE... AND RUNS INTO UNEXPECTED ACTION AS HE LEAVES THE BRINY DEEP, AND BECOMES A FISH OUT OF WATER WHEN—
"AQUAMAN GOES TO COLLEGE!"

AQUAMAN, SOVEREIGN OF THE SEVEN SEAS SAYS GOODBYE TO HIS MANY FRIENDS FROM THE OCEAN'S DEPTHS...
FELLOWS, I'M LEAVING THE OCEAN—FOR A WHILE, THAT IS.'

IT'S BECAUSE OF SOMETHING THAT HAPPENED THE OTHER DAY! I SAW A STRANGE KIND OF FISH I HAD NEVER SEEN BEFORE...
"WANTING TO GET ACQUAINTED, I SWAM AFTER IT, AND SUDDENLY..."
OWWW... THOSE SPINES HURT!
"SECONDS LATER..."
MY ARM'S BURNING! THOSE SPINES ARE POISONOUS!
I WAS PRETTY SICK FOR A FEW DAYS... SIMPLY BECAUSE I HADN'T KNOWN ABOUT THOSE SPINES!
THE OCEAN'S TOO BIG FOR A MAN TO LEARN ALL ABOUT IT FROM HIS OWN EXPERIENCE! SO I'VE DECIDED TO GO TO COLLEGE TO STUDY ABOUT FISH!
SO LONG, PAL... I'LL KEEP IN TOUCH WITH YOU!
2

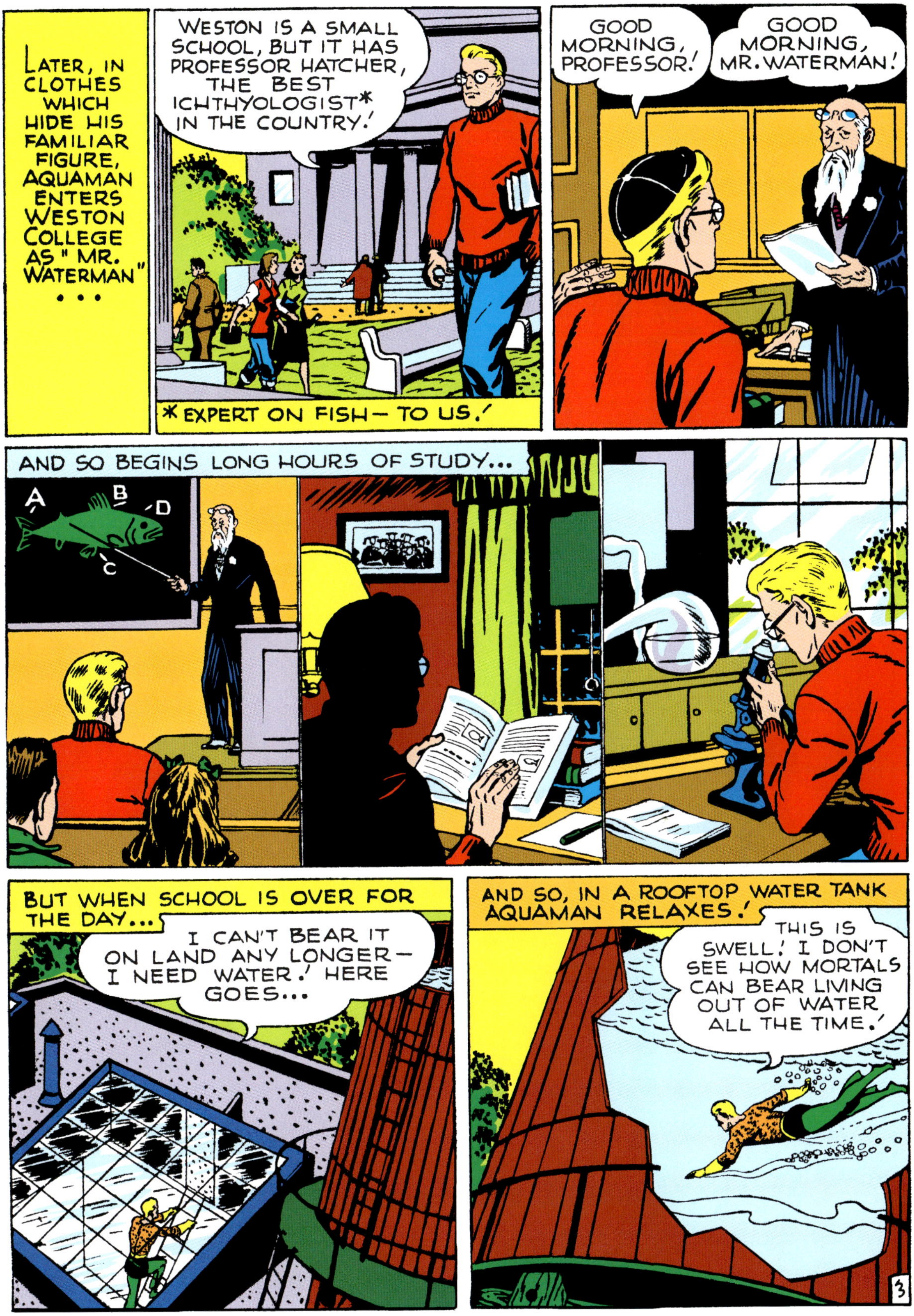
LATER, IN CLOTHES WHICH HIDE HIS FAMILIAR FIGURE, AQUAMAN ENTERS WESTON COLLEGE AS " MR. WATERMAN" • • •
WESTON IS A SMALL SCHOOL, BUT IT HAS PROFESSOR HATCHER, THE BEST ICHTHYOLOGIST* IN THE COUNTRY!
* EXPERT ON FISH— TO US!
GOOD MORNING, PROFESSOR!
GOOD MORNING, MR. WATERMAN!
AND SO BEGINS LONG HOURS OF STUDY...
A
B
D
C
BUT WHEN SCHOOL IS OVER FOR THE DAY...
I CAN'T BEAR IT ON LAND ANY LONGER— I NEED WATER! HERE GOES...
AND SO, IN A ROOFTOP WATER TANK AQUAMAN RELAXES!
THIS IS SWELL! I DON'T SEE HOW MORTALS CAN BEAR LIVING OUT OF WATER ALL THE TIME!
3

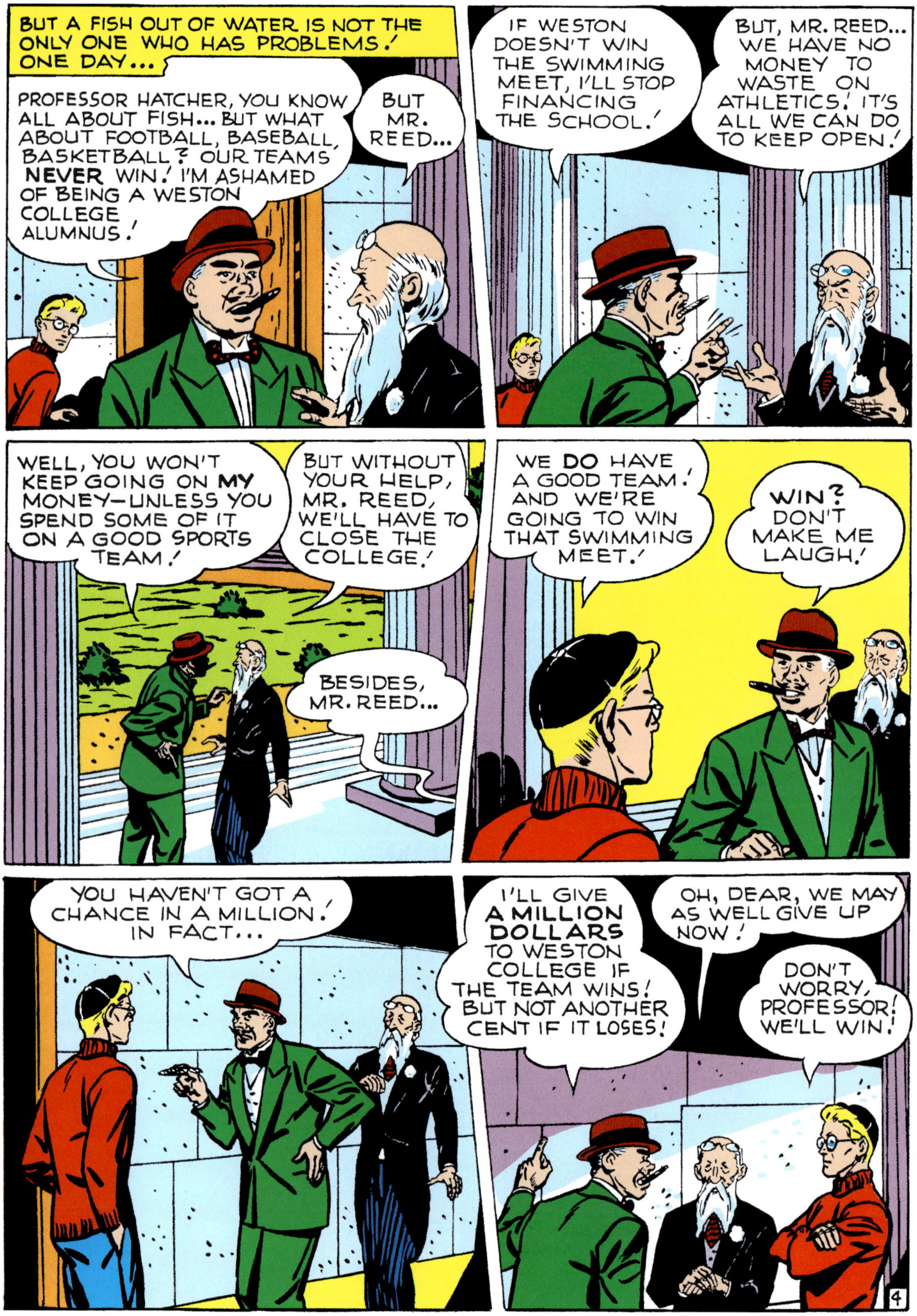
BUT A FISH OUT OF WATER IS NOT THE ONLY ONE WHO HAS PROBLEMS! ONE DAY...
PROFESSOR HATCHER, YOU KNOW ALL ABOUT FISH... BUT WHAT ABOUT FOOTBALL, BASEBALL, BASKETBALL? OUR TEAMS NEVER WIN! I'M ASHAMED OF BEING A WESTON COLLEGE ALUMNUS!
BUT MR. REED...
IF WESTON DOESN'T WIN THE SWIMMING MEET, I'LL STOP FINANCING THE SCHOOL!
BUT, MR. REED... WE HAVE NO MONEY TO WASTE ON ATHLETICS! IT'S ALL WE CAN DO TO KEEP OPEN!
WELL, YOU WON'T KEEP GOING ON MY MONEY—UNLESS YOU SPEND SOME OF IT ON A GOOD SPORTS TEAM!
BUT WITHOUT YOUR HELP, MR. REED, WE'LL HAVE TO CLOSE THE COLLEGE!
BESIDES, MR. REED...
WE DO HAVE A GOOD TEAM! AND WE'RE GOING TO WIN THAT SWIMMING MEET!
WIN? DON'T MAKE ME LAUGH!
YOU HAVEN'T GOT A CHANCE IN A MILLION! IN FACT...
I'LL GIVE A MILLION DOLLARS TO WESTON COLLEGE IF THE TEAM WINS! BUT NOT ANOTHER CENT IF IT LOSES!
OH, DEAR, WE MAY AS WELL GIVE UP NOW!
DON'T WORRY, PROFESSOR! WE'LL WIN!
4

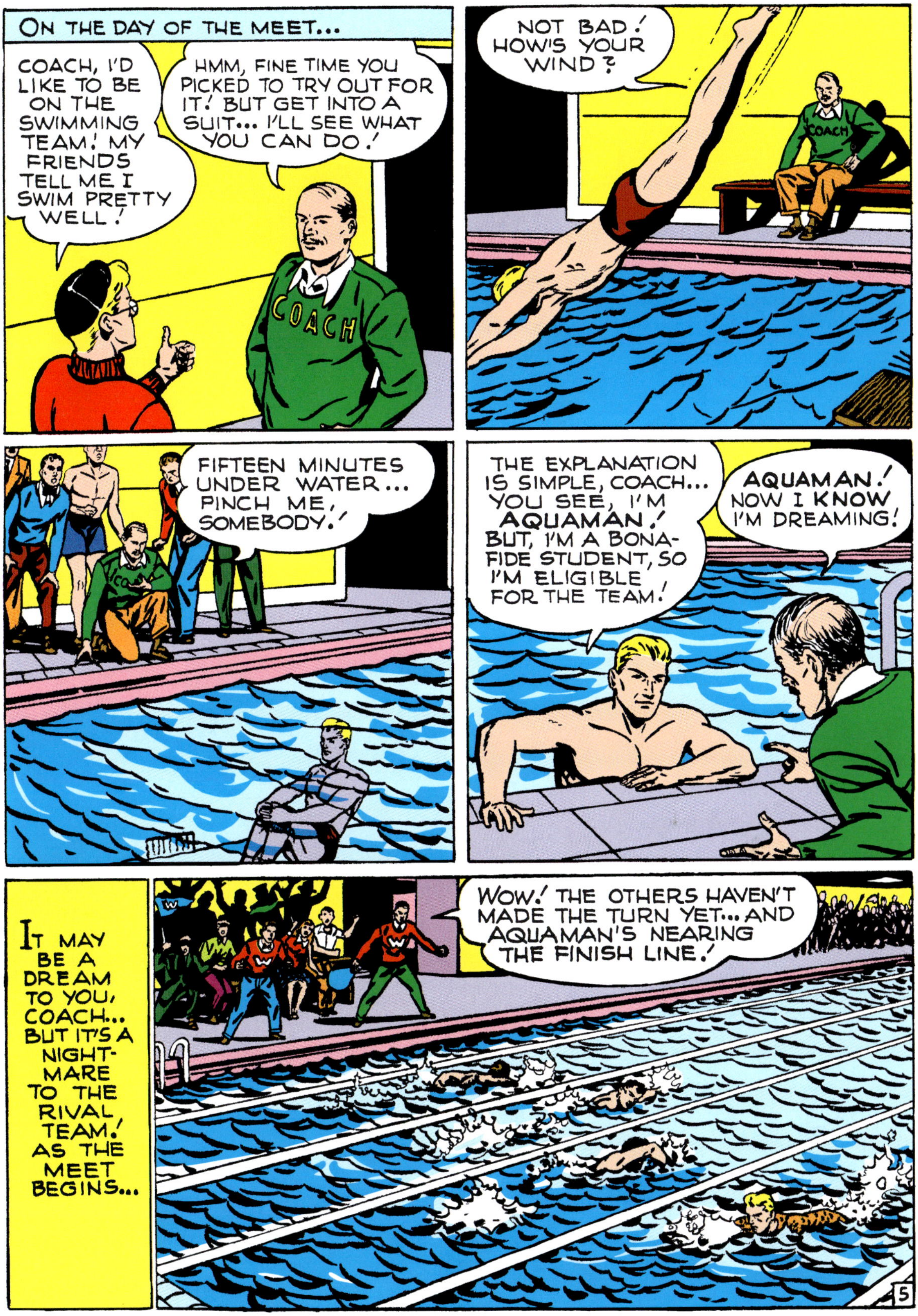
ON THE DAY OF THE MEET...
COACH, I'D LIKE TO BE ON THE SWIMMING TEAM! MY FRIENDS TELL ME I SWIM PRETTY WELL!
HMM, FINE TIME YOU PICKED TO TRY OUT FOR IT! BUT GET INTO A SUIT... I'LL SEE WHAT YOU CAN DO!
COACH
NOT BAD! HOW'S YOUR WIND?
COACH
FIFTEEN MINUTES UNDER WATER... PINCH ME, SOMEBODY!
THE EXPLANATION IS SIMPLE, COACH... YOU SEE, I'M AQUAMAN! BUT, I'M A BONA-FIDE STUDENT, SO I'M ELIGIBLE FOR THE TEAM!
AQUAMAN! NOW I KNOW I'M DREAMING!
IT MAY BE A DREAM TO YOU, COACH... BUT IT'S A NIGHTMARE TO THE RIVAL TEAM! AS THE MEET BEGINS...
WOW! THE OTHERS HAVEN'T MADE THE TURN YET... AND AQUAMAN'S NEARING THE FINISH LINE!
5

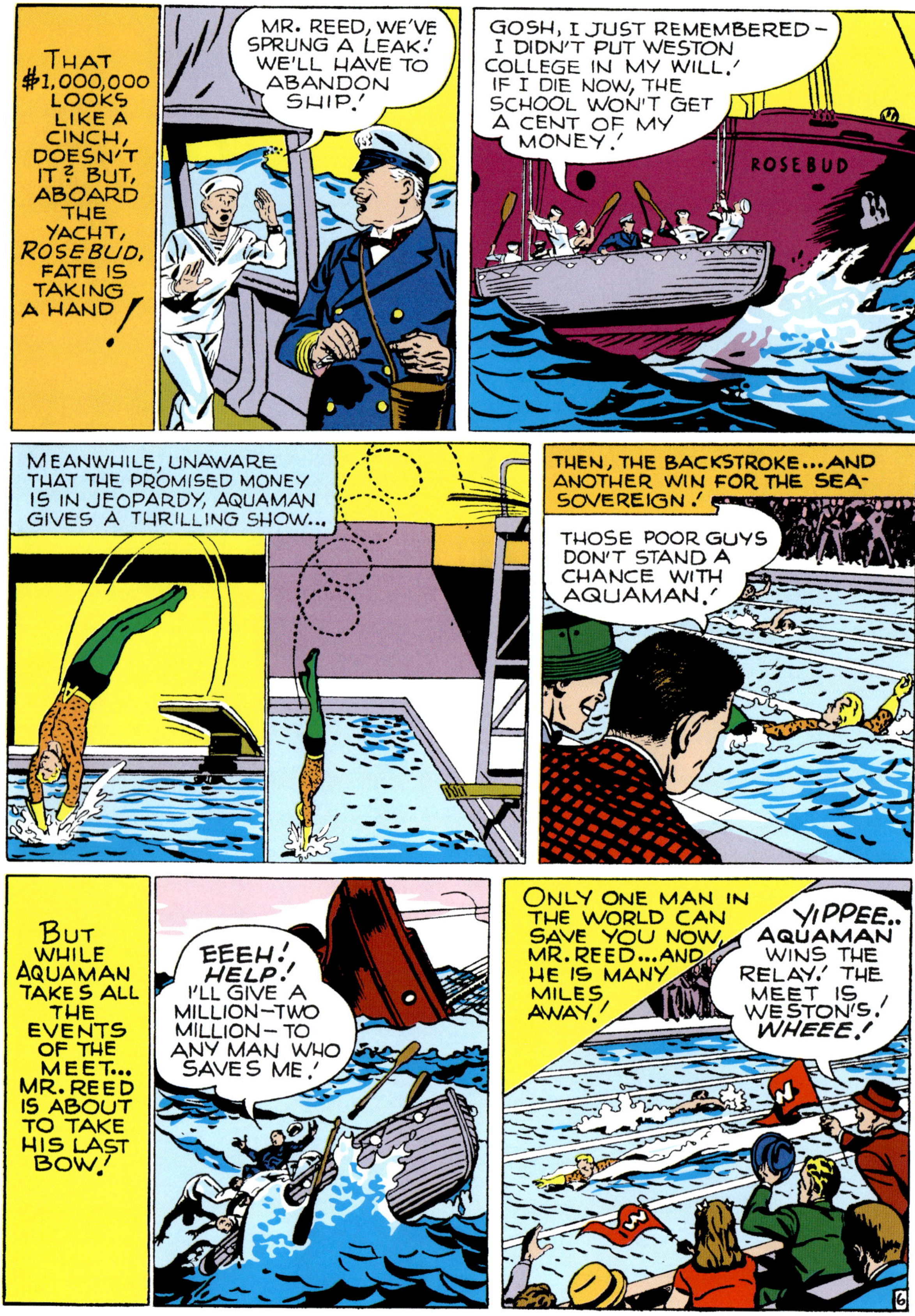
THAT $1,000,000 LOOKS LIKE A CINCH, DOESN'T IT? BUT, ABOARD THE YACHT, ROSEBUD, FATE IS TAKING A HAND!
MR. REED, WE'VE SPRUNG A LEAK! WE'LL HAVE TO ABANDON SHIP!
GOSH, I JUST REMEMBERED - I DIDN'T PUT WESTON COLLEGE IN MY WILL! IF I DIE NOW, THE SCHOOL WON'T GET A CENT OF MY MONEY!
ROSEBUD
MEANWHILE, UNAWARE THAT THE PROMISED MONEY IS IN JEOPARDY, AQUAMAN GIVES A THRILLING SHOW...
THEN, THE BACKSTROKE...AND ANOTHER WIN FOR THE SEA-SOVEREIGN!
THOSE POOR GUYS DON'T STAND A CHANCE WITH AQUAMAN!
BUT WHILE AQUAMAN TAKES ALL THE EVENTS OF THE MEET... MR. REED IS ABOUT TO TAKE HIS LAST BOW!
EEEH! HELP! I'LL GIVE A MILLION—TWO MILLION—TO ANY MAN WHO SAVES ME!
ONLY ONE MAN IN THE WORLD CAN SAVE YOU NOW, MR. REED...AND HE IS MANY MILES AWAY!
YIPPEE.. AQUAMAN WINS THE RELAY! THE MEET IS WESTON'S! WHEEE!
6

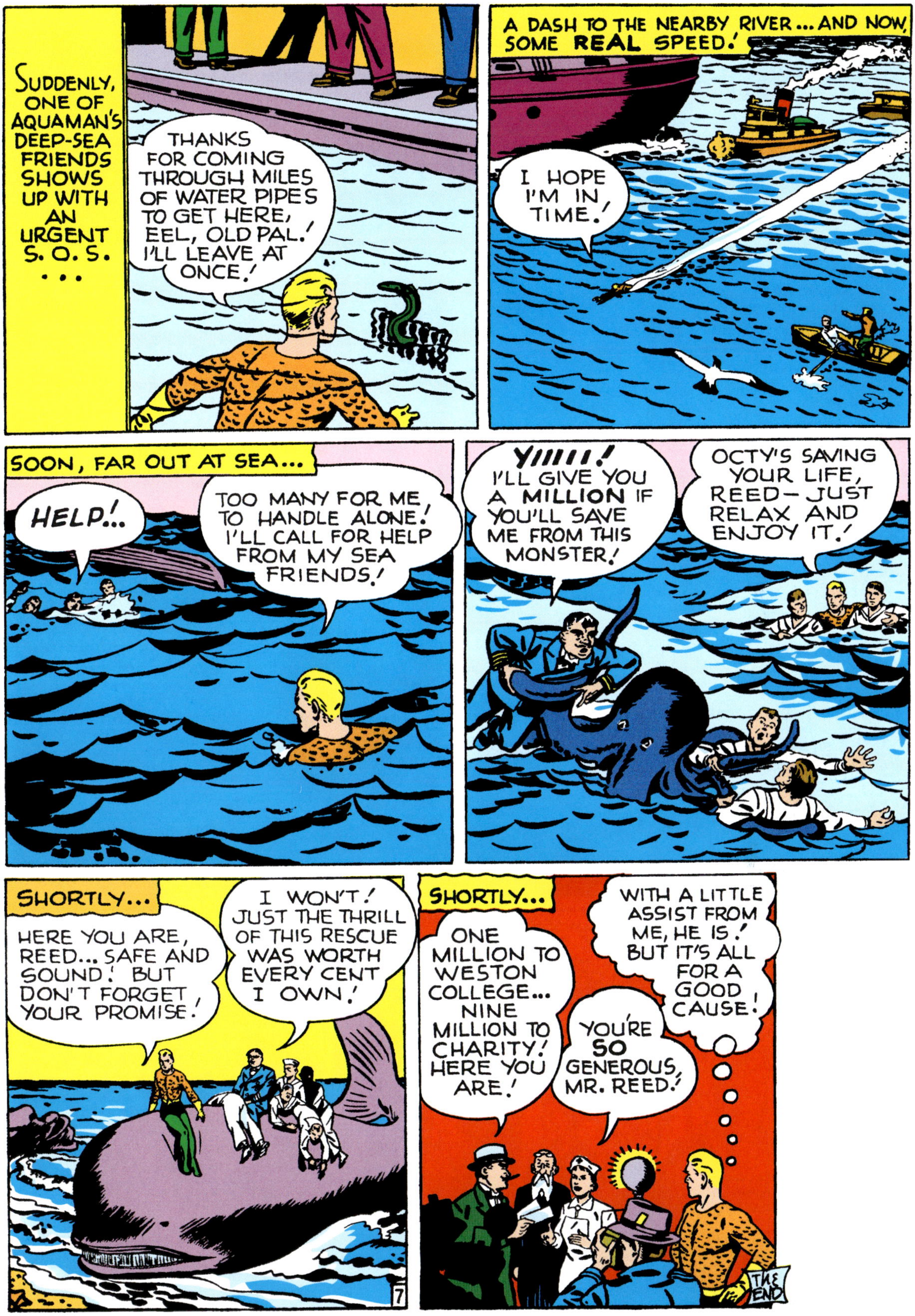

SUDDENLY, ONE OF AQUAMAN'S DEEP-SEA FRIENDS SHOWS UP WITH AN URGENT S.O.S. . . .
THANKS FOR COMING THROUGH MILES OF WATER PIPES TO GET HERE, EEL, OLD PAL! I'LL LEAVE AT ONCE!
A DASH TO THE NEARBY RIVER ... AND NOW, SOME REAL SPEED!
I HOPE I'M IN TIME!
SOON, FAR OUT AT SEA...
HELP!..
TOO MANY FOR ME TO HANDLE ALONE! I'LL CALL FOR HELP FROM MY SEA FRIENDS!
YIIIII! I'LL GIVE YOU A MILLION IF YOU'LL SAVE ME FROM THIS MONSTER!
OCTY'S SAVING YOUR LIFE, REED—JUST RELAX AND ENJOY IT!
SHORTLY...
HERE YOU ARE, REED... SAFE AND SOUND! BUT DON'T FORGET YOUR PROMISE!
I WON'T! JUST THE THRILL OF THIS RESCUE WAS WORTH EVERY CENT I OWN!
7
SHORTLY...
ONE MILLION TO WESTON COLLEGE... NINE MILLION TO CHARITY! HERE YOU ARE!
YOU'RE SO GENEROUS, MR. REED!
WITH A LITTLE ASSIST FROM ME, HE IS! BUT IT'S ALL FOR A GOOD CAUSE!
THE END

AQUAMAN
THE NORTH POLE HAS BEEN DISCOVERED! THE ANTARCTIC WASTES HAVE BEEN CHARTED! DARKEST AFRICA HAS BEEN MAPPED! HAVE EXPLORERS RUN OUT OF WORLDS TO CONQUER? BUT NO! THERE IS YET A MUCH VASTER AND MORE MYSTERIOUS LAND TO BE EXPLORED AND CLAIMED-- THE OCEAN FLOOR! AND AQUAMAN, KING OF THE SEA, GUIDES THE FIRST EXPEDITION INTO THE UNKNOWN SUBSEA WILDERNESS...
The UNDERSEA LOST WORLD!

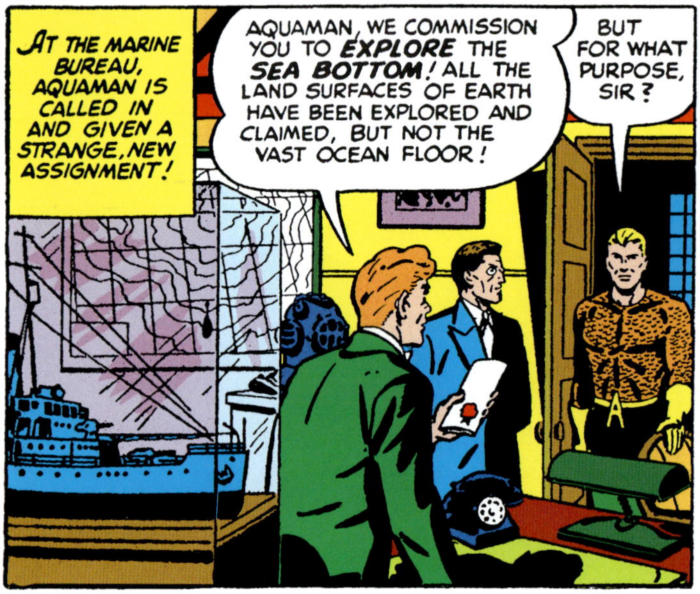
AT THE MARINE BUREAU, AQUAMAN IS CALLED IN AND GIVEN A STRANGE, NEW ASSIGNMENT!
AQUAMAN, WE COMMISSION YOU TO EXPLORE THE SEA BOTTOM! ALL THE LAND SURFACES OF EARTH HAVE BEEN EXPLORED AND CLAIMED, BUT NOT THE VAST OCEAN FLOOR!
BUT FOR WHAT PURPOSE, SIR?

THIS IS PROFESSOR PEABODY, OCEANOLOGIST. HE WILL EXPLAIN!
I BELIEVE THAT VALUABLE MINERAL DEPOSITS LIE ON THE OCEAN FLOOR! THE WORLD WOULD BENEFIT GREATLY FROM THEIR DISCOVERY AND EXTRACTION!

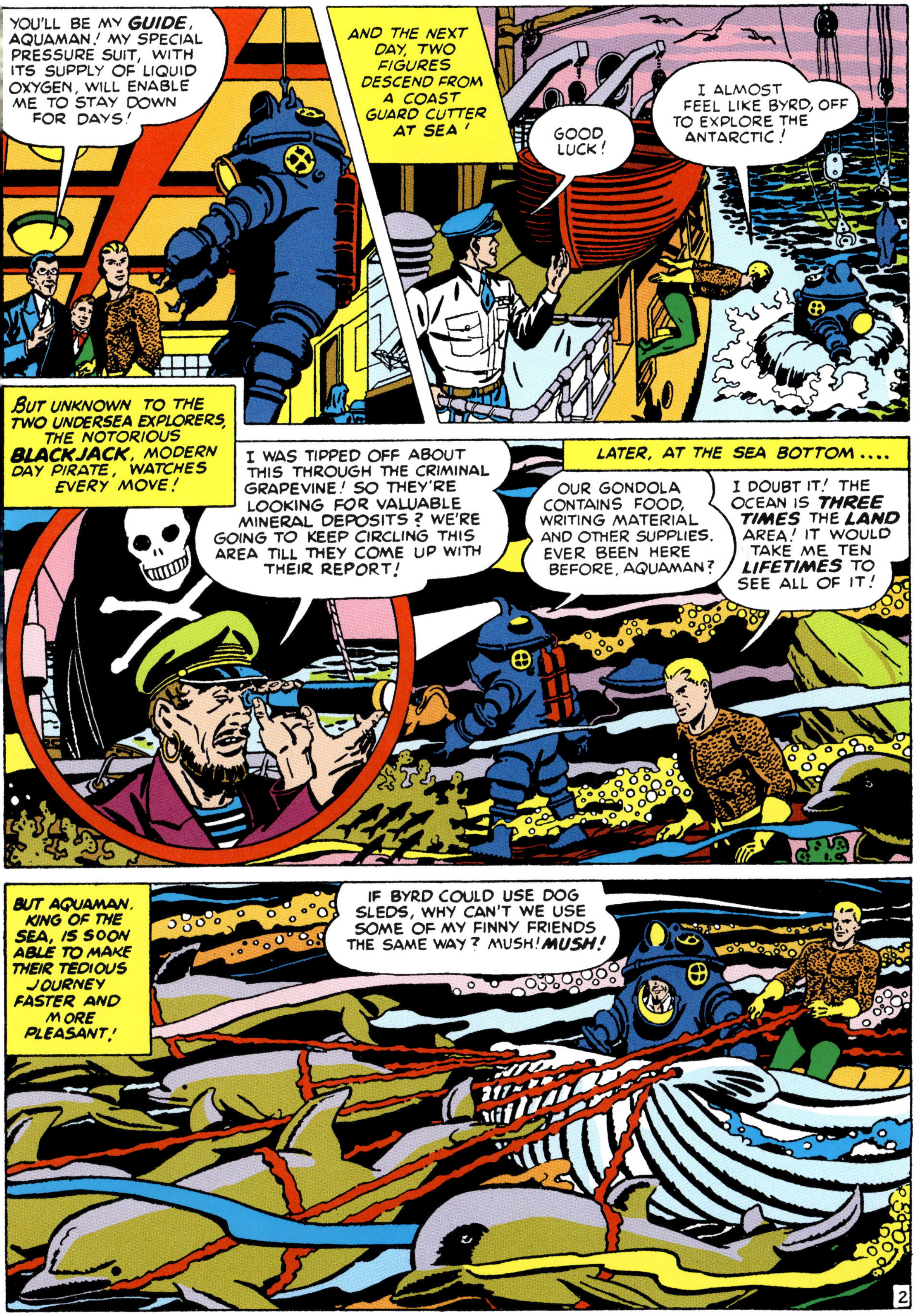
YOU'LL BE MY GUIDE, AQUAMAN! MY SPECIAL PRESSURE SUIT, WITH ITS SUPPLY OF LIQUID OXYGEN, WILL ENABLE ME TO STAY DOWN FOR DAYS!
AND THE NEXT DAY, TWO FIGURES DESCEND FROM A COAST GUARD CUTTER AT SEA!
GOOD LUCK!
I ALMOST FEEL LIKE BYRD, OFF TO EXPLORE THE ANTARCTIC!
BUT UNKNOWN TO THE TWO UNDERSEA EXPLORERS, THE NOTORIOUS BLACKJACK, MODERN DAY PIRATE, WATCHES EVERY MOVE!
I WAS TIPPED OFF ABOUT THIS THROUGH THE CRIMINAL GRAPEVINE! SO THEY'RE LOOKING FOR VALUABLE MINERAL DEPOSITS? WE'RE GOING TO KEEP CIRCLING THIS AREA TILL THEY COME UP WITH THEIR REPORT!
LATER, AT THE SEA BOTTOM....
OUR GONDOLA CONTAINS FOOD, WRITING MATERIAL AND OTHER SUPPLIES. EVER BEEN HERE BEFORE, AQUAMAN?
I DOUBT IT! THE OCEAN IS THREE TIMES THE LAND AREA! IT WOULD TAKE ME TEN LIFETIMES TO SEE ALL OF IT!
BUT AQUAMAN, KING OF THE SEA, IS SOON ABLE TO MAKE THEIR TEDIOUS JOURNEY FASTER AND MORE PLEASANT!
IF BYRD COULD USE DOG SLEDS, WHY CAN'T WE USE SOME OF MY FINNY FRIENDS THE SAME WAY? MUSH! MUSH!
2

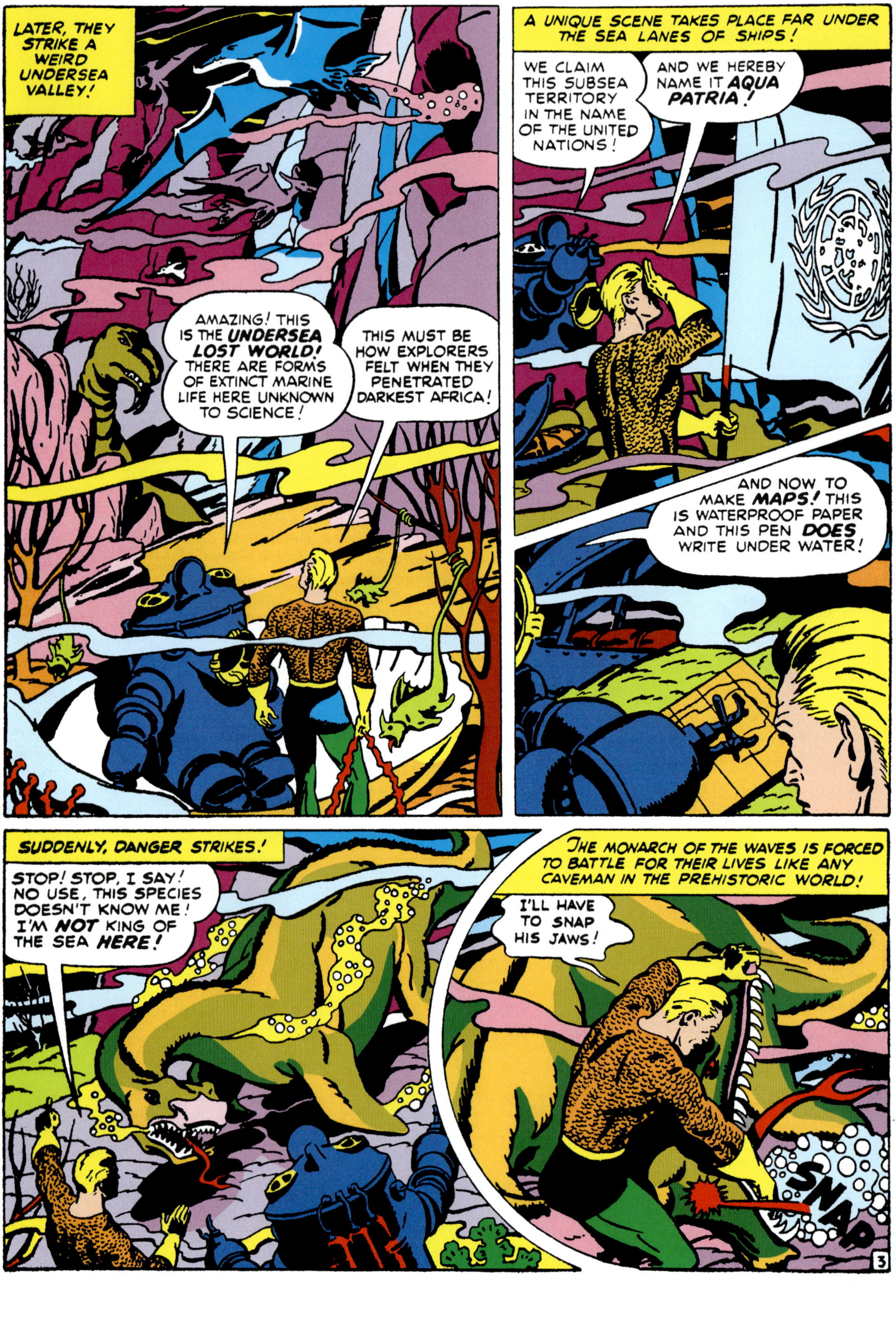
LATER, THEY STRIKE A WEIRD UNDERSEA VALLEY!
AMAZING! THIS IS THE UNDERSEA LOST WORLD! THERE ARE FORMS OF EXTINCT MARINE LIFE HERE UNKNOWN TO SCIENCE!
THIS MUST BE HOW EXPLORERS FELT WHEN THEY PENETRATED DARKEST AFRICA!
A UNIQUE SCENE TAKES PLACE FAR UNDER THE SEA LANES OF SHIPS!
WE CLAIM THIS SUBSEA TERRITORY IN THE NAME OF THE UNITED NATIONS!
AND WE HEREBY NAME IT AQUA PATRIA!
AND NOW TO MAKE MAPS! THIS IS WATERPROOF PAPER AND THIS PEN DOES WRITE UNDER WATER!
SUDDENLY, DANGER STRIKES!
STOP! STOP, I SAY! NO USE, THIS SPECIES DOESN'T KNOW ME! I'M NOT KING OF THE SEA HERE!
THE MONARCH OF THE WAVES IS FORCED TO BATTLE FOR THEIR LIVES LIKE ANY CAVEMAN IN THE PREHISTORIC WORLD!
I'LL HAVE TO SNAP HIS JAWS!
SNAP
3

BUT AS THE MONSTER THRASHES IN ITS DYING AGONY...
OHHHH!
THE TAIL STRUCK THE PROFESSOR!
OXYGEN CUT OFF--- CAN'T BREATHE! GASP! GET ME TO THE SURFACE--- HURRY!
MEANWHILE...
AH! AQUAMAN AND THE PROFESSOR CAME UP! WHAT ARE THEY DOING AT THAT SMALL ISLAND? FULL STEAM AHEAD!
THIS BREATHING TUBE WAS BENT. I'LL HAVE IT FIXED SHORTLY!
TAKE AN HOUR OR SO AND REST UP, PROFESSOR! NO NEED TO HURRY BACK! I'M GOING TO STROLL AROUND MYSELF!
BLACKJACK COMES UPON THE SCIENTIST, ALONE!
NOW'S OUR CHANCE, WITH AQUAMAN AWAY! KNOCK HIM OUT AND HIDE HIM IN THE BUSHES, MEN! I'M GOING TO LOOK AROUND UNDERSEA MYSELF, AND AQUAMAN WON'T KNOW THE DIFFERENCE!
LATER
READY TO GO DOWN AGAIN, PROFESSOR?
RIGHT!
4

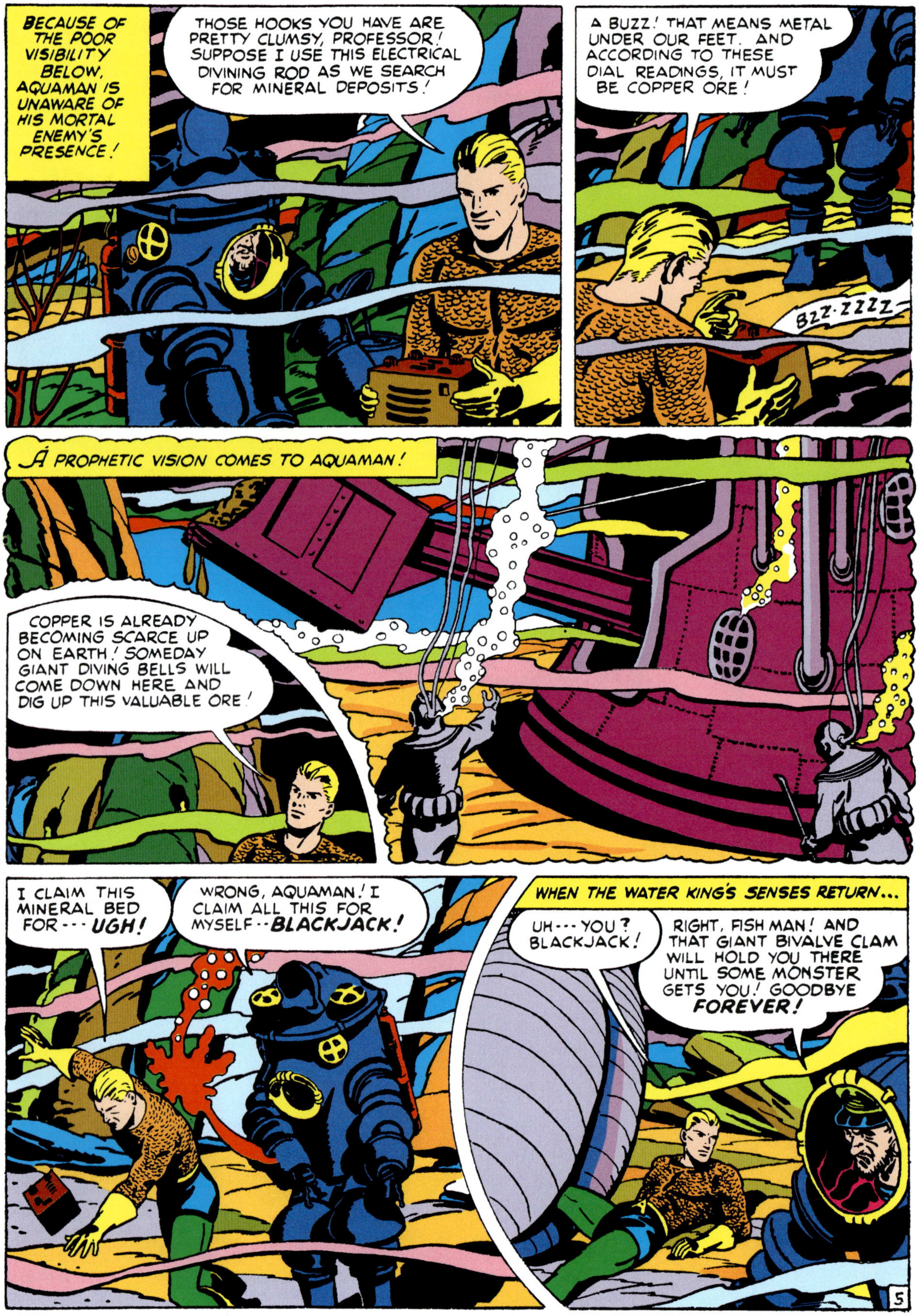
BECAUSE OF THE POOR VISIBILITY BELOW, AQUAMAN IS UNAWARE OF HIS MORTAL ENEMY'S PRESENCE!
THOSE HOOKS YOU HAVE ARE PRETTY CLUMSY, PROFESSOR! SUPPOSE I USE THIS ELECTRICAL DIVINING ROD AS WE SEARCH FOR MINERAL DEPOSITS!
A BUZZ! THAT MEANS METAL UNDER OUR FEET. AND ACCORDING TO THESE DIAL READINGS, IT MUST BE COPPER ORE!
BZZ-ZZZZ
A PROPHETIC VISION COMES TO AQUAMAN!
COPPER IS ALREADY BECOMING SCARCE UP ON EARTH! SOMEDAY GIANT DIVING BELLS WILL COME DOWN HERE AND DIG UP THIS VALUABLE ORE!
I CLAIM THIS MINERAL BED FOR--- UGH!
WRONG, AQUAMAN! I CLAIM ALL THIS FOR MYSELF--BLACKJACK!
WHEN THE WATER KING'S SENSES RETURN...
UH--- YOU? BLACKJACK!
RIGHT, FISH MAN! AND THAT GIANT BIVALVE CLAM WILL HOLD YOU THERE UNTIL SOME MONSTER GETS YOU! GOODBYE FOREVER!
5

BUT AQUAMAN SENDS OUT A CALL AND ONE OF HIS FINNY FRIENDS FEARLESSLY ARRIVES, TO AID!
HURRY! SAW THROUGH THAT CLAM'S MUSCLES, SO THE TWO SHELLS WILL OPEN UP AND LET ME FREE! HURRY!
FREE! AND MY BEAKED PAL IS TAKING CARE OF THAT HUNGRY MONSTROSITY!
SOON, ON THE ISLAND, ABOVE....
I'LL SELL OUT THAT UNDERSEA COPPER FIELD TO THE HIGHEST BIDDER!
MAY I MAKE A BID NOW?
I BID YOU GOOD NIGHT!
AHHHHH-
GREAT WORK! THE NAME OF AQUAMAN WILL GO DOWN IN HISTORY ALONGSIDE THOSE OF AMUNDSEN, PERRY AND BYRD, FOR THE FIRST EXPLORATION AND DISCOVERY OF UNDERSEA REGIONS!
THEY GAVE ME A BIG PARADE AND ALL, AND I'M PROUD OF THAT MEDAL!
AQUAMAN AWARDED MARINE MEDAL FOR DARING DEEP SEA EXPLORATION!
6
THE END

AQUAMAN
THE U.S. NAVY IS ALWAYS ON THE LOOKOUT FOR BRIGHT AND BRAVE YOUNG MEN TO MAN ITS SHIPS... BUT NEVER IN THE HISTORY OF OUR MARITIME SERVICE HAS IT EVER HAD A SEAMAN LIKE AQUAMAN! THAT'S WHY BLUEJACKETS WILL ALWAYS REMEMBER THE AMAZING EVENTS THAT OCCUR WHEN...
"AQUAMAN JOINS THE NAVY!"
I'LL MAKE A GOOD SEAMAN OF YOU, IF IT'S THE LAST THING I EVER DO!
Y-YES, SIR!
ONE DAY, AS AQUAMAN PATROLS THE WATERS, ABOARD HIS TRUSTED SEA STEED, TOPO THE OCTOPUS...
THREE ROCKET FLARES SHOT AT DIFFERENT LEVELS... THAT'S ADMIRAL HANLEY'S SECRET SIGNAL TO ME! HOPE NOTHING'S WRONG! LET'S MAKE TRACKS, TOPO...
SOON AFTER, ON THE ADMIRAL'S FLAGSHIP...
HELLO, ADMIRAL HANLEY! NO TROUBLE, I HOPE?
NONE AT ALL, AQUAMAN! I JUST WANTED TO ASK IF YOU'D DO ME A PERSONAL FAVOR BY JOINING THE NAVY-- AS AN ORDINARY SEAMAN!

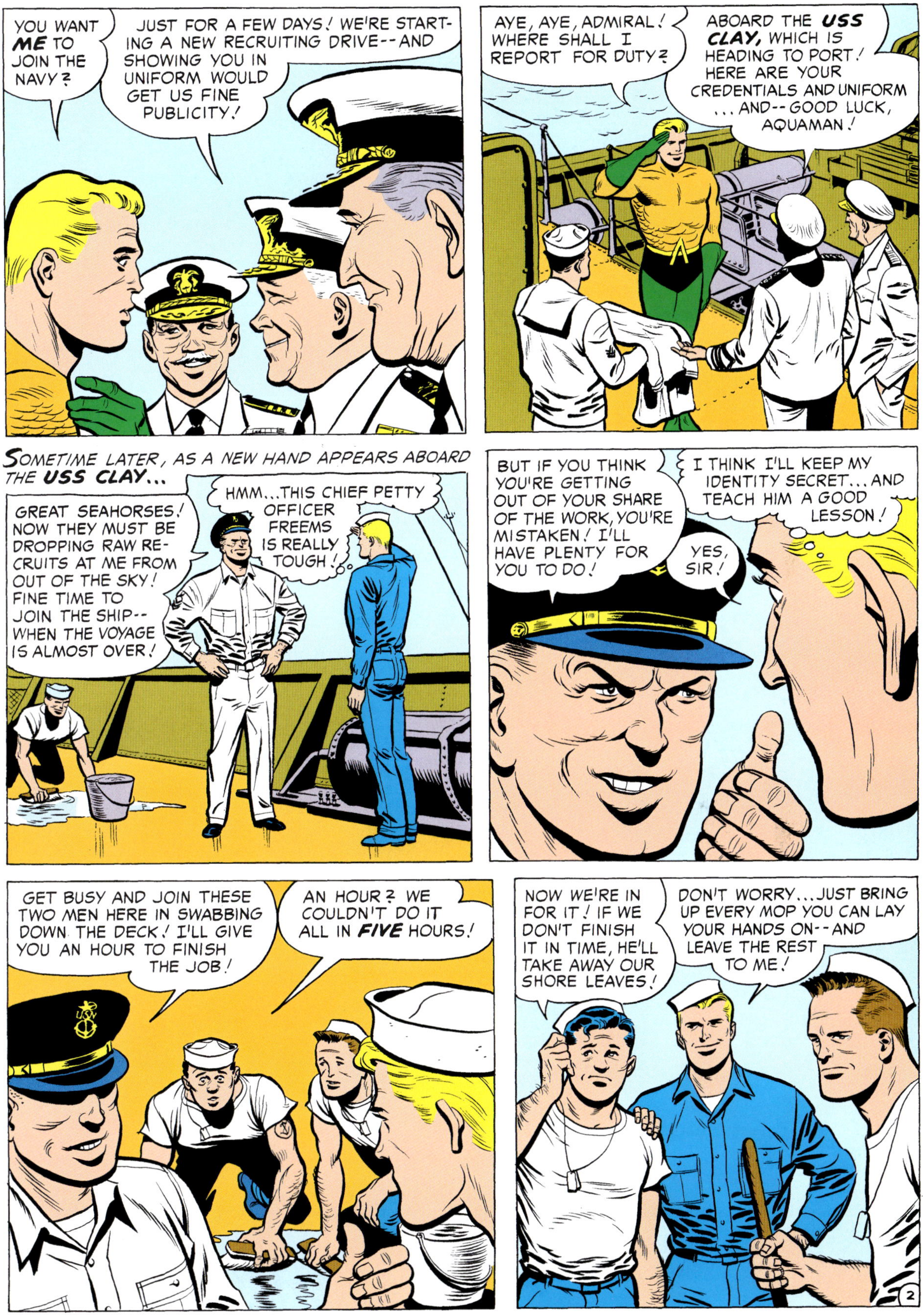
YOU WANT ME TO JOIN THE NAVY?
JUST FOR A FEW DAYS! WE'RE STARTING A NEW RECRUITING DRIVE--AND SHOWING YOU IN UNIFORM WOULD GET US FINE PUBLICITY!
AYE, AYE, ADMIRAL! WHERE SHALL I REPORT FOR DUTY?
ABOARD THE USS CLAY, WHICH IS HEADING TO PORT! HERE ARE YOUR CREDENTIALS AND UNIFORM ...AND--GOOD LUCK, AQUAMAN!
SOMETIME LATER, AS A NEW HAND APPEARS ABOARD THE USS CLAY...
GREAT SEAHORSES! NOW THEY MUST BE DROPPING RAW RECRUITS AT ME FROM OUT OF THE SKY! FINE TIME TO JOIN THE SHIP--WHEN THE VOYAGE IS ALMOST OVER!
HMM...THIS CHIEF PETTY OFFICER FREEMS IS REALLY TOUGH!
BUT IF YOU THINK YOU'RE GETTING OUT OF YOUR SHARE OF THE WORK, YOU'RE MISTAKEN! I'LL HAVE PLENTY FOR YOU TO DO!
YES, SIR!
I THINK I'LL KEEP MY IDENTITY SECRET...AND TEACH HIM A GOOD LESSON!
GET BUSY AND JOIN THESE TWO MEN HERE IN SWABBING DOWN THE DECK! I'LL GIVE YOU AN HOUR TO FINISH THE JOB!
AN HOUR? WE COULDN'T DO IT ALL IN FIVE HOURS!
NOW WE'RE IN FOR IT! IF WE DON'T FINISH IT IN TIME, HE'LL TAKE AWAY OUR SHORE LEAVES!
DON'T WORRY...JUST BRING UP EVERY MOP YOU CAN LAY YOUR HANDS ON--AND LEAVE THE REST TO ME!
2

SHORTLY...
THERE ARE THE BUCKETS AND MOPS... BUT WHAT'S THE GOOD? WE'VE STILL ONLY GOT TWO HANDS APIECE!
THAT'S TRUE...
...BUT MY FRIENDS HAVE A LOT MORE!
OCTOPUSES! DOZENS OF 'EM!
NEXT INSTANT, AS THE SEA KING'S SUBJECTS GO INTO ACTION...
THIS IS SURE ONE FOR THE BOOKS! SAY, WHO ARE YOU ANYWAY-- AQUAMAN?
DO I LOOK LIKE AQUAMAN?
THE DECK'S ALL SOAPED UP FINE! BUT HOW'LL WE GET IT RINSED OFF?
THAT'S EVEN EASIER...
ANOTHER SIGNAL TO HIS FINNY FRIENDS, AND...
WHEW! CLEAN AS A WHISTLE... AND ALL IT TOOK WAS MINUTES!
I'M GETTING FREEMS... WAIT'LL HE SEES THIS!
BUT WHEN THE CHIEF PETTY OFFICER ARRIVES...
YOU COULDN'T HAVE GOTTEN IT THIS CLEAN IN SUCH A SHORT TIME, WITHOUT PUTTING THE WHOLE CREW TO WORK! ADMIT IT!
NO, SIR--THE CREW WASN'T EVEN ON DECK, SIR!
3

JUST THEN...
SIR--THE DISHWASHING MACHINE BROKE DOWN! LAST NIGHT'S DINNERWARE IS STILL STACKED TO THE CEILING!
OH, NO! FOLLOW ME, MEN!
SOON, BELOW DECK...
THIS IS TERRIBLE, SIR! WE'RE DUE IN PORT, FOR INSPECTION, IN A COUPLE OF HOURS--AND WHEN THE ADMIRAL SPOTS THIS MESS, WE'LL BE DISGRACED!
NO, WE WON'T--BECAUSE THEY'LL BE WASHED BY HAND! AND SINCE YOU'RE SUCH A SPEED DEMON, SAILOR, I'M PLACING YOU IN CHARGE!
THERE ARE THOUSANDS OF THESE GREASY DISHES! WE'LL NEVER GET THEM CLEAN IN TIME!
RELAX, BOYS... I'VE GOT THE BEST KITCHEN DETAIL IN THE WORLD!
AND ONCE AGAIN, AS AQUAMAN USES HIS AMAZING POWERS TO SUMMON HIS SUBJECTS FROM THE SEA...
NOW I'VE SEEN EVERYTHING! A CHUTE MADE OF ATTACHED EELS! BUT THE COLD SEA WATER WILL NEVER GET THE GREASE OFF THOSE DISHES!
I KNOW!.. THAT'S WHY I'M HAVING THEM SENT DOWN A COUPLE OF FATHOMS, WHERE THERE'S A LAYER OF WARM GULFSTREAM WATER!
ARE YOU KIDDING?
JUST STAY PUT--AND YOU'LL FIND OUT...
SOON, FATHOMS BELOW...
THE SPONGES, MOVING BACK AND FORTH ACROSS THE PLATES, ARE DOING A FINE JOB!
4

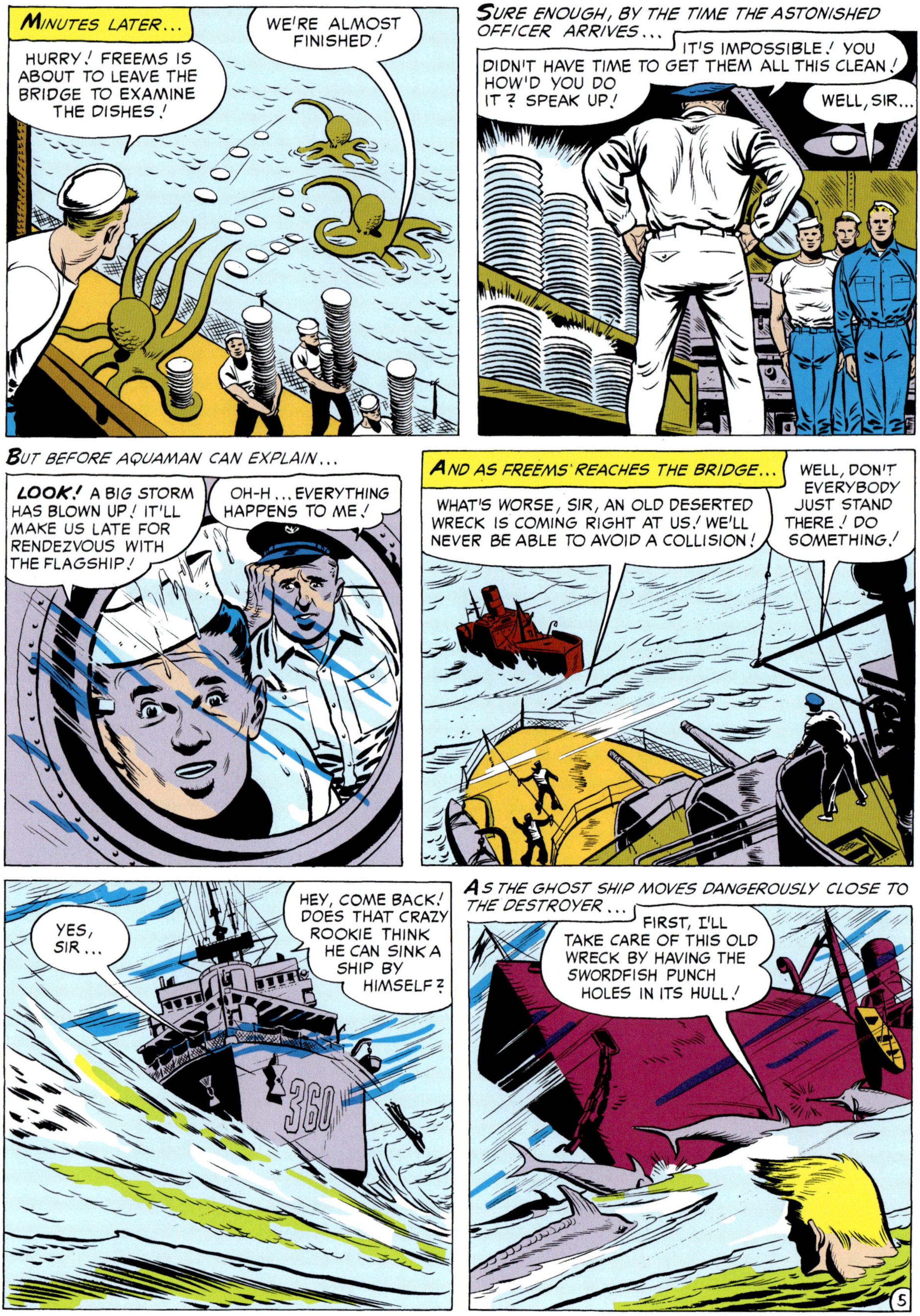
MINUTES LATER...
HURRY! FREEMS IS ABOUT TO LEAVE THE BRIDGE TO EXAMINE THE DISHES!
WE'RE ALMOST FINISHED!
SURE ENOUGH, BY THE TIME THE ASTONISHED OFFICER ARRIVES...
IT'S IMPOSSIBLE! YOU DIDN'T HAVE TIME TO GET THEM ALL THIS CLEAN! HOW'D YOU DO IT? SPEAK UP!
WELL, SIR...
BUT BEFORE AQUAMAN CAN EXPLAIN...
LOOK! A BIG STORM HAS BLOWN UP! IT'LL MAKE US LATE FOR RENDEZVOUS WITH THE FLAGSHIP!
OH-H... EVERYTHING HAPPENS TO ME!
AND AS FREEMS REACHES THE BRIDGE...
WHAT'S WORSE, SIR, AN OLD DESERTED WRECK IS COMING RIGHT AT US! WE'LL NEVER BE ABLE TO AVOID A COLLISION!
WELL, DON'T EVERYBODY JUST STAND THERE! DO SOMETHING!
YES, SIR...
HEY, COME BACK! DOES THAT CRAZY ROOKIE THINK HE CAN SINK A SHIP BY HIMSELF?
360
AS THE GHOST SHIP MOVES DANGEROUSLY CLOSE TO THE DESTROYER...
FIRST, I'LL TAKE CARE OF THIS OLD WRECK BY HAVING THE SWORDFISH PUNCH HOLES IN ITS HULL!
5

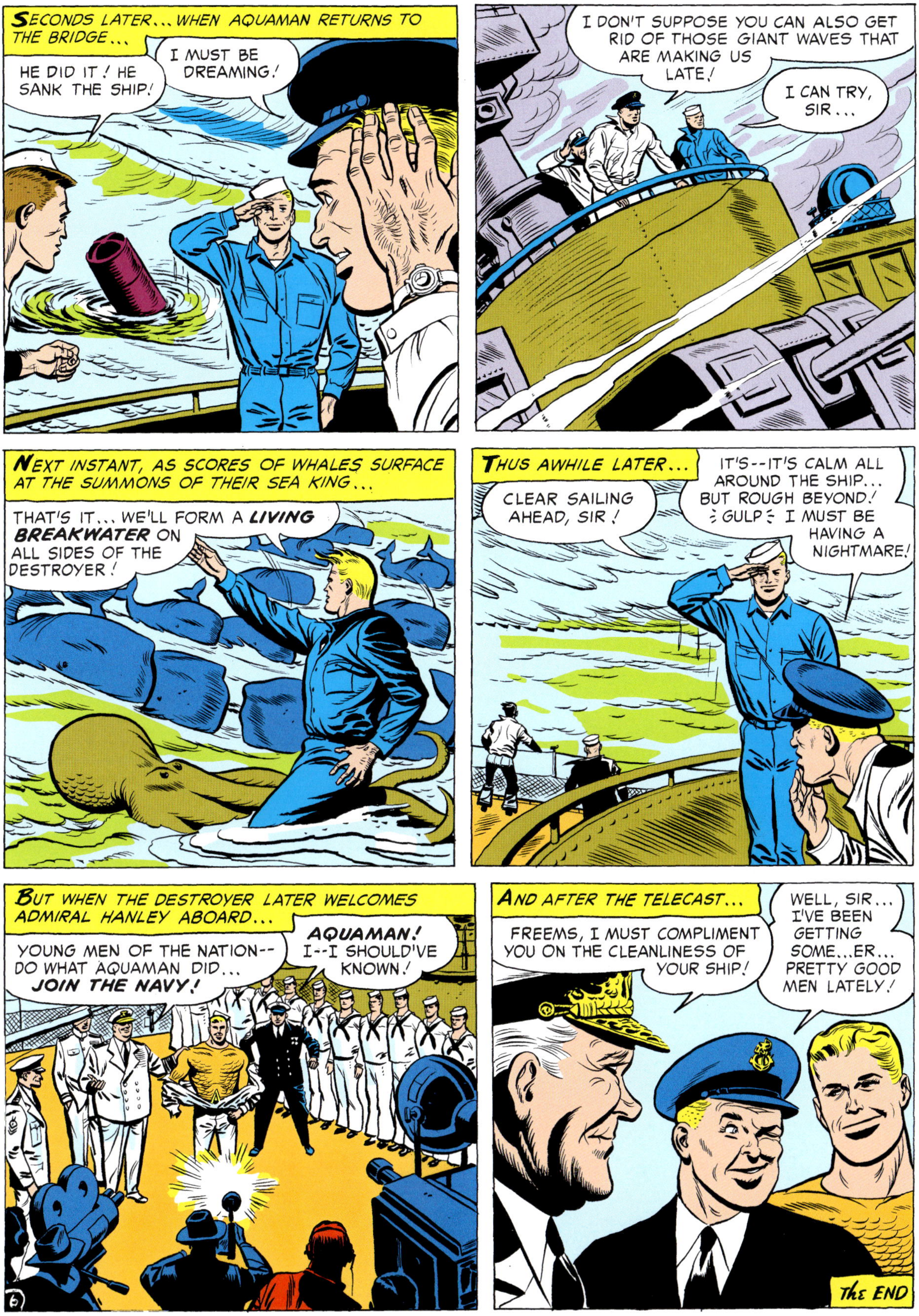

SECONDS LATER... WHEN AQUAMAN RETURNS TO THE BRIDGE...
HE DID IT! HE SANK THE SHIP!
I MUST BE DREAMING!
I DON'T SUPPOSE YOU CAN ALSO GET RID OF THOSE GIANT WAVES THAT ARE MAKING US LATE!
I CAN TRY, SIR...
NEXT INSTANT, AS SCORES OF WHALES SURFACE AT THE SUMMONS OF THEIR SEA KING...
THAT'S IT... WE'LL FORM A LIVING BREAKWATER ON ALL SIDES OF THE DESTROYER!
THUS AWHILE LATER...
CLEAR SAILING AHEAD, SIR!
IT'S--IT'S CALM ALL AROUND THE SHIP... BUT ROUGH BEYOND! GULP I MUST BE HAVING A NIGHTMARE!
BUT WHEN THE DESTROYER LATER WELCOMES ADMIRAL HANLEY ABOARD...
YOUNG MEN OF THE NATION-- DO WHAT AQUAMAN DID... JOIN THE NAVY!
AQUAMAN! I--I SHOULD'VE KNOWN!
6
AND AFTER THE TELECAST...
FREEMS, I MUST COMPLIMENT YOU ON THE CLEANLINESS OF YOUR SHIP!
WELL, SIR... I'VE BEEN GETTING SOME...ER... PRETTY GOOD MEN LATELY!
THE END

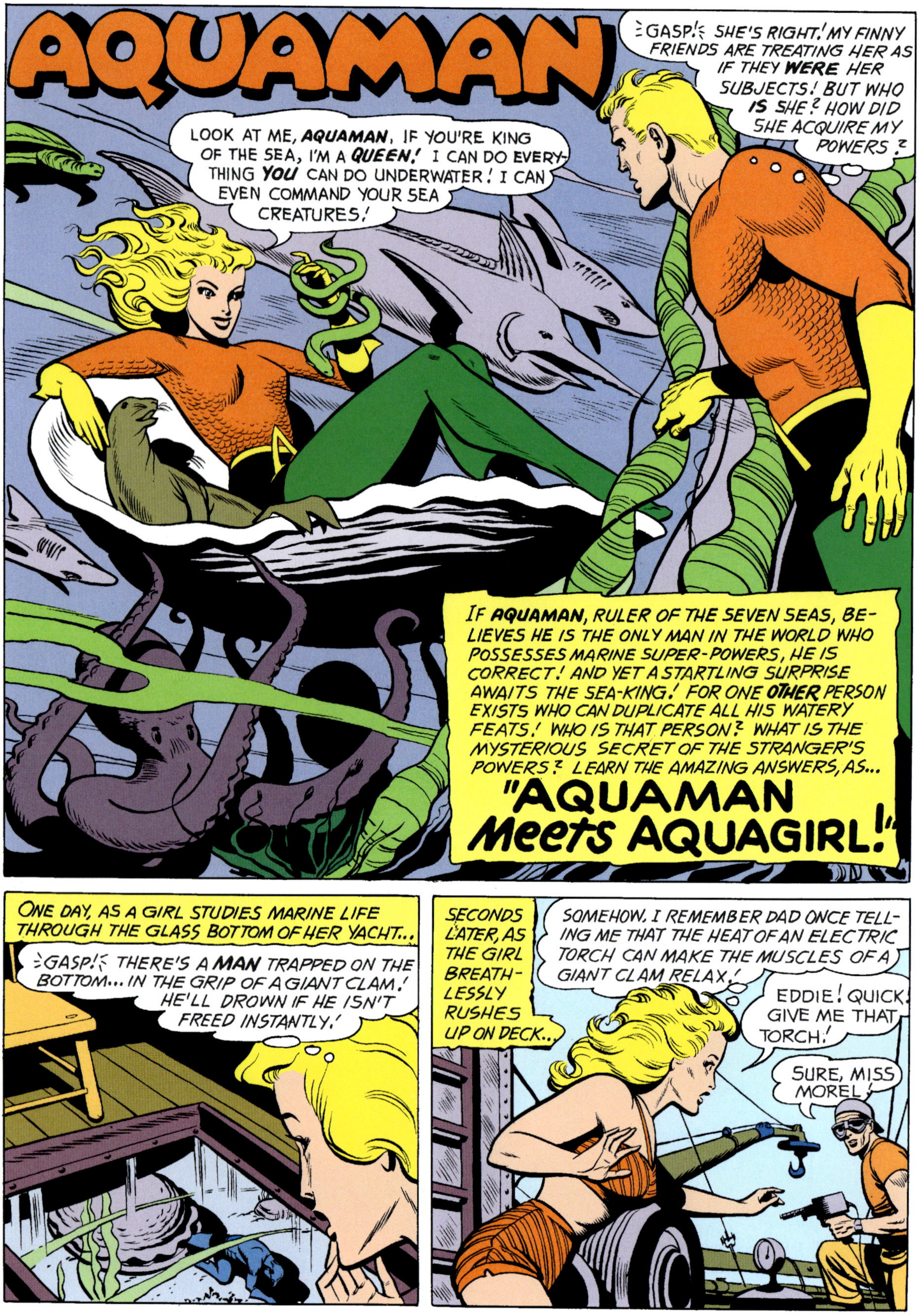
AQUAMAN
LOOK AT ME, AQUAMAN, IF YOU'RE KING OF THE SEA, I'M A QUEEN! I CAN DO EVERYTHING YOU CAN DO UNDERWATER! I CAN EVEN COMMAND YOUR SEA CREATURES!
GASP! SHE'S RIGHT! MY FINNY FRIENDS ARE TREATING HER AS IF THEY WERE HER SUBJECTS! BUT WHO IS SHE? HOW DID SHE ACQUIRE MY POWERS?
IF AQUAMAN, RULER OF THE SEVEN SEAS, BELIEVES HE IS THE ONLY MAN IN THE WORLD WHO POSSESSES MARINE SUPER-POWERS, HE IS CORRECT! AND YET A STARTLING SURPRISE AWAITS THE SEA-KING! FOR ONE OTHER PERSON EXISTS WHO CAN DUPLICATE ALL HIS WATERY FEATS! WHO IS THAT PERSON? WHAT IS THE MYSTERIOUS SECRET OF THE STRANGER'S POWERS? LEARN THE AMAZING ANSWERS, AS...
"AQUAMAN Meets AQUAGIRL!"
ONE DAY, AS A GIRL STUDIES MARINE LIFE THROUGH THE GLASS BOTTOM OF HER YACHT...
GASP! THERE'S A MAN TRAPPED ON THE BOTTOM... IN THE GRIP OF A GIANT CLAM! HE'LL DROWN IF HE ISN'T FREED INSTANTLY!
SECONDS LATER, AS THE GIRL BREATHLESSLY RUSHES UP ON DECK..
SOMEHOW, I REMEMBER DAD ONCE TELLING ME THAT THE HEAT OF AN ELECTRIC TORCH CAN MAKE THE MUSCLES OF A GIANT CLAM RELAX!
EDDIE! QUICK! GIVE ME THAT TORCH!
SURE, MISS MOREL!

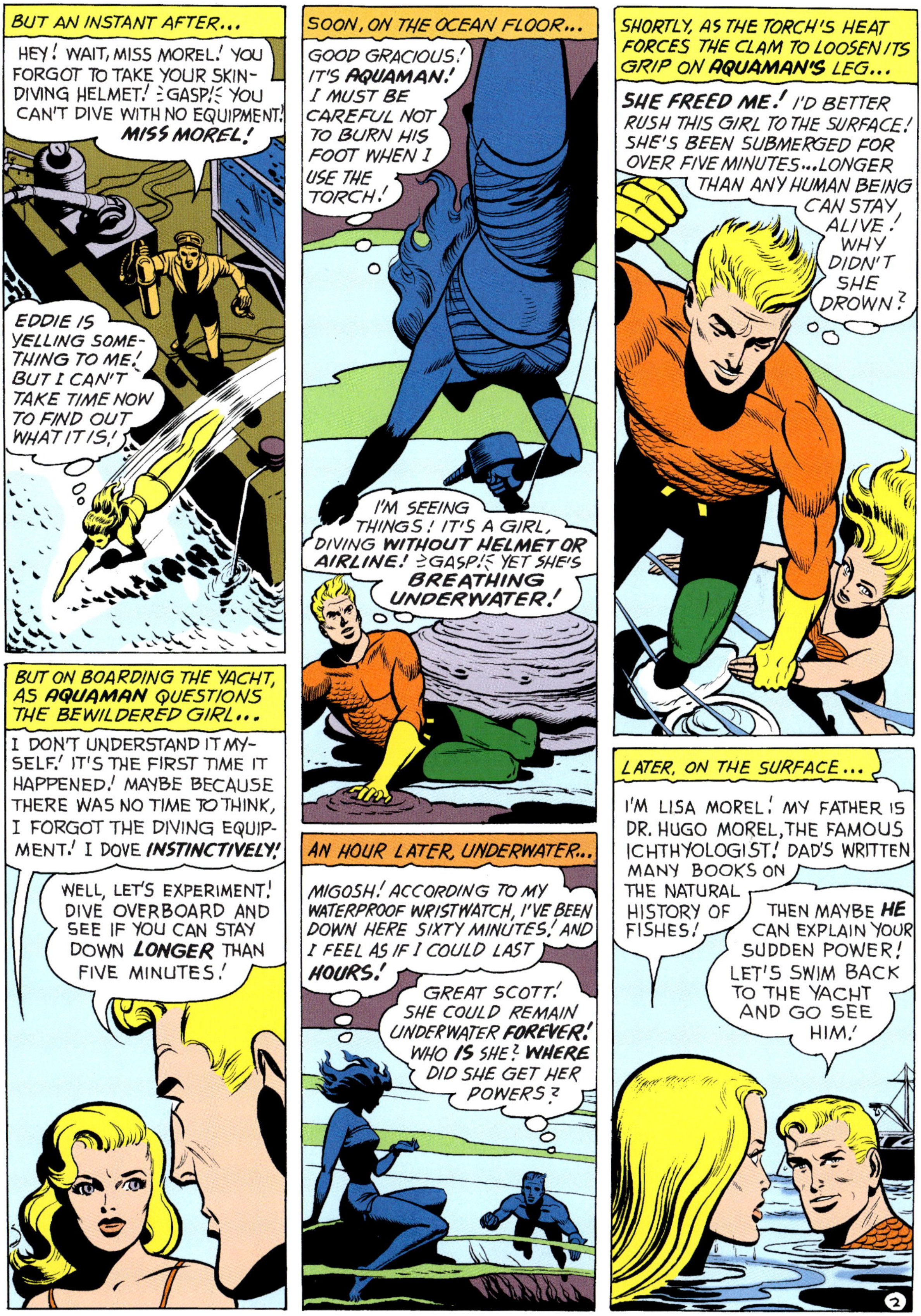
BUT AN INSTANT AFTER...
HEY! WAIT, MISS MOREL! YOU FORGOT TO TAKE YOUR SKIN-DIVING HELMET! ≥GASP!≤ YOU CAN'T DIVE WITH NO EQUIPMENT! MISS MOREL!
EDDIE IS YELLING SOMETHING TO ME! BUT I CAN'T TAKE TIME NOW TO FIND OUT WHAT IT IS!
SOON, ON THE OCEAN FLOOR...
GOOD GRACIOUS! IT'S AQUAMAN! I MUST BE CAREFUL NOT TO BURN HIS FOOT WHEN I USE THE TORCH!
I'M SEEING THINGS! IT'S A GIRL, DIVING WITHOUT HELMET OR AIRLINE! ≥GASP!≤ YET SHE'S BREATHING UNDERWATER!
SHORTLY, AS THE TORCH'S HEAT FORCES THE CLAM TO LOOSEN ITS GRIP ON AQUAMAN'S LEG...
SHE FREED ME! I'D BETTER RUSH THIS GIRL TO THE SURFACE! SHE'S BEEN SUBMERGED FOR OVER FIVE MINUTES...LONGER THAN ANY HUMAN BEING CAN STAY ALIVE! WHY DIDN'T SHE DROWN?
BUT ON BOARDING THE YACHT, AS AQUAMAN QUESTIONS THE BEWILDERED GIRL...
I DON'T UNDERSTAND IT MYSELF! IT'S THE FIRST TIME IT HAPPENED! MAYBE BECAUSE THERE WAS NO TIME TO THINK, I FORGOT THE DIVING EQUIPMENT! I DOVE INSTINCTIVELY!
WELL, LET'S EXPERIMENT! DIVE OVERBOARD AND SEE IF YOU CAN STAY DOWN LONGER THAN FIVE MINUTES!
AN HOUR LATER, UNDERWATER...
MIGOSH! ACCORDING TO MY WATERPROOF WRISTWATCH, I'VE BEEN DOWN HERE SIXTY MINUTES! AND I FEEL AS IF I COULD LAST HOURS!
GREAT SCOTT! SHE COULD REMAIN UNDERWATER FOREVER! WHO IS SHE? WHERE DID SHE GET HER POWERS?
LATER, ON THE SURFACE...
I'M LISA MOREL! MY FATHER IS DR. HUGO MOREL, THE FAMOUS ICHTHYOLOGIST! DAD'S WRITTEN MANY BOOKS ON THE NATURAL HISTORY OF FISHES!
THEN MAYBE HE CAN EXPLAIN YOUR SUDDEN POWER! LET'S SWIM BACK TO THE YACHT AND GO SEE HIM!
2

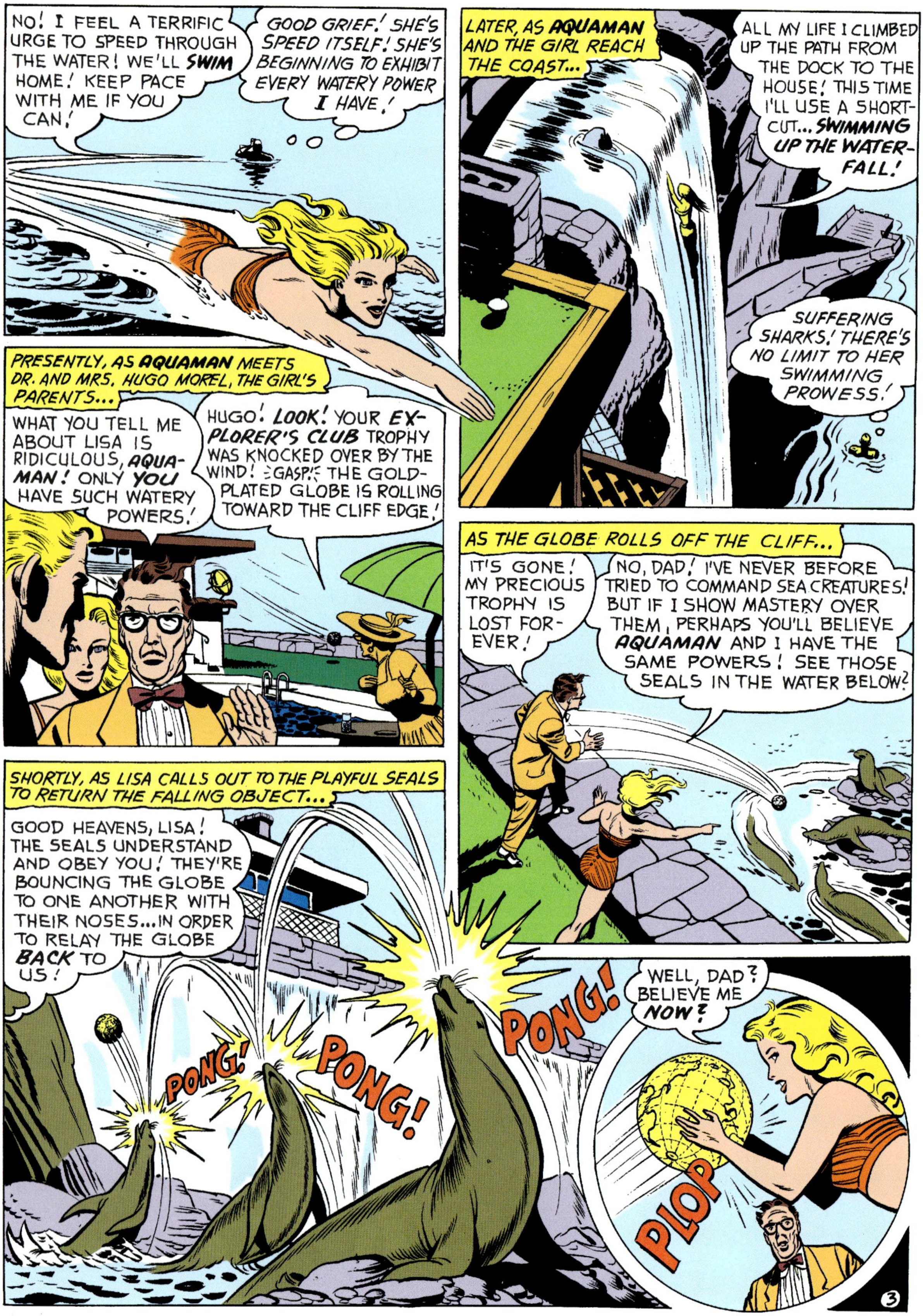

NO! I FEEL A TERRIFIC URGE TO SPEED THROUGH THE WATER! WE'LL SWIM HOME! KEEP PACE WITH ME IF YOU CAN!
GOOD GRIEF! SHE'S SPEED ITSELF! SHE'S BEGINNING TO EXHIBIT EVERY WATERY POWER I HAVE!
LATER, AS AQUAMAN AND THE GIRL REACH THE COAST...
ALL MY LIFE I CLIMBED UP THE PATH FROM THE DOCK TO THE HOUSE! THIS TIME I'LL USE A SHORT-CUT... SWIMMING UP THE WATER-FALL!
SUFFERING SHARKS! THERE'S NO LIMIT TO HER SWIMMING PROWESS!
PRESENTLY, AS AQUAMAN MEETS DR. AND MRS. HUGO MOREL, THE GIRL'S PARENTS...
WHAT YOU TELL ME ABOUT LISA IS RIDICULOUS, AQUA-MAN! ONLY YOU HAVE SUCH WATERY POWERS!
HUGO! LOOK! YOUR EX-PLORER'S CLUB TROPHY WAS KNOCKED OVER BY THE WIND! GASP! THE GOLD-PLATED GLOBE IS ROLLING TOWARD THE CLIFF EDGE!
AS THE GLOBE ROLLS OFF THE CLIFF...
IT'S GONE! MY PRECIOUS TROPHY IS LOST FOR-EVER!
NO, DAD! I'VE NEVER BEFORE TRIED TO COMMAND SEA CREATURES! BUT IF I SHOW MASTERY OVER THEM, PERHAPS YOU'LL BELIEVE AQUAMAN AND I HAVE THE SAME POWERS! SEE THOSE SEALS IN THE WATER BELOW?
SHORTLY, AS LISA CALLS OUT TO THE PLAYFUL SEALS TO RETURN THE FALLING OBJECT...
GOOD HEAVENS, LISA! THE SEALS UNDERSTAND AND OBEY YOU! THEY'RE BOUNCING THE GLOBE TO ONE ANOTHER WITH THEIR NOSES...IN ORDER TO RELAY THE GLOBE BACK TO US!
PONG!
PONG!
PONG!
WELL, DAD? BELIEVE ME NOW?
PLOP
3

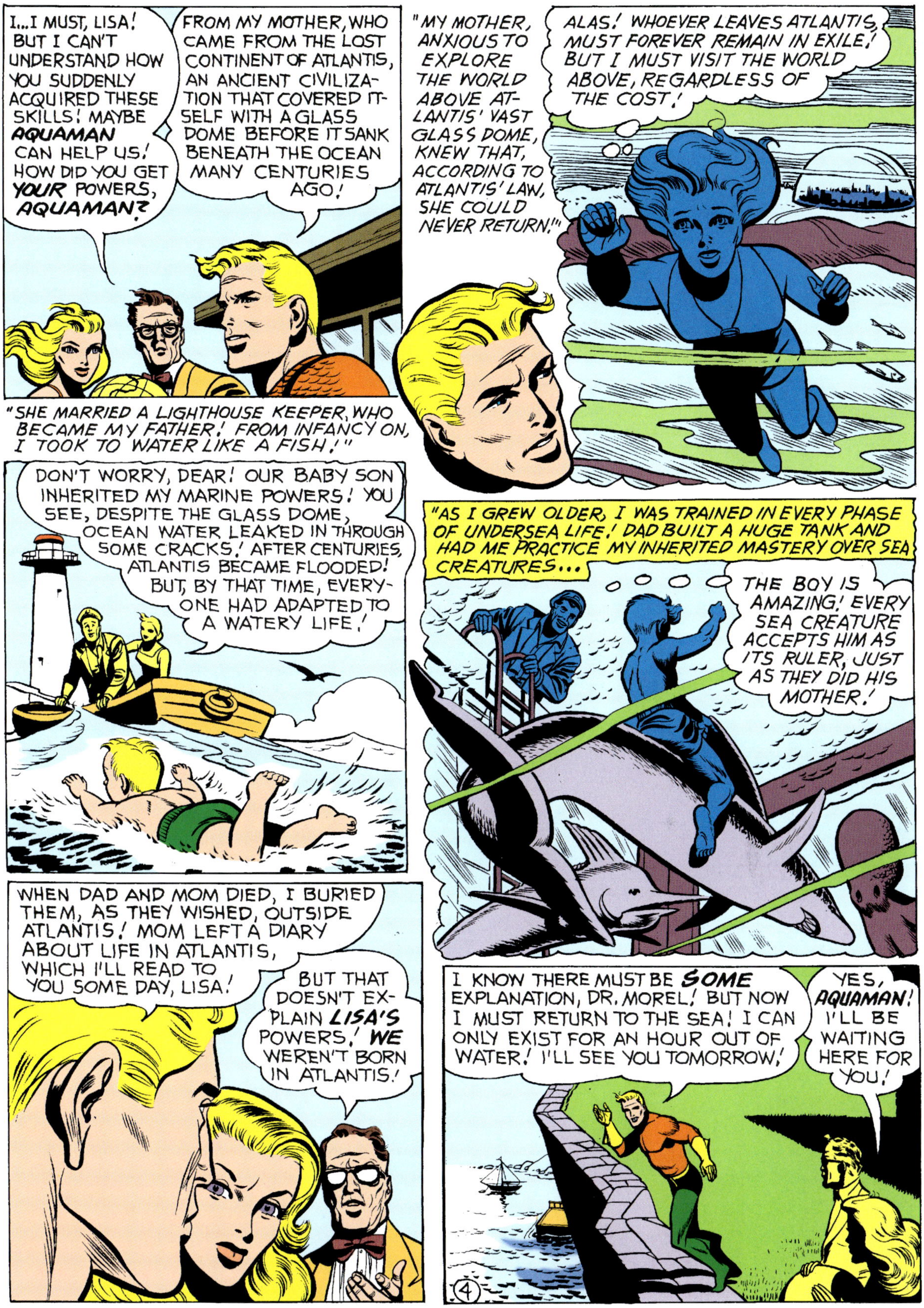

I...I MUST, LISA! BUT I CAN'T UNDERSTAND HOW YOU SUDDENLY ACQUIRED THESE SKILLS! MAYBE AQUAMAN CAN HELP US! HOW DID YOU GET YOUR POWERS, AQUAMAN?
FROM MY MOTHER, WHO CAME FROM THE LOST CONTINENT OF ATLANTIS, AN ANCIENT CIVILIZATION THAT COVERED ITSELF WITH A GLASS DOME BEFORE IT SANK BENEATH THE OCEAN MANY CENTURIES AGO!
"MY MOTHER, ANXIOUS TO EXPLORE THE WORLD ABOVE ATLANTIS' VAST GLASS DOME, KNEW THAT, ACCORDING TO ATLANTIS' LAW, SHE COULD NEVER RETURN!"
ALAS! WHOEVER LEAVES ATLANTIS MUST FOREVER REMAIN IN EXILE! BUT I MUST VISIT THE WORLD ABOVE, REGARDLESS OF THE COST!
"SHE MARRIED A LIGHTHOUSE KEEPER, WHO BECAME MY FATHER! FROM INFANCY ON, I TOOK TO WATER LIKE A FISH!"
DON'T WORRY, DEAR! OUR BABY SON INHERITED MY MARINE POWERS! YOU SEE, DESPITE THE GLASS DOME, OCEAN WATER LEAKED IN THROUGH SOME CRACKS! AFTER CENTURIES, ATLANTIS BECAME FLOODED! BUT, BY THAT TIME, EVERYONE HAD ADAPTED TO A WATERY LIFE!
"AS I GREW OLDER, I WAS TRAINED IN EVERY PHASE OF UNDERSEA LIFE! DAD BUILT A HUGE TANK AND HAD ME PRACTICE MY INHERITED MASTERY OVER SEA CREATURES...
THE BOY IS AMAZING! EVERY SEA CREATURE ACCEPTS HIM AS ITS RULER, JUST AS THEY DID HIS MOTHER!
WHEN DAD AND MOM DIED, I BURIED THEM, AS THEY WISHED, OUTSIDE ATLANTIS! MOM LEFT A DIARY ABOUT LIFE IN ATLANTIS, WHICH I'LL READ TO YOU SOME DAY, LISA!
BUT THAT DOESN'T EXPLAIN LISA'S POWERS! WE WEREN'T BORN IN ATLANTIS!
I KNOW THERE MUST BE SOME EXPLANATION, DR. MOREL! BUT NOW I MUST RETURN TO THE SEA! I CAN ONLY EXIST FOR AN HOUR OUT OF WATER! I'LL SEE YOU TOMORROW!
YES, AQUAMAN! I'LL BE WAITING HERE FOR YOU!
4

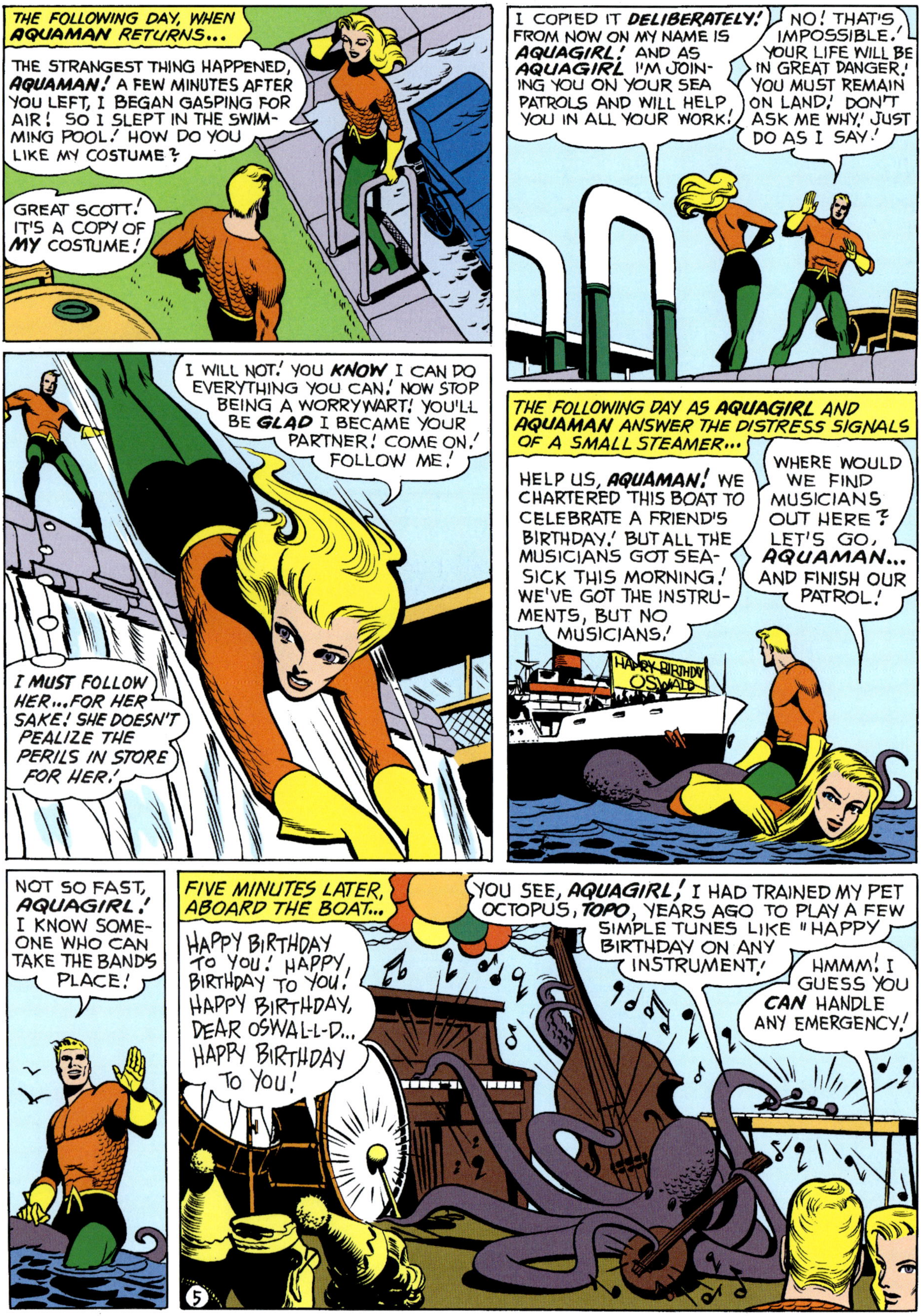

THE FOLLOWING DAY, WHEN AQUAMAN RETURNS...
THE STRANGEST THING HAPPENED, AQUAMAN! A FEW MINUTES AFTER YOU LEFT, I BEGAN GASPING FOR AIR! SO I SLEPT IN THE SWIMMING POOL! HOW DO YOU LIKE MY COSTUME?
GREAT SCOTT! IT'S A COPY OF MY COSTUME!
I COPIED IT DELIBERATELY! FROM NOW ON MY NAME IS AQUAGIRL! AND AS AQUAGIRL I'M JOINING YOU ON YOUR SEA PATROLS AND WILL HELP YOU IN ALL YOUR WORK!
NO! THAT'S IMPOSSIBLE! YOUR LIFE WILL BE IN GREAT DANGER! YOU MUST REMAIN ON LAND! DON'T ASK ME WHY! JUST DO AS I SAY!
I WILL NOT! YOU KNOW I CAN DO EVERYTHING YOU CAN! NOW STOP BEING A WORRYWART! YOU'LL BE GLAD I BECAME YOUR PARTNER! COME ON! FOLLOW ME!
I MUST FOLLOW HER...FOR HER SAKE! SHE DOESN'T PEALIZE THE PERILS IN STORE FOR HER!
THE FOLLOWING DAY AS AQUAGIRL AND AQUAMAN ANSWER THE DISTRESS SIGNALS OF A SMALL STEAMER...
HELP US, AQUAMAN! WE CHARTERED THIS BOAT TO CELEBRATE A FRIEND'S BIRTHDAY! BUT ALL THE MUSICIANS GOT SEA-SICK THIS MORNING! WE'VE GOT THE INSTRUMENTS, BUT NO MUSICIANS!
WHERE WOULD WE FIND MUSICIANS OUT HERE? LET'S GO, AQUAMAN... AND FINISH OUR PATROL!
HAPPY BIRTHDAY OSWALD
NOT SO FAST, AQUAGIRL! I KNOW SOMEONE WHO CAN TAKE THE BAND'S PLACE!
FIVE MINUTES LATER, ABOARD THE BOAT...
HAPPY BIRTHDAY TO YOU! HAPPY BIRTHDAY TO YOU! HAPPY BIRTHDAY, DEAR OSWAL-L-D... HAPPY BIRTHDAY TO YOU!
YOU SEE, AQUAGIRL, I HAD TRAINED MY PET OCTOPUS, TOPO, YEARS AGO TO PLAY A FEW SIMPLE TUNES LIKE "HAPPY BIRTHDAY ON ANY INSTRUMENT!
HMMM! I GUESS YOU CAN HANDLE ANY EMERGENCY!
5

THE NEXT EVENING, AS AQUAMAN SPOTS AN ICEBERG...
THIS BERG HAS FLOATED INTO A BUSY SHIPPING LANE! IT'S A MENACE! WHAT WOULD YOU DO ABOUT IT, AQUAGIRL, IF YOU WERE ALONE ON SEA PATROL?
TRYING TO TEST ME, EH? OKAY! WATCH!
PRESENTLY, AS AQUAGIRL RETURNS WITH SEVERAL WHALES...
THERE! NO MORE ICEBERG!
CRASHH! CRRACKK!
YOU FORGET THAT MOST OF ANY ICEBERG LIES BENEATH THE WAVES! THIS ONE IS TOO HUGE AND HEAVY TO BE MOVED BY WHALES! AND A SHIP'S COMING!
AS AQUAMAN SWIMS RAPIDLY TO THE FREIGHTER'S SIDE...
IT'S NO GOOD SHOUTING A WARNING! THE SHIP'S ENGINE THRUMS SO LOUDLY, THE SAILORS COULD NEVER HEAR ME! I MUST WARN THE VESSEL IN SOME OTHER WAY! HMM... I'VE GOT AN IDEA!
PUMM! PUMM! PUMM!
AS AQUAMAN HASTILY SUMMONS HUNDREDS OF LUMINOUS FISH AND ARRANGES THEM AROUND THE ICEBERG...
LOOK! IT'S AQUAMAN! HE GOT HIS LUMINOUS FISH TO LIGHT UP A SUNKEN ICEBERG! TURN HARD LEFT! WE CAN JUST MANAGE TO AVOID A COLLISION!
THE NEXT DAY, AS AQUAGIRL EXPLORES AN UNDERSEA GROTTO TO COLLECT RARE SHELLS FOR HER FATHER...
I FEARED THIS WOULD HAPPEN! I MUST BRING HER TO THE SURFACE... BUT FAST!
GOOD GRIEF! GASP! SUDDENLY I...I CAN'T BREATHE! I CAN'T SWIM! I FEEL A CRUSHING WEIGHT ON ME! THE PRESSURE OF TONS OF WATER!
SOON AFTER AQUAMAN CARRIES THE GASPING GIRL INTO THE AIR...
WHAT HAPPENED? I FELT AS IF I WOULD DROWN DOWN THERE!
YES, LISA! I EXPECTED IT! THAT'S WHY I WARNED YOU AGAINST PATROLLING WITH ME! YOU SEE, YOU'VE LOST YOUR UNDERWATER POWERS!
6

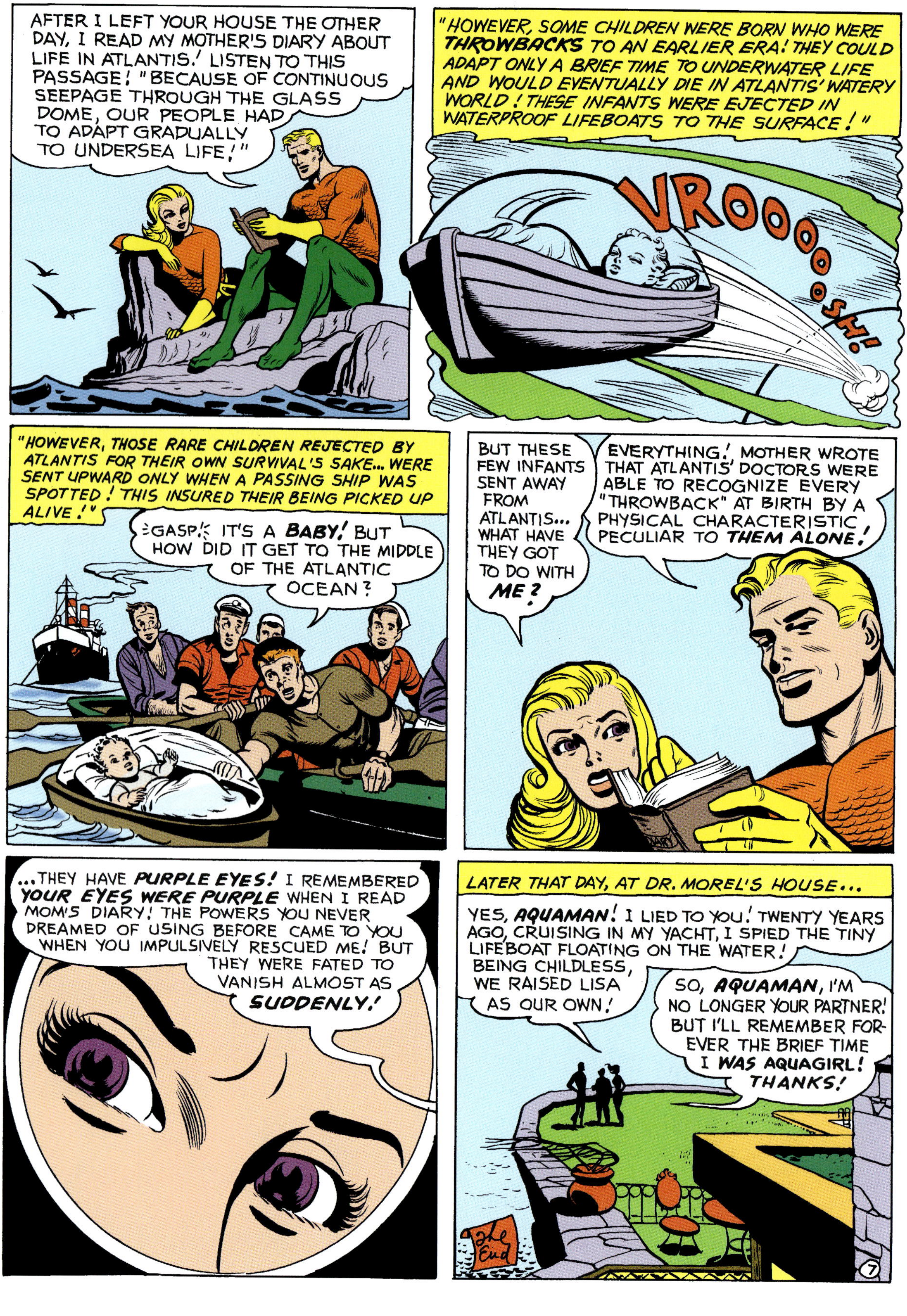
AFTER I LEFT YOUR HOUSE THE OTHER DAY, I READ MY MOTHER'S DIARY ABOUT LIFE IN ATLANTIS! LISTEN TO THIS PASSAGE! "BECAUSE OF CONTINUOUS SEEPAGE THROUGH THE GLASS DOME, OUR PEOPLE HAD TO ADAPT GRADUALLY TO UNDERSEA LIFE!"
"HOWEVER, SOME CHILDREN WERE BORN WHO WERE THROWBACKS TO AN EARLIER ERA! THEY COULD ADAPT ONLY A BRIEF TIME TO UNDERWATER LIFE AND WOULD EVENTUALLY DIE IN ATLANTIS' WATERY WORLD! THESE INFANTS WERE EJECTED IN WATERPROOF LIFEBOATS TO THE SURFACE!"
VROOOOOOSH!
"HOWEVER, THOSE RARE CHILDREN REJECTED BY ATLANTIS FOR THEIR OWN SURVIVAL'S SAKE... WERE SENT UPWARD ONLY WHEN A PASSING SHIP WAS SPOTTED! THIS INSURED THEIR BEING PICKED UP ALIVE!"
GASP! IT'S A BABY! BUT HOW DID IT GET TO THE MIDDLE OF THE ATLANTIC OCEAN?
BUT THESE FEW INFANTS SENT AWAY FROM ATLANTIS... WHAT HAVE THEY GOT TO DO WITH ME?
EVERYTHING! MOTHER WROTE THAT ATLANTIS' DOCTORS WERE ABLE TO RECOGNIZE EVERY "THROWBACK" AT BIRTH BY A PHYSICAL CHARACTERISTIC PECULIAR TO THEM ALONE!
...THEY HAVE PURPLE EYES! I REMEMBERED YOUR EYES WERE PURPLE WHEN I READ MOM'S DIARY! THE POWERS YOU NEVER DREAMED OF USING BEFORE CAME TO YOU WHEN YOU IMPULSIVELY RESCUED ME! BUT THEY WERE FATED TO VANISH ALMOST AS SUDDENLY!
LATER THAT DAY, AT DR. MOREL'S HOUSE...
YES, AQUAMAN! I LIED TO YOU! TWENTY YEARS AGO, CRUISING IN MY YACHT, I SPIED THE TINY LIFEBOAT FLOATING ON THE WATER! BEING CHILDLESS, WE RAISED LISA AS OUR OWN!
SO, AQUAMAN, I'M NO LONGER YOUR PARTNER! BUT I'LL REMEMBER FOREVER THE BRIEF TIME I WAS AQUAGIRL! THANKS!
The End
7

AQUAMAN
SOME PEOPLE ON EARTH HAVE A FEAR OF WATER (HYDROPHOBIA) OR A FEAR OF CROWDS (AGORAPHOBIA) OR A FEAR OF NARROW PLACES (CLAUSTROPHOBIA!) BUT ONE DAY AQUAMAN MEETS A TERRIFIED YOUTH FROM THE STRANGE WORLD OF ATLANTIS WHO HAS AN INCURABLE FEAR OF FISH... A PHOBIA FOR WHICH OUR WORLD HAS NO NAME! BUT WHATEVER THIS NAMELESS DREAD IS, THE KING OF THE SEA KNOWS THAT FINDING A CURE FOR THIS PHOBIA IS A MATTER OF LIFE AND DEATH TO... The KID FROM ATLANTIS!
GASP! W-WHY DOESN'T AQUAMAN SEND THE FISH AWAY? HE KNOWS I'M DEATHLY AFRAID OF FISH! I-IF THEY COME ANY CLOSER, I'LL FAINT!
HMMM...EVEN THE SMALLEST, MOST HARMLESS FISH TERRIFY THE POOR LAD! I MUST MAKE HIM OVERCOME HIS FEAR BEFORE HE DIES OF SHEER TERROR!
ONE DAY, AS AQUAMAN'S SEA PATROL HASTILY SUMMONS HIM...
GASP! THEY FOUND A SEALED CAPSULE WITH A YOUNG BOY INSIDE! WHERE ON EARTH COULD IT HAVE COME FROM?
BUT AS AQUAMAN OPENS THE STRANGE CAPSULE...
HE'S STILL DAZED FROM HIS CONFINEMENT IN THE CAPSULE! BUT THE FRESH AIR WILL SOON REVIVE HIM!
OHHHH...

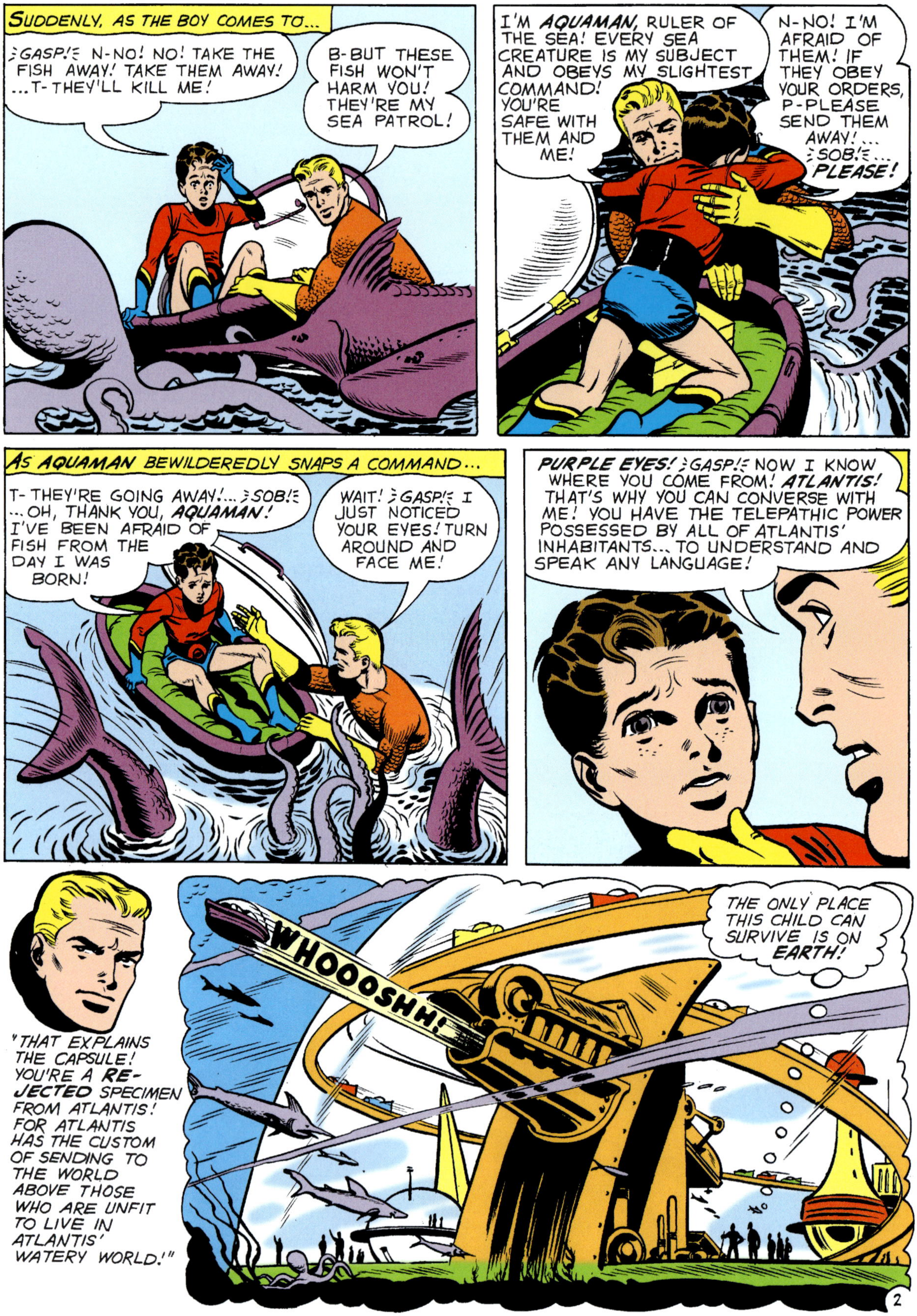
SUDDENLY, AS THE BOY COMES TO...
:GASP!: N-NO! NO! TAKE THE FISH AWAY! TAKE THEM AWAY! ...T-THEY'LL KILL ME!
B-BUT THESE FISH WON'T HARM YOU! THEY'RE MY SEA PATROL!
I'M AQUAMAN, RULER OF THE SEA! EVERY SEA CREATURE IS MY SUBJECT AND OBEYS MY SLIGHTEST COMMAND! YOU'RE SAFE WITH THEM AND ME!
N-NO! I'M AFRAID OF THEM! IF THEY OBEY YOUR ORDERS, P-PLEASE SEND THEM AWAY!... :SOB:... PLEASE!
AS AQUAMAN BEWILDEREDLY SNAPS A COMMAND...
T-THEY'RE GOING AWAY!... :SOB!: ...OH, THANK YOU, AQUAMAN! I'VE BEEN AFRAID OF FISH FROM THE DAY I WAS BORN!
WAIT! :GASP!: I JUST NOTICED YOUR EYES! TURN AROUND AND FACE ME!
PURPLE EYES! :GASP!: NOW I KNOW WHERE YOU COME FROM! ATLANTIS! THAT'S WHY YOU CAN CONVERSE WITH ME! YOU HAVE THE TELEPATHIC POWER POSSESSED BY ALL OF ATLANTIS' INHABITANTS... TO UNDERSTAND AND SPEAK ANY LANGUAGE!
"THAT EXPLAINS THE CAPSULE! YOU'RE A REJECTED SPECIMEN FROM ATLANTIS! FOR ATLANTIS HAS THE CUSTOM OF SENDING TO THE WORLD ABOVE THOSE WHO ARE UNFIT TO LIVE IN ATLANTIS' WATERY WORLD!"
WHOOOOSHH!
THE ONLY PLACE THIS CHILD CAN SURVIVE IS ON EARTH!
2

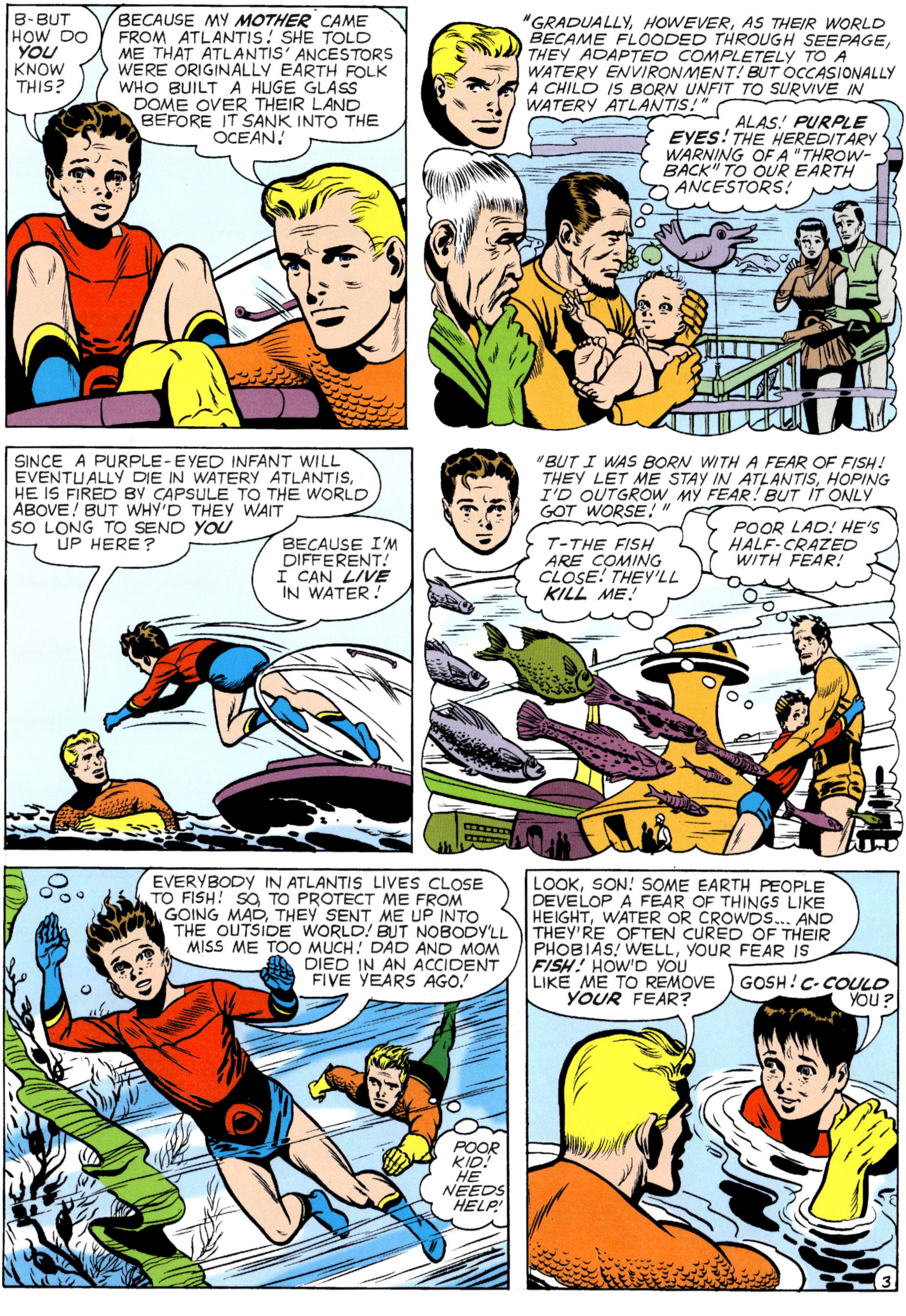
B-BUT HOW DO YOU KNOW THIS?
BECAUSE MY MOTHER CAME FROM ATLANTIS! SHE TOLD ME THAT ATLANTIS' ANCESTORS WERE ORIGINALLY EARTH FOLK WHO BUILT A HUGE GLASS DOME OVER THEIR LAND BEFORE IT SANK INTO THE OCEAN!
"GRADUALLY, HOWEVER, AS THEIR WORLD BECAME FLOODED THROUGH SEEPAGE, THEY ADAPTED COMPLETELY TO A WATERY ENVIRONMENT! BUT OCCASIONALLY A CHILD IS BORN UNFIT TO SURVIVE IN WATERY ATLANTIS!"
ALAS! PURPLE EYES! THE HEREDITARY WARNING OF A "THROW-BACK" TO OUR EARTH ANCESTORS!
SINCE A PURPLE-EYED INFANT WILL EVENTUALLY DIE IN WATERY ATLANTIS, HE IS FIRED BY CAPSULE TO THE WORLD ABOVE! BUT WHY'D THEY WAIT SO LONG TO SEND YOU UP HERE?
BECAUSE I'M DIFFERENT! I CAN LIVE IN WATER!
"BUT I WAS BORN WITH A FEAR OF FISH! THEY LET ME STAY IN ATLANTIS, HOPING I'D OUTGROW MY FEAR! BUT IT ONLY GOT WORSE!"
T-THE FISH ARE COMING CLOSE! THEY'LL KILL ME!
POOR LAD! HE'S HALF-CRAZED WITH FEAR!
EVERYBODY IN ATLANTIS LIVES CLOSE TO FISH! SO, TO PROTECT ME FROM GOING MAD, THEY SENT ME UP INTO THE OUTSIDE WORLD! BUT NOBODY'LL MISS ME TOO MUCH! DAD AND MOM DIED IN AN ACCIDENT FIVE YEARS AGO!
POOR KID! HE NEEDS HELP!
LOOK, SON! SOME EARTH PEOPLE DEVELOP A FEAR OF THINGS LIKE HEIGHT, WATER OR CROWDS... AND THEY'RE OFTEN CURED OF THEIR PHOBIAS! WELL, YOUR FEAR IS FISH! HOW'D YOU LIKE ME TO REMOVE YOUR FEAR?
GOSH! C-COULD YOU?
3

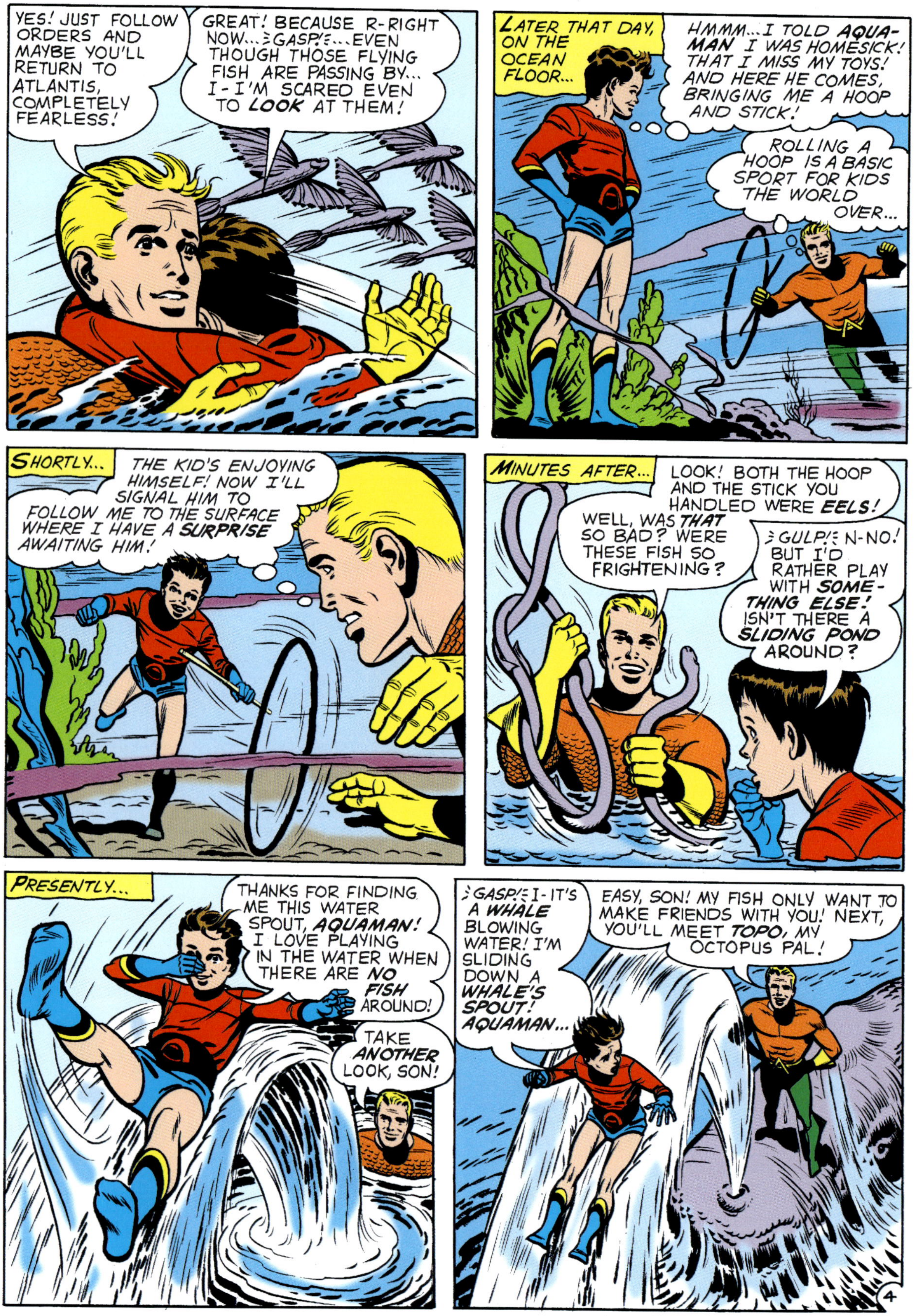
YES! JUST FOLLOW ORDERS AND MAYBE YOU'LL RETURN TO ATLANTIS, COMPLETELY FEARLESS!
GREAT! BECAUSE R-RIGHT NOW... GASP! ...EVEN THOUGH THOSE FLYING FISH ARE PASSING BY... I-I'M SCARED EVEN TO LOOK AT THEM!
LATER THAT DAY, ON THE OCEAN FLOOR...
HMMM... I TOLD AQUAMAN I WAS HOMESICK! THAT I MISS MY TOYS! AND HERE HE COMES, BRINGING ME A HOOP AND STICK!
ROLLING A HOOP IS A BASIC SPORT FOR KIDS THE WORLD OVER...
SHORTLY...
THE KID'S ENJOYING HIMSELF! NOW I'LL SIGNAL HIM TO FOLLOW ME TO THE SURFACE WHERE I HAVE A SURPRISE AWAITING HIM!
MINUTES AFTER...
LOOK! BOTH THE HOOP AND THE STICK YOU HANDLED WERE EELS!
WELL, WAS THAT SO BAD? WERE THESE FISH SO FRIGHTENING?
GULP! N-NO! BUT I'D RATHER PLAY WITH SOMETHING ELSE! ISN'T THERE A SLIDING POND AROUND?
PRESENTLY...
THANKS FOR FINDING ME THIS WATER SPOUT, AQUAMAN! I LOVE PLAYING IN THE WATER WHEN THERE ARE NO FISH AROUND!
TAKE ANOTHER LOOK, SON!
GASP! I-IT'S A WHALE BLOWING WATER! I'M SLIDING DOWN A WHALE'S SPOUT! AQUAMAN...
EASY, SON! MY FISH ONLY WANT TO MAKE FRIENDS WITH YOU! NEXT, YOU'LL MEET TOPO, MY OCTOPUS PAL!
4

SOON AFTER...
GOSH, TOPO MAKES A SWELL--WHAT IS IT YOU CALL IT--A MERRY-GO-ROUND! I'M NOT AFRAID OF FISH...ER...AS LONG AS YOU'RE NEAR ME, AQUAMAN!
WELL, AS IT HAPPENS, SON, I MUST GO OUT NOW ON PATROL! YOU'LL BE SAFE HERE WITH TOPO!
OH, NO, YOU DON'T, AQUAMAN! WHEREVER YOU GO, I GO! I'M COMING ALONG!
OKAY! MAYBE YOU'LL SEE HOW VALUABLE SEA CREATURES ARE TO PEOPLE! THEN YOU WON'T BE SO AFRAID OF CREATURES WHO ARE YOUR FRIENDS, NOT YOUR ENEMIES!
PRESENTLY, AS AQUAMAN DISCOVERS A SAIL-BOAT IN DISTRESS...
OUR SAIL WAS RIPPED TO SHREDS IN A GALE! WE NEED A NEW SAIL TO MAKE PORT, AQUAMAN!
A NEW SAIL, EH? I'LL HAVE ONE FOR YOU IN A FEW MINUTES!
AS AQUAMAN ORDERS A HUGE MANTA RAY TO FASTEN ITSELF TO THE SAILBOAT'S MAST...
THE MANTA RAY'S BODY IS THIN AND FLEXIBLE ENOUGH TO CATCH THE WIND! BUT THE SECOND YOU REACH LAND, RELEASE HIM!
OF COURSE! YOUR FINNY FRIENDS ARE OUR FRIENDS, AQUAMAN!
GOSH, AQUAMAN! I DON'T KNOW WHAT I WAS AFRAID OF! I WAS SO WRONG ABOUT FISH! FISH DON'T WANT TO HURT ANYBODY!
YOU HAVEN'T SEEN ANYTHING YET, SON! LET'S CONTINUE OUR PATROL!
AT SUNDOWN, THAT DAY...
WE'RE AFRAID TO PROCEED, AQUAMAN! OUR PILOT WAS KNOCKED UNCONSCIOUS IN A DECK ACCIDENT...AND THE ROUTE AHEAD IS FULL OF JAGGED REEFS! WITHOUT A PILOT, WE'RE SUNK!
ISABELLE
I'LL GET A HUNDRED PILOTS FOR YOU!
5

PRESENTLY, AS AQUAMAN SUMMONS HIS PILOT FISH FRIENDS...
NORMALLY, PILOT FISH ACT AS THE GUIDES AND PROTECTORS OF SHARKS, WARNING THEM OF DANGER! THIS TIME, THE PILOT FISH WILL GUIDE A FREIGHTER TO SAFETY!
I-IT'S AMAZING WHAT A HELP FISH CAN BE!
BUT THAT NIGHT...
LOOK, SON! A PLANE IS BLINKING A DISTRESS SIGNAL! IT MUST MAKE AN EMERGENCY LANDING BUT CAN'T SEE IN THE DARK! EVERY INHABITANT OF ATLANTIS HAS THE TELEPATHIC POWER TO COMMAND FISH! SO YOU GO TO WORK!
M-ME?
AS THE YOUNG EXILE FROM ATLANTIS UNEASILY ISSUES ORDERS TO SOME OF AQUAMAN'S SEA CREATURES...
YOU DID IT, SON! YOU FEARLESSLY APPROACHED A SCHOOL OF LUMINOUS FISH AND MADE THEM LIGHT UP THE OCEAN LIKE A LANDING FIELD! YOU'VE CONQUERED YOUR FEAR OF FISH! NOW YOU CAN GO BACK TO ATLANTIS!
B-BUT I DON'T WANT TO GO BACK!
I'VE NOBODY TO RETURN TO! YOU'RE LIKE A FATHER TO ME! I WANT TO STAY HERE AND HELP YOU!
IMPOSSIBLE! I CAN'T PROVIDE A HOME FOR YOU! YOUR HOME IS ATLANTIS! YOU'LL RE-ENTER ATLANTIS BY THE SAME LOCK THROUGH WHICH YOUR CAPSULE WAS FIRED! NOW LET'S GO!
MANY HOURS LATER, OUTSIDE ATLANTIS...
POOR KID! HOW SLOWLY HE'S SWIMMING TO THE LOCK, LOOKING BACK, HOPING I'LL CHANGE MY MIND! BUT I CAN'T! I MUST DO WHAT'S BEST FOR HIM! I CAN'T OFFER HIM MUCH OF A LIFE, AWAY FROM HIS WORLD!
6

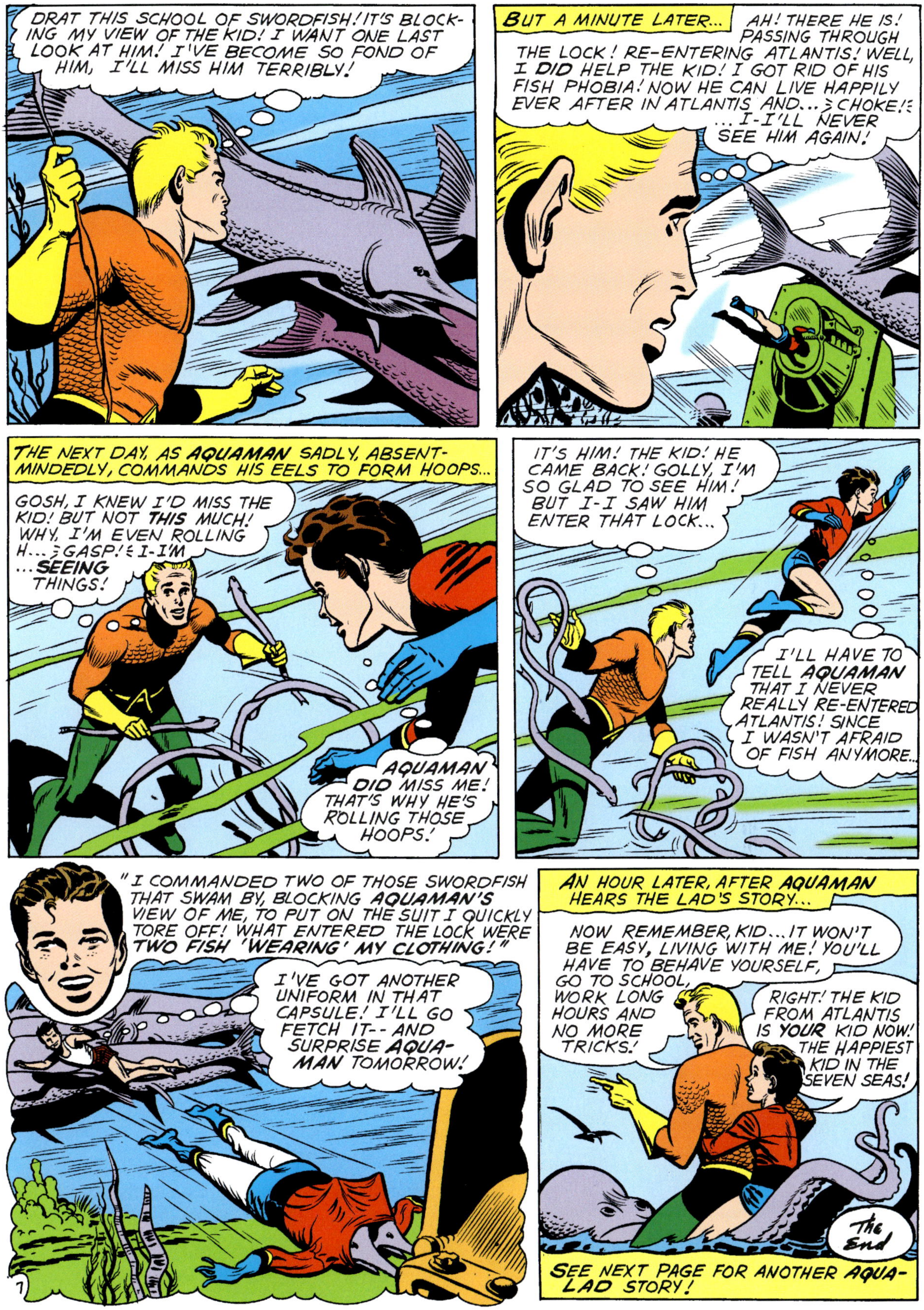
DRAT THIS SCHOOL OF SWORDFISH! IT'S BLOCKING MY VIEW OF THE KID! I WANT ONE LAST LOOK AT HIM! I'VE BECOME SO FOND OF HIM, I'LL MISS HIM TERRIBLY!
BUT A MINUTE LATER...
AH! THERE HE IS! PASSING THROUGH THE LOCK! RE-ENTERING ATLANTIS! WELL, I DID HELP THE KID! I GOT RID OF HIS FISH PHOBIA! NOW HE CAN LIVE HAPPILY EVER AFTER IN ATLANTIS AND... CHOKE! ... I-I'LL NEVER SEE HIM AGAIN!
THE NEXT DAY, AS AQUAMAN SADLY, ABSENT-MINDEDLY, COMMANDS HIS EELS TO FORM HOOPS...
GOSH, I KNEW I'D MISS THE KID! BUT NOT THIS MUCH! WHY, I'M EVEN ROLLING H... GASP! I-I'M ...SEEING THINGS!
AQUAMAN DID MISS ME! THAT'S WHY HE'S ROLLING THOSE HOOPS!
IT'S HIM! THE KID! HE CAME BACK! GOLLY, I'M SO GLAD TO SEE HIM! BUT I-I SAW HIM ENTER THAT LOCK...
I'LL HAVE TO TELL AQUAMAN THAT I NEVER REALLY RE-ENTERED ATLANTIS! SINCE I WASN'T AFRAID OF FISH ANYMORE...
"I COMMANDED TWO OF THOSE SWORDFISH THAT SWAM BY, BLOCKING AQUAMAN'S VIEW OF ME, TO PUT ON THE SUIT I QUICKLY TORE OFF! WHAT ENTERED THE LOCK WERE TWO FISH 'WEARING' MY CLOTHING!"
I'VE GOT ANOTHER UNIFORM IN THAT CAPSULE! I'LL GO FETCH IT-- AND SURPRISE AQUAMAN TOMORROW!
7
AN HOUR LATER, AFTER AQUAMAN HEARS THE LAD'S STORY...
NOW REMEMBER, KID... IT WON'T BE EASY, LIVING WITH ME! YOU'LL HAVE TO BEHAVE YOURSELF, GO TO SCHOOL, WORK LONG HOURS AND NO MORE TRICKS!
RIGHT! THE KID FROM ATLANTIS IS YOUR KID NOW! THE HAPPIEST KID IN THE SEVEN SEAS!
The End
SEE NEXT PAGE FOR ANOTHER AQUALAD STORY!

AQUAMAN
GENESIS
AQUAMAN
AQUAMAN
JUSTICE LEAGUE OF AMERICA

KING of ATLANTIS

by **PAUL KUPPERBERG**

Aquaman swam into the 1960s like a minnow but finished the decade like a sea lion.

Just the fact that he was one of only *five* superheroes in the entire comics industry (along with Superman, Batman, Wonder Woman, and Green Arrow) to survive being continuously published from the 1940s and into the 1960s while the rest of the four-color world gave way to funny animals, Westerns, romance, and other genres proved Aquaman was no superhero slouch.

And he came into his third decade in a pretty good place. He graduated from backup feature to his own title in 1962 after a successful four-issue tryout in *Showcase*. He was also a founding member of the Justice League of America; the first superhero to get married in comics (*Aquaman* #18, December 1964), Arthur and Mera (whose first appearance follows) beating out the Richards' over at Marvel by almost a year; and it was the Sea King who was selected to co-star on the 1967-1968 CBS Saturday morning Filmation animated show, *The Superman/Aquaman Hour of Adventure*.

WESTON
P
W

For most of the 1960s, comics were still being written and drawn for an audience of eight- to 12-year-olds, stories full of action and adventure but no real consequences. Aquaman was no exception: during a time when Superman fought crooks in suits; Batman tangled with aliens; and Wonder Woman contended with dragons, genies, and Mer-Boys; the Sea King was swimming up against fire-trolls, aliens, evil sorcerers, a lot of monsters and sea creatures, the imminent destruction of Atlantis and/or some foe's attempt to usurp his throne, and a surprising number of Aquaman, Aqualad, and Mera duplicates. Also, I suppose because Superman had Mr. Mxyzptlk and Batman had Bat-Mite, Aquaman was given Quisp, a magical water sprite who alternately aided or hindered the heroes. He even died in "The Death of Aquaman" in #30 (November/December 1966), a tearjerker of a tale guest-starring his JLA colleagues as mourners and pallbearers. (Spoiler: It was really an Aquaman duplicate that got killed.)

Fortunately, no matter how wacky and silly the situations writers Jack Miller and Bob Haney dreamt up, artist Nick Cardy had it covered. Nick was already a veteran artist when he drew his first Aquaman story in 1961. Born Nicholas Viscardi in 1913, he was already working as a professional artist while attending the Art Student League of New York. He entered comics in 1940, hired by the art packaging studio of Will Eisner and Jerry Eiger, and in 1941, the 21-year-old artist was assigned to draw the adventures of Lady Luck, a backup strip in Eisner's groundbreaking *Spirit Sunday Section*.

Following a stint in the army during World War II (where Nick won two Purple Hearts for

AQUAMAN
BATMAN
AQUAMAN
AQUAMAN
AQUAMAN
IS THIS MY FOE?
AQUAMAN
JABBER

wounds received driving tanks in the 66th Infantry Cavalry Division), he went into advertising and magazine art. In 1950, he was hired as the artist on Burne Hogarth's *Tarzan* daily strip. That same year he started working for DC Comics on such features as *Gang Busters* (based on a radio program) and *Tomahawk*, the adventures of a Revolutionary War resistance fighter.

Cardy's smooth, flowing style was a perfect fit for Aquaman's undersea world, and the man could draw anything, from absurd little Quisp to magnificent underwater seascapes. He was especially adept at capturing facial expressions, bringing an extra bit of warmth to his characters. By the late 1960s and into the 1970s, Nick was DC's main cover artist, contributing over 400 covers by his own count, along with such assignments as the comedy Western series *Bat Lash* and the *Teen Titans*.

Cardy manned the artistic helm for six years and 39 issues of *Aquaman*, guiding the Sea King from those early 1960s kids adventure stories right up to the cusp of the age of "relevance." During his tenure, Aquaman married, became a father, first encountered his two greatest foes—half brother Orm, also known as Ocean Master (*Aquaman* #29, September 1966), and Black Manta (whose debut followed)—and began to assemble the pieces of what would become the Aquaman family legacy. I would later script solo backup features in *Aquaman* and *Adventure Comics* that touched on both Mera's and Aqualad's histories that grew out of the conversation between the two outcast characters on panel five of page six of *Aquaman* #11.

Taking over from Cardy (and writer Bob Haney) in 1968 were artist Jim Aparo and writer Steve Skeates. Over the next three years, they infused a new depth and intensity to Aquaman and crew, adding a third dimension to the characters that had been missing from those earlier adventures. Aquaman turned inward, a troubled, brooding monarch with the weight of the Seven Seas on his shoulders, and Mera was established as something infinitely more than an underwater damsel in distress needing rescue by her man, as she proved in "The Explanation," which follows. *Aquaman* was canceled after #56 but returned for a brief seven-issue run half a dozen years later with Aparo back on the art and David Michelinie as writer; I stepped in to write the last two issues with the title's third and final artist, Don Newton, including winding up the controversial death of Aquababy storyline.

The '60s and '70s were tough times for Aquaman to be sure, his adolescence and young adult phase following the innocent, kid-friendly stories of the previous decades. But like the rest of the superhero world, Aquaman was finally growing up and becoming a more mature and well-rounded character.

***Paul Kupperberg** is a former DC Comics editor and one-time writer of* Aquaman, *as well as scores of other heroes of the DCU, including Superman, Supergirl, and Peacemaker. He is also the author of* Paul Kupperberg's Illustrated Guide to Writing Comics *(Charlton Neo Press) and the comic book-industry-based mystery novel,* The Same Old Story *(Crazy 8 Press).*

SUPERMAN
DC
NATIONAL COMICS
12¢
OCT.
NO. 11
APPROVED BY THE COMICS CODE AUTHORITY
AQUAMAN
THIS FANTASTIC WHIRLPOOL IS ENDLESS, MERA! THOSE CRIMINALS FROM YOUR WATER WORLD HAVE US AT THEIR MERCY!
"DOOM from DIMENSION AQUA!"

AQUAMAN
AND AQUALAD
CHAPTER 1
GREAT WAVES! LOOK, MERA... THAT PAL OF YOURS IS FIRING SUBMARINES AT US--LIKE MISSILES!

A DEADLY MENACE STRIKES SUDDENLY FROM A FANTASTIC WATER-WORLD-- AND **AQUAMAN** AND **AQUALAD** SOON FIND THEMSELVES UP AGAINST THE INCREDIBLE POWERS OF THE STRANGE SEA-PEOPLE WHO BRING...

the DOOM from DIMENSION AQUA

ON A ROUTINE PATROL OF THE OCEAN, AQUAMAN, KING OF THE SEAS, AND HIS YOUNG ALLY, AQUALAD, ENCOUNTER AN OMINOUS SIGHT...
AQUAMAN-- LOOK! AN ABANDONED SHIP-- AND IT'S RUNNING WILD
COME ON, AQUALAD! WE'VE GOT TO GET THAT SHIP OFF THE SEA LANES, BEFORE IT RAMS ANOTHER VESSEL!
BUT, BEFORE THEY CAN EVEN GET CLOSE, A FANTASTIC PHENOMENON OCCURS...
SUFFERING SARDINES! AM I SEEING THINGS?
NO, AQUALAD!... I SEE IT, TOO! A GIANT PINCERS, BEING FORMED OUT OF THAT CORAL REEF!
YIPES! IT'S COMING AFTER US!
FULL SPEED AHEAD!
BUT THE CLUTCHING PINCERS MOVE FASTER, AND...
IT'S --IT'S GOT US!
2

IN THE NEXT TERRIFYING MOMENT...
AQUAMAN! WH-WHERE'S IT TAKING US?
STEADY, AQUALAD... WE CAN SQUEEZE THROUGH THIS SMALL SPACE!
BUT WHAT'S THE USE?... NOT EVEN WE CAN MOVE FAST ENOUGH TO ESCAPE IT!
TO THEIR SURPRISED RELIEF...
NO--WAIT! IT'S BREAKING UP NOW! BUT WHAT IS IT?
NO TIME TO WORRY ABOUT THAT NOW! LET'S GET BACK TO THAT SHIP!
BUT, AS THEY TURN BACK TO THE VESSEL...
AQUALAD! A WAVE -- IT'S BEING SUSPENDED OVER THE SHIP, AND ACTING LIKE A GIANT MAGNIFYING GLASS!
3

BLAM
GREAT WAVES! THE HOLD OF THAT SHIP MUST'VE BEEN LOADED WITH DYNAMITE--AND THE MAGNIFIED RAYS OF THE SUN SET IT OFF!
WATCH OUT FOR THAT BURNING OIL, AQUALAD!
B-BUT WHAT'S BEHIND IT ALL?
JUST THEN, AS IF IN ANSWER TO AQUALAD...
LOOK! A--A GIRL, SWIMMING AT FANTASTIC SPEED! BUT NOBODY CAN SWIM THAT FAST!
NOBODY BUT US! COME ON!
AND AS THE SWIFTEST MORTALS IN THE SEA GIVE CHASE...
SHE MUST BE A--A SEA WITCH, OR SOMETHING, AQUAMAN! SHE MUST'VE BEEN BEHIND THE PINCERS THAT GRABBED US!
YES--AND THE "MAGNIFYING GLASS" THAT DESTROYED THE SHIP! KEEP GOING, AQUALAD!
SLOWLY BUT SURELY, THE GAP IS NARROWED...
CAREFUL... SHE MAY HAVE SOME OTHER POWERS TO USE ON US!
4

SURE ENOUGH, AS THEY REACH OUT FOR THEIR FEMALE QUARRY...
OH, NO! SHE-- SHE FORMED A BUBBLE OUT OF THE WATER-- AND IS FLOATING UP OUT OF REACH!
NOW I'M SURE SHE'S A WITCH!
BUT, A FEW SECONDS LATER...
FUNNY... NOW SHE SEEMS TO BE WEAKENING INSIDE HER WATER BUBBLE!
POP
IT BURST! MUST CATCH HER!
THEN, TO THEIR ASTONISHMENT...
I'VE LOST ALL MY POWERS! PLEASE... PLEASE DON'T HURT ME!
HUH--! LOOK WHO'S TALKING ABOUT HURTING PEOPLE!
YOU DON'T UNDERSTAND... I SAVED YOU! I WAS NEARBY WHEN THE CREW ABANDONED THAT SHIP--BECAUSE THE FIRE IN THE HOLD WENT OUT OF CONTROL AND THREATENED TO BLOW UP THE EXPLOSIVE CARGO!
5

HMM... SO AFTER GETTING US OUT OF THE WAY, YOU EXPLODED THE SHIP WITH THAT WATERY MAGNIFYING GLASS! BUT WHO ARE YOU?... AND HOW DID YOU GET THOSE POWERS?
I AM--OR WAS--QUEEN MERA OF A WATERY WORLD IN ANOTHER DIMENSION! YOU SEE, EVERYONE IN MY WORLD HAS THE ABILITY TO WILL THE WATER TO DO HIS BIDDING!
"UPON MY FATHER'S DEATH, I BECAME QUEEN, BUT..."
MY QUEEN--THE EVIL PRETENDER, LERON, HAS REACHED THE CASTLE GATES! YOU MUST FLEE FOR YOUR LIFE!
BUT WHERE CAN I GO?
OUR SCIENTIST, XEBEL, HAS JUST FOUND THE ANSWER TO THAT! COME WITH ME...
"SOON, IN THE TOWER OF A NEARBY LABORATORY..."
THIS IS A DIMENSIONAL WARP, MY QUEEN--LEADING TO ANOTHER WORLD! ALTHOUGH THE OPENING IS ONLY TEMPORARY, IT WILL KEEP YOU SAFE FOR A WHILE!
SOB! THERE WAS ONLY TIME FOR ME TO STEAL THROUGH--BEFORE LERON CAPTURED THE KINGDOM!
DON'T FEEL BAD, MERA... I WAS CAST OUT OF MY HOMELAND, ATLANTIS, YEARS AGO--BUT NOW I VISIT IT OFTEN!
BUT TELL ME, MERA--WHY HAVE YOU SUDDENLY LOST YOUR POWER TO CONTROL WATER?
I DON'T KNOW... IT--IT SIMPLY VANISHED, WITHOUT A TRACE!
6

DON'T WORRY, MERA... WE'LL TAKE GOOD CARE OF YOU WHILE YOU'RE A VISITOR IN THIS DIMENSION!
BUT NEXT INSTANT...
GREAT GUPPIES!... LOOK! A SUBMARINE-- IT'S BEING HURTLED THROUGH THE AIR!
THERE'S A WHOLE FLEET OF THEM--CONVERTED INTO MISSILES... AND WE'RE THE TARGET! MAKE SEA-TRACKS!
M-MERA... ARE YOU SURE YOU LOST YOUR POWERS?
YOU MUST BELIEVE ME--I'M NOT RESPONSIBLE FOR THIS!
I DO BELIEVE YOU-- BUT WHO IS?
OH, NO!... THERE'S THE ANSWER!
7

A... A SEA-MAN--RIDING A WATER-SPOUT--! HE'S GOT MERA'S POWERS!
IT'S LERON--THE USURPER TO MY THRONE!
HE PROBABLY FOLLOWED YOU THROUGH THE WARP--TO MAKE SURE YOU NEVER COME BACK! HURRY!
BUT JUST THEN...
SUFFERING SNAILS! HE TURNED THE WATER AROUND US AS HARD AS STEEL! WE CAN'T MOVE!
8
PROMISE TO HAND OVER THE QUEEN--OR I SHALL LEAVE YOU ALL WHERE YOU ARE, TO PERISH!
CONTINUED IN CHAPTER 2

AQUAMAN

CHAPTER 2
WHY-- THIS AQUAMAN HAS POWERS EQUAL TO OUR OWN! HE HAS TURNED A WAVE INTO A--A FLYING RAFT!
I--I MUST BE DREAMING! H-HOW'S HE DOING IT?
9
NOW LERON AND HIS FOLLOWERS COMBINE THEIR AWESOME POWERS TO DEFEAT MERA AND HER FAMILIAR FRIENDS--BUT AQUAMAN IS EQUAL TO THE MIGHTY CHALLENGE AS HE BECOMES...
the SUPER SEA SLEUTH

ENCASED IN A TRAP OF HARDENED WATER, AQUAMAN GRAVELY CONSIDERS LERON'S ULTIMATUM...
WELL?...YOUR ANSWER! WILL YOU SAVE YOUR OWN LIFE, AND HAND HER OVER TO ME?
HMM...IT SEEMS I HAVE NO CHOICE!
B-BUT, AQUAMAN--YOU CAN'T! YOU KNOW WHAT HE'LL DO TO MERA IF WE TURN HER OVER TO HIM!
AQUAMAN ;SOB; I CAN'T EXPECT YOU TO SACRIFICE YOUR OWN LIFE TO SAVE ME--A MERE STRANGER!
ENOUGH IDLE TALK! YOUR DECISION!
VERY WELL, LERON--HERE IS MY ANSWER...
NEXT INSTANT, THE VERY SURFACE OF THE SEA BUBBLES UP WITH ENDLESS MASSES OF TWISTING FORMS...
HUH?
THE SUDDEN DIVERSION MOMENTARILY LOOSENS LERON'S THOUGHT-CONTROL OVER THE WATER, AND...
DIVE!
10

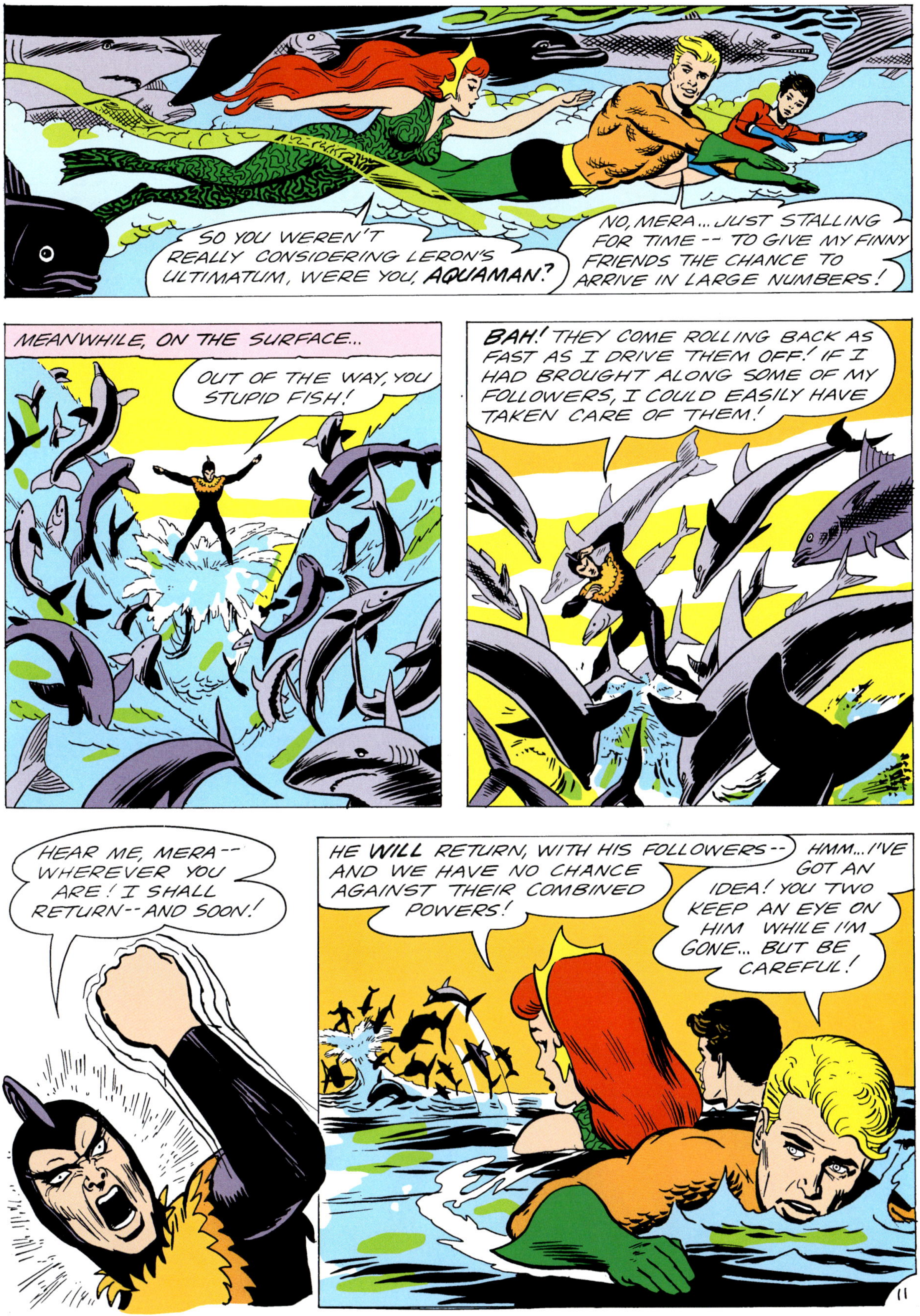
SO YOU WEREN'T REALLY CONSIDERING LERON'S ULTIMATUM, WERE YOU, AQUAMAN?
NO, MERA... JUST STALLING FOR TIME -- TO GIVE MY FINNY FRIENDS THE CHANCE TO ARRIVE IN LARGE NUMBERS!
MEANWHILE, ON THE SURFACE...
OUT OF THE WAY, YOU STUPID FISH!
BAH! THEY COME ROLLING BACK AS FAST AS I DRIVE THEM OFF! IF I HAD BROUGHT ALONG SOME OF MY FOLLOWERS, I COULD EASILY HAVE TAKEN CARE OF THEM!
HEAR ME, MERA-- WHEREVER YOU ARE! I SHALL RETURN--AND SOON!
HE WILL RETURN, WITH HIS FOLLOWERS-- AND WE HAVE NO CHANCE AGAINST THEIR COMBINED POWERS!
HMM...I'VE GOT AN IDEA! YOU TWO KEEP AN EYE ON HIM WHILE I'M GONE... BUT BE CAREFUL!
11

SHORTLY...
THAT'S THE WARP, AQUALAD! IF--IF THERE WERE ONLY SOME WAY OF BLOCKING IT UP, SO LERON AND HIS FOLLOWERS COULDN'T RETURN!
I'M AFRAID THERE'S NO WAY, MERA!
JUST THEN...
HERE THEY COME, MERA! HURRY--BEFORE THEY SPOT US!
BUT...
HELP ME, AQUALAD! I--I CAN'T SWIM THAT FAST ANYMORE!
I FORGOT! HERE-- I'LL GIVE YOU A HAND!
AND AS AQUAMAN RE-JOINS THE PAIR...
AH! THERE IS MERA AND TWO OF HER FRIENDS!
POWERFUL MENTAL IMPULSES CRACKLE, AND...
SUFFERING SNAILS! THEY OPENED UP A BIG, SWIRLING PIT IN THE SEA! WE'LL FALL A-- A MILE!
12

HANG ON TIGHT, MERA... I--I'LL TRY AND PLUNGE INTO THE WATER WALL!
¡WHEW! MADE IT! BUT--WHY DIDN'T THEY FOLLOW US DOWN HERE?
NO SOONER DOES THE TRIO SURFACE THAN...
AQUAMAN!... HE'S RECKLESSLY SWIMMING RIGHT TOWARD THEM!
GO BACK WHERE YOU CAME FROM--UNLESS YOU WANT A SAMPLE OF MY POWERS!
HUH?
YOUR POWERS?
YES! I TEMPORARILY LOST THEM BEFORE... BUT MY POWERS HAVE RETURNED IN FULL!
WE SHALL SEE ABOUT THAT...
13

NEXT INSTANT...
GREAT GUPPIES! LERON FORMED A GIANT SWORD FROM THE WATER--AND HE'S ABOUT TO HURL IT AT AQUAMAN!
YES, BUT LOOK! AQUAMAN HAS FORMED A--A WATERY SHIELD!
CRASH
TH-THIS IS CRAZY!
NOW AQUAMAN IS LIFTING HIMSELF OUT OF THE SEA ON A--A WATERY MAGIC CARPET!
SWISH
HE-HE HAS MIGHTY POWERS OVER THE WATER, INDEED!
14

THEN, AS THE SEA SLEUTH DEMONSTRATES MORE OF HIS NEW SUPER-POWERS...
YIPPEE! THOSE GIANT WATER BALLS AQUAMAN FORMED... THEY'RE FORCING LERON AND HIS PALS TO RETREAT!
WE CAN KEEP DESTROYING THE MISSILES -- BUT MORE KEEP COMING!
HMM...IT SEEMS ODD THAT IF PEOPLE FROM THIS DIMENSION POSSESS SUCH POWERS, THE YOUNG ONE DID NOT USE THEM AGAINST US! KEEP RETREATING!
MEANWHILE
THOSE WATER BALLS ARE SENDING THEM BACK A MILE! BUT WHERE DID YOU GET THOSE POWERS, AQUAMAN?
I'LL BE GLAD TO LET YOU IN ON THE SECRET OF MY NEW POWERS, AQUALAD...
QUISP-- WORKING HIS OWN WATER-MAGIC, BY REMOTE CONTROL!
SO THAT'S WHERE YOU WENT BEFORE-- TO BRING BACK OUR WATER-SPRITE FRIEND!
ALWAYS HAPPY TO HELP... TEE-HEE!
AND I'VE JUST GOT ANOTHER IDEA, QUISP! LISTEN...
15

IF WE HAD A **WHOLE ARMY** OF WATER SPRITES, WE COULD EVEN WIN BACK MERA'S KINGDOM FOR HER!
GOOD IDEA! I'LL BRING BACK AN ARMY RIGHT AWAY!
BUT, AS THE LOYAL WATER SPRITE SPEEDS OFF, A SHADOWY FIGURE DARTS AFTER HIM...
HA, HA! THEY DIDN'T REALIZE THIS BIG "FISH" IS ONLY A WATER MASQUERADE I CREATED!
NOW TO STOP THAT WATER SPRITE BEFORE HE CAN BRING HELP!
16
CONCLUDED IN CHAPTER 3

AQUAMAN

CHAPTER 3
INTO DIMENSION-AQUA HURTLE THE DARING DUO OF THE DEEP AND THE BEAUTIFUL QUEEN MERA! BUT THEY ENTER, NOT AS RETURNING HEROES AND CONQUERORS, BUT AS...
PRISONERS of the WATER WORLD
GIVE ME THE SECRET OF THE DIMENSION-WARP, XEBEL -- OR THE QUEEN AND HER FRIENDS ARE DOOMED!
NO, XEBEL -- DON'T TRUST HIM! LERON INTENDS TO DESTROY US, ANYWAY!
17

UNAWARE OF THE APPROACHING MENACE FROM BEHIND, QUISP IS CAUGHT OFF-GUARD WHEN...
WHOOSH
BY THE TIME HE RECOVERS, IT WILL BE TOO LATE FOR HIM AND HIS PEOPLE TO HELP MERA!
CRACK
HA, HA! MERA AND HER FRIENDS ARE EXPECTING HELP FROM THAT LITTLE CREATURE! INSTEAD, THEY WILL BE GETTING SOMETHING FROM US!
SOME MINUTES LATER...
LOOK... THAT SIGNAL FISH-- WARNING US THAT LERON AND HIS PALS ARE HEADING THIS WAY!
YOU CAN SAY THAT AGAIN! HERE THEY COME!
HEAD FOR THE SURFACE! WE'LL TRY TO REACH DRY LAND!
18

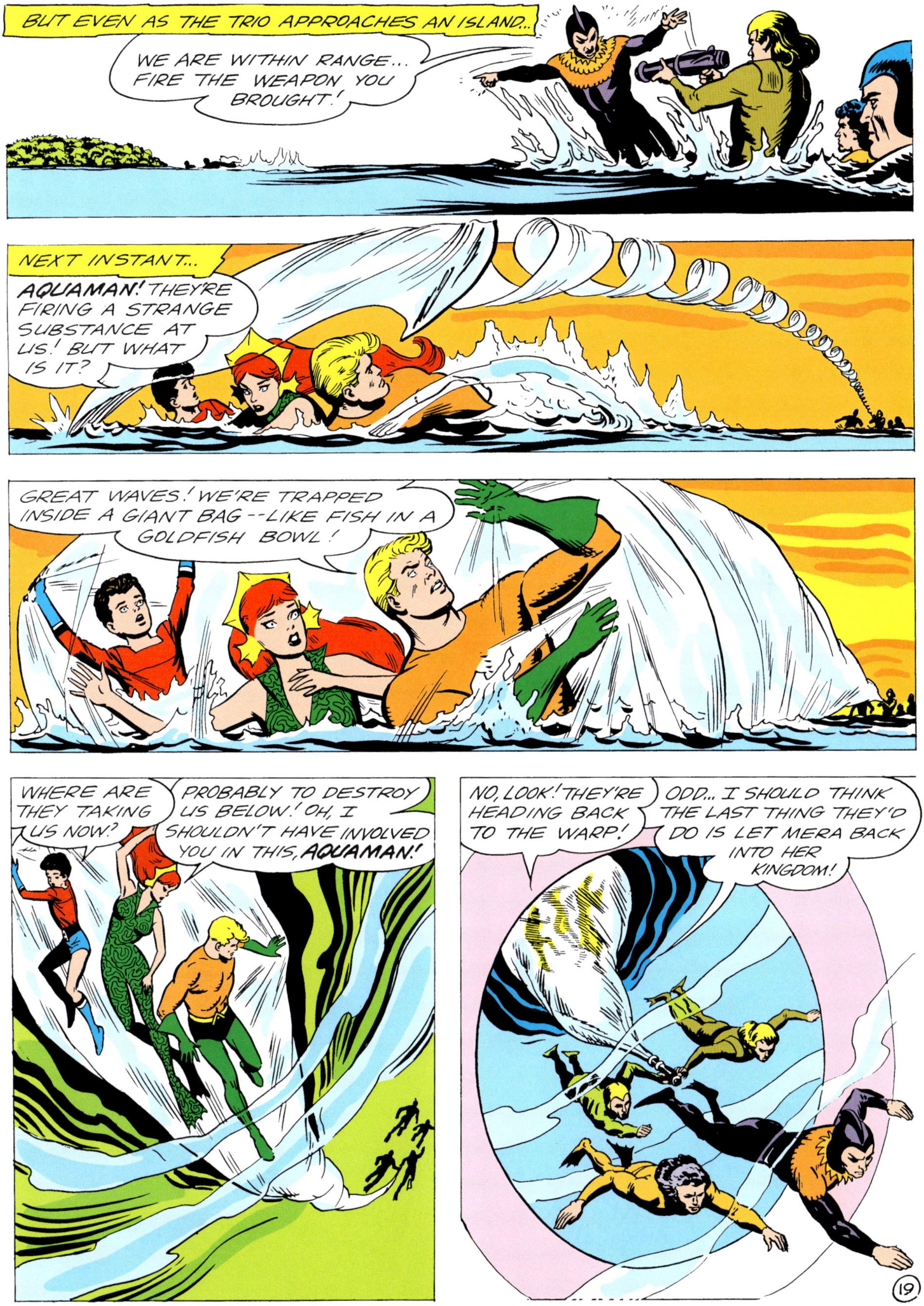

BUT EVEN AS THE TRIO APPROACHES AN ISLAND...
WE ARE WITHIN RANGE... FIRE THE WEAPON YOU BROUGHT!
NEXT INSTANT...
AQUAMAN! THEY'RE FIRING A STRANGE SUBSTANCE AT US! BUT WHAT IS IT?
GREAT WAVES! WE'RE TRAPPED INSIDE A GIANT BAG--LIKE FISH IN A GOLDFISH BOWL!
WHERE ARE THEY TAKING US NOW?
PROBABLY TO DESTROY US BELOW! OH, I SHOULDN'T HAVE INVOLVED YOU IN THIS, AQUAMAN!
NO, LOOK! THEY'RE HEADING BACK TO THE WARP!
ODD... I SHOULD THINK THE LAST THING THEY'D DO IS LET MERA BACK INTO HER KINGDOM!
19

BUT THAT'S EXACTLY WHAT THEY'RE DOING, AQUAMAN!
SHORTLY...
W-WE'RE BEING LOCKED IN A--A CORAL CAGE!
WHAT'S THE IDEA, LERON?
YOU WILL SOON HAVE YOUR ANSWER, AQUAMAN-- AND YOU, TOO, MERA! BRING XEBEL HERE!
WHY, XEBEL IS THE SCIENTIST WHO CREATED THE WARP!
SOON...
MY QUEEN!
YES, XEBEL... YOUR QUEEN-- AT MY MERCY! NOW, IF YOU REVEAL THE SECRET OF HOW YOU CONTROL THE WARP, SHE LIVES! OTHERWISE--SHE PERISHES!
NO, NO--YOU MUST NOT HARM HER!
DON'T TRUST HIM, XEBEL! EVEN IF YOU TELL HIM WHAT HE WANTS TO KNOW...
...HE WILL STILL DESTROY ME-- AND MY FRIENDS!
SHE LIES! WE WILL GIVE YOU A SHORT TIME TO DECIDE, XEBEL! TAKE HIM AWAY!
20

AS THE BEWILDERED SCIENTIST IS DRAGGED OFF...
OH, AQUAMAN-- IS THERE NO WAY TO STOP LERON FROM FORCING XEBEL TO SPEAK?
YES--BY REMOVING THEIR TRUMP CARD, MERA... YOU! WHILE THE WARP IS STILL OPEN, THAT SHOULD BE EASY!
A TELEPATHIC MESSAGE CRACKLES FROM THE SEA KING--AND BEFORE LONG...
HUH? ALL THOSE FISH... MUST WARN LERON!
BUT BEFORE THE SENTRY CAN TAKE OFF...
OOF!
AFTERWARD...
WAIT'LL I TIE THIS ON TIGHT--THEN MY FINNY FRIENDS CAN GO INTO ACTION!
WHY--YOUR FISH ARE WHIRLING US ABOUT!
YES, MERA--HOLD ONTO ME, TIGHTLY!
21

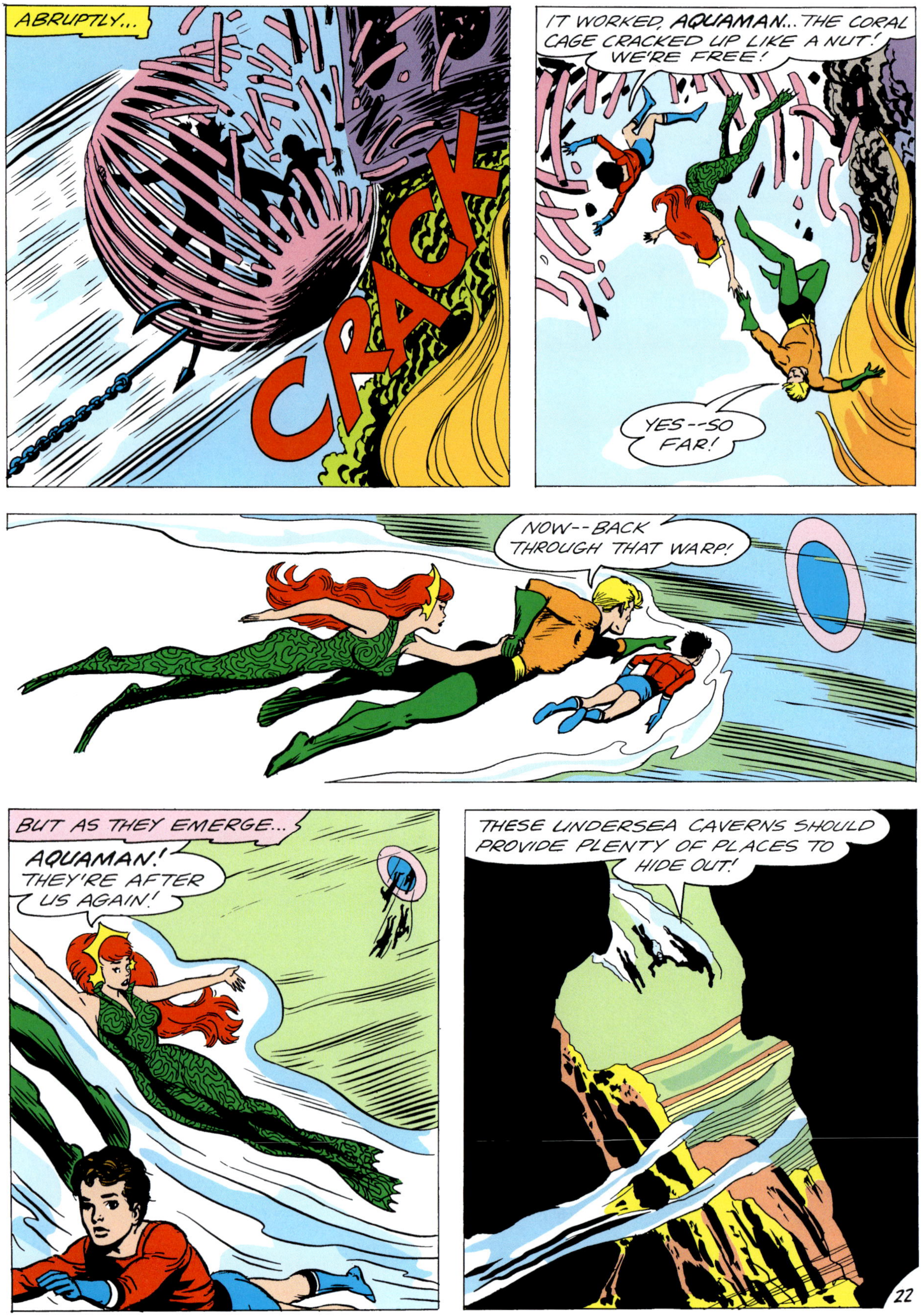
ABRUPTLY...
CRACK
IT WORKED, AQUAMAN... THE CORAL CAGE CRACKED UP LIKE A NUT! WE'RE FREE!
YES--SO FAR!
NOW--BACK THROUGH THAT WARP!
BUT AS THEY EMERGE...
AQUAMAN! THEY'RE AFTER US AGAIN!
THESE UNDERSEA CAVERNS SHOULD PROVIDE PLENTY OF PLACES TO HIDE OUT!
22

BUT, UPON ENTERING...
OH, NO! THERE'S BEEN AN UNDERWATER LANDSLIDE-- BLOCKING OFF THE INTERIOR CAVERNS! WE'RE TRAPPED IN A NARROW CAVE!
NOW WE ARE SURELY DOOMED!
DON'T GIVE UP, MERA! HERE, LET ME WIPE THIS SMUDGE OFF YOUR ARM!
SUDDENLY...
THEY'RE IN!
BUT, TO THE AMAZEMENT OF THE DARING DUO OF THE DEEP...
A--A GREAT WAVE--HURLING THEM BACK! IT MUST BE QUISP!
WHOOSH
NO--IT'S ME! SOMEHOW, MY POWERS HAVE RETURNED!
THAT'S GREAT... BUT WE'RE STILL OUTNUMBERED! LET'S GO--WHILE THE GOING IS GOOD!
ON THE SURFACE...
THEY'RE CATCHING UP AGAIN, AQUAMAN-- AND THIS TIME, I WON'T BE ABLE TO TAKE THEM BY SURPRISE!
HMM... THAT OIL TANKER! I--I THINK I'VE GOT THE ANSWER! YOU TWO HIDE IN THAT SEAWEED!
23

ANOTHER TELEPATHIC COMMAND GOES OUT-- AND NEXT MOMENT...
WHY--AQUAMAN IS RIDING A COUPLE OF SWORDFISH TOWARD THAT TANKER--LURING LERON AND HIS MEN AFTER HIM!
NOW--NOW HE DROVE THEIR SWORDS RIGHT INTO THE TANKER'S SIDES, CAUSING IT TO SPRING A LEAK!
AS LERON AND HIS BAND RACE THROUGH THE OIL-DRENCHED WATERS...
HUH? I--I'VE BEEN SLOWED DOWN TO A CRAWL!
THE REST OF US, TOO!
OUR POWERS--THEY HAVE VANISHED!
YES THANKS TO THE OIL ON THEIR BODIES! IT WAS OIL THAT ROBBED YOU OF YOUR POWERS--WHICH RETURNED WHEN I RUBBED THE OIL SMUDGE OFF YOUR ARM!
OIL? BUT OIL HAS NO SUCH EFFECT ON US! ONLY LEAD WOULD WEAKEN OUR POWERS--AND THERE IS NO LEAD ANYWHERE AROUND!
OH, YES, THERE IS! PRACTICALLY ALL REFINED OIL CONTAINS A HIGH PERCENTAGE OF LEAD!
24

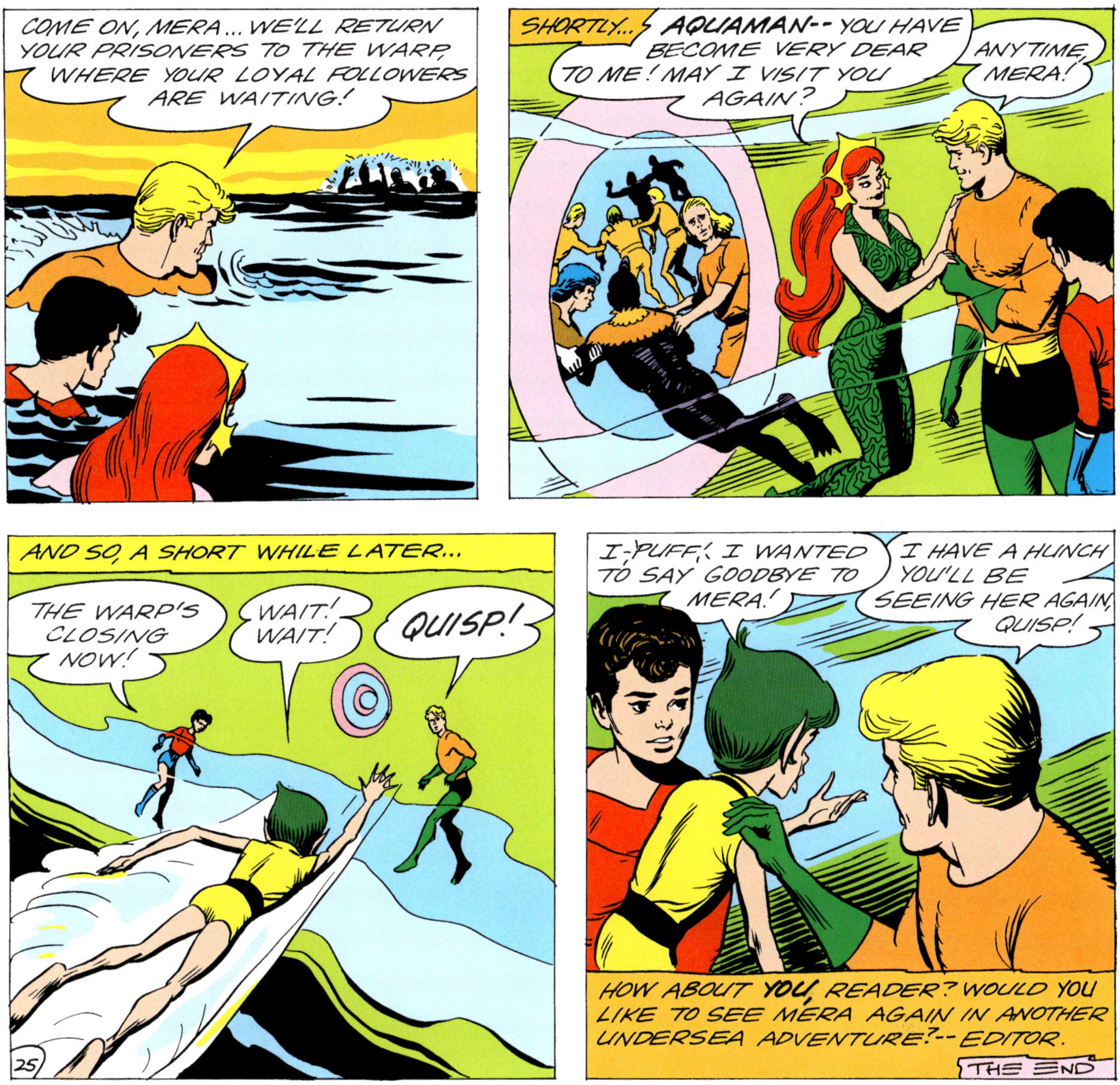
COME ON, MERA... WE'LL RETURN YOUR PRISONERS TO THE WARP, WHERE YOUR LOYAL FOLLOWERS ARE WAITING!
SHORTLY...
AQUAMAN-- YOU HAVE BECOME VERY DEAR TO ME! MAY I VISIT YOU AGAIN?
ANYTIME, MERA!
AND SO, A SHORT WHILE LATER...
THE WARP'S CLOSING NOW!
WAIT! WAIT!
QUISP!
25
I-PUFF!- I WANTED TO SAY GOODBYE TO MERA!
I HAVE A HUNCH YOU'LL BE SEEING HER AGAIN, QUISP!
HOW ABOUT YOU, READER? WOULD YOU LIKE TO SEE MERA AGAIN IN ANOTHER UNDERSEA ADVENTURE?--EDITOR.
THE END

AQUAMAN

SUPERMAN DC NATIONAL COMICS
AQUAMAN
OCT. NO. 35
APPROVED BY THE COMICS CODE AUTHORITY
12¢
WHO DESTROYS the SEA KING?
The OCEAN MASTER or BLACK MANTA?

AQUAMAN AND AQUALAD
BEFORE YOU STAND THE TOPLESS TOWERS OF ATLANTIS, UNDER THE GREAT SHIMMERING DOME THAT NOTHING HAS EVER PENETRATED--AS THE WORLD'S ONLY WATER-BREATHING HUMANS WAKE TO THE SEA'S DIM DAY! BUT NOW THEY HEAR IT--SEE IT--THE SINISTER OBJECT ORBITING AT AMAZING SPEED AROUND THEIR UNDERWATER HOME!
between TWO DOOMS!
LIKE ALL THE CITIZENS OF ATLANTIS, ITS ROYAL FAMILY WATCHES IN SHOCK AND WONDER...
HOLY HADDOCKS!
WH-WHAT IS IT, AQUAMAN?
WAH-WAH-WAH!
I DON'T KNOW, MERA HONEY--BUT I'M GOING OUT TO SEE!

NO, DARLING, YOU'RE NOT GOING OUT THERE ALONE!
EASY, SWEETHEART... WHO'S THE GUARDIAN OF ATLANTIS? YOU'RE LOOKING AT HIM... THE GUY YOU MARRIED-- ME!
DA-DA!
MERA'S RIGHT, AQUAMAN... LET ME GO WITH YOU!
LOVE TO HAVE YOU, TADPOLE, BUT I WOULDN'T BE WORTH A BUSTED CLAM-SHELL OUT THERE, IF I DIDN'T KNOW THE GREATEST BACK-UP MAN A GUY EVER HAD WAS HERE, TAKING CARE OF THINGS! CHECK?
CHECK!
NOW, SO AS NOT TO GIVE THE STRANGE ORBITING MACHINE THE SLIGHTEST CHANCE OF BREACHING THE DEFENSES OF ATLANTIS...
SPECIAL EJECTION TUBE... FIRE!
PA-TOOOSH
WHOOMA
WHOOMA
OKAY, GIZMO, HERE'S WHERE I LATCH ON AND SEE WHAT MAKES YOU TICK!
2

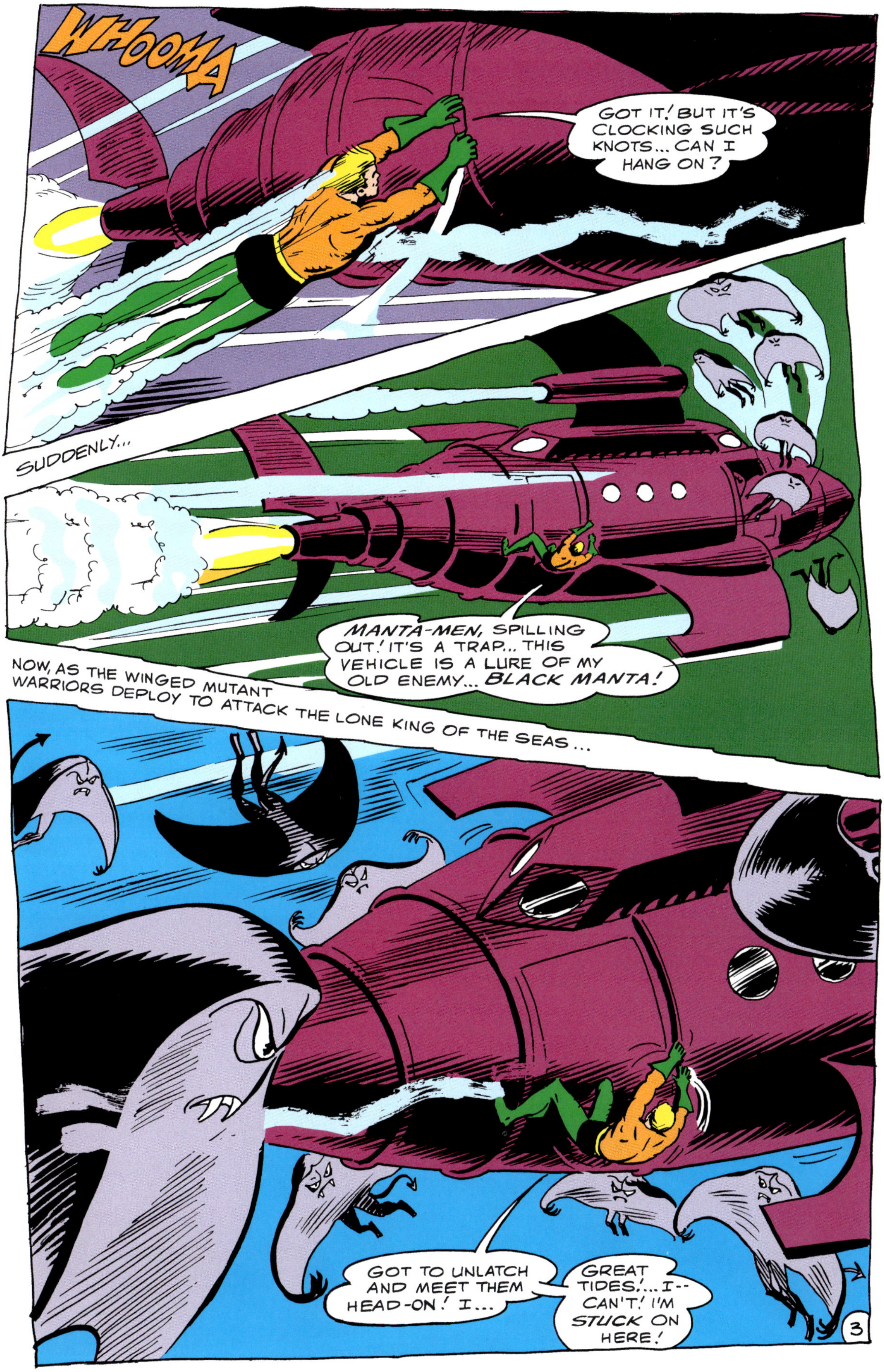
WHOOMA
GOT IT! BUT IT'S CLOCKING SUCH KNOTS... CAN I HANG ON?
SUDDENLY...
MANTA-MEN, SPILLING OUT! IT'S A TRAP... THIS VEHICLE IS A LURE OF MY OLD ENEMY... BLACK MANTA!
NOW, AS THE WINGED MUTANT WARRIORS DEPLOY TO ATTACK THE LONE KING OF THE SEAS...
GOT TO UNLATCH AND MEET THEM HEAD-ON! I...
GREAT TIDES!... I-- CAN'T! I'M STUCK ON HERE!
3

BLACK MANTA... HE DECOYED ME! NO WONDER I LATCHED ONTO THIS THING SO EASILY... IT'S BIO-MAGNETIC!
NOW, AS THE MUTANT MANTA-MEN CLOSE IN ON THE ORBITING SEA KING -- WITH EVERY FORWARD SWEEP OF THEIR WINGS EMITTING DEADLY STUN BLASTS...
KRA CCLE
KRA CCLE
BLAZING BLUE WHALES! I'M PASTED ON THIS THING LIKE A HUMAN BULL'S-EYE!
I FELL FOR THE OLDEST TRICK IN THE BOOK... BLACK MANTA WANTED ME OUT OF ATLANTIS -- KEPT BUSY -- WHILE HE DOES... WHAT?
THUNNG
THUNNG
FOR THE SEA-SHAKING ANSWER, LET'S WATCH AS A SINISTER-SHAPED SHIP GLIDES TOWARD ATLANTIS...
IT HAS SUCCEEDED! THE WAY IS OPEN... THE WAY TO ULTIMATE POWER AND TO AQUAMAN'S DESTRUCTION IS ASSURED!
THE FOOL -- HE WAS LURED SO EASILY... HE DISAPPOINTS ME!
4

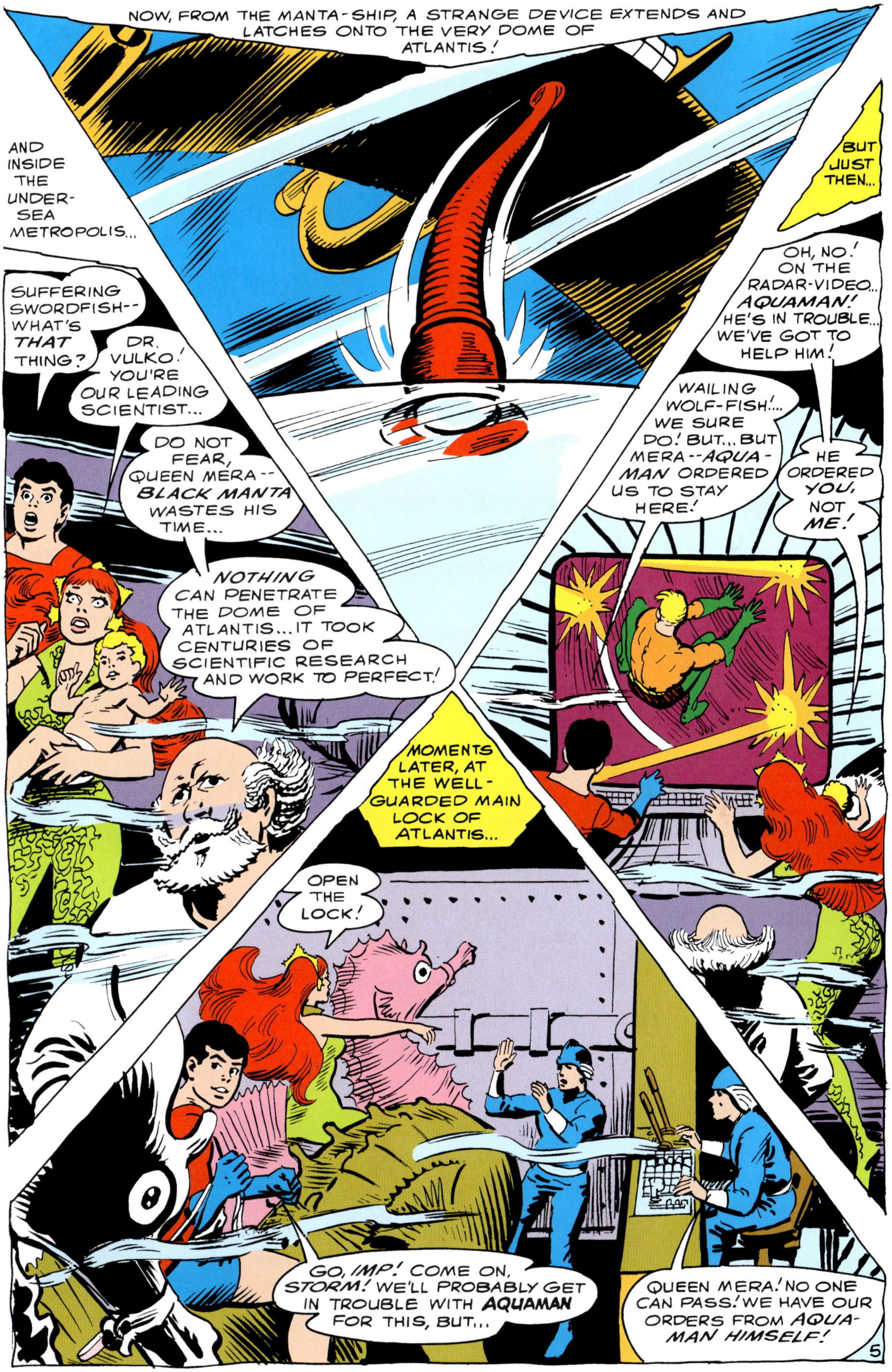

NOW, FROM THE MANTA-SHIP, A STRANGE DEVICE EXTENDS AND LATCHES ONTO THE VERY DOME OF ATLANTIS!
AND INSIDE THE UNDER-SEA METROPOLIS...
SUFFERING SWORDFISH-- WHAT'S THAT THING?
DR. VULKO! YOU'RE OUR LEADING SCIENTIST...
DO NOT FEAR, QUEEN MERA-- BLACK MANTA WASTES HIS TIME...
NOTHING CAN PENETRATE THE DOME OF ATLANTIS... IT TOOK CENTURIES OF SCIENTIFIC RESEARCH AND WORK TO PERFECT!
BUT JUST THEN...
OH, NO! ON THE RADAR-VIDEO... AQUAMAN! HE'S IN TROUBLE... WE'VE GOT TO HELP HIM!
WAILING WOLF-FISH!... WE SURE DO! BUT... BUT MERA--AQUAMAN ORDERED US TO STAY HERE!
HE ORDERED YOU, NOT ME!
MOMENTS LATER, AT THE WELL-GUARDED MAIN LOCK OF ATLANTIS...
OPEN THE LOCK!
GO, IMP! COME ON, STORM! WE'LL PROBABLY GET IN TROUBLE WITH AQUAMAN FOR THIS, BUT...
QUEEN MERA! NO ONE CAN PASS! WE HAVE OUR ORDERS FROM AQUAMAN HIMSELF!
5

NEXT INSTANT...
HERE ARE YOUR NEW ORDERS! ONE SIDE!
A HARD-WATER HAND, WORKING THE CONTROLS!
AND AS MERA USES THE SPECIAL POWERS OF HER OWN HOME-DIMENSIONAL WATER WORLD...
THEY'RE GONE!
WHAT COULD WE DO? I'D RATHER FACE AQUAMAN'S FURY THAN HERS!
CLOSE THE LOCK... INSTANTLY!
MEANTIME, AS AQUAMAN ORBITS ATLANTIS--A PRISONER OF THE DECOY MACHINE...
BY MAKING... MY BODY... A COUNTER-WEIGHT... I'VE GOT THIS GADGET ROTATING... GIVING THESE BUSTERS A TOUGHER TARGET!
THUNG
KRACLE
THUNG
BUT HOW LONG CAN I KEEP THIS UP?
HOW LONG? JUST LONG ENOUGH, AQUAMAN, AS...
A GIANT HARD-WATER HAMMER, CLOBBERING THE MACHINE! IT'S... MERA!
THWAANNG
6

AT THIS VERY MOMENT, IN ATLANTIS...
DR. VULKO! THAT STRANGE CONE OF LIGHT...
REMAIN CALM! THE DOME, OF COURSE, IS TRANSPARENT... THUS LIGHT CAN PASS THROUGH IT--BUT THAT IS ALL!
IT RESISTS ALL HEAT, STUN, OR OTHER DESTRUCTO-RAYS!
DR. VULKO IS THE LEADING SCIENTIST OF ATLANTIS--BUT EVEN HE ISN'T CLUED IN TO WHAT HAPPENS NOW...
DR. VULKO! THE CONE OF LIGHT... PARTICLES FORMING WITHIN IT--HURTLING TOWARD THE DOME!
AS MORE AND MORE PARTICLES FORM INSIDE THE LIGHT CONE AND THEN HURTLE TO COAT THEMSELVES ON THE DOME'S INSIDE...
BLURRGLEE
BLRSSLLLSSH
THE WATER INSIDE THE CITY... IT'S BOILING--GOING BERSERK!
BLACK MANTA HAS SOME NEW PHOTON TRANS-DUCER RAY REACTING WITH WATER... BUT WE'RE READY FOR HIM!
ACTI-VATE ALL EXHAUST PUMPS AND VALVES!
THROUGH UNDERGROUND GRATES AND VENTS, POWERFUL PUMPS QUICKLY BEGIN TO EMPTY THE GREAT UNDERSEA CITY OF THE LIFE-GIVING WATER...
THE WATER RECEDES... BLACK MANTA'S DIABOLICAL PLAN IS THWARTED FOR THE MOMENT! BUT AS WATER-BREATHERS, OUR PEOPLE CAN ONLY SURVIVE NOW FOR ONE HOUR INSIDE THE CITY!
PERHAPS THE EFFECT OF THAT PHOTON SUB-STANCE WILL HAVE WORN OFF BY THEN!
IT HAD BETTER, OR WE SHALL HAVE TO EVACUATE EVERYONE AND FACE BLACK MANTA'S WRATH OUTSIDE THE DOME'S PRO-TECTION!
7

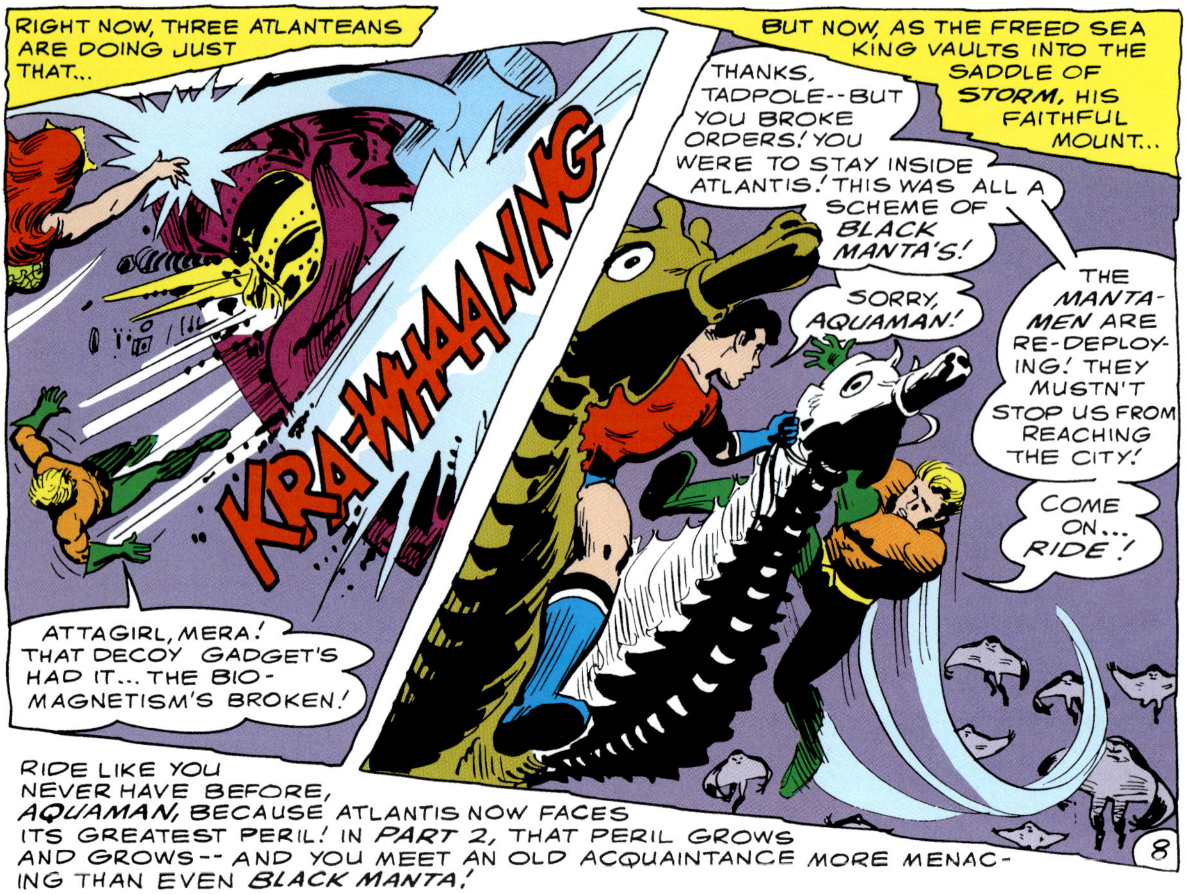

RIGHT NOW, THREE ATLANTEANS ARE DOING JUST THAT...
KRA-WHAANNG
ATTAGIRL, MERA! THAT DECOY GADGET'S HAD IT... THE BIO-MAGNETISM'S BROKEN!
BUT NOW, AS THE FREED SEA KING VAULTS INTO THE SADDLE OF STORM, HIS FAITHFUL MOUNT...
THANKS, TADPOLE--BUT YOU BROKE ORDERS! YOU WERE TO STAY INSIDE ATLANTIS! THIS WAS ALL A SCHEME OF BLACK MANTA'S!
SORRY, AQUAMAN!
THE MANTA-MEN ARE RE-DEPLOYING! THEY MUSTN'T STOP US FROM REACHING THE CITY!
COME ON... RIDE!
8
RIDE LIKE YOU NEVER HAVE BEFORE, AQUAMAN, BECAUSE ATLANTIS NOW FACES ITS GREATEST PERIL! IN PART 2, THAT PERIL GROWS AND GROWS-- AND YOU MEET AN OLD ACQUAINTANCE MORE MENACING THAN EVEN BLACK MANTA!

AQUAMAN

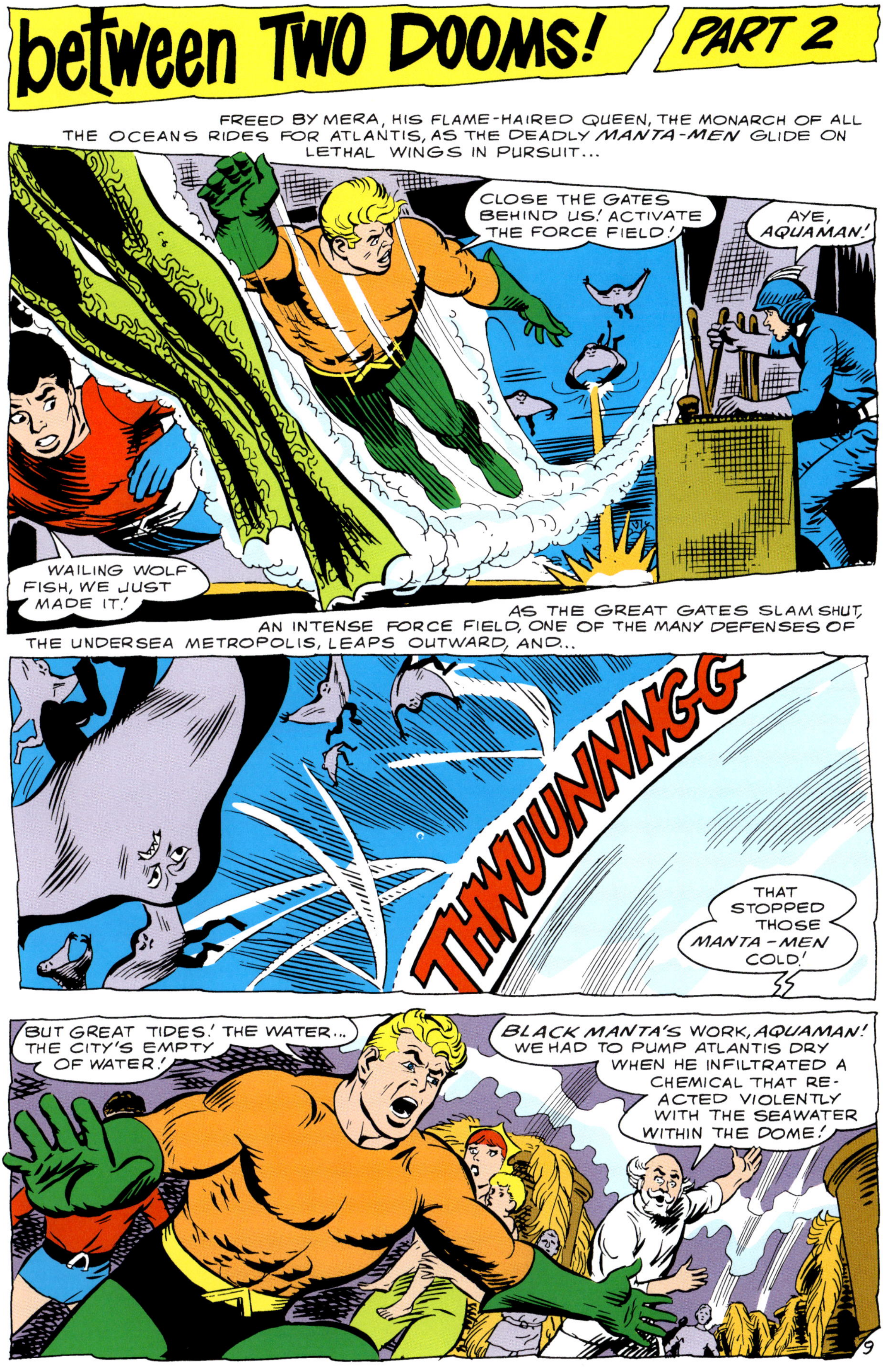
between TWO DOOMS! PART 2
FREED BY MERA, HIS FLAME-HAIRED QUEEN, THE MONARCH OF ALL THE OCEANS RIDES FOR ATLANTIS, AS THE DEADLY MANTA-MEN GLIDE ON LETHAL WINGS IN PURSUIT...
CLOSE THE GATES BEHIND US! ACTIVATE THE FORCE FIELD!
AYE, AQUAMAN!
WAILING WOLF-FISH, WE JUST MADE IT!
AS THE GREAT GATES SLAM SHUT, AN INTENSE FORCE FIELD, ONE OF THE MANY DEFENSES OF THE UNDERSEA METROPOLIS, LEAPS OUTWARD, AND...
THWUUNNNGG
THAT STOPPED THOSE MANTA-MEN COLD!
BUT GREAT TIDES! THE WATER... THE CITY'S EMPTY OF WATER!
BLACK MANTA'S WORK, AQUAMAN! WE HAD TO PUMP ATLANTIS DRY WHEN HE INFILTRATED A CHEMICAL THAT RE-ACTED VIOLENTLY WITH THE SEAWATER WITHIN THE DOME!
9

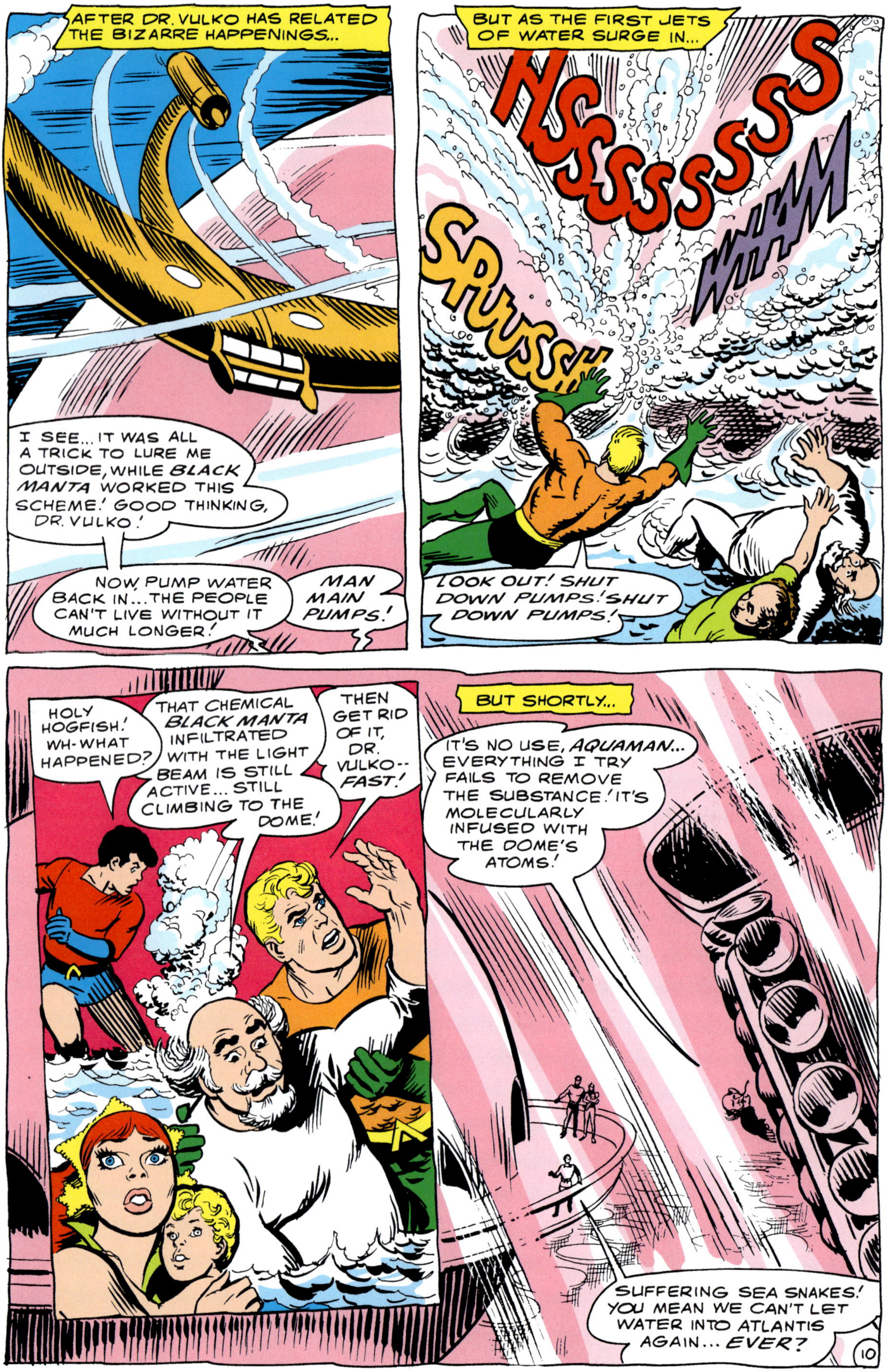
AFTER DR. VULKO HAS RELATED THE BIZARRE HAPPENINGS...
I SEE... IT WAS ALL A TRICK TO LURE ME OUTSIDE, WHILE BLACK MANTA WORKED THIS SCHEME! GOOD THINKING, DR. VULKO!
NOW PUMP WATER BACK IN... THE PEOPLE CAN'T LIVE WITHOUT IT MUCH LONGER!
MAN MAIN PUMPS!
BUT AS THE FIRST JETS OF WATER SURGE IN...
HSSSSSSSS
WHAM
SPLUSSH
LOOK OUT! SHUT DOWN PUMPS! SHUT DOWN PUMPS!
HOLY HOGFISH! WH-WHAT HAPPENED?
THAT CHEMICAL BLACK MANTA INFILTRATED WITH THE LIGHT BEAM IS STILL ACTIVE... STILL CLIMBING TO THE DOME!
THEN GET RID OF IT, DR. VULKO-- FAST!
BUT SHORTLY...
IT'S NO USE, AQUAMAN... EVERYTHING I TRY FAILS TO REMOVE THE SUBSTANCE! IT'S MOLECULARLY INFUSED WITH THE DOME'S ATOMS!
SUFFERING SEA SNAKES! YOU MEAN WE CAN'T LET WATER INTO ATLANTIS AGAIN... EVER?
10

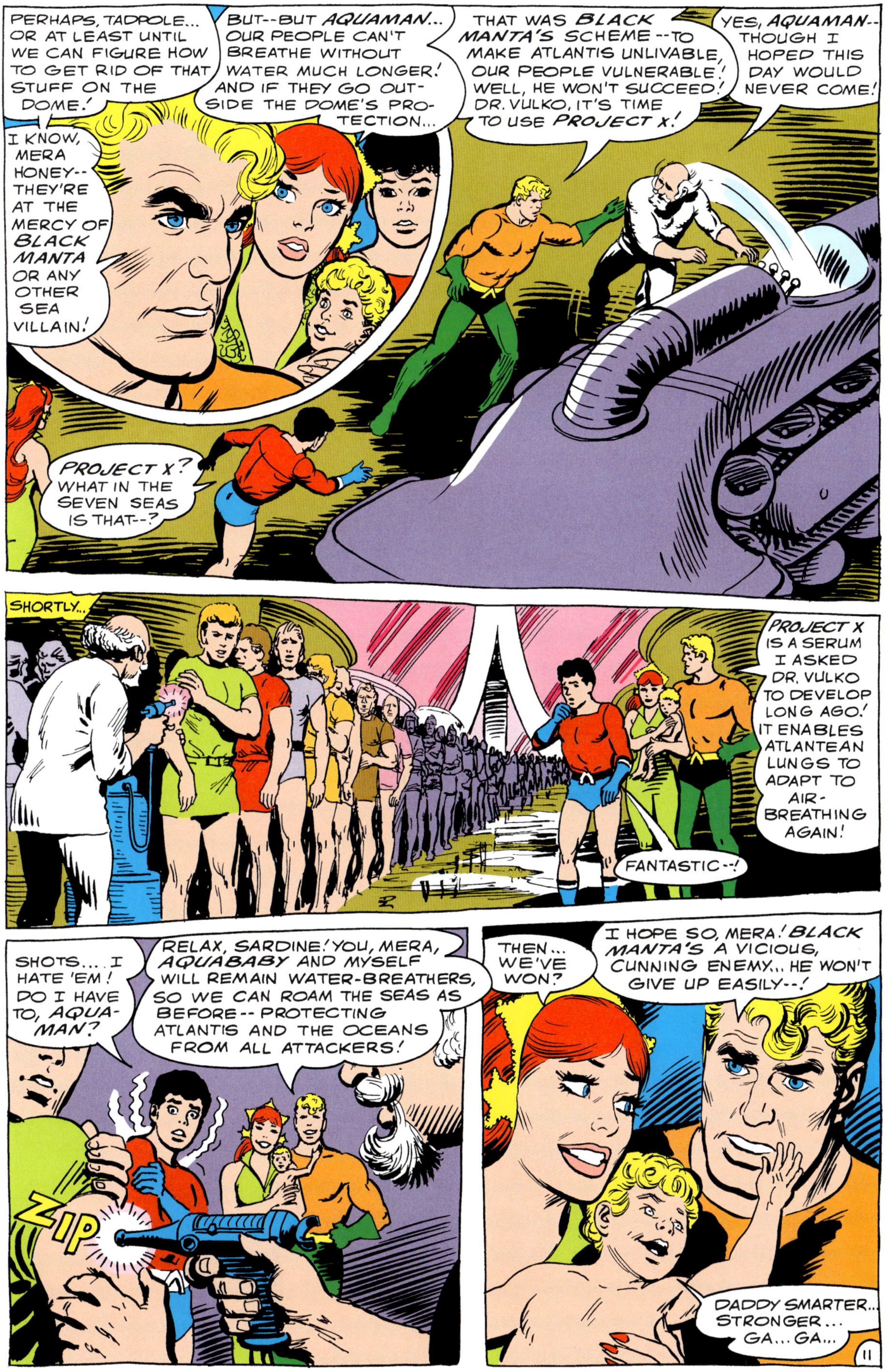
PERHAPS, TADPOLE... OR AT LEAST UNTIL WE CAN FIGURE HOW TO GET RID OF THAT STUFF ON THE DOME!
BUT--BUT AQUAMAN... OUR PEOPLE CAN'T BREATHE WITHOUT WATER MUCH LONGER! AND IF THEY GO OUTSIDE THE DOME'S PROTECTION...
I KNOW, MERA HONEY-- THEY'RE AT THE MERCY OF BLACK MANTA OR ANY OTHER SEA VILLAIN!
THAT WAS BLACK MANTA'S SCHEME--TO MAKE ATLANTIS UNLIVABLE, OUR PEOPLE VULNERABLE! WELL, HE WON'T SUCCEED! DR. VULKO, IT'S TIME TO USE PROJECT X!
YES, AQUAMAN-- THOUGH I HOPED THIS DAY WOULD NEVER COME!
PROJECT X? WHAT IN THE SEVEN SEAS IS THAT--?
SHORTLY...
PROJECT X IS A SERUM I ASKED DR. VULKO TO DEVELOP LONG AGO! IT ENABLES ATLANTEAN LUNGS TO ADAPT TO AIR-BREATHING AGAIN!
FANTASTIC--!
SHOTS... I HATE 'EM! DO I HAVE TO, AQUAMAN?
RELAX, SARDINE! YOU, MERA, AQUABABY AND MYSELF WILL REMAIN WATER-BREATHERS, SO WE CAN ROAM THE SEAS AS BEFORE--PROTECTING ATLANTIS AND THE OCEANS FROM ALL ATTACKERS!
ZIP
THEN... WE'VE WON?
I HOPE SO, MERA! BLACK MANTA'S A VICIOUS, CUNNING ENEMY... HE WON'T GIVE UP EASILY--!
DADDY SMARTER... STRONGER... GA... GA...
11

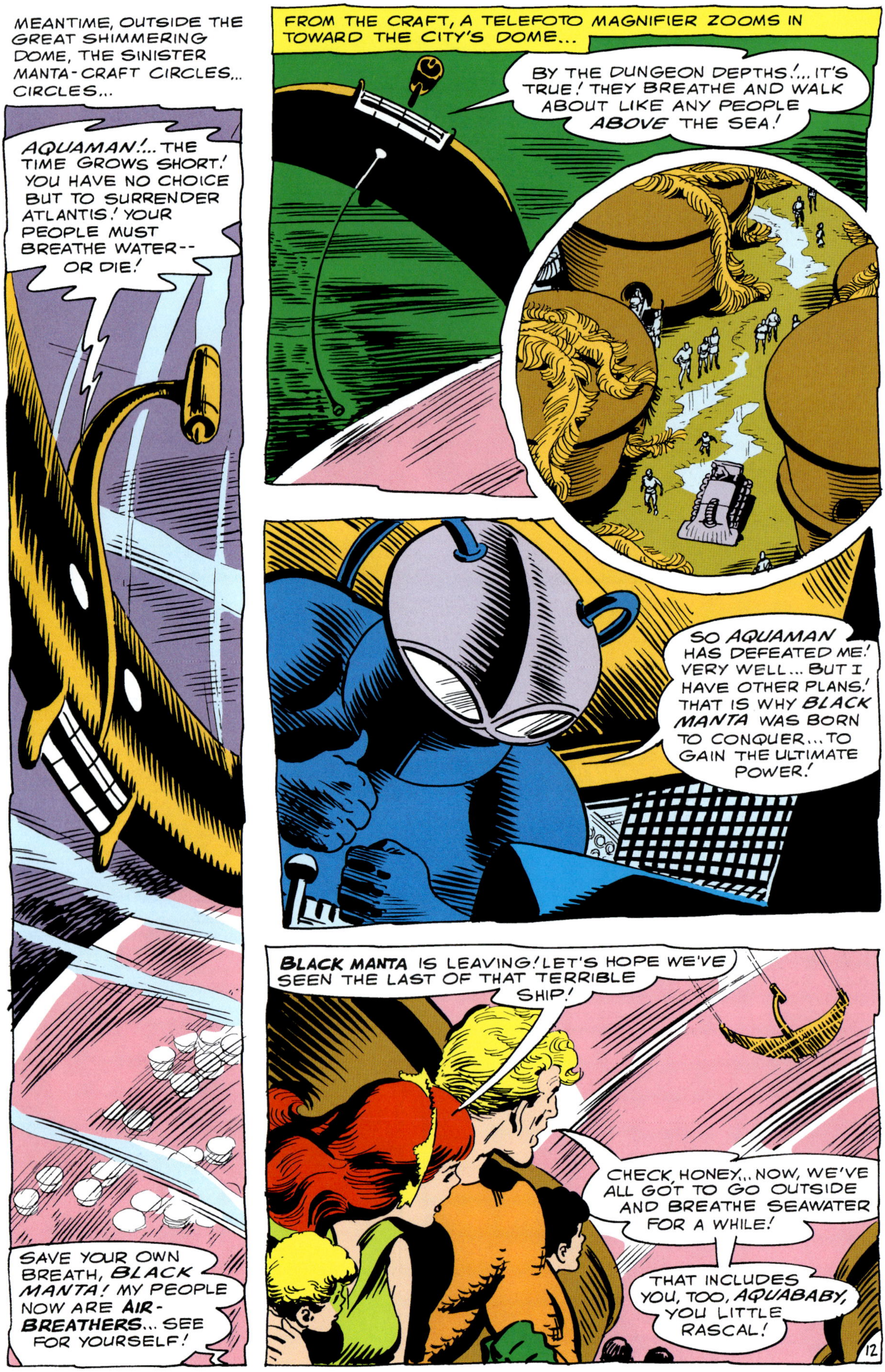
MEANTIME, OUTSIDE THE GREAT SHIMMERING DOME, THE SINISTER MANTA-CRAFT CIRCLES... CIRCLES...
AQUAMAN!... THE TIME GROWS SHORT! YOU HAVE NO CHOICE BUT TO SURRENDER ATLANTIS! YOUR PEOPLE MUST BREATHE WATER-- OR DIE!
SAVE YOUR OWN BREATH, BLACK MANTA! MY PEOPLE NOW ARE AIR-BREATHERS... SEE FOR YOURSELF!
FROM THE CRAFT, A TELEFOTO MAGNIFIER ZOOMS IN TOWARD THE CITY'S DOME...
BY THE DUNGEON DEPTHS!... IT'S TRUE! THEY BREATHE AND WALK ABOUT LIKE ANY PEOPLE ABOVE THE SEA!
SO AQUAMAN HAS DEFEATED ME! VERY WELL... BUT I HAVE OTHER PLANS! THAT IS WHY BLACK MANTA WAS BORN TO CONQUER... TO GAIN THE ULTIMATE POWER!
BLACK MANTA IS LEAVING! LET'S HOPE WE'VE SEEN THE LAST OF THAT TERRIBLE SHIP!
CHECK, HONEY... NOW, WE'VE ALL GOT TO GO OUTSIDE AND BREATHE SEAWATER FOR A WHILE!
THAT INCLUDES YOU, TOO, AQUABABY, YOU LITTLE RASCAL!
12

SHORTLY, OUTSIDE THE CITY...
MERA, YOU REMAIN HERE WITH THE GUARDS, WHILE AQUALAD AND I GO ON RECON PATROL, JUST TO MAKE SURE BLACK MANTA IS REALLY GONE!
BYE-BYE, DADDY...
SOON AFTER THE TWO AQUATIC ACES RIDE OFF...
QUEEN MERA!... A STRANGE MISSILE APPROACH-ING ATLANTIS!
IT CAN'T PENETRATE THE DOME -- BUT YOU'D BETTER INVESTIGATE IT!
AQUABABY AND I WILL BE ALL RIGHT... REMEMBER, I HAVE MY HARD-WATER POWERS!
BUT MOMENTS LATER...
OH, NO! BLACK MANTA'S SHIP!
IT WAS ALL A TRICK... BUT I'LL TORPEDO HIM RIGHT BACK WHERE HE CAME FROM!
BUT AS MERA'S HARD-WATER "TORP" STREAKS AT THE ONCOMING CRAFT...
ZAAAP
WHAAAM
13

THAT STRANGE MIST SPURTING TOWARD ME... OOOH!
IT IS SOME TIME LATER WHEN SOBS ECHO THROUGH THE ROYAL PALACE OF ATLANTIS...
MY PRECIOUS AQUABABY... GONE... STOLEN BY THAT FIEND!
EASY, HONEY-- WE'LL GET HIM BACK! I'LL TURN THE SEVEN SEAS INSIDE OUT IF I HAVE TO!
SUDDENLY, FROM OUTSIDE THE SORROWING CITY...
HEAR ME, AQUAMAN! I HAVE YOUR SON! SURRENDER TO ME-- AND I WILL RETURN HIM SAFELY!
AN ULTIMATUM!
NEVER HAS THE SEA KING FACED SUCH A CRUEL DECISION! NEVER HAS THE FLAME-HAIRED MERA KNOWN SUCH ANGUISH...
MY BABY... I CAN'T LIVE WITHOUT MY BABY!
THERE'S ONLY ONE WAY-- ONLY ONE THING TO DO...
BUT NOW, ANOTHER SINISTER CRAFT APPROACHES ATLANTIS...
ATLANTIS--MY GOAL... THE HOME OF MY GREATEST FOE, AQUAMAN! YET WHY DO I NOT FEEL JOY AT THE IDEA OF MEETING HIM IN A BATTLE AGAIN?
14

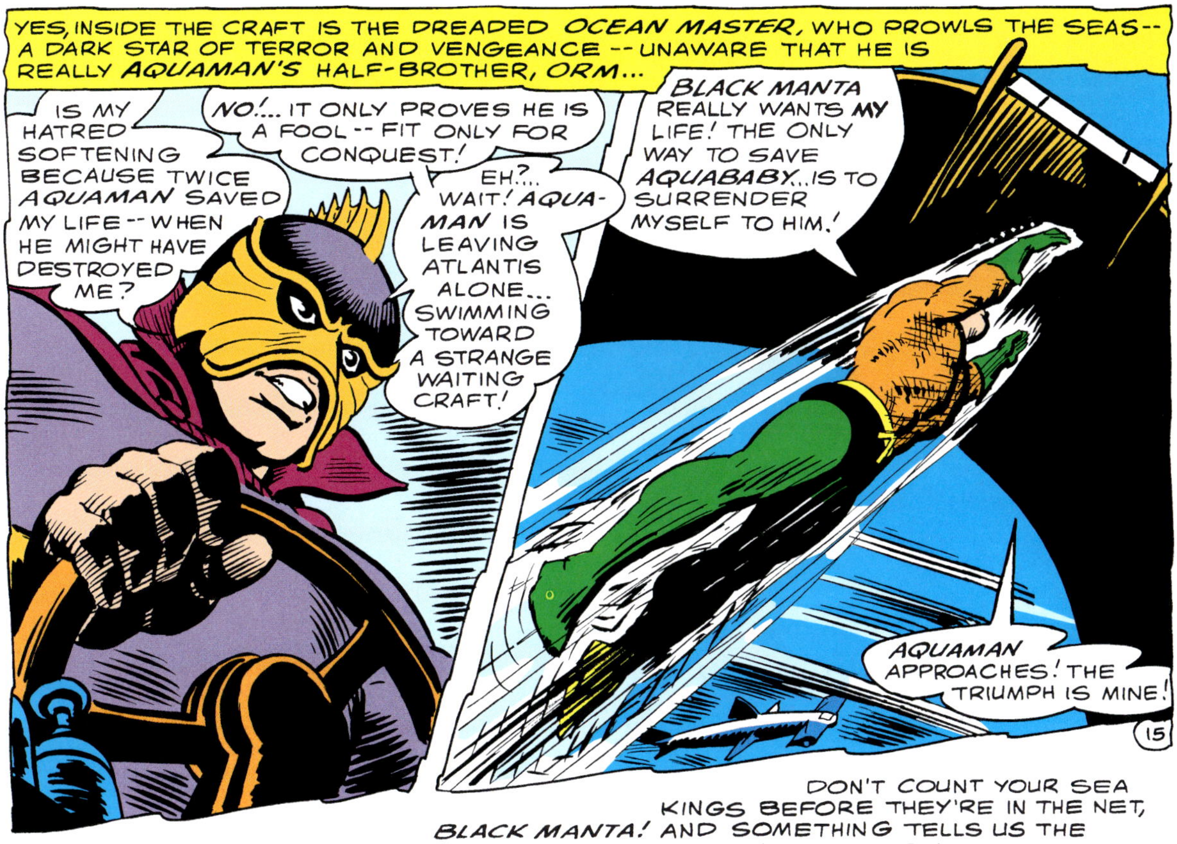
YES, INSIDE THE CRAFT IS THE DREADED OCEAN MASTER, WHO PROWLS THE SEAS-- A DARK STAR OF TERROR AND VENGEANCE -- UNAWARE THAT HE IS REALLY AQUAMAN'S HALF-BROTHER, ORM...
IS MY HATRED SOFTENING BECAUSE TWICE AQUAMAN SAVED MY LIFE -- WHEN HE MIGHT HAVE DESTROYED ME?
NO!... IT ONLY PROVES HE IS A FOOL -- FIT ONLY FOR CONQUEST!
EH?... WAIT! AQUAMAN IS LEAVING ATLANTIS ALONE... SWIMMING TOWARD A STRANGE WAITING CRAFT!
BLACK MANTA REALLY WANTS MY LIFE! THE ONLY WAY TO SAVE AQUABABY... IS TO SURRENDER MYSELF TO HIM!
AQUAMAN APPROACHES! THE TRIUMPH IS MINE!
15

DON'T COUNT YOUR SEA KINGS BEFORE THEY'RE IN THE NET, *BLACK MANTA!* AND SOMETHING TELLS US THE *OCEAN MASTER* IS GOING TO HAVE A HAND IN THE FANTASTIC UNDERSEA SHOCK WAVES THAT HIT YOU IN *PART 3*

AQUAMAN

between TWO DOOMS! PART 3

IF THE SEA ITSELF COULD WEEP, IT WOULD WEEP NOW FOR *AQUAMAN!* FOR WITH HIS GREAT STRENGTH USELESS, HIS FIGHTING COURAGE SMOTHERED, HE HUMBLY SURRENDERS HIMSELF TO HIS ARCH FOE, *BLACK MANTA*, TO SAVE HIS SON...

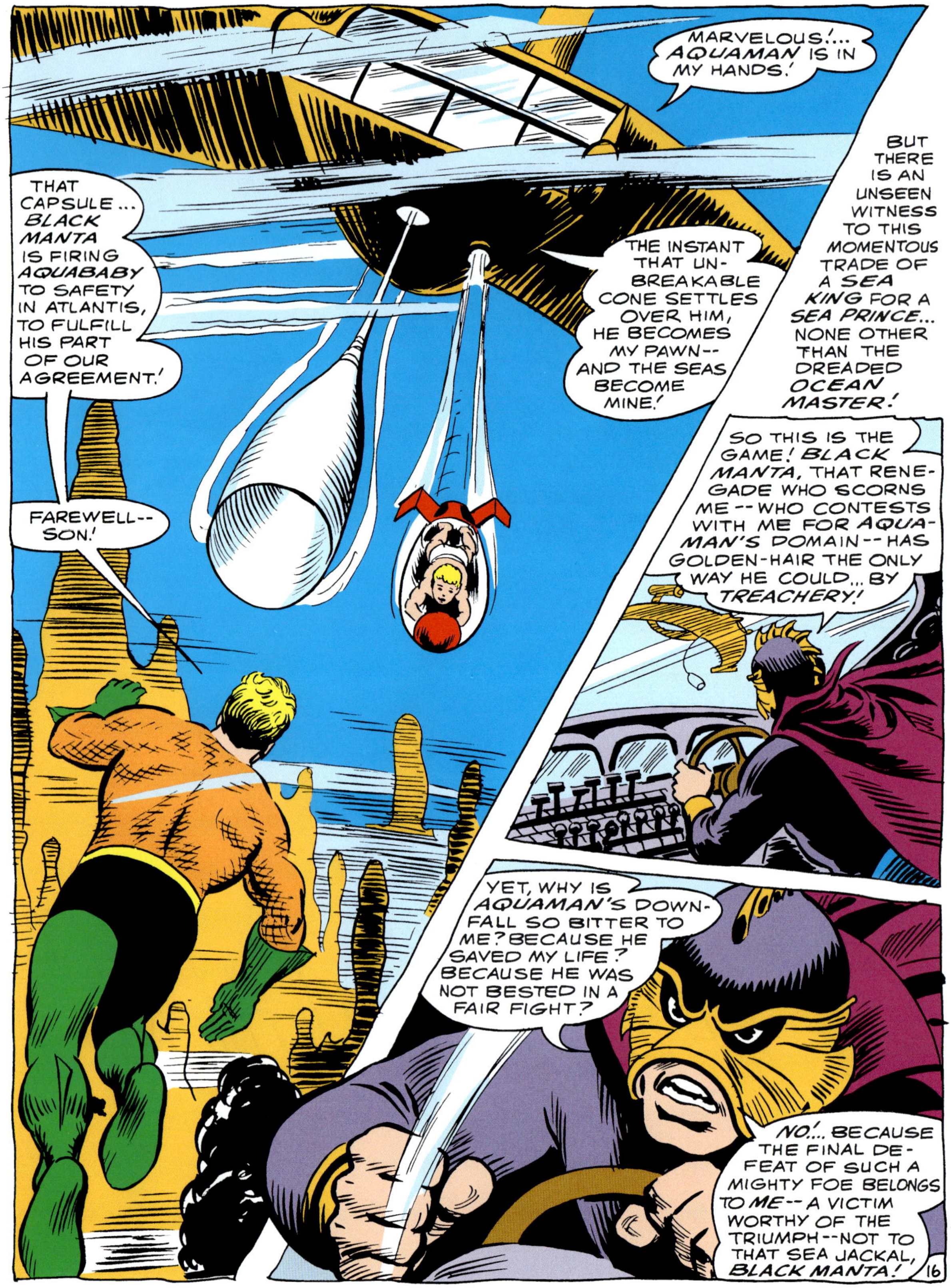

MARVELOUS!... AQUAMAN IS IN MY HANDS!
THAT CAPSULE... BLACK MANTA IS FIRING AQUABABY TO SAFETY IN ATLANTIS, TO FULFILL HIS PART OF OUR AGREEMENT!
THE INSTANT THAT UNBREAKABLE CONE SETTLES OVER HIM, HE BECOMES MY PAWN-- AND THE SEAS BECOME MINE!
FAREWELL-- SON!
BUT THERE IS AN UNSEEN WITNESS TO THIS MOMENTOUS TRADE OF A SEA KING FOR A SEA PRINCE... NONE OTHER THAN THE DREADED OCEAN MASTER!
SO THIS IS THE GAME! BLACK MANTA, THAT RENEGADE WHO SCORNS ME--WHO CONTESTS WITH ME FOR AQUAMAN'S DOMAIN--HAS GOLDEN-HAIR THE ONLY WAY HE COULD... BY TREACHERY!
YET, WHY IS AQUAMAN'S DOWNFALL SO BITTER TO ME? BECAUSE HE SAVED MY LIFE? BECAUSE HE WAS NOT BESTED IN A FAIR FIGHT?
NO!... BECAUSE THE FINAL DEFEAT OF SUCH A MIGHTY FOE BELONGS TO ME--A VICTIM WORTHY OF THE TRIUMPH--NOT TO THAT SEA JACKAL, BLACK MANTA!
16

NEXT MOMENT, AS THE CONE DROPS OVER AQUAMAN...
NOW, OCEAN MASTER TAKES A HAND IN THE GAME!
GREAT WAVES!... THE CAPSULE -- TURNING BACK TOWARD BLACK MANTA'S SHIP! HE DOUBLE-CROSSED ME!
BUT--THAT LONG CLAW ARM, FROM BEYOND THOSE ROCKS...
AQUABABY-- THE CAPSULE -- BEING INTERCEPTED! THAT SHIP -- IT CAN ONLY BE ... THE OCEAN MASTER!
NOW THAT I HAVE AQUAMAN'S SON, WE SHALL SEE WHAT IS BLACK MANTA'S NEXT MOVE IN THIS DEADLY GAME!
BLACK MANTA IS MOVING, ALL RIGHT-- AND VERY QUICKLY...
HELLO, MANS...
HE ATTACKS! BLACK MANTA DARES TO ATTACK!
THE FOOL! HE HAS FIRED THE OPENING SALVO OF HIS LAST BATTLE!
17

NOW, AS THE TWO CRAFT JOCKEY FOR POSITION IN THIS DUEL TO THE DEATH...
ZAAP
GREAT TIDES! MY TWO WORST ENEMIES FIGHTING IT OUT -- AND AQUABABY A TARGET INSIDE THE OCEAN MASTER'S SHIP!
THE OCEAN MASTER DOESN'T KNOW HE'S REALLY ORM, MY HALF-BROTHER, SO AQUABABY MEANS NOTHING TO HIM!
MUST TRY TO BREAK OUT OF THIS THING... MUST!
AND WHILE AQUAMAN STRUGGLES MIGHTILY AGAINST THE CONFINES OF HIS STRANGE PRISON...
HA-HA... AS BLACK MANTA STEERS IN A PATTERN TO EVADE MY FIRE, HE PLAYS RIGHT INTO MY HANDS!
ZAPP
NOW LET US SEE HIM EVADE THOSE CORAL SHAFTS IN HIS PATH!
18

MY SHIP--DAMAGED... OUT OF CONTROL!
KRUUNG
CRAANG
WHRAAM...
MEANWHILE, WHERE TWO WHALES ANSWER A UNIQUE TELEPATHIC COMMAND...
THAT'S IT, BIG BUSTERS... CRACK THIS NUTSHELL! AQUABABY NEEDS ME!
HA! HA! HA! HE'S FINISHED! BLACK MANTA IS FINISHED!
MANS-- LOOK!
TOO LATE, AQUABABY! OCEAN MASTER DOES NOT SEE THAT LAST DESPERATE SHOT FIRED FROM THE WRECK OF BLACK MANTA'S CRAFT...
WRAAAANG
19

A MOMENT LATER...
MANS HURT... POOR MANS...
MANTA-MEN! FINISH OFF THAT ARROGANT UPSTART, AND RETURN THE CHILD TO ME!
BUT AS THE DEADLY MUTANTS GLIDE IN...
WHAT--? AQUABABY HURLED MY MANTA-MEN BACK WITH A HARD-WATER ATTACK!
AS ALL LOYAL AQUA-FANS KNOW, AQUABABY INHERITED HARD-WATER POWERS FROM MERA, HIS BEAUTIFUL MOM...
TIME I ENTERED THE... AQUAMAN--! BUT HOW--?
HOW DID I GET FREE, CHUM? BETTER WORRY HOW YOU'RE GOING TO ESCAPE WHAT'S COMING TO YOU!
FIRST, SEA KING, HAVE WHAT'S COMING TO YOU!
WHILE NEARBY...
YOU SAVED MY LIFE, CHILD-- JUST LIKE YOUR NOBLE, PRECIOUS FATHER DID!
WHAT HUMILITY... TO OWE MY LIFE TO AN INFANT-- THE SON OF MY WORST ENEMY!
NICE MANS... I LIKE HIMS...
20

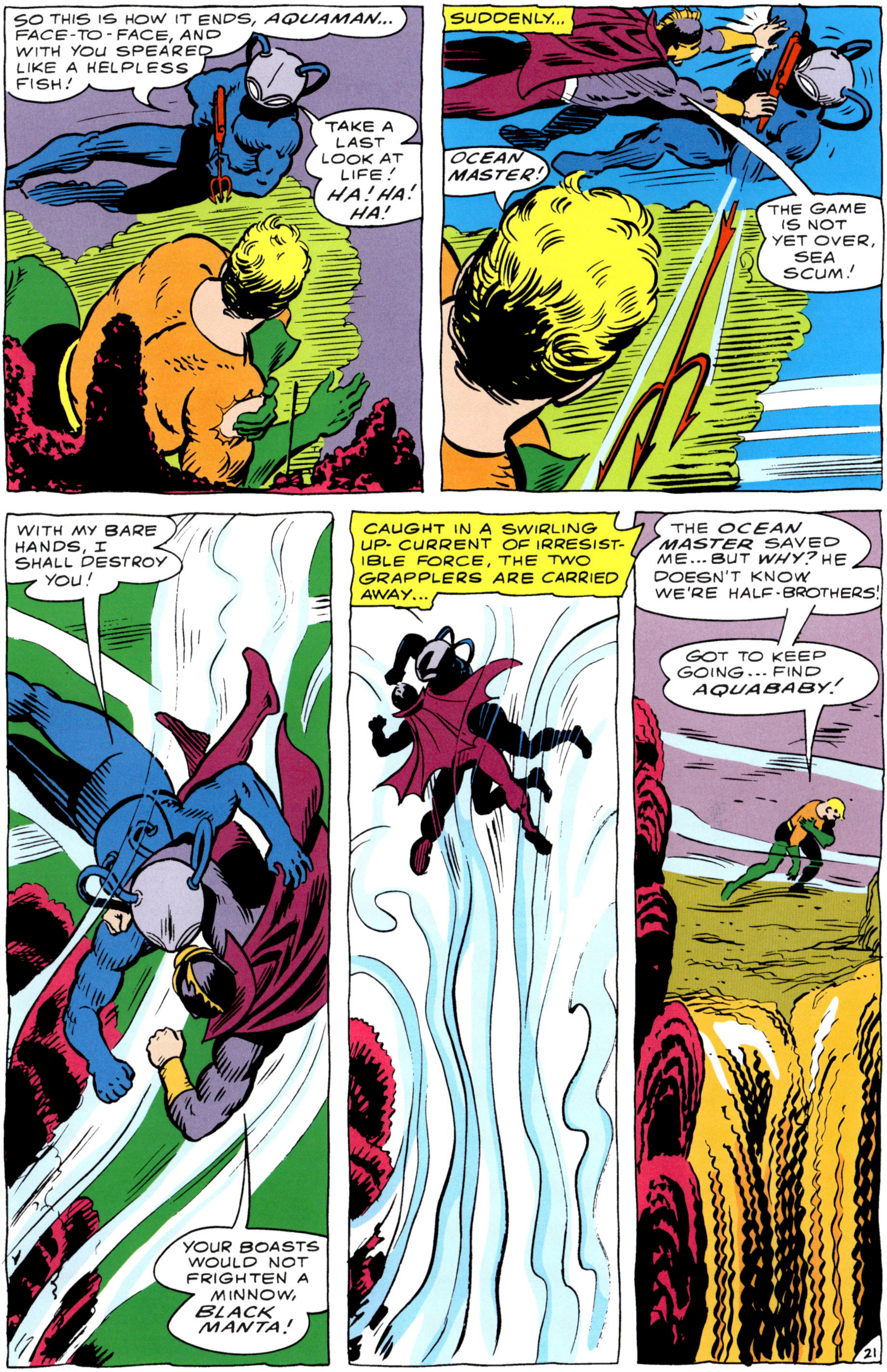
SO THIS IS HOW IT ENDS, AQUAMAN... FACE-TO-FACE, AND WITH YOU SPEARED LIKE A HELPLESS FISH!
TAKE A LAST LOOK AT LIFE! HA! HA! HA!
SUDDENLY...
OCEAN MASTER!
THE GAME IS NOT YET OVER, SEA SCUM!
WITH MY BARE HANDS, I SHALL DESTROY YOU!
YOUR BOASTS WOULD NOT FRIGHTEN A MINNOW, BLACK MANTA!
CAUGHT IN A SWIRLING UP-CURRENT OF IRRESISTIBLE FORCE, THE TWO GRAPPLERS ARE CARRIED AWAY...
THE OCEAN MASTER SAVED ME... BUT WHY? HE DOESN'T KNOW WE'RE HALF-BROTHERS!
GOT TO KEEP GOING... FIND AQUABABY!
21

MUST FIND HIM... MUST FIND MY SON... UUHHH...
AT THE SAME TIME, NEARBY...
BLACK MANTA... HE ELUDED MY GRASP-- ESCAPED INTO THE DEPTHS!
EH--? WHAT'S THAT? AQUABABY ...CRAWLING ALONE!
NOW, AS THE DREAD FIGHTER SCOOPS UP THE CRAWLING PRINCE OF ATLANTIS...
NICE MANS AGAIN...
THAT FIGURE... IT'S AQUAMAN! HE MUST HAVE BEEN WOUNDED BY BLACK MANTA!
THUS I RETURN YOUR SON TO YOU, SEA KING! THOUGH IF YOU WERE NOT HELPLESS, THERE WOULD BE ONLY BATTLE BETWEEN US!
FAREWELL!
DADDY!
AS THE TOUCH OF A TINY, FAMILIAR HAND REVIVES THE FALLEN AQUAMAN...
AQUABABY!... YOU'RE ALL RIGHT! THANK THE SEVEN SEAS!
THERE THEY ARE, MERA! NO SIGN OF EITHER BLACK MANTA OR THE OCEAN MASTER!
22

BOTH OF YOU ALIVE! IT'S A MIRACLE!
A MIRACLE? PERHAPS, MERA-- OR MAYBE JUST A CERTAIN UNDERSEA MENACE FINDING HE HAS SOMETHING ELSE IN HIS HEART BESIDES HATRED AND A LUST FOR POWER!
NOW, AS A HAPPY PROCESSION STARTS BACK TOWARD ATLANTIS...
WHY DO MY EYES TURN TOWARD THEM? WHY SHOULD I ENVY *AQUAMAN*?
THE *OCEAN MASTER'S* DESTINY IS DIFFERENT FROM ALL OTHERS! MY GOAL IS CLEAR... ABSOLUTE COMMAND OF THE SEAS-- AND SOME DAY, IT SHALL BE MINE!
AND SOME DAY, *AQUA-FANATICS*, WE'LL BRING BACK THE VILLAIN YOU LOVE TO HATE--*AQUAMAN'S* FOE OF FOES--THE DREAD BUT COMPLEX *OCEAN MASTER*! MEANTIME, STAY WET!
.23
THE END

AQUAMAN

SUPERMAN DC NATIONAL COMICS
AUG.
NO. 46
APPROVED BY THE COMICS CODE AUTHORITY
15¢
AQUAMAN
YOU!
YOU DID THIS TO HER!
AND NOW... YOU DIE!!

THE FOLLOWING STORY WAS WRITTEN BY STEVE SKEATES, DRAWN BY JIM APARO, INKED BY AN INKER AND EDITED BY DICK GIORDANO
AQUAMAN
THE EXPLANATION!
G-127
1

AS THE RISING SUN HERALDS THE DAWN OF A NEW DAY, AN AMBULANCE RACES THROUGH THE SLEEPING CITY...
...AND SLOWLY, THE MOTION OF THE CAREENING VEHICLE JARS THE SEA KING BACK TO CONSCIOUSNESS...
MERA! IT...IT IS YOU!
BUT... BUT HOW? HOW DID YOU GET HERE? WHAT...
HUSH... I'LL TELL YOU EVERYTHING LATER... AFTER THE DOCTOR'S EXAMINED YOU! NOW, TRY TO REST...
AS AQUAMAN DRIFTS INTO A TROUBLED REST, THE SEA QUEEN'S THOUGHTS FLOAT BACK... AND, IN HER MIND, RELIVES THE SHOCK AND THE HORROR OF THE EVENTS GONE BY...
IT SEEMS UNREAL NOW... A NIGHTMARE!
AND YET... IT REALLY DID HAPPEN! IT WAS ALL REAL!
KEEP A FIRM GRIP ON AQUABABY, TADPOLE! WE MUST FIND A WAY OUT OF THIS SWIRLING MADNESS!
2

I'M CUT OFF FROM THE OTHERS...
...CAN HARDLY SEE! WHERE'S AQUAMAN... AQUALAD? WHERE...
GRAB HER!!
WHA-?
THESE MEN...THIEVES! AQUAMAN HAD THEM BANISHED FROM ATLANTIS YEARS AGO! HOW--?
CAN'T... BREAK LOOSE FROM THEIR HOLDS... TO USE MY HARD-WATER POWER! MUST CALL AQUAMAN!
AQUAMAN! HELP! HELP!!
SHE'S STOPPED STRUGGLING! WE'VE GOT HER NOW!!
THANK GOD HE'S HEARD ME! NOW I SHOULD BE SAFE!
3

"AS AQUAMAN QUICKLY CLOSED THE DISTANCE BETWEEN US, ONE OF MY CAPTORS HUNG BACK, AND AQUAMAN, WEAKENED BY THE WHIRLPOOL, WAS RENDERED UNCONSCIOUS WITH A SINGLE PUNCH AND I WAS PULLED AWAY... UNTIL, AT LAST, AQUAMAN WAS NO LONGER IN SIGHT..."
A SUB! THEY MUST HAVE USED IT TO CREATE THE SWIRLING WATER! AND SURFACE MEN-- THEY'RE THE ONES BEHIND THIS!
QUICK! GIT HER ABOARD!
STILL TOO WEAK...CAN'T FIGHT BACK!
THAT'S IT! MAKE IT REAL TIGHT!
NOW, LISTEN, SISTER!...WE KNOW ABOUT YOUR ONE HOUR LIMIT! AND, IF YOU GIVE US ANY HASSLE, WE'LL LEAVE YUH OUTTA WATER TILL YOU DIE! UNDERSTAND??
WHAT OF OUR REWARD? WE WERE TOLD WE WOULD BE PAID WELL!
DON'T BUG ME ABOUT THAT! TALK TO NARKRAN... HE'S YOUR BOSS!
NARKRAN??
THE ATLANTEAN OFFICIAL AQUAMAN TRUSTS ABOVE ALL OTHERS... THE ONE HE MADE DEPUTY LEADER!
THIS CAN'T BE! NONE OF THIS MAKES SENSE!
4

SOMETIME LATER...
OUR TIMING IS PERFECT! THE HOUR IS ALMOST UP! AND SHE'S TOO WEAK TO PUT UP ANY RESISTANCE!
HERE'S YOUR CELL, SISTER!
I SUGGEST YOU DON'T FOOL AROUND WITH YOUR HARD-WATER POWER! THIS CELL IS MONITORED! AND IF YOU TRY TO BREAK OUT, WE'LL PUMP ALL THE WATER OUT, AND LEAVE IT OUT!
...THEN THEY LEFT ME TO WAIT... HOURS AND HOURS-WONDERING WHY I WAS THERE... WONDERING WHAT THEY WERE PLANNING...
Editor's Note: WHAT WERE THEY PLANNING? WELL, THROUGH THE POWER OF OUR IMAGINATIONS, LET US GO BACK AND FIND OUT EXACTLY WHAT THESE BADDIES HAD UP THEIR SLEEVES...
GOOD WORK! HER HARD-WATER POWER COUPLED WITH OUR ARTIFICIAL WHIRLPOOLS WILL MAKE IT A CINCH FOR US TO CAPTURE ANY SHIP WHOSE CARGO WE WANT! WHEN THAT BIG GOLD SHIPMENT NEARS THE HARBOR, WE GRAB IT!
I STILL SAY WE SHOULDA GRABBED AQUAMAN, TOO!
5

HE WOULDA BEEN TOO HARD TO HANDLE!
BESIDES WE DON'T NEED HIM! ALL WE GOTTA DO IS CONVINCE HIS CHICK THAT WE'VE GOT THE GREAT SEA KING HELD CAPTIVE! NOW, C'MON--LET'S GET IN THERE AND GIVE HER THE NEWS!
WHAT?? YOU'RE OUT OF YOUR MIND IF YOU THINK I'M GOING TO HELP YOU COMMIT PIRACY!
YOU'LL HELP US... OR AQUAMAN DIES!
YES! WE'VE GOT HIM, TOO! IN A SPECIAL LEAD-LINED ROOM SO HE CAN'T COMMUNICATE WITH HIS FISH FRIENDS!
AND IT'D BE VERY EASY FOR US TO PUMP THE WATER OUTTA THERE... SO...
I DON'T BELIEVE YOU! IF YOU TOOK HIM CAPTIVE WHY DIDN'T I SEE HIM ON THE WAY HERE?!? WHY DON'T YOU LET ME SEE HIM NOW!
YOU DIDN'T SEE HIM, BECAUSE WE KEPT HIM IN ANOTHER PART OF THE SHIP! AND I'D HAVE TO BE A REAL DUMMY TO LET THE TWO OF YOU GET TOGETHER NOW!..
6
I STILL DON'T BELIEVE YOU!
HAVE IT YOUR OWN WAY! BUT, YOU'VE GOT FIFTEEN MINUTES TO DECIDE! IF YOU'RE SO SURE WE DON'T HAVE HIM, THEN YOU HAVE NOTHING TO WORRY ABOUT... DO YOU?

AQUAMAN

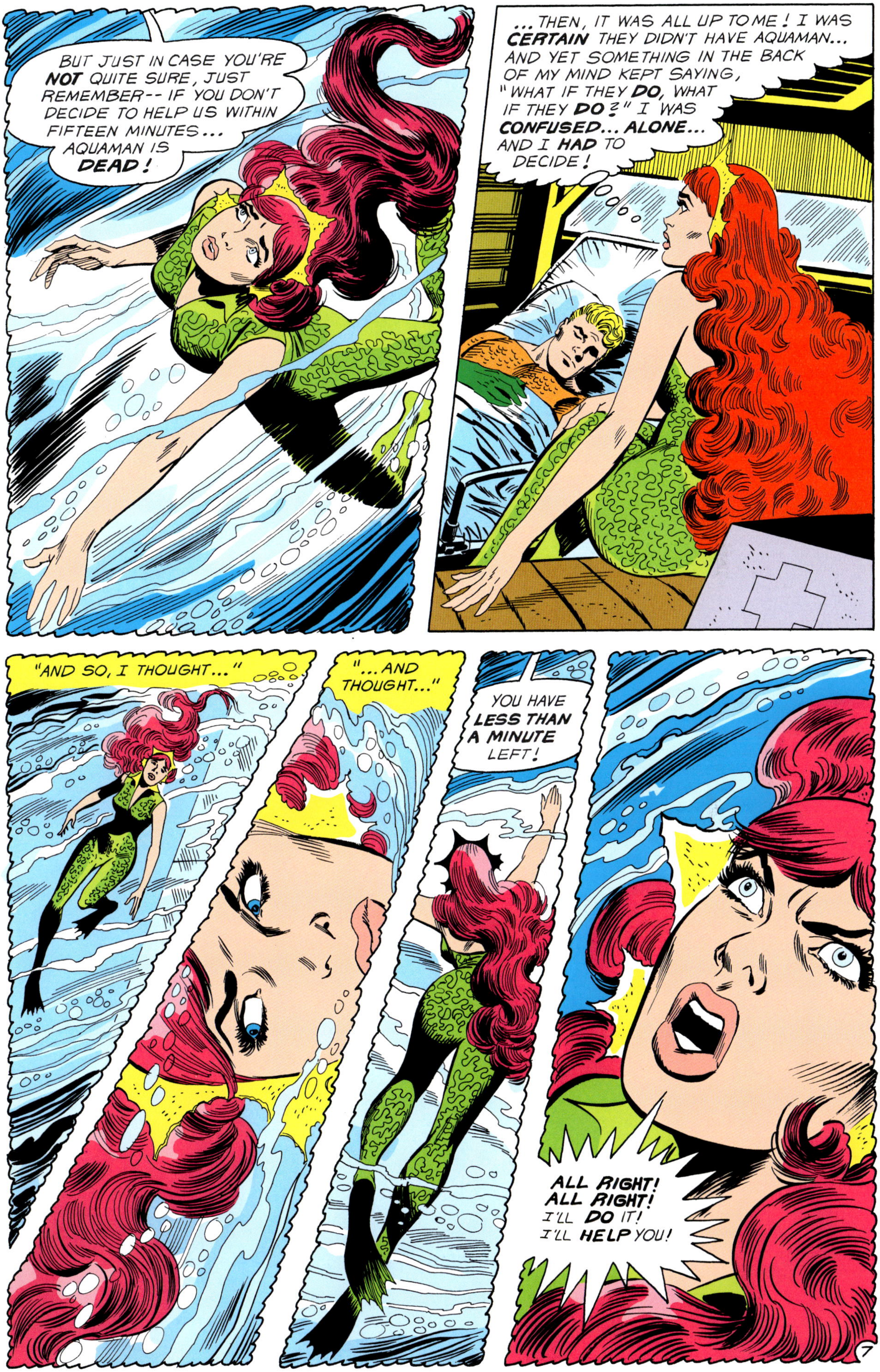
BUT JUST IN CASE YOU'RE NOT QUITE SURE, JUST REMEMBER-- IF YOU DON'T DECIDE TO HELP US WITHIN FIFTEEN MINUTES... AQUAMAN IS DEAD!
...THEN, IT WAS ALL UP TO ME! I WAS CERTAIN THEY DIDN'T HAVE AQUAMAN... AND YET SOMETHING IN THE BACK OF MY MIND KEPT SAYING, "WHAT IF THEY DO, WHAT IF THEY DO?" I WAS CONFUSED... ALONE... AND I HAD TO DECIDE!
"AND SO, I THOUGHT..."
"...AND THOUGHT..."
YOU HAVE LESS THAN A MINUTE LEFT!
ALL RIGHT! ALL RIGHT! I'LL DO IT! I'LL HELP YOU!
7

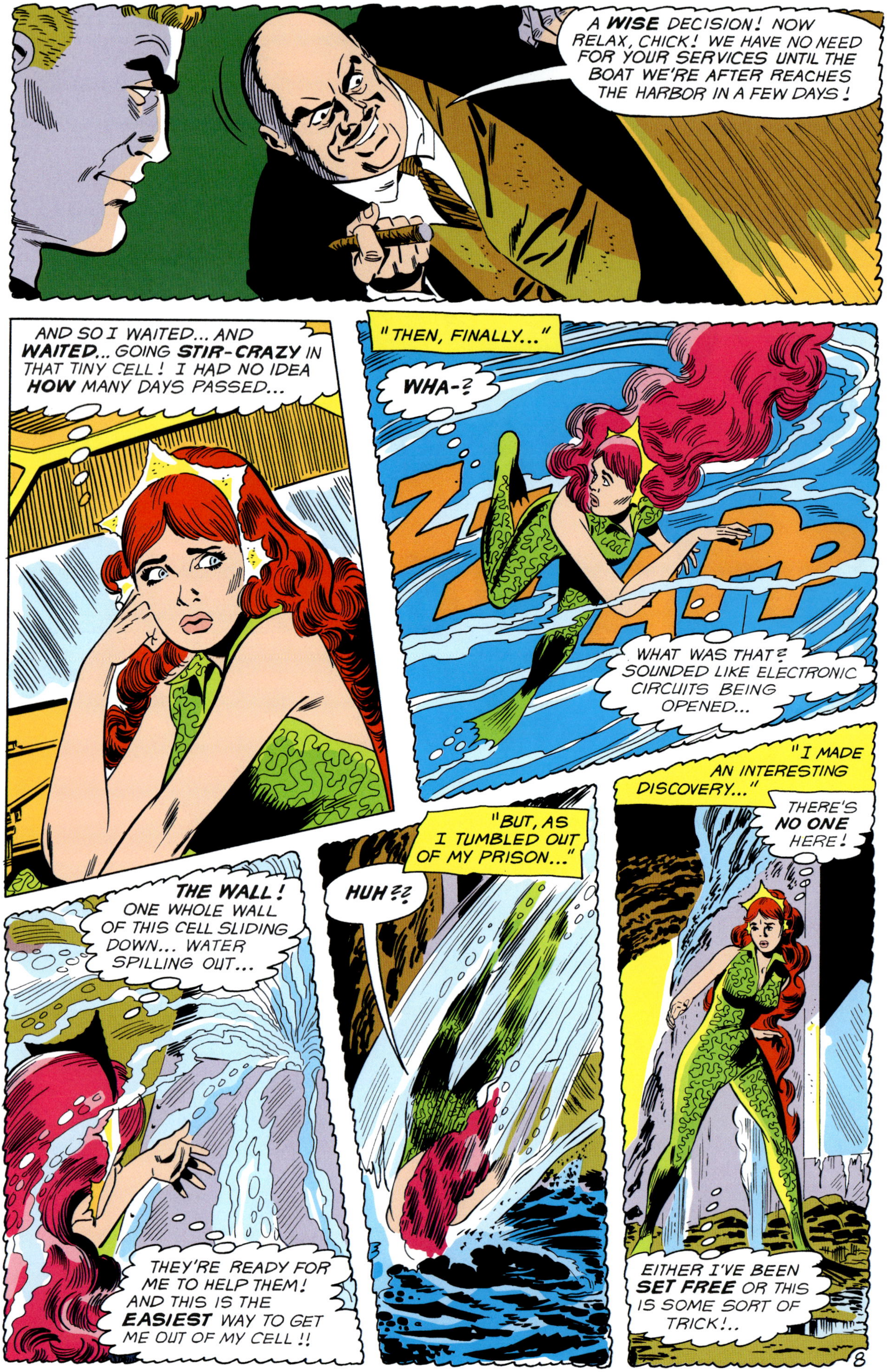
A WISE DECISION! NOW RELAX, CHICK! WE HAVE NO NEED FOR YOUR SERVICES UNTIL THE BOAT WE'RE AFTER REACHES THE HARBOR IN A FEW DAYS!
AND SO I WAITED... AND WAITED... GOING STIR-CRAZY IN THAT TINY CELL! I HAD NO IDEA HOW MANY DAYS PASSED...
"THEN, FINALLY..."
WHA-?
ZZAPP
WHAT WAS THAT? SOUNDED LIKE ELECTRONIC CIRCUITS BEING OPENED...
THE WALL! ONE WHOLE WALL OF THIS CELL SLIDING DOWN... WATER SPILLING OUT...
THEY'RE READY FOR ME TO HELP THEM! AND THIS IS THE EASIEST WAY TO GET ME OUT OF MY CELL!!
"BUT, AS I TUMBLED OUT OF MY PRISON..."
HUH??
"I MADE AN INTERESTING DISCOVERY..."
THERE'S NO ONE HERE!
EITHER I'VE BEEN SET FREE OR THIS IS SOME SORT OF TRICK!..
8

COULD IT... HAVE BEEN AN ACCIDENT?? WAS THE WALL TO THE CELL SOMEHOW OPENED ACCIDENTALLY??
Editor's Note: MERA RAN FROM HER CELL UNAWARE THAT AQUAMAN HAD A HAND IN HER ESCAPE. DURING THE FIGHT, AS SEEN LAST ISSUE, THE MECHANISM THAT CONTROLLED THE SLIDING WALL WAS SET INTO OPERATION WHEN ONE OF AQUAMAN'S OPPONENTS SLAMMED INTO A MAIN CONTROL PANEL...
KLAK
NO MATTER HOW IT HAPPENED, THIS IS MY CHANCE TO GET AWAY AND FIND MY WAY BACK TO THE SEA WHERE I'LL BE ABLE TO FIGHT OFF ANY ONE WHO COMES AFTER ME WITH MY HARD-WATER POWER!
I HAVE TO FIND THAT ROOM IN WHICH THE SUB SURFACED...
BUT, JUST THEN...
UH-OH-- TROUBLE!
HUH?
9

HALT RIGHT WHERE Y--YOW!
NO ONE'S STOPPING ME!
WAK
NO ONE!
UNNGH
NOT NOW!
I MUST GET OUT!
I MUST!!
WAK
10

AND SHORTLY...
IF AQUAMAN IS HERE, I'VE GOT TO FIND SOME WAY TO RESCUE HIM!
AHH, THIS IS THE ROOM I WAS LOOKING FOR!
THE LOCK'S OPEN! I'M OUT! FREE!
BUT...
BUT NOW WHAT DO I DO?
I CAN'T JUST LEAVE! NOT IF AQUAMAN'S IN THERE!
GOT TO GET HIM OUT OF THERE! BUT I CAN'T DO IT ALONE! NEED HELP! BUT WHERE--
11

"SUDDENLY..."
WHA-? AQUAMAN!
KA-BLAM
HE'S HURT! GOT TO GET TO HIM!
HE HASN'T SEEN ME YET, BUT...
OH! A WHIRLPOOL! HEADING TOWARD HIM MUCH FASTER THAN I AM!
THAT EXPLOSION MUST'VE SET THE ARTIFICIAL WHIRLPOOL MACHINERY INTO OPERATION!
Editor's Note: REMEMBER?-- WE WITNESSED THIS EXPLOSION LAST ISH!
GOTTA STOP IT FROM GRABBING HIM! MY HARD-WATER POWER...
NO! MY POWER HAS NO EFFECT ON IT AT ALL! IT'S TOO STRONG! THE WATER MUST BE WHIRLING ABOUT AT A FANTASTIC RATE!
AND NOW IT'S GOT AQUAMAN!!
GOT TO FIND SOME WAY TO GET HIM OUT!
HE... HE SEES ME! BUT...
HE...HE'S SHAKING HIS HEAD... AS THOUGH HE DOESN'T BELIEVE I'M HERE!
12

"BUT, BEFORE I COULD MAKE ANOTHER MOVE... THERE WAS A SUDDEN BLINDING FLASH, THE GIANT UNDERWATER FORTRESS I HAD JUST ESCAPED EXPLODED..."
UNNNGH
OOOOOO...
13

AQUAMAN

"THE EXPLOSION NEUTRALIZED THE WHIRLPOOL! AND AQUAMAN WAS FREED FROM THAT..."
BUT... WE... WE'RE SHOOTING THROUGH... WATER TOO QUICKLY! CAN'T TAKE IT!
AQUAMAN CLOSER TO THE EXPLOSION... ALREADY PASSED OUT! I'M NEXT... UNLESS...
G-GOT TO FORM... A PROTECTIVE SHELL OF HARD-WATER AROUND ME...
AQUAMAN STILL MOVING TOO QUICKLY! HAVE TO EXTEND THE SHELL TO HIM!
14

"I STRAINED... THINKING ONLY OF AQUAMAN'S FATE, EXTENDING MY POWER FURTHER THAN EVER BEFORE...
THERE! WE'VE SLOWED DOWN ENOUGH! NOW I CAN **REMOVE** THE HARD-WATER SHELLS AND **CHECK** ON AQUAMAN! I **PRAY** THAT HE HASN'T--
THANK GOD! HE'S **ALL RIGHT**! JUST **UNCONSCIOUS**!
HE'S **BREATHING** REGULARILY! DOESN'T SEEM INJURED-- **NO! WAIT!! HE'S...**
...HE'S **GASPING**! SOMETHING'S **WRONG**! HE CAN'T SEEM TO **CATCH HIS BREATH**!
HAVE TO **DO** SOMETHING... GET **HELP**! BUT... **HOW**? **WHERE**?
15

UP AHEAD-- A **BEACH**! THAT **COULD** BE THE ANSWER!
SOMETIMES, AIR HAS A REVIVING EFFECT ON ATLANTEANS, JUST AS PURE OXYGEN HAS ON ORDINARY HUMANS!
16

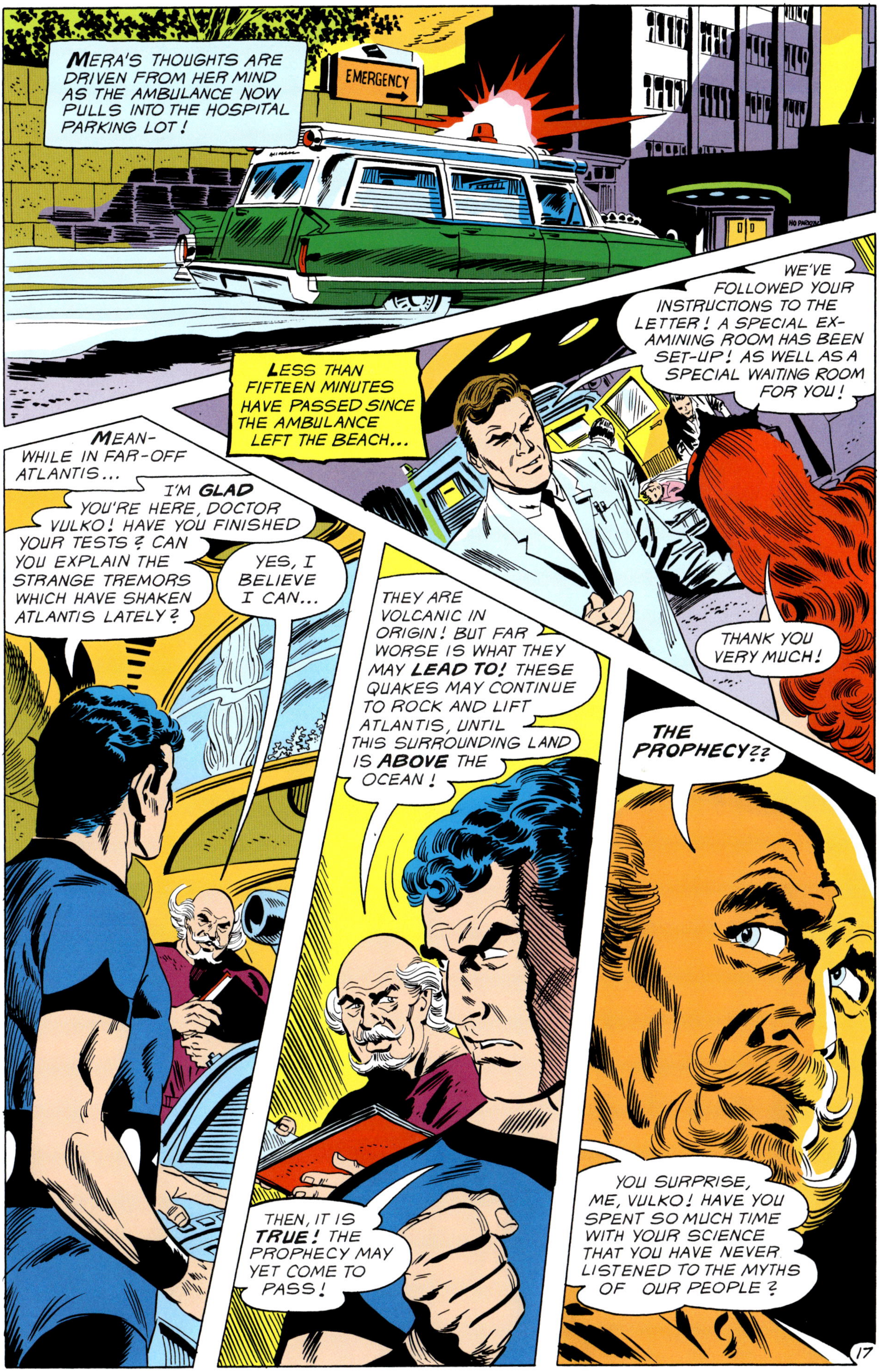

MERA'S THOUGHTS ARE DRIVEN FROM HER MIND AS THE AMBULANCE NOW PULLS INTO THE HOSPITAL PARKING LOT!
EMERGENCY
LESS THAN FIFTEEN MINUTES HAVE PASSED SINCE THE AMBULANCE LEFT THE BEACH...
WE'VE FOLLOWED YOUR INSTRUCTIONS TO THE LETTER! A SPECIAL EXAMINING ROOM HAS BEEN SET-UP! AS WELL AS A SPECIAL WAITING ROOM FOR YOU!
THANK YOU VERY MUCH!
MEANWHILE IN FAR-OFF ATLANTIS...
I'M GLAD YOU'RE HERE, DOCTOR VULKO! HAVE YOU FINISHED YOUR TESTS? CAN YOU EXPLAIN THE STRANGE TREMORS WHICH HAVE SHAKEN ATLANTIS LATELY?
YES, I BELIEVE I CAN...
THEY ARE VOLCANIC IN ORIGIN! BUT FAR WORSE IS WHAT THEY MAY LEAD TO! THESE QUAKES MAY CONTINUE TO ROCK AND LIFT ATLANTIS, UNTIL THIS SURROUNDING LAND IS ABOVE THE OCEAN!
THEN, IT IS TRUE! THE PROPHECY MAY YET COME TO PASS!
THE PROPHECY??
YOU SURPRISE, ME, VULKO! HAVE YOU SPENT SO MUCH TIME WITH YOUR SCIENCE THAT YOU HAVE NEVER LISTENED TO THE MYTHS OF OUR PEOPLE?
17

IT IS SAID THAT AT THE END OF THIS CENTURY, ATLANTIS SHALL RISE TO THE SURFACE! AND WE SHALL TAKE OUR PLACE AMONG THE KINGDOMS OF THE SURFACE WORLD-- THE PLACE THAT ONCE WAS OURS EONS AGO!
WHEN WE DO RISE, IT SHALL BE THE GREATEST DAY FOR ALL ATLANTIS! AND I-- I WILL BE THE RULER OF THE GREAT DOMED KINGDOM!
HUH? BUT... WHAT OF AQUAMAN? SURELY, HE WILL RETURN SOON... AND RECLAIM HIS KINGDOM!
NO! HE WILL NOT RETURN!
...ER... THAT IS... I DOUBT THAT HE'LL RETURN! HE'S BEEN GONE TOO LONG! I...I HAVE A FEELING SOME DISASTER MAY HAVE BEFALLEN HIM!
ENOUGH, DOCTOR VULKO-- YOU HAVE ANSWERED MY QUESTION! YOU NEED STAY NO LONGER!
I WISH TO BE ALONE! THERE IS MUCH I MUST THINK ABOUT!
AS YOU WISH!
WITH EACH DAY, HIS MADNESS GROWS! HE BECOMES MORE AND MORE A TYRANT! SOMETHING MUST BE DONE!
BUT... WHAT?
AND IN ANOTHER SECTOR OF ATLANTIS, SIMILAR THOUGHTS PASS THROUGH ANOTHER'S MIND...
IF ONLY AQUAMAN WERE HERE! IF ONLY THERE WERE SOMEONE HERE WHO COULD PUT AN END TO NARKRAN'S RULE!
18

HEY-? WHAT'S GOING ON OVER THERE?
SOMETHING'S UP! THOSE TWO ARE BEHAVING TOO SNEAKY FOR THEM TO BE ON THE UP AND UP!
I'LL FOLLOW HIM AND GET TO THE BOTTOM OF THIS! I'VE BEEN KEEPING MY EYES OPEN LATELY AND I'VE NOTICED AN AWFUL LOT OF PUSSY-FOOTING AROUND GOING ON! HOPE I'M WRONG...
CAN'T JUST GO BARGING IN RIGHT AFTER HIM! I'LL TRY TO SNEAK IN...
SOMETHING TELLS ME I SHOULDN'T BE DOING THIS, BUT...
SUDDENLY...
COME ON RIGHT IN, YOU LITTLE SPY!!
WHOOOP!
19

OOOMPHF
STOP THE FIGHTING! THIS IS SENSELESS!
WAK
UNNGH!
BUT, MUPO-- SHE DOESN'T BELONG HERE! SHE FOLLOWED ME! IT--
DON'T YOU REALIZE WHO THIS IS! THIS IS AQUAGIRL, DEVOTED FOLLOWER OF THE TRUE KING OF ATLANTIS! SHE IS NO ENEMY! IF ANYTHING, SHE IS ON OUR SIDE!
YOUR SIDE??
YES... I AM THE LEADER OF THE REVOLUTIONARIES! WE HAVE GROUPED TOGETHER BECAUSE WE HAVE LIKE MINDS... LIKE PURPOSE.
OUR NUMBER HAVE GROWN AND GROWN! WE ARE NOW STRONG ENOUGH TO OVERTHROW THE TYRANT, NARKRAN! THIS IS OUR PURPOSE!
THEN, I WAS RIGHT... SOMETHING HAS BEEN GOING ON!
20

WH-WHEN IS THIS GOING TO TAKE PLACE?
NO! DON'T TELL HER! I STILL SAY WE SHOULDN'T TRUST HER!
PERHAPS YOU'RE RIGHT! WE SHOULD ACT WITH CAUTION!
BUT THERE'S ONE THING I WILL SAY-- IT WILL BE SOON -- VERY SOON!!
BUT...YOU CAN'T! YOU MUSTN'T! IT'S TOO DANGEROUS! TOO MANY LIVES WILL BE LOST!
AT LEAST, WAIT A FEW WEEKS! AQUAMAN MAY BE RETURNING HOME AT THIS VERY MOMENT!
21
NO! WE'VE WAITED LONG ENOUGH! WE MUST STRIKE!
AND IF LIVES ARE LOST, THAT'S THE PRICE THAT HAS TO BE PAID IF A TYRANT IS TO BE OVERTHROWN!

AQUAMAN

EPILOGUE: THE SUN THAT HOURS BEFORE HAD LENT PROMISE TO THE NEW DAWNING DAY, NOW SINKS GENTLY IN THE WEST AND AS DUSK SETTLES UPON THE CITY A MAN AND A WOMAN IN STRANGE GARB LEAVE A HOSPITAL AND WALK AWAY HAND IN HAND...
STRANGE--! I NEVER SUSPECTED YOUR CAPTORS WERE ATLANTEANS! FROM THE WAY THEY HIT ME, I FELT THEY MUST HAVE HAD SOME SORT OF SUPER-STRENGTH!
AN HOSPITAL
THE SWIRLING WATER MUST HAVE WEAKENED ME FAR MORE THAN I THOUGHT!
HOSPITAL ZONE
AS FOR THE MAARZON RING WHICH ONE OF THEM WORE...
...I SUPPOSE THE EXPLANATION FOR THAT IS QUITE SIMPLE! PROBABLY, AFTER BEING EXILED FROM ATLANTIS, ONE OF THE MEN VISITED THE COLONY OF THE MAARZONS AND PICKED UP THE RING THERE!
I WASTED A LOT OF TIME TRYING TO TRACE THAT RING! BUT THEN, IT WAS THE ONLY CLUE I HAD TO WORK ON!
ONCE THINGS HAVE BEEN SETTLED BACK IN ATLANTIS, I'LL HAVE TO TELL YOU ABOUT THE STRANGE LANDS I VISITED!
THERE WAS THE LAND OF THE SORCERERS, WHOSE QUEEN LOOKED EXACTLY LIKE YOU... AND...
WELL, OF ALL THE--!
THIS IS THE FIRST TIME WE'VE SEEN EACH OTHER IN WEEKS, AND ALL YOU CAN DO IS TALK ABOUT OTHER WOMEN!
22

OKAY, OKAY-- I THINK WE'VE SPENT JUST ABOUT ENOUGH TIME ON SMALL TALK! C'MON!
WE HAVE TO GET BACK TO ATLANTIS AND SEE TO IT THAT NARKRAN RECEIVES THE JUSTICE HE SO RICHLY DESERVES!
OF COURSE, EVERYTHING HAS IT'S BRIGHTER SIDE! IT CERTAINLY IS GOING TO BE GREAT TO SEE TULA, AQUALAD AND AQUABABY AGAIN!
BUT AT THE MOMENT, AQUALAD IS NOT BACK HOME! HE IS, JUST IN CASE YOU'VE FORGOTTEN (WE HAVEN'T FORGOTTEN--HONEST!), NOW FAR FROM ATLANTIS, ENGAGED IN COMBAT WITH THE DREAD MONSTER CALLED THE BUGALA...
NEXT ISSUE:
ATLANTEAN SHOW-DOWN!
23

AQUAMAN
AFTER THE BLACK MANTA'S LAST TWO ATTACKS, I'M EXHAUSTED! THE MONITORS DON'T SHOW ANY DANGERS, SO I CAN TAKE A RELAXING SWIM AROUND THE REALM!
IT'S BEEN A LONG TIME SINCE I WAS ABLE TO VISIT MY PEOPLE--BETWEEN JUSTICE LEAGUE MISSIONS AND ALL MY OTHER DUTIES.
I'VE GOT TO DO THIS MORE--
ZZZSSSHH
UGH!
WHEN YOU'RE THE MONARCH OF THE SEVEN SEAS, AND A CRUSADING SUPER-HERO IN YOUR SPARE TIME, YOU DON'T GET MANY VACATIONS--AS A MATTER OF FACT, THERE'S NEVER...
A QUIET DAY IN ATLANTIS
SCRIPT ~ PAUL LEVITZ
ART ~ MIKE GRELL

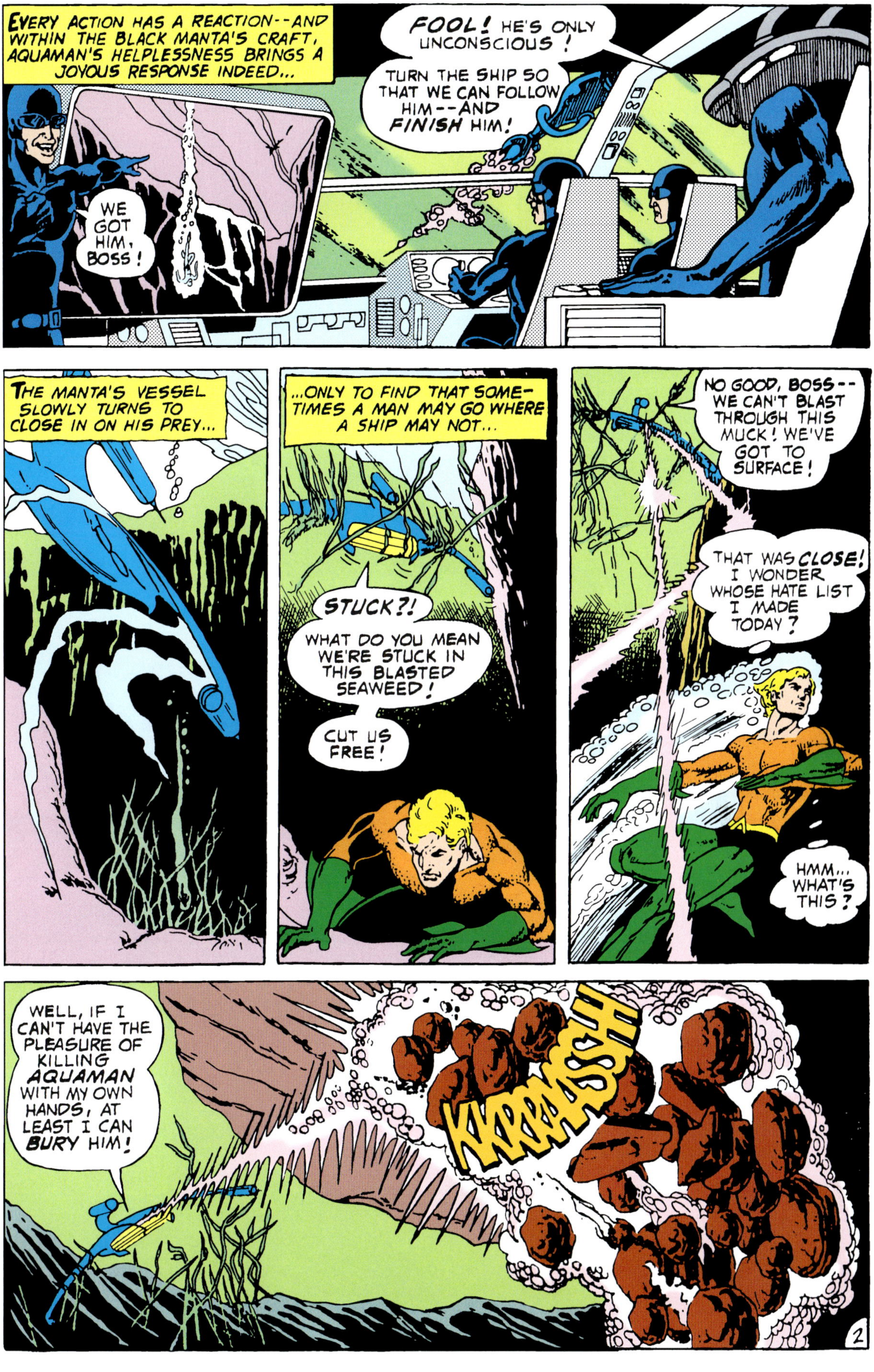
EVERY ACTION HAS A REACTION--AND WITHIN THE BLACK MANTA'S CRAFT, AQUAMAN'S HELPLESSNESS BRINGS A JOYOUS RESPONSE INDEED...
WE GOT HIM, BOSS!
FOOL! HE'S ONLY UNCONSCIOUS!
TURN THE SHIP SO THAT WE CAN FOLLOW HIM--AND FINISH HIM!
THE MANTA'S VESSEL SLOWLY TURNS TO CLOSE IN ON HIS PREY...
...ONLY TO FIND THAT SOMETIMES A MAN MAY GO WHERE A SHIP MAY NOT...
STUCK?!
WHAT DO YOU MEAN WE'RE STUCK IN THIS BLASTED SEAWEED!
CUT US FREE!
NO GOOD, BOSS--WE CAN'T BLAST THROUGH THIS MUCK! WE'VE GOT TO SURFACE!
THAT WAS CLOSE! I WONDER WHOSE HATE LIST I MADE TODAY?
HMM... WHAT'S THIS?
WELL, IF I CAN'T HAVE THE PLEASURE OF KILLING AQUAMAN WITH MY OWN HANDS, AT LEAST I CAN BURY HIM!
KKRAASSH
2

THE WATER STEAMS FOR A MOMENT... THEN SETTLES...AND ALL IS STILL...
...OR IS IT?
IF THIS CAVE WASN'T HERE, I'D HAVE BEEN GROUND TO DUST!
BUT I'M STILL IN TROUBLE UNLESS THERE'S ANOTHER EXIT SOMEWHERE!
IT'S NOT LIKELY TO HAVE AN OPENING BIG ENOUGH FOR ME TO SWIM THROUGH, BUT MAYBE THERE'S ONE I CAN ENLARGE!
MINUTES LATER, AQUAMAN MEETS SOME FISH WHO INHABIT THE CAVE AND USES HIS AMAZING TELEPATHIC POWERS TO ASK THEM FOR DIRECTIONS...
--THIS TUNNEL PASSES THROUGH A CAVERN AND THEN LEADS OUT TO THE OPEN SEA FARM?
THANK YOU, MY FRIENDS!
3

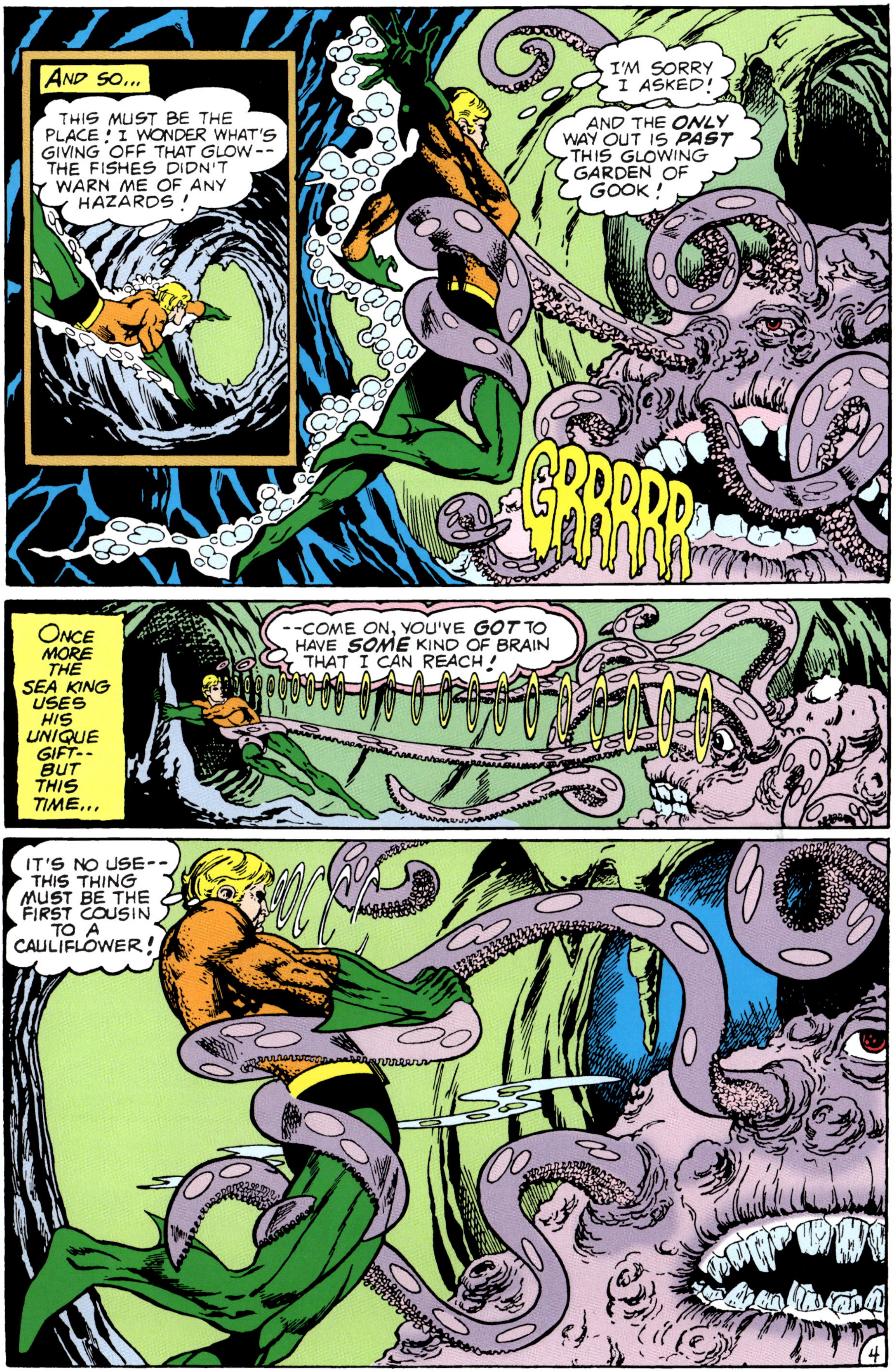
AND SO...
THIS MUST BE THE PLACE! I WONDER WHAT'S GIVING OFF THAT GLOW-- THE FISHES DIDN'T WARN ME OF ANY HAZARDS!
I'M SORRY I ASKED!
AND THE ONLY WAY OUT IS PAST THIS GLOWING GARDEN OF GOOK!
GRRRRR
ONCE MORE THE SEA KING USES HIS UNIQUE GIFT-- BUT THIS TIME...
--COME ON, YOU'VE GOT TO HAVE SOME KIND OF BRAIN THAT I CAN REACH!
IT'S NO USE-- THIS THING MUST BE THE FIRST COUSIN TO A CAULIFLOWER!
4

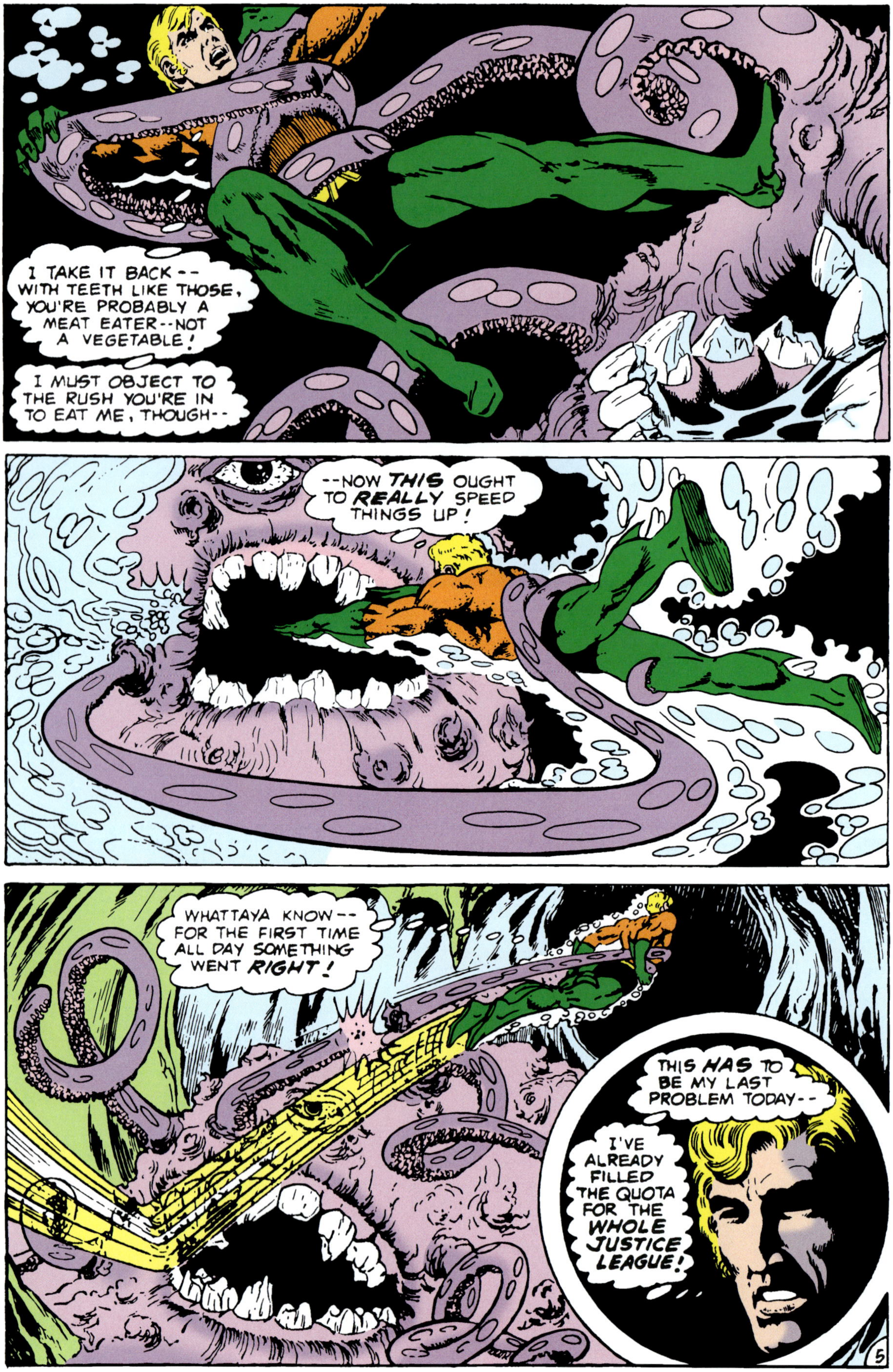
I TAKE IT BACK -- WITH TEETH LIKE THOSE, YOU'RE PROBABLY A MEAT EATER--NOT A VEGETABLE!
I MUST OBJECT TO THE RUSH YOU'RE IN TO EAT ME, THOUGH--
--NOW THIS OUGHT TO REALLY SPEED THINGS UP!
WHATTAYA KNOW -- FOR THE FIRST TIME ALL DAY SOMETHING WENT RIGHT!
THIS HAS TO BE MY LAST PROBLEM TODAY--
I'VE ALREADY FILLED THE QUOTA FOR THE WHOLE JUSTICE LEAGUE!
5

LATER THAT AFTERNOON, HIS BODY WEARY AND WORN, AQUAMAN FINALLY REACHES THE END OF THE CAVERN...
...BUT NOT THE END OF HIS LABORS...
OH, NO! THAT KID'S ABOUT TO WALK RIGHT IN FRONT OF THAT MECHANIZED HARVESTER!
STOP!
"HERO: A LEGENDARY FIGURE OF GREAT STRENGTH...
...OR ABILITIES...
...OR DETERMINATION."
OF SUCH FABRIC ARE LEGENDS WOVEN.
6

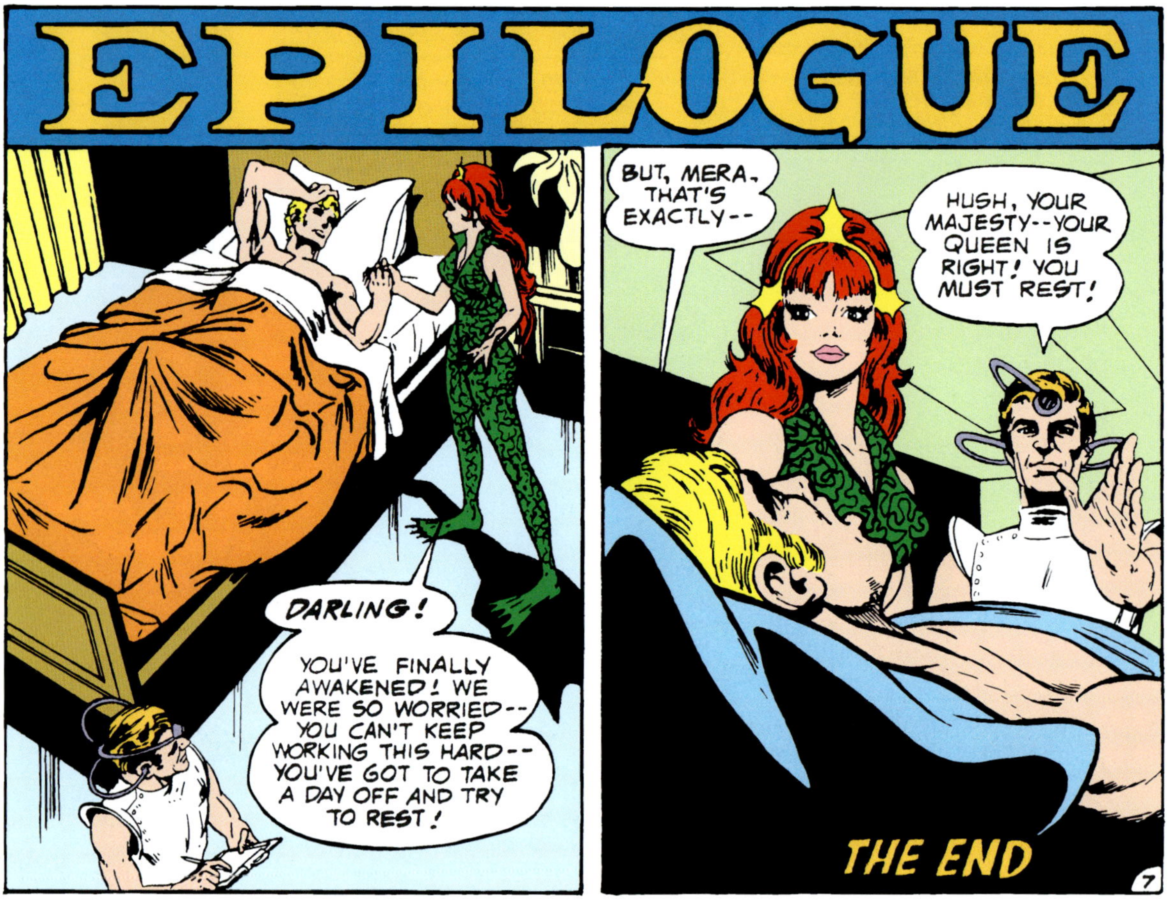
EPILOGUE
DARLING!
YOU'VE FINALLY AWAKENED! WE WERE SO WORRIED--YOU CAN'T KEEP WORKING THIS HARD--YOU'VE GOT TO TAKE A DAY OFF AND TRY TO REST!
BUT, MERA, THAT'S EXACTLY--
HUSH, YOUR MAJESTY--YOUR QUEEN IS RIGHT! YOU MUST REST!
THE END
7

AQUAMAN

NO. 62
30425
35¢
AQUAMAN
APPROVED BY THE COMICS CODE AUTHORITY
MY SON IS DEAD-- AND IT'S ALL YOUR FAULT, AQUAMAN!
ARTHUR CURRY JUNIOR 1973 1978
A NOVEL-LENGTH SEA SPECTACULAR!
WITH A SPECIAL SURPRISE VILLAIN!

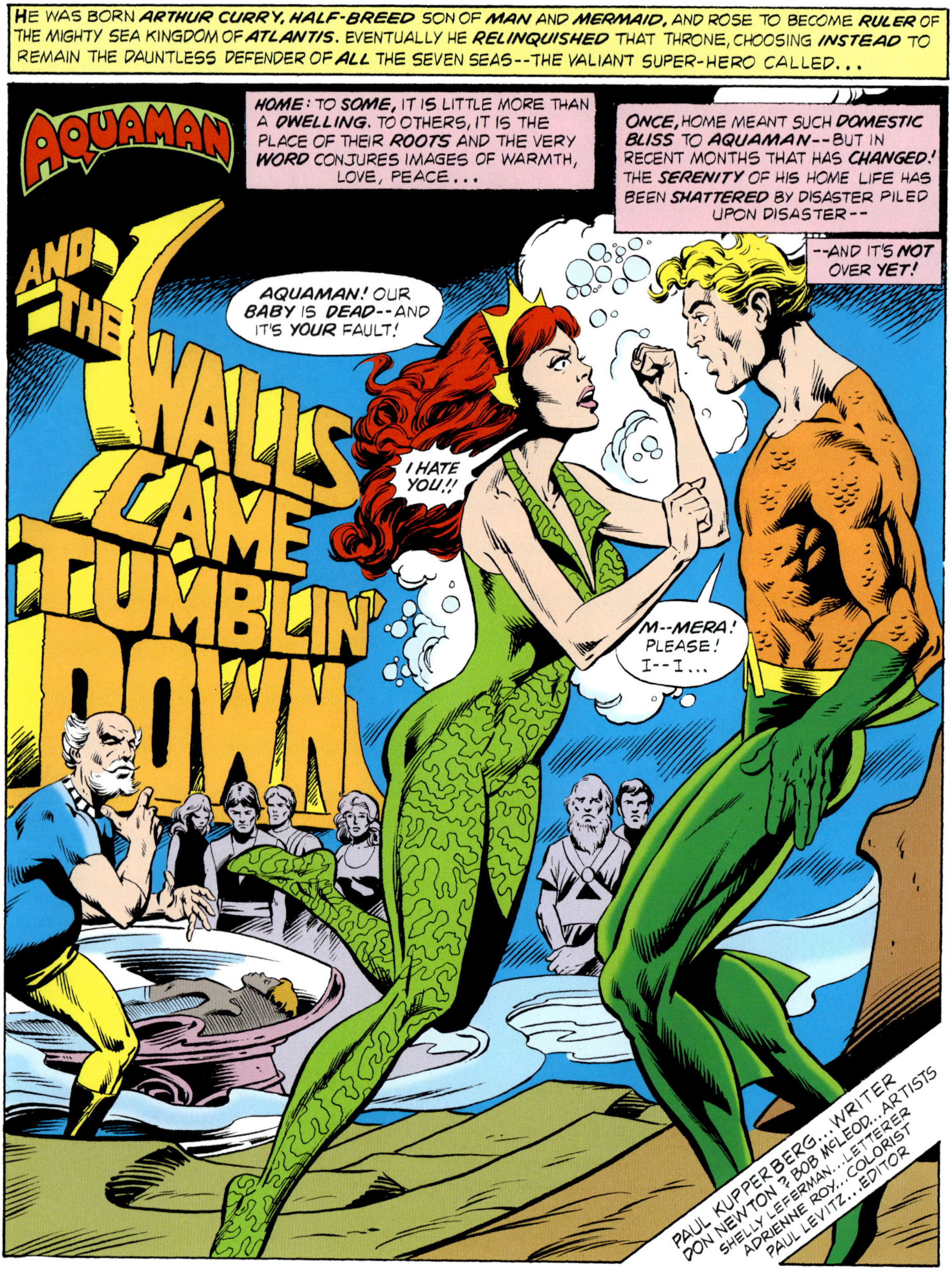
HE WAS BORN ARTHUR CURRY, HALF-BREED SON OF MAN AND MERMAID, AND ROSE TO BECOME RULER OF THE MIGHTY SEA KINGDOM OF ATLANTIS. EVENTUALLY HE RELINQUISHED THAT THRONE, CHOOSING INSTEAD TO REMAIN THE DAUNTLESS DEFENDER OF ALL THE SEVEN SEAS--THE VALIANT SUPER-HERO CALLED...
AQUAMAN
HOME: TO SOME, IT IS LITTLE MORE THAN A DWELLING. TO OTHERS, IT IS THE PLACE OF THEIR ROOTS AND THE VERY WORD CONJURES IMAGES OF WARMTH, LOVE, PEACE...
ONCE, HOME MEANT SUCH DOMESTIC BLISS TO AQUAMAN--BUT IN RECENT MONTHS THAT HAS CHANGED! THE SERENITY OF HIS HOME LIFE HAS BEEN SHATTERED BY DISASTER PILED UPON DISASTER--
--AND IT'S NOT OVER YET!
AND THE WALLS CAME TUMBLIN' DOWN
AQUAMAN! OUR BABY IS DEAD--AND IT'S YOUR FAULT!
I HATE YOU!!
M--MERA! PLEASE! I--I...
PAUL KUPPERBERG...WRITER
DON NEWTON & BOB McLEOD...ARTISTS
SHELLY LEFERMAN...LETTERER
ADRIENNE ROY...COLORIST
PAUL LEVITZ...EDITOR

PLEASE, MERA...LET ME EXPLAIN...
YOU CAN EXPLAIN NOTHING! YOU CARE MORE FOR YOUR STUPID HEROICS THAN FOR ME--OR OUR CHILD!
SHE'S HYSTERICAL... NOT THINKING STRAIGHT! I CAN'T REASON WITH HER LIKE THIS!
IF YOU HAD STAYED, ARTHUR JR. WOULD STILL BE ALIVE! YOU KILLED HIM!
MERA...CONTROL YOURSELF! YOU DON'T KNOW WHAT YOU'RE DOING!
GREAT NEPTUNE! I--I THOUGHT HE WAS ALREADY DEAD...
IT IS SAID THE LINE SEPARATING LOVE FROM HATE IS A THIN ONE...
NO!
YOU ARE HIS FRIEND, VULKO... ON HIS SIDE! STAY AWAY FROM ME!
WHOOOSSH
OOOFF!
...BUT NEVER HAS AQUAMAN SEEN THAT LINE BREACHED SO SWIFTLY--SO SUDDENLY--BY ONE SO CLOSE...
IT WAS YOUR INVOLVEMENT WITH BLACK MANTA THAT PLACED OUR SON IN DANGER --
--IT WAS YOUR PRIDE THAT SENT YOU CHASING AFTER HIM INSTEAD OF REMAINING WITH US--
--AND AIDING IN SAVING YOUR CHILD'S LIFE!
YOU KILLED MY BABY, DAMN YOU, AND FOR THAT--
--I'LL KILL YOU TOO!
SHOCK: PSYCHIC PAIN WHICH OBLITERATES ALL PHYSICAL SENSATION IN AQUAMAN, LEAVING HIM WITH BUT A SINGLE NAGGING DOUBT...
2

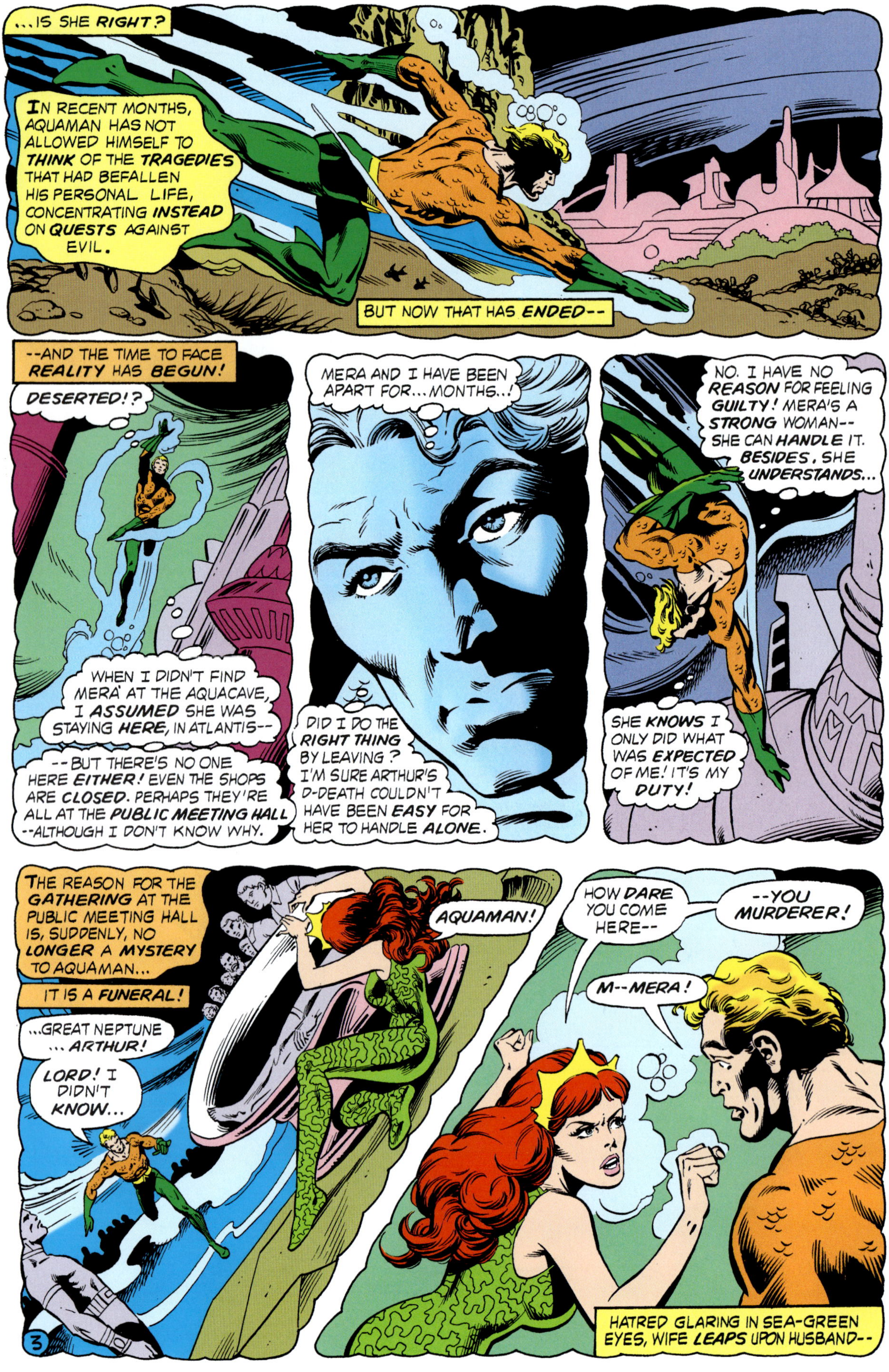
...IS SHE RIGHT?
IN RECENT MONTHS, AQUAMAN HAS NOT ALLOWED HIMSELF TO THINK OF THE TRAGEDIES THAT HAD BEFALLEN HIS PERSONAL LIFE, CONCENTRATING INSTEAD ON QUESTS AGAINST EVIL.
BUT NOW THAT HAS ENDED--
--AND THE TIME TO FACE REALITY HAS BEGUN!
DESERTED!?
WHEN I DIDN'T FIND MERA AT THE AQUACAVE, I ASSUMED SHE WAS STAYING HERE, IN ATLANTIS--
--BUT THERE'S NO ONE HERE EITHER! EVEN THE SHOPS ARE CLOSED. PERHAPS THEY'RE ALL AT THE PUBLIC MEETING HALL --ALTHOUGH I DON'T KNOW WHY.
MERA AND I HAVE BEEN APART FOR... MONTHS...!
DID I DO THE RIGHT THING BY LEAVING? I'M SURE ARTHUR'S D-DEATH COULDN'T HAVE BEEN EASY FOR HER TO HANDLE ALONE.
NO. I HAVE NO REASON FOR FEELING GUILTY! MERA'S A STRONG WOMAN-- SHE CAN HANDLE IT. BESIDES, SHE UNDERSTANDS...
SHE KNOWS I ONLY DID WHAT WAS EXPECTED OF ME! IT'S MY DUTY!
THE REASON FOR THE GATHERING AT THE PUBLIC MEETING HALL IS, SUDDENLY, NO LONGER A MYSTERY TO AQUAMAN...
IT IS A FUNERAL!
...GREAT NEPTUNE ...ARTHUR!
LORD! I DIDN'T KNOW...
AQUAMAN!
HOW DARE YOU COME HERE--
--YOU MURDERER!
M--MERA!
HATRED GLARING IN SEA-GREEN EYES, WIFE LEAPS UPON HUSBAND--
3

--IN AN ATTACK AS VICIOUS AS IT IS HEART-FELT!
UGH!
WHAM
I'VE LONGED FOR THIS MOMENT, AQUAMAN--WAITED TO PAY BACK THE PAIN AND SUFFERING YOUR HEROICS HAVE CAUSED!
MERA'S LOST CONTROL-- NO TELLING WHAT SHE MIGHT DO! I HAVE TO STOP HER, BUT WITHOUT HURTING HER!
LINES OF CONCENTRATION ETCH THEMSELVES ON THE SEA KING'S FOREHEAD AS TELEPATHIC COMMANDS RADIATE OUTWARD--
--AND ARE IMMEDIATELY ANSWERED BY...
TOPO! GENTLY, OLD FRIEND... DON'T HURT HER!
NEPTUNE'S TRIDENT! WHAT ARE YOU DOING HERE, AQUAMAN?
IN CASE YOU'VE FORGOTTEN, VULKO, THAT'S MY SON YOU'RE EULOGIZING OVER! WHAT KIND OF STUPID QUESTION IS...
BUT YOU'RE UPSETTING MERA--AS WELL AS EVERY-ONE ELSE! IT WOULD BE BEST IF YOU LEFT... AT LEAST UNTIL EMOTIONS COOL DOWN!
4
THEN YOU CAN ALL GO TO BLAZES! I'LL BE BACK LATER TO SEE MY... MY SON--ALONE!
COME ON, TOPO!
THERE IS A RAGE DEEP WITHIN THE SEA KING--A RAGE FAR GREATER THAN ANY HE HAS EXPERIENCED AGAINST HIMSELF! BUT HE LEAVES NONETHELESS--

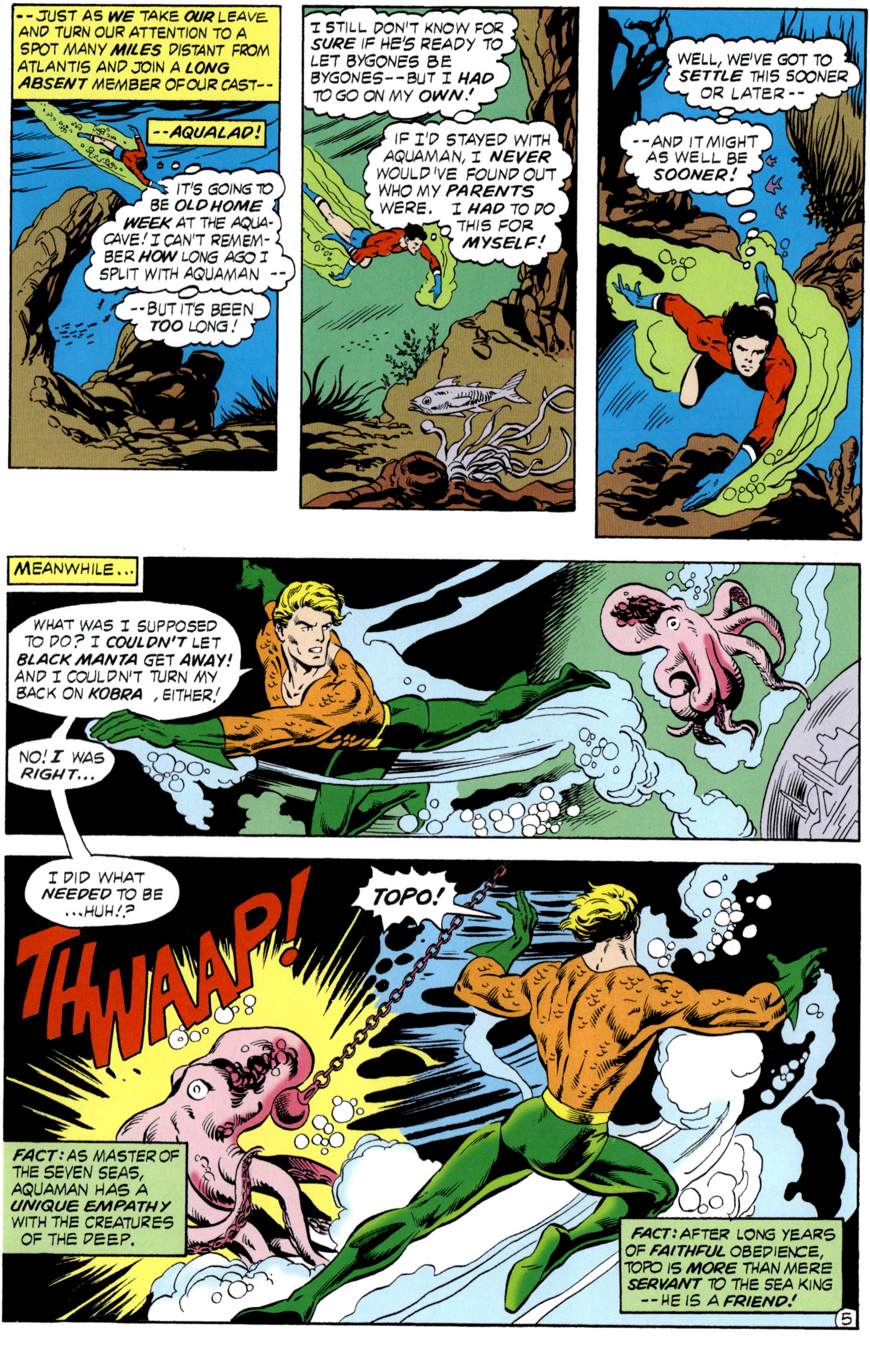
--JUST AS WE TAKE OUR LEAVE AND TURN OUR ATTENTION TO A SPOT MANY MILES DISTANT FROM ATLANTIS AND JOIN A LONG ABSENT MEMBER OF OUR CAST--
--AQUALAD!
IT'S GOING TO BE OLD HOME WEEK AT THE AQUACAVE! I CAN'T REMEMBER HOW LONG AGO I SPLIT WITH AQUAMAN --
--BUT IT'S BEEN TOO LONG!
I STILL DON'T KNOW FOR SURE IF HE'S READY TO LET BYGONES BE BYGONES--BUT I HAD TO GO ON MY OWN!
IF I'D STAYED WITH AQUAMAN, I NEVER WOULD'VE FOUND OUT WHO MY PARENTS WERE. I HAD TO DO THIS FOR MYSELF!
WELL, WE'VE GOT TO SETTLE THIS SOONER OR LATER--
--AND IT MIGHT AS WELL BE SOONER!
MEANWHILE...
WHAT WAS I SUPPOSED TO DO? I COULDN'T LET BLACK MANTA GET AWAY! AND I COULDN'T TURN MY BACK ON KOBRA, EITHER!
NO! I WAS RIGHT...
I DID WHAT NEEDED TO BE ...HUH!?
THWAAP!
TOPO!
FACT: AS MASTER OF THE SEVEN SEAS, AQUAMAN HAS A UNIQUE EMPATHY WITH THE CREATURES OF THE DEEP.
FACT: AFTER LONG YEARS OF FAITHFUL OBEDIENCE, TOPO IS MORE THAN MERE SERVANT TO THE SEA KING --HE IS A FRIEND!
5

FACT: SINCE RETURNING, AQUAMAN HAS WITNESSED HIS CHILD'S FUNERAL, HAS BEEN REJECTED BY HIS WIFE--
--AND NOW HIS ONLY REMAINING FRIEND IN THE SEA HAS BEEN SAVAGELY AND UNJUSTLY ATTACKED!
FACT: THESE EVENTS HAVE BUILT UP A DEEP ANGER WITHIN AQUAMAN--AND THERE HAS BEEN NO RELEASE FOR THIS ANGER--
--UNTIL NOW!
THAT HE DOES NOT RECOGNIZE THIS FOE IS OF LITTLE CONCERN TO AQUAMAN. FOR HIM, THESE ROBOTS ARE BUT A CONVENIENT OBJECT ON WHICH HE MAY...
--VENT HIS RAGE!
KER-KRASH
6

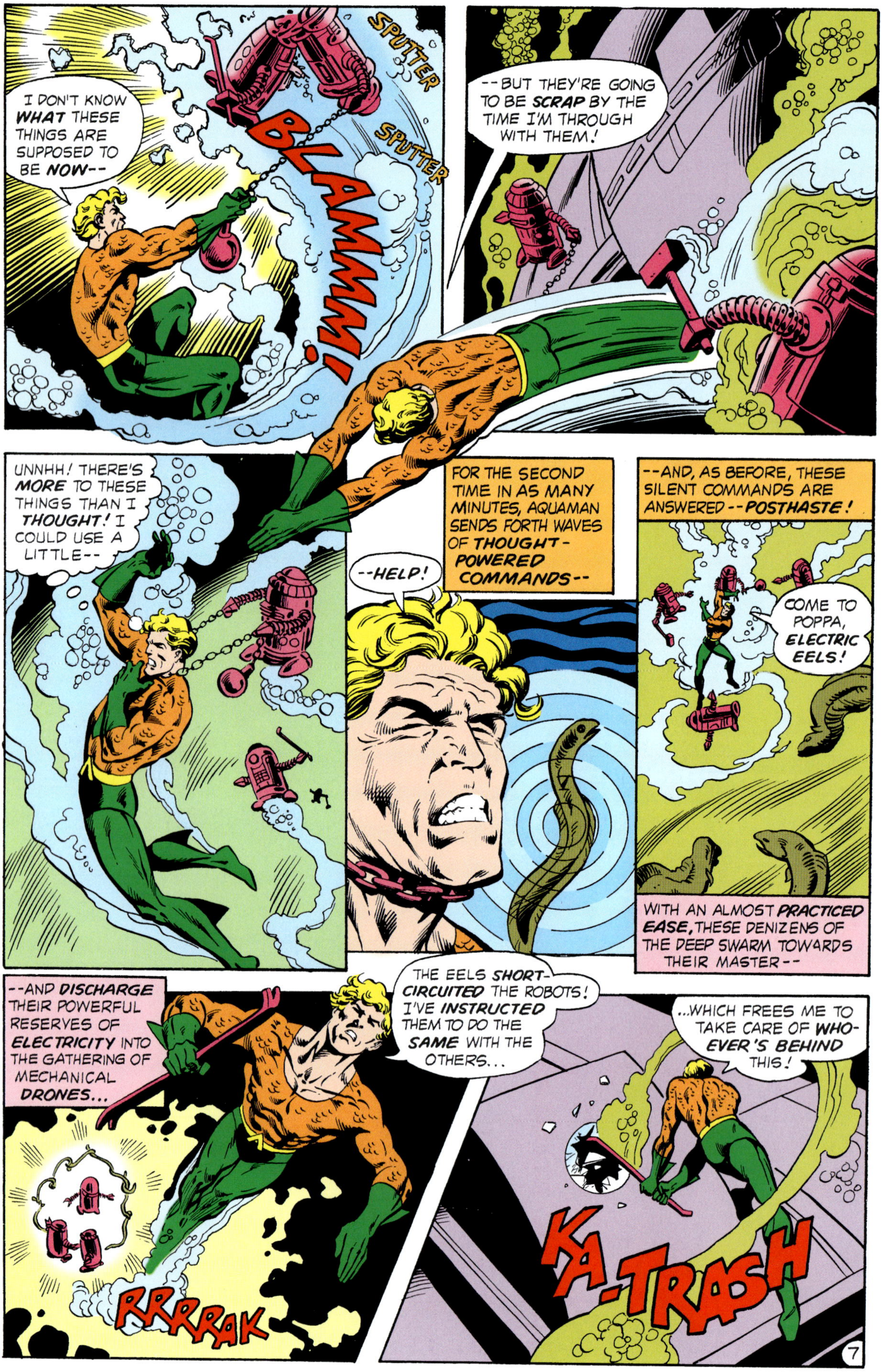
SPUTTER
SPUTTER
I DON'T KNOW WHAT THESE THINGS ARE SUPPOSED TO BE NOW--
BLAMMM!
--BUT THEY'RE GOING TO BE SCRAP BY THE TIME I'M THROUGH WITH THEM!
UNNHH! THERE'S MORE TO THESE THINGS THAN I THOUGHT! I COULD USE A LITTLE--
--HELP!
FOR THE SECOND TIME IN AS MANY MINUTES, AQUAMAN SENDS FORTH WAVES OF THOUGHT-POWERED COMMANDS--
--AND, AS BEFORE, THESE SILENT COMMANDS ARE ANSWERED--POSTHASTE!
COME TO POPPA, ELECTRIC EELS!
WITH AN ALMOST PRACTICED EASE, THESE DENIZENS OF THE DEEP SWARM TOWARDS THEIR MASTER--
--AND DISCHARGE THEIR POWERFUL RESERVES OF ELECTRICITY INTO THE GATHERING OF MECHANICAL DRONES...
RRRRAK
THE EELS SHORT-CIRCUITED THE ROBOTS! I'VE INSTRUCTED THEM TO DO THE SAME WITH THE OTHERS...
...WHICH FREES ME TO TAKE CARE OF WHO-EVER'S BEHIND THIS!
KA-TRASH
7

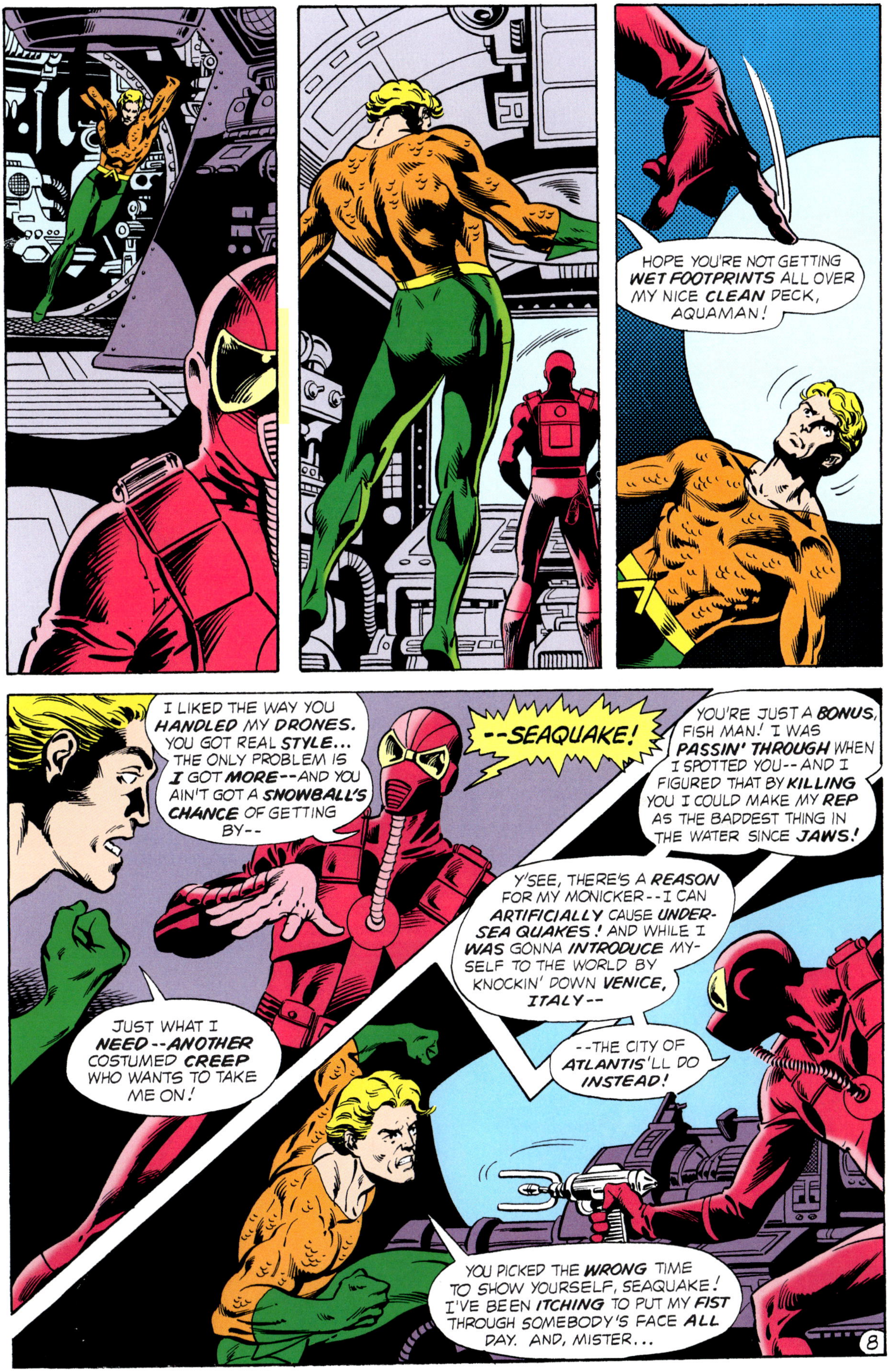
HOPE YOU'RE NOT GETTING WET FOOTPRINTS ALL OVER MY NICE CLEAN DECK, AQUAMAN!
I LIKED THE WAY YOU HANDLED MY DRONES. YOU GOT REAL STYLE... THE ONLY PROBLEM IS I GOT MORE--AND YOU AIN'T GOT A SNOWBALL'S CHANCE OF GETTING BY--
--SEAQUAKE!
JUST WHAT I NEED--ANOTHER COSTUMED CREEP WHO WANTS TO TAKE ME ON!
YOU'RE JUST A BONUS, FISH MAN! I WAS PASSIN' THROUGH WHEN I SPOTTED YOU--AND I FIGURED THAT BY KILLING YOU I COULD MAKE MY REP AS THE BADDEST THING IN THE WATER SINCE JAWS!
Y'SEE, THERE'S A REASON FOR MY MONICKER--I CAN ARTIFICIALLY CAUSE UNDER-SEA QUAKES! AND WHILE I WAS GONNA INTRODUCE MY-SELF TO THE WORLD BY KNOCKIN' DOWN VENICE, ITALY--
--THE CITY OF ATLANTIS'LL DO INSTEAD!
YOU PICKED THE WRONG TIME TO SHOW YOURSELF, SEAQUAKE! I'VE BEEN ITCHING TO PUT MY FIST THROUGH SOMEBODY'S FACE ALL DAY. AND, MISTER...
8

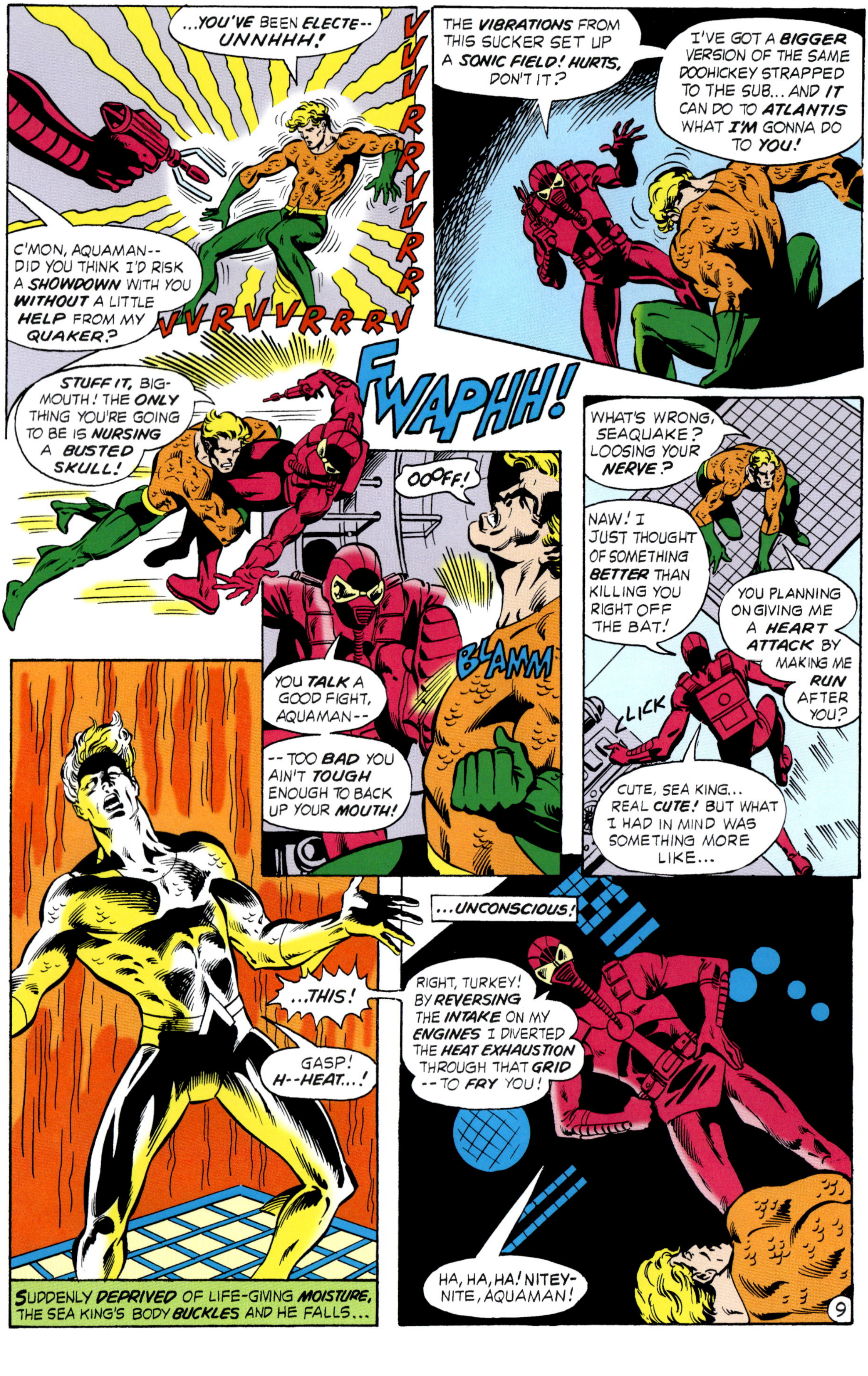
...YOU'VE BEEN ELECTE-- UNNHHH!
VVVRRVVRRR
C'MON, AQUAMAN-- DID YOU THINK I'D RISK A SHOWDOWN WITH YOU WITHOUT A LITTLE HELP FROM MY QUAKER?
VVRVVRRRRV
THE VIBRATIONS FROM THIS SUCKER SET UP A SONIC FIELD! HURTS, DON'T IT?
I'VE GOT A BIGGER VERSION OF THE SAME DOOHICKEY STRAPPED TO THE SUB... AND IT CAN DO TO ATLANTIS WHAT I'M GONNA DO TO YOU!
STUFF IT, BIG-MOUTH! THE ONLY THING YOU'RE GOING TO BE IS NURSING A BUSTED SKULL!
FWAPHH!
OOOFF!
BLAMM
YOU TALK A GOOD FIGHT, AQUAMAN--
-- TOO BAD YOU AIN'T TOUGH ENOUGH TO BACK UP YOUR MOUTH!
WHAT'S WRONG, SEAQUAKE? LOOSING YOUR NERVE?
NAW! I JUST THOUGHT OF SOMETHING BETTER THAN KILLING YOU RIGHT OFF THE BAT!
YOU PLANNING ON GIVING ME A HEART ATTACK BY MAKING ME RUN AFTER YOU?
CLICK
CUTE, SEA KING... REAL CUTE! BUT WHAT I HAD IN MIND WAS SOMETHING MORE LIKE...
...THIS!
GASP! H--HEAT...!
SUDDENLY DEPRIVED OF LIFE-GIVING MOISTURE, THE SEA KING'S BODY BUCKLES AND HE FALLS...
...UNCONSCIOUS!
RIGHT, TURKEY! BY REVERSING THE INTAKE ON MY ENGINES I DIVERTED THE HEAT EXHAUSTION THROUGH THAT GRID --TO FRY YOU!
HA, HA, HA! NITEY-NITE, AQUAMAN!
9

WATER!
...OOOHH...
FOR AQUAMAN, IT IS THE GIVER OF LIFE...REVITALIZING HIS EVERY TORTURED CELL AND RETURNING HIM TO CONSCIOUS-NESS...
YOU LOUSY SCUM! I'D...
WELCOME BACK TO THE LAND OF THE LIVING, AQUAMAN--
--ALTHOUGH I CAN'T GUARANTEE YOU'LL STAY HERE VERY LONG! HA, HA, HA!
LET'S NOT BE NASTY, AQUA-MAN! AFTER ALL, YOU WOULDN'T WANT MY LAST MEMORY OF YOU TO BE A BITTER ONE, WOULD YOU?
NOW I GOTTA WARM UP THE QUAKER! IT TAKES A WHILE TO GET THAT THING WORKING, BUT DON'T WORRY--YOU'LL BE THE FIRST TO KNOW WHEN IT IS!
I'M GOING TO NEED LOTS OF ASSISTANCE TO BREAK LOOSE! THESE CHAINS ARE TITANIUM STEEL!
IF ONLY THERE'S TIME...!
FASTER, MY FRIENDS! YOU MUST BREAK ME LOOSE BEFORE WE REACH--
--ATLANTIS!
NEPTUNE! WE WERE CLOSER THAN I THOUGHT! FASTER!
IT'S STARTED! AND IF THESE TORTOISES AREN'T ABLE TO SNAP THESE CHAINS IN AN-OTHER FEW SECONDS, I'M FINISHED!
VVVVRVVVVVRRRRVRVVRP
10

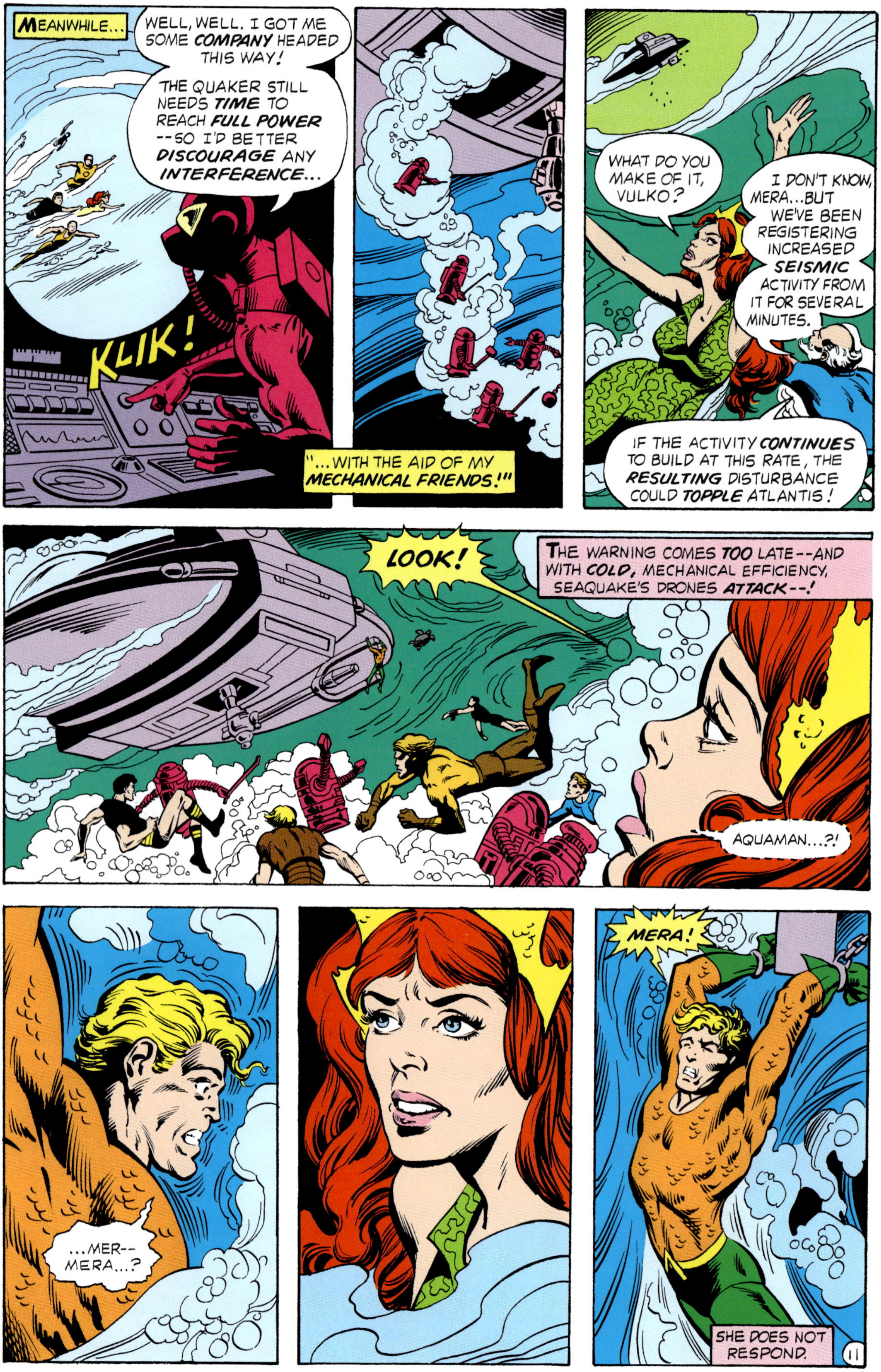
MEANWHILE...
WELL, WELL. I GOT ME SOME COMPANY HEADED THIS WAY!
THE QUAKER STILL NEEDS TIME TO REACH FULL POWER --SO I'D BETTER DISCOURAGE ANY INTERFERENCE...
KLIK!
"...WITH THE AID OF MY MECHANICAL FRIENDS!"
WHAT DO YOU MAKE OF IT, VULKO?
I DON'T KNOW, MERA...BUT WE'VE BEEN REGISTERING INCREASED SEISMIC ACTIVITY FROM IT FOR SEVERAL MINUTES.
IF THE ACTIVITY CONTINUES TO BUILD AT THIS RATE, THE RESULTING DISTURBANCE COULD TOPPLE ATLANTIS!
LOOK!
THE WARNING COMES TOO LATE--AND WITH COLD, MECHANICAL EFFICIENCY, SEAQUAKE'S DRONES ATTACK--!
AQUAMAN...?!
...MER-- MERA...?
MERA!
SHE DOES NOT RESPOND.
11

INSTEAD, SHE TURNS TO PURSUE THE DEADLY DRONES--
SHOOM
--AND SAVE HER ATLANTEAN COMPANIONS--
--BEFORE RETURNING TO THE CITY--
--WITHOUT HER HUSBAND!
I'VE NEVER TRIED PLACING THE QUAKER IN THE MIDDLE OF MY, AH... TEST AREA.
SO LET'S SEE WHAT HAPPENS WHEN I TAKE THIS DOOHICKEY--
--RIGHT INTO THEIR LAPS!
KAW-THOOMM!
T-TIME'S RUN O-OUT! VI-VIBRATIONS ARE KE-KEEPING THE F-FISH FROM CO-COMING TO HELP--
--AND TE-TEARING ME TO P-PIECES IN THE PRO-PROCESS!
VVRRVVRRVVRR
12

VVVRRRRRVVVVVRVR
VIBRATIONS SP--SPEEDING UP--THE PA-PAIN--GO-GOTTA BR- BREAK FR-FREE!
VVVRRRVRVVVVRRRRRRR
FOR MOST OF HIS LIFE AQUAMAN HAS LIVED AT THE OCEAN'S FLOOR --DEVELOPING MUSCLES TO COPE WITH THE BONE-CRUSHING PRESSURES OF THE DEEP--
YET EVEN THIS GREAT STRENGTH RAPIDLY EBBS FROM THE PAIN-RACKED SEA-KING AS THOSE MUSCLES BEGIN TO TEAR WITH STRAIN--
AAARRRGGHHH!
AND AS THE VIBRATIONS INCREASE WITH A DEAFENING WHINE, AQUAMAN LUNGES FORWARD WITH A FINAL, DESPERATE SURGE OF RAW POWER--
VVRREEEEEEEEEEEEEEEEEEE
--SNAPPING CHAINS ALREADY WEAKENED BY THE HIGH FREQUENCY VIBRATIONS!
BUT HIS ESCAPE IS A MOMENTARY THING--
--FOR IN THE NEXT INSTANT, THE WORLD IS SHUT FROM AQUAMAN'S VIEW AS TONS OF RUBBLE SHOWER DOWN TO BURY HIM!
13

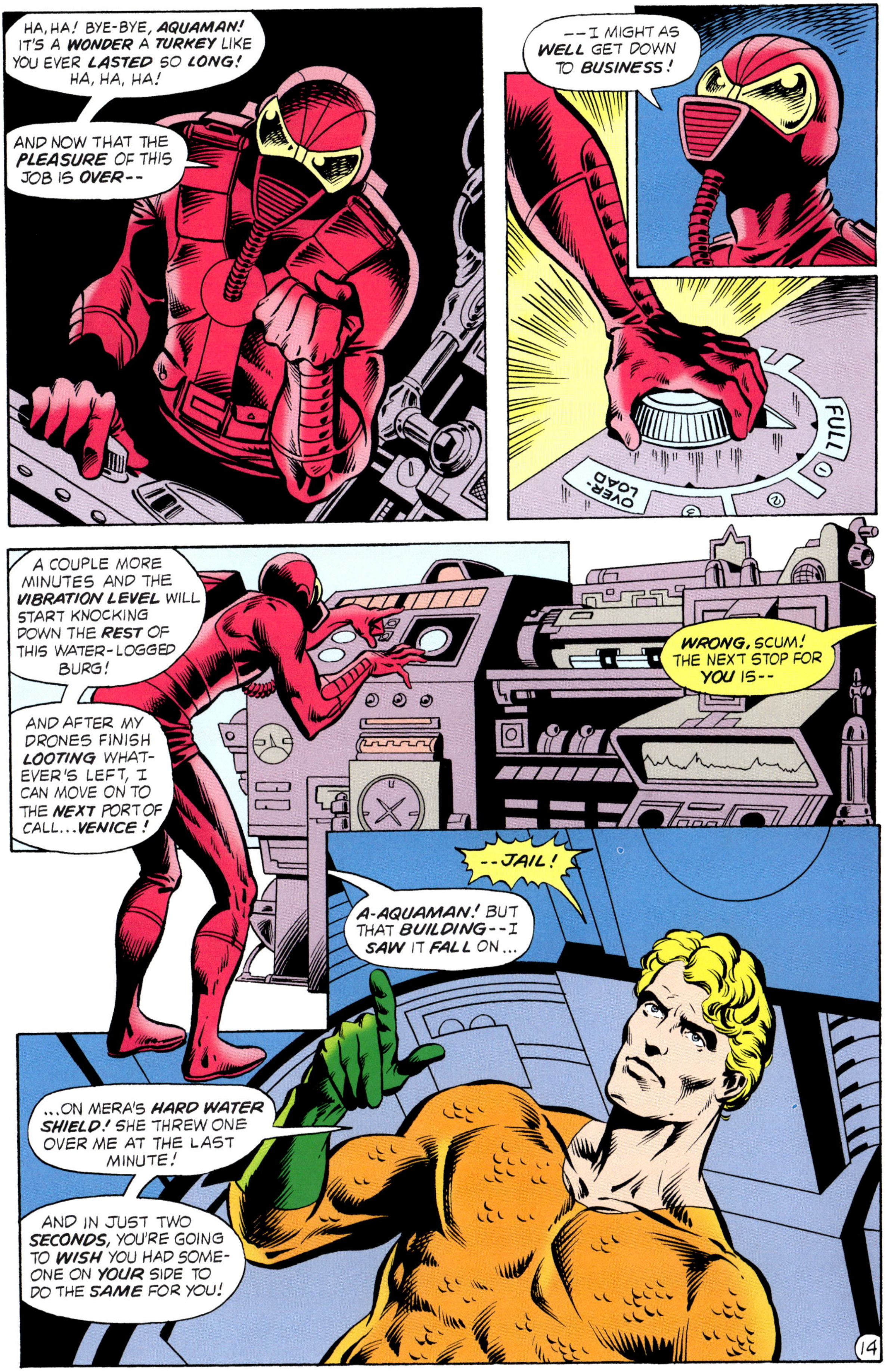
HA, HA! BYE-BYE, AQUAMAN! IT'S A WONDER A TURKEY LIKE YOU EVER LASTED SO LONG! HA, HA, HA!
AND NOW THAT THE PLEASURE OF THIS JOB IS OVER--
--I MIGHT AS WELL GET DOWN TO BUSINESS!
FULL
1
2
3
OVER-LOAD
A COUPLE MORE MINUTES AND THE VIBRATION LEVEL WILL START KNOCKING DOWN THE REST OF THIS WATER-LOGGED BURG!
AND AFTER MY DRONES FINISH LOOTING WHATEVER'S LEFT, I CAN MOVE ON TO THE NEXT PORT OF CALL...VENICE!
WRONG, SCUM! THE NEXT STOP FOR YOU IS--
--JAIL!
A-AQUAMAN! BUT THAT BUILDING--I SAW IT FALL ON...
...ON MERA'S HARD WATER SHIELD! SHE THREW ONE OVER ME AT THE LAST MINUTE!
AND IN JUST TWO SECONDS, YOU'RE GOING TO WISH YOU HAD SOMEONE ON YOUR SIDE TO DO THE SAME FOR YOU!
14

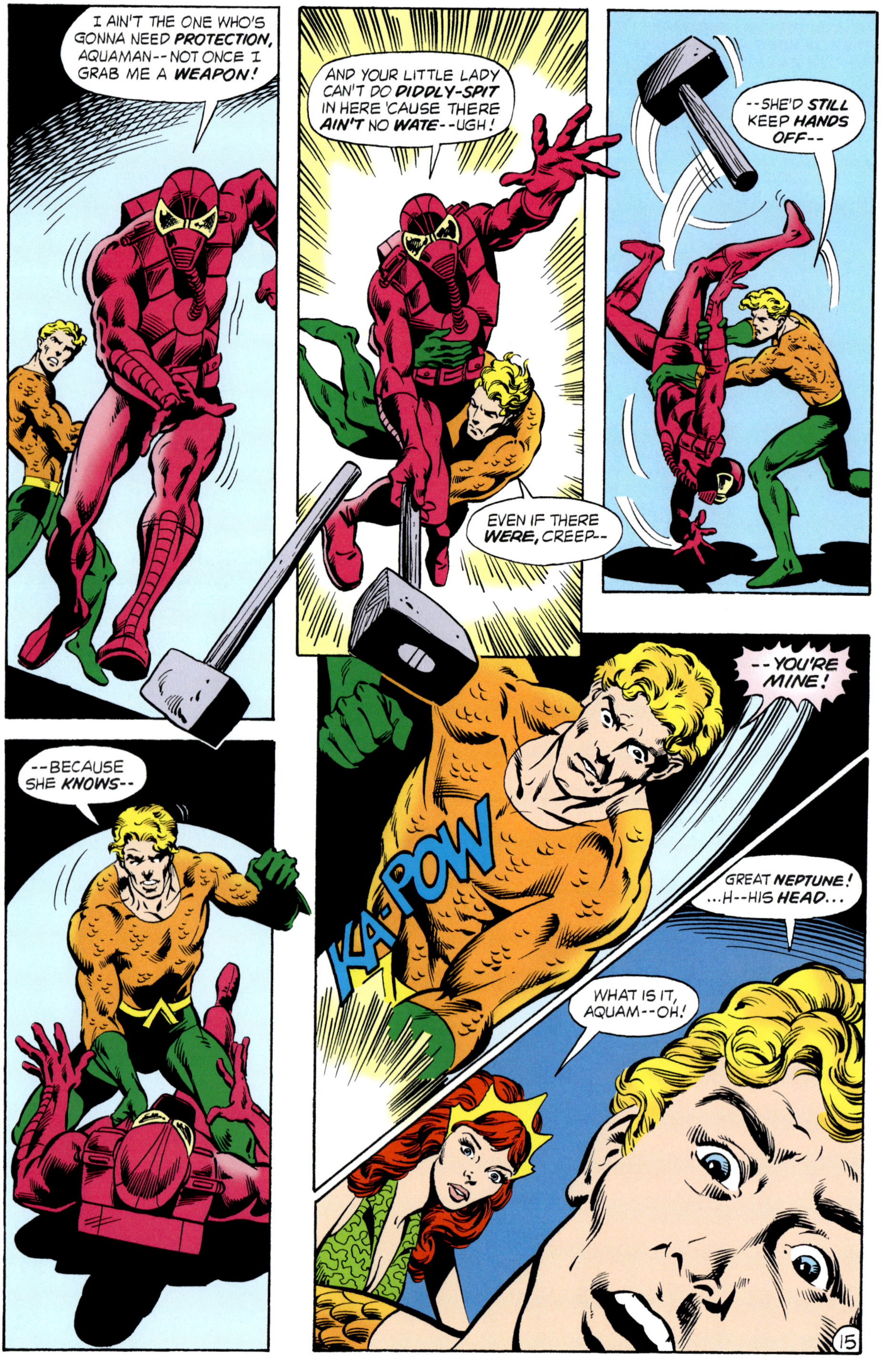
I AIN'T THE ONE WHO'S GONNA NEED PROTECTION, AQUAMAN--NOT ONCE I GRAB ME A WEAPON!
AND YOUR LITTLE LADY CAN'T DO DIDDLY-SPIT IN HERE 'CAUSE THERE AIN'T NO WATE--UGH!
EVEN IF THERE WERE, CREEP--
--SHE'D STILL KEEP HANDS OFF--
--BECAUSE SHE KNOWS--
--YOU'RE MINE!
KA-POW
GREAT NEPTUNE! ...H--HIS HEAD...
WHAT IS IT, AQUAM--OH!
15

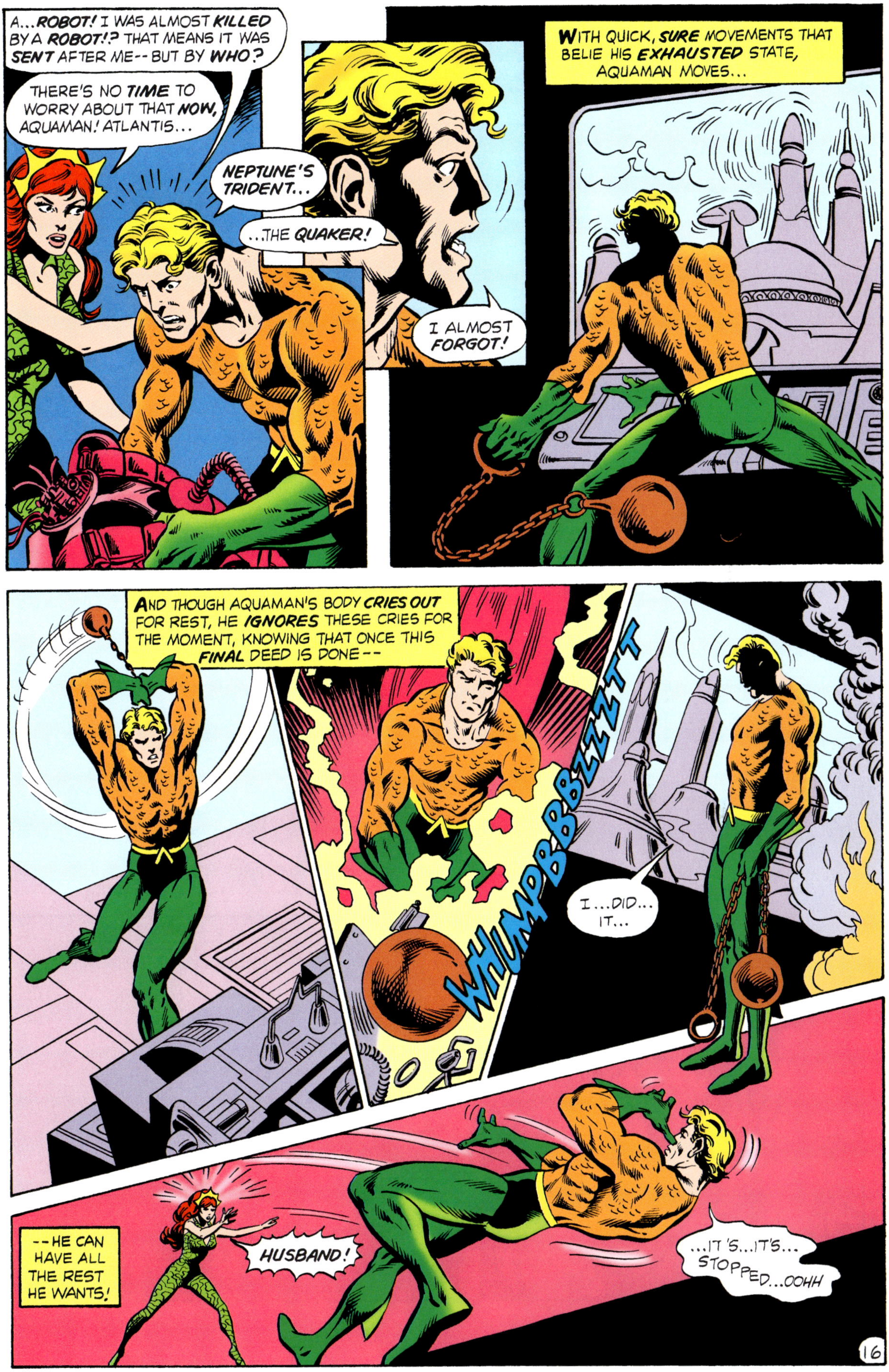
A...ROBOT! I WAS ALMOST KILLED BY A ROBOT!? THAT MEANS IT WAS SENT AFTER ME-- BUT BY WHO?
THERE'S NO TIME TO WORRY ABOUT THAT NOW, AQUAMAN! ATLANTIS...
NEPTUNE'S TRIDENT...
...THE QUAKER!
I ALMOST FORGOT!
WITH QUICK, SURE MOVEMENTS THAT BELIE HIS EXHAUSTED STATE, AQUAMAN MOVES...
AND THOUGH AQUAMAN'S BODY CRIES OUT FOR REST, HE IGNORES THESE CRIES FOR THE MOMENT, KNOWING THAT ONCE THIS FINAL DEED IS DONE--
WHUMPBBBZZZTTT
I...DID... IT...
--HE CAN HAVE ALL THE REST HE WANTS!
HUSBAND!
...IT'S...IT'S... STOPPED...OOHH
16

EPILOGUE
LATER...
YOU'LL BE FINE AQUAMAN-- AFTER A LOT OF REST!
YOU DON'T HAVE TO TELL ME THAT TWICE, VULKO! IT FEELS LIKE EVERY BONE IN MY BODY'S BEEN GROUND TO DUST!
EXCUSE ME, VULKO... HUSBAND.
MERA!
MERA, I...
PLEASE, AQUAMAN ...LET ME SPEAK!
I REALIZE NOW THAT WHAT YOU DID, YOU DID BECAUSE YOU FELT IT WAS YOUR DUTY! YOU WERE A SUPER-HERO BEFORE WE WED AND YOU SHALL REMAIN ONE--REGARDLESS OF WHAT I SAY.
BUT...I CANNOT FORGIVE YOU FOR THAT REASON!
BUT WHAT OF ALL THE YEARS WE HAD TOGETHER? SURELY THAT COUNTS FOR SOMETHING!
I--IT DOES, HUSBAND. AND BECAUSE OF THOSE YEARS OF HAPPINESS, I FIND THAT NO MATTER HOW HARD I TRY TO HATE YOU...
...I CANNOT!
IT WILL NOT BE EASY, HUSBAND... BUT WE MUST TRY!
WE WILL, MY DARLING--AND WE WILL MAKE IT WORK...
MY, MY...ISN'T THIS A TOUCHING SCENE!
WHO...?
IT'S ALMOST A PITY THAT I MUST END THIS TENDER TABLEAU, DEAR BROTHER--
--BY KILLING YOU BOTH!
OCEAN MASTER!

EXTRA!
8 ALL-NEW PAGES STARRING
AQUAMAN
50¢
ALL NEW!
NO. 475
SEPT.
APPROVED BY THE COMICS CODE AUTHORITY
ADVENTURE COMICS
NOW THREE FABULOUS FEATURES!
C-409
BOLLAND

DEADMAN LIVES AGAIN!
AQUAMAN STANDS ALONE!
LEGEND OF AQUAMAN
JUSTICE LEAGUE OF AMERICA
STARRO THE CONQUEROR!
METAMORPHO
AQUAMAN
SUPER FRIENDS
Adventure Comics
AQUAMAN
Manhunter
Mars
Hawkman
AQUAMAN
AQUAMAN
AQUAMAN
DOOM From DIMENSION AQUA!
AQUAMAN
URBAN RENEWAL!
UNDERWORLD
REBIRTH
AQUAMAN
DC UNIVERSE REBIRTH
AQUAMAN
AQUAMAN
Who Destroys the Sea King
The OCEAN MASTER or BLACK MANTA?
AQUAMAN
ARTHUR CURRY JUNIOR
DC COMICS
THE NEW 52!
AQUAMAN
IS THIS MY FOE!
AQUAMAN
AQUAMAN
JABBERJAW
CAPTAIN CAVEMAN
the BRAVE and the BOLD
presents
BATMAN
AQUAMAN
The SLEEP-WALKER from the SEA!
THE NEW 52!
JUSTICE LEAGUE
AQUAMAN
AQUAMAN
AQUAMAN A COWARD? IS HE REALLY IN TERROR OF... The OCEAN MASTER?
THE BEGINNING OF TOMORROW!
AQUAMAN
AQUAMAN
IN THE SHADOWY DEPTHS OF ATLANTIS, HIS LIFE WILL CHANGE FOREVER!
DC COMICS
THE NEW 52!
AQUAMAN
YEAR ONE
AQUAMAN
AQUAMAN
Who Destroys the Sea King
GENESIS
AQUAMAN
AQUAMAN
SWORD OF ATLANTIS
KURT BUSIEK
BUTCH GUICE
AQUAMAN
LEADS HIS ARMY TO BATTLE!
AQUAMAN
YOU!
YOU DID THIS TO HER!
AND NOW... YOU DIE!!
AQUAMAN

HE WAS BORN ARTHUR CURRY, HALF-BREED SON OF MAN AND MERMAID, AND ROSE TO BECOME RULER OF THE MIGHTY SEA KINGDOM OF ATLANTIS. EVENTUALLY HE RELINQUISHED THAT THRONE, CHOOSING INSTEAD TO REMAIN THE DAUNTLESS DEFEADER OF ALL THE SEVEN SEAS-- THE VALIANT SUPER-HERO CALLED...
AQUAMAN®
FOR THE MAN WHO HAS CHOSEN A LIFE OF COURAGEOUS ACTION, MOMENTS OF TENDERNESS AND SOFT PLEASURE ARE ALL TOO RARE. NO ONE KNOWS THIS BETTER THAN AQUAMAN, WHO HAS FOLLOWED THE PATH OF THE HERO SINCE HIS YOUTH...
IMAGINE THEN THE MARINE MARVEL'S CONSTERNATION WHEN ONE OF THESE MOST FRAGILE MOMENTS OF PEACE AND QUIETUDE IS SHATTERED BY HIS WIFE'S SUDDEN, PAIN-WRACKED CRY...
HUSBAND...
...HELP ME...!
MERA-- WHAT IS IT?
WHAT'S WRONG?!
J-6713
SCAVENGER HUNT!
J. M. DeMATTEIS writer • DICK GIORDANO artist • JOHN COSTANZA letterer • ADRIENNE ROY colorist • LEN WEIN editor
...FEEL... SO COLD...
COLD?! HER BODY IS SO HOT THAT IT'S ACTUALLY BOILING THE WATER AROUND HER!
DON'T WORRY, DARLING...
...I'LL SWIM TO ATLANTIS-- GET DOCTOR VULKO...
POLIC
...AND NEPTUNE HELP ANY FOOL WHO GETS IN MY WAY!

I SET UP THIS NEW VENICE BASE SO THAT MERA COULD HAVE A SAFE HAVEN FOR REST-- AWAY FROM ANY THREATS FROM MY ENEMIES...
...WHILE VULKO ATTEMPTS TO ASCERTAIN THE NATURE OF HER MYSTERIOUS AILMENT...
...BUT WHAT IF IT'S ALREADY TOO LATE? WHAT IF--NO! I CAN'T ALLOW MYSELF SUCH THOUGHTS!
MERA WILL BE ALL RIGHT! SHE'S GOT TO BE! FACING LIFE WITHOUT MY SON HAS BEEN HARD ENOUGH--BUT LIFE WITHOUT MY WIFE WOULD BE...
...IMPOSSIBLE...?!
LIKE A HANGMAN'S NOOSE, THE VISCOUS TENTACLE WRAPS ITSELF AROUND THE SEA KING'S PALE THROAT...
...BUT THE FORMER MONARCH OF ATLANTIS IS NOT ONE EASILY NUMBED BY SURPRISE!
HE STRIKES...
...HE WHIRLS...
...HE...
...STOPS!
TOPO!?!
I'M PLEASED TO SEE YOU, OLD FRIEND--BUT I HAVEN'T GOT TIME TO PLAY! MERA'S ILL!
2

THE LOYAL OCTOPUS' ONLY RESPONSE IS TO TURN AND FORCIBLY DRAG ITS MASTER DOWN INTO THE EVER-DARKENING DEPTHS...
THIS HAD BETTER BE VERY IMPORTANT, TOPO! BECAUSE IF IT'S NOT, THERE'S GOING TO BE THE DEVIL TO...
...PAY..!
THE WORD DISSOLVES ON AQUAMAN'S TONGUE AS HIS WONDERING EYES DRINK IN THE HOARY, GLITTERING SIGHT BEFORE HIM...
ITS VERY SURFACE RADIATES IMMENSE POWER, THE LIGHTEST TOUCH SENDING GENTLY UNDULATING WAVES OF ENERGY COURSING THROUGH THE OCEAN LORD'S STURDY FRAME, WHICH SOMEHOW SEEM TO RELEASE A HERETOFORE UNTAPPED RACIAL MEMORY...
INSTANTLY, AQUAMAN KNOWS...
TOPO--YOU'VE FOUND IT! THE ANCIENT ATLANTEAN MACHINERY I'VE BEEN SEARCHING FOR!
AND INSTANTLY, AQUAMAN REMEMBERS...
...REMEMBERS THE SIREN CALL OF THE WOMAN CALLED ATLENA, SOLE SURVIVOR OF THE ORIGINAL ATLANTIS...*
*WORLD'S FINEST #262.--LEN.
IN SEEKING A MEANS TO SAVE HER PEOPLE BEFORE THE FABLED LOST CONTINENT WAS SWALLOWED BY THE SEA, ATLENA CREATED A DEVICE CAPABLE OF PIERCING THE MISTY VEILS BETWEEN DIMENSIONS--
--A DEVICE THAT TRANSPORTED ITS INVENTOR AND THEN SANK WITH ATLENA'S HOMELAND, LEAVING THE WOMAN TRAPPED AND ALONE IN AN EERIE, OTHERWORLDLY REALM...
BUT ATLENA DID NOT REMAIN ALONE FOR LONG. ALTHOUGH LOST TO THE AGES, HER DEVICE STILL FUNCTIONED, PERIODICALLY DRAWING MAN...AND AQUAMAN THROUGH THE SWIRLING VORTEX LINKING THE DIMENSIONS...
WHEN HIS ATTEMPTS TO LIBERATE ATLENA AND HER CHARGES FAILED DISMALLY, AQUAMAN VOWED TO SCOUR THE OCEAN FLOOR FOR THE MISSING MACHINERY...
3

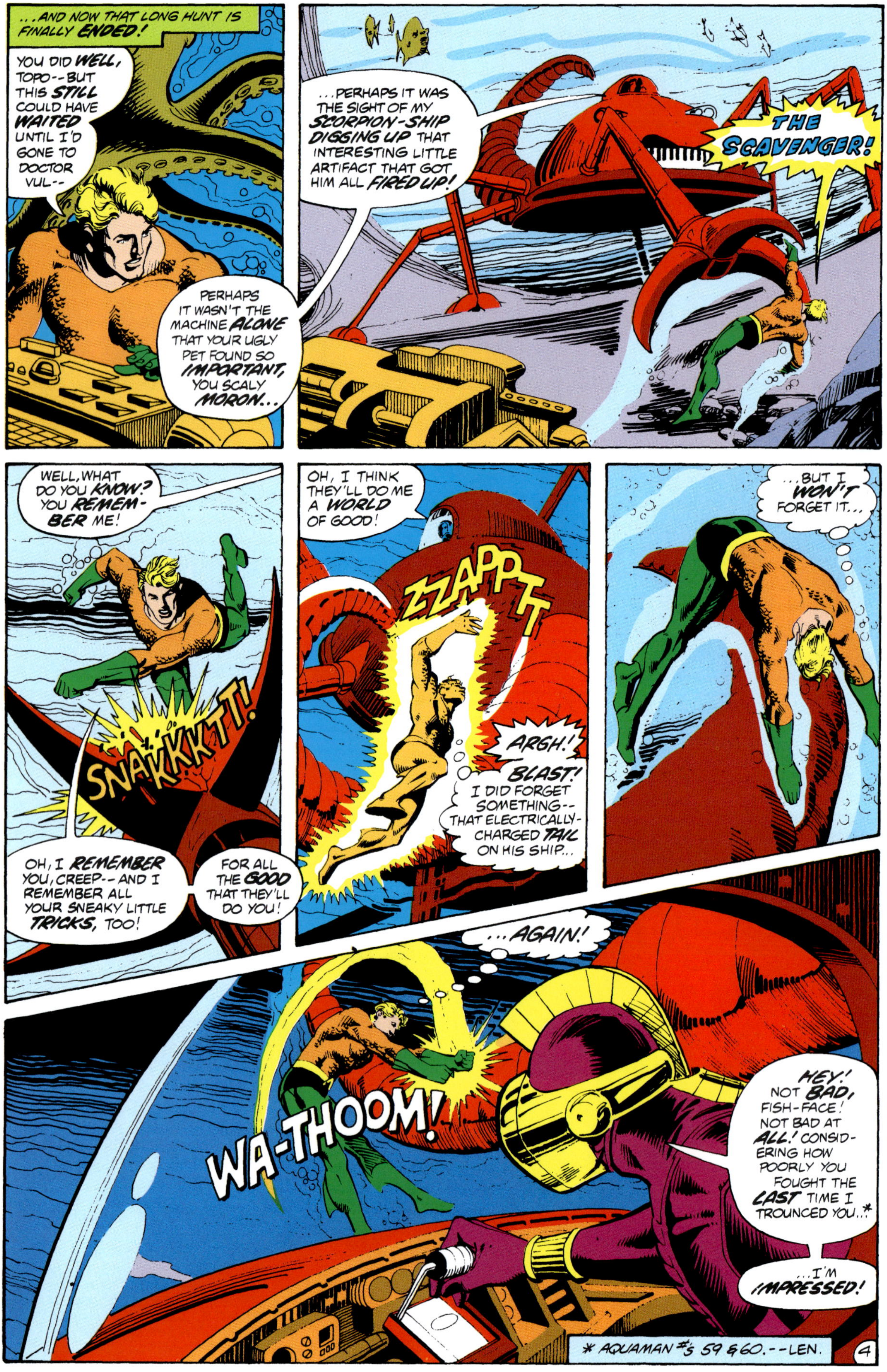

...AND NOW THAT LONG HUNT IS FINALLY ENDED!
YOU DID WELL, TOPO--BUT THIS STILL COULD HAVE WAITED UNTIL I'D GONE TO DOCTOR VUL--
PERHAPS IT WASN'T THE MACHINE ALONE THAT YOUR UGLY PET FOUND SO IMPORTANT, YOU SCALY MORON...
...PERHAPS IT WAS THE SIGHT OF MY SCORPION-SHIP DIGGING UP THAT INTERESTING LITTLE ARTIFACT THAT GOT HIM ALL FIRED UP!
THE SCAVENGER!
WELL, WHAT DO YOU KNOW? YOU REMEMBER ME!
SNAKKKTT!
OH, I REMEMBER YOU, CREEP--AND I REMEMBER ALL YOUR SNEAKY LITTLE TRICKS, TOO!
FOR ALL THE GOOD THAT THEY'LL DO YOU!
OH, I THINK THEY'LL DO ME A WORLD OF GOOD!
ZZAPPTT
ARGH!
BLAST! I DID FORGET SOMETHING--THAT ELECTRICALLY-CHARGED TAIL ON HIS SHIP...
...BUT I WON'T FORGET IT...
...AGAIN!
WA-THOOM!
HEY! NOT BAD, FISH-FACE! NOT BAD AT ALL! CONSIDERING HOW POORLY YOU FOUGHT THE LAST TIME I TROUNCED YOU...*
...I'M IMPRESSED!
* AQUAMAN #'S 59 & 60.--LEN.
4

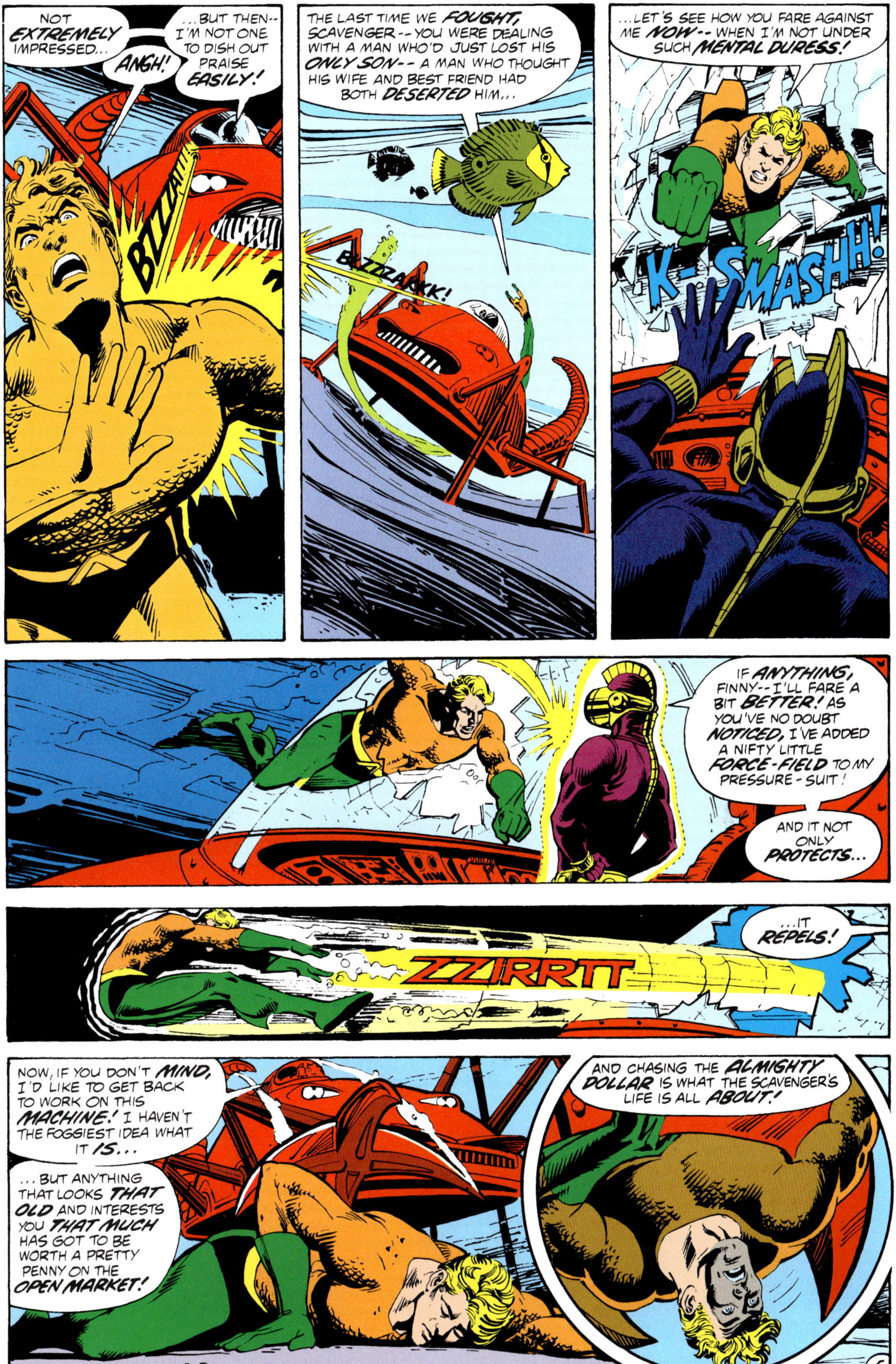
NOT EXTREMELY IMPRESSED...
ANGH!
...BUT THEN-- I'M NOT ONE TO DISH OUT PRAISE EASILY!
BZZZAAT!
THE LAST TIME WE FOUGHT, SCAVENGER -- YOU WERE DEALING WITH A MAN WHO'D JUST LOST HIS ONLY SON -- A MAN WHO THOUGHT HIS WIFE AND BEST FRIEND HAD BOTH DESERTED HIM...
BZZZRAKK!
...LET'S SEE HOW YOU FARE AGAINST ME NOW -- WHEN I'M NOT UNDER SUCH MENTAL DURESS!
K-SMASHH!
IF ANYTHING, FINNY-- I'LL FARE A BIT BETTER! AS YOU'VE NO DOUBT NOTICED, I'VE ADDED A NIFTY LITTLE FORCE-FIELD TO MY PRESSURE-SUIT!
AND IT NOT ONLY PROTECTS...
...IT REPELS!
ZZIRRTT
NOW, IF YOU DON'T MIND, I'D LIKE TO GET BACK TO WORK ON THIS MACHINE! I HAVEN'T THE FOGGIEST IDEA WHAT IT IS...
...BUT ANYTHING THAT LOOKS THAT OLD AND INTERESTS YOU THAT MUCH HAS GOT TO BE WORTH A PRETTY PENNY ON THE OPEN MARKET!
AND CHASING THE ALMIGHTY DOLLAR IS WHAT THE SCAVENGER'S LIFE IS ALL ABOUT!
5

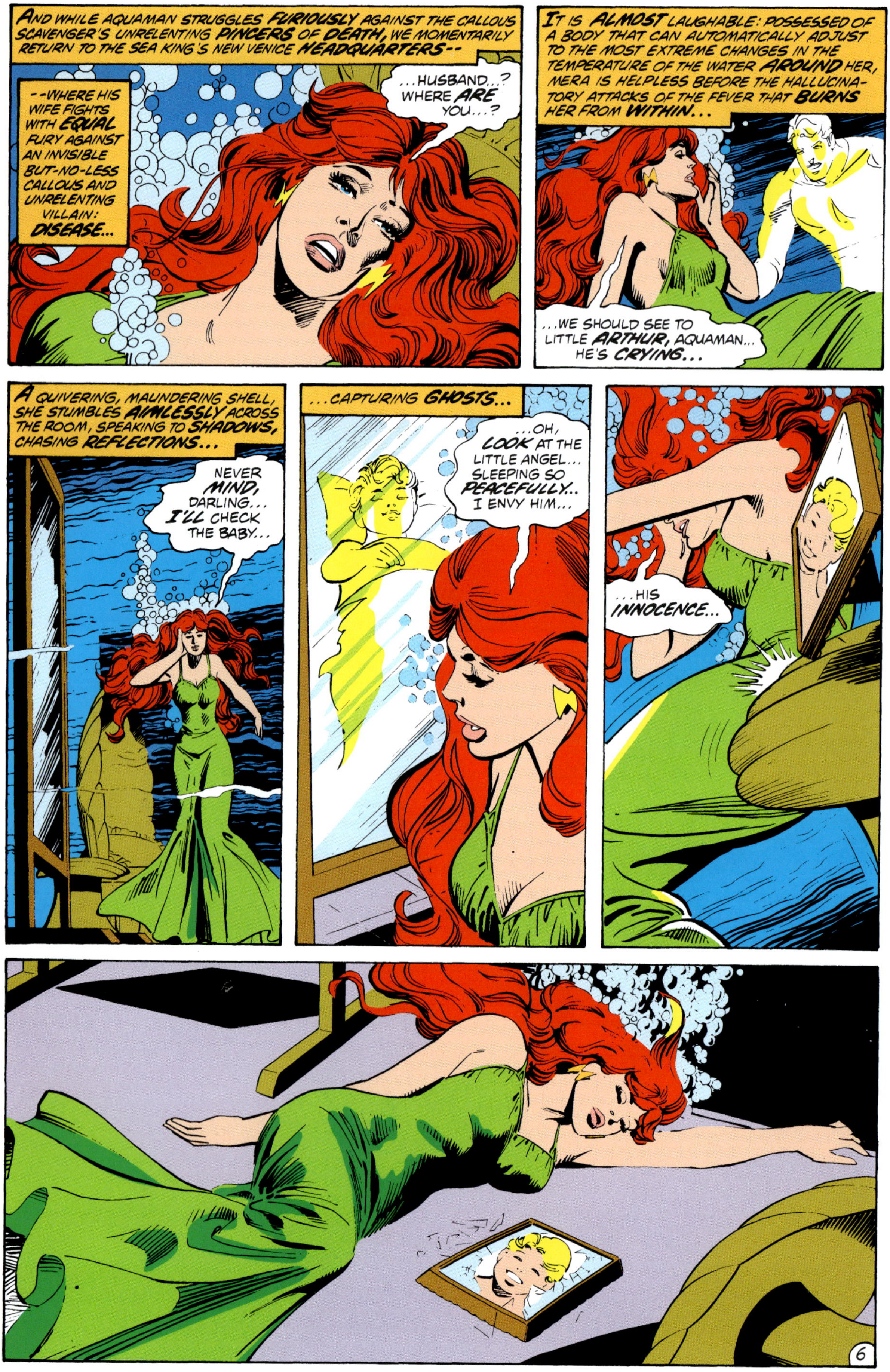
AND WHILE AQUAMAN STRUGGLES FURIOUSLY AGAINST THE CALLOUS SCAVENGER'S UNRELENTING PINCERS OF DEATH, WE MOMENTARILY RETURN TO THE SEA KING'S NEW VENICE HEADQUARTERS--
--WHERE HIS WIFE FIGHTS WITH EQUAL FURY AGAINST AN INVISIBLE BUT-NO-LESS CALLOUS AND UNRELENTING VILLAIN: DISEASE...
...HUSBAND...? WHERE ARE YOU...?
IT IS ALMOST LAUGHABLE: POSSESSED OF A BODY THAT CAN AUTOMATICALLY ADJUST TO THE MOST EXTREME CHANGES IN THE TEMPERATURE OF THE WATER AROUND HER, MERA IS HELPLESS BEFORE THE HALLUCINATORY ATTACKS OF THE FEVER THAT BURNS HER FROM WITHIN...
...WE SHOULD SEE TO LITTLE ARTHUR, AQUAMAN... HE'S CRYING...
A QUIVERING, MAUNDERING SHELL, SHE STUMBLES AIMLESSLY ACROSS THE ROOM, SPEAKING TO SHADOWS, CHASING REFLECTIONS...
NEVER MIND, DARLING... I'LL CHECK THE BABY...
...CAPTURING GHOSTS...
...OH, LOOK AT THE LITTLE ANGEL... SLEEPING SO PEACEFULLY... I ENVY HIM...
...HIS INNOCENCE...
6

BUT WHILE ONE BATTLE SEEMS HOPELESSLY LOST, THE OTHER HAS REACHED AN EXPLOSIVE TURNING POINT...
ALL RIGHT, SCAVENGER-- ENOUGH IS ENOUGH! YOU'VE TROTTED OUT ALL YOUR NEW AND OLD GIZMOS-- YOU'VE MOUTHED OFF ENOUGH FOR A NINETY-MINUTE TALK SHOW...
...AND I'M REALLY GETTING BORED!
K-RAKKK!
WHAT?!
SO I THINK I'LL JUST SHORT OUT THAT FORCE-FIELD YOU'RE SO BLASTED PROUD OF-- WITH A LITTLE HELP FROM MY ELECTRIC FRIENDS, OF COURSE...
ZZZZZZTTT
...AND THEN I'M CANCELLING THIS PROGRAM!
OW!-- THAT'S NOT FAIR! I WAS WINNING! I HAD YOU BEATEN!
WHAP!
BEATEN? I KNOW THERE ARE CERTAIN BENIGHTED SOULS WHO THINK I'M SOME KIND OF THIRD-RATE HERO, SCAVENGER-- BUT I'D THINK THAT YOU-- OF ALL PEOPLE-- WOULD KNOW BETTER!
BUT SINCE YOU SEEM A BIT CONFUSED-- LET ME MAKE THIS PERFECTLY CLEAR...
...I WAS IN THE WORLD-SAVING GAME WHEN PEOPLE LIKE FIRESTORM AND BLACK LIGHTNING WERE STILL IN DIAPERS...
BROOOMF!
...I'VE WORKED HARD TO EARN THE RESPECT AND TRUST OF EVERY LIVING CREATURE BENEATH THE WAVES-- AND I TAKE MY JOB VERY SERIOUSLY...
...SO GET THIS THROUGH YOUR HEAD, PUNK...
SPLAKK
...I'M AQUAMAN, KING OF THE SEVEN SEAS...
THAAM!
...AND I'M THE BEST!
7

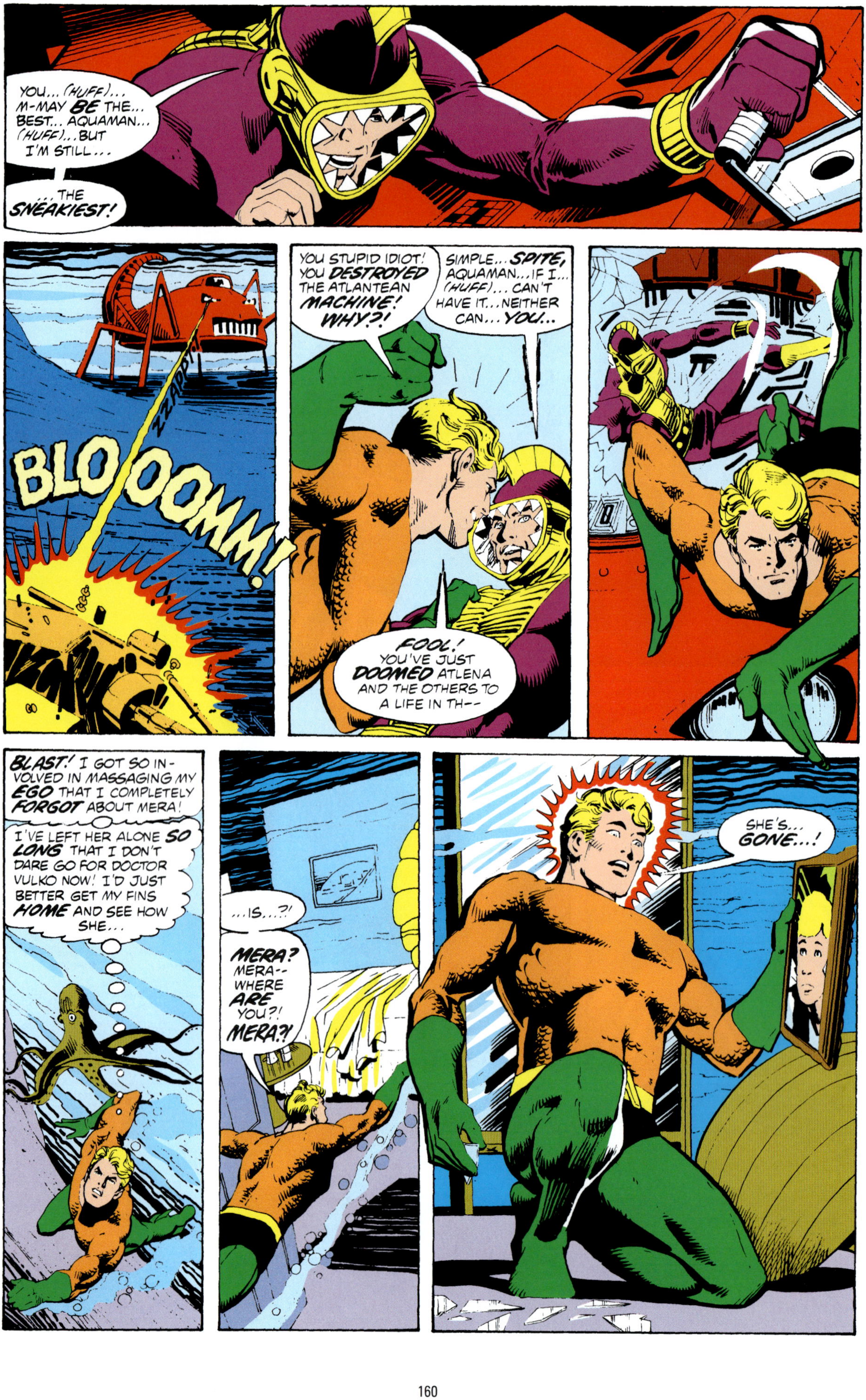
YOU... (HUFF)... M-MAY BE THE... BEST... AQUAMAN... (HUFF)... BUT I'M STILL...
...THE SNEAKIEST!
ZZAPPP
BLOOOMM!
YOU STUPID IDIOT! YOU DESTROYED THE ATLANTEAN MACHINE! WHY?!
SIMPLE... SPITE, AQUAMAN... IF I... (HUFF)... CAN'T HAVE IT... NEITHER CAN... YOU...
FOOL! YOU'VE JUST DOOMED ATLENA AND THE OTHERS TO A LIFE IN TH--
BLAST! I GOT SO IN-VOLVED IN MASSAGING MY EGO THAT I COMPLETELY FORGOT ABOUT MERA!
I'VE LEFT HER ALONE SO LONG THAT I DON'T DARE GO FOR DOCTOR VULKO NOW! I'D JUST BETTER GET MY FINS HOME AND SEE HOW SHE...
...IS...?!
MERA? MERA-- WHERE ARE YOU?! MERA?!
SHE'S... GONE...!

AQUAMAN
GENESIS
AQUAMAN
AQUAMAN
AQUAMAN
AQUAMAN
YOU!
YOU DID THIS TO HER!
AND NOW... YOU DIE!!
LIVES AGAIN!

THE RULER of THE DEEP GAINS DEPTH

by **ROBERT GREENBERGER**

The 1985 Crisis on Infinite Earths allowed DC's editorial team to rethink their heroes and villains. When executive editor Dick Giordano invited Neal Pozner, who was then the company's design director, to pitch for an available character even before the 50th-anniversary event, he was drawn to the King of the Seven Seas.

In his proposal, he stated, "Atlantis was a vague concept which had never been explored in depth. Or perhaps I should say, several vague concepts within the framework of the DC Universe which had never been related." In his mind, the Atlantis of Lori Lemaris, Aquaman, Arion, and Warlord could and should be integrated. From this point on, mysticism and Arthur's character would remain works in progress well into the 21st century.

The miniseries, illustrated by newcomer Craig Hamilton, finally arrived just as *Crisis* was winding down. Here, Pozner used Aquaman's half brother, Ocean Master, as a touchstone to the past while sending his hero to Thierna Na Oge, a newly discovered city, a place of magic. This series brought renewed interest in Aquaman with fans divided over the new blue-and-white-camo costume, but most appreciating Hamilton's work. The miniseries sold well enough to have a follow-up commissioned that never happened due to artist delays and Pozner leaving DC.

Interest in a follow-up remained within the offices, so a one-shot was commissioned from the writing team of Dan Mishkin and Gary Cohn, with art from George Freeman and Mark Pacella. *Aquaman Special* #1 (1988) continued themes from the miniseries but felt as if it was marking time, waiting for an energized new status quo.

During this period, DC was retelling the post-Crisis origins of their heroes, mostly in the pages of *Secret Origins*. Karl Kesel turned to the writing partnership of Keith Giffen and Robert Loren Fleming to try their hand at miniseries and as work progressed, it was decided a *Secret Origins* launch would help sales. After editor Mark Waid put Eric Shanower on to ink Curt Swan's pencils, the superlative look inspired management to upgrade the project. *The Legend of Aquaman Special* (1989) retold the origin while adding new details such as naming Mercy Reef and that the Atlanteans are born with fins on the backs of their legs. The underbelly of Atlantean politics was explored with Vulko a political prisoner and later Arthur being imprisoned, donning the familiar orange-and-green uniform. It was received with critical acclaim, which paved the way for the successful follow-up miniseries *Aquaman* (1989) with Al Vey replacing Shanower on inks. Here, Vulko is presumed dead, and Queen Mera is struggling to hold things together until former prisoner Aquaman arrives on the scene, leading an underground rebellion. Giffen intended Mera to die here but was overruled by Giordano, who once edited the character and *really* liked her.

While all this was happening, Peter David and Esteban Maroto had been working on their upscale format *Atlantis Chronicles*, a seven-issue

AQUAMAN
LIVES AGAIN!
AQUAMAN STANDS ALONE!
BATMAN
AQUAMAN
HE'S THE DEADLIEST MAN ALIVE
AQUAMAN
ARTHUR CURRY JUNIOR
AQUAMAN
IS THIS MY FOE!
AQUAMAN
SUPER FRIENDS
Adventure COMICS
AQUAMAN
AQUAMAN
AQUAMAN

series that told the full history of Atlantis from its sinking through the birth of Arthur Curry. When it arrived in 1990, it was praised for its sophisticated storytelling and how it works as a continuity implant and standalone epic fantasy.

A new *Aquaman* ongoing series was launched under editor Kevin Dooley, from newcomers Shaun McLaughlin and Ken Hooper. Debuting in 1991, events pick up where the previous Aquaman miniseries ended, with Mera back in her home dimension and Aquaman a solo act, without ties to either Atlantis or the Justice League. The initial storyline involved a war between the surface North Sea country of Oumland and Atlantis's capital city of Poseidonis, and as the bubbles settled, Aquaman found himself appointed by King Thesily to represent the undersea kingdom at the United Nations, a fresh angle to explore. Surface and undersea political shenanigans along with personal challenges carried the series for the rest of McLaughlin's run.

Peter David took over the writing and intended to show the king some respect and in turn, get him respect from the rest of the DCU. David explored threads from *Atlantis Chronicles* while also resetting Aquaman's relationships with those around him. David also built on material left over from both Giffen's and McLaughlin's runs, notably the relationship between Aquaman and Prom, the dolphin who helped the infant survive the deep. He decided the Sea King also needed a revised look, so he sent him to dwell in the Aquacave until he emerged with the beard and long hair, as replicated in Jason Momoa's live-action take on the hero.

David also developed a romance between Arthur and Dolphin, which was upended with the later introduction of Koryak, a son Aquaman didn't know he had from a long-ago romance with Kako, an Inuit woman.

All was not peaceful when the terrorist Charybdis arrived and brought piranhas to consume the hero's hand, which was subsequently replaced with a harpoon, completing the visual remaking of the character. David and artists Martin Englund and Jim Caliafiore's efforts were rewarded with buzz among the fan community and a rise in sales.

Writer Dan Jurgens and artist Steve Epting were later brought in to shift the tone. In Jurgens's mind, Arthur was King Arthur, and he told grand epic tales, including a war with Cerdia and fresh supporting players. When Cerdia was defeated, Atlantis annexed it, giving the undersea kingdom its first toehold into the surface world. And when Garth, now the hero Tempest, had gone missing, Aquaman and the entire Atlantean army went to his rescue in the series's 75th and final issue.

With the increased interest in the hero, Aquaman began appearing in other titles, resuming his role within the JLA and getting himself embroiled in events both on the surface and across the galaxy. Atlantis had gained stature and respect, while Aquaman had finally shown depth and complexity in fresh, exciting ways.

A former editor and executive for DC Comics, ***Robert Greenberger*** *may be best remembered for his editorial work on series such as* Suicide Squad, Doom Patrol, *and* Atlantis Chronicles. *He has worked at Marvel Comics, Starlog Press, and* Weekly World News *in addition to writing numerous works of fiction and nonfiction. He remains a comics historian when not teaching high school English in Maryland.*

MINUTES LATER, AQUAMAN MEETS SOME FISH WHO INHABIT THE CAVE AND USES HIS AMAZING TELEPATHIC POWERS TO ASK THEM FOR DIRECTIONS...
--THIS TUNNEL PASSES THROUGH A CAVERN AND THEN LEADS OUT TO THE OPEN SEA FARM ?
THANK YOU, MY FRIENDS!

4 PART MINI-SERIES
AQUAMAN
75¢
NO.1
FEB. 86
APPROVED BY THE COMICS CODE AUTHORITY
craig. hamilton.
IN THE SHADOWY DEPTHS OF ATLANTIS, HIS LIFE WILL CHANGE FOREVER!

LIVES AGAIN!
AQUAMAN STANDS ALONE!
LEGEND OF AQUAMAN
JUSTICE LEAGUE of AMERICA
STARRO THE CONQUEROR!
METAMORPHO
AQUAMAN
THE SUPER FRIENDS
Adventure COMICS
AQUAMAN
Manhunter Mars Hawkman
AQUAMAN
AQUAMAN
DOOM from DIMENSION AQUA!
AQUAMAN
URBAN RENEWAL!
UNDERWORLD
DC UNIVERSE REBIRTH
AQUAMAN
DC UNIVERSE REBIRTH
AQUAMAN
AQUAMAN
WHO DESTROYS THE SEA KING
The OCEAN MASTER or BLACK MANTA?
AQUAMAN
ARTHUR CURRY JUNIOR
A NOVEL-LENGTH SEA SPECTACULAR!
DC COMICS
THE NEW 52!
AQUAMAN
AQUAMAN
IS THIS MY FOE?
AQUAMAN
AQUAMAN
JABBERJAW
CAPTAIN CAVEMAN
the BRAVE and the BOLD
BATMAN
AQUAMAN
The SLEEP-WALKER from the SEA!
DC COMICS
JUSTICE LEAGUE
AQUAMAN
"The WEDDING of AQUAMAN!"
AQUAMAN
AQUAMAN A COWARD? IS HE REALLY IN TERROR OF... The OCEAN MASTER?
THE BEGINNING OF TOMORROW
AQUAMAN
AQUAMAN
IN THE SHADOWY DEPTHS OF ATLANTIS, HIS LIFE WILL CHANGE FOREVER!
DC COMICS
THE NEW 52!
AQUAMAN
YEAR ONE
AQUAMAN
1995 ANNUAL
AQUAMAN
WHO DESTROYS THE SEA KING
GENESIS
AQUAMAN
AQUAMAN
SWORD OF ATLANTIS
KURT BUSIEK
BUTCH GUICE
The King of the Seas
AQUAMAN
LEADS HIS ARMY TO BATTLE!
AQUAMAN
YOU!
YOU DID THIS TO HER!
AND NOW... YOU DIE!!
AQUAMAN

...and the great cities flourished o'er the mighty continent of Atlantis. The fathers of our race brought splendor where'er they went. As humanity crawled from caves, our ancestors thrived in an oasis of civilization.
A time will come, millennia hence, when we are buried 'neath the waves and humanity will worship the scientific arts.
Yet the beauty and harmony of this first Atlantis grew out of magicks, pure and potent. Here, magic reigned supreme...
A lattice of mystical multicolored threads wove magic through the very air, as the mage Calculha discovered.
But far greater magicks lay ready to be tapped.

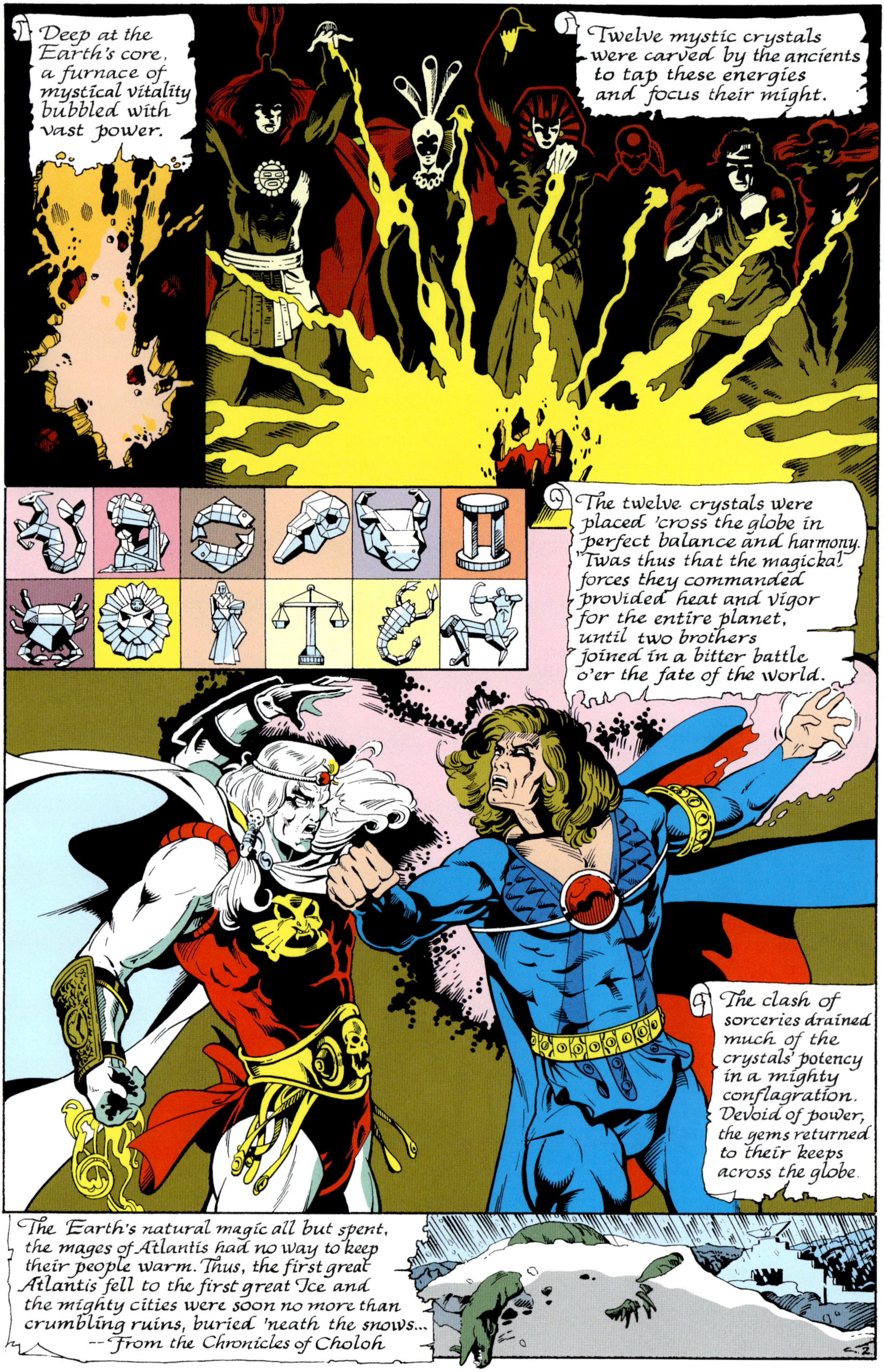
Deep at the Earth's core, a furnace of mystical vitality bubbled with vast power.
Twelve mystic crystals were carved by the ancients to tap these energies and focus their might.
The twelve crystals were placed 'cross the globe in perfect balance and harmony. 'Twas thus that the magickal forces they commanded provided heat and vigor for the entire planet, until two brothers joined in a bitter battle o'er the fate of the world.
The clash of sorceries drained much of the crystals' potency in a mighty conflagration. Devoid of power, the gems returned to their keeps across the globe.
The Earth's natural magic all but spent, the mages of Atlantis had no way to keep their people warm. Thus, the first great Atlantis fell to the first great Ice and the mighty cities were soon no more than crumbling ruins, buried 'neath the snows...
--From the Chronicles of Choloh

NEW VENICE, FLORIDA. TODAY BEGAN LIKE ANY OTHER DAY IN THIS PEACEFUL COMMUNITY.
POLICE
NEW VENICE · FLORIDA · DEPARTMENT
FRANKIE SAY WAR
SANDWICHES
HMMMKCHHRRR
KRRRA-BLAAAMM
3.

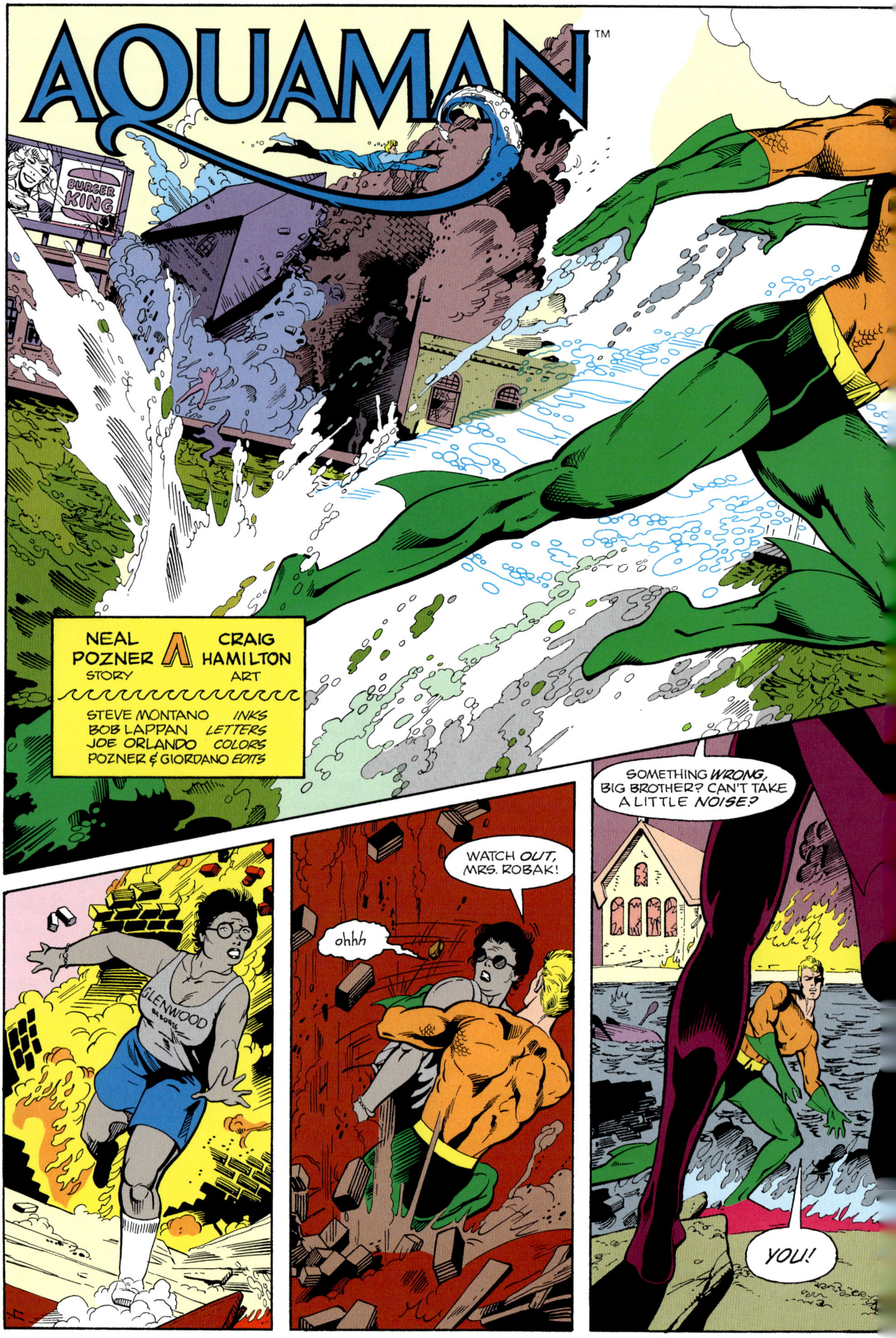
AQUAMAN™
BURGER KING
NEAL POZNER STORY
CRAIG HAMILTON ART
STEVE MONTANO INKS
BOB LAPPAN LETTERS
JOE ORLANDO COLORS
POZNER & GIORDANO EDITS
SOMETHING WRONG, BIG BROTHER? CAN'T TAKE A LITTLE NOISE?
GLENWOOD
WATCH OUT, MRS. ROBAK!
ohhh
YOU!

WHO'S RESPONSIBLE FOR THIS CARNAGE? MY HOME...DESTROYED!
NEVER MIND THAT, ARTHUR. WE MUST SAVE OUR FRIENDS!
YOU SHOULD THANK THE OCEAN MASTER FOR GETTING RID OF THIS DISGUSTING SLUM YOU LIVE IN!
ORM, HOW COULD YOU DO THIS?
YOU'VE POINTLESSLY DEMOLISHED MY HOME, ENDANGERED MY COMMUNITY...
WHY, YOU MANIAC?
WHY?!
NEW VENICE POLICE DEPT
5

WELL, WELL! WHAT'S ALL THIS?
DADDY DEAR ACTUALLY TAUGHT YOU TO DO SOMETHING NASTY?
ORM...
WHY DO YOU DESTROY WHAT IS MINE? JEOPARDIZE INNOCENTS?
YOU'RE SO SMART, FIGURE IT OUUUUF
ARE YOU TRYING AGAIN TO PROVE TO YOURSELF THAT WE'RE EQUALS?
CAN'T YOU GET IT THROUGH YOUR HEAD THAT WE'RE NOT...
...WE NEVER WILL BE...
...AND THAT'S NO REFLECTION ON YOU?
AN ACCIDENT OF BIRTH LEFT ME WITH SPECIAL POWERS RATHER THAN YOU, YOU PATHETIC LUNATIC!
6.

HUSBAND, NEVER MIND ORM! MY POWER TO SOLIDIFY WATER CAN SAVE MANY OF OUR FRIENDS--
--BUT THE CITY IS COLLAPSING AROUND US!
WE NEED YOUR HELP, TOO!
ARTHUR?

ARTHUR, DO YOU HEAR ME?
AN ACCIDENT OF BIRTH MADE YOU SUPERIOR, EH?
IN THAT CASE IF I CAN BEAT YOU, IT'LL BE A DOUBLE VICTORY, WON'T IT, ARTIE?
NOT ONLY WILL I BE YOUR BETTER, BUT IT'LL BE BECAUSE I MADE IT SO, NOT BECAUSE I WAS BORN LUCKY!
WH...WHAT ARE YOU DOING?
JUST SHOWING YOU WHO'S BOSS!
8.

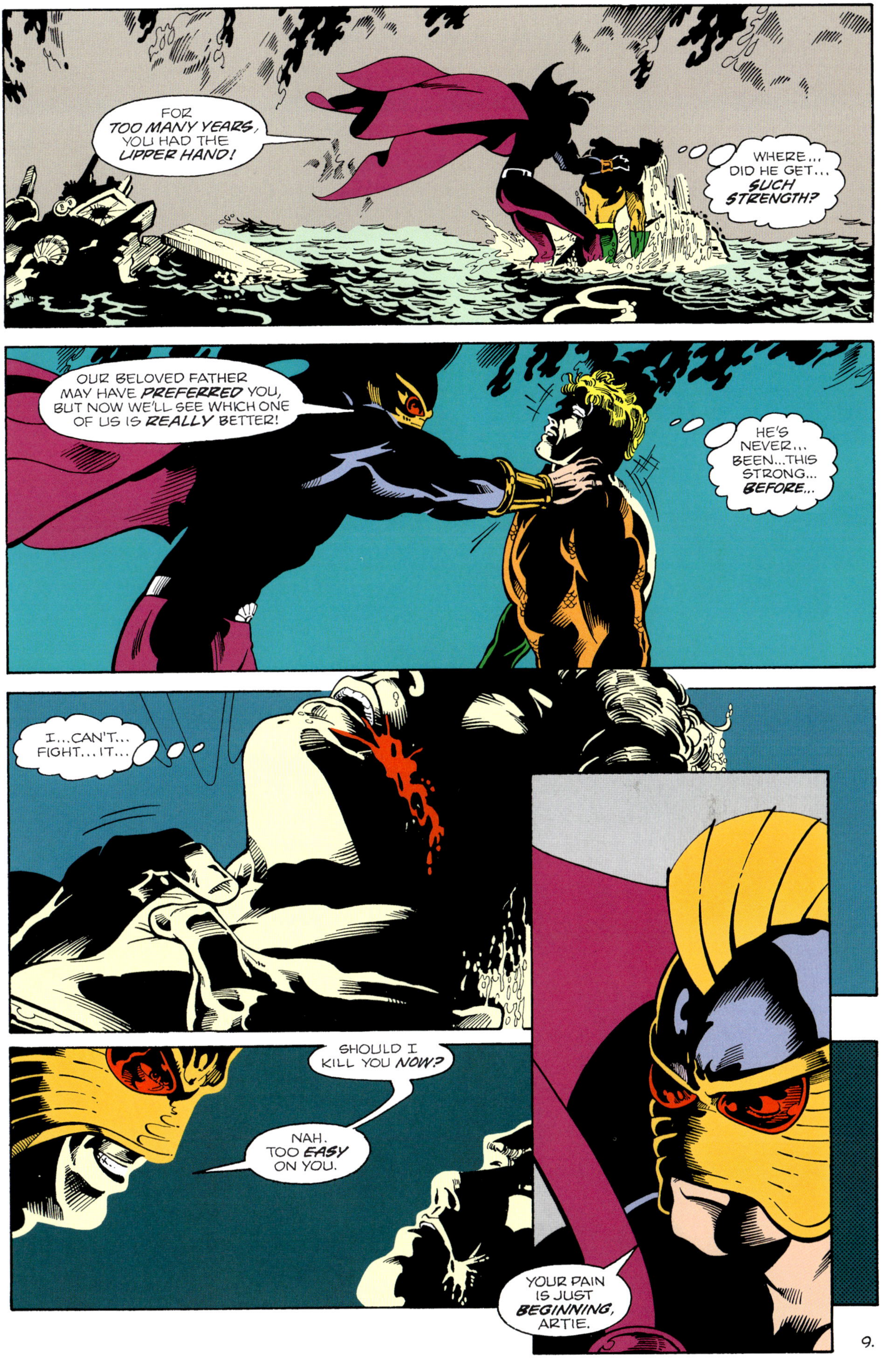
FOR TOO MANY YEARS, YOU HAD THE UPPER HAND!
WHERE... DID HE GET... SUCH STRENGTH?
OUR BELOVED FATHER MAY HAVE PREFERRED YOU, BUT NOW WE'LL SEE WHICH ONE OF US IS REALLY BETTER!
HE'S NEVER... BEEN...THIS STRONG... BEFORE...
I...CAN'T... FIGHT... IT...
SHOULD I KILL YOU NOW?
NAH. TOO EASY ON YOU.
YOUR PAIN IS JUST BEGINNING, ARTIE.
9.

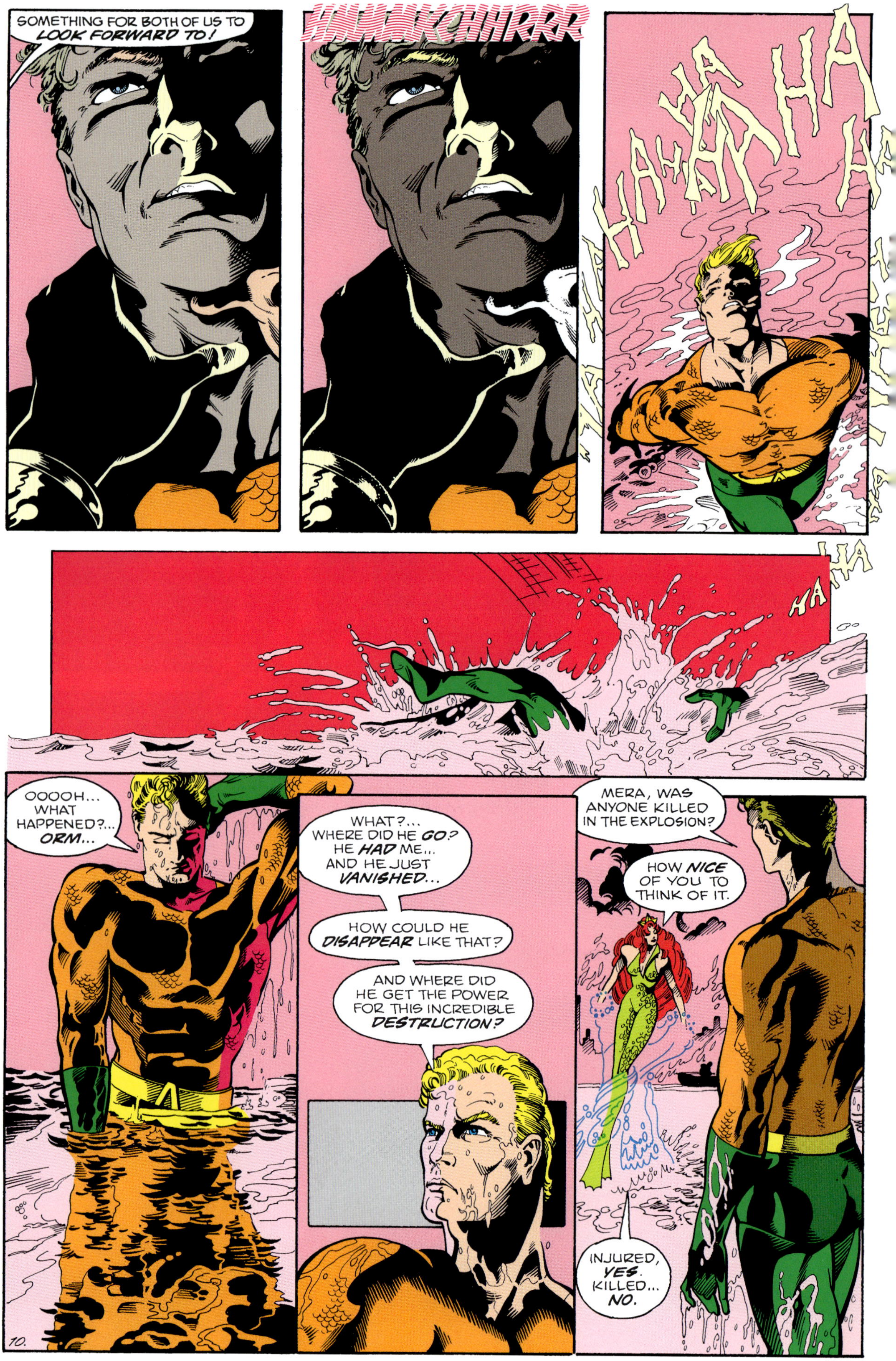
SOMETHING FOR BOTH OF US TO LOOK FORWARD TO!
HHHAAKCHHRRR
HAHAHAHAHAHA
OOOOH... WHAT HAPPENED?... ORM...
WHAT?... WHERE DID HE GO? HE HAD ME... AND HE JUST VANISHED...
HOW COULD HE DISAPPEAR LIKE THAT?
AND WHERE DID HE GET THE POWER FOR THIS INCREDIBLE DESTRUCTION?
MERA, WAS ANYONE KILLED IN THE EXPLOSION?
HOW NICE OF YOU TO THINK OF IT.
INJURED, YES. KILLED... NO.
10.

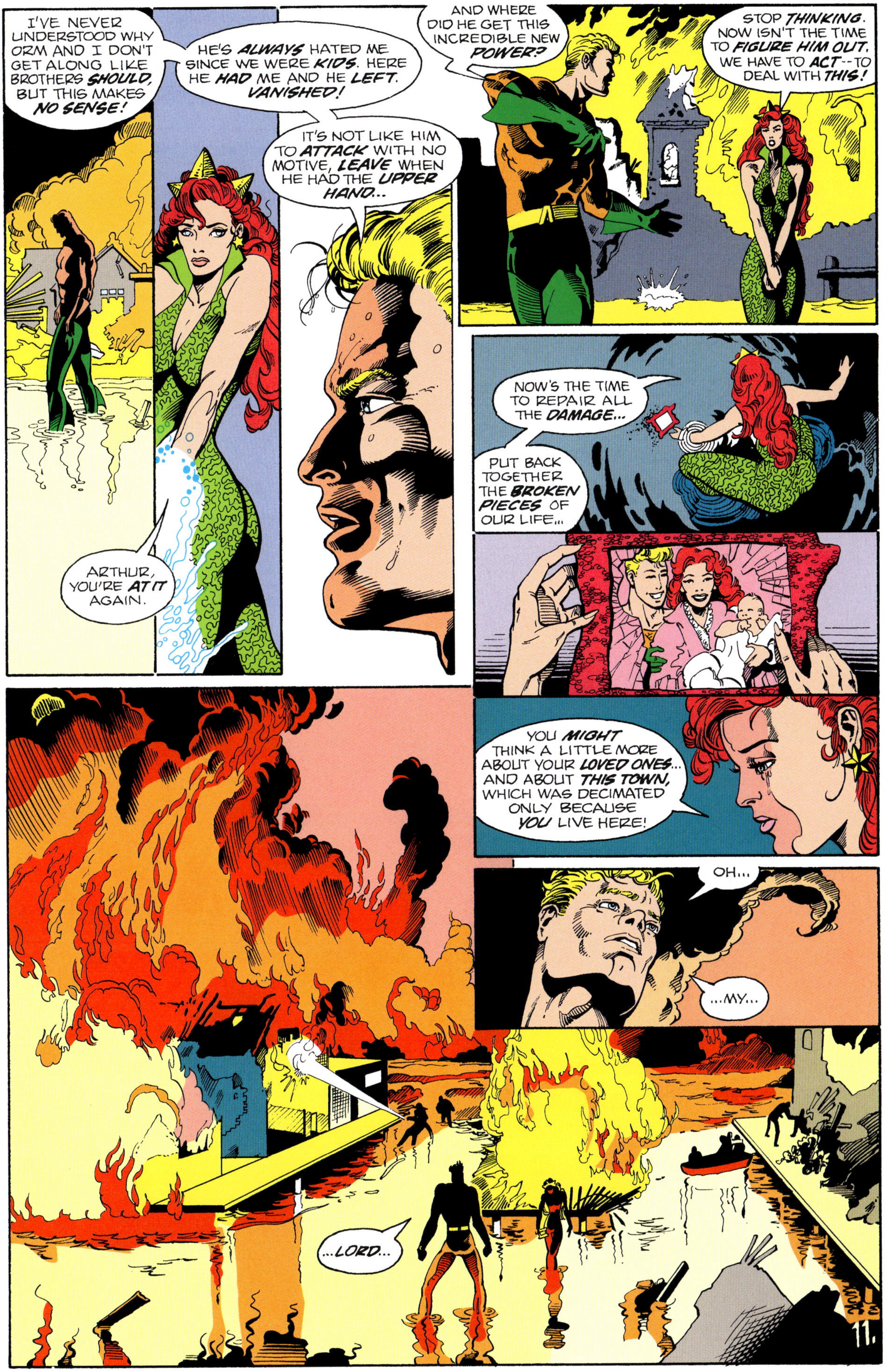
I'VE NEVER UNDERSTOOD WHY ORM AND I DON'T GET ALONG LIKE BROTHERS SHOULD, BUT THIS MAKES NO SENSE!
HE'S ALWAYS HATED ME SINCE WE WERE KIDS. HERE HE HAD ME AND HE LEFT. VANISHED!
IT'S NOT LIKE HIM TO ATTACK WITH NO MOTIVE, LEAVE WHEN HE HAD THE UPPER HAND...
ARTHUR, YOU'RE AT IT AGAIN.
AND WHERE DID HE GET THIS INCREDIBLE NEW POWER?
STOP THINKING. NOW ISN'T THE TIME TO FIGURE HIM OUT. WE HAVE TO ACT--TO DEAL WITH THIS!
NOW'S THE TIME TO REPAIR ALL THE DAMAGE...
PUT BACK TOGETHER THE BROKEN PIECES OF OUR LIFE...
YOU MIGHT THINK A LITTLE MORE ABOUT YOUR LOVED ONES... AND ABOUT THIS TOWN, WHICH WAS DECIMATED ONLY BECAUSE YOU LIVE HERE!
OH...
...MY...
...LORD...
11.

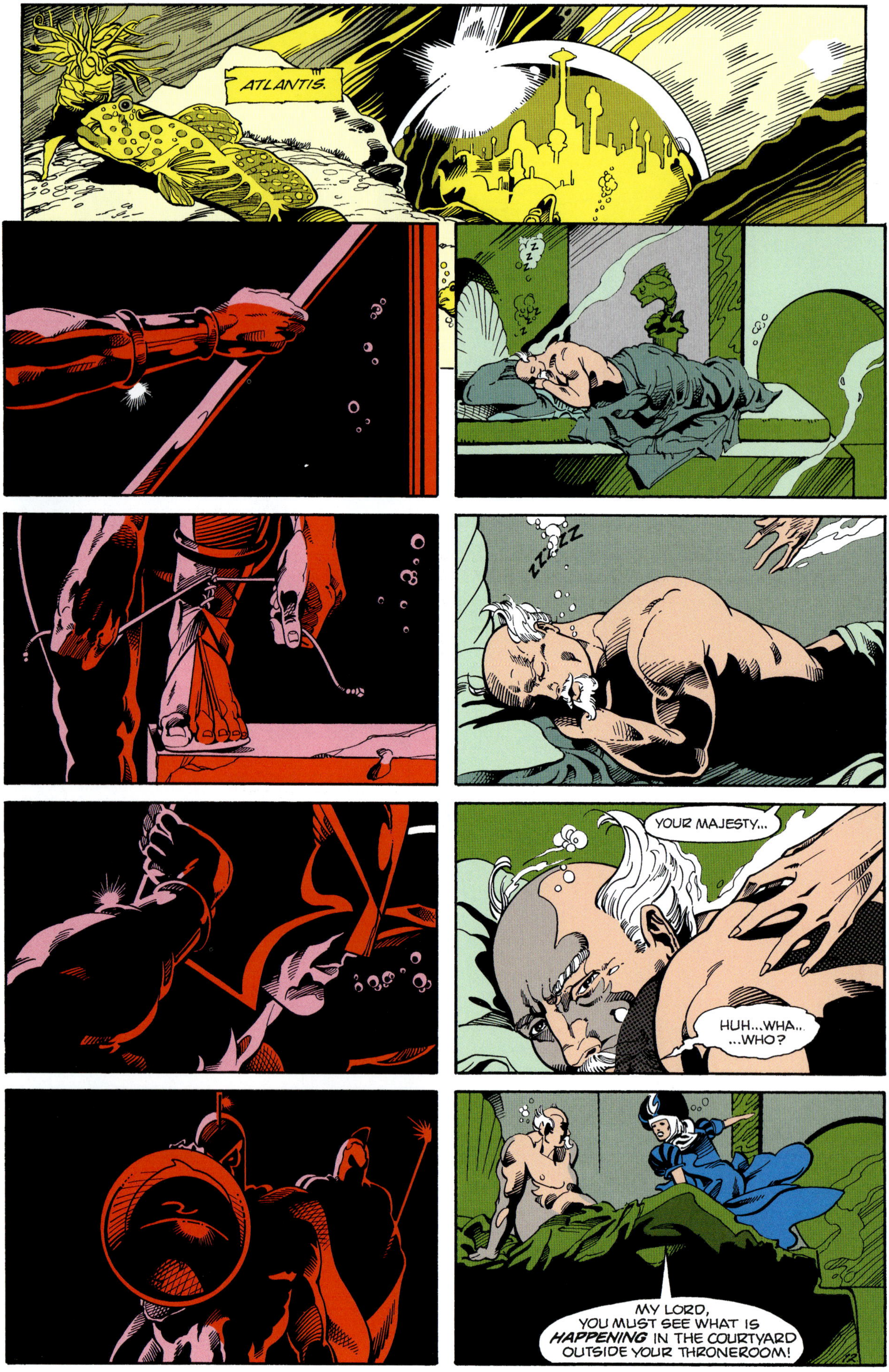
ATLANTIS.
Z
Z
Z
ZZZZZ
YOUR MAJESTY...
HUH...WHA...
...WHO?
MY LORD, YOU MUST SEE WHAT IS HAPPENING IN THE COURTYARD OUTSIDE YOUR THRONEROOM!

THE COUNCIL AGAIN REQUESTS THAT YOU SANCTION MILITARY ACTION.
CAN'T YOU TELL THEM THAT I'M STILL DELIBERATING?
KING VULKO! ARE YOU PREPARED TO MARCH ON THE BLASPHEMERS?
THEY FIND THAT REPLY... NO LONGER ACCEPTABLE, MY LORD.
I...SEE.
BUT I CAN'T GIVE THEM THE ANSWER THEY WANT.
STILL, IF I DON'T DECLARE WAR, THEY'LL APPOINT ANOTHER KING IN MY PLACE WHO WILL!
WILL AQUAMAN RESPOND TO YOUR CALL FOR AID?
I PITY THE SURFACE WORLD IF HE DOESN'T.
HE'S THE ONLY ONE WHO COULD HELP US...
...IF ONLY HIS TEMPER DOESN'T GET IN THE WAY OF THE MISSION...
13.

MID-ATLANTIC.
I WONDER WHY VULKO SUMMONED ME SO URGENTLY AFTER ALL THIS TIME...?
THERE WASN'T EVEN TIME TO HELP MERA REPAIR THE DAMAGE IN NEW VENICE.
STILL, SHE'S MORE THAN CAPABLE.
AS COMMITTED AS I AM TO MY FRIENDS ON THE SURFACE WORLD, MY HEART BELONGS HERE...
AH, THE SPLENDORS OF THE SEA! THE FREEDOM! THE CALM!
EACH TIME I RETURN TO THE OCEAN, I APPRECIATE IT MORE!
THIS IS WHERE I AM AT PEACE, WHERE I BELONG! WHY DO I LIVE ANYWHERE ELSE?

THESE ARE MY FRIENDS AS MUCH AS ANY SURFACE MAN!
HOW GOES IT?
HAVE YOU LOCATED THE OCEAN MASTER YET, FRIEND GURNARD?
HOW COULD HE AVOID BEING SEEN BY A MILLION EYES?
ALL OF YOU KEEP LOOKING, AND LET ME KNOW WHEN YOU FIND HIM!
I STILL CAN'T FATHOM WHY HE ATTACKED.
WHAT DID HE HAVE TO GAIN?
AND WHERE DID HE GET THE POWER TO CAUSE SUCH DAMAGE AND TO OVERWHELM ME LIKE... HUH?
ALGAE FARMS!
I MUST BE NEAR THE CITY ALREADY.
FUNNY... EVEN THOUGH I FIRST SAW ATLANTIS AS AN ADULT, I STILL FEEL LIKE I'M COMING HOME.
15.

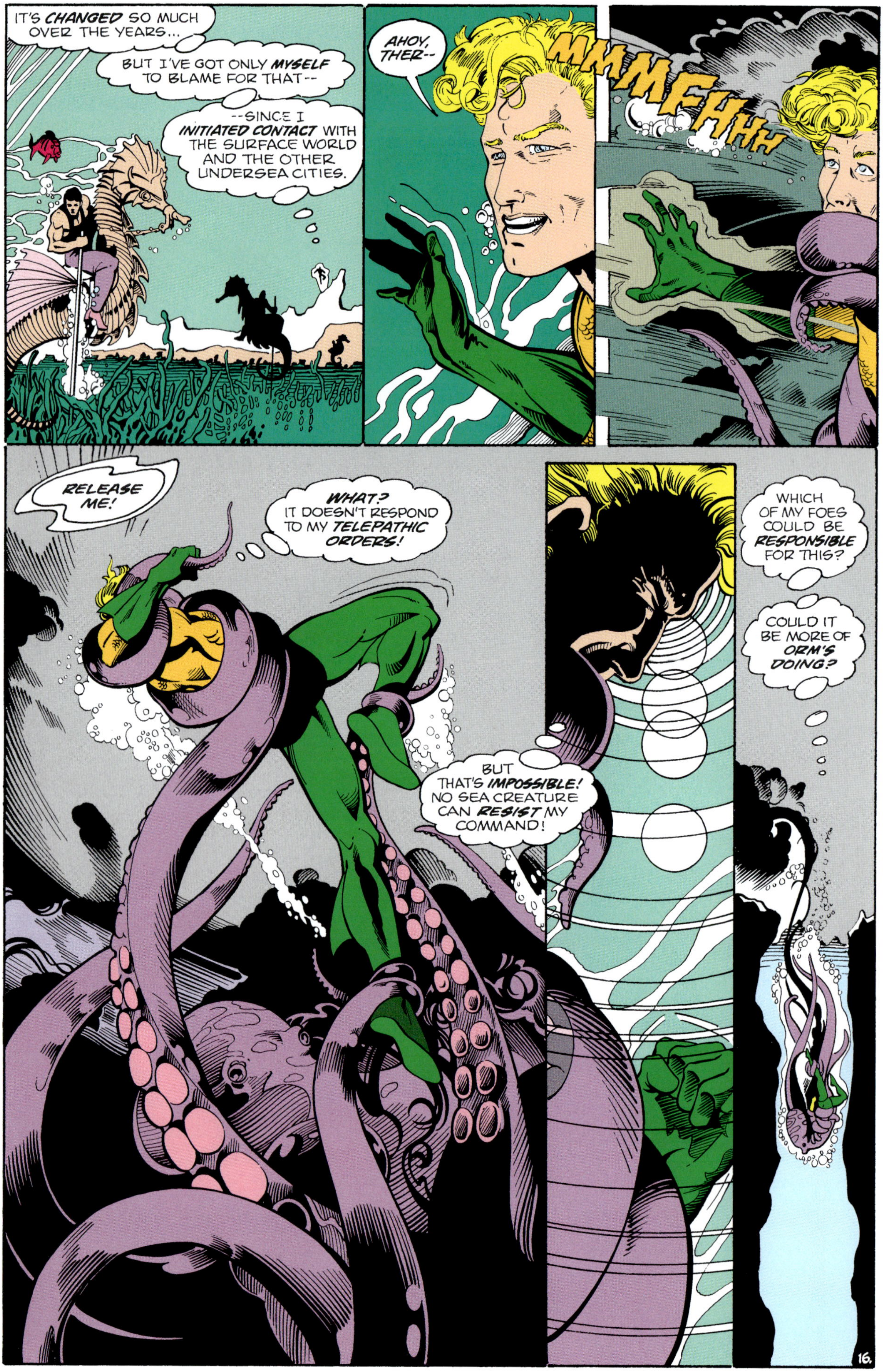
IT'S CHANGED SO MUCH OVER THE YEARS...
BUT I'VE GOT ONLY MYSELF TO BLAME FOR THAT--
--SINCE I INITIATED CONTACT WITH THE SURFACE WORLD AND THE OTHER UNDERSEA CITIES.
AHOY, THER--
MMMMFHHHH
RELEASE ME!
WHAT? IT DOESN'T RESPOND TO MY TELEPATHIC ORDERS!
BUT THAT'S IMPOSSIBLE! NO SEA CREATURE CAN RESIST MY COMMAND!
WHICH OF MY FOES COULD BE RESPONSIBLE FOR THIS?
COULD IT BE MORE OF ORM'S DOING?
16.

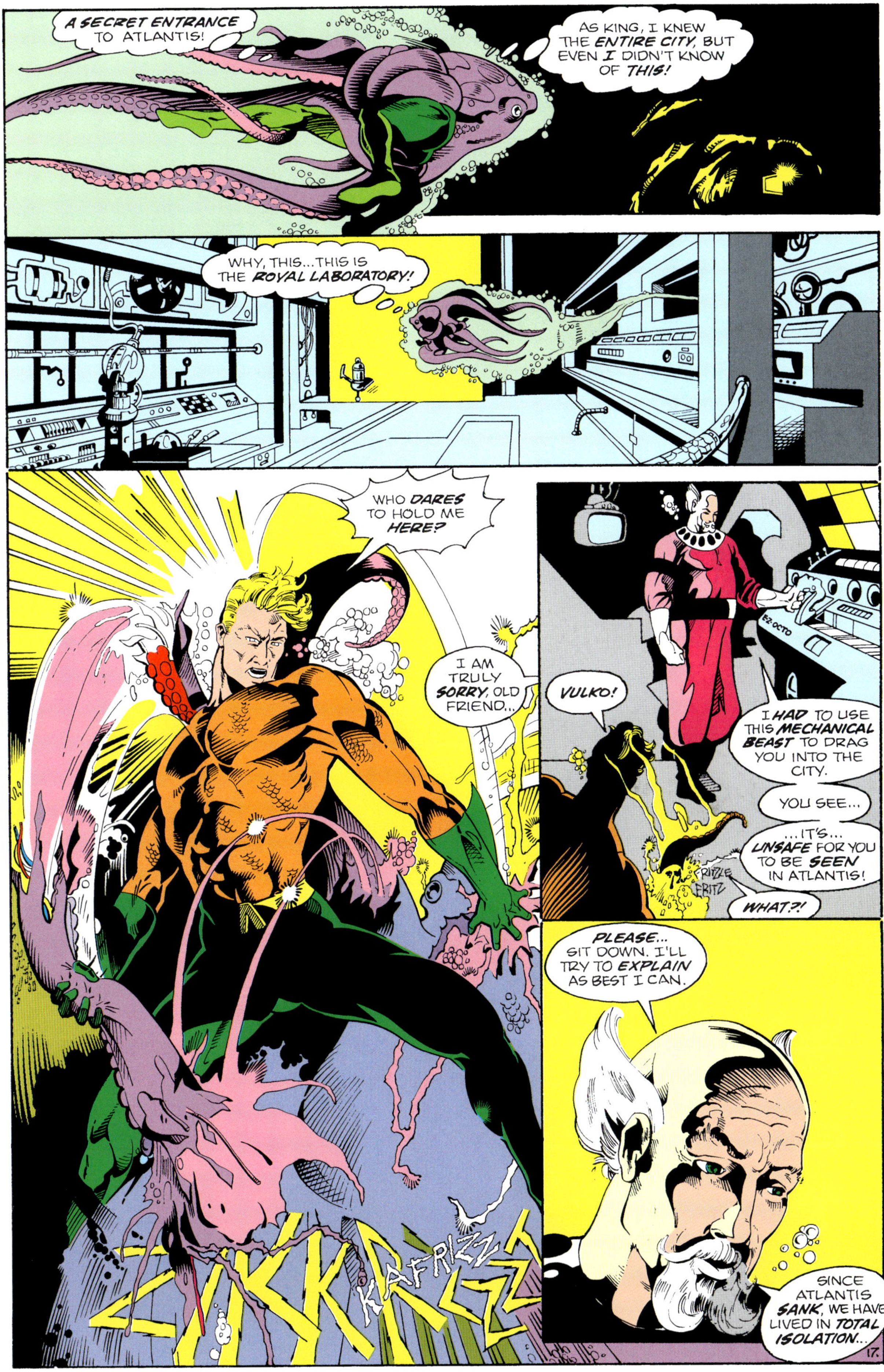
A SECRET ENTRANCE TO ATLANTIS!
AS KING, I KNEW THE ENTIRE CITY, BUT EVEN I DIDN'T KNOW OF THIS!
WHY, THIS...THIS IS THE ROYAL LABORATORY!
WHO DARES TO HOLD ME HERE?
I AM TRULY SORRY, OLD FRIEND...
KAFRIZZ
VULKO!
I HAD TO USE THIS MECHANICAL BEAST TO DRAG YOU INTO THE CITY.
YOU SEE...
...IT'S... UNSAFE FOR YOU TO BE SEEN IN ATLANTIS!
WHAT?!
PLEASE... SIT DOWN. I'LL TRY TO EXPLAIN AS BEST I CAN.
SINCE ATLANTIS SANK, WE HAVE LIVED IN TOTAL ISOLATION...
17.

YOUR RULE CHANGED ALL THAT, WHEN YOU ESTABLISHED TIES TO OTHER ATLANTEAN CITIES AND THE SURFACE WORLD...
BUT YOUR LIFE HAS LEFT YOU FAR MORE WORLDLY THAN US.
PERHAPS YOU DIDN'T REALIZE IT, BUT WE WERE A SMALL, INSULAR COMMUNITY.
ALL THESE NEW IDEAS HAVE SHOCKED AND SCARED OUR PEOPLE...
AND THEY BLAME YOU FOR UPSETTING THE BALANCE.
WHAT IS ALL THIS?
THE ROYAL SEAL HAS BEEN STOLEN!
IT HAS LONG BEEN A NATIONAL TREASURE, A SYMBOL OF THE OLD WAYS.
AND WITHOUT IT, I CAN PERFORM NO OFFICIAL ACT.
DEATH TO AQUAMAN!
RETURN THE SEA
SURFACE MEN SHALL DIE!
THIS WAS THE LAST STRAW! ALL THE STRANGE NEW WAYS OF LIFE WE'VE SEEN OF LATE HAVE DISRUPTED THINGS, BUT THE PEOPLE ARE SURE THE SEAL WAS TAKEN BY ONE OF THE SURFACE WORLD DIPLOMATS WHO WERE SO RECENTLY HERE.
18

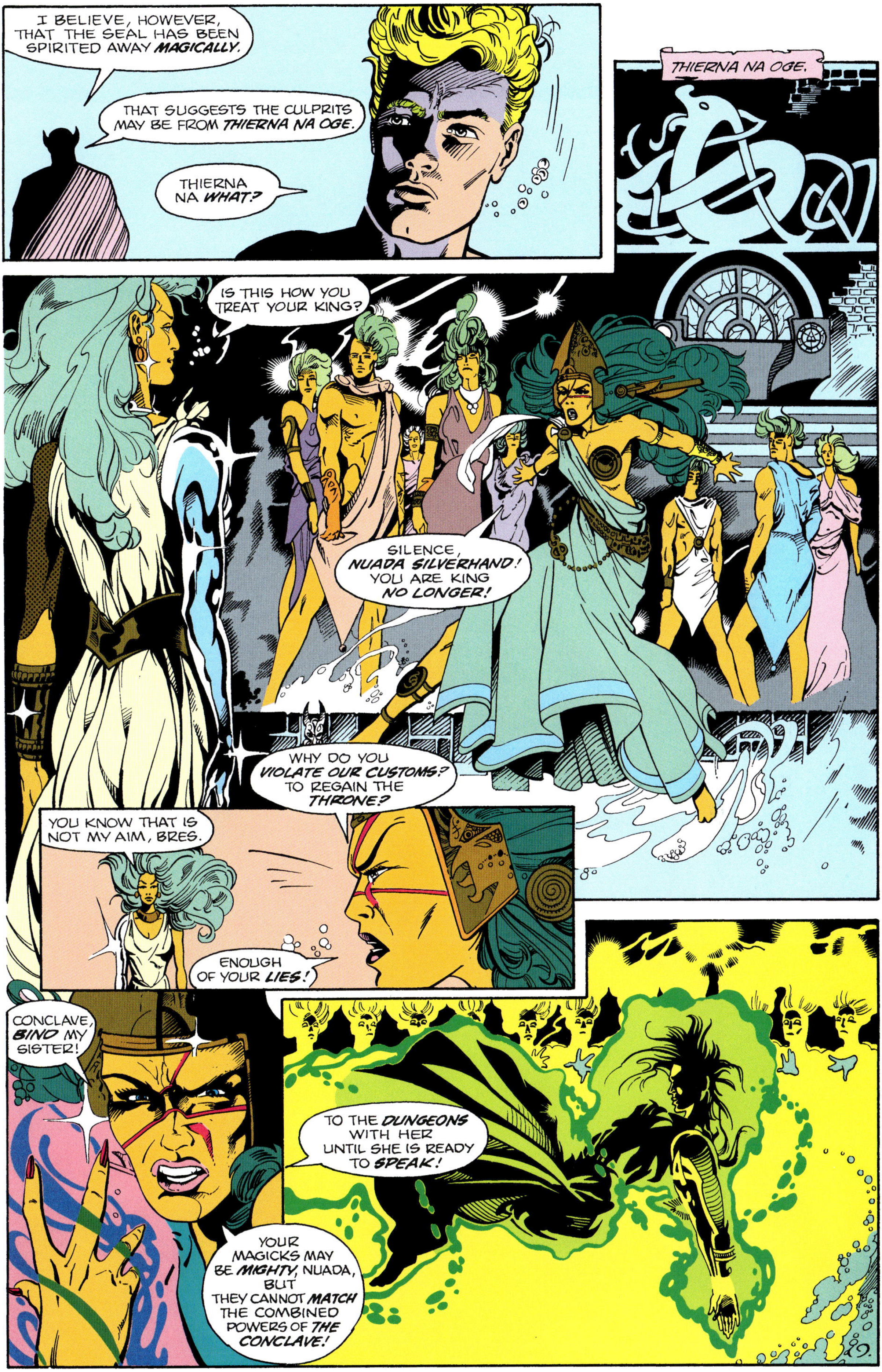
I BELIEVE, HOWEVER, THAT THE SEAL HAS BEEN SPIRITED AWAY MAGICALLY.
THAT SUGGESTS THE CULPRITS MAY BE FROM THIERNA NA OGE.
THIERNA NA WHAT?
THIERNA NA OGE.
IS THIS HOW YOU TREAT YOUR KING?
SILENCE, NUADA SILVERHAND! YOU ARE KING NO LONGER!
WHY DO YOU VIOLATE OUR CUSTOMS? TO REGAIN THE THRONE?
YOU KNOW THAT IS NOT MY AIM, BRES.
ENOUGH OF YOUR LIES!
CONCLAVE, BIND MY SISTER!
TO THE DUNGEONS WITH HER UNTIL SHE IS READY TO SPEAK!
YOUR MAGICKS MAY BE MIGHTY, NUADA, BUT THEY CANNOT MATCH THE COMBINED POWERS OF THE CONCLAVE!

MID-ATLANTIC.
SO FAR, SO GOOD. I'VE BEEN TRAVELING FOR HOURS AND NO ONE HAS RECOGNIZED ME YET!
STILL NO WORD ABOUT ORM, THOUGH. HOW COULD HE VANISH SO COMPLETELY?
I SHOULD REALLY CONCENTRATE ON MY MISSION AT HAND.
VULKO ONLY JUST DISCOVERED THIS THIERNA NA OGE. HE CAN'T ACCUSE THEIR KING BRES OF TAKING THE SEAL WITHOUT MORE EVIDENCE.
IT'S UP TO ME TO FIND THAT EVIDENCE--
--OR VULKO WILL HAVE TO ACCEDE TO HIS PEOPLE'S WISHES AND DECLARE WAR ON THE SURFACE WORLD!
MY DUTY IS TO HELP VULKO...
...NOT ONLY BECAUSE HE'S MY FRIEND, BUT BECAUSE MY POLICIES ARE RESPONSIBLE FOR THIS MESS!
HE CERTAINLY HAD THIS MISSION ALL PLANNED...
20

...AND WITH YOUR SKILL, KNOWLEDGE, EXPERIENCE, AND STRENGTH, ONLY YOU COULD SUCCESSFULLY INFILTRATE THIERNA NA OGE AND FIND THE SEAL!
BUT YOU MUST BE DISGUISED! I CANNOT BE LINKED WITH YOUR MISSION, AND YOU ARE KNOWN TO BE MY ALLY.
BESIDES, THAT MOB WILL HANG YOU ON THE SPOT IF THEY RECOGNIZE YOU.
THIS CAMOUFLAGE SUIT WILL CAUSE YOU TO BLEND IN WITH UNDERSEA CURRENTS AS WELL AS OBSCURING YOUR TRUE IDENTITY.
MAKAIRA! CAN IT BE YOU?!
NO TIME FOR A REUNION NOW, ARTHUR. YOU HAVE A JOB TO DO.
HERE. GO CHANGE BEHIND THE THRONE.
IS THERE ANYTHING YOU'LL NEED FROM YOUR OLD UNIFORM?
NO, THE ONLY USEFUL THING HERE IS MY SIGNAL DEVICE FOR THE JUSTICE LEAGUE...
...AND I CERTAINLY WON'T NEED THEIR HELP DOWN HERE!
WHOOA! WHO WAS THAT?
SOME BLOND GUY! NEVER SAW HIM BEFORE!
I HOPE IT WASN'T SOMEONE WITH ANOTHER SHIPMENT FROM THE SURFACE WORLD.
I KNOW WHAT YOU MEAN! PLEASE--NO MORE LAVA LAMPS!
OR HAIR DRYERS!
THAT WALLED CITY MUST BE THIERNA NA OGE.
FUNNY HOW EACH UNDERSEA CITY HAS DEVELOPED ITS OWN UNIQUE CULTURE, ISOLATED AS EACH HAS BEEN SINCE THE CONTINENT SANK.

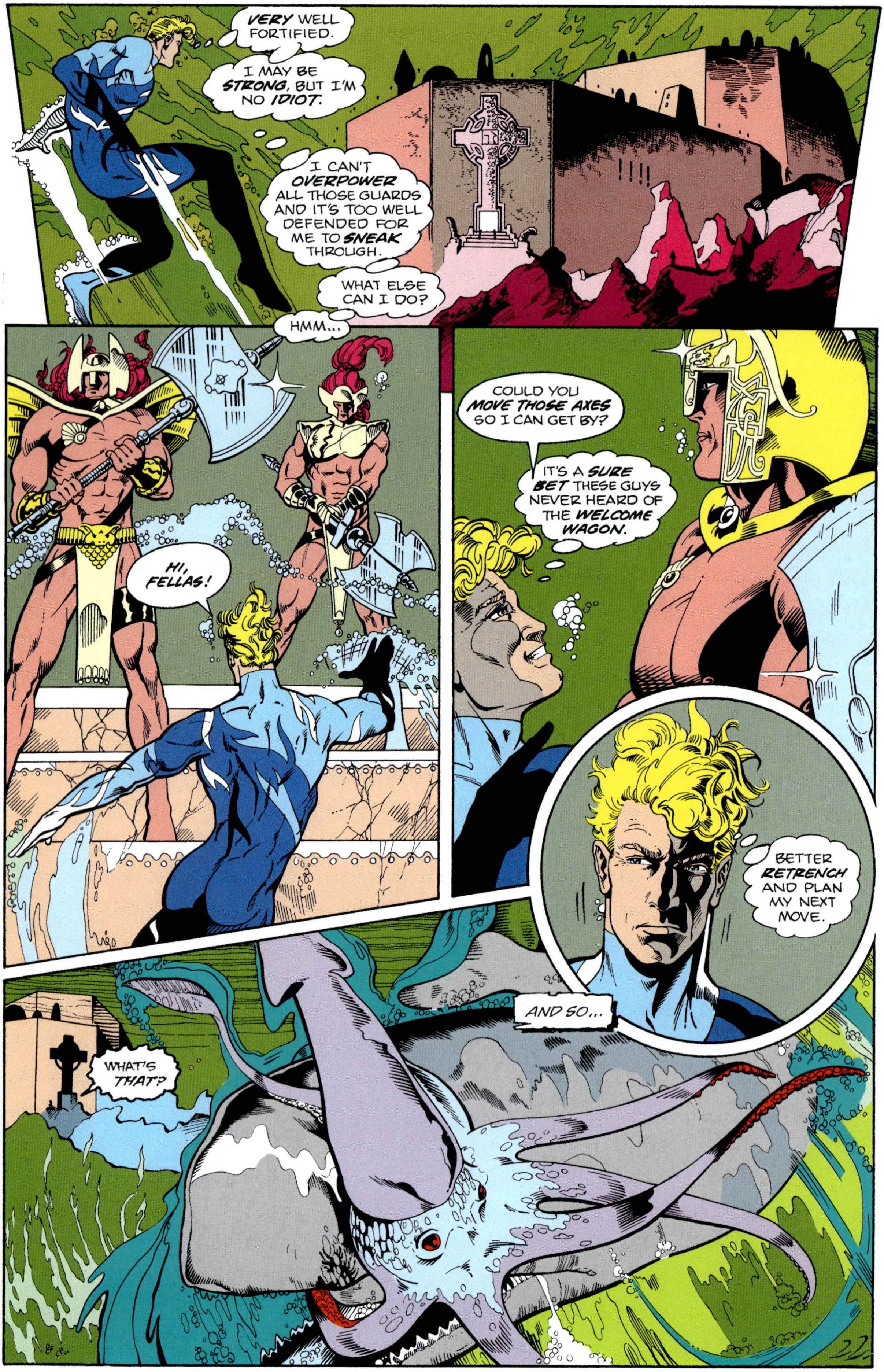

VERY WELL FORTIFIED.
I MAY BE STRONG, BUT I'M NO IDIOT.
I CAN'T OVERPOWER ALL THOSE GUARDS AND IT'S TOO WELL DEFENDED FOR ME TO SNEAK THROUGH.
WHAT ELSE CAN I DO?
HMM...
HI, FELLAS!
COULD YOU MOVE THOSE AXES SO I CAN GET BY?
IT'S A SURE BET THESE GUYS NEVER HEARD OF THE WELCOME WAGON.
BETTER RETRENCH AND PLAN MY NEXT MOVE.
AND SO...
WHAT'S THAT?

A SPERM WHALE AND A GIANT SQUID!
ATTEND!
MY DISTRACTION SEEMS TO HAVE WORKED. THE GUARDS ARE GOING FOR A CLOSER LOOK.
AND MY SQUID AND WHALE ALLIES WILL BE NONE THE WORSE FOR WEAR WHEN I'M PAST THE GATE.
THANKS, FRIENDS!
THE STRANGER. HE RETURNS.
HALT, FOREIGNER!
HOW DID THEY BOTH KNOW TO TURN AROUND JUST THEN? I MADE NO SOUND.
NOT THAT IT MATTERS. THEY'LL NEVER BE ABLE TO REACH ME IN TIME.
AND I SHOULD BE ABLE TO HIDE ONCE I'M INSIDE...
...THE CITY...
NO FURTHER.
AAARGHH

OOOOH. WHERE AM I?
HAVE I BEEN CHEWING COTTON?
WHAT HAPPENED? MY ACHING HEAD!
WHO...
...ooooh...
NEXT
Thierna na Oge

THE LEGEND OF
AQUAMAN
NEW FORMAT
SPECIAL
1
1989
US $2.00
CAN $2.50
UK £ 1.20
APPROVED BY THE COMICS CODE AUTHORITY
GIFFEN • FLEMING • SWAN • SHANOWER

THE LEGEND OF
AQUAMAN™
KEITH GIFFEN PLOT & BREAKDOWNS
CURT SWAN PENCILS
ROBERT LOREN FLEMING SCRIPT
ERIC SHANOWER INKS
AGUSTIN MAS LETTERING
TOM McCRAW COLORING
MARK WAID EDITING

HE WASN'T SUPPOSED TO LIVE.
WHEN THE ATLANTEANS EXPOSED HIM TO THE OPEN AIR ON THE FLAT PINNACLE OF MERCY REEF, IT WAS LOW TIDE. THEY EXPECTED THE SUN ALONE TO KILL HIM.
INSTEAD, THE LOVELY WARMTH AND CLEAN SEA BREEZES LULLED HIM TO SLEEP. WHEN HE AWOKE, HE FOUND HIMSELF ABANDONED, LEFT TO FEND FOR HIMSELF AGAINST THE EXQUISITE CRUELTY OF NATURE.
AND THAT WAS HIS SALVATION.
IN ATLANTIS HE WOULD HAVE BEEN RAISED TO THINK OF HIMSELF AS A FREAK. HIS SKIN, PALE AS THE ALABASTER OF A CONCH SHELL, WOULD HAVE MADE HIM A TARGET OF RIDICULE AND DERISION. HIS BLOND CURLS, TRICKLING DOWN HIS FOREHEAD IN RIVULETS OF GOLD, WOULD HAVE BEEN SHAVED OFF AND BURIED.
YET THE ONE TRAIT THAT MADE HIM MOST DIFFERENT HAD BEEN MISSED BY THE ATLANTEANS... HE COULD BREATHE AIR. HE COULD STAND UNBLINKING IN THE BRILLIANCE OF PURE SUNLIGHT AND FEEL THE OXYGEN FILLING HIS CHEST, GIVING HIM LIFE AND POWER. HE COULD GO ANYWHERE. HE WAS FREE.
IT WAS HIS ABILITY TO LEAVE THE OCEANS THAT MADE HIM THEIR KING.

BUT FOR NOW HE WAS COLD AND HUNGRY.
AND HE WANTED HIS MOTHER.
THE SHARK THAT BORE DOWN ON HIM STOPPED SHORT WHEN IT MET HIS EYES.
IT WAS THE KING'S FIRST COMMAND. HE TOLD IT TO GO AWAY.
HE TOLD THE SHARK THAT IT WAS NOT HIS MOTHER.

THE CRIB MEMORY OF HER FACE WAS ALL HE KEPT FROM HIS TIME IN ATLANTIS.
ALL OTHER THINGS HE TOOK FROM THE SEA.
KILLING ONLY WHAT HE COULD CATCH, HE OFTEN WENT HUNGRY.
THE FISH OBEYED ALL OF HIS COMMANDS, BUT HE COULDN'T BRING HIMSELF TO DEMAND OF THEM SELF-SACRIFICE.
HE WAS THE TRUE SON OF THE LAW OF SURVIVAL AND WOULD NOT BETRAY IT.

PANT
PANT
PANT
CAW! CAW!
CAW!
CAW!
CAW! CAW!
CAW!
ALTHOUGH SURVIVAL BY ITSELF COULD BE A VERY LONELY LEGACY.

CAW! CAW! CAW!
CLANK!
NOT BAD, NOT BAD. YOU'LL DO FOR MY DINNER TONIGHT, AND THAT'S A FACT!
NOW LET'S SEE ABOUT TOMORROW'S LUNCH...
EH?

★!@#!!✱!!!
ALL RIGHT, ALL RIGHT, HERE I COME...
WHAT'S HOLDING YOU? COME ALONG...
COME ALONG!
--ULP!

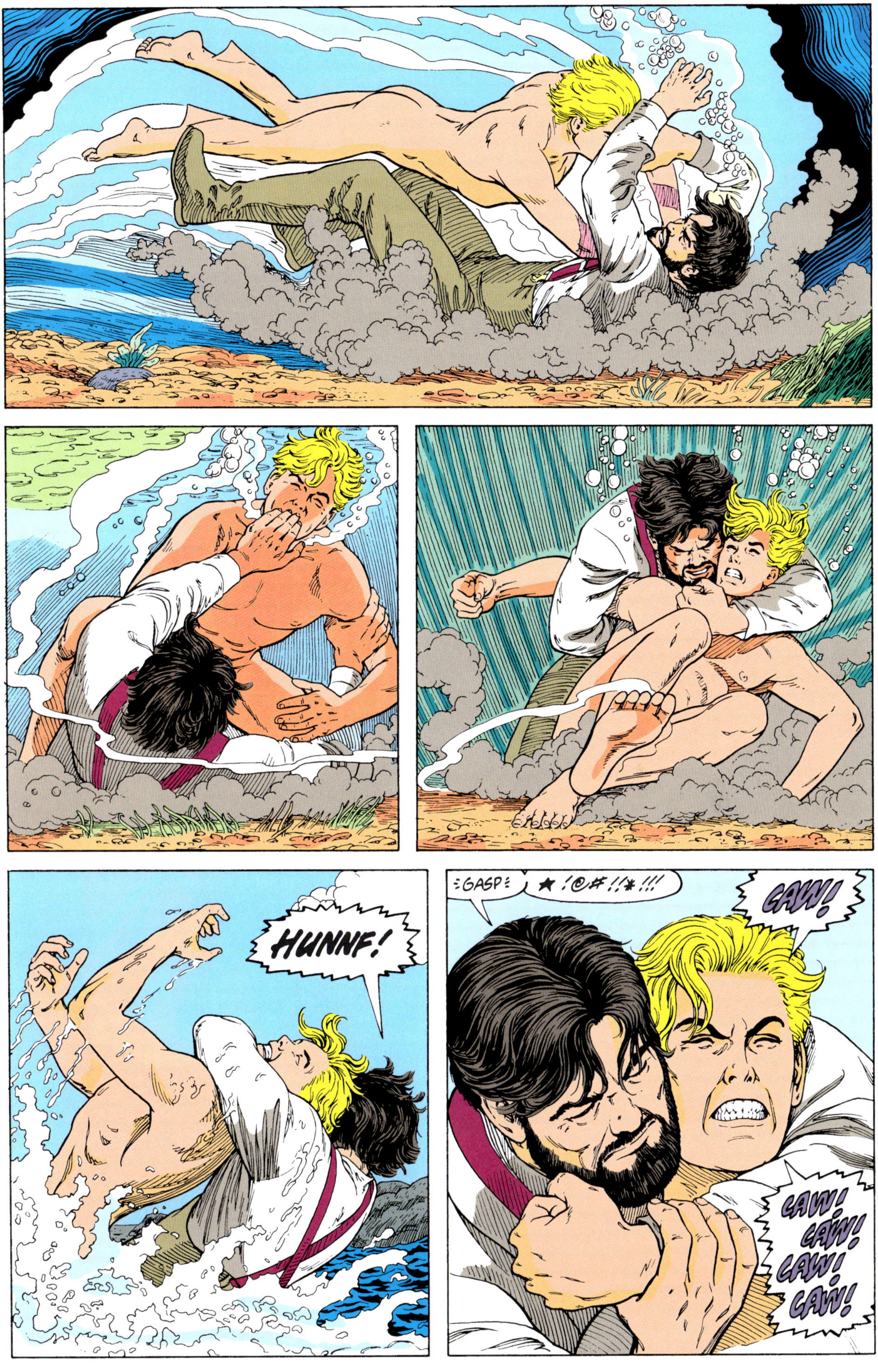
HUNNF!
GASP
★ !@#!!*!!!
CAW!
CAW! CAW! CAW! CAW!

BE STILL!!
CAW! CAW! CAW!
CAW! CAW!
CAW!

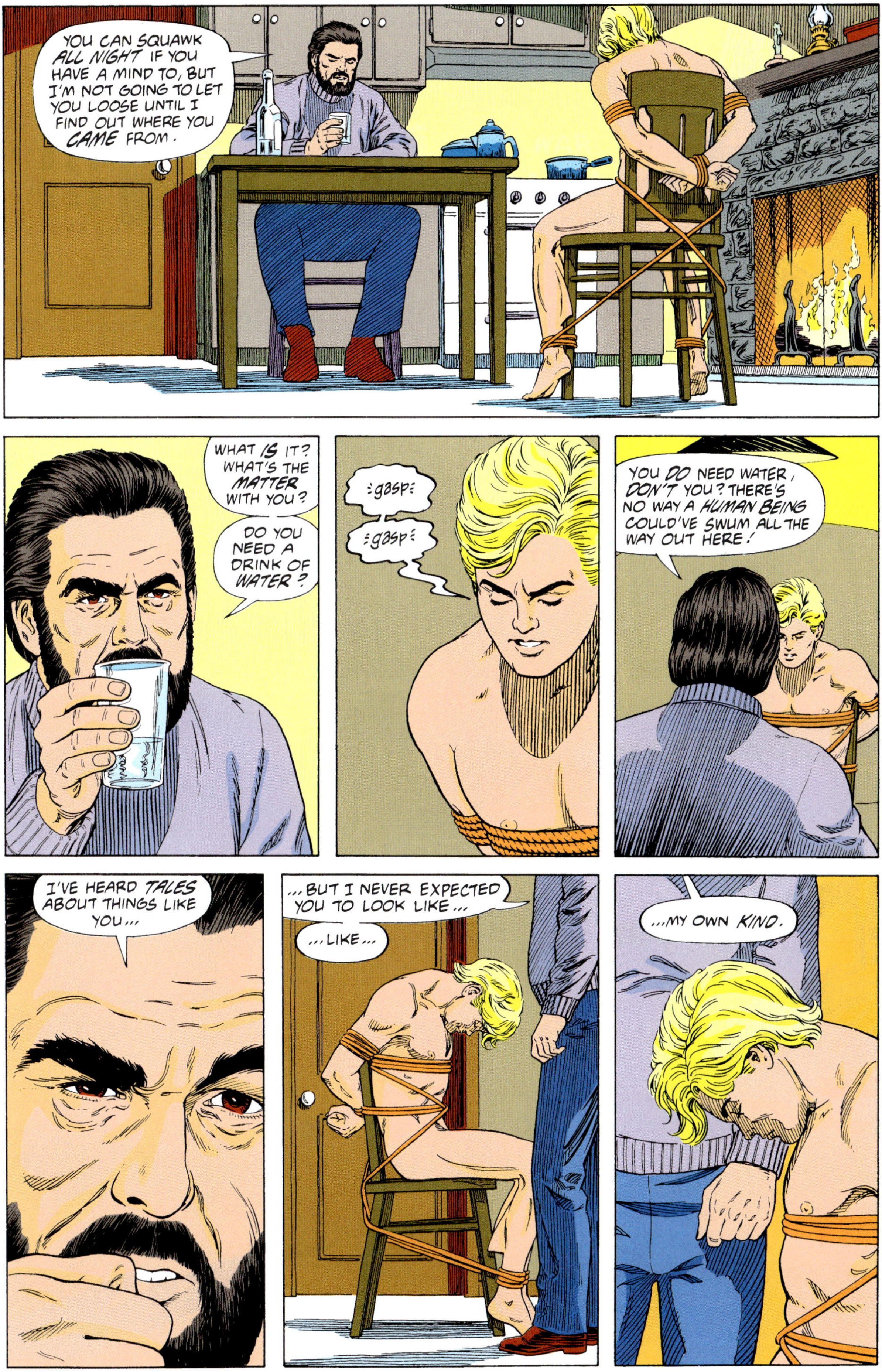
YOU CAN SQUAWK ALL NIGHT IF YOU HAVE A MIND TO, BUT I'M NOT GOING TO LET YOU LOOSE UNTIL I FIND OUT WHERE YOU CAME FROM.
WHAT IS IT? WHAT'S THE MATTER WITH YOU?
DO YOU NEED A DRINK OF WATER?
:gasp:
:gasp:
YOU DO NEED WATER, DON'T YOU? THERE'S NO WAY A HUMAN BEING COULD'VE SWUM ALL THE WAY OUT HERE!
I'VE HEARD TALES ABOUT THINGS LIKE YOU...
...BUT I NEVER EXPECTED YOU TO LOOK LIKE...
...LIKE...
...MY OWN KIND.

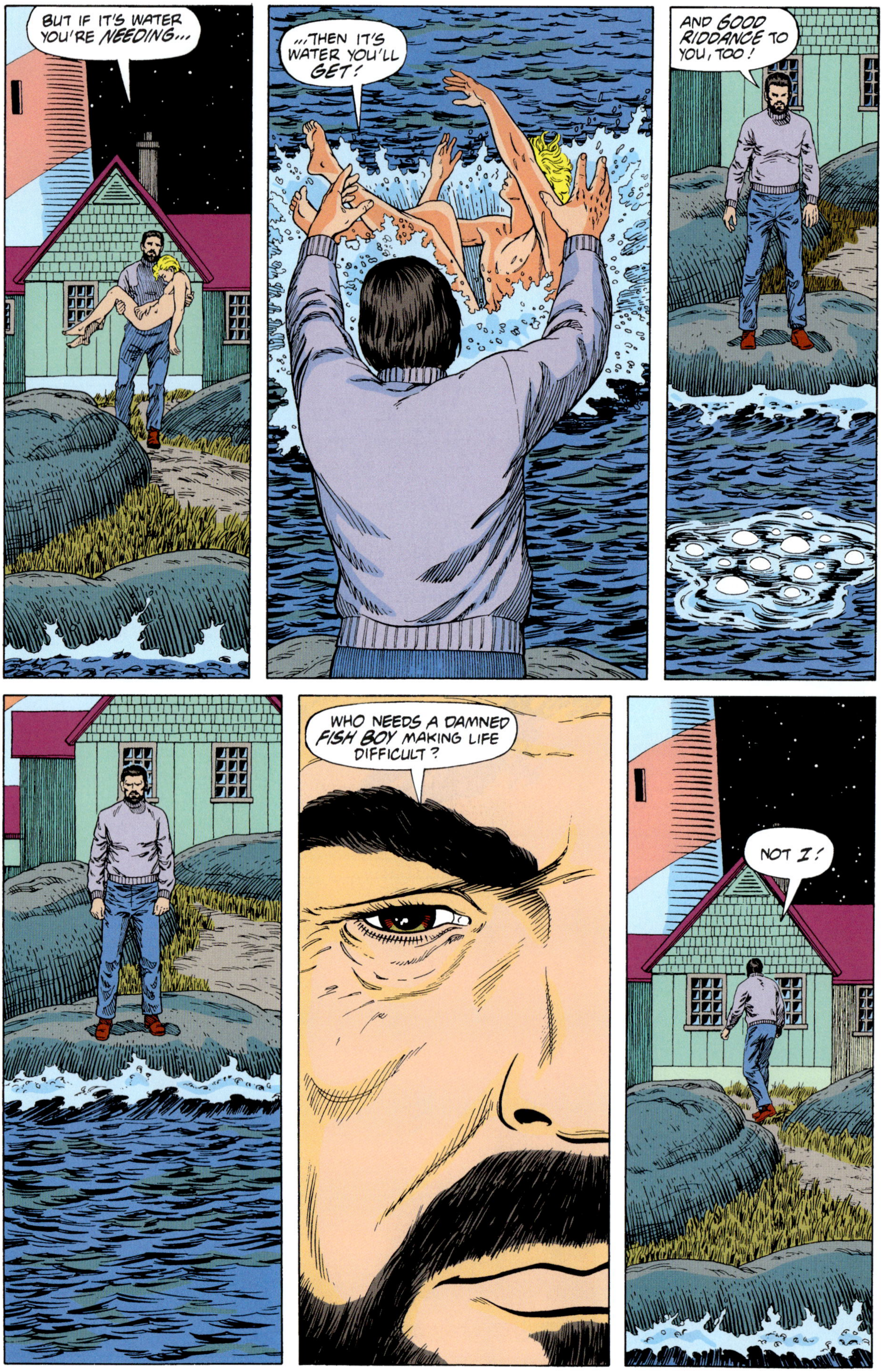

BUT IF IT'S WATER YOU'RE NEEDING...
...THEN IT'S WATER YOU'LL GET!
AND GOOD RIDDANCE TO YOU, TOO!
WHO NEEDS A DAMNED FISH BOY MAKING LIFE DIFFICULT?
NOT I!

HOWEVER, THE VERY NEXT MORNING...
YOU!
DID YOU PUT THESE FISH HERE?
ANSWER ME!
WHAT DO YOU WANT HERE? IS THIS SOME SORT OF TRICK? IF YOU'RE LOOKING TO SABOTAGE THE LIGHTHOUSE SO AS TO BRING UNSUSPECTING SHIPS ONTO THE REEFS, THEN I WARN YOU I'M ON MY GUARD AGAINST YOU!
IS THAT IT? IS THAT YOUR PLAN?
!@#!!!!! I'M TALKING TO YOU!!
I'LL BE SQUAWKING LIKE A GULL NEXT!

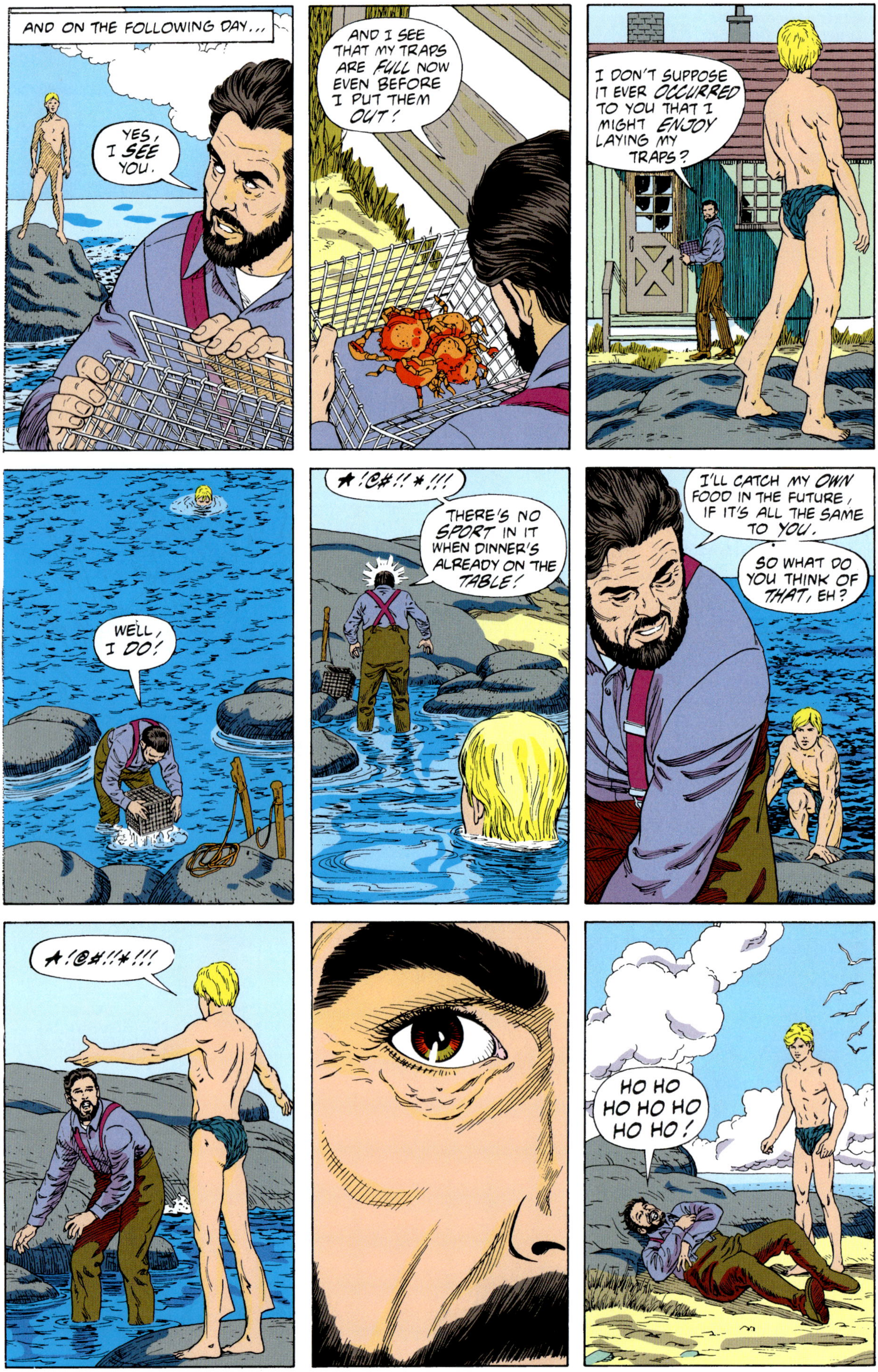
AND ON THE FOLLOWING DAY...
YES, I SEE YOU.
AND I SEE THAT MY TRAPS ARE FULL NOW EVEN BEFORE I PUT THEM OUT!
I DON'T SUPPOSE IT EVER OCCURRED TO YOU THAT I MIGHT ENJOY LAYING MY TRAPS?
WELL, I DO!
!@#!!!!!
THERE'S NO SPORT IN IT WHEN DINNER'S ALREADY ON THE TABLE!
I'LL CATCH MY OWN FOOD IN THE FUTURE, IF IT'S ALL THE SAME TO YOU.
SO WHAT DO YOU THINK OF THAT, EH?
!@#!!!!!
HO HO HO HO HO HO HO!

FROM THAT MOMENT THEY WERE INSEPARABLE.
THEY BECAME LIKE FATHER AND SON...
TEACHER AND PUPIL...
Aa Bb
Apple
Ball
THEY BECAME FRIENDS.
THE LIGHTHOUSE KEEPER FOUND IN HIS YOUNG COMPANION THE ONE THING THAT HAD ELUDED HIM IN EVERYTHING HE DID.
HE FOUND HAPPINESS.

AND BECAUSE HAPPY YEARS PASS LIKE WEEKS, THE OLD MAN WAS SOON MUCH OLDER AND THE YOUNG MAN STRONG AND TALL.
AND ONE DAY THE YOUNG MAN WENT FOR HIS DAILY SWIM AND THE LIGHTHOUSE KEEPER KNEW THAT IT WAS THE LAST TIME THEY'D EVER SEE EACH OTHER.
HE STOOD THERE WATCHING UNTIL HIS COMPANION VANISHED BEYOND THE HORIZON.
THEN HE WENT INSIDE AND WAITED FOR WHAT HE KNEW WOULD HAPPEN.
I'M BACK!
HELLO?

FATHER!!!

Dear son,
I believe that this will be my last entry in the journal, which is why I am hiding it in our secret place. For two weeks now I have been seeing creatures in the waters surrounding the island, and yesterday they showed themselves openly.
They are the stuff of legends, true fish but with the limbs of man, and their purpose here is clear. They are watching you, son. You are related to them in some way that I cannot understand. Once they have gauged your strength and abilities they will try to capture or kill you; of this I am certain.
Now I am out of the way. I apologize for cheating you of the opportunity to defend me against them. I felt that my presence would impair your ability to fight successfully. In fact, I would rather that you not fight at all. Escape while you can. Forget about me and run as far from this island as you...
Well, who am I kidding? You are of the sea and could never run from it. You will always triumph over any foe and do your old father proud. But just in case you should ever wish to brave the world of my people, I give you as a parting gift the one thing you lack-a name. You can have mine.
With love,
Arthur Curry
JOURNAL

AND SO, YOUNG ARTHUR CURRY FOUND HIMSELF ALONE AGAIN. AND WITH NOWHERE ELSE TO GO, HE RETURNED TO THE ONLY OTHER HOME HE'D EVER KNOWN...
...MERCY REEF.
THERE HE SAT FOR MANY DAYS, THINKING OF A FACE WHICH WAS A CRIB MEMORY AND WONDERING HOW TO FIND HER.
FOR HE KNEW THAT ONLY BY LOCATING HIS MOTHER COULD HE FIND HIMSELF. NOW, THIS WAS ALL THAT MATTERED TO HIM.
HE HAD TO FIND OUT WHO HE WAS.

REMEMBERING THE LIGHTHOUSE KEEPER'S TALES OF A LEGENDARY SUNKEN CITY CALLED ATLANTIS, THE YOUNG MAN SCOURED THE SEVEN SEAS FOR SOME PROOF OF ITS EXISTENCE.
HE COULD NO LONGER BRING HIMSELF TO FEED ON THE FISH, SO HE WAS FORCED TO TAKE SUSTENANCE FROM KELP... WHICH GREW AND LIVED, BUT WITH WHICH HE SHARED NO PSYCHIC CONNECTION.
THEN ONE DAY, A MIGHTY SHIP APPEARED.
IN FOLLOWING THE VESSEL, THE YOUNG MAN ENCOUNTERED SCENES FAMILIAR FROM THE PICTURE BOOKS OF HIS FATHER.
AT LAST THE SHIP DOCKED, AND YOUNG ARTHUR CURRY BRACED HIMSELF FOR A GREAT ADVENTURE.

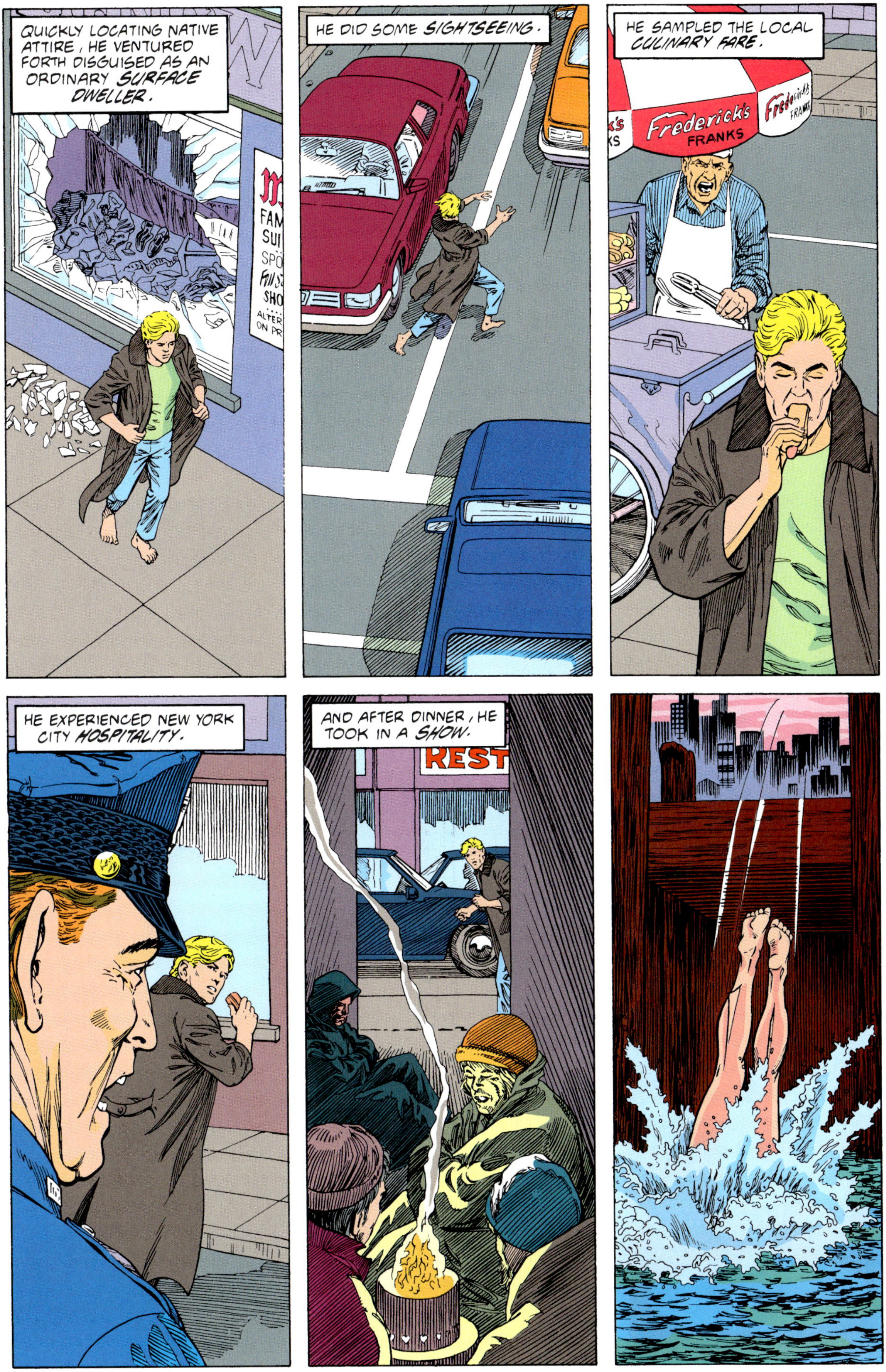
QUICKLY LOCATING NATIVE ATTIRE, HE VENTURED FORTH DISGUISED AS AN ORDINARY SURFACE DWELLER.
HE DID SOME SIGHTSEEING.
HE SAMPLED THE LOCAL CULINARY FARE.
Frederick's FRANKS
HE EXPERIENCED NEW YORK CITY HOSPITALITY.
AND AFTER DINNER, HE TOOK IN A SHOW.
REST

ONCE SAFELY AWAY FROM CIVILIZED SOCIETY, ARTHUR CURRY RESUMED HIS SEARCH FOR HIS BIRTHPLACE.
AND ONE DAY, QUITE BY CHANCE...
...HE FOUND IT!
ATLANTIS!
HIDDEN ON THE BOTTOM OF THE SEA AT A DEPTH NOT YET ATTAINED BY THE SUBMARINES AND BATHY-SPHERES OF THE SURFACE WORLD, IT WAS AS PURELY FOREIGN AS THE CULTURE OF A FAR DISTANT PLANET!

BUT TO YOUNG ARTHUR, IT REPRESENTED THE POSSIBILITY OF A HOME HE'D NEVER KNOWN, AND IN HIS EAGERNESS TO KNOW MORE, HE FORGOT WHAT HE'D ALREADY LEARNED.
HE FORGOT TO BE CAREFUL.
HE FORGOT WHAT THE ATLANTEANS HAD DONE TO HIM AS A CHILD.
HE FORGOT WHAT THEY DID TO HIS FATHER.
AND HE FORGOT HIS TRUE FATHER, THE LAW OF SURVIVAL!

ARTHUR CURRY SPENT THE NEXT THREE YEARS IN SOLITARY CONFINEMENT IN THE PRISON FACILITY KNOWN AS AQUARIUM.
EVENTUALLY HE WAS RELEASED INTO THE YARD...
...WHERE HE SPENT ALL OF HIS FREE TIME STARING THROUGH THE PLEXIGLASS WALL AT THE FEMALE ATLANTEANS...
...LOOKING FOR HIS MOTHER.

AND THEN ONE DAY, QUITE BY CHANCE...
...HE FOUND HER.
YOU HAVE TO KNOW THE LANGUAGE TO MEET THE LADIES, FRIEND!
I AM VULKO, FORMER PROFESSOR OF ADVANCED CULTURE AT THE ATLANTIS INSTITUTE. MIGHT I BE OF SERVICE?

IT WAS SLOW GOING AT FIRST, BUT VULKO RELISHED THE UNEXPECTED CHALLENGE OF HIS NEW PUPIL.
GOOD! YOU'RE MAKING PROGRESS!
NOW...THESE ARE THE TWELVE ALCERIPS USED IN ALL WORDS: ZI, UR, TA, YS, PR, VX, CL, JV, BO, EK, GN, AND NF.
FALL IN FOR WORK DETAIL!
WE'LL CONTINUE THIS TOMORROW.
EVERY DAY THE PRISONERS WERE MARCHED OUT TO FORCED LABOR IN THE SALT MINES.
MOVE!!
THE TWELVE ALCERIPS ARE: ZI, UR, TA, YS, PR, VX, CL, JV, BO, EK...GN...
...AND...
CHUK!
SHUT UP, FREAK!
ZAXX
UHH!

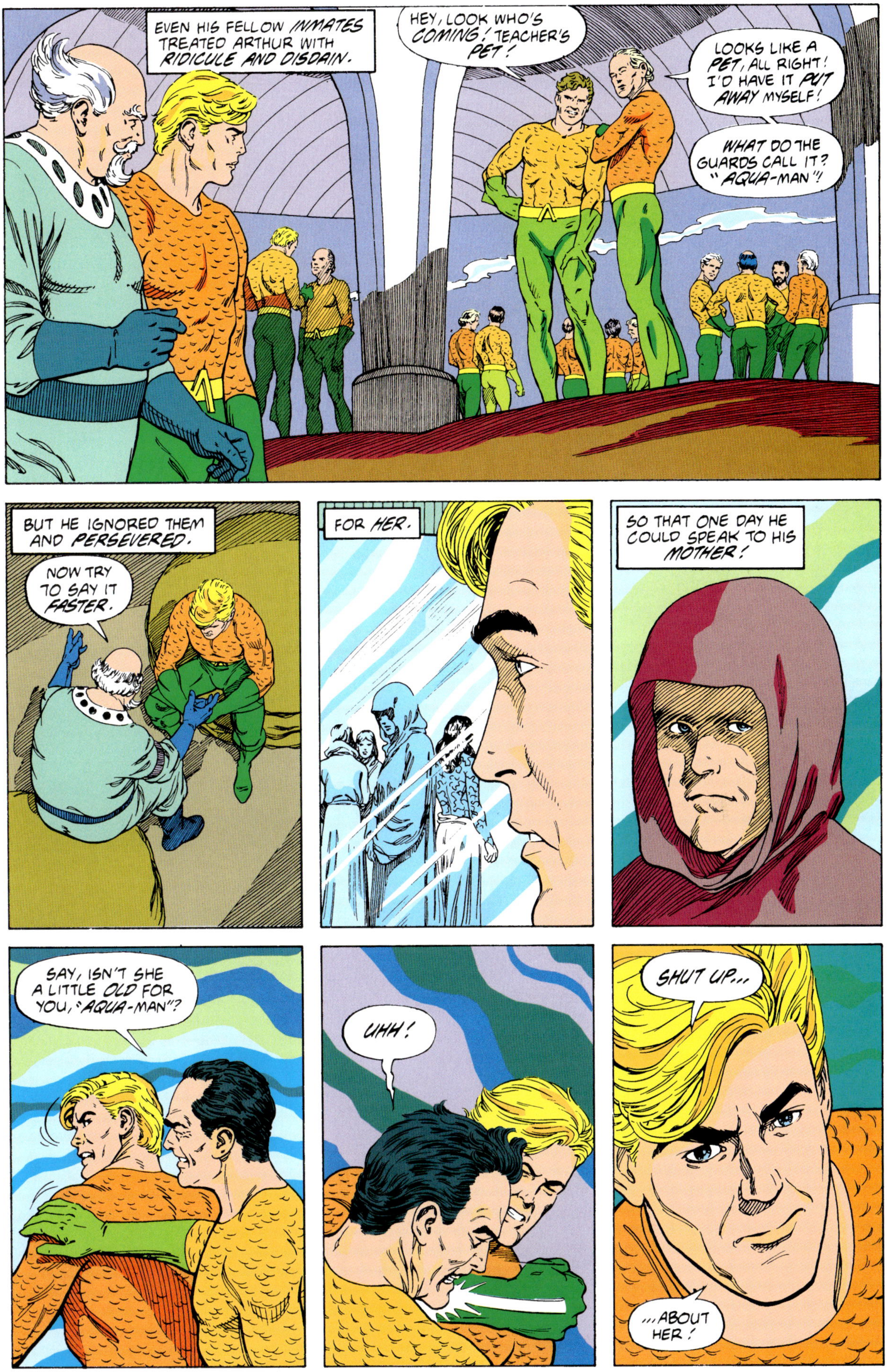
EVEN HIS FELLOW INMATES TREATED ARTHUR WITH RIDICULE AND DISDAIN.
HEY, LOOK WHO'S COMING! TEACHER'S PET!
LOOKS LIKE A PET, ALL RIGHT! I'D HAVE IT PUT AWAY MYSELF!
WHAT DO THE GUARDS CALL IT? "AQUA-MAN"!
BUT HE IGNORED THEM AND PERSEVERED.
NOW TRY TO SAY IT FASTER.
FOR HER.
SO THAT ONE DAY HE COULD SPEAK TO HIS MOTHER!
SAY, ISN'T SHE A LITTLE OLD FOR YOU, "AQUA-MAN"?
UHH!
SHUT UP...
...ABOUT HER!

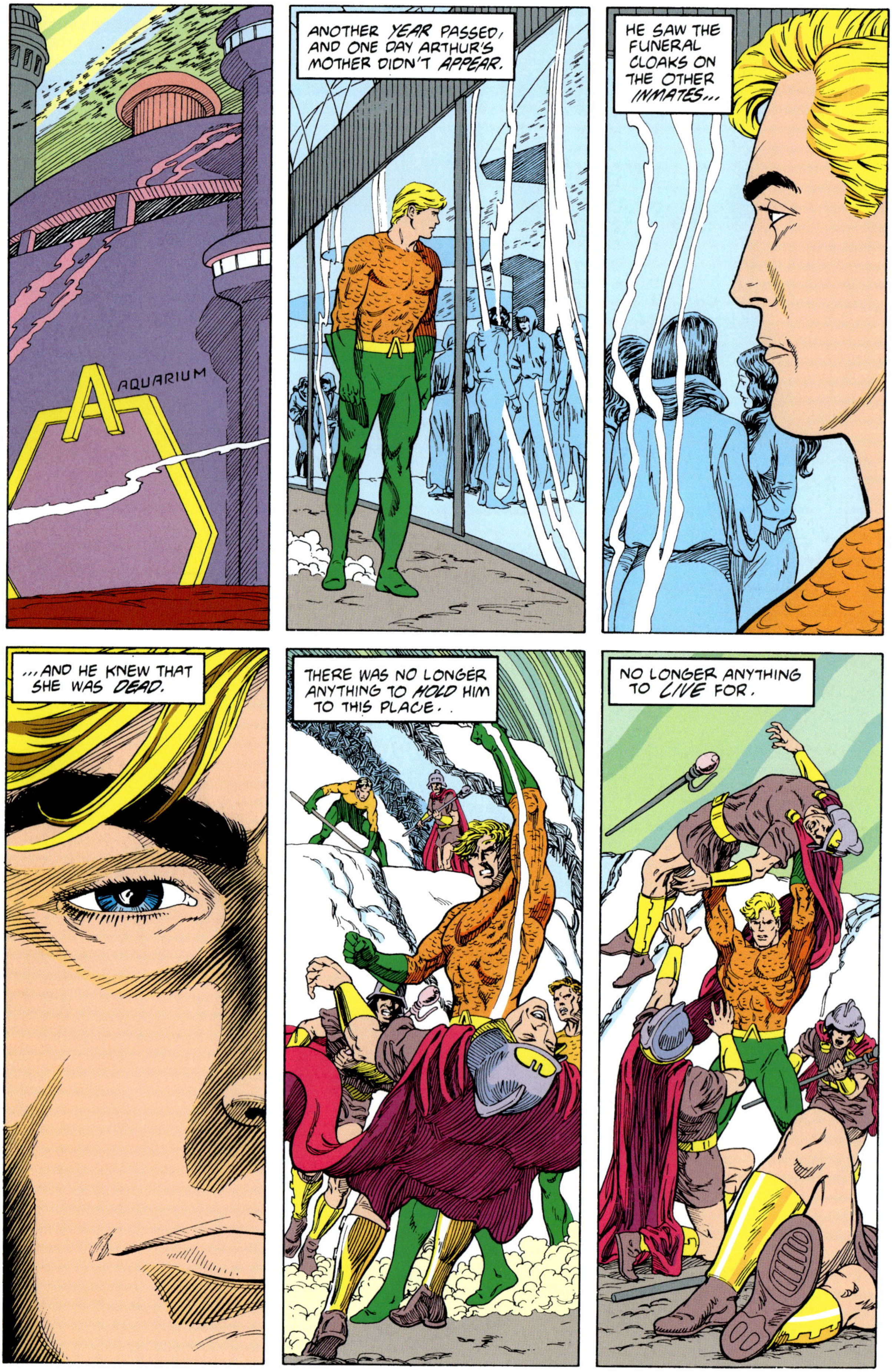
AQUARIUM
ANOTHER YEAR PASSED, AND ONE DAY ARTHUR'S MOTHER DIDN'T APPEAR.
HE SAW THE FUNERAL CLOAKS ON THE OTHER INMATES...
...AND HE KNEW THAT SHE WAS DEAD.
THERE WAS NO LONGER ANYTHING TO HOLD HIM TO THIS PLACE.
NO LONGER ANYTHING TO LIVE FOR.

I DON'T UNDERSTAND.
IF YOU COULD DO THIS... THEN WHY DID YOU REMAIN A PRISONER ALL THESE YEARS?
I DIDN'T KNOW WHAT I WAS CAPABLE OF...
...UNTIL TODAY.
YOU MUST LEAVE NOW! THERE WILL BE REINFORCEMENTS! THEY'LL KILL YOU!
VULKO...
WILL YOU COME WITH ME?
I CAN'T! I BELONG HERE... WITH MY PEOPLE!
BUT YOU... YOU BELONG TO THE SEAS!
GODSPEED...
...AQUAMAN!

IN THE YEARS THAT FOLLOWED, AQUAMAN STRENGTHENED HIS CONTROL OVER ALL THE SEA'S CREATURES.
HE USED HIS NEWFOUND EXPERTISE TO FIGHT THOSE SURFACE DWELLERS WHO POLLUTED HIS KINGDOM.
HIS EXPLOITS EARNED HIM A REPUTATION THAT LED TO HIS INAUGURATION AS A CHARTER MEMBER OF THE ORIGINAL JUSTICE LEAGUE OF AMERICA.

WHEN HE RETURNED TO HIS BIRTHPLACE, ATLANTIS, IT WAS AS A HERO.
THIS WAS THE ONE PLACE ON EARTH WHERE HE HAD YET TO PROVE HIMSELF.
HERE HE'D BEEN CONSIDERED A FREAK AND MADE A COMMON PRISONER.
BUT TODAY THOSE MEMORIES WOULD END.
TODAY ALL PAST DEBTS CAME DUE!
TODAY I'LL SEE MY OLD FRIEND VULKO AGAIN... AND HELP HIM FREE HIS PEOPLE!

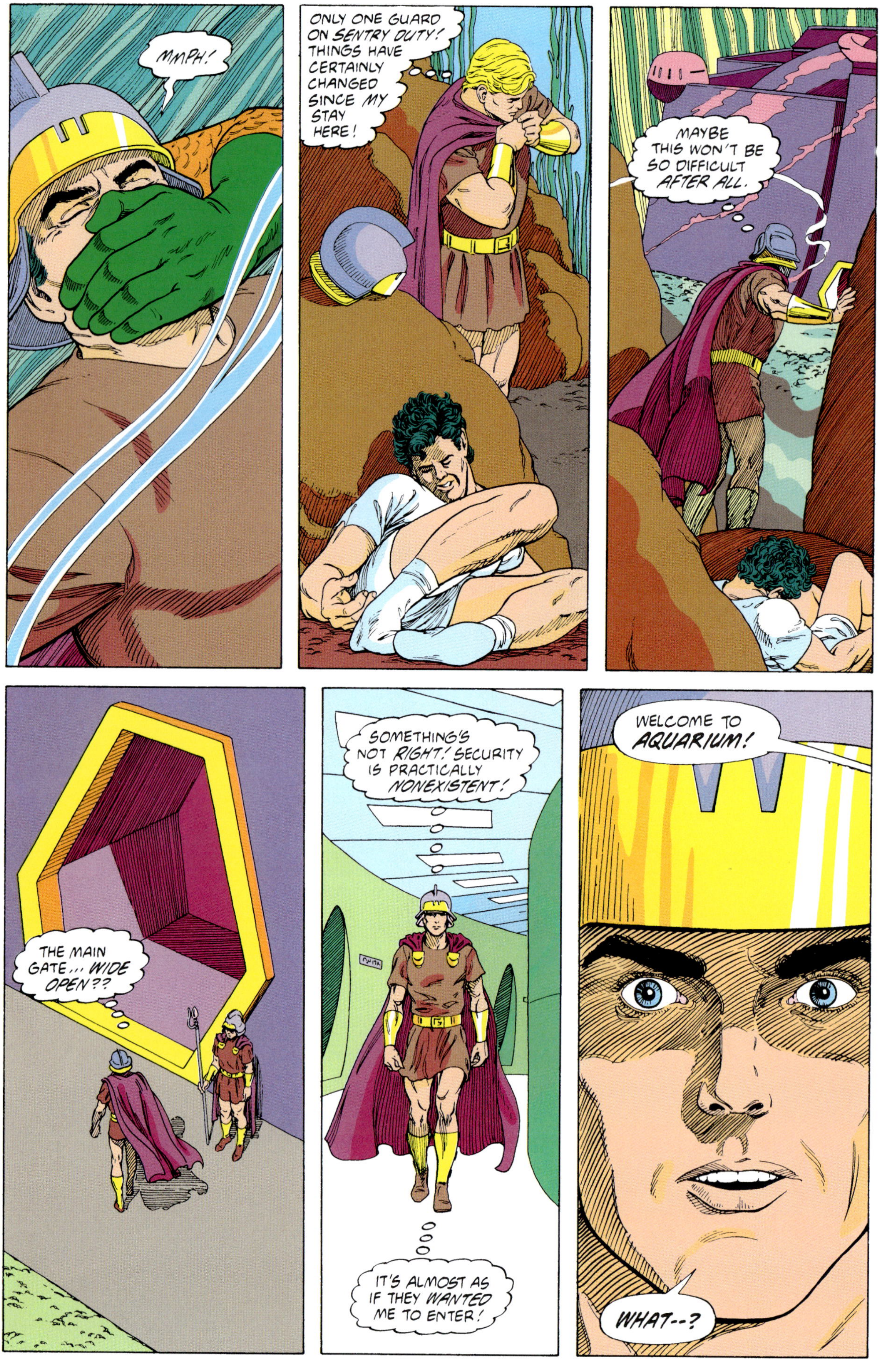

MMPH!
ONLY ONE GUARD ON SENTRY DUTY! THINGS HAVE CERTAINLY CHANGED SINCE MY STAY HERE!
MAYBE THIS WON'T BE SO DIFFICULT AFTER ALL.
THE MAIN GATE... WIDE OPEN??
SOMETHING'S NOT RIGHT! SECURITY IS PRACTICALLY NONEXISTENT!
IT'S ALMOST AS IF THEY WANTED ME TO ENTER!
WELCOME TO AQUARIUM!
WHAT--?

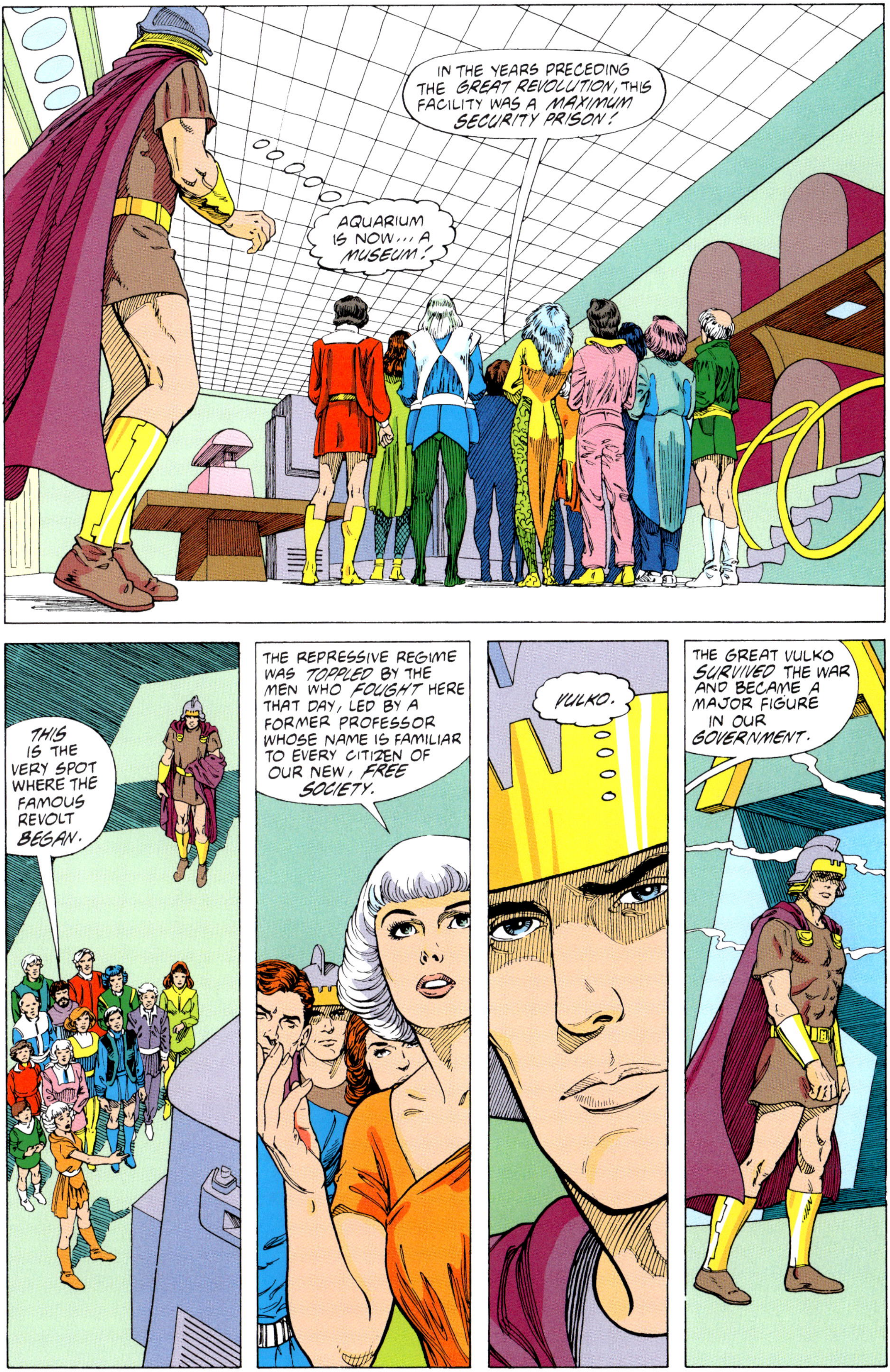
IN THE YEARS PRECEDING THE GREAT REVOLUTION, THIS FACILITY WAS A MAXIMUM SECURITY PRISON!
AQUARIUM IS NOW... A MUSEUM!
THIS IS THE VERY SPOT WHERE THE FAMOUS REVOLT BEGAN.
THE REPRESSIVE REGIME WAS TOPPLED BY THE MEN WHO FOUGHT HERE THAT DAY, LED BY A FORMER PROFESSOR WHOSE NAME IS FAMILIAR TO EVERY CITIZEN OF OUR NEW, FREE SOCIETY.
VULKO.
THE GREAT VULKO SURVIVED THE WAR AND BECAME A MAJOR FIGURE IN OUR GOVERNMENT.

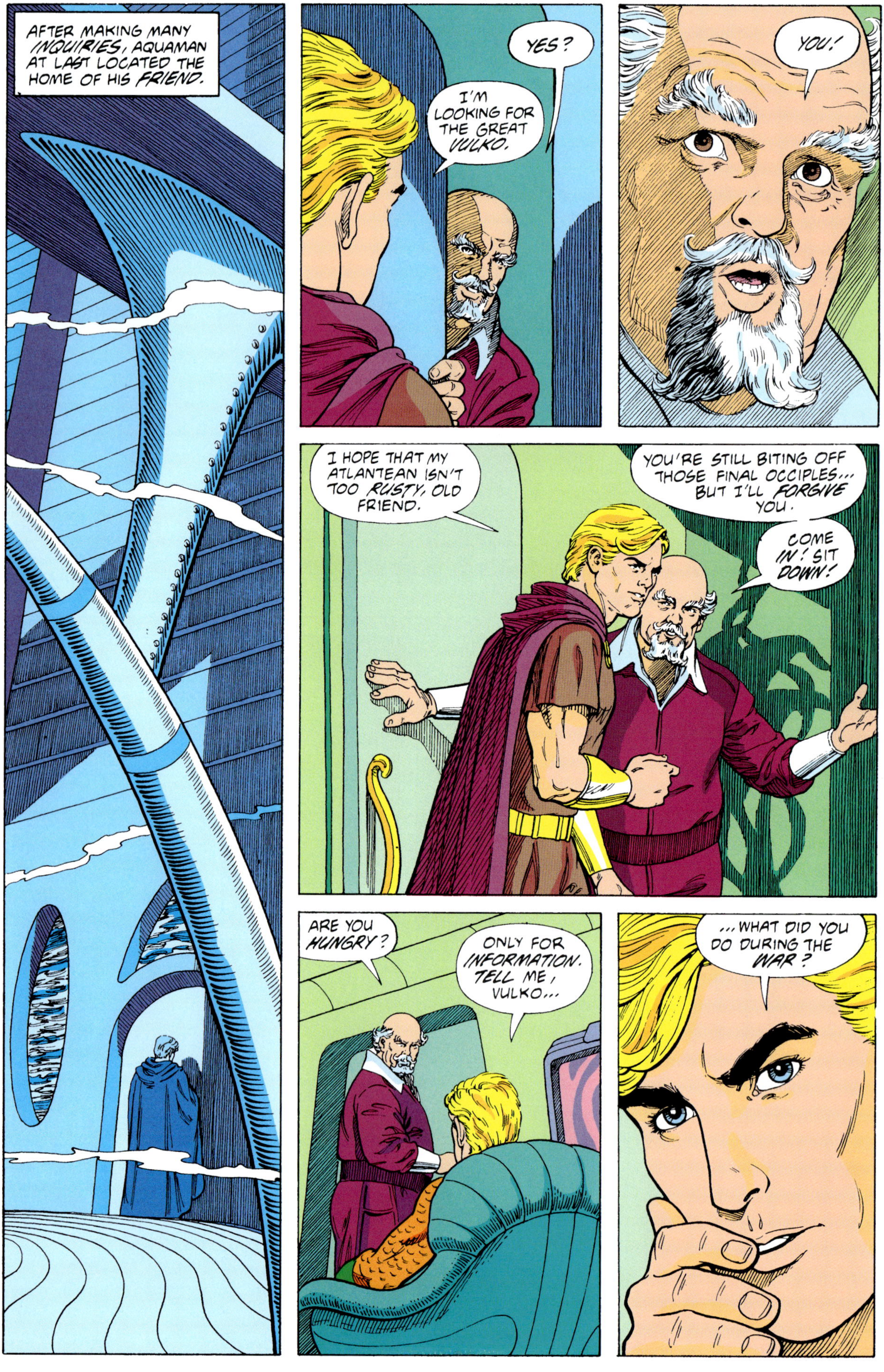
AFTER MAKING MANY INQUIRIES, AQUAMAN AT LAST LOCATED THE HOME OF HIS FRIEND.
YES?
I'M LOOKING FOR THE GREAT VULKO.
YOU!
I HOPE THAT MY ATLANTEAN ISN'T TOO RUSTY, OLD FRIEND.
YOU'RE STILL BITING OFF THOSE FINAL OCCIPLES... BUT I'LL FORGIVE YOU.
COME IN! SIT DOWN!
ARE YOU HUNGRY?
ONLY FOR INFORMATION. TELL ME, VULKO...
...WHAT DID YOU DO DURING THE WAR?

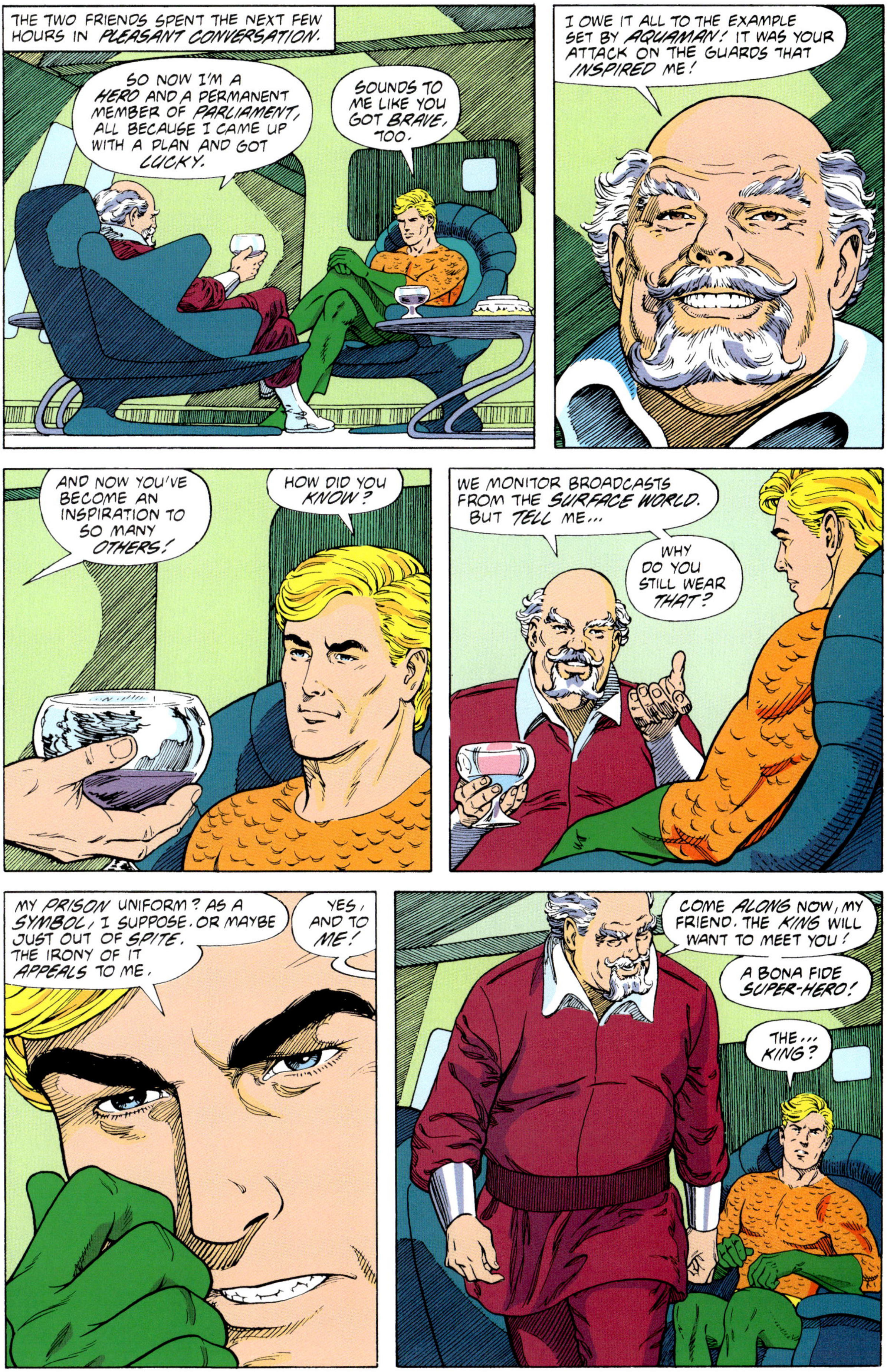

THE TWO FRIENDS SPENT THE NEXT FEW HOURS IN PLEASANT CONVERSATION.
SO NOW I'M A HERO AND A PERMANENT MEMBER OF PARLIAMENT, ALL BECAUSE I CAME UP WITH A PLAN AND GOT LUCKY.
SOUNDS TO ME LIKE YOU GOT BRAVE, TOO.
I OWE IT ALL TO THE EXAMPLE SET BY AQUAMAN! IT WAS YOUR ATTACK ON THE GUARDS THAT INSPIRED ME!
AND NOW YOU'VE BECOME AN INSPIRATION TO SO MANY OTHERS!
HOW DID YOU KNOW?
WE MONITOR BROADCASTS FROM THE SURFACE WORLD. BUT TELL ME...
WHY DO YOU STILL WEAR THAT?
MY PRISON UNIFORM? AS A SYMBOL, I SUPPOSE. OR MAYBE JUST OUT OF SPITE. THE IRONY OF IT APPEALS TO ME.
YES, AND TO ME!
COME ALONG NOW, MY FRIEND. THE KING WILL WANT TO MEET YOU!
A BONA FIDE SUPER-HERO!
THE... KING?

SOON AQUAMAN FOUND HIMSELF IN THE THRONE ROOM OF A MAGNIFICENT PALACE, PREPARING FOR AN AUDIENCE WITH ROYALTY.
VULKO, I'VE NEVER MET A KING BEFORE! WHAT SHOULD I DO?
JUST FOLLOW MY LEAD.
SO... THIS IS THE FAMOUS AQUAMAN!
YOUR HIGHNESS.
PLEASE...
IT IS I WHO SHOULD KNEEL!

WE HAVE HEARD TALES OF YOUR EXPLOITS! YOU CAN IMAGINE OUR PRIDE IN SUCH AN ILLUSTRIOUS NATIVE SON!
I MEAN NO DISRESPECT, YOUR HIGHNESS, BUT I MAKE NO CLAIM TO AN ATLANTEAN HERITAGE. NOR AM I A SURFACE DWELLER. I FALL SOMEWHERE IN BETWEEN.
YOU'LL EXCUSE ME, BUT I DON'T UNDERSTAND.
EXPLAIN IT TO ME.
I WAS BORN IN THIS CITY, ONLY TO BE LEFT TO PERISH ON MERCY REEF!
I AM AN OUTCAST.
THAT IS AS MAY BE, BUT THIS IS A DIFFERENT DAY, MY DEAR AQUAMAN.
I AM NOW KING OF ATLANTIS, AND IT IS MY DECREE THAT YOU BE ACCORDED THE PRIVILEGES OF FULL AND UNCONDITIONAL CITIZENSHIP!
SO BE IT!

NOW THAT YOU'RE ONE OF US, WE'D BETTER CONTINUE YOUR EDUCATION. THESE ARE PAST RULERS, FROM THE TIME BEFORE THE REPRESSIVE REGIME OVERTHREW OUR LEGITIMATE GOVERNMENT.
OUR PRESENT KING WAS HEIR TO THE THRONE. HIS AUNT, OUR QUEEN, DIED IN AQUARIUM JUST BEFORE THE REVOLT.
VULKO... WAIT!
WHO... IS THAT?
WHY, THAT'S HER. OUR LATE QUEEN.
MY MOTHER!

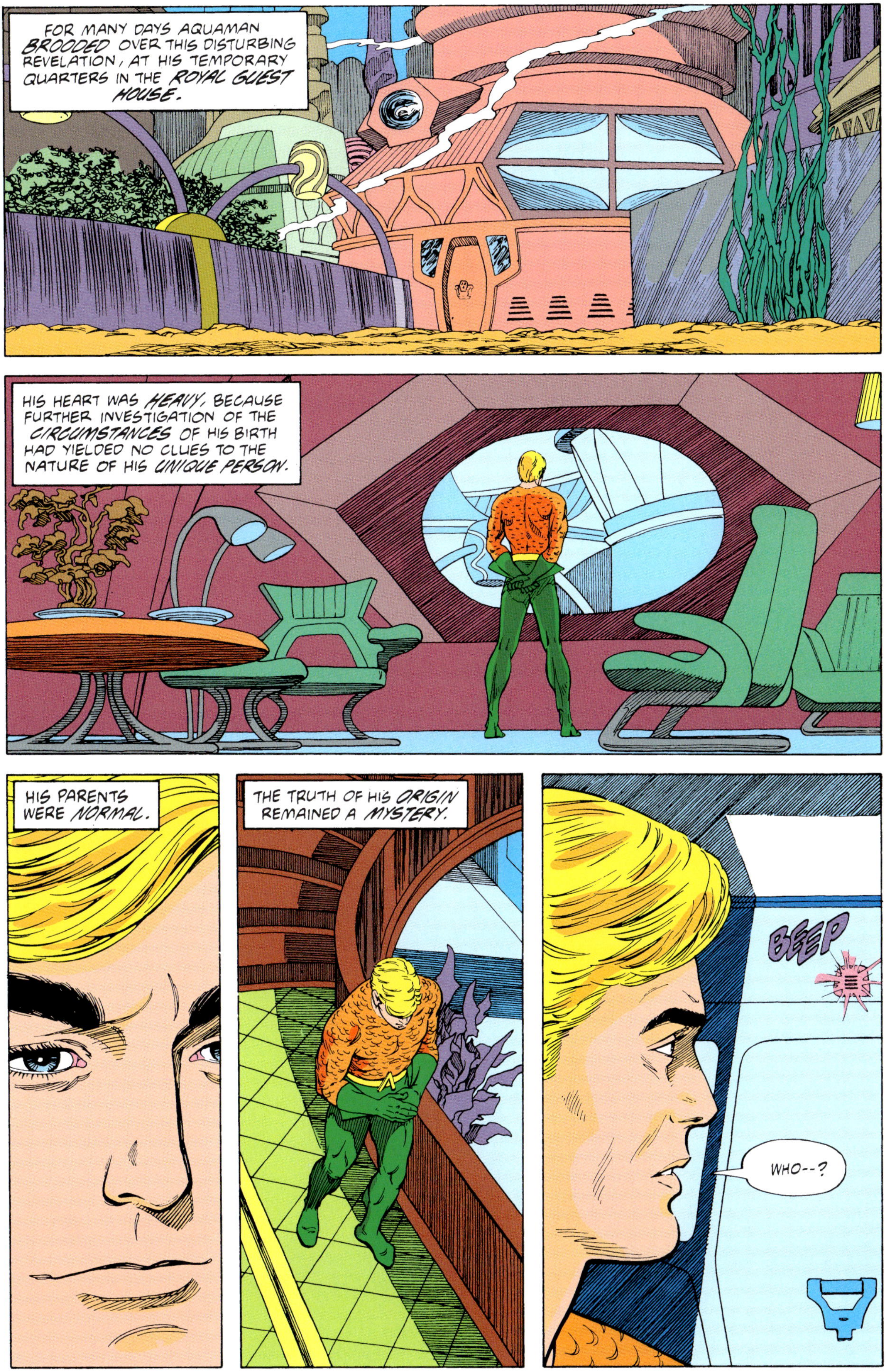
FOR MANY DAYS AQUAMAN BROODED OVER THIS DISTURBING REVELATION, AT HIS TEMPORARY QUARTERS IN THE ROYAL GUEST HOUSE.
HIS HEART WAS HEAVY, BECAUSE FURTHER INVESTIGATION OF THE CIRCUMSTANCES OF HIS BIRTH HAD YIELDED NO CLUES TO THE NATURE OF HIS UNIQUE PERSON.
HIS PARENTS WERE NORMAL.
THE TRUTH OF HIS ORIGIN REMAINED A MYSTERY.
BEEP
WHO--?

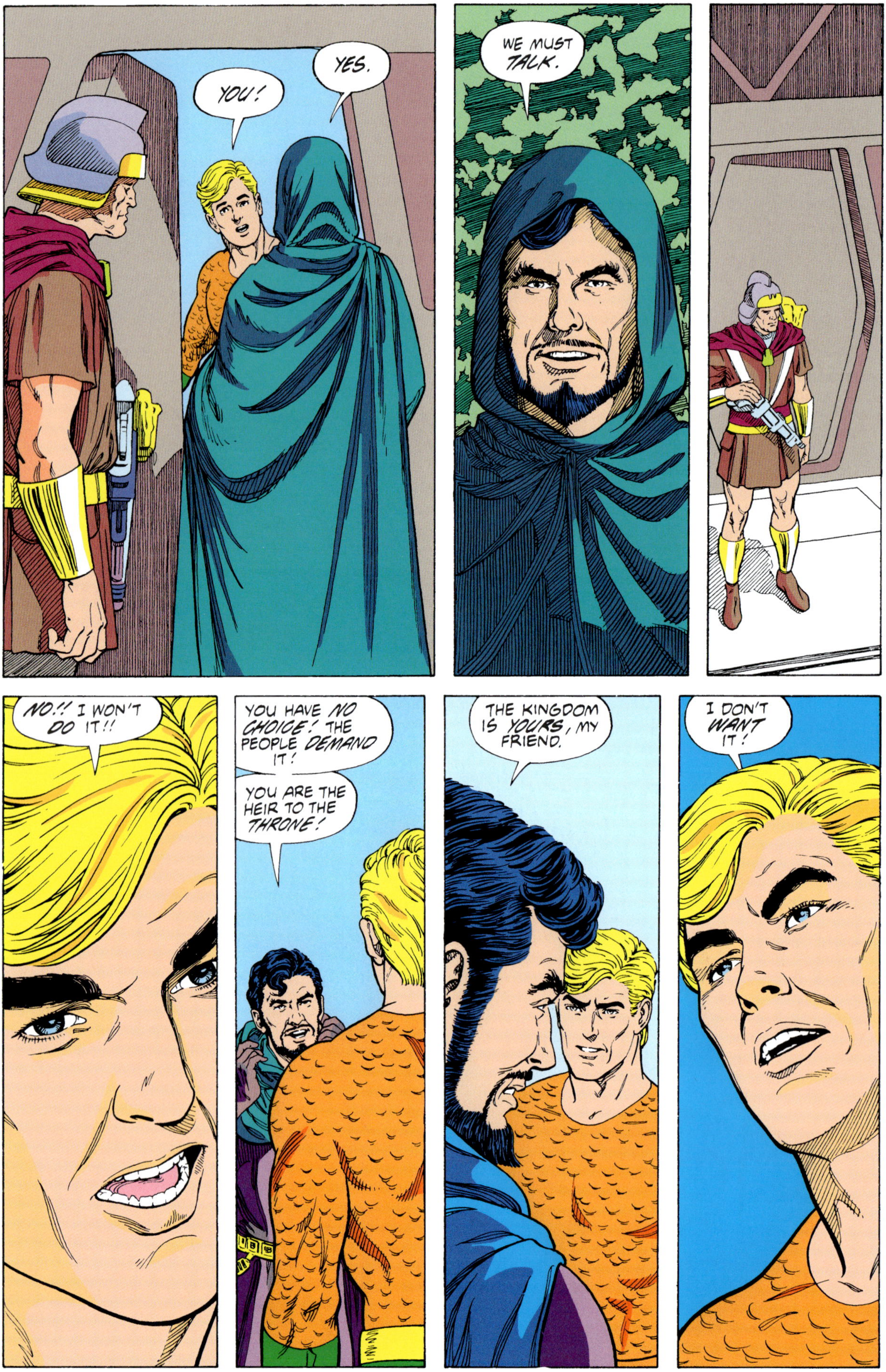
YOU!
YES.
WE MUST TALK.
NO.!! I WON'T DO IT!!
YOU HAVE NO CHOICE! THE PEOPLE DEMAND IT!
YOU ARE THE HEIR TO THE THRONE!
THE KINGDOM IS YOURS, MY FRIEND.
I DON'T WANT IT!

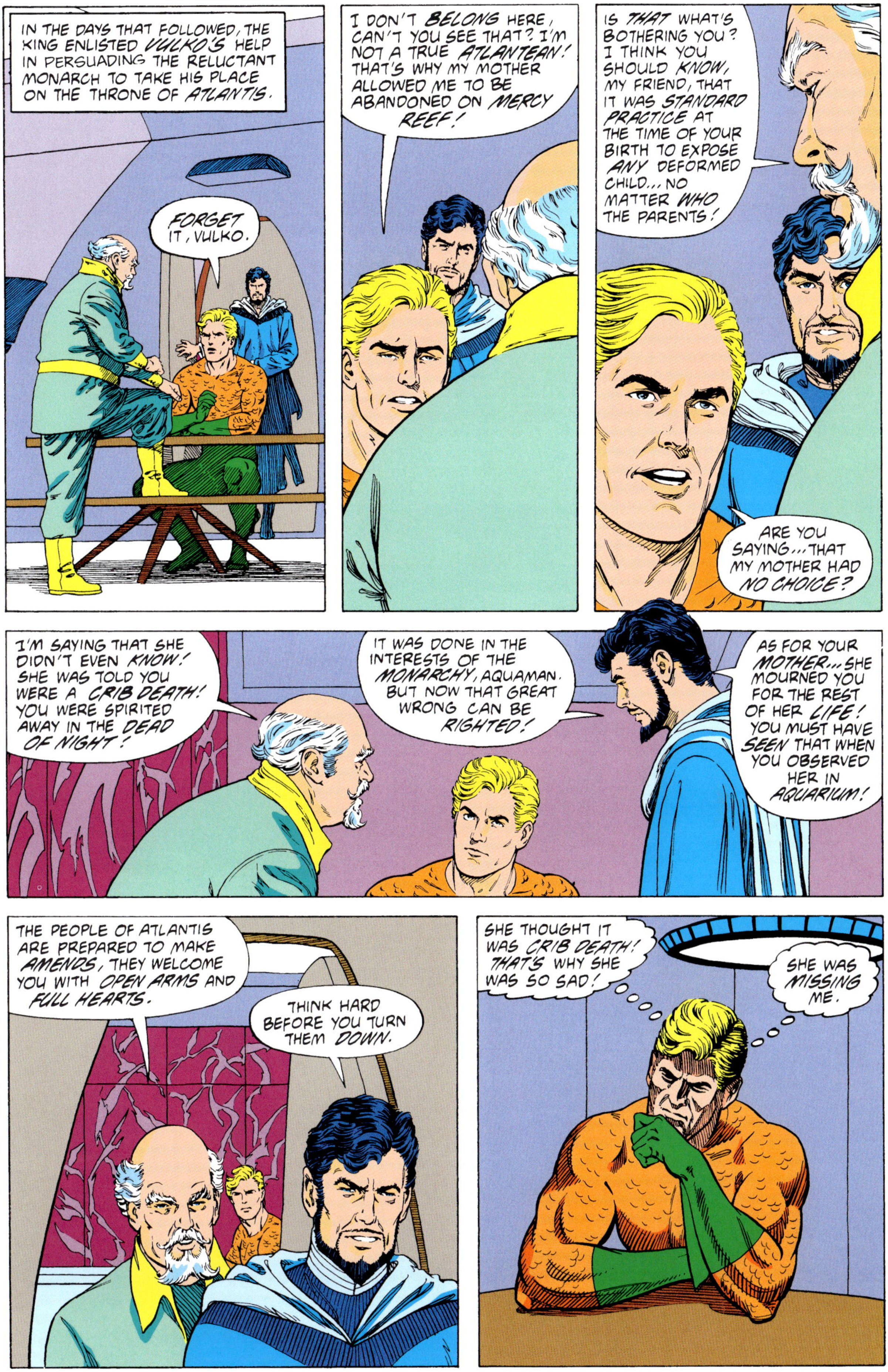
IN THE DAYS THAT FOLLOWED, THE KING ENLISTED VULKO'S HELP IN PERSUADING THE RELUCTANT MONARCH TO TAKE HIS PLACE ON THE THRONE OF ATLANTIS.
FORGET IT, VULKO.
I DON'T BELONG HERE, CAN'T YOU SEE THAT? I'M NOT A TRUE ATLANTEAN! THAT'S WHY MY MOTHER ALLOWED ME TO BE ABANDONED ON MERCY REEF!
IS THAT WHAT'S BOTHERING YOU? I THINK YOU SHOULD KNOW, MY FRIEND, THAT IT WAS STANDARD PRACTICE AT THE TIME OF YOUR BIRTH TO EXPOSE ANY DEFORMED CHILD... NO MATTER WHO THE PARENTS!
ARE YOU SAYING... THAT MY MOTHER HAD NO CHOICE?
I'M SAYING THAT SHE DIDN'T EVEN KNOW! SHE WAS TOLD YOU WERE A CRIB DEATH! YOU WERE SPIRITED AWAY IN THE DEAD OF NIGHT!
IT WAS DONE IN THE INTERESTS OF THE MONARCHY, AQUAMAN. BUT NOW THAT GREAT WRONG CAN BE RIGHTED!
AS FOR YOUR MOTHER... SHE MOURNED YOU FOR THE REST OF HER LIFE! YOU MUST HAVE SEEN THAT WHEN YOU OBSERVED HER IN AQUARIUM!
THE PEOPLE OF ATLANTIS ARE PREPARED TO MAKE AMENDS, THEY WELCOME YOU WITH OPEN ARMS AND FULL HEARTS.
THINK HARD BEFORE YOU TURN THEM DOWN.
SHE THOUGHT IT WAS CRIB DEATH! THAT'S WHY SHE WAS SO SAD!
SHE WAS MISSING ME.

FOR YOU, MOTHER.

EPILOGUE
AQUAMAN CONTINUED TO SERVE IN THE JUSTICE LEAGUE OF AMERICA, SAFEGUARDING THE WORLD OF HIS BELOVED FOSTER FATHER.
HIS RELATIONSHIP WITH THE BOY WHO BECAME KNOWN AS AQUALAD WAS A PARTIAL REPAYMENT FOR THE KINDNESS HE'D BEEN SHOWN BY THE CRUSTY OLD LIGHTHOUSE KEEPER.
THE TWO BECAME FAST FRIENDS.
AND ON ONE PARTICULARLY SPLENDID DAY, AQUAMAN MET HIS QUEEN. MERA WAS A VISITOR FROM AN OTHER-DIMENSIONAL WATER WORLD. SHE SOON BECAME AQUAMAN'S BRIDE.
WITH VULKO AS HIS ADVISOR, HANDLING ALL THE DAY-TO-DAY BUSINESS OF GOVERNING THE KINGDOM, AQUAMAN'S LIFE WAS IDEAL.

THEN SOMETHING HAPPENED WHICH MADE IT EVEN BETTER...
DA-DA HIGH!
HIGH!
LOOK, MERA! THE LITTLE KING DELIVERS A COMMAND!
HA HA HA!

BUT HAPPY YEARS PASS LIKE WEEKS.
AQUAMAN'S INFANT SON WAS KILLED ON A BITTERLY COLD DAY SHORTLY BEFORE HIS SECOND BIRTHDAY. HE WAS BURIED ON MERCY REEF.
IN MEMORY ARTHUR CURRY III
WITHOUT A WORD OR A TEAR, AQUAMAN ABANDONED ALL HE HELD DEAR. THERE WAS NOTHING TO SAY, NOTHING THAT COULD POSSIBLY MATTER. ONLY FLIGHT WAS LEFT TO HIM NOW.
THE COLD SEAS WELCOMED THEIR FAVORITE SON.

THE BEGINNING OF TOMORROW!
AQUAMAN
0
OCT 94
$1.50 US
$2.10 CAN
70p UK
APPROVED BY THE COMICS CODE AUTHORITY
DAVID
EGELAND
VANCATA

A CRASH OF SYMBOLS
PETER DAVID WRITER
MARTIN EGELAND PENCILLER
BRAD VANCATA & HOWARD M. SHUM INKERS
TOM McCRAW COLORIST
DAN NAKROSIS LETTERER
EDDIE BERGANZA ASST. EDITOR
KEVIN DOOLEY EDITOR
ZERO.
IT IS THE NUMBER THAT FLOATS THROUGH DOLPHIN'S MIND.
ZERO BEING THE CHANCE THAT HER TWO SUDDEN CHARGES WILL SURVIVE UNLESS IMMEDIATE HELP IS FOUND.

Up ahead... just ... little further...
SLEEKSKIN... YOUR MATE STIRS.
HE DOES NOT HAVE MUCH LONGER, I THINK.
BUT WE WILL BRING HIM NO FURTHER...
WE WILL NOT GO TO THE BAD PLACE.
YOU MEAN ATLANTIS? BUT... THERE'S NOTHING "BAD" THERE. HE WOULDN'T BRING YOU SOMEWHERE BAD.
HE DOES NOT KNOW...
IT IS NOT HIS FAULT. HE IS ONLY HUMAN.
AQUAMAN IS NOT MY MATE.
NOT YET.
YOU'RE LEAVING ME NO CHOICE. I SEE.
I'LL BRING THEM.
SWIFT CURRENT, SLEEKSKIN, TO YOU AND YOUR MATE.

THE WOMAN CALLED DOLPHIN, WHEN IT COMES TO TALKING, IS MUCH LIKE THE OCEANS THAT ARE HER HOME.
OFTENTIMES SILENT AND REFLECTIVE, AND DIFFICULT TO KNOW...
BENEATH HER SURFACE THERE ARE MANY DARK THINGS... THE MOST RECENT BEING HER SHOOTING THE VILLAIN CALLED CHARYBDIS, SO THAT AQUAMAN MIGHT SURVIVE.
SHE DID WHAT SHE HAD TO.
SHE WOULD DO IT AGAIN.
HOW SHE FEELS ABOUT HER ACTIONS REMAINS... AS DOES THE OCEAN... UNFATHOMABLE.
BUT WHEN SHE DOES FEEL THE NEED TO EXPRESS HERSELF VERBALLY, THEN... LIKE A STORMY SEA...
...IT COMES IN WAVES.
OH MY LORD! I...
I'D HEARD ABOUT IT, BUT I... I NEVER DREAMED...

NO... I TAKE THAT BACK. I DID DREAM.
I JUST NEVER DARED BELIEVE, THAT'S ALL.
HALT!
STATE YOUR BUSINESS!
CALM DOWN, MERO. I DON'T THINK SHE'S CARRYING ANY CONCEALED WEAPONS!
SIR! IT'S AQUAMAN!
AND AQUALAD, TOO!
THEY LOOK IN BAD SHAPE!
HOW BAD?
Pr...pretty bad...

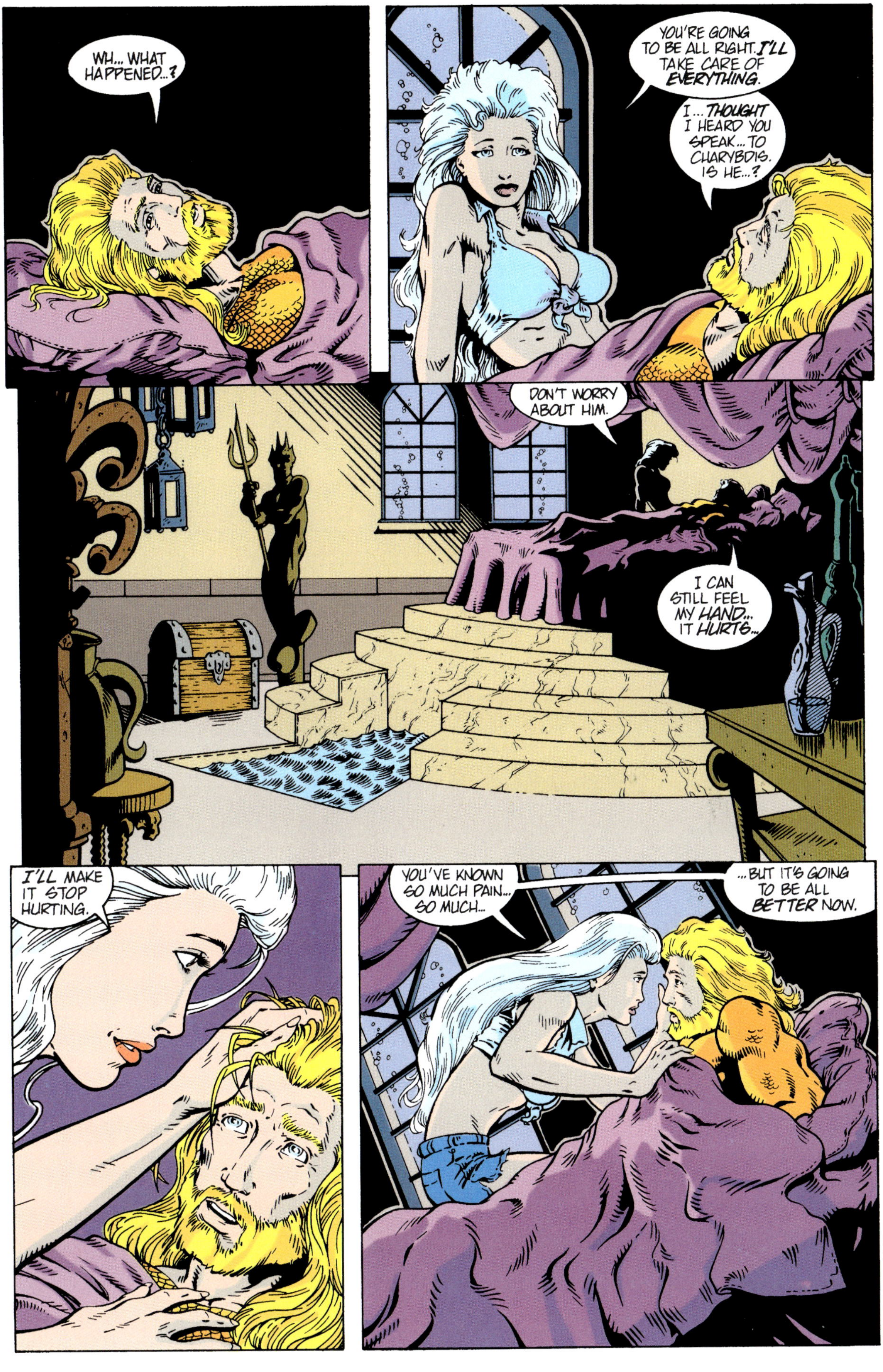
WH... WHAT HAPPENED...?
YOU'RE GOING TO BE ALL RIGHT. I'LL TAKE CARE OF EVERYTHING.
I... THOUGHT I HEARD YOU SPEAK... TO CHARYBDIS. IS HE...?
DON'T WORRY ABOUT HIM.
I CAN STILL FEEL MY HAND... IT HURTS...
I'LL MAKE IT STOP HURTING.
YOU'VE KNOWN SO MUCH PAIN... SO MUCH...
...BUT IT'S GOING TO BE ALL BETTER NOW.

PROMISE?
PROMISE, DEAR HEART...
DEAR, DEAR HEART...
MY... CHEST...
WH-WHAT ARE YOU DOING TO MY CH-ARRGGHHHH!!!
WHAT'S WRONG? DIDN'T YOU EVER HAVE A GIRL STEAL YOUR HEART BEFORE?
SEE! I KEPT MY PROMISE! BET YOU'VE FORGOTTEN ALL ABOUT YOUR HAND HURTING!

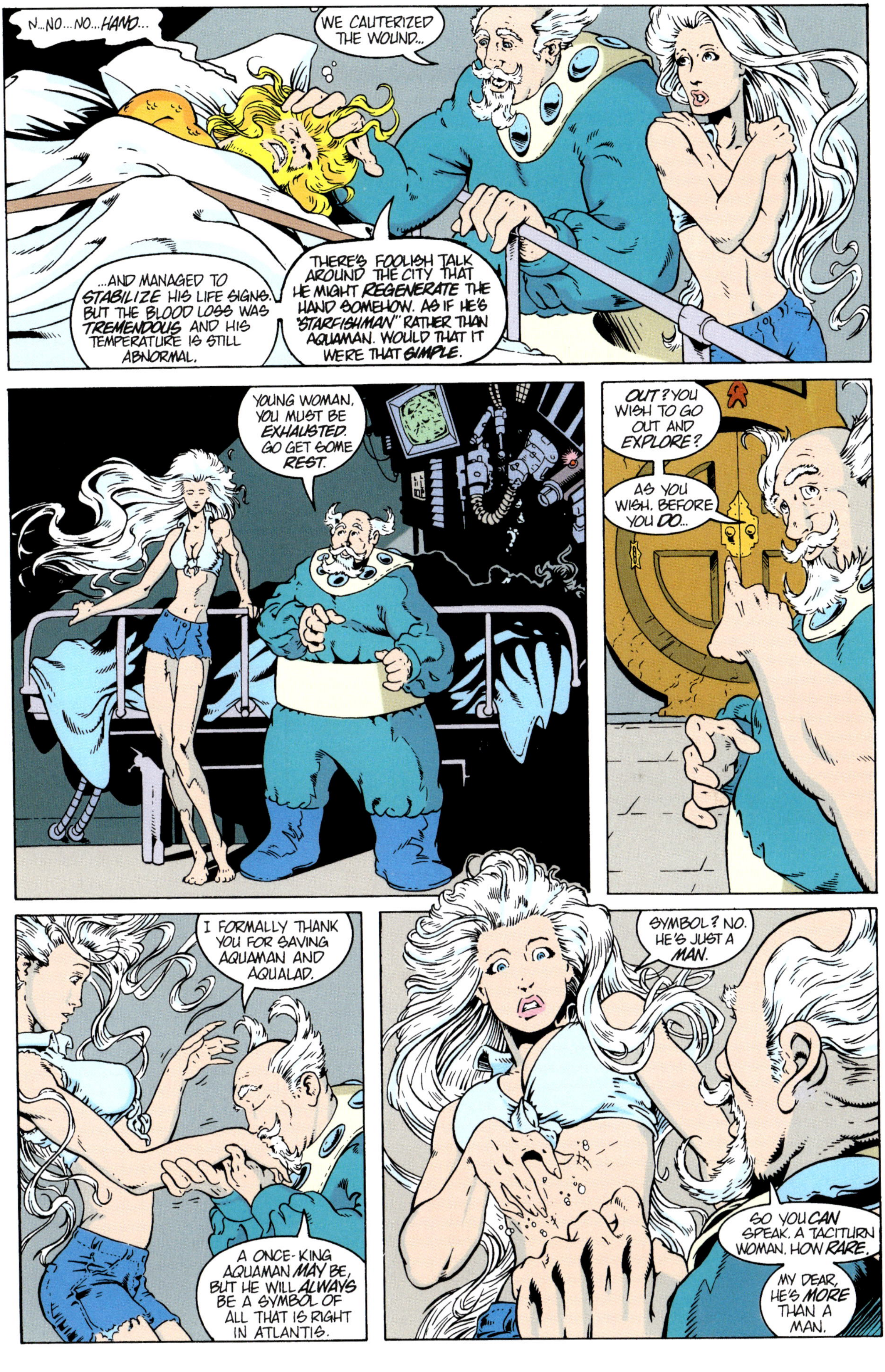
N...NO...NO...HAND...
WE CAUTERIZED THE WOUND...
...AND MANAGED TO STABILIZE HIS LIFE SIGNS. BUT THE BLOOD LOSS WAS TREMENDOUS AND HIS TEMPERATURE IS STILL ABNORMAL.
THERE'S FOOLISH TALK AROUND THE CITY THAT HE MIGHT REGENERATE THE HAND SOMEHOW. AS IF HE'S "STARFISHMAN" RATHER THAN AQUAMAN. WOULD THAT IT WERE THAT SIMPLE.
YOUNG WOMAN, YOU MUST BE EXHAUSTED. GO GET SOME REST.
OUT? YOU WISH TO GO OUT AND EXPLORE?
AS YOU WISH. BEFORE YOU DO...
I FORMALLY THANK YOU FOR SAVING AQUAMAN AND AQUALAD.
A ONCE-KING AQUAMAN MAY BE, BUT HE WILL ALWAYS BE A SYMBOL OF ALL THAT IS RIGHT IN ATLANTIS.
SYMBOL? NO. HE'S JUST A MAN.
SO YOU CAN SPEAK. A TACITURN WOMAN. HOW RARE.
MY DEAR, HE'S MORE THAN A MAN.

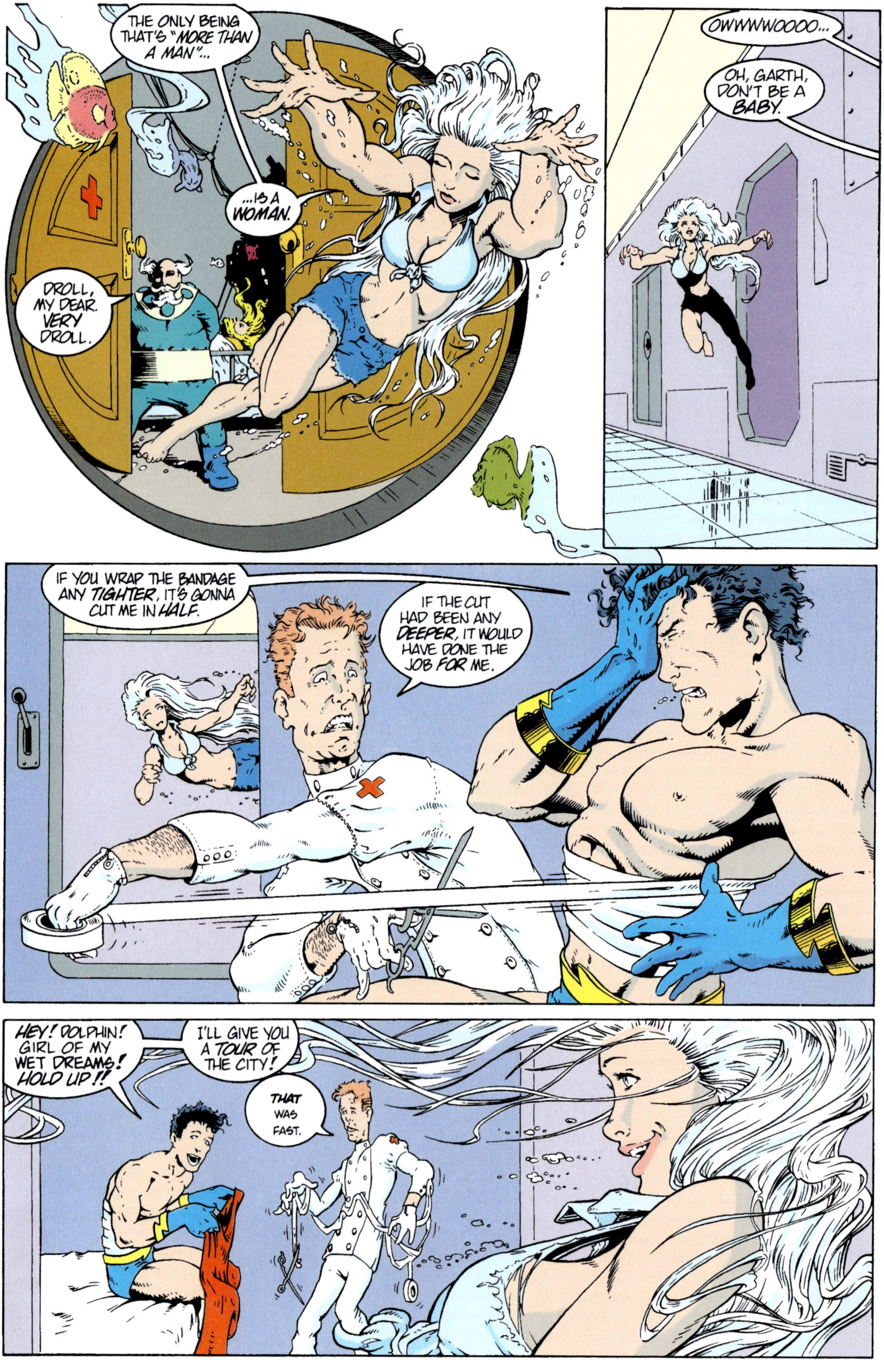
THE ONLY BEING THAT'S "MORE THAN A MAN"...
...IS A WOMAN.
DROLL, MY DEAR. VERY DROLL.
OWWWWOOOO...
OH, GARTH, DON'T BE A BABY.
IF YOU WRAP THE BANDAGE ANY TIGHTER, IT'S GONNA CUT ME IN HALF.
IF THE CUT HAD BEEN ANY DEEPER, IT WOULD HAVE DONE THE JOB FOR ME.
HEY! DOLPHIN! GIRL OF MY WET DREAMS! HOLD UP!!
I'LL GIVE YOU A TOUR OF THE CITY!
THAT WAS FAST.

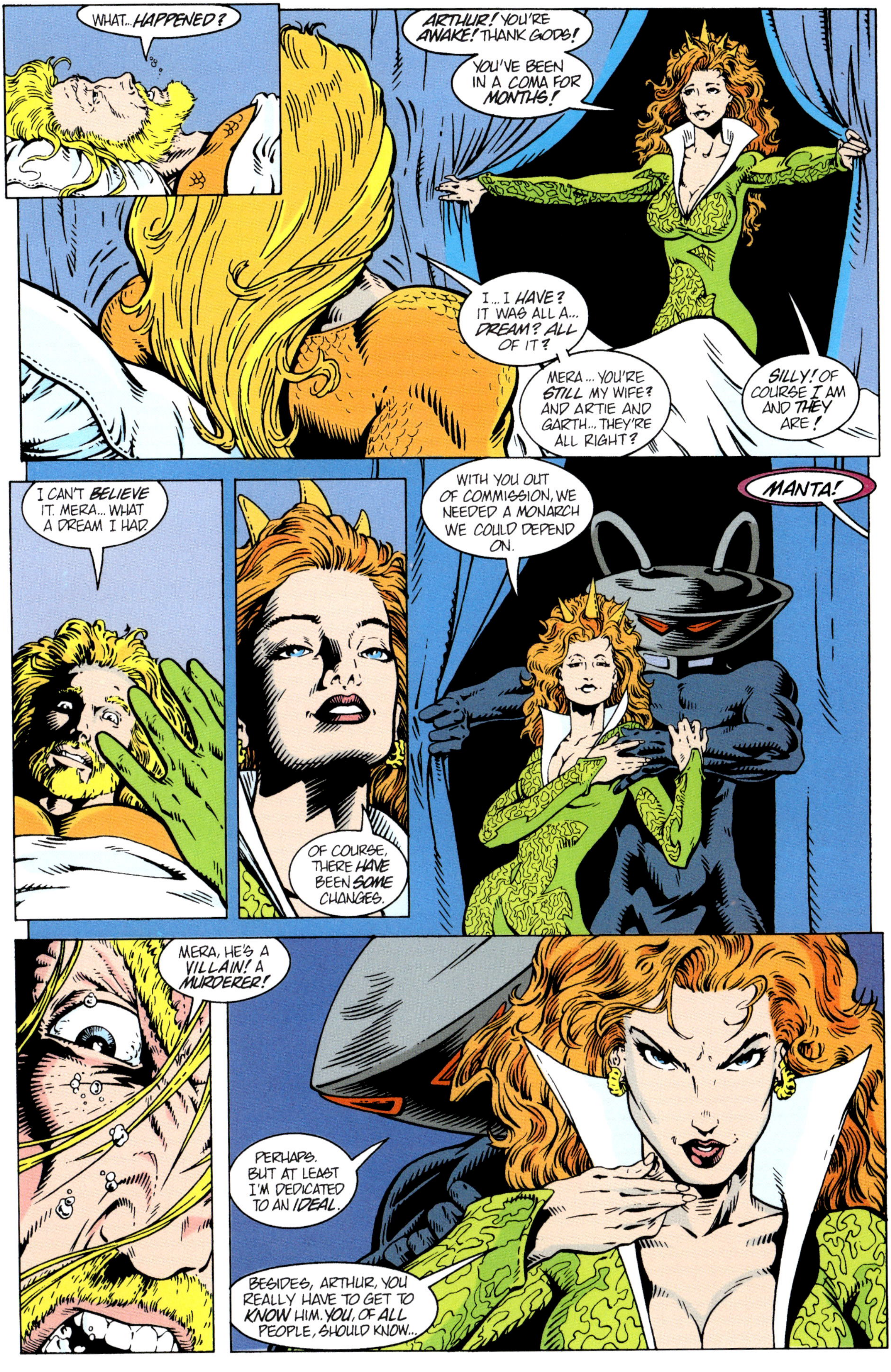

WHAT... HAPPENED?
ARTHUR! YOU'RE AWAKE! THANK GODS!
YOU'VE BEEN IN A COMA FOR MONTHS!
I... I HAVE? IT WAS ALL A... DREAM? ALL OF IT?
MERA... YOU'RE STILL MY WIFE? AND ARTIE AND GARTH... THEY'RE ALL RIGHT?
SILLY! OF COURSE I AM AND THEY ARE!
I CAN'T BELIEVE IT. MERA... WHAT A DREAM I HAD.
OF COURSE, THERE HAVE BEEN SOME CHANGES.
WITH YOU OUT OF COMMISSION, WE NEEDED A MONARCH WE COULD DEPEND ON.
MANTA!
MERA, HE'S A VILLAIN! A MURDERER!
PERHAPS. BUT AT LEAST I'M DEDICATED TO AN IDEAL.
BESIDES, ARTHUR, YOU REALLY HAVE TO GET TO KNOW HIM. YOU, OF ALL PEOPLE, SHOULD KNOW...

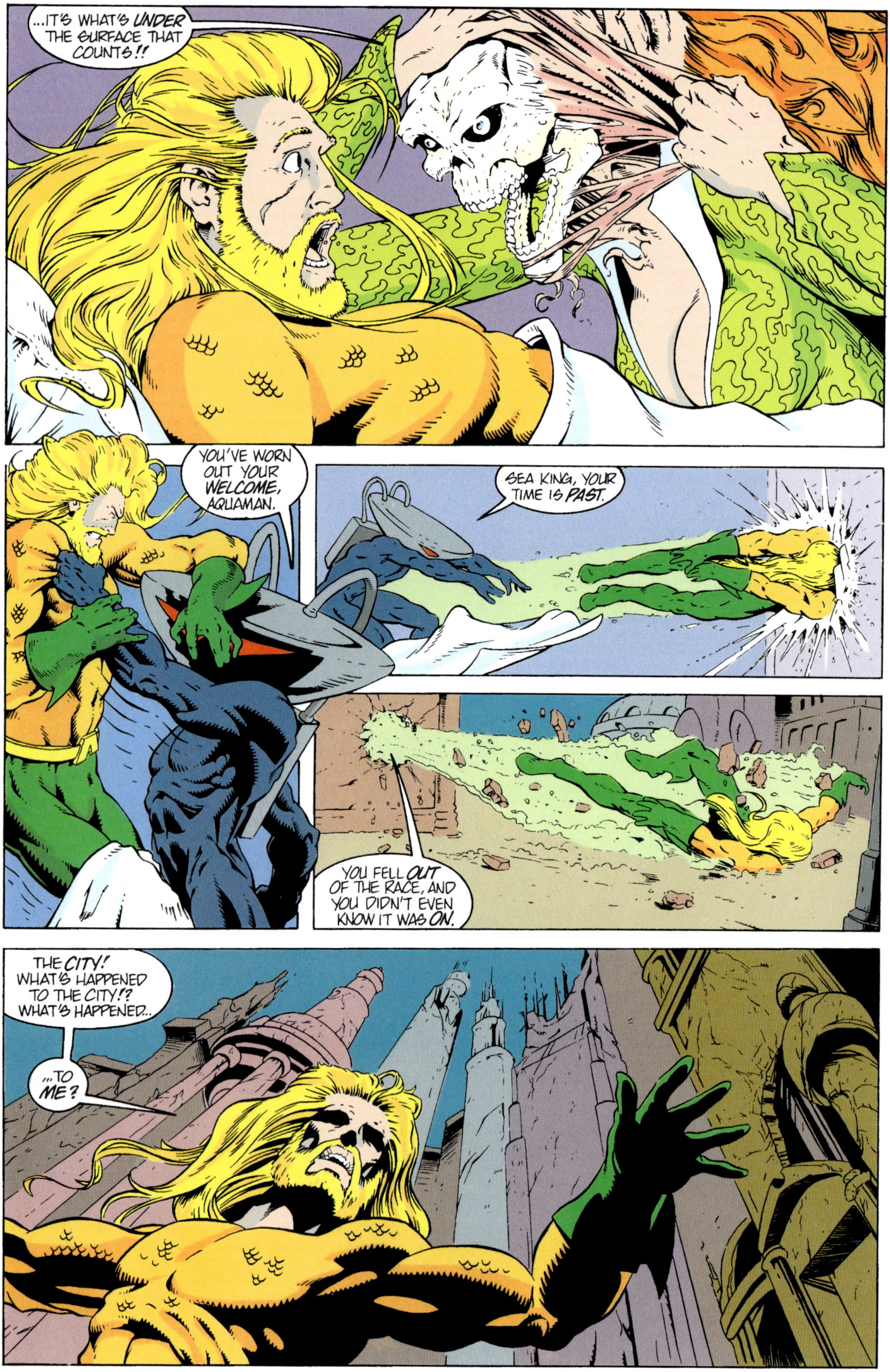

...IT'S WHAT'S UNDER THE SURFACE THAT COUNTS!!
YOU'VE WORN OUT YOUR WELCOME, AQUAMAN.
SEA KING, YOUR TIME IS PAST.
YOU FELL OUT OF THE RACE, AND YOU DIDN'T EVEN KNOW IT WAS ON.
THE CITY! WHAT'S HAPPENED TO THE CITY!? WHAT'S HAPPENED...
...TO ME?

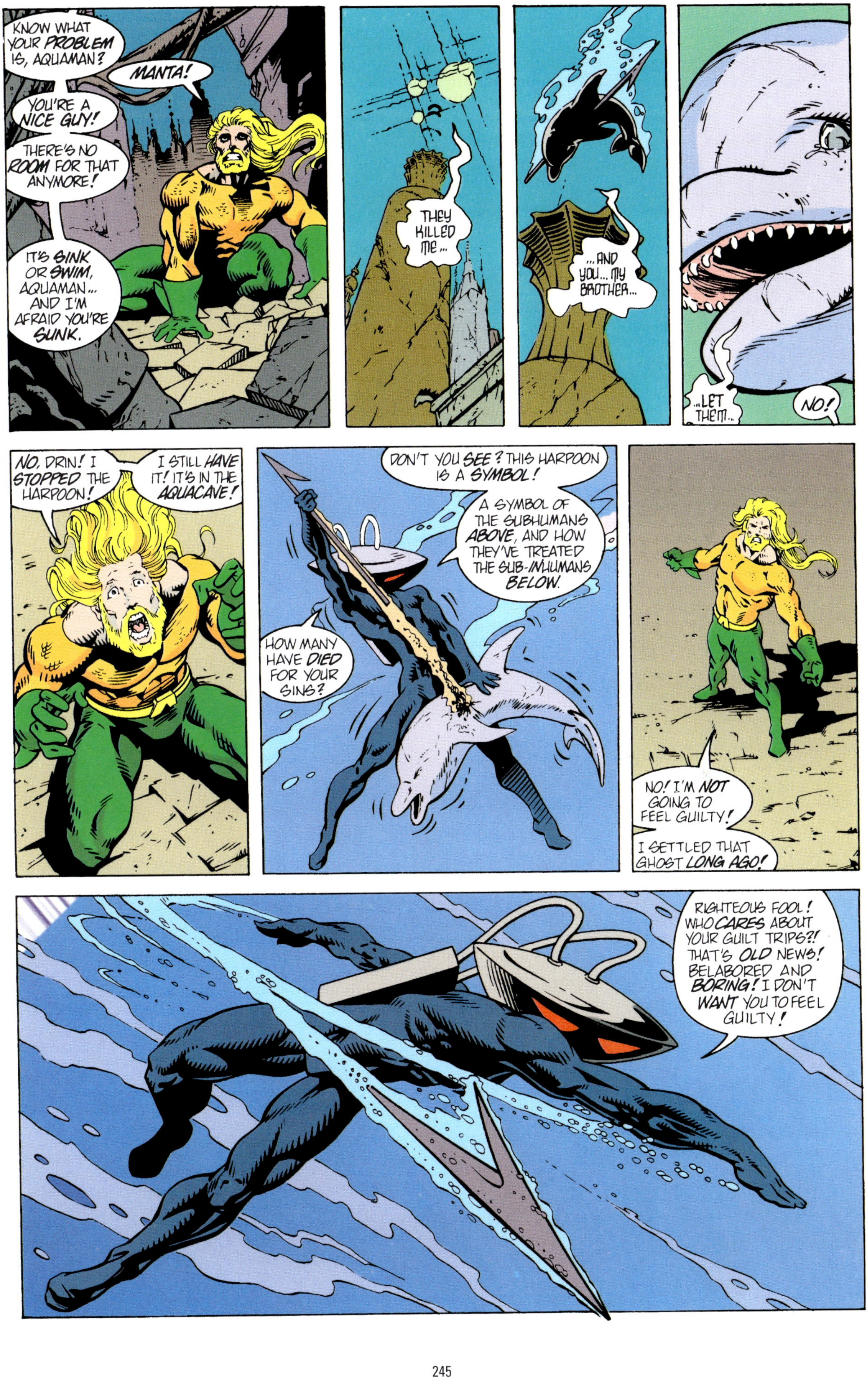
KNOW WHAT YOUR PROBLEM IS, AQUAMAN?
MANTA!
YOU'RE A NICE GUY!
THERE'S NO ROOM FOR THAT ANYMORE!
IT'S SINK OR SWIM, AQUAMAN... AND I'M AFRAID YOU'RE SUNK.
THEY KILLED ME...
...AND YOU... MY BROTHER...
...LET THEM...
NO!
NO, DRIN! I STOPPED THE HARPOON!
I STILL HAVE IT! IT'S IN THE AQUACAVE!
DON'T YOU SEE? THIS HARPOON IS A SYMBOL!
A SYMBOL OF THE SUBHUMANS ABOVE, AND HOW THEY'VE TREATED THE SUB-INHUMANS BELOW.
HOW MANY HAVE DIED FOR YOUR SINS?
NO! I'M NOT GOING TO FEEL GUILTY!
I SETTLED THAT GHOST LONG AGO!
RIGHTEOUS FOOL! WHO CARES ABOUT YOUR GUILT TRIPS?! THAT'S OLD NEWS! BELABORED AND BORING! I DON'T WANT YOU TO FEEL GUILTY!

I WANT YOU TO FEEL PAIN!!
NO! KEEP IT AW--
ARRRRHHHH!
I KNOW IT HURTS. I KNOW IT'S TOUGH. BUT AS YOU CAN SEE...
WE ALL HAVE TO MAKE SACRIFICES.
ARRRHHHHHH!

AQUAMAN SAVED ME FROM GETTIN' KILLED!
HOW'D HE DO THAT, CHUBB?
WHY YA WANNA KNOW?
I JUST DO.
HOW DID WALLY PUT IT?
OH YEAH. "VAST TRACTS OF LAND"...
WELL, THIS WAS BACK WHEN I WAS A LITTLE KID... NOT BIG LIKE NOW. WE WERE PLAYIN' CATCH, AND...
CATCH IT, CHUBB!
I GOT IT! I--
OOOOFF!
WATCH WHERE YA GOIN'! YA BIG DUMB--

OHHHHH BOY....
YOU HAVE STRUCK AND INSULTED THE KING, BOY! THE PENALTY IS... UMM...
VULKO? WHAT'S THE PENALTY?
DEATH.
NO OTHER WAY?
NONE, SIRE. YOU NEED MERELY NAME THE PLACE OF EXECUTION.
THE LAW LEAVES NO ROOM FOR MERCY OR--
I AM THE LAW!
YES, SIRE! OF COURSE!
WATCH WHERE YOU'RE GOING NEXT TIME?
YESSIR.
GO.

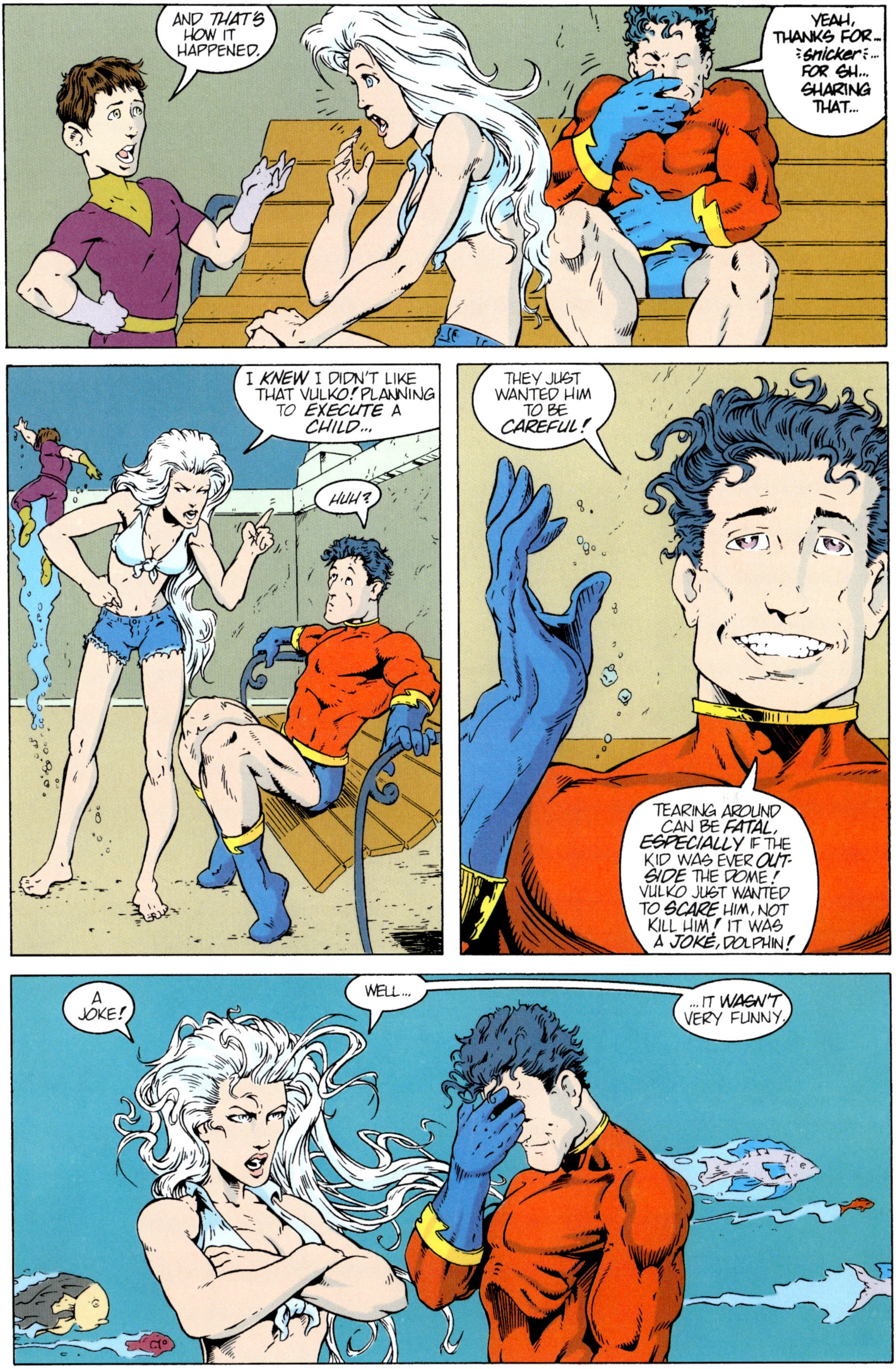
AND THAT'S HOW IT HAPPENED.
YEAH, THANKS FOR... snicker... FOR SH... SHARING THAT...
I KNEW I DIDN'T LIKE THAT VULKO! PLANNING TO EXECUTE A CHILD...
HUH?
THEY JUST WANTED HIM TO BE CAREFUL!
TEARING AROUND CAN BE FATAL, ESPECIALLY IF THE KID WAS EVER OUT-SIDE THE DOME! VULKO JUST WANTED TO SCARE HIM, NOT KILL HIM! IT WAS A JOKE, DOLPHIN!
A JOKE!
WELL...
...IT WASN'T VERY FUNNY.

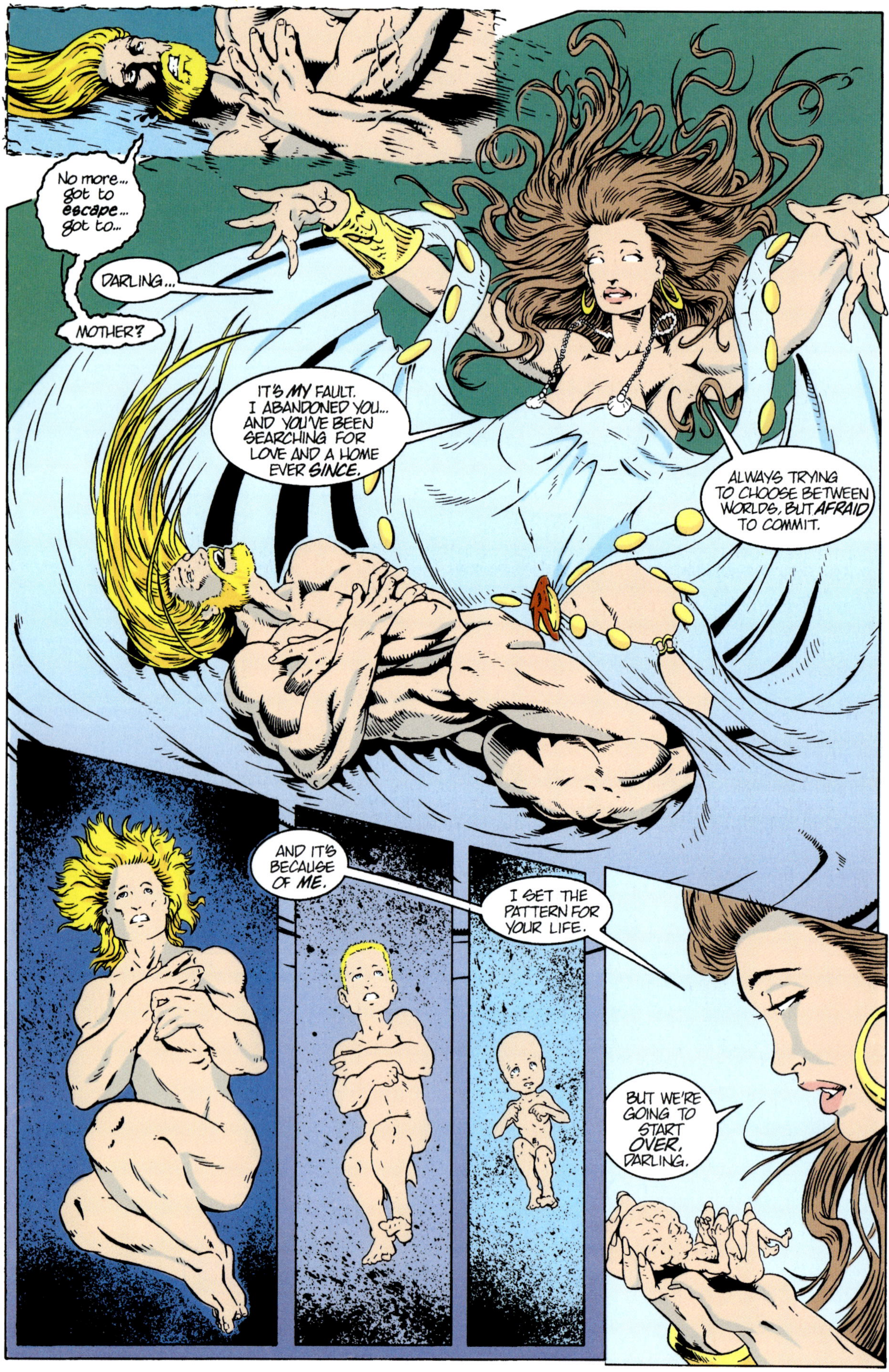
No more... got to escape... got to...
DARLING...
MOTHER?
IT'S MY FAULT. I ABANDONED YOU... AND YOU'VE BEEN SEARCHING FOR LOVE AND A HOME EVER SINCE.
ALWAYS TRYING TO CHOOSE BETWEEN WORLDS, BUT AFRAID TO COMMIT.
AND IT'S BECAUSE OF ME.
I SET THE PATTERN FOR YOUR LIFE.
BUT WE'RE GOING TO START OVER, DARLING.

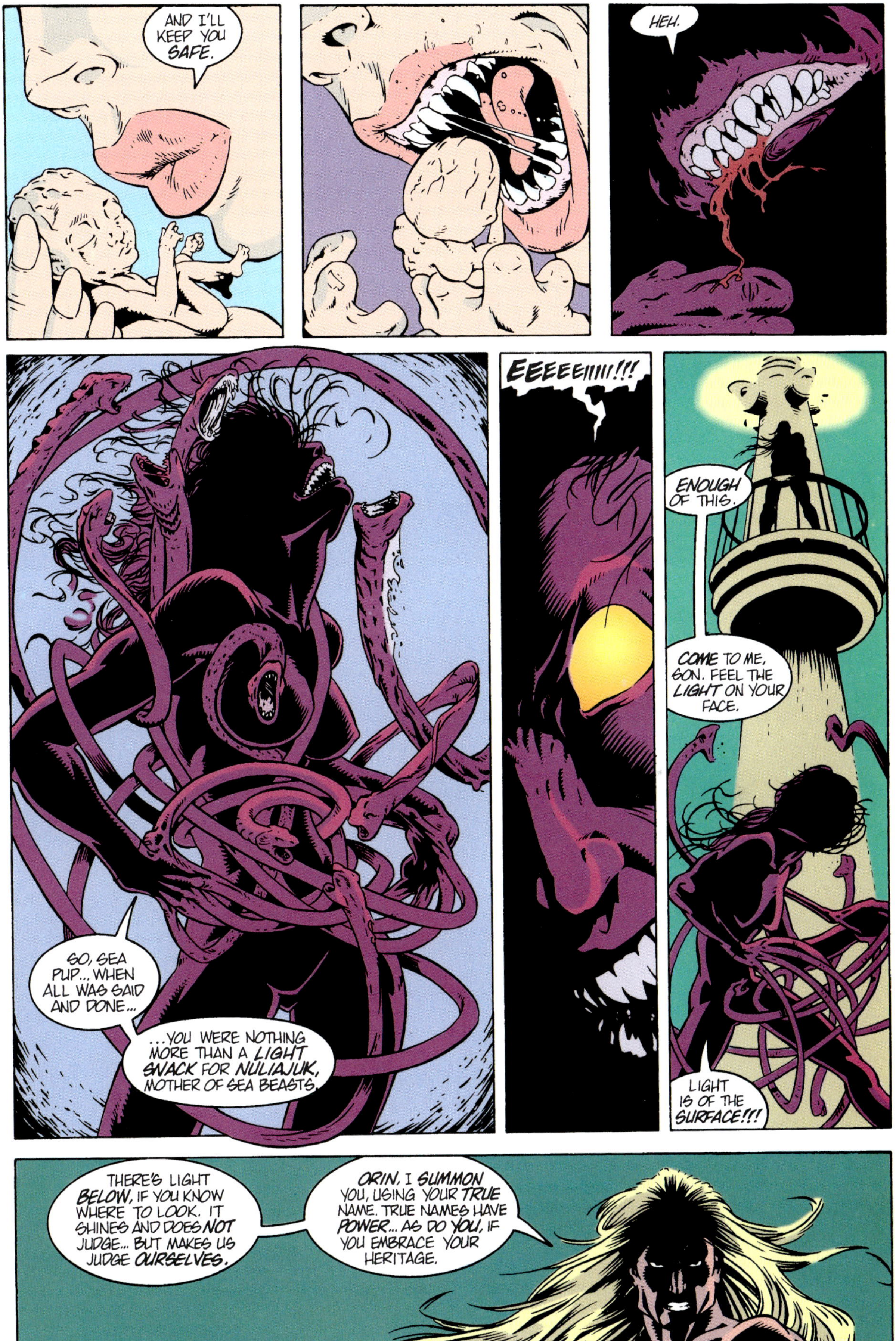
AND I'LL KEEP YOU SAFE.
HEH.
SO, SEA PUP... WHEN ALL WAS SAID AND DONE...
...YOU WERE NOTHING MORE THAN A LIGHT SNACK FOR NULIAJUK, MOTHER OF SEA BEASTS.
EEEEEIIIII!!!
ENOUGH OF THIS.
COME TO ME, SON. FEEL THE LIGHT ON YOUR FACE.
LIGHT IS OF THE SURFACE!!!
THERE'S LIGHT BELOW, IF YOU KNOW WHERE TO LOOK. IT SHINES AND DOES NOT JUDGE... BUT MAKES US JUDGE OURSELVES.
ORIN, I SUMMON YOU, USING YOUR TRUE NAME. TRUE NAMES HAVE POWER... AS DO YOU, IF YOU EMBRACE YOUR HERITAGE.

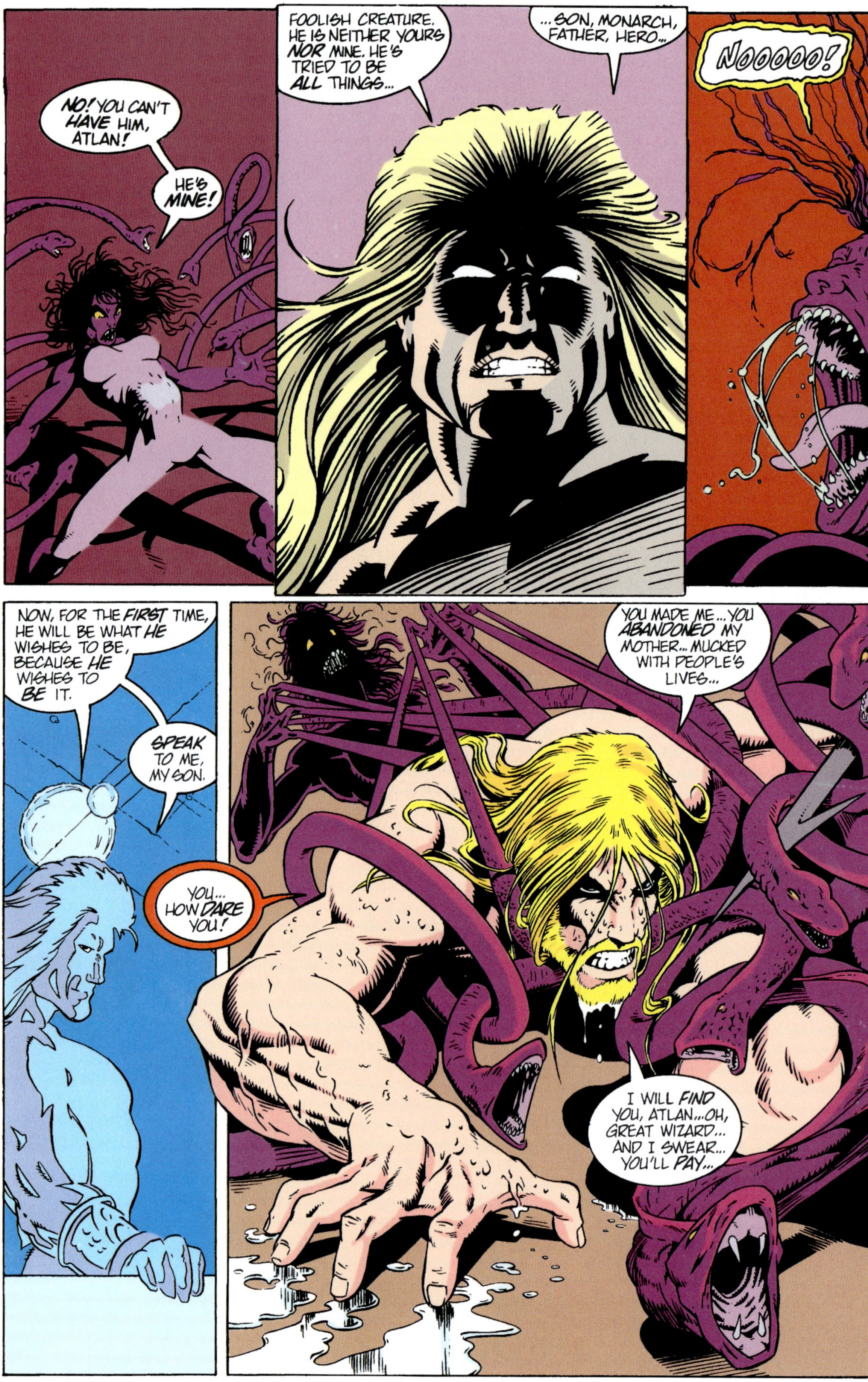

NO! YOU CAN'T HAVE HIM, ATLAN!
HE'S MINE!
FOOLISH CREATURE. HE IS NEITHER YOURS NOR MINE. HE'S TRIED TO BE ALL THINGS...
...SON, MONARCH, FATHER, HERO...
NOOOOO!
NOW, FOR THE FIRST TIME, HE WILL BE WHAT HE WISHES TO BE, BECAUSE HE WISHES TO BE IT.
SPEAK TO ME, MY SON.
YOU... HOW DARE YOU!
YOU MADE ME... YOU ABANDONED MY MOTHER... MUCKED WITH PEOPLE'S LIVES...
I WILL FIND YOU, ATLAN... OH, GREAT WIZARD... AND I SWEAR... YOU'LL PAY...

THANK GOD YOU'VE COME!
THEY'VE BEEN SURROUNDING HIS BED, MORE AND MORE... AND NOW THEY WON'T LET ME GET THROUGH!
I... I THINK I SEE HIM! BUT IS HE CONTROLLING THEM, OR...??!
LOOK OUT!

UNFFF!!!
DOL'! BACK OFF! WE GOT ZERO CHANCE HERE!

SHOOOOMM

NOW WHAT?
NOW?

NOW WE FOLLOW THE FISH POLICE AND SEE WHERE THEY'RE TAKING HIM.

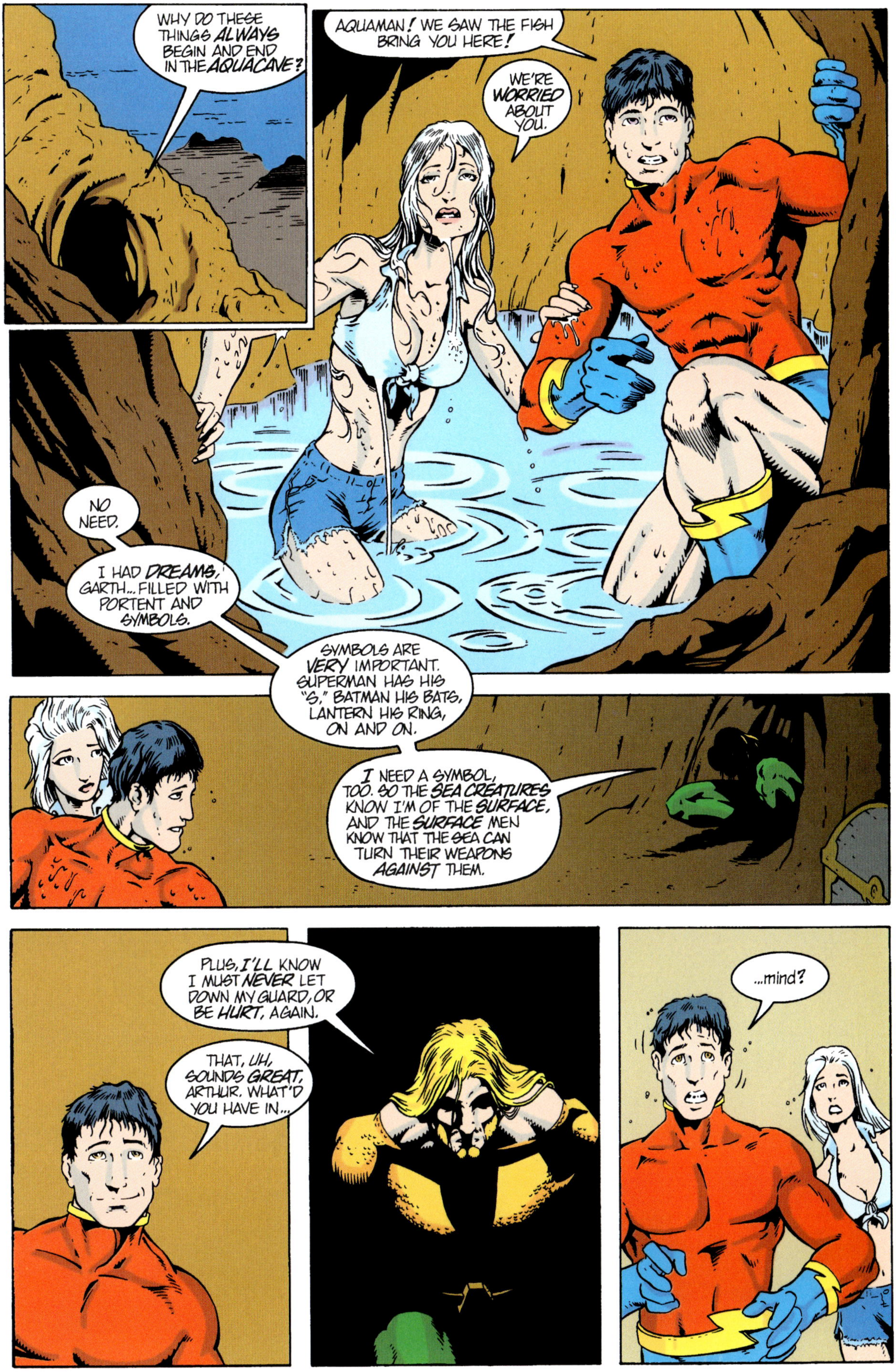
WHY DO THESE THINGS ALWAYS BEGIN AND END IN THE AQUACAVE?
AQUAMAN! WE SAW THE FISH BRING YOU HERE!
WE'RE WORRIED ABOUT YOU.
NO NEED.
I HAD DREAMS, GARTH... FILLED WITH PORTENT AND SYMBOLS.
SYMBOLS ARE VERY IMPORTANT. SUPERMAN HAS HIS "S," BATMAN HIS BATS, LANTERN HIS RING, ON AND ON.
I NEED A SYMBOL, TOO. SO THE SEA CREATURES KNOW I'M OF THE SURFACE, AND THE SURFACE MEN KNOW THAT THE SEA CAN TURN THEIR WEAPONS AGAINST THEM.
PLUS, I'LL KNOW I MUST NEVER LET DOWN MY GUARD, OR BE HURT, AGAIN.
THAT, UH, SOUNDS GREAT, ARTHUR. WHAT'D YOU HAVE IN...
...mind?

BE HONEST NOW:
DO YOU THINK IT'S TOO MUCH?
NEXT:
SUPERBOY

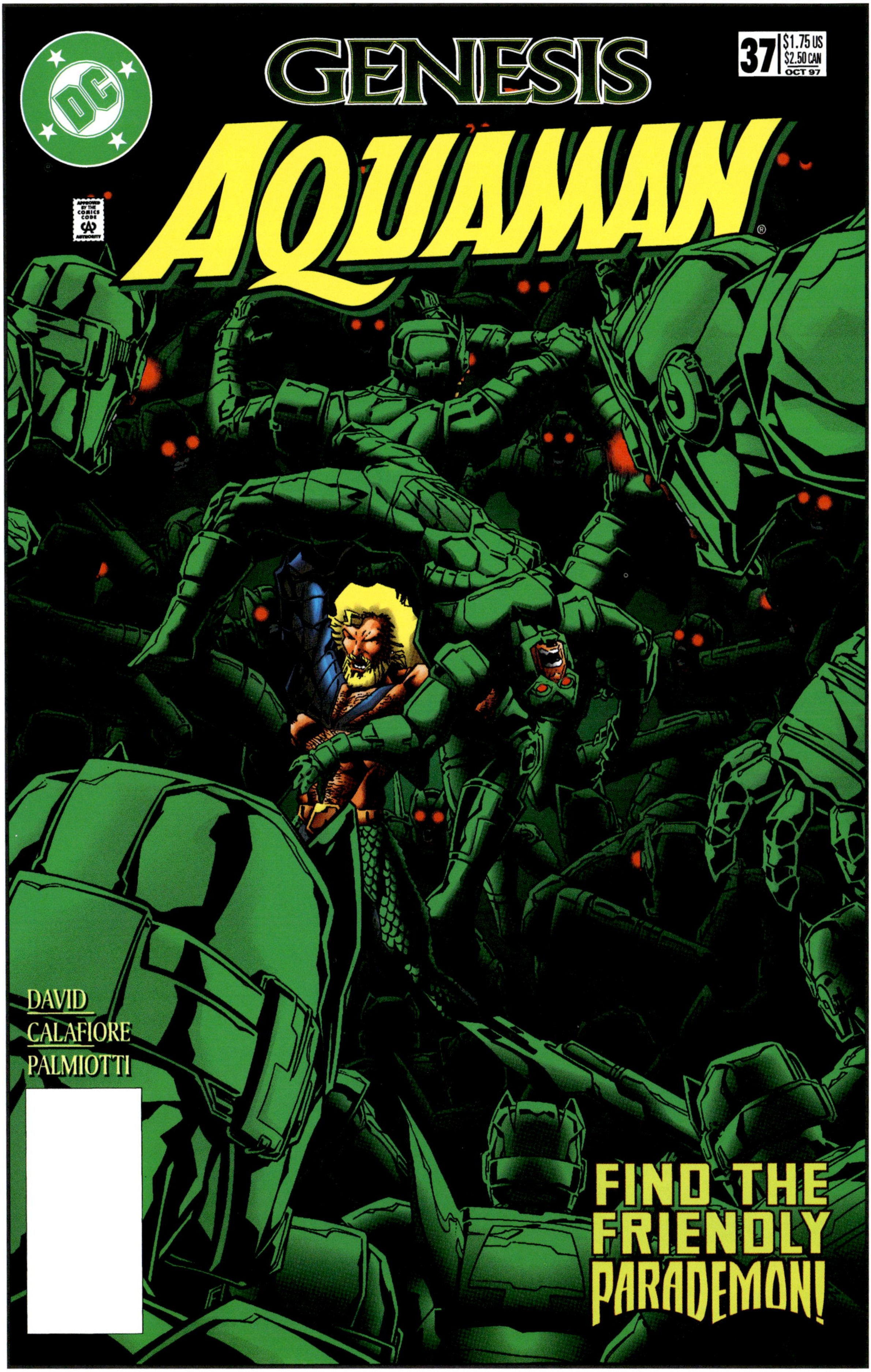
GENESIS
37 $1.75 US $2.50 CAN OCT 97
AQUAMAN
DAVID
CALAFIORE
PALMIOTTI
FIND THE FRIENDLY PARADEMON!

LIVES AGAIN!
THE LEGEND OF AQUAMAN
JUSTICE LEAGUE of AMERICA
METAMORPHO AQUAMAN
SUPER FRIENDS
Adventure COMICS
AQUAMAN
AQUAMAN
AQUAMAN
DOOM from DIMENSION AQUA!
AQUAMAN
URBAN RENEWAL!
UNDERWORLD
REBIRTH
AQUAMAN
DC UNIVERSE REBIRTH
AQUAMAN
AQUAMAN
Who DESTROYS the SEA KING
The OCEAN MASTER
BLACK MANTA?
AQUAMAN
ARTHUR CURRY JUNIOR
AQUAMAN
THE NEW 52!
IS THIS MY FOE!
AQUAMAN
AQUAMAN
JABBERJAW
CAPTAIN CAVEMAN
the BRAVE and the BOLD
BATMAN
AQUAMAN
The SLEEP-WALKER from the SEA!
JUSTICE LEAGUE
AQUAMAN
AQUAMAN
AQUAMAN A COWARD? IS HE REALLY IN TERROR OF The OCEAN MASTER?
THE BEGINNING OF TOMORROW
AQUAMAN
AQUAMAN
IN THE SHADOWY DEPTHS OF ATLANTIS, HIS LIFE WILL CHANGE FOREVER!
AQUAMAN
THE NEW 52!
YEAR ONE
AQUAMAN
AQUAMAN
Who DESTROYS the SEA KING
GENESIS
AQUAMAN
AQUAMAN
SWORD OF ATLANTIS
KURT BUSIEK
BUTCH GUICE
The King of the Seas
AQUAMAN
AQUAMAN
YOU DID THIS TO HER!
YOU!
YOU DIE!!
AQUAMAN

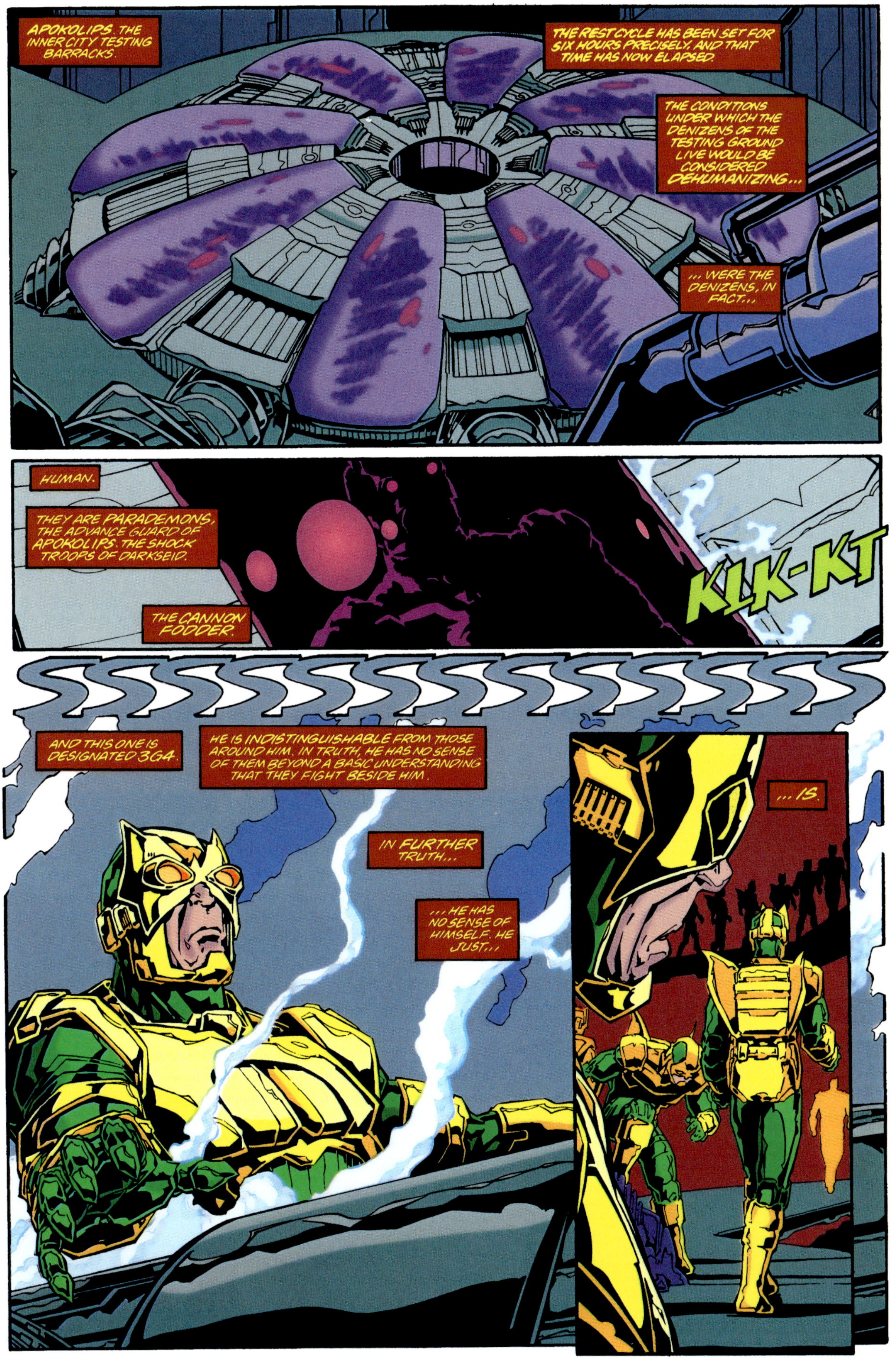
APOKOLIPS. THE INNER CITY TESTING BARRACKS.
THE REST CYCLE HAS BEEN SET FOR SIX HOURS PRECISELY, AND THAT TIME HAS NOW ELAPSED.
THE CONDITIONS UNDER WHICH THE DENIZENS OF THE TESTING GROUND LIVE WOULD BE CONSIDERED DEHUMANIZING...
...WERE THE DENIZENS, IN FACT...
HUMAN.
THEY ARE PARADEMONS, THE ADVANCE GUARD OF APOKOLIPS. THE SHOCK TROOPS OF DARKSEID.
THE CANNON FODDER.
KLK-KT
SSSSSSSSSSSSSS
AND THIS ONE IS DESIGNATED 3G4.
HE IS INDISTINGUISHABLE FROM THOSE AROUND HIM. IN TRUTH, HE HAS NO SENSE OF THEM BEYOND A BASIC UNDERSTANDING THAT THEY FIGHT BESIDE HIM.
IN FURTHER TRUTH...
...HE HAS NO SENSE OF HIMSELF. HE JUST...
...IS.

AND THAT IS SUFFICIENT FOR THE PURPOSES OF...
ONE DEMON LIFE

PETER DAVID
Writer
J. CALAFIORE
Penciller
P.L. PALMIOTTI
Inker
TOM McCRAW
Colorist
ALBERT DE GUZMAN
Letterer
DANA KURTIN
Associate
KEVIN DOOLEY
Drill Sergeant

AFTER A QUICK MEAL OF PROTEIN CAPSULES, THEY MOVE TO THE PROVING GROUND, THERE TO DEMONSTRATE THEIR FACILITY FOR FLYING TO THE RATHER STRICT STANDARDS OF...
...TOPKICK.
NEXT!
NEXT!
NEXT!
YER FORM BITES!
SHOOM

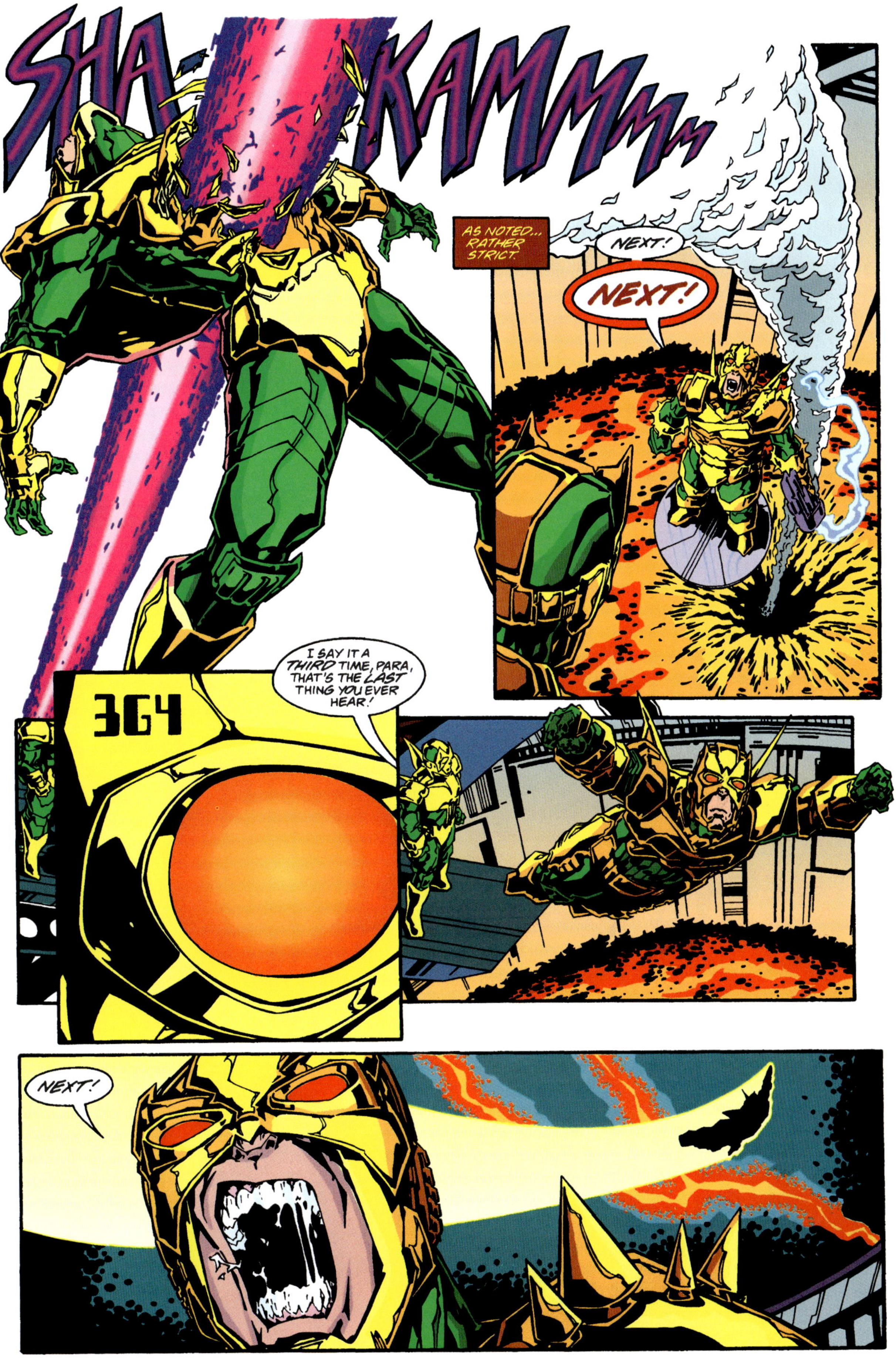
SHA-KAMMMM
AS NOTED... RATHER STRICT.
NEXT!
NEXT!
I SAY IT A THIRD TIME, PARA, THAT'S THE LAST THING YOU EVER HEAR!
3G4
NEXT!

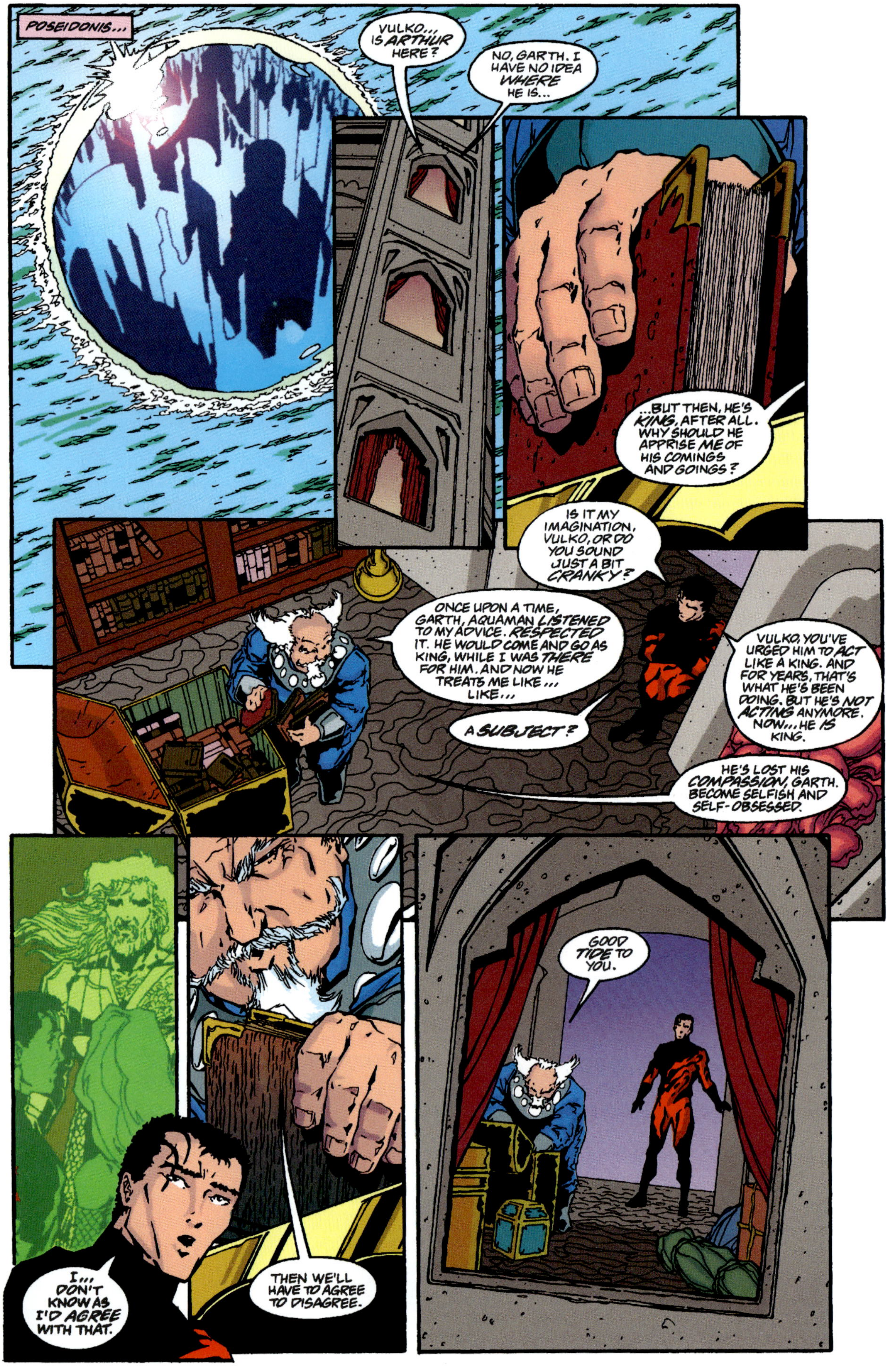
POSEIDONIS...
VULKO... IS ARTHUR HERE?
NO, GARTH. I HAVE NO IDEA WHERE HE IS...
...BUT THEN, HE'S KING, AFTER ALL. WHY SHOULD HE APPRISE ME OF HIS COMINGS AND GOINGS?
IS IT MY IMAGINATION, VULKO, OR DO YOU SOUND JUST A BIT CRANKY?
ONCE UPON A TIME, GARTH, AQUAMAN LISTENED TO MY ADVICE. RESPECTED IT. HE WOULD COME AND GO AS KING, WHILE I WAS THERE FOR HIM. AND NOW HE TREATS ME LIKE... LIKE...
A SUBJECT?
VULKO, YOU'VE URGED HIM TO ACT LIKE A KING. AND FOR YEARS, THAT'S WHAT HE'S BEEN DOING. BUT HE'S NOT ACTING ANYMORE. NOW... HE IS KING.
HE'S LOST HIS COMPASSION, GARTH. BECOME SELFISH AND SELF-OBSESSED.
I... DON'T KNOW AS I'D AGREE WITH THAT.
THEN WE'LL HAVE TO AGREE TO DISAGREE.
GOOD TIDE TO YOU.

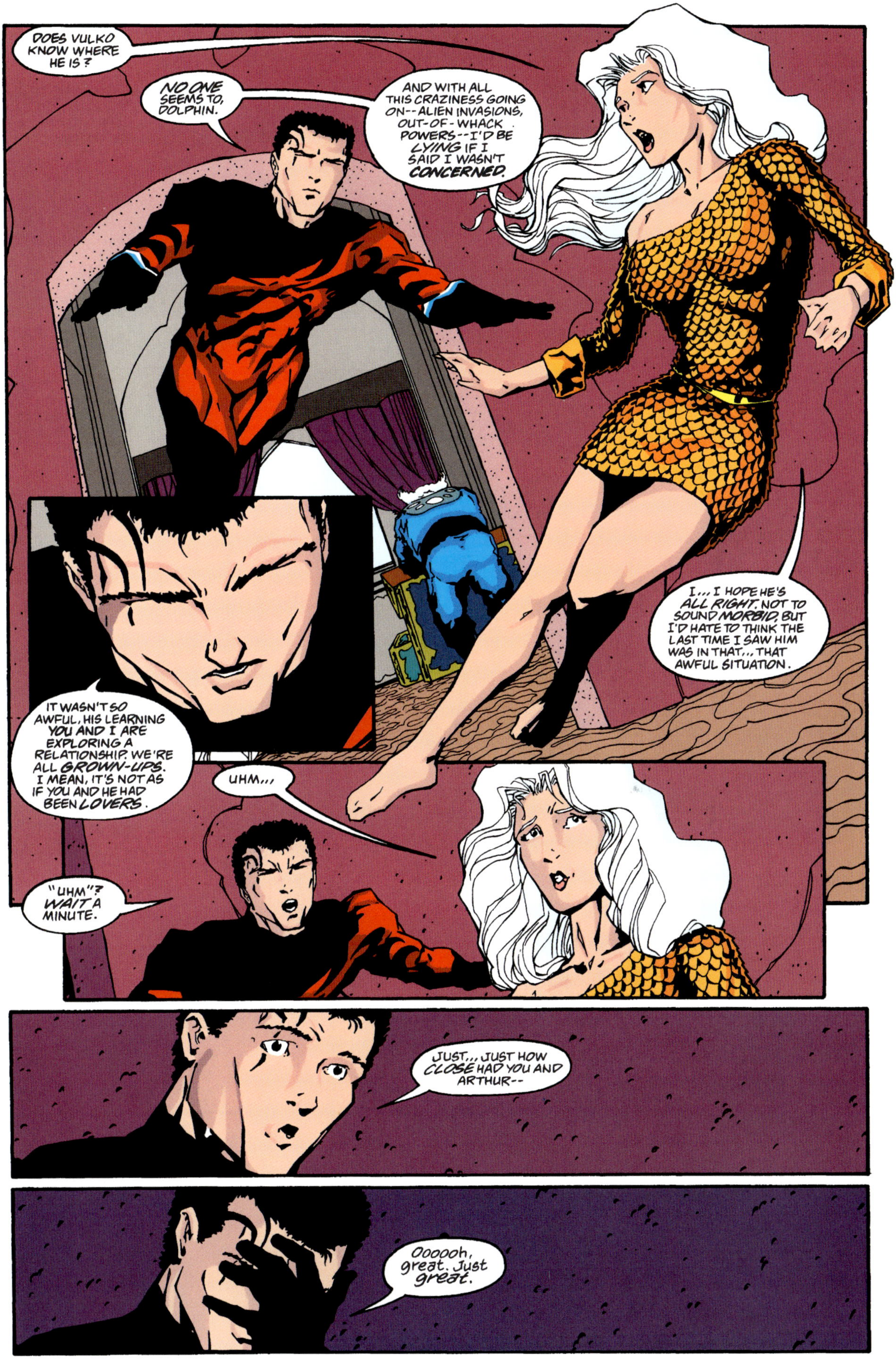
DOES VULKO KNOW WHERE HE IS?
NO ONE SEEMS TO, DOLPHIN.
AND WITH ALL THIS CRAZINESS GOING ON-- ALIEN INVASIONS, OUT-OF-WHACK POWERS--I'D BE LYING IF I SAID I WASN'T CONCERNED.
I... I HOPE HE'S ALL RIGHT. NOT TO SOUND MORBID, BUT I'D HATE TO THINK THE LAST TIME I SAW HIM WAS IN THAT... THAT AWFUL SITUATION.
IT WASN'T SO AWFUL, HIS LEARNING YOU AND I ARE EXPLORING A RELATIONSHIP. WE'RE ALL GROWN-UPS. I MEAN, IT'S NOT AS IF YOU AND HE HAD BEEN LOVERS.
UHM...
"UHM"? WAIT A MINUTE.
JUST... JUST HOW CLOSE HAD YOU AND ARTHUR--
Oooooh, great. Just great.

BOOOM
KEEP FROSTY, PARAS. WE'RE ON LIMITED VISIBILITY WITH THE DENSE--
INCOMING!!!
WHAT THE HELL?!?
WHAT IS THAT, GEESE?!? IN ARMOR?!
TURN! TURN!
WHAK
TOPKICK BARELY AFFORDS A GLANCE AT THE PARADEMON-- 394 HE THINKS-- WHO IS CLIPPED BY THE JUMBO JET'S WING. PARADEMON IS TOO SLOW. PARADEMON IS OUT. IT'S JUST THAT SIMPLE.

THEY DO NOT ATTACK OR PURSUE THE AIRPLANE, FOR THEIR MISSION IS TO ATTACK POSEIDONIS AND KILL AQUAMAN. ALL ELSE IS A WASTE.
AS FOR 3g4...
...HE LIES UPON A CORAL REEF, UNABLE TO DEFEND HIMSELF AGAINST THE ADVANCING PREDATOR.
BACK AWAY FROM HIM.
AWWW. CAN I BUTT HIM, AT LEAST?
NO. I SAID GET AWAY. NO IFS, ANDS, OR BUTTS.
ARE YOU OKAY?
DON'T BE ALARMED. I'M AQUAMAN. I CAN HELP YOU... SOON AS I KNOW WHO, OR WHAT, YOU ARE.

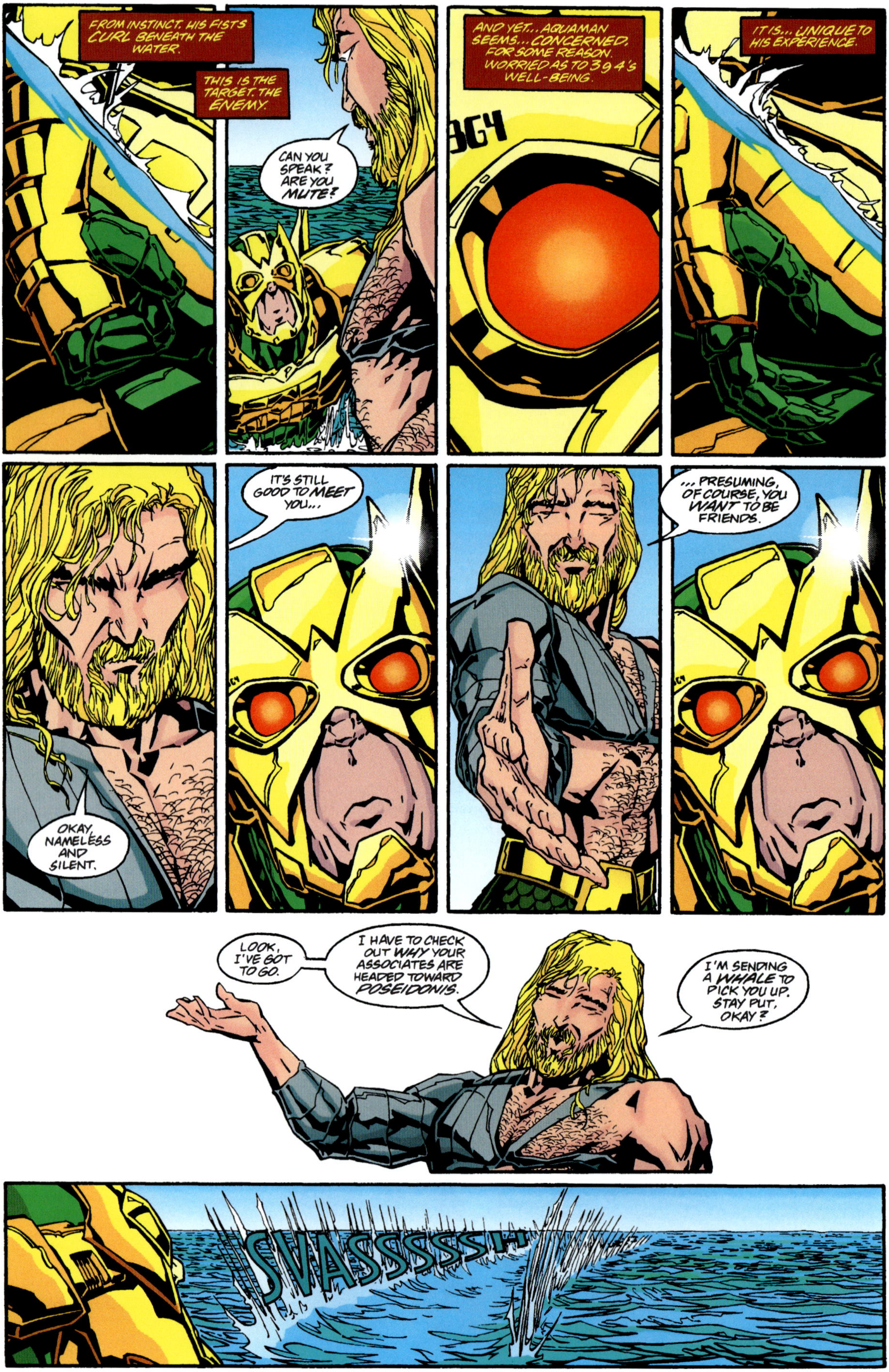
FROM INSTINCT, HIS FISTS CURL BENEATH THE WATER.
THIS IS THE TARGET. THE ENEMY.
CAN YOU SPEAK? ARE YOU MUTE?
AND YET... AQUAMAN SEEMS... CONCERNED, FOR SOME REASON. WORRIED AS TO 394's WELL-BEING.
IT IS... UNIQUE TO HIS EXPERIENCE.
OKAY, NAMELESS AND SILENT.
IT'S STILL GOOD TO MEET YOU...
...PRESUMING, OF COURSE, YOU WANT TO BE FRIENDS.
LOOK, I'VE GOT TO GO.
I HAVE TO CHECK OUT WHY YOUR ASSOCIATES ARE HEADED TOWARD POSEIDONIS.
I'M SENDING A WHALE TO PICK YOU UP. STAY PUT, OKAY?
SVASSSSSH

BUT HE MUST HAVE TOLD YOU!
AND WHAT ABOUT ATLAN? ISN'T HE AN ALL-SEEING WIZARD?
ALL-SEEING DOESN'T MEAN VOYEURISTIC.
AND NO, ARTHUR DIDN'T TELL ME. MAYBE HE THOUGHT IT'D SOUND LIKE BOASTING...
I'M WEARING ONE OF HIS OLD SHIRTS! DIDN'T THAT TELL YOU SOMETHING?
I LENT ROBIN A BATHING SUIT ONCE. DIDN'T MEAN WE WERE LOVERS.
I KNOW YOU SAY IT'S OVER, BUT HAVE YOU DISCUSSED IT WITH ARTHUR?
NOT IN SO MANY WORDS...
MAYBE HE DOESN'T KNOW THEN! HE'S NOT TELEPATHIC!
YES, HE IS!
OKAY, OKAY, POINT TAKEN. BUT STILL, I--
I... THINK WE HAVE A PROBLEM.
ATTAAAAACK!

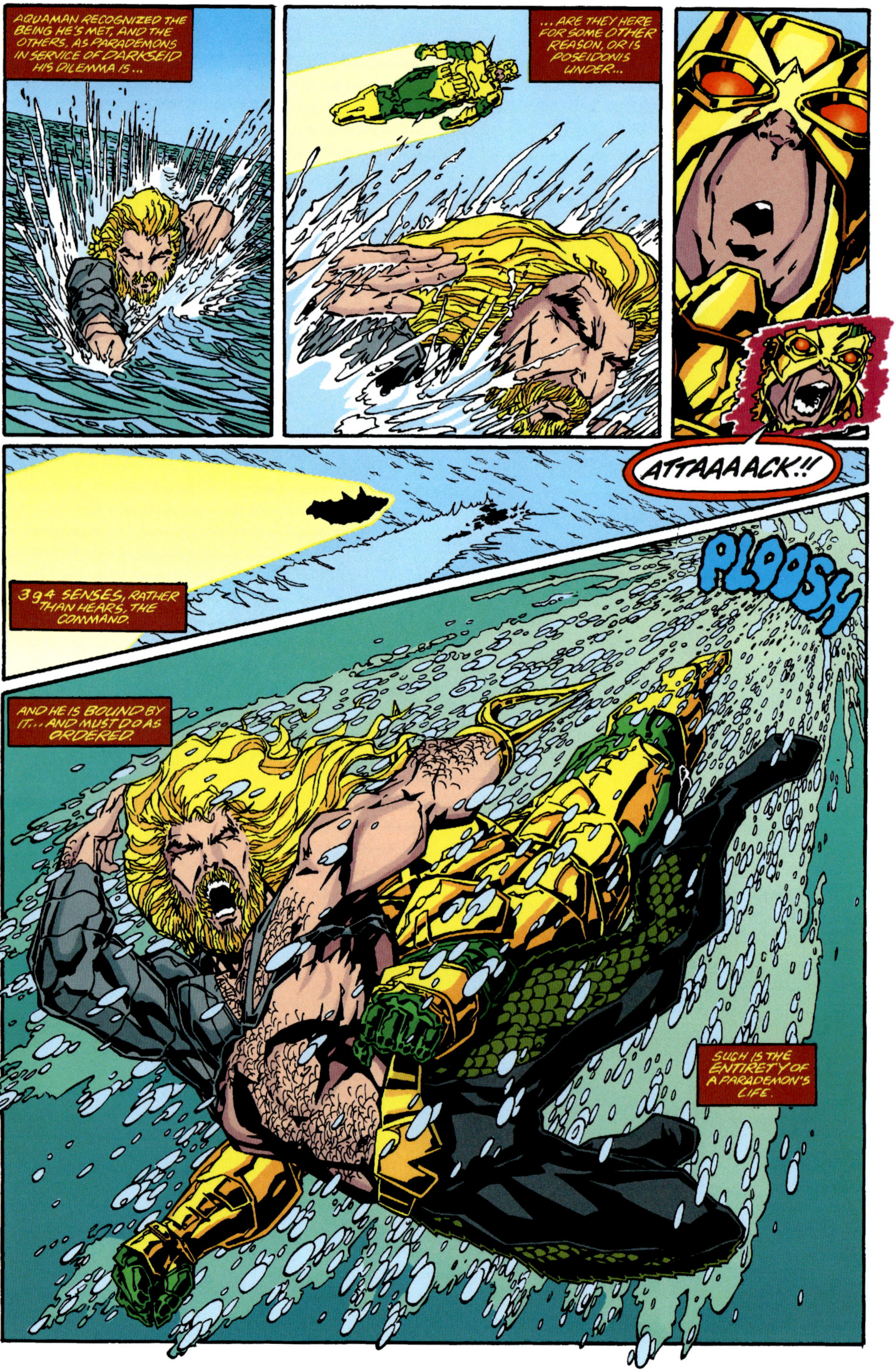
AQUAMAN RECOGNIZED THE BEING HE'S MET, AND THE OTHERS, AS PARADEMONS IN SERVICE OF DARKSEID. HIS DILEMMA IS...
...ARE THEY HERE FOR SOME OTHER REASON, OR IS POSEIDONIS UNDER...
ATTAAAACK!!
394 SENSES, RATHER THAN HEARS, THE COMMAND.
PLOOSH
AND HE IS BOUND BY IT... AND MUST DO AS ORDERED.
SUCH IS THE ENTIRETY OF A PARADEMON'S LIFE.

I SHOULD THANK YOU, I SUPPOSE.
CONSIDERING THAT YOU ATTACKED ME WITHOUT PROVOCATION, I CAN ASSUME THE REST OF YOUR "BRETHREN" MEAN NO GOOD TO MY PEOPLE.
SO AS SOON AS I DISPOSE OF YOU--
--I CAN GET DOWN TO THE BUSINESS OF MAKING MY PEOPLE SAFE.
BOK
SOMETHING STIRS WITHIN 3g4. LIKE SOME UNFAMILIAR CREATURE STRUGGLING TO BREAK LOOSE.
AND THEN... HIS MOUTH OPENS FOR A REASON OTHER THAN MEAL INTAKE.
HIS TONGUE TREMBLES WITH THE EXERTION... AND HE MANAGES TO FORM...

...A QUESTION.
WHY?
HUH?
WHY... WHAT?
WHAT ARE YOU, ANYWAY?
SOME SORT OF SYNTHETIC BEING? A MINDLESS CONSTRUCT?
YOU PROBABLY DON'T KNOW HOW TO DO ANYTHING EXCEPT WHAT YOU'RE TOLD.
AND PARDON ME FOR BEING SKITTISH REGARDING MINDLESS SLAVES.
THERE'S TROUBLE AT POSEIDONIS. I CAN'T BOTHER WITH YOU.
STAY HERE AND STAY OUT OF TROUBLE.
MAKE ONE MOVE ON ME, AND YOU'RE FISH FOOD.

WHAT ARE THEY?! WHAT ARE THEY?!?
FWOOSH
OKAY, KORMAK. LET'S SEE IF WE CAN ACTUALLY WORK TOGETHER. YOU TAKE THE RIGHT, I'LL TAKE THE LEFT.
DONE!
UNDER ORDINARY CIRCUMSTANCES, THE ICE GENERATED BY TEMPEST WOULD BE ENOUGH TO--AT THE VERY LEAST--GIVE THE PARADEMONS PAUSE.
BUT THE FIRES OF APOKOLIPS BURN WITHIN TOPKICK...
KA-VOOM
...RENDERING THE CIRCUMSTANCES FAR FROM ORDINARY.

COME ON, KORYAK. SHOW THEM WHAT YOU'RE MADE OF.
SHOW THEM YOUR--
--OHHH MY...
MOVE, VULKO!
NO ARGUMENT THERE, MY DEAR!
WELL NOW! A NEW "RECRUIT!"
OKAY, BLONDIE! LET'S SEE WHAT YOU'VE GOT!
AND FOR YOUR SAKE, IT BETTER BE A LOT MORE THAN WHAT IT LOOKS LIKE!

THE BATTLE, UNEQUAL AS IT IS, SEESAWS NONETHELESS.
KRAK
AND THEN KORYAK SPOTS A PARADEMON, DESCENDING BEHIND TEMPEST'S BACK.
TEMPEST, HIS ATTENTION DRAWN ELSEWHERE, DOESN'T SEE IT.
FOR A MOMENT STRETCHING TO ETERNITY, KORYAK IS ABOUT TO SHOUT A WARNING...
...BUT FINDS HIS LIPS WON'T FORM THE WORDS.
AND THEN...
...IT BECOMES MOOT.
HUH?
AH. NICE TIMING, ARTHUR.

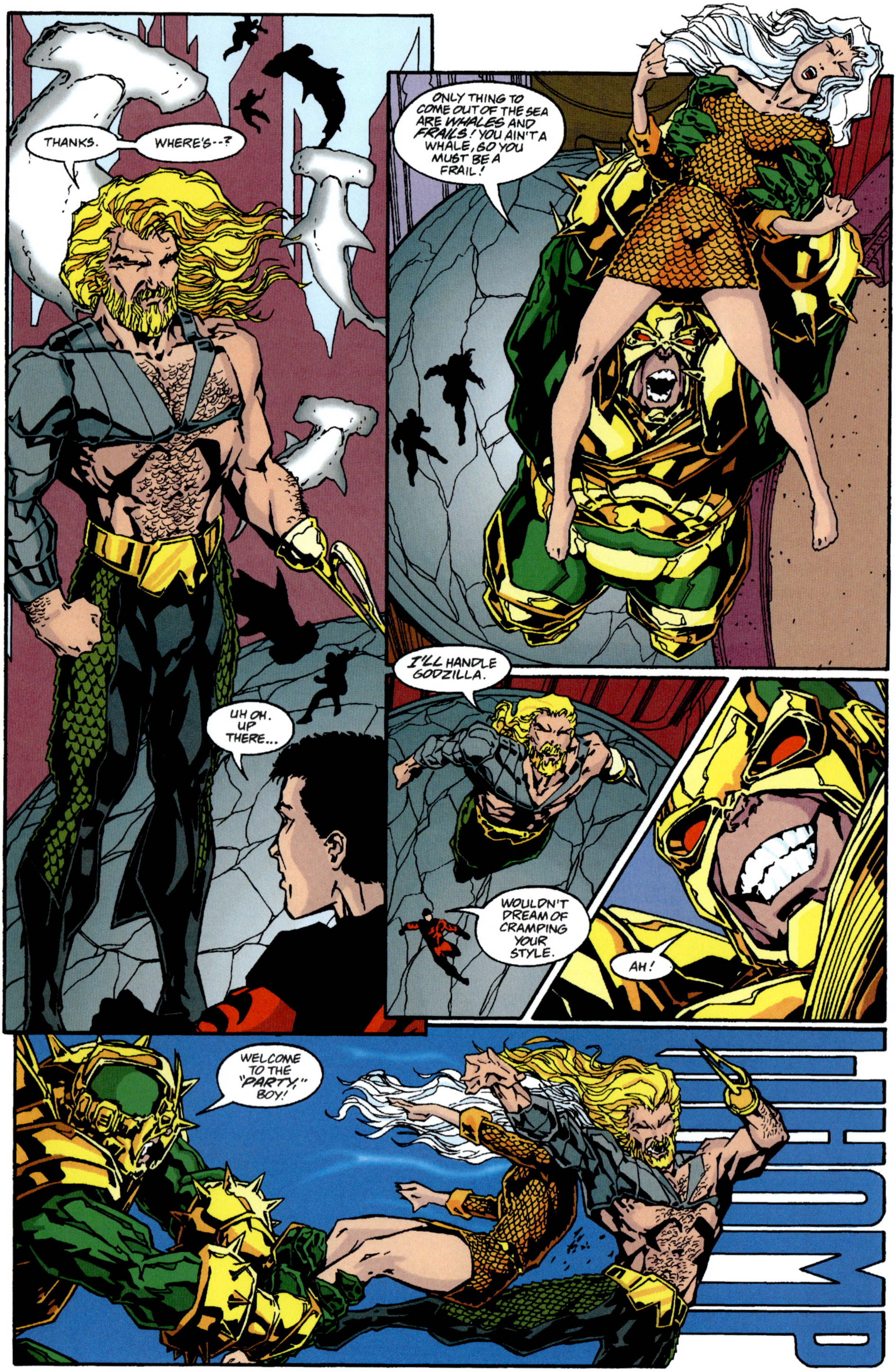
THANKS.
WHERE'S--?
ONLY THING TO COME OUT OF THE SEA ARE WHALES AND FRAILS! YOU AIN'T A WHALE, SO YOU MUST BE A FRAIL!
UH OH. UP THERE...
I'LL HANDLE GODZILLA.
WOULDN'T DREAM OF CRAMPING YOUR STYLE.
AH!
WELCOME TO THE "PARTY," BOY!
THOMP

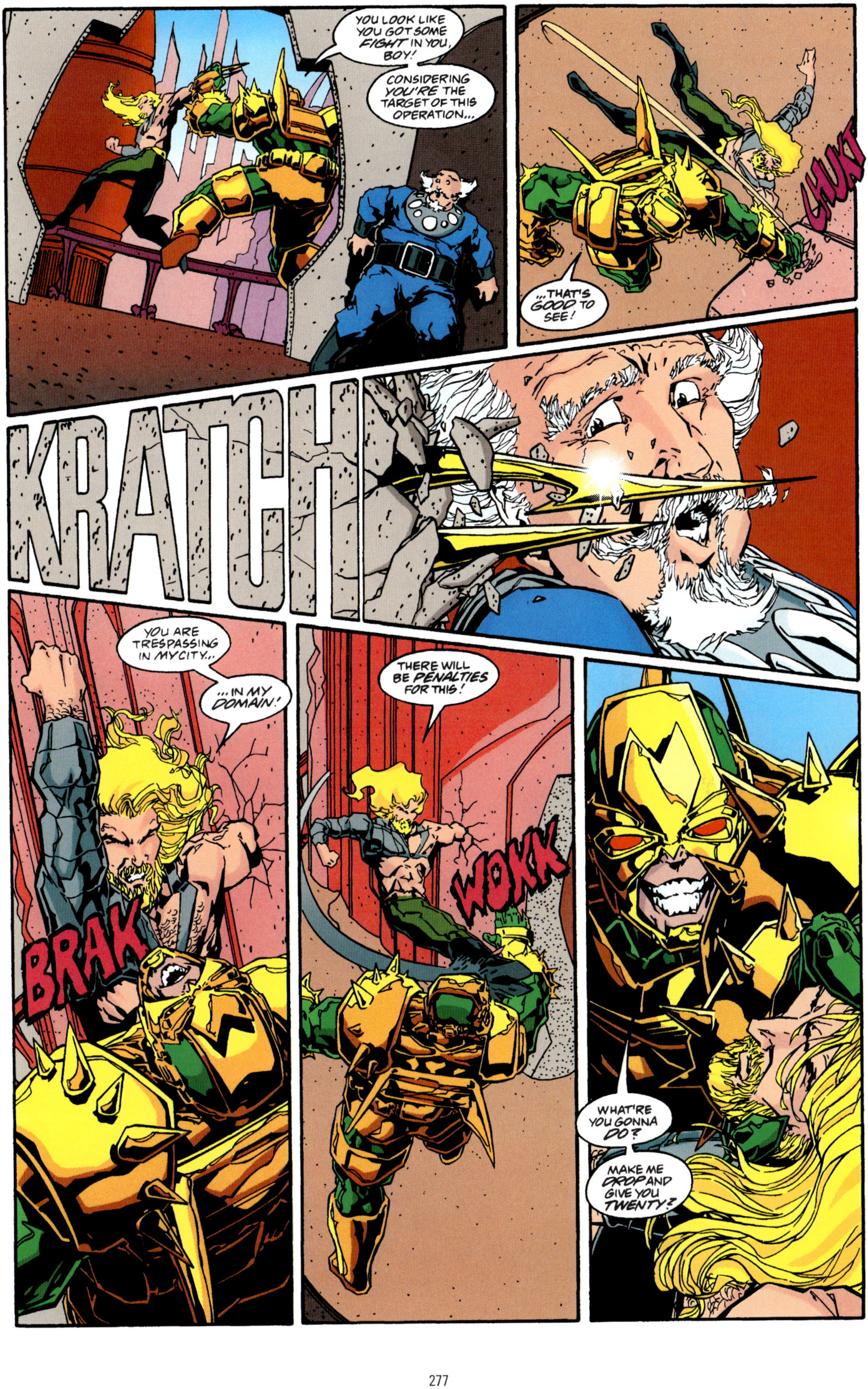
YOU LOOK LIKE YOU GOT SOME FIGHT IN YOU, BOY!
CONSIDERING YOU'RE THE TARGET OF THIS OPERATION...
CHUKT
...THAT'S GOOD TO SEE!
KRATCH
YOU ARE TRESPASSING IN MY CITY...
...IN MY DOMAIN!
BRAK
THERE WILL BE PENALTIES FOR THIS!
WOKK
WHAT'RE YOU GONNA DO?
MAKE ME DROP AND GIVE YOU TWENTY?

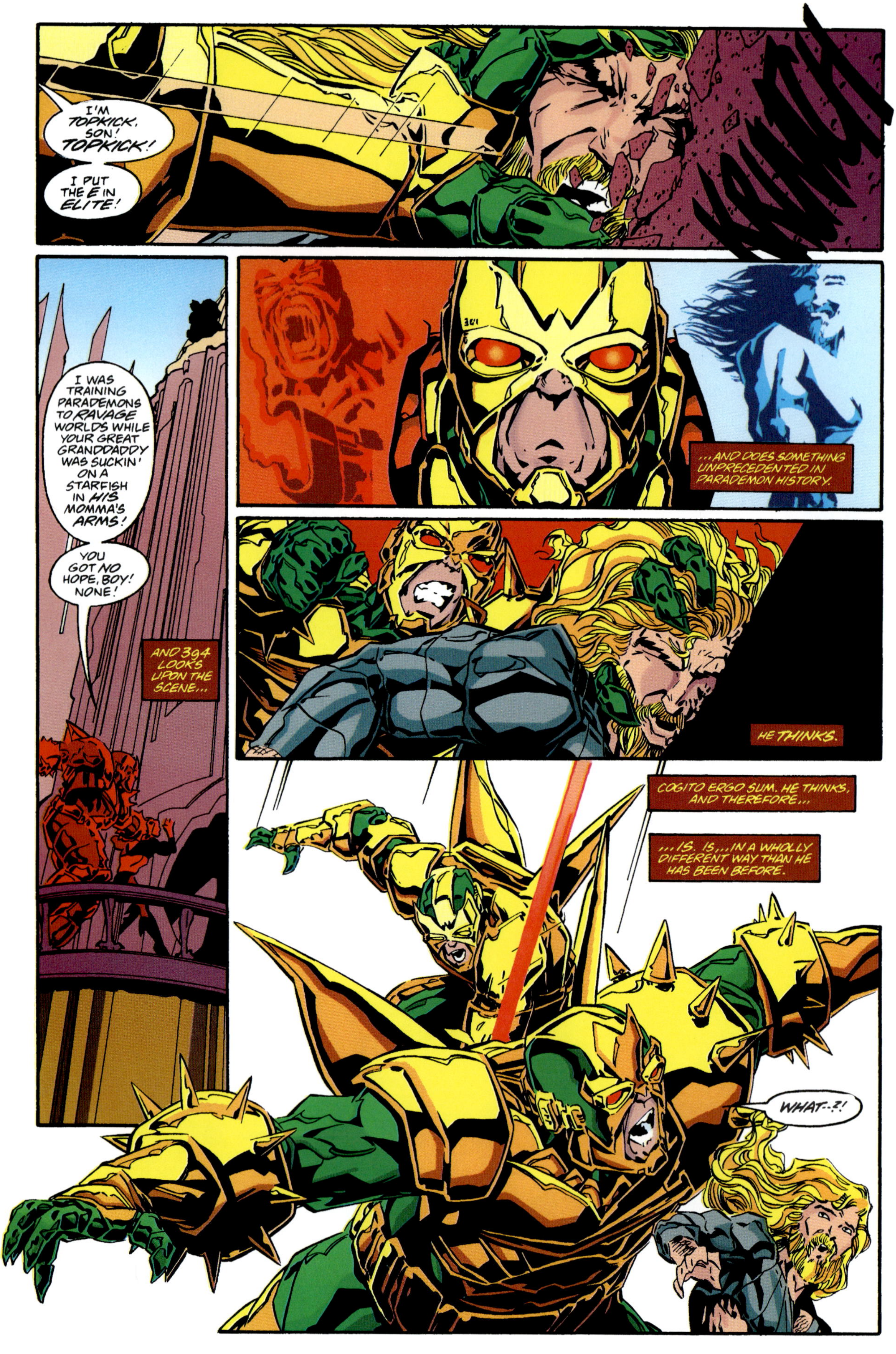
I'M TOPKICK, SON! TOPKICK!
I PUT THE E IN ELITE!
I WAS TRAINING PARADEMONS TO RAVAGE WORLDS WHILE YOUR GREAT GRANDDADDY WAS SUCKIN' ON A STARFISH IN HIS MOMMA'S ARMS!
YOU GOT NO HOPE, BOY! NONE!
AND 394 LOOKS UPON THE SCENE...
...AND DOES SOMETHING UNPRECEDENTED IN PARADEMON HISTORY.
HE THINKS.
COGITO ERGO SUM. HE THINKS, AND THEREFORE...
...IS. IS...IN A WHOLLY DIFFERENT WAY THAN HE HAS BEEN BEFORE.
WHAT--?!

GET OFF ME! WHO IS THAT?
SCHRUNNCH
3g4? SON, YOU ARE STUPID, EVEN FOR A PARADEMON!
3g4 HAS THOUGHT.
HE HAS EXISTED.
AND THEN, A HEARTBEAT LATER...
KTHAM
...HE EXISTS NO MORE.

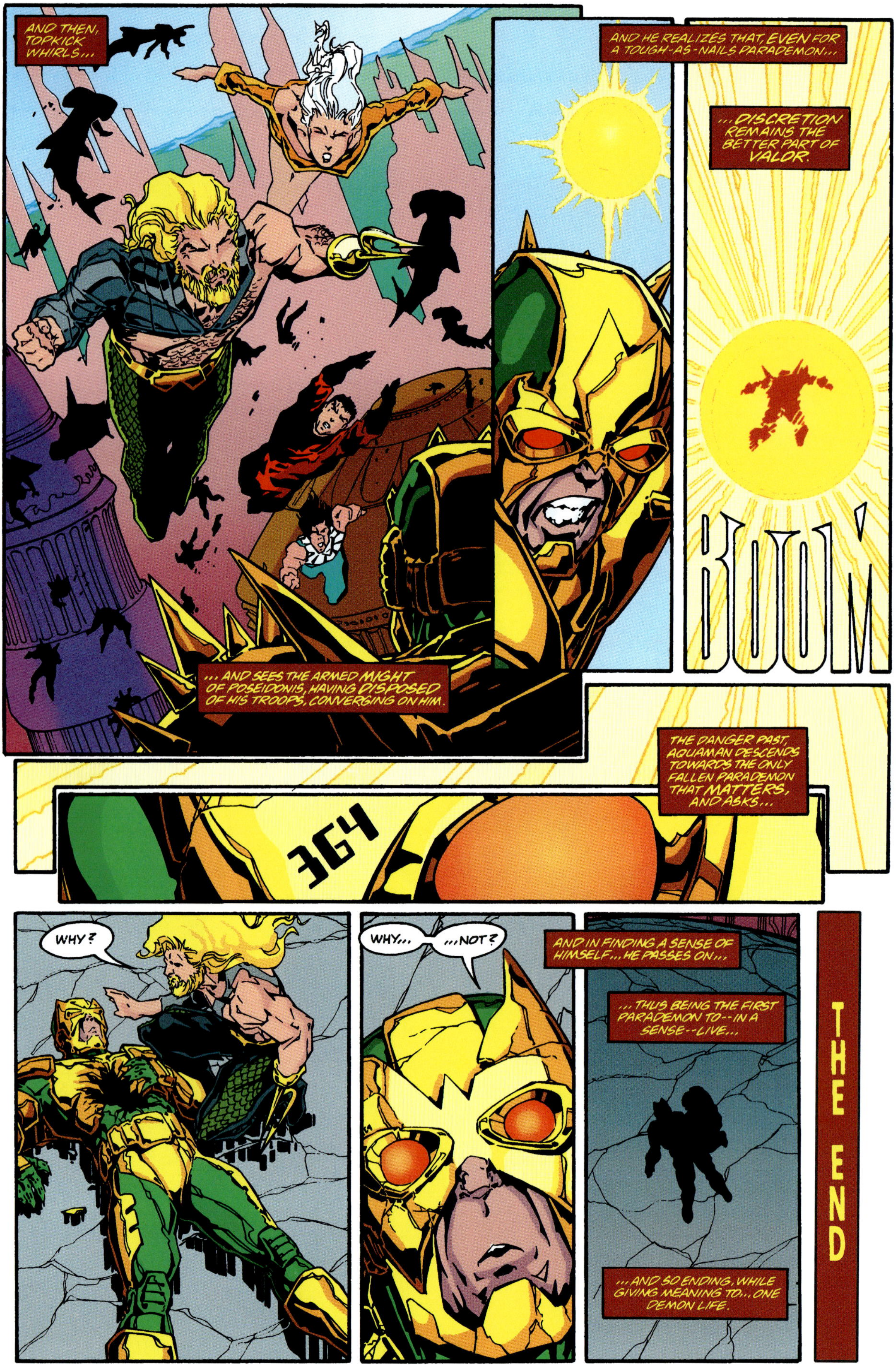
AND THEN, TOPKICK WHIRLS...
...AND SEES THE ARMED MIGHT OF POSEIDONIS, HAVING DISPOSED OF HIS TROOPS, CONVERGING ON HIM.
AND HE REALIZES THAT, EVEN FOR A TOUGH-AS-NAILS PARADEMON...
...DISCRETION REMAINS THE BETTER PART OF VALOR.
BOOM!
THE DANGER PAST, AQUAMAN DESCENDS TOWARDS THE ONLY FALLEN PARADEMON THAT MATTERS, AND ASKS...
364
WHY?
WHY...
...NOT?
AND IN FINDING A SENSE OF HIMSELF... HE PASSES ON...
...THUS BEING THE FIRST PARADEMON TO--IN A SENSE--LIVE...
...AND SO ENDING, WHILE GIVING MEANING TO... ONE DEMON LIFE.
THE END

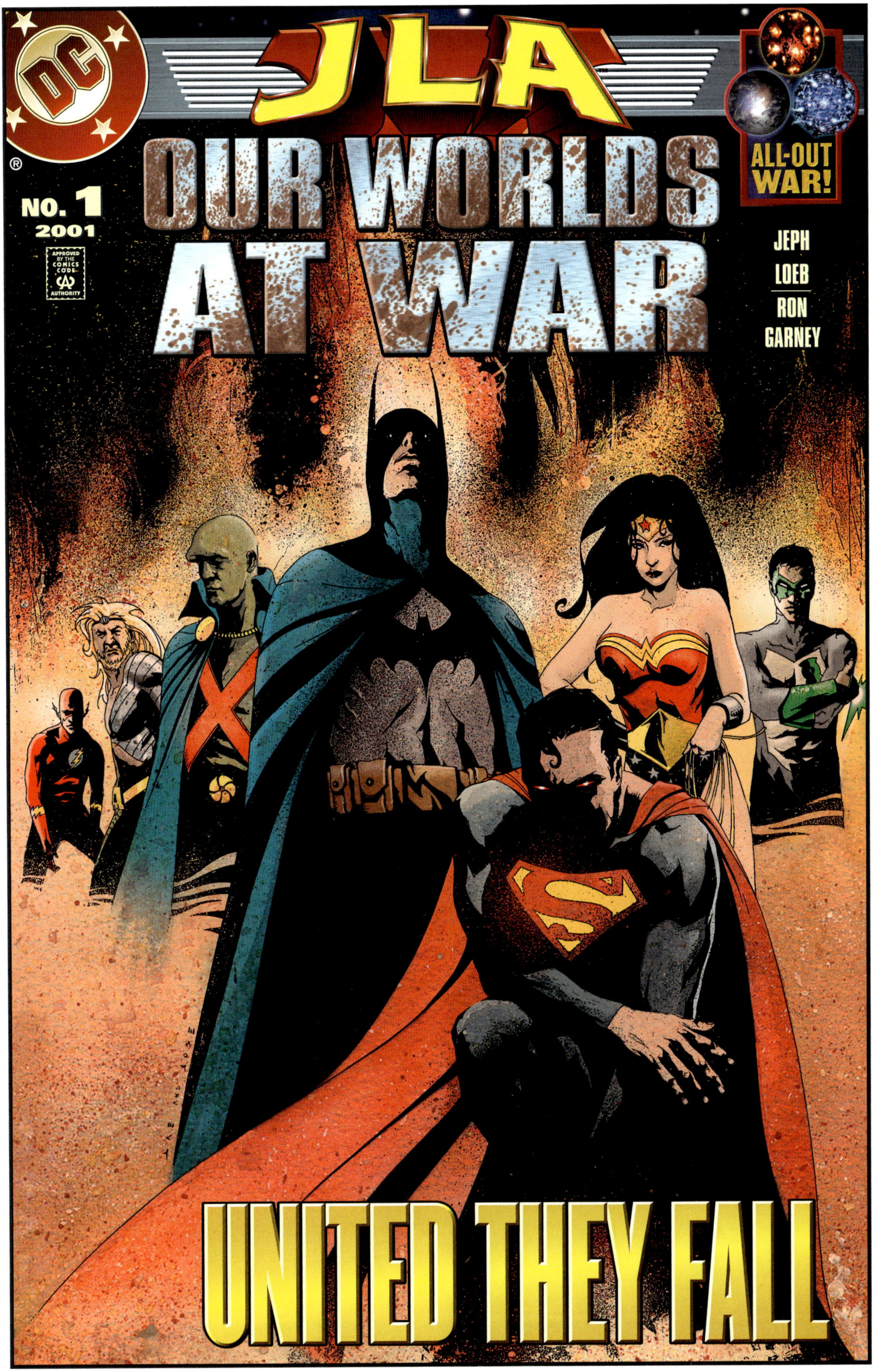
DC
JLA
OUR WORLDS AT WAR
NO. 1
2001
APPROVED BY THE COMICS CODE AUTHORITY
ALL-OUT WAR!
JEPH LOEB
RON GARNEY
UNITED THEY FALL

DEADMAN LIVES AGAIN!
AQUAMAN STANDS ALONE!
JUSTICE LEAGUE of AMERICA
STARRO THE CONQUEROR
METAMORPHO
AQUAMAN
SUPER FRIENDS
Adventure COMICS
AQUAMAN
Manhunter Mars Hawkman
AQUAMAN
DOOM from DIMENSION AQUA!
AQUAMAN
URBAN RENEWAL!
UNDERWORLD
DC UNIVERSE REBIRTH
AQUAMAN
DC UNIVERSE REBIRTH
AQUAMAN
AQUAMAN
WHO DESTROYS THE SEA KING
THE OCEAN MASTER OR BLACK MANTA?
AQUAMAN
ARTHUR CURRY JUNIOR
THE NEW 52!
AQUAMAN
IS THIS MY FOE?
AQUAMAN
AQUAMAN
JABBERJAW
CAPTAIN CAVEMAN
the BRAVE and the BOLD
BATMAN
AQUAMAN
THE SLEEP-WALKER FROM THE SEA!
THE NEW 52!
JUSTICE LEAGUE
AQUAMAN
AQUAMAN
AQUAMAN A COWARD?
THE OCEAN MASTER!
THE BEGINNING OF TOMORROW
AQUAMAN
AQUAMAN
IN THE SHADOWY DEPTHS OF ATLANTIS, HIS LIFE WILL CHANGE FOREVER!
THE NEW 52!
AQUAMAN
YEAR ONE
AQUAMAN
1995 ANNUAL
AQUAMAN
WHO DESTROYS THE SEA KING
GENESIS
AQUAMAN
AQUAMAN
SWORD OF ATLANTIS
KURT BUSIEK
BUTCH GUICE
the King of the Seas
AQUAMAN
LEADS THE ARMY TO BATTLE!
AQUAMAN
YOU DIP THIS TO HER!
AND NOW... YOU DIE!!
AQUAMAN

ON DECEMBER 7, 1941, JAPAN BOMBED PEARL HARBOR IN HAWAII.
IT WAS THE FIRST TIME IN MODERN AMERICAN HISTORY THAT A FOREIGN COUNTRY MADE AN ATTACK ON U.S. SOIL.
AMERICA WOULD THEN ENTER WORLD WAR II. BEFORE IT WAS OVER, MILLIONS WOULD DIE THROUGHOUT THE WORLD; ALLIANCES WOULD BE FORGED AND BROKEN; AND THE FUTURE IRREVOCABLY ALTERED.
HELP.
ON THE FOLLOWING DAY, PRESIDENT FRANKLIN DELANO ROOSEVELT DELIVERED TO CONGRESS "THE PEARL HARBOR SPEECH."

"To the Congress of The United States:
"Yesterday, December 7, 1941 -- a date which will live in infamy...

MARTIAN MANHUNTER IS DOWN. I'M AFRAID WE LET ANOTHER ONE GET BY US!
DON'T KNOW HOW LONG J'ONN WILL MAINTAIN THE TELEPATHIC LINK. WE MIGHT HAVE TO GO ELECTRONIC --
THIS STORY TAKES PLACE RIGHT AFTER SUPERMAN #172 -- ED.

"-- the United States was suddenly and deliberately attacked by naval and air forces of the Empire of Japan.
NNNNGGNNN
FLASH I CAN'T KEEP THIS UP --!
I'M ON IT, GL!

THE ALIEN ALLIANCE
MIGHT'VE SUFFERED A SETBACK --

EXTRA!!
DEADMAN LIVES AGAIN!
AQUAMAN STANDS ALONE
HE'S THE DEADLIEST MAN ALIVE
ARTHUR CURRY JUNIOR
THE LEGEND OF AQUAMAN
The Brave and the Bold
JUSTICE LEAGUE OF AMERICA
"STARRO THE CONQUEROR!"
METAMORPHO
AQUAMAN
SUPER FRIENDS
Adventure Comics
AQUAMAN
Manhunter
Mars
Hawkman
AQUAMAN
AQUAMAN
AQUAMAN
URBAN RENEWAL!
UNDERWORLD
DC UNIVERSE REBIRTH
AQUAMAN
DC UNIVERSE REBIRTH
AQUAMAN
AQUAMAN
WHO DESTROYS THE SEA KING
The OCEAN MASTER or... BLACK MANTA?
DOOM from DIMENSION "AQUA"
AQUAMAN
DC COMICS
THE NEW 52!
AQUAMAN
JOHNS
REIS
PRADO
AQUAMAN
IS THIS MY FOE!
AQUAMAN
AQUAMAN
JABBERJAW
CAPTAIN CAVEMAN
the BRAVE and the BOLD
BATMAN
AQUAMAN
The SLEEP-WALKER from the SEA!
DC COMICS
THE NEW 52!
JUSTICE LEAGUE
JOHNS
LEE
WILLIAMS
AQUAMAN
AQUAMAN
AQUAMAN A COWARD? IS HE REALLY IN TERROR OF The OCEAN MASTER?
THE BEGINNING OF TOMORROW!
AQUAMAN
AQUAMAN
IN THE SHADOWY DEPTHS OF ATLANTIS, HIS LIFE WILL CHANGE FOREVER!
DC COMICS
THE NEW 52!
AQUAMAN
JOHNS
REIS
PRADO
YEAR ONE
AQUAMAN
1995 ANNUAL
AQUAMAN
WHO DESTROYS THE SEA KING
GENESIS
AQUAMAN
AQUAMAN
SWORD OF ATLANTIS
KURT BUSIEK
BUTCH GUICE
The KING of the SEAS
AQUAMAN
AQUAMAN
YOU!
YOU DID THIS TO HER!
AND NOW... YOU DIE!!
AQUAMAN

"The United States was at peace with that nation and...
-- BUT THE JUSTICE LEAGUE IS THE BEST LINE OF DEFENSE FOR EARTH!
ROOM
AAAAG!

"...at the solicitation of Japan, was still in conversation with the government and its Emperor looking toward the maintenance of peace in the Pacific."
WHY DO YOU RESIST?
YOU COULD NO MORE STOP THE HOLLOWING THAN YOUR OWN SUN FROM RISING.
CALL US "WACKY." BUT, THE WAY WE HEARD IT --
-- OUR SUPERMAN HAS ALREADY STOPPED YOUR UNSTOPPABLE PLANS ONCE.*
ER... HOW MANY OF THEM ARE YOU?

ZZRAKK
GAAAH!!
* SEE SUPERMAN #153

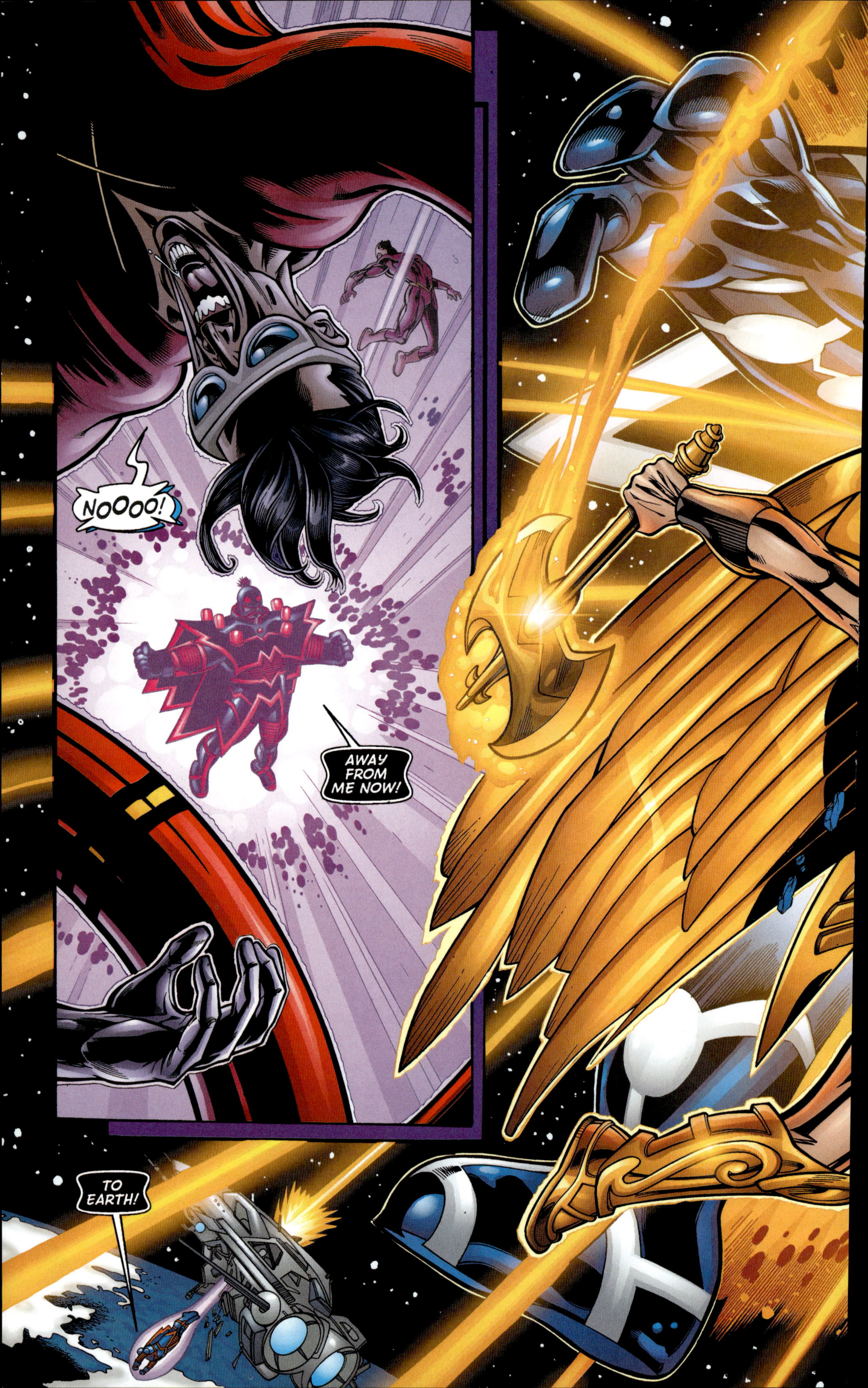
NOOOO!
AWAY FROM ME NOW!
TO EARTH!

SINCE THE DAWN OF TIME, THE WILL OF IMPERIEX HAS BEEN HEEDED.
TO FIGHT THIS IS MERELY TO HASTEN YOUR OWN DEMISE.
HAVE AT HIM, AQUAMAN! THE LEAGUE CANNOT HAVE FALLEN IN VAIN.
I WOULD NEVER DO OTHERWISE, WONDER WOMAN!
ALL I WANT TO KNOW IS --
-- WHERE THE DEVIL ARE BATMAN AND SUPERMAN?!
"Indeed, one hour after Japanese air squadrons had commenced bombing in Oahu, the Japanese ambassador to the United States and his colleagues delivered to the Secretary of State a formal reply to a recent American message."

LIVES AGAIN!
AQUAMAN STANDS ALONE!
LEGEND OF AQUAMAN
JUSTICE LEAGUE of AMERICA
METAMORPHO
AQUAMAN
SUPER FRIENDS
Adventure COMICS
AQUAMAN
Manhunter Mars Hawkman
AQUAMAN
AQUAMAN
DOOM from DIMENSION AQUA!
AQUAMAN
URBAN RENEWAL!
UNDERWORLD
REBIRTH
AQUAMAN
DC UNIVERSE REBIRTH
AQUAMAN
AQUAMAN
Who Destroys the Sea King
The OCEAN MASTER or BLACK MANTA?
AQUAMAN
ARTHUR CURRY JUNIOR
THE NEW 52!
AQUAMAN
IS THIS MY FOE!
AQUAMAN
AQUAMAN
JABBERJAW
CAPTAIN CAVEMAN
the BRAVE and the BOLD
BATMAN
AQUAMAN
The SLEEP-WALKER From the SEA!
THE NEW 52!
JUSTICE LEAGUE
AQUAMAN
AQUAMAN
AQUAMAN, A COWARD? IS HE REALLY IN TERROR OF... The OCEAN MASTER?
THE BEGINNING OF TOMORROW!
AQUAMAN
AQUAMAN
IN THE SHADOWY DEPTHS OF ATLANTIS, HIS LIFE WILL CHANGE FOREVER!
THE NEW 52!
AQUAMAN
YEAR ONE
1995 ANNUAL
AQUAMAN
AQUAMAN
Who Destroys the Sea King
GENESIS
AQUAMAN
AQUAMAN
SWORD OF ATLANTIS
KURT BUSIEK
BUTCH GUICE
The King of the Seas
AQUAMAN
Leads the Army to Battle!
AQUAMAN
YOU!
YOU DID THIS TO HER!
AND NOW... YOU DIE!!
AQUAMAN

DEAD!
BECAUSE OF YOUR "SUPERMAN" THE DEMOLITION OF THIS GALAXY HAS BEEN WAYLAID.
HE WAS ONLY THE FIRST OF MANY TARGETS STRUCK UPON THIS DAY!*
THERE CANNOT BE -- THERE WILL NOT BE ANY FURTHER DELAYS.
"While this reply stated that it seemed useless to continue the existing diplomatic negotiations, it contained no threat or hint of war or armed attack."
* SEE SUPERMAN #172 -- ON SALE NOW!

GOTHAM CITY. NOW.
ORACLE?
I'M ZZTZZ ONLINE ZZTTZ BATMAN. ZZTZ APPARENTLY ZZTTZ WE'RE NOT THE ONLY ZTZZ PLACE THAT'S ZZTZZ BEEN HIT.
SOMETHING TOOK ZTZZ TOPEKA, KANSAS OFF ZTTZZ THE MAP.
KANSAS...?
FIND NIGHTWING. ROBIN. BATGIRL. HUNTRESS, IF YOU HAVE TO.
AND CONTACT THE J.L.A. TELL THEM GOTHAM CITY HAS TO BE MY PRIORITY RIGHT NOW...
"It will be recorded that the distance of Hawaii from Japan makes it obvious that the attack was deliberately planned many days or even weeks ago."

SMALLVILLE, KANSAS. NOW.
THE KENTS
51
"During the intervening time, The Japanese Government has deliberately sought to deceive the United States by false statements and expressions of hope for continued peace."
THIS IS THE EMERGENCY BROADCASTING SYSTEM. WE ARE GETTING REPORTS NOW THAT A MASSIVE EXPLOSION HAS OCCURRED IN TOPEKA, KANSAS.
AFTERSHOCKS HAVE BEEN FELT AS FAR WEST AS SALINA AND AS FAR SOUTH AS WICHITA. DAMAGE IS EXTREMELY HIGH.
STAY INDOORS. REPEAT. STAY INDOORS. THOSE OF YOU WITH TORNADO CELLARS, REMAIN THERE.
THIS IS THE EMERGENCY BROADCASTING SYSTEM.

J'ONN.
TELL THE LEAGUE.
I'M ON MY WAY.
"The attack yesterday on the Hawaiian Islands has caused severe damage to American naval and military forces."

DEADMAN LIVES AGAIN!
AQUAMAN STANDS ALONE!
JUSTICE LEAGUE of AMERICA
STARRO THE CONQUEROR!
METAMORPHO AQUAMAN
SUPER FRIENDS
Adventure Comics
AQUAMAN
AQUAMAN
AQUAMAN
DOOM from DIMENSION AQUA!
AQUAMAN
URBAN RENEWAL!
UNDERWORLD
DC UNIVERSE REBIRTH
AQUAMAN
DC UNIVERSE REBIRTH
AQUAMAN
AQUAMAN
WHO DESTROYS THE SEA KING
The OCEAN MASTER or BLACK MANTA?
ARTHUR CURRY JUNIOR
A NOVEL-LENGTH SEA SPECTACULAR!
DC COMICS
THE NEW 52!
AQUAMAN
IS THIS MY FOE!
AQUAMAN
AQUAMAN
JABBERJAW
CAPTAIN CAVEMAN
the BRAVE and the BOLD
BATMAN
AQUAMAN
The SLEEP-WALKER From the SEA!
DC COMICS
THE NEW 52!
JUSTICE LEAGUE
AQUAMAN
AQUAMAN A COWARD? IS HE REALLY IN TERROR OF... The OCEAN MASTER?
THE BEGINNING OF TOMORROW!
AQUAMAN
AQUAMAN
IN THE SHADOWY DEPTHS OF ATLANTIS, HIS LIFE WILL CHANGE FOREVER!
DC COMICS
THE NEW 52!
AQUAMAN
YEAR ONE
1995 ANNUAL
AQUAMAN
WHO DESTROYS THE SEA KING
GENESIS
AQUAMAN
AQUAMAN
SWORD OF ATLANTIS
KURT BUSIEK
BUTCH GUICE
The King of the Seas
AQUAMAN
Leads his army to Battle!
AQUAMAN
YOU!
YOU DID THIS TO HER!
AND NOW... YOU DIE!!
AQUAMAN

"Very many American lives have been lost."
HE CAN INTERCEPT OUR TELEPATHIC LINK!
IMPERIEX CAN ACHIEVE ANYTHING!
AGGG!
NO.
NO, YOU CAN'T.
SCHBOOM
NNNYAH!
YOU'VE DEALT WITH THESE BEFORE?
"THESE"? THERE WAS ONE!
NOT ANY-MORE.

THE ARMOR WILL CRACK-- BUT IT'S FOR ENERGY CONTAINMENT.
IF I HADN'T CAUTERIZED IT AS I SNATCHED YOU, ARTHUR--
THEN, WE'LL RIP THIS ONE OPEN AND HEAD AFTER THE OTHERS!
JACAKK
DIANA, NO! IT'LL EXPLODE!
"In addition, American ships have been reported torpedoed on the high seas between San Francisco and Honolulu."

"Yesterday, the Japanese government also launched an attack against Malaya."

I CAN'T HEAR A HEARTBEAT.

NOT DIANA... PLEASE... NOT DIANA...
CLARK.
WE HAVE TO GET HER AND THE OTHERS TO SAFETY.
OTHERS...?
"Last night, Japanese forces attacked Hong Kong."

"Last night, Japanese forces attacked Guam."
WE CAN HELP GET YOUR WOUNDED TO SAFETY.
A TRIAGE CENTER AND MEDICAL SERVICES ARE AVAILABLE ABOARD THE PARADOCS.*
GOOD ENOUGH. I... SINCE WONDER WOMAN NEEDS THE MOST IMMEDIATE ATTENTION, I'LL TAKE HER IN FIRST.
MAXIMA AND STARFIRE. STRANGE ALLIANCES, INDEED.
* SEE MAN OF STEEL #115 AND YOUNG JUSTICE #35.
I'LL BE BACK AS QUICKLY AS I CAN.
HE CARES FOR HER, THAT ONE.
OF COURSE, WE ALL CARE FOR DIANA.
AQUAMAN, I'M A LITTLE SURPRISED TO FIND YOU HERE WITH WHAT'S HAPPENED.
AN IMPERIEX PROBE HIT OUTSIDE THE CAPITAL CITY IN ATLANTIS.
WHAT? GET ME TO A JLA TELEPORTER.
AND REMIND SUPERMAN...
...THE OCEANS COVER THREE FOURTHS OF THE PLANET.
IF ATLANTIS FALLS -- SO FALL THE REST OF YOU!
NOT TOO ARROGANT.
IS IT ARROGANCE TO SPEAK THE TRUTH?
IF SO, I LIKE THAT IN A MAN...

THE PARADOCS. SPACE ARK. NOW.
"Last night, Japanese forces attacked the Philippine Islands."
THE J.S.A. WAS ASSEMBLED-- BUT I CAME UP HERE AS SOON AS I HEARD.
HOW IS MY DAUGHTER --?
GAEA..

HIPPOLYTA.
DIANA... SHE NEEDS YOUR HELP.
"Last night, Japanese forces attacked Wake Island."

"This morning, Japanese forces attacked Midway Island."
WASHINGTON, D.C. NOW.
MR. PRESIDENT.
WHILE THEY SUCCEEDED IN TURNING BACK ONE IMPERIEX PROBE --
-- THE JUSTICE LEAGUE GOT THEIR HEADS HANDED TO THEM.
THE BOYS AT N.O.R.A.D. REPORT IMPERIEX PROBES HAVE SO FAR TARGETED SEVERAL MAJOR CITIES.
TOPEKA. KRASNOYARSK. FRANKFURT. ATLANTIS --
I KNOW, DAMMIT!
SIR --?
-- HOW COULD YOU KNOW? THIS INFO JUST CAME IN HOT FROM N.O.R.A.D.
AS PRESIDENT, IT IS MY JOB TO KNOW.
NOW, GENERAL ROCK. TELL ME SOMETHING I DON'T KNOW.

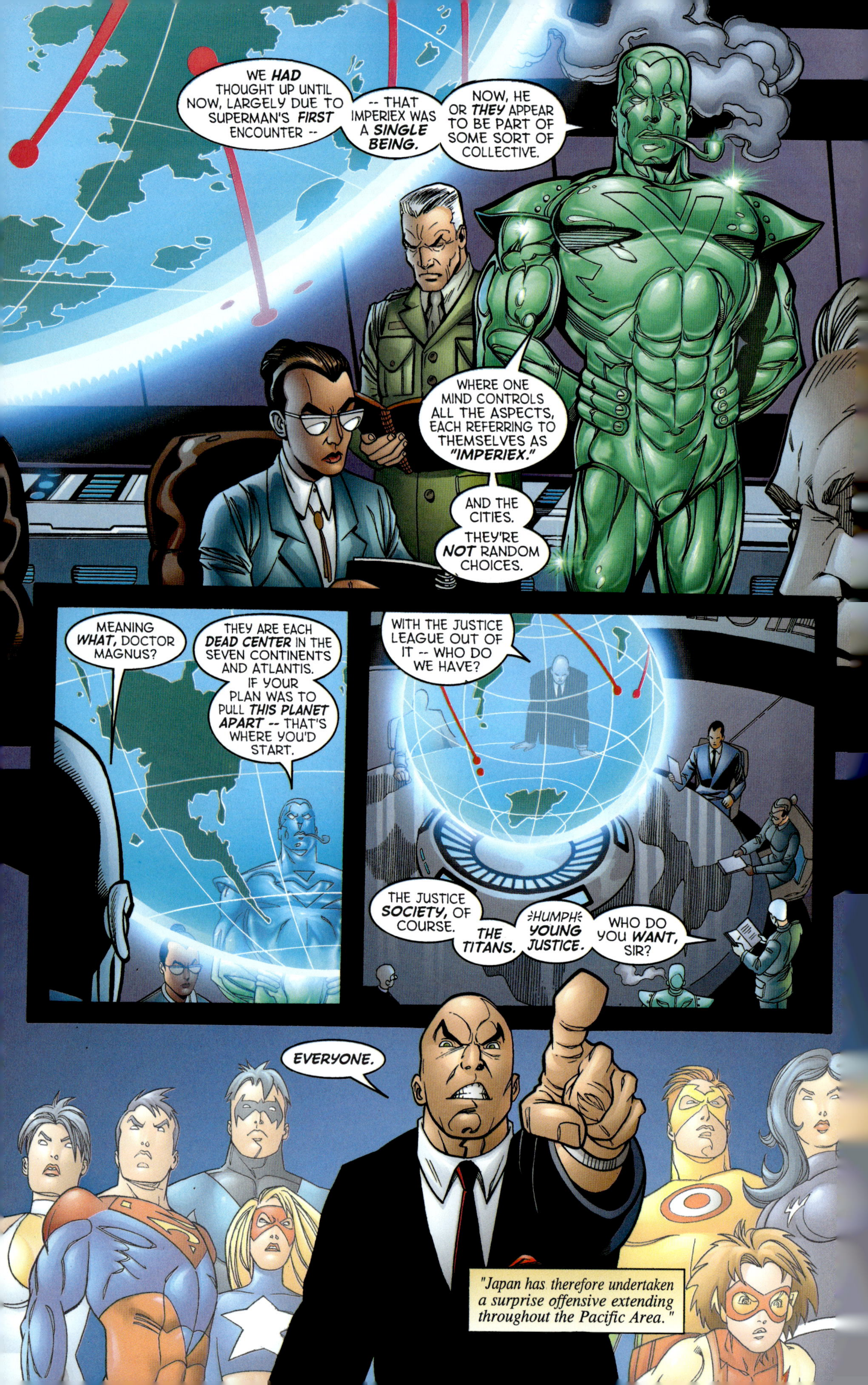
WE HAD THOUGHT UP UNTIL NOW, LARGELY DUE TO SUPERMAN'S FIRST ENCOUNTER --
-- THAT IMPERIEX WAS A SINGLE BEING.
NOW, HE OR THEY APPEAR TO BE PART OF SOME SORT OF COLLECTIVE.
WHERE ONE MIND CONTROLS ALL THE ASPECTS, EACH REFERRING TO THEMSELVES AS "IMPERIEX."
AND THE CITIES. THEY'RE NOT RANDOM CHOICES.
MEANING WHAT, DOCTOR MAGNUS?
THEY ARE EACH DEAD CENTER IN THE SEVEN CONTINENTS AND ATLANTIS. IF YOUR PLAN WAS TO PULL THIS PLANET APART -- THAT'S WHERE YOU'D START.
WITH THE JUSTICE LEAGUE OUT OF IT -- WHO DO WE HAVE?
THE JUSTICE SOCIETY, OF COURSE.
THE TITANS.
HUMPH YOUNG JUSTICE.
WHO DO YOU WANT, SIR?
EVERYONE.
"Japan has therefore undertaken a surprise offensive extending throughout the Pacific Area."

KRASNOYARSK, RUSSIA. NOW.
URK--
I KNEW THIS WAS A BAD IDEA.
THE MOMENT I HEARD "SEND IN GUY GARDNER, BOOSTER GOLD AND BLUE BEETLE--"
--I JUST KNEW IT. THE JUSTICE LEAGUE RESERVES.
RESERVED FOR WHAT?!
BEETLE! HE'S KILLED GUY!
JUST TELL ME HOW TO KILL THIS THING!
"The facts of yesterday speak for themselves."

"The people of the United States have already formed their opinions and well understand the implications to the very life and safety of our nation."
FRANKFURT, GERMANY. GENERAL ZOD AND IGNITION.
ZAIRE, AFRICA. THE TITANS.
SOUTH POLE; ANTARCTICA. THE OUTSIDERS.

"As Commander in Chief of the Army and Navy, I have directed all measures be taken for our defense."
THE PARADOCS. SPACE ARK. DEEP SPACE. NOW.
DID WE WIN?
GET SOME REST, KYLE.
WELL... WE'LL GET 'EM NEXT TIME, RIGHT?
RIGHT, WALLY?
Y'KNOW, I WAS JUST THINKING ABOUT HOW LONELY IT IS UP HERE, BUT THE TERRIBLE FOOD MORE THAN MAKES UP FOR IT.
LOIS...

"Always remember the character of the onslaught against us."
YOU OKAY, SMALLVILLE...?
SMALLVILLE.
LOIS... I...
CLARK. WHAT IS IT? WHAT'S HAPPENED?
ATLANTIS IS UNDER ATTACK. AQUAMAN NEEDS YOU. NOW!
ATLANTIS!
I HAVE TO GO.
TIME IS BEING WASTED HERE!
YES. IS...
...IS THERE ANYTHING YOU NEED ME TO DO FOR YOU?

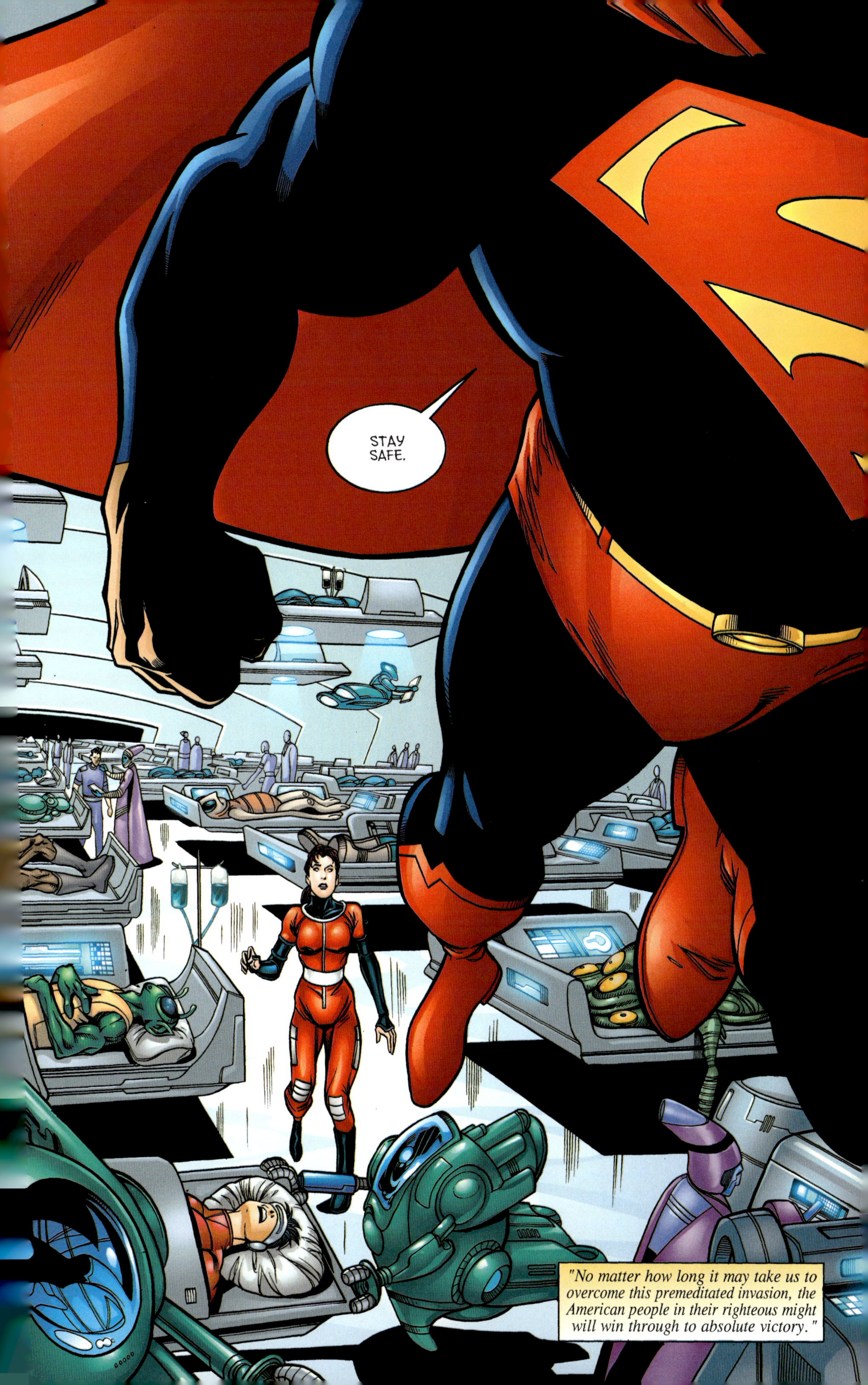
STAY SAFE.
"No matter how long it may take us to overcome this premeditated invasion, the American people in their righteous might will win through to absolute victory."

ATLANTIS. UNDER THE SEA. NOW.
"I believe I interpret the will of Congress of the People..."
MERA --
THERE ARE NO WORDS FOR US TO SAY.
THE SITUATION IS TOO DIRE FOR ANYTHING OTHER THAN DOING WHAT IS BEST FOR ATLANTIS AND HER PEOPLE.
"...when I assert that we will not only defend ourselves to the uttermost..."
TEMPEST.
GARTH.
IF I SHOULD FALL-- YOU KNOW WHAT YOU MUST DO TO SAVE ATLANTIS.
YOU WILL NOT FALL.
"...but will make certain that this form of treachery shall never endanger us again."
MAY FATHER NEPTUNE WATCH OVER YOU. MAY HIS TRIDENT'S POWER BE YOUR POWER.
MAY HE WATCH OVER US ALL.

"Hostilities exist."
WHETHER IN THE OCEAN OF SPACE OR THE SEA --
-- IT MATTERS LITTLE.
IMPERIEX WILL NOT BE DENIED.
THIS WORLD WILL DIE.
FOR ATLANTIS!
KLANG

LIVES AGAIN!
LEGEND OF AQUAMAN
JUSTICE LEAGUE of AMERICA
STARRO THE CONQUEROR!
METAMORPHO AQUAMAN
SUPER FRIENDS
Adventure COMICS
AQUAMAN
Manhunter Mars vs HAWKMAN
AQUAMAN
AQUAMAN
DOOM from DIMENSION AQUA!
AQUAMAN
URBAN RENEWAL!
UNDERWORLD
REBIRTH
AQUAMAN
DC UNIVERSE REBIRTH
AQUAMAN
AQUAMAN
Who Destroys the Sea King
The OCEAN MASTER? or BLACK MANTA?
AQUAMAN
ARTHUR CURRY JUNIOR
A NOVEL-LENGTH SEA SPECTACULAR!
DC COMICS THE NEW 52!
AQUAMAN
AQUAMAN
IS THIS MY FOE!
AQUAMAN
AQUAMAN
JABBERJAW
CAPTAIN CAVEMAN
the BRAVE and the BOLD presents
BATMAN
AQUAMAN
The SLEEP-WALKER from the SEA!
DC COMICS THE NEW 52!
JUSTICE LEAGUE
AQUAMAN
The WEDDING of AQUAMAN!
AQUAMAN
AQUAMAN A COWARD? IS HE REALLY IN TERROR OF... The OCEAN MASTER?
THE BEGINNING OF TOMORROW!
AQUAMAN
AQUAMAN
IN THE SHADOWY DEPTHS OF ATLANTIS, HIS LIFE WILL CHANGE FOREVER!
DC COMICS THE NEW 52!
AQUAMAN
YEAR ONE
1995 ANNUAL
AQUAMAN
AQUAMAN
Who Destroys the Sea King
GENESIS
AQUAMAN
AQUAMAN
SWORD OF ATLANTIS
KURT BUSIEK BUTCH GUICE
The KING of the SEAS
AQUAMAN
Leads his Army to Battle!
AQUAMAN
YOU!
YOU DID THIS TO HER!
AND NOW YOU DIE!!
AQUAMAN

"There is no blinking at the fact that our people, our territory, and our interests are in grave danger."
FATHER NEPTUNE!
CHANK
GRANT ME THE STRENGTH TO VANQUISH THE FOES OF ATLANTIS --
-- AND TO PROTECT THE KINGDOM OF THE SEVEN SEAS!
SZRAK

THY WILL BE DONE!

"With confidence in our armed forces -- with the unbounding determination of our people -- we will gain the inevitable triumph."

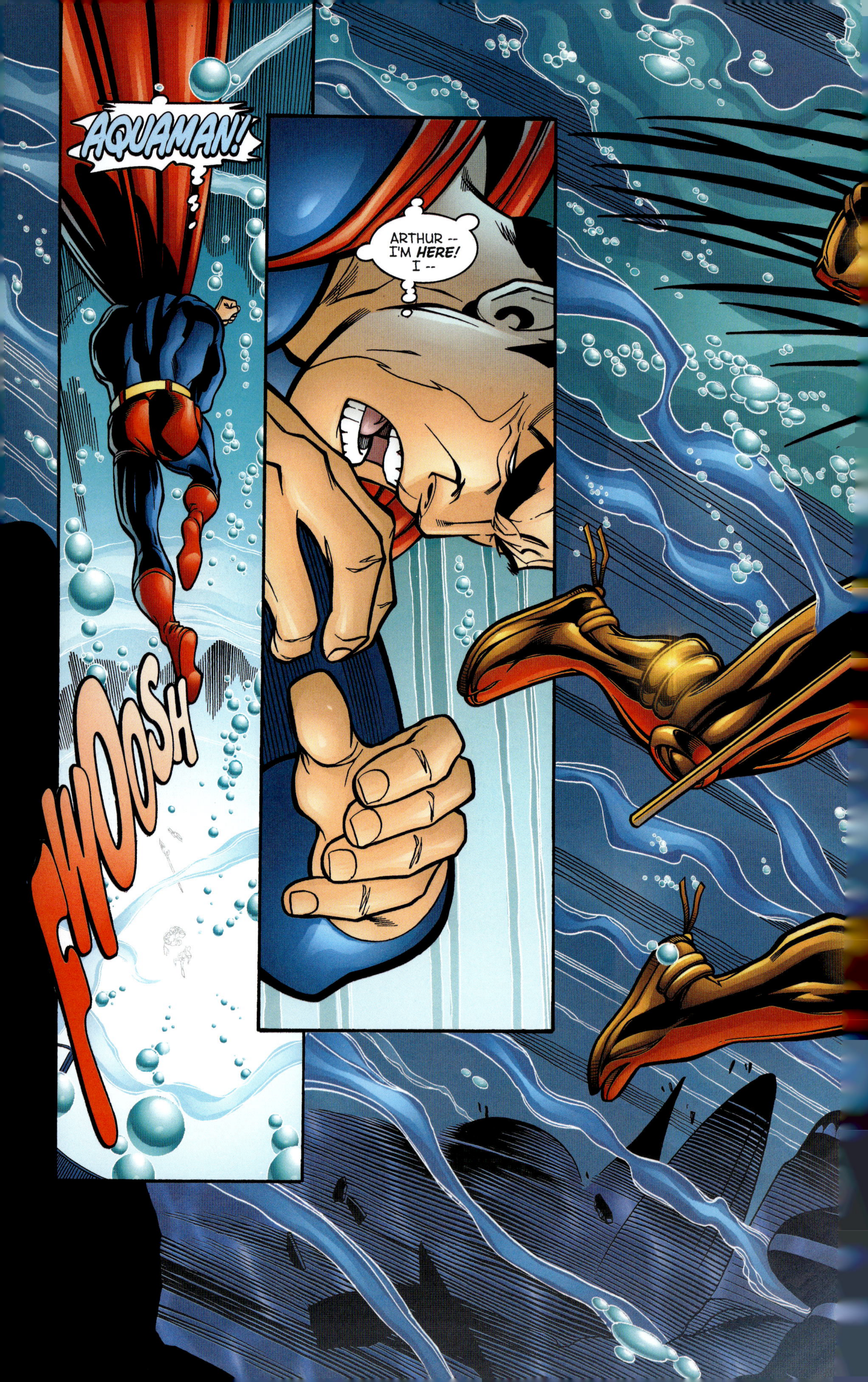
AQUAMAN!
ARTHUR -- I'M HERE! I --
FWOOSH

"So help us God."
SWOOSH

"I ask that Congress declare that since the unprovoked and dastardly attack by Japan on Sunday, December 7, a state of war has existed between the United States and the Japanese Empire." President Franklin Delano Roosevelt War Message to Congress December 8, 1941
IMPERIEX! IF YOU WANT WAR--
--I'LL GIVE YOU WAR!
A DATE WHICH WILL LIVE IN INFAMY
SUPERMAN created by: JERRY SIEGEL & JOE SHUSTER
BATMAN created by BOB KANE
JEPH LOEB writer
RON GARNEY penciller
MARK MORALES inker
TANYA & RICH HORIE colors
RICHARD STARKINGS letters
TOM PALMER jr ass't editor
EDDIE BERGANZA editor

AQUAMAN
GENESIS
AQUAMAN
AQUAMAN
AQUAMAN
AQUAMAN
YOU!
YOU DIE!!
LIVES AGAIN

THE NEXT EIGHT DECADES

by **PAUL LEVITZ**

Aquaman's had it rough. He's been exiled, dethroned, and amputated, and faced the ultimate parental nightmare of his child being killed. That's not even mentioning lousy periods in his life like a year-long quest for his missing wife. Or being made into a running joke on *Entourage*. But he survived.

He might be the ultimate survivor of the Golden Age of comics. Legend has it that he was created by Paul Norris and Mort Weisinger on Mort's first day on the job at DC, along with Green Arrow and Johnny Quick (a trifecta that makes the tale even less likely no matter how fast a writer Mort was). It's likely that parental pride kept the Sea King alive through the disappearance of the superheroes in the postwar years. Squeezed out of *More Fun Comics* when it gave up on heroic stories, he followed Superboy to a safe new berth in *Adventure Comics.* Only Superman, Batman, and Wonder Woman continued to star in their own comics through that drought, but Aquaman (and his buddy Green Arrow) quietly kept going in little six-pagers in the back of *Adventure*. Edited, probably not coincidentally, by Weisinger.

He'd last almost 200 issues in *Adventure*, and get a shot (finally) at full-length tales in four issues of *Showcase* as the *Adventure* run ended. But unlike any other heroic character in the first *40* issues of that title, he wasn't quickly awarded his own comic or even a lead feature in one of DC's many anthology titles. There were a couple of consolation prizes: after 19 years he got to be the cover feature of those four issues (the longest any significant DC hero had to wait to show up on a cover), and the talented Nick Cardy alternated with the uniquely gifted Ramona Fradon on the art.

When he did get his own comic, he had to do double and even triple duty; his short stories kept showing up in the back of unlikely places like *Detective Comics* and *World's Finest.* Maybe those were inventory already drawn before he got his own comic, or maybe his proud poppa was still pushing his creation in DC's editorial halls. In any case, that original run of *Aquaman* would see the first big superhero wedding in comics (almost a year before Reed and Sue Richards would tie the knot). So his life wasn't without some bright spots.

And maybe the brightest of those spots was becoming the first superhero other than Superman and Batman to get his own original television series (the limited animation of the *Marvel Super Heroes* cartoons by Gantray-Lawrence the year before are really the first "motion comics" rather than genuine original productions). He even got to lord it over his fellow heroes like Green Lantern and the Atom, who were relegated to filler cartoons between his.

AQUAMAN
LIVES AGAIN!
AQUAMAN STANDS ALONE!
IS THIS MY FOE?
SUPER FRIENDS

That first television run proved vital to Aquaman's long run for survival, for when his comic was canceled in 1971 (coincidentally just after the retirement of Weisinger?), he was relegated to the perpetual fish-out-of-water member of the Justice League, and might have faded into the background of the DC Universe. But television loves to draw upon its own, and when the *Super Friends* show was being developed, Aquaman's brief life on the screen was enough to promote him to the original and long last-lasting team, along with the more famous trinity of heroes (and Robin, for his kid appeal). *Super Friends* would have a 13-year run on Saturday mornings (the second-longest-running series in that kiddie prime time, after *Scooby-Doo*) and permanently ensure his status as one of DC's superstars of comics, toys, and media.

All this is long enough ago that I hadn't arrived at DC, and there are almost five decades more of Aquaman's triumphs and tragedies, many of which are beautifully recaptured in these pages. I got to write a few of them (he was my first super-heroic assignment), edit a couple (making me a co-conspirator in Aquababy's death), and mostly enjoy them as a reader. Through all the challenges, Aquaman's been a survivor, tough enough not only to endure the awesome pressures in the sea's depths but the mental and physical terrors he's had to face. Here's hoping he's got another 80 years ahead.

***Paul Levitz** has been a comics fan (*The Comic Reader*), writer (*Legion of Super-Heroes*), editor (*Batman*), executive (decades at DC ending as president and publisher from 2002-2009), educator (Columbia University), and historian (*75 Years of DC Comics: The Art of Modern Myth-Making*). His latest graphic novel is* Unfinished Business.

I TAKE IT BACK -- WITH TEETH LIKE THOSE, YOU'RE PROBABLY A MEAT EATER--NOT A VEGETABLE!
I MUST OBJECT TO THE RUSH YOU'RE IN TO EAT ME, THOUGH--

DC
AQUAMAN
NO.17
JUNE '04
PFEIFER
GLEASON
ALAMY
URBAN RENEWAL!

LIVES AGAIN!
LEGEND OF AQUAMAN
JUSTICE LEAGUE of AMERICA
STARRO THE CONQUEROR!
METAMORPHO AQUAMAN
SUPER FRIENDS
Adventure COMICS
AQUAMAN
AQUAMAN
AQUAMAN
AQUAMAN
DOOM From DIMENSION AQUA!
AQUAMAN
URBAN RENEWAL!
UNDERWORLD
DC UNIVERSE REBIRTH
AQUAMAN
DC UNIVERSE REBIRTH
AQUAMAN
AQUAMAN
Who Destroys the Sea King
The OCEAN MASTER or BLACK MANTA?
AQUAMAN
ARTHUR CURRY JUNIOR
DC COMICS
THE NEW 52!
AQUAMAN
AQUAMAN
IS THIS MY FOE!
AQUAMAN
AQUAMAN
JABBERJAW
CAPTAIN CAVEMAN
the BRAVE and the BOLD
BATMAN
AQUAMAN
The SLEEP-WALKER from the SEA!
DC COMICS
THE NEW 52!
JUSTICE LEAGUE
AQUAMAN
AQUAMAN
AQUAMAN A COWARD? IS HE REALLY IN TERROR OF... The OCEAN MASTER?
THE BEGINNING OF TOMORROW!
AQUAMAN
AQUAMAN
IN THE SHADOWY DEPTHS OF ATLANTIS, HIS LIFE WILL CHANGE FOREVER!
DC COMICS
THE NEW 52!
AQUAMAN
YEAR ONE
AQUAMAN
AQUAMAN
Who Destroys the Sea King
GENESIS
AQUAMAN
AQUAMAN
SWORD OF ATLANTIS
KURT BUSIEK
BUTCH GUICE
AQUAMAN
Leads his army to Battle!
AQUAMAN
YOU!
YOU DID THIS TO HER!
AND NOW YOU DIE!!
AQUAMAN

JUST OFF THE NEW COAST OF SAN DIEGO...
FIVE WEEKS AFTER MUCH OF THE CITY PLUNGED INTO THE SEA...
50
50
HELLO.

I NEED YOU TO CALM DOWN. YOU'RE NOT GOING MAD. I'M THE ONE TALKING TO YOU, AND I'M GOING TO HELP YOU.
I'M AQUAMAN.
WITH THE HELP OF THE JLA'S MARTIAN MANHUNTER, I'VE SET UP A TELEPATHIC LINK SO WE CAN TALK...
...BUT RIGHT NOW, I NEED YOU TO LISTEN.
I'M GOING TO GET YOU OUT OF HERE. BUT WHEN I DO, WHATEVER YOU DO...
...DO NOT SWIM TO THE SURFACE.
DO NOT LEAVE THE OCEAN.
IF YOU DO, YOU WILL DIE.
NOW, PLEASE STAND BACK.

AMERICAN
TIDAL
PART 3
WILL PFEIFER
WRITER
PATRICK GLEASON
PENCILLER
CHRISTIAN ALAMY INKER
NATHAN EYRING- COLORIST
ROB LEIGH- LETTERER
STEPHEN WACKER- ASSOC. EDITOR
PETER TOMASI- EDITOR
AQUAMAN CREATED BY PAUL NORRIS

I KNOW SOME OF YOU ARE INJURED, AND ALL OF YOU ARE HUNGRY AND FRIGHTENED...
HELP...
AIR!
AIR!
AIR!
AIR!
...IS ON THE WAY.
AIR!
AIR!
NICK!
JEFF!
NO!
DON'T WORRY.
THEY WON'T GET FAR.

AIR!
AIR!
AIR!
AIR!
AIR!
AIR!
PHAT-PHARM

THOSE SHARKS WON'T HURT YOU.
THEY'RE THERE TO KEEP YOU SAFE, BELIEVE IT OR NOT.
OF COURSE, YOU'VE BOTH GOT A LOT OF CUTS AND SCRATCHES...
...THERE'S BOUND TO BE AT LEAST A LITTLE BLOOD IN THE WATER.
RIGHT NOW, THOSE SHARKS ARE OBEYING MY COMMANDS...
BUT THERE'S A LIMIT TO MY CONTROL.
MAYBE YOU'D BETTER JOIN THE REST OF US.
GOOD...
NOW, I WANT YOU ALL TO LISTEN...

SOMETHING TERRIBLE HAS HAPPENED.
YOU KNOW THIS.
HERE'S WHAT YOU PROBABLY DON'T KNOW.
FIVE WEEKS AGO, A QUAKE STRUCK SAN DIEGO.
AT LEAST HALF THE CITY PLUNGED INTO THE WATER.
THOUSANDS WERE KILLED. CRUSHED IN THE QUAKE OR DROWNED IN THE OCEAN.
ABOVE, WE ASSUMED EVERYONE HAD DIED. THAT THERE WERE NO SURVIVORS.
"IN OTHER WORDS...
...YOU ARE BEING MOURNED."
R.I.P.

THAT'S NOT THE WORST NEWS, THOUGH.
THAT'S NOT WHY I'M KEEPING YOU DOWN HERE.
SOMETHING-- AND I'M NOT SURE WHAT--HAPPENED AT THE SAME TIME THE QUAKE HIT.
SOMETHING CHANGED ALL OF YOU.
YOU CAN BREATHE IN WATER...
...BUT NOT AIR.
THAT MEANS YOU CAN NEVER LEAVE THE OCEAN. YOU CAN NEVER GO BACK TO THE SURFACE.
YOU CAN NEVER GO HOME.

NO!
NO!
I'M SORRY.
NO!
NO!
NO!
NO!
NO!
NO!
NO!
NO!
NO!
NO!
NO!
NO!
NO!
NO!
NO!
NO!

NO!
NO!
NO!
Uhhhhh...
W-WHERE AM I?
LORENA, PLEASE RELAX.
MY NAME IS...
YAHHHHHHH!!
PLEASE! DON'T HURT ME!
JUST TELL ME WHERE I AM!!
IN THE JUSTICE LEAGUE WATCHTOWER.
ON THE MOON.
MY NAME IS JOHN.

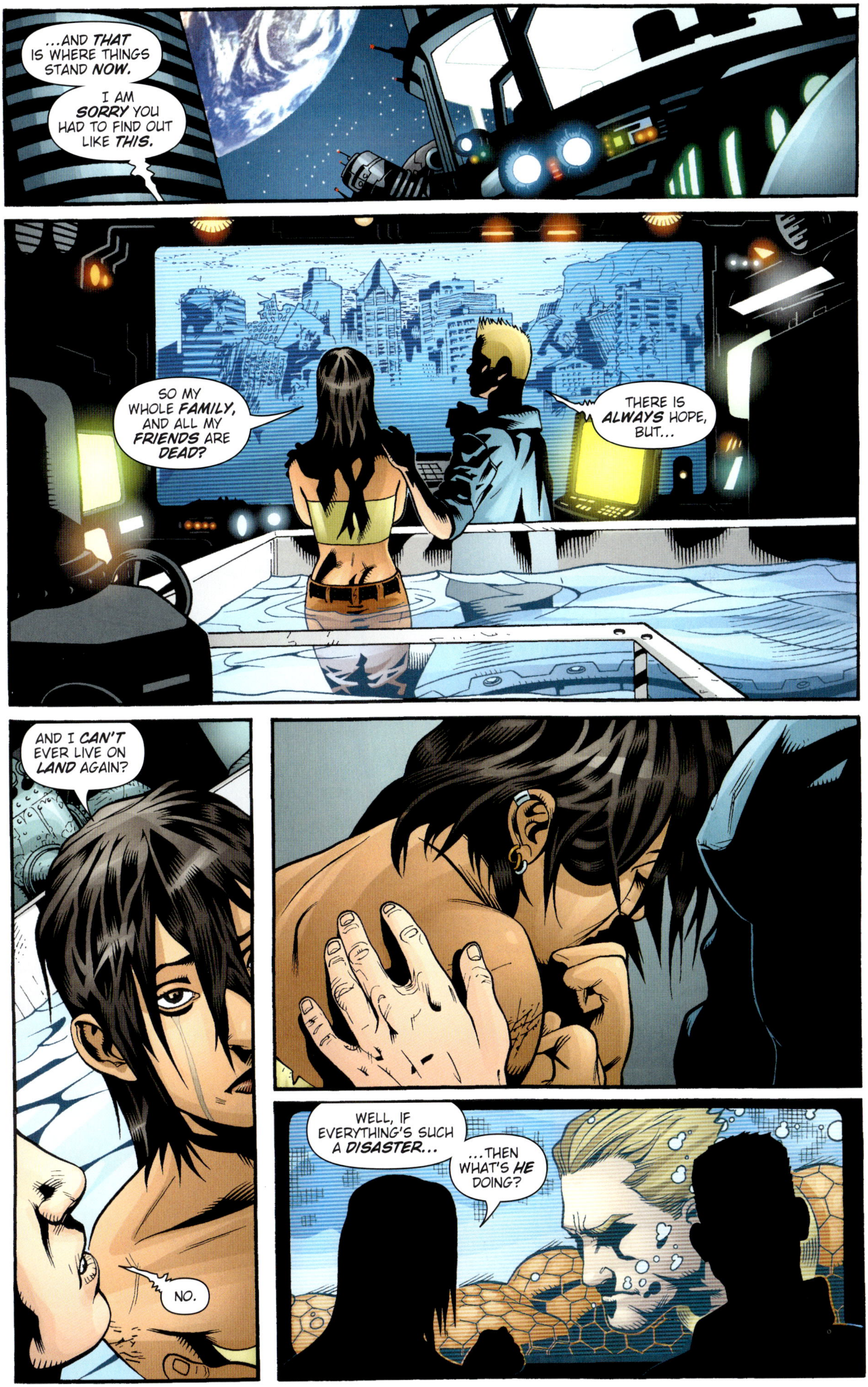
...AND THAT IS WHERE THINGS STAND NOW.
I AM SORRY YOU HAD TO FIND OUT LIKE THIS.
SO MY WHOLE FAMILY, AND ALL MY FRIENDS ARE DEAD?
THERE IS ALWAYS HOPE, BUT...
AND I CAN'T EVER LIVE ON LAND AGAIN?
NO.
WELL, IF EVERYTHING'S SUCH A DISASTER...
...THEN WHAT'S HE DOING?

HE'S DOING WHAT HE ALWAYS DOES.
HE'S SAVING LIVES.
LORENA?
HAVEN'T YOU BEEN LISTENING? YOU'RE GOING TO DIE IF YOU DON'T GET BACK IN THE WATER!
THEN YOU'D BETTER FIND A WAY TO GET ME BACK HOME...
...BECAUSE I'M NOT GETTING BACK INTO THAT TANK.
BESIDES...
HE LOOKS LIKE HE COULD USE A LITTLE HELP.

YOU CAN TALK DOWN HERE, YOU KNOW.

I CAN...?
OH MY GOD! I CAN! HOW?
YOU'VE ALL CHANGED. YOU CAN DO THINGS NOW YOU WOULDN'T HAVE DREAMED OF DOING BEFORE.
THE SONIC WAVES OF YOUR WORDS CAN BE HEARD BY SPECIAL EARS.
AND OF COURSE, YOU'VE GOT "SPECIAL EARS"?
YOU ALL DO. RIGHT NOW, YOU'RE THE ONLY ONE CALM ENOUGH TO REALIZE IT.
I GUESS...
...I JUST THOUGHT MAYBE YOU COULD USE SOME HELP.
I CAN.
WHILE I SEARCH FOR SURVIVORS, YOU TRY AND CALM DOWN THE ONES I'VE FREED. THEY'RE PRETTY SHAKEN UP.
I KNOW HOW THEY FEEL.
WHAT HAPPENED... IT'S SO BIG!
IT JUST SEEMS OVERWHELMING... WHERE DO WE EVEN START?
WE START BY GETTING SOME HELP.
DID YOU CONTACT THOSE ORGANIZATIONS, J'ONN?
THEY'RE ON THE WAY, ARTHUR.

Gaslamp Quarter
HISTORIC HEART OF SAN DIEGO
...YOU WEREN'T KIDDING, WERE YOU?
AT TIMES LIKE THIS, IT'S EASY TO GET HELP.

WHAT WORRIES ME IS WHAT WE'LL DO LATER, WHEN THE HELP LEAVES AND THESE PEOPLE REALIZE THEY CAN'T.
EVER.
WHAT WILL YOU DO THEN?
DO? THERE'S NOT MUCH I CAN DO, ASIDE FROM HELP THEM ADJUST.
WILL THEY?
YOU DID.
YES. WHERE? SHOW ME.
Huh? WHAT ARE--
I WASN'T TALKING TO YOU.

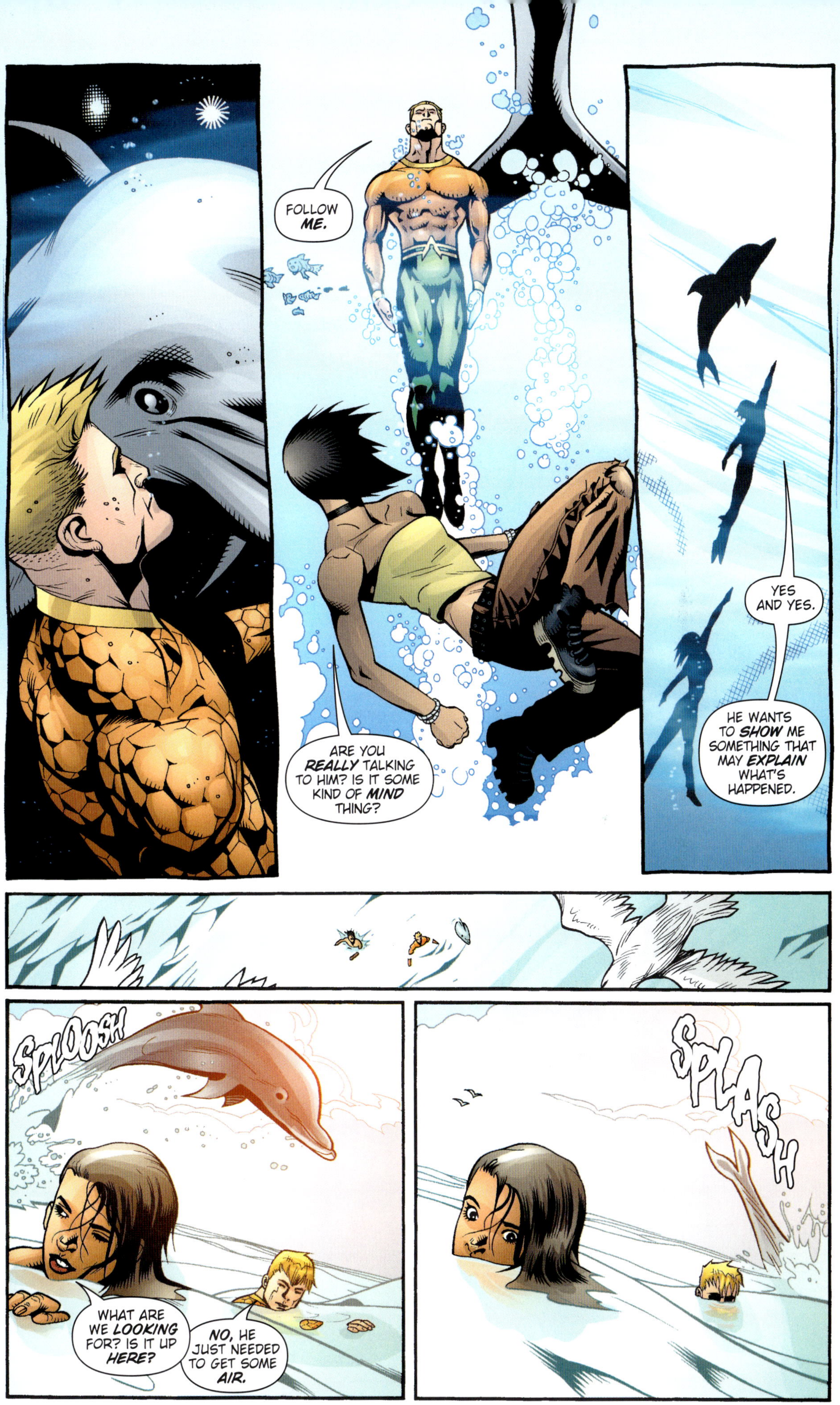
FOLLOW ME.
ARE YOU REALLY TALKING TO HIM? IS IT SOME KIND OF MIND THING?
YES AND YES.
HE WANTS TO SHOW ME SOMETHING THAT MAY EXPLAIN WHAT'S HAPPENED.
SPLOOSH
WHAT ARE WE LOOKING FOR? IS IT UP HERE?
NO, HE JUST NEEDED TO GET SOME AIR.
SPLASH

ARE YOU GUYS TALKING NOW? WHAT'S HE SAYING? WHERE ARE WE GOING?
HE SAYS HE AND HIS FAMILY FOUND A MACHINE.
A MACHINE? WHAT KIND OF MACHINE?
IT WAS PLAYING HAVOC WITH THEIR SONAR, SO THEY DECIDED TO INVESTIGATE.
A BIG ONE.
AT FIRST, THEY THOUGHT IT WAS JUST GARBAGE FROM UP TOP...
GARBAGE?
WOULDN'T BE THE FIRST TIME. BUT THEN, THEY REALIZED IT HADN'T BEEN DROPPED.
IT HAD BEEN PLACED...
...AND THEN ACTIVATED.
VENT

HE SAYS THE HUM IT GIVES OFF IS A QUIETER VERSION OF THE SOUND THEY HEARD THAT DAY.
W-WHAT'S HE SAYIN' NOW?
WHAT DAY IS--
OH... RIGHT.
QUESTION IS, WHO ACTIVATED IT?

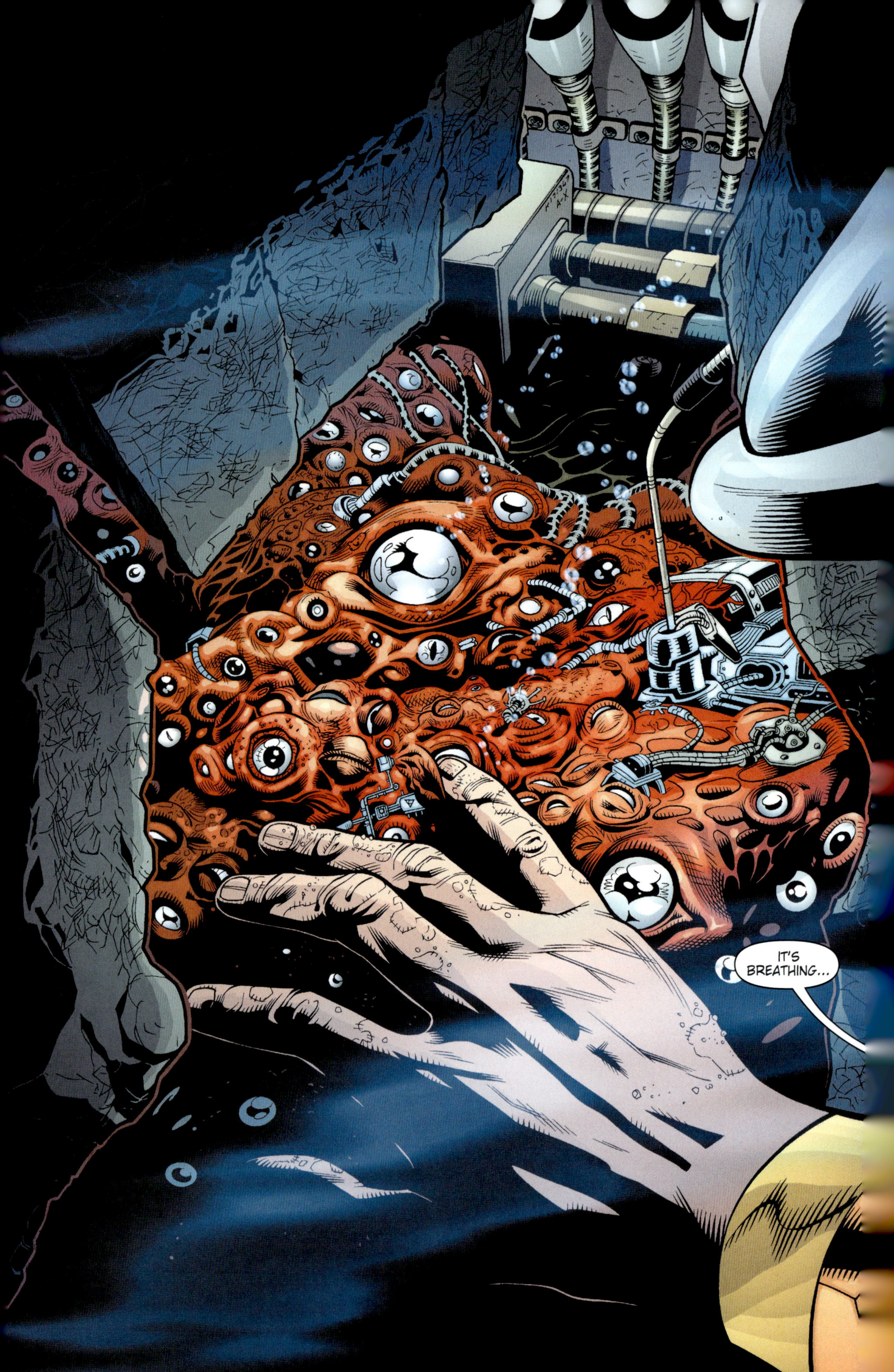
IT'S BREATHING...

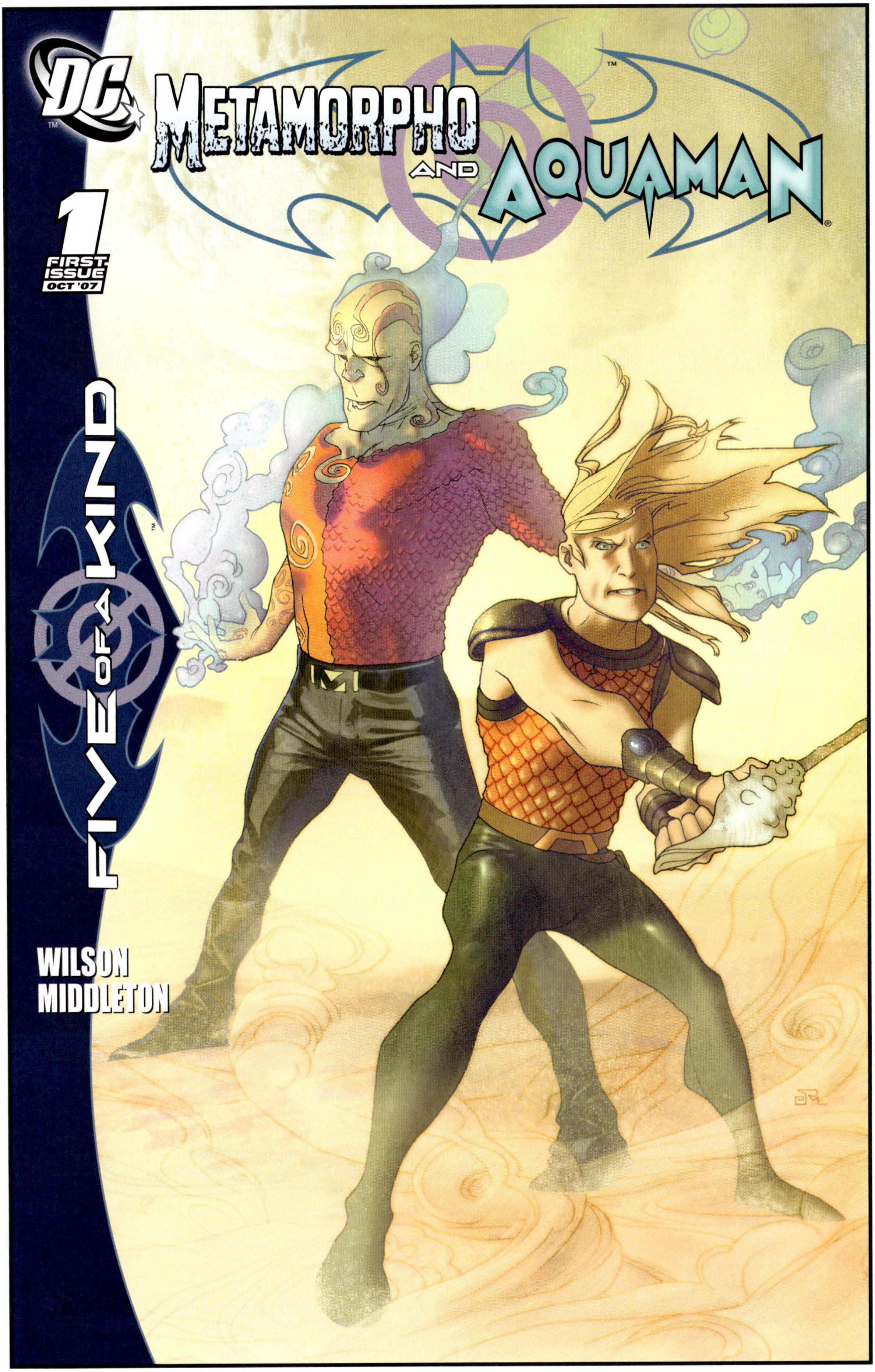
DC
METAMORPHO AND AQUAMAN
1
FIRST ISSUE
OCT '07
FIVE OF A KIND
WILSON
MIDDLETON

AQUAMAN STANDS ALONE!
LIVES AGAIN!
JUSTICE LEAGUE of AMERICA
STARRO THE CONQUEROR
METAMORPHO
AQUAMAN
THE SUPER FRIENDS
Adventure COMICS
AQUAMAN
Manhunter Mars Hawkman
AQUAMAN
DOOM from DIMENSION AQUA!
AQUAMAN
URBAN RENEWAL!
DC UNIVERSE REBIRTH
AQUAMAN
DC UNIVERSE REBIRTH
AQUAMAN
AQUAMAN
Who DESTROYS the SEA KING
The OCEAN MASTER or BLACK MANTA?
ARTHUR CURRY JUNIOR
VILLAIN!
THE NEW 52!
AQUAMAN
IS THIS MY FOE!
AQUAMAN
AQUAMAN
JABBERJAW
CAPTAIN CAVEMAN
the BRAVE and the BOLD
BATMAN
AQUAMAN
The SLEEP-WALKER From the SEA!
JUSTICE LEAGUE
AQUAMAN
AQUAMAN
AQUAMAN A COWARD? IS HE REALLY IN TERROR OF... The OCEAN MASTER?
THE BEGINNING OF TOMORROW!
AQUAMAN
AQUAMAN
IN THE SHADOWY DEPTHS OF ATLANTIS, HIS LIFE WILL CHANGE FOREVER!
THE NEW 52!
AQUAMAN
YEAR ONE
AQUAMAN
Who DESTROYS the SEA KING
GENESIS
AQUAMAN
AQUAMAN SWORD of ATLANTIS
KURT BUSIEK BUTCH GUICE
AQUAMAN
Leads his army to Battle!
AQUAMAN
YOU!
YOU DID THIS TO HER!
YOU DIE!!
AQUAMAN

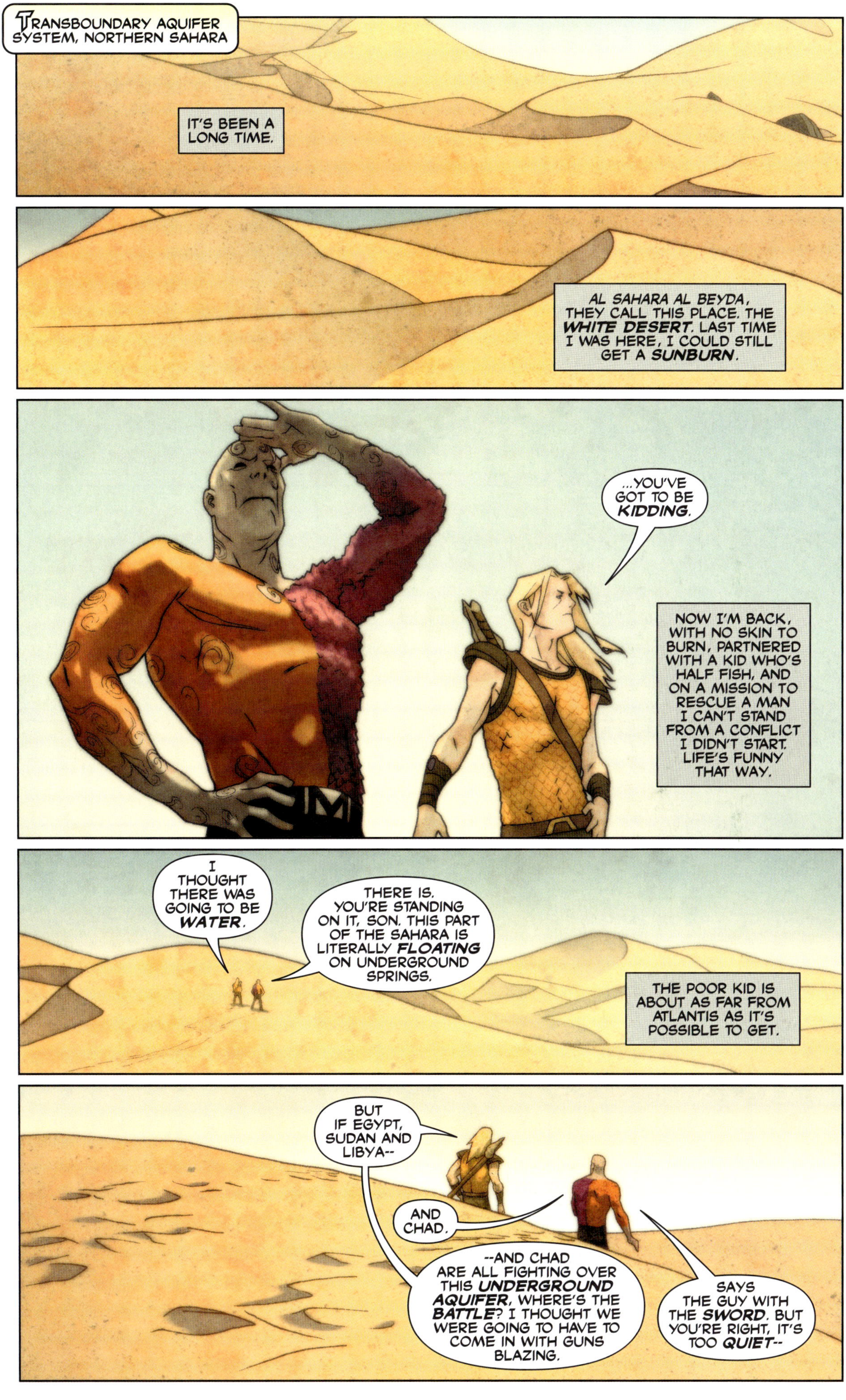

TRANSBOUNDARY AQUIFER SYSTEM, NORTHERN SAHARA
IT'S BEEN A LONG TIME.
AL SAHARA AL BEYDA, THEY CALL THIS PLACE. THE WHITE DESERT. LAST TIME I WAS HERE, I COULD STILL GET A SUNBURN.
...YOU'VE GOT TO BE KIDDING.
NOW I'M BACK, WITH NO SKIN TO BURN, PARTNERED WITH A KID WHO'S HALF FISH, AND ON A MISSION TO RESCUE A MAN I CAN'T STAND FROM A CONFLICT I DIDN'T START. LIFE'S FUNNY THAT WAY.
I THOUGHT THERE WAS GOING TO BE WATER.
THERE IS. YOU'RE STANDING ON IT, SON. THIS PART OF THE SAHARA IS LITERALLY FLOATING ON UNDERGROUND SPRINGS.
THE POOR KID IS ABOUT AS FAR FROM ATLANTIS AS IT'S POSSIBLE TO GET.
BUT IF EGYPT, SUDAN AND LIBYA--
AND CHAD.
--AND CHAD ARE ALL FIGHTING OVER THIS UNDERGROUND AQUIFER, WHERE'S THE BATTLE? I THOUGHT WE WERE GOING TO HAVE TO COME IN WITH GUNS BLAZING.
SAYS THE GUY WITH THE SWORD. BUT YOU'RE RIGHT, IT'S TOO QUIET--

FIVE OF A KIND PART 4
ROGUE ELEMENTS
G. WILLOW WILSON WRITER
JOSH MIDDLETON ARTIST
JOHN J. HILL LETTERER
RACHEL GLUCKSTERN ASSOCIATE EDITOR
JOAN HILTY EDITOR
MY GOD...
NO WEAPON COULD HAVE DONE THIS. THIS IS--
META-HUMAN. ONE WITH POWERS ON A SCALE I'VE NEVER SEEN BEFORE.
DOESN'T SEEM LIKE THERE'S MUCH LEFT OF THE STAGG ENTERPRISES CONTINGENT TO SAVE. WHOEVER CAME THROUGH HERE CLEARLY WASN'T ON A "SIDE." HE'S FRIED EVERYBODY.

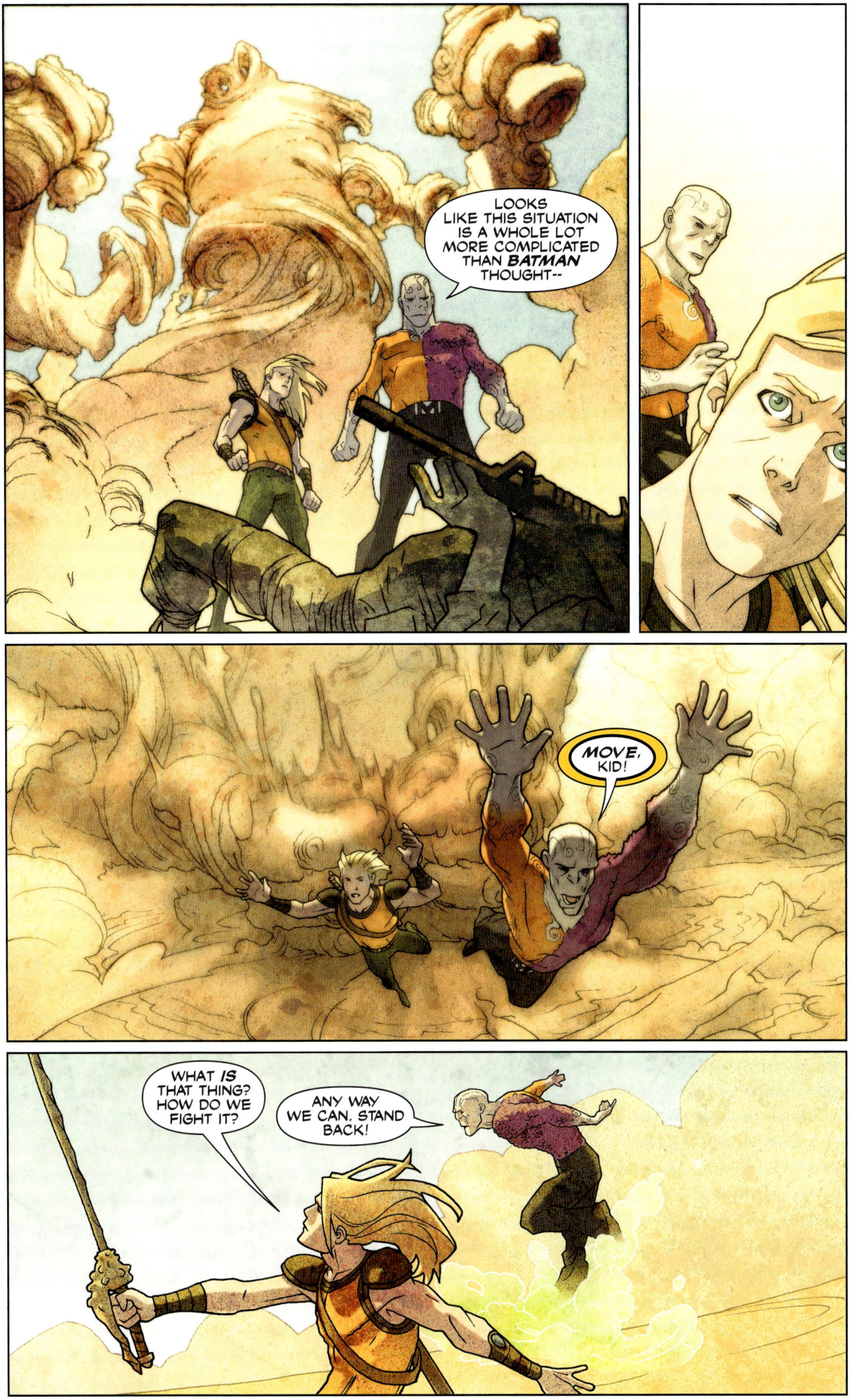
LOOKS LIKE THIS SITUATION IS A WHOLE LOT MORE COMPLICATED THAN *BATMAN* THOUGHT--
MOVE, KID!
WHAT *IS* THAT THING? HOW DO WE FIGHT IT?
ANY WAY WE CAN. STAND BACK!

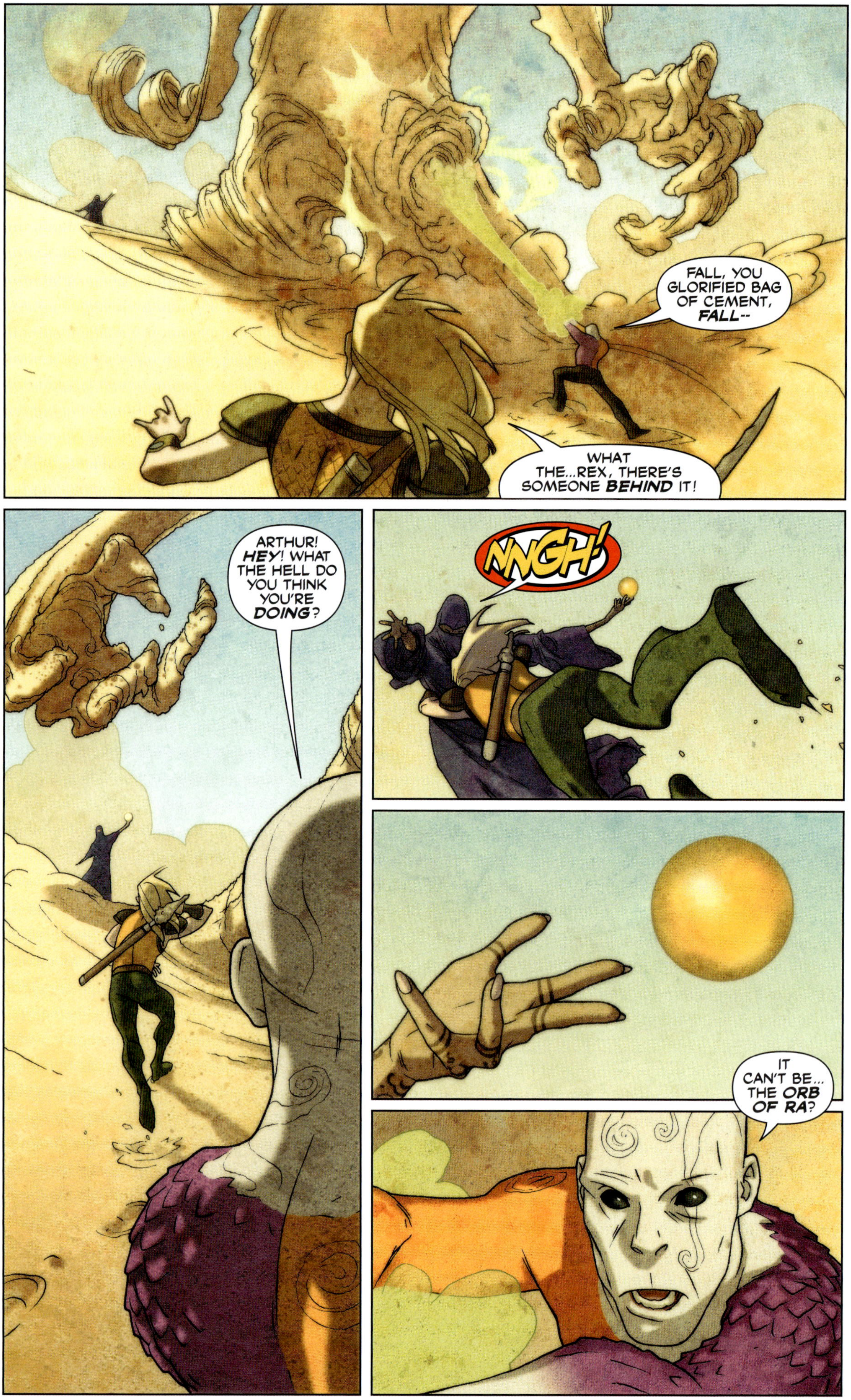

FALL, YOU GLORIFIED BAG OF CEMENT, FALL--
WHAT THE...REX, THERE'S SOMEONE BEHIND IT!
ARTHUR! HEY! WHAT THE HELL DO YOU THINK YOU'RE DOING?
NNGH!
IT CAN'T BE... THE ORB OF RA?

YA 'AJNABI Y'IBN IL KELB...
...A GIRL?
HUNH?
WOAH!
ARTHUR? ARTHUR!

OH NO...
THE KID WAS GONE. PULLED STRAIGHT INTO THE SAND BY WHATEVER-IT-WAS. PULLED BY MAGIC.
"MAGIC." ONE OF MANKIND'S LITTLE WORDS FOR A BIG SCARY IDEA IT DOESN'T QUITE UNDERSTAND.
A LITTLE WORD.
NOW YOU WILL DROWN IN THE EARTH-LAKE, AND I WILL FEED YOUR BONES TO THE SAND.
YOU WISH, LADY. YOU'VE JUST DONE ME A HUGE FAVOR.
PEOPLE CALL ME AQUAMAN. MAYBE YOU'VE HEARD OF ME.
I'M THE ONE WITH GILLS.

YOU MAY BREATHE THE WATER, AQUAMAN-- BUT HALCYON COMMANDS IT.
IF BY "COMMAND" YOU MEAN THIS WUSSY LITTLE WATER MONSTER--
NNGH!
NOW, DEFILER, I WILL BREAK YOU--
--AND IT WILL HURT.
WOOOAH!

HOLD ON, KID... JUST HOLD ON...
SSSSSSSS
HUH?
I'LL BE DAMNED--YOU'RE ALL RIGHT! I THOUGHT I WAS GOING TO HAVE TO HAVE A BAD CONVERSATION WITH BATMAN ABOUT YOUR UNTIMELY DEATH--
SHE'S COMING.
SHE?

THERE IT WAS: THE ORB, LIKE A SMALL SUN. IT TUGGED AT MY BLOOD.
AND THERE WAS A GLAZED LOOK IN THE WOMAN'S EYES THAT TOLD ME SOMETHING WAS VERY WRONG...
YOU BEASTS BROUGHT THE ORB OF RA HERE TO FIGHT YOUR WAR OVER THE EARTH-LAKE, A PRECIOUS PLACE WHICH YOUR VERY PRESENCE CORRUPTS... BUT NOW I HAVE THE ORB, AND I WILL USE IT TO FIGHT YOU.
WHAT THE--
YOU'RE WRONG. WE'VE BEEN SENT HERE TO STOP THIS WAR.
AND THAT ORB IS DANGEROUS. YOU WANT TO END UP LOOKING LIKE ME? DO YOU?

AND THEN I REALIZED WHAT WAS GOING ON.
WOULD THAT... BE SO BAD... REX MASON? THE POWER I GAVE YOU, I WILL GIVE TO HER ALSO...
THE ORB...IT'S SPEAKING THROUGH HER!
WHA--?
AH!
ARTHUR!
WITH PLEASURE.
KRAK

WELCOME BACK. WE HAVE TO TALK.
I HAVE NOTHING TO SAY TO YOU.
WELL I HAVE SOMETHING TO SAY TO YOU.
THE ORB IS CONTROLLING YOUR MIND, LADY--IT'S USING YOU TO KILL SOLDIERS. I WANT TO KNOW WHO BROUGHT IT HERE AND WHAT YOU'VE DONE WITH HIM. AND THEN I WANT YOUR HELP TO DESTROY IT.

TELL ME WHY I SHOULD DO ANY PART OF WHAT YOU ASK.
BECAUSE IF YOU DO, I WILL HELP YOU PROTECT THIS AQUIFER AND END THIS WAR.
SWEAR IT ON YOUR LIFE.
I SWEAR IT ON YOURS.
THEN UNTIE ME--AND I WILL SHOW YOU WHAT YOU SHOULD SEE.
HEY, 'MORPHO...NOT TO BE A DRAG, BUT I COULD USE SOME WATER.
RIGHT, SORRY. YOU SHOULD HAVE SPOKEN UP SOONER, KID.
YOU CAN MAKE WATER? OUT OF AIR?
NOT EXACTLY. I CAN MAKE WATER OUT OF MYSELF, AND THEN MAKE MORE OF MYSELF OUT OF THE SAND.
THIS IS A BLESSING, AND A GIFT IN A DESERT. YOU ARE VERY LUCKY.
YEAH, LUCKY.

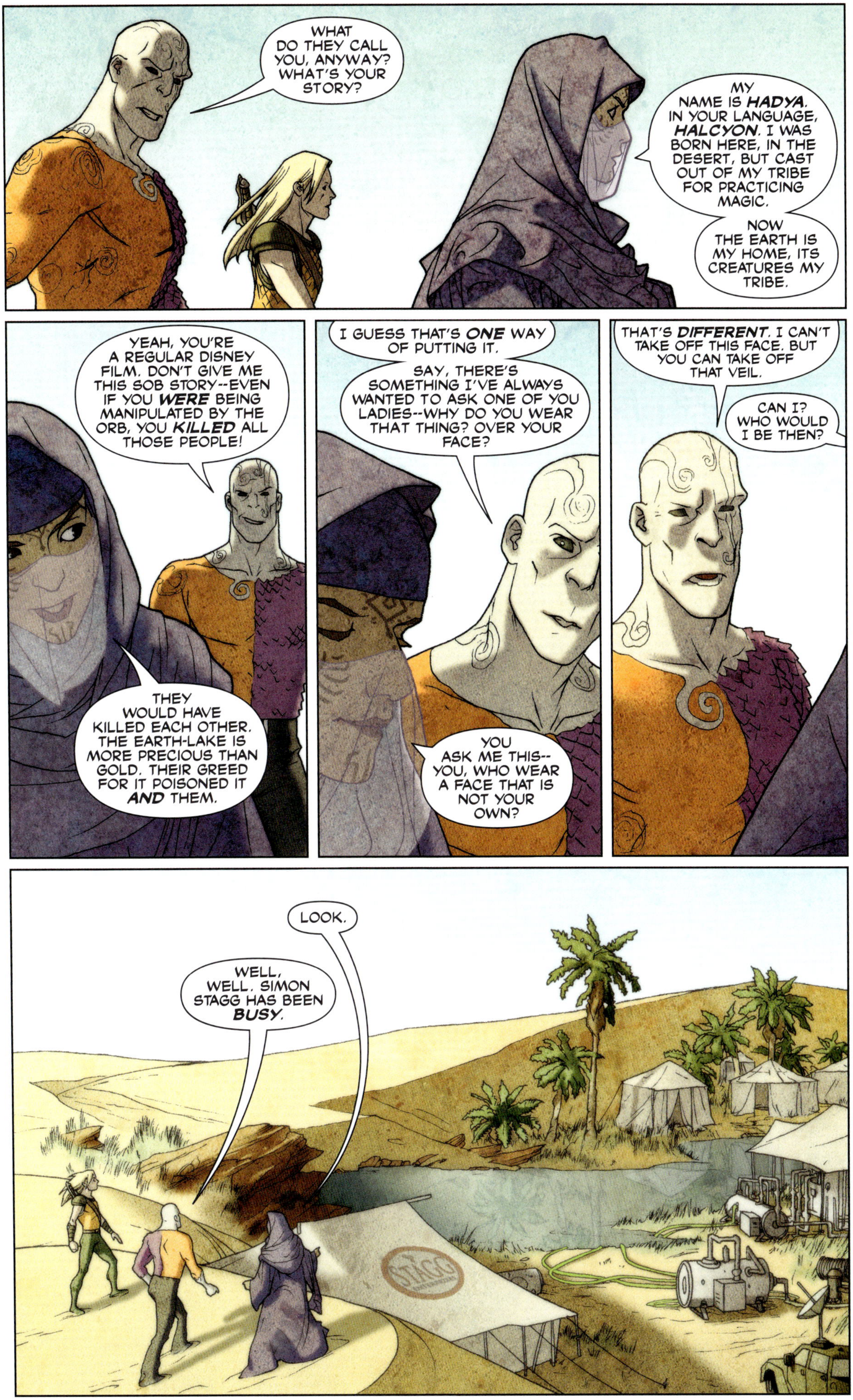

WHAT DO THEY CALL YOU, ANYWAY? WHAT'S YOUR STORY?
MY NAME IS **HADYA**. IN YOUR LANGUAGE, **HALCYON**. I WAS BORN HERE, IN THE DESERT, BUT CAST OUT OF MY TRIBE FOR PRACTICING MAGIC.
NOW THE EARTH IS MY HOME, ITS CREATURES MY TRIBE.
YEAH, YOU'RE A REGULAR DISNEY FILM. DON'T GIVE ME THIS SOB STORY--EVEN IF YOU **WERE** BEING MANIPULATED BY THE ORB, YOU **KILLED** ALL THOSE PEOPLE!
THEY WOULD HAVE KILLED EACH OTHER. THE EARTH-LAKE IS MORE PRECIOUS THAN GOLD. THEIR GREED FOR IT POISONED IT **AND** THEM.
I GUESS THAT'S **ONE** WAY OF PUTTING IT.
SAY, THERE'S SOMETHING I'VE ALWAYS WANTED TO ASK ONE OF YOU LADIES--WHY DO YOU WEAR THAT THING? OVER YOUR FACE?
YOU ASK ME THIS-- YOU, WHO WEAR A FACE THAT IS NOT YOUR OWN?
THAT'S **DIFFERENT**. I CAN'T TAKE OFF THIS FACE. BUT YOU CAN TAKE OFF THAT VEIL.
CAN I? WHO WOULD I BE THEN?
LOOK.
WELL, WELL. SIMON STAGG HAS BEEN **BUSY**.
STAGG

WHAT IS THIS STUFF?
I DON'T KNOW. IT IS STRANGE...IT DOES NOT BEHAVE LIKE WATER, OR LIKE OIL.
IT IS SEEPING INTO THE SAND AND ROCK ITSELF. SOON IT WILL REACH THE MAIN CHAMBER OF THE WATER BELOW. IT WAS PUT HERE BY THE FOREIGNER WHO BROUGHT THE ORB.
SIMON BROUGHT THE ORB HERE? CHRIST, I SHOULD HAVE KNOWN.
WE GET SENT TO SAVE HIS BUTT AND HE TURNS OUT TO BE THE SOURCE OF HIS OWN PROBLEM. WHERE IS HE NOW?
I WILL SHOW YOU.
KID? YOU OKAY? YOU COMING?
YEAH. IT'S JUST...I CAN'T TELL YOU WHAT IT'S LIKE DOWN THERE, REX. IT'S HUGE. LIKE A DARK SEA. IT'S BEAUTIFUL. I JUST DON'T KNOW WHY ANYONE WOULD TREAT IT THIS WAY.
YOUTHFUL IDEALISM.
WHAT? WHAT'D I SAY WRONG?
NOTHING AT ALL. IT'S ONLY THAT YOU REMIND ME OF--I HAVE A SON, SEE, WHO WOULD BE ABOUT YOUR AGE BY NOW. I HAVEN'T SEEN HIM IN A LONG TIME.
...OH. I DIDN'T KNOW.
IT'S OKAY. LET'S KEEP MOVING.
I NEED TO KNOW WHAT OUR FRIEND HERE HAS DONE WITH MY EX-FATHER-IN-LAW.

DON'T WORRY, THEY'RE COMFORTABLE.
NOT TO DRAG UP OLD FAMILY HISTORY, BUT LET'S JUST SAY MY EX-WIFE'S FATHER AND I DON'T SEE EYE TO EYE. AND NOT BECAUSE I'M TALLER...
...BUT I STILL WASN'T PREPARED TO SEE HIM LIKE THIS.
HELPLESS.
COMFORTABLE. YEAH. COULD YOU LET THEM GO, PLEASE?
AS YOU WISH.
NNGH!
HUH?

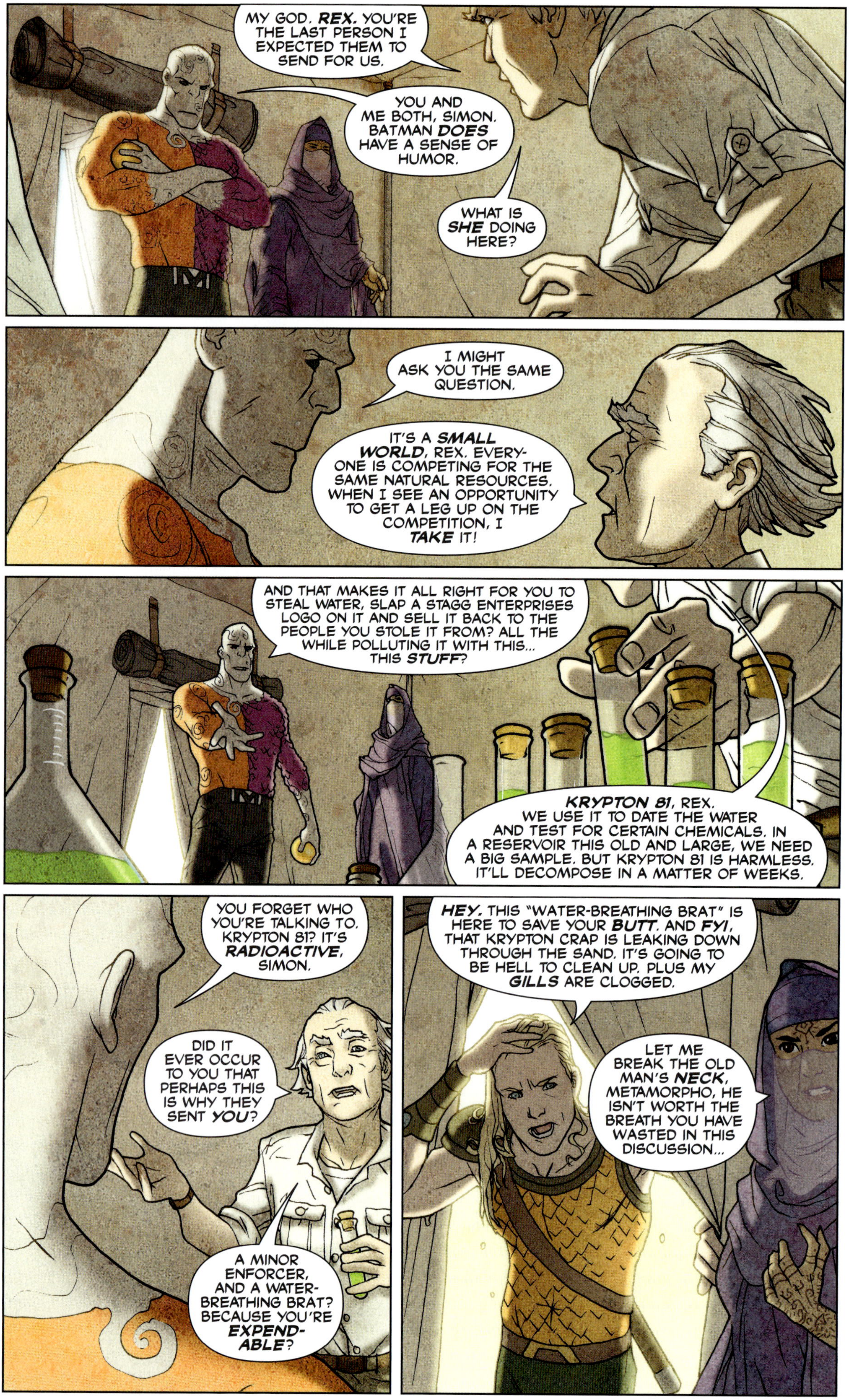

MY GOD. REX. YOU'RE THE LAST PERSON I EXPECTED THEM TO SEND FOR US.
YOU AND ME BOTH, SIMON. BATMAN DOES HAVE A SENSE OF HUMOR.
WHAT IS SHE DOING HERE?
I MIGHT ASK YOU THE SAME QUESTION.
IT'S A SMALL WORLD, REX. EVERY-ONE IS COMPETING FOR THE SAME NATURAL RESOURCES. WHEN I SEE AN OPPORTUNITY TO GET A LEG UP ON THE COMPETITION, I TAKE IT!
AND THAT MAKES IT ALL RIGHT FOR YOU TO STEAL WATER, SLAP A STAGG ENTERPRISES LOGO ON IT AND SELL IT BACK TO THE PEOPLE YOU STOLE IT FROM? ALL THE WHILE POLLUTING IT WITH THIS... THIS STUFF?
KRYPTON 81, REX. WE USE IT TO DATE THE WATER AND TEST FOR CERTAIN CHEMICALS. IN A RESERVOIR THIS OLD AND LARGE, WE NEED A BIG SAMPLE. BUT KRYPTON 81 IS HARMLESS. IT'LL DECOMPOSE IN A MATTER OF WEEKS.
YOU FORGET WHO YOU'RE TALKING TO. KRYPTON 81? IT'S RADIOACTIVE, SIMON.
DID IT EVER OCCUR TO YOU THAT PERHAPS THIS IS WHY THEY SENT YOU?
A MINOR ENFORCER, AND A WATER-BREATHING BRAT? BECAUSE YOU'RE EXPEND-ABLE?
HEY. THIS "WATER-BREATHING BRAT" IS HERE TO SAVE YOUR BUTT. AND FYI, THAT KRYPTON CRAP IS LEAKING DOWN THROUGH THE SAND. IT'S GOING TO BE HELL TO CLEAN UP. PLUS MY GILLS ARE CLOGGED.
LET ME BREAK THE OLD MAN'S NECK, METAMORPHO. HE ISN'T WORTH THE BREATH YOU HAVE WASTED IN THIS DISCUSSION...

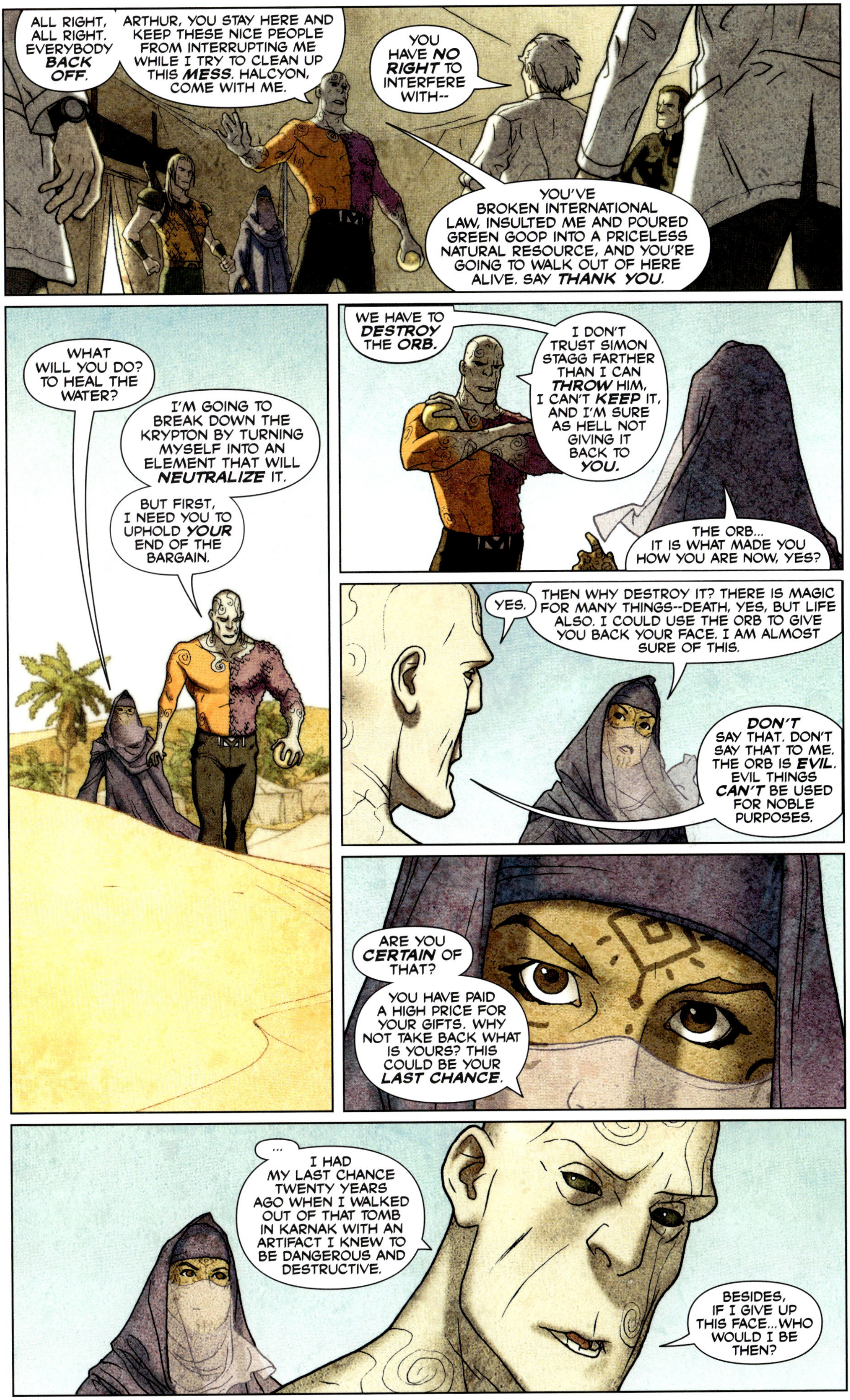
ALL RIGHT, ALL RIGHT. EVERYBODY BACK OFF.
ARTHUR, YOU STAY HERE AND KEEP THESE NICE PEOPLE FROM INTERRUPTING ME WHILE I TRY TO CLEAN UP THIS MESS. HALCYON, COME WITH ME.
YOU HAVE NO RIGHT TO INTERFERE WITH--
YOU'VE BROKEN INTERNATIONAL LAW, INSULTED ME AND POURED GREEN GOOP INTO A PRICELESS NATURAL RESOURCE, AND YOU'RE GOING TO WALK OUT OF HERE ALIVE. SAY THANK YOU.
WHAT WILL YOU DO? TO HEAL THE WATER?
I'M GOING TO BREAK DOWN THE KRYPTON BY TURNING MYSELF INTO AN ELEMENT THAT WILL NEUTRALIZE IT.
BUT FIRST, I NEED YOU TO UPHOLD YOUR END OF THE BARGAIN.
WE HAVE TO DESTROY THE ORB.
I DON'T TRUST SIMON STAGG FARTHER THAN I CAN THROW HIM, I CAN'T KEEP IT, AND I'M SURE AS HELL NOT GIVING IT BACK TO YOU.
THE ORB... IT IS WHAT MADE YOU HOW YOU ARE NOW, YES?
YES.
THEN WHY DESTROY IT? THERE IS MAGIC FOR MANY THINGS--DEATH, YES, BUT LIFE ALSO. I COULD USE THE ORB TO GIVE YOU BACK YOUR FACE. I AM ALMOST SURE OF THIS.
DON'T SAY THAT. DON'T SAY THAT TO ME. THE ORB IS EVIL. EVIL THINGS CAN'T BE USED FOR NOBLE PURPOSES.
ARE YOU CERTAIN OF THAT?
YOU HAVE PAID A HIGH PRICE FOR YOUR GIFTS. WHY NOT TAKE BACK WHAT IS YOURS? THIS COULD BE YOUR LAST CHANCE.
...
I HAD MY LAST CHANCE TWENTY YEARS AGO WHEN I WALKED OUT OF THAT TOMB IN KARNAK WITH AN ARTIFACT I KNEW TO BE DANGEROUS AND DESTRUCTIVE.
BESIDES, IF I GIVE UP THIS FACE...WHO WOULD I BE THEN?

I UNDER-STAND.
GOOD. THEN LET'S GIVE THIS CHUNK OF SPACE-ROCK A RUN FOR ITS MONEY. I'LL TRY TO BREAK IT DOWN, BUT IF THERE'S TROUBLE, I'LL NEED YOU TO CONTAIN IT--
NOT SO FAST, REX!
THE ORB OF RA IS A VALUABLE ARTIFACT! ITS POTENTIAL USES ARE ENDLESS! A CURE FOR CANCER? ADVANCED CHEMICAL WARFARE? RESOURCE PRODUCTION? NONE OF THAT'S OUTSIDE THE REALM OF POSSIBILITY HERE!
I WON'T ALLOW YOU TO DESTROY IT!
SORRY, REX, HE SAID HE NEEDED TO TALK TO YOU--
IT'S ALL RIGHT, KID.
SIMON, YOU BROUGHT THE ORB HERE TO HELP YOU WIN THIS WAR--TO WEAPONIZE IT.
BUT YOU FORGOT THAT ANY AND ALL WEAPONS CAN BE USED AGAINST THEIR MAKERS. NO MORE, SIMON. I'M GOING TO TURN IT INTO A SMALL PILE OF SALT.
SO TAKE A GOOD LAST LOOK.
AND I'LL LOOK TOO. AND REMEMBER WHO I USED TO BE. FOR THE LAST TIME.

...DAMN THING IS DENSE...
THE SWORD DOESN'T LOOK SO CHEESY WHEN IT'S IN YOUR FACE, HUH?
AAAAH!
REX! HALCYON, HELP HIM!
I CAN'T... HOLD THEM MUCH LONGER...

I DON'T THINK SO.
REX! HEY! YOU ALIVE?
YEAH. I'M ALIVE.

AND THE ORB?
...GONE.
IT'S GONE.
SOON...
IT'S SETTLED, THEN. STAGG ENTERPRISES WILL LEAVE THE AREA IMMEDIATELY, AND CHECKMATE HAS AGREED TO STEP IN AND HELP EGYPT, LIBYA, SUDAN AND CHAD NEGOTIATE SHARED RIGHTS TO THE TRANSBOUNDARY AQUIFER.
AND THE WITCH? SHE MUST BE BROUGHT TO JUSTICE.
OF COURSE. HALCYON, I'M AFRAID IT'S MY DUTY TO PLACE YOU UNDER ARREST.
YOU LIAR, YOU SWORE, YOU SWORE TO ME--
CALM DOWN.
GO. QUICKLY.
YOU...YOU WILL HEAL THE WATER? AS YOU PROMISED?
I'M NOT LEAVING UNTIL I DO. I DON'T LIE. GO.

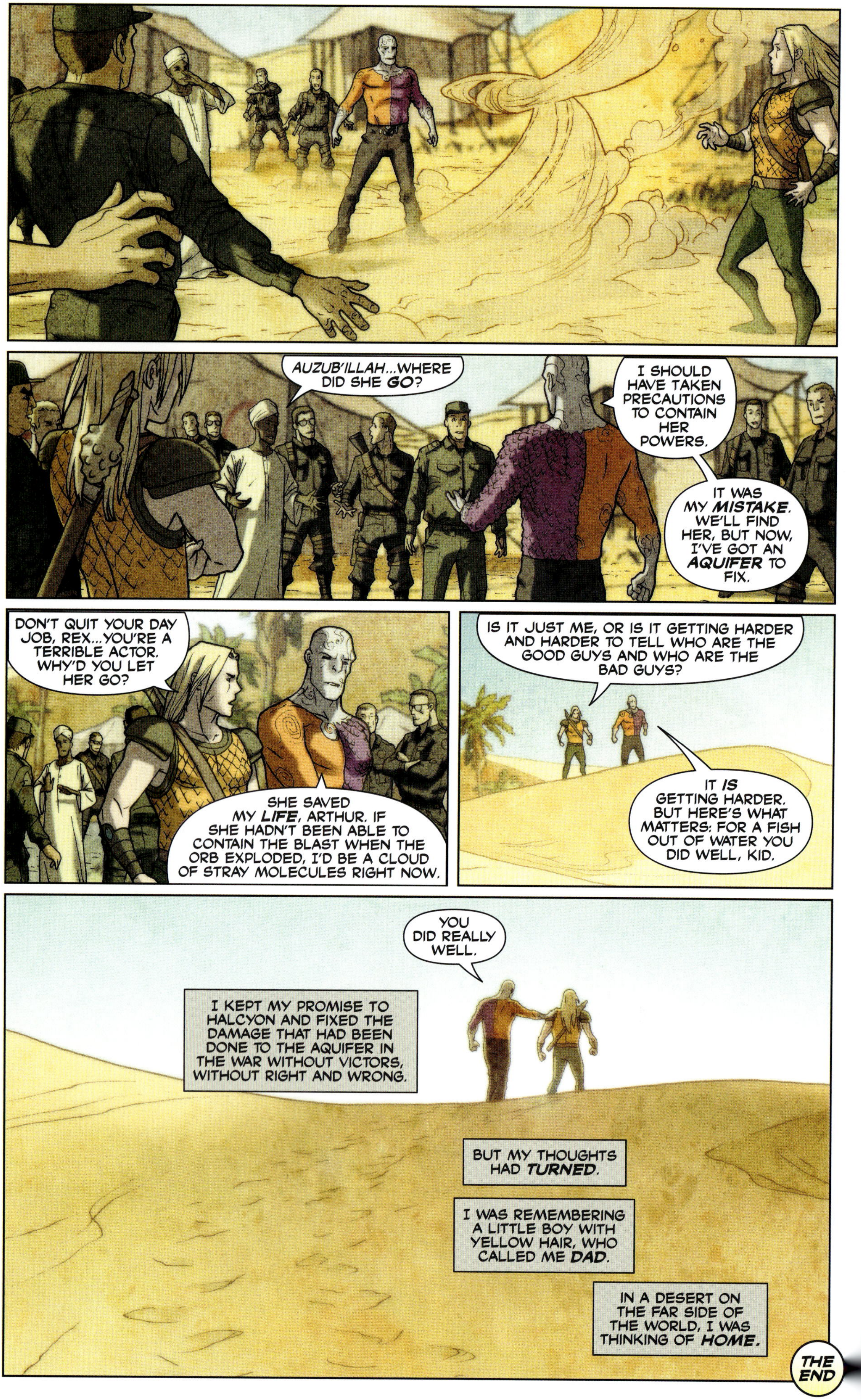
AUZUB'ILLAH...WHERE DID SHE GO?
I SHOULD HAVE TAKEN PRECAUTIONS TO CONTAIN HER POWERS.
IT WAS MY MISTAKE. WE'LL FIND HER, BUT NOW, I'VE GOT AN AQUIFER TO FIX.
DON'T QUIT YOUR DAY JOB, REX...YOU'RE A TERRIBLE ACTOR. WHY'D YOU LET HER GO?
SHE SAVED MY LIFE, ARTHUR. IF SHE HADN'T BEEN ABLE TO CONTAIN THE BLAST WHEN THE ORB EXPLODED, I'D BE A CLOUD OF STRAY MOLECULES RIGHT NOW.
IS IT JUST ME, OR IS IT GETTING HARDER AND HARDER TO TELL WHO ARE THE GOOD GUYS AND WHO ARE THE BAD GUYS?
IT IS GETTING HARDER. BUT HERE'S WHAT MATTERS: FOR A FISH OUT OF WATER YOU DID WELL, KID.
YOU DID REALLY WELL.
I KEPT MY PROMISE TO HALCYON AND FIXED THE DAMAGE THAT HAD BEEN DONE TO THE AQUIFER IN THE WAR WITHOUT VICTORS, WITHOUT RIGHT AND WRONG.
BUT MY THOUGHTS HAD TURNED.
I WAS REMEMBERING A LITTLE BOY WITH YELLOW HAIR, WHO CALLED ME DAD.
IN A DESERT ON THE FAR SIDE OF THE WORLD, I WAS THINKING OF HOME.
THE END

BEDARD WRITER
MIDDLETON ARTIST
HILL LETTERER
GLUCKSTERN ASSOC. EDITOR
HILTY EDITOR
SO, HOW ABOUT IT, BATMAN? ARE WE IN?
WE GO BACK A LONG WAY, REX. I WENT INTO THIS EXPECTING YOU TO DO WELL...
...BUT LETTING HALCYON GO? DESTROYING THE ORB OF RA?
YOU SAYIN' I SCREWED UP?
I'M SAYING YOU PLAYED IT PERFECTLY.
HALCYON WILL SPREAD THE WORD, AND WE'LL MAKE INROADS WITH ANY UNDERWORLD TYPES IN THIS PART OF THE WORLD.
YOU WANT TO MAKE FRIENDS WITH CRIMINALS?
THIS CONVERSATION CAN WAIT A COUPLE OF HOURS UNTIL AFTER WE'VE DROPPED HIM OFF OVER ATLANTIS.
HUH?
WHY, BATS? THE KID DID FINE!
I NEED BETTER THAN "FINE," REX. I WANTED TO SEE HOW HE MEASURED UP TO HIS PREDECESSOR--A MAN WHOSE HIDDEN STRENGTHS NEVER FAILED TO AMAZE ME.
I'M SORRY, ARTHUR. YOU'RE A GOOD KID, BUT YOU'RE NO AQUAMAN.

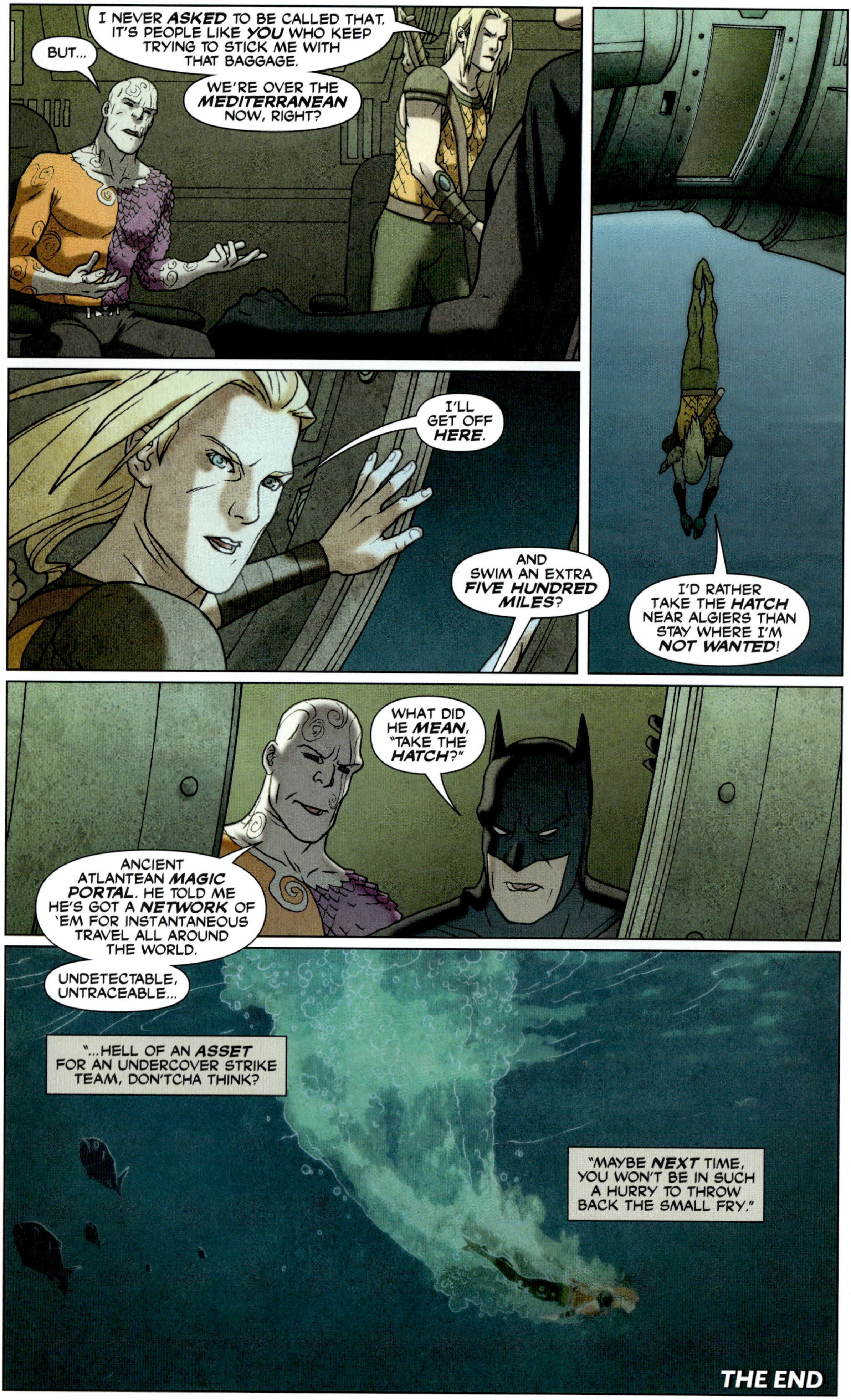
BUT...
I NEVER ASKED TO BE CALLED THAT. IT'S PEOPLE LIKE YOU WHO KEEP TRYING TO STICK ME WITH THAT BAGGAGE.
WE'RE OVER THE MEDITERRANEAN NOW, RIGHT?
I'LL GET OFF HERE.
AND SWIM AN EXTRA FIVE HUNDRED MILES?
I'D RATHER TAKE THE HATCH NEAR ALGIERS THAN STAY WHERE I'M NOT WANTED!
WHAT DID HE MEAN, "TAKE THE HATCH?"
ANCIENT ATLANTEAN MAGIC PORTAL. HE TOLD ME HE'S GOT A NETWORK OF 'EM FOR INSTANTANEOUS TRAVEL ALL AROUND THE WORLD.
UNDETECTABLE, UNTRACEABLE...
"...HELL OF AN ASSET FOR AN UNDERCOVER STRIKE TEAM, DON'TCHA THINK?
"MAYBE NEXT TIME, YOU WON'T BE IN SUCH A HURRY TO THROW BACK THE SMALL FRY."
THE END

DC COMICS
THE NEW 52!
#1
AQUAMAN
$2.99 US/CAN
GEOFF JOHNS
IVAN REIS
JOE PRADO
ROD REIS

DEADMAN LIVES AGAIN!
AQUAMAN STANDS ALONE!
THE LEGEND OF AQUAMAN
JUSTICE LEAGUE of AMERICA
METAMORPHO AQUAMAN
SUPER FRIENDS
Adventure COMICS
AQUAMAN
DOOM from DIMENSION AQUA
URBAN RENEWAL!
UNDERWORLD
DC UNIVERSE REBIRTH
WHO DESTROYS THE SEA KING
The OCEAN MASTER or BLACK MANTA?
ARTHUR CURRY JUNIOR
THE NEW 52!
IS THIS MY FOE!
JABBERJAW
the BRAVE and the BOLD
BATMAN
The SLEEP-WALKER from the SEA!
JUSTICE LEAGUE
AQUAMAN A COWARD? IS HE REALLY IN TERROR OF The OCEAN MASTER?
THE BEGINNING OF TOMORROW
IN THE SHADOWY DEPTHS OF ATLANTIS, HIS LIFE WILL CHANGE FOREVER!
YEAR ONE
GENESIS
KURT BUSIEK BUTCH GUICE
YOU DID THIS TO HER!
AND NOW... YOU DIE!!

THE BOTTOM OF THE ATLANTIC OCEAN.

IT IS TRUE. THERE IS AN ABOVE.
WHERE DO WE GO?
UP.

BOSTON.
WEEEEOO WEEEEOO WEEEEOO
GO, MAN! GO!
BAMMMM
DON'T LOSE THEM!
BOSTON POLICE
BPD
THOOOMMM
WHAT THE HELL IS THAT?

THE TRENCH
PART ONE
GEOFF JOHNS
WRITER
IVAN REIS
PENCILLER
JOE PRADO: INKER
ROD REIS: COLORIST
NICK J. NAPOLITANO: LETTERER
SEAN MACKIEWICZ
ASST. EDITOR
PATRICK MCCALLUM
EDITOR
COVER BY
IVAN REIS, JOE PRADO
& ROD REIS

DUDE, IS THAT...?
AQUAMAN?
HAHAHAHA!
AW, HELL. WHAT'S AQUAMAN DOING HERE?
WE'RE NOT IN THE OCEAN AND I DON'T SEE ANY FISH AROUND--
--SO WHAT THE HELL'S HE THINK HE'S GONNA DO?
WHO KNOWS? FLOOR IT!
BYE-BYE, TUNA MAN.

KRANNNKK
BAMMMM
BAMMM

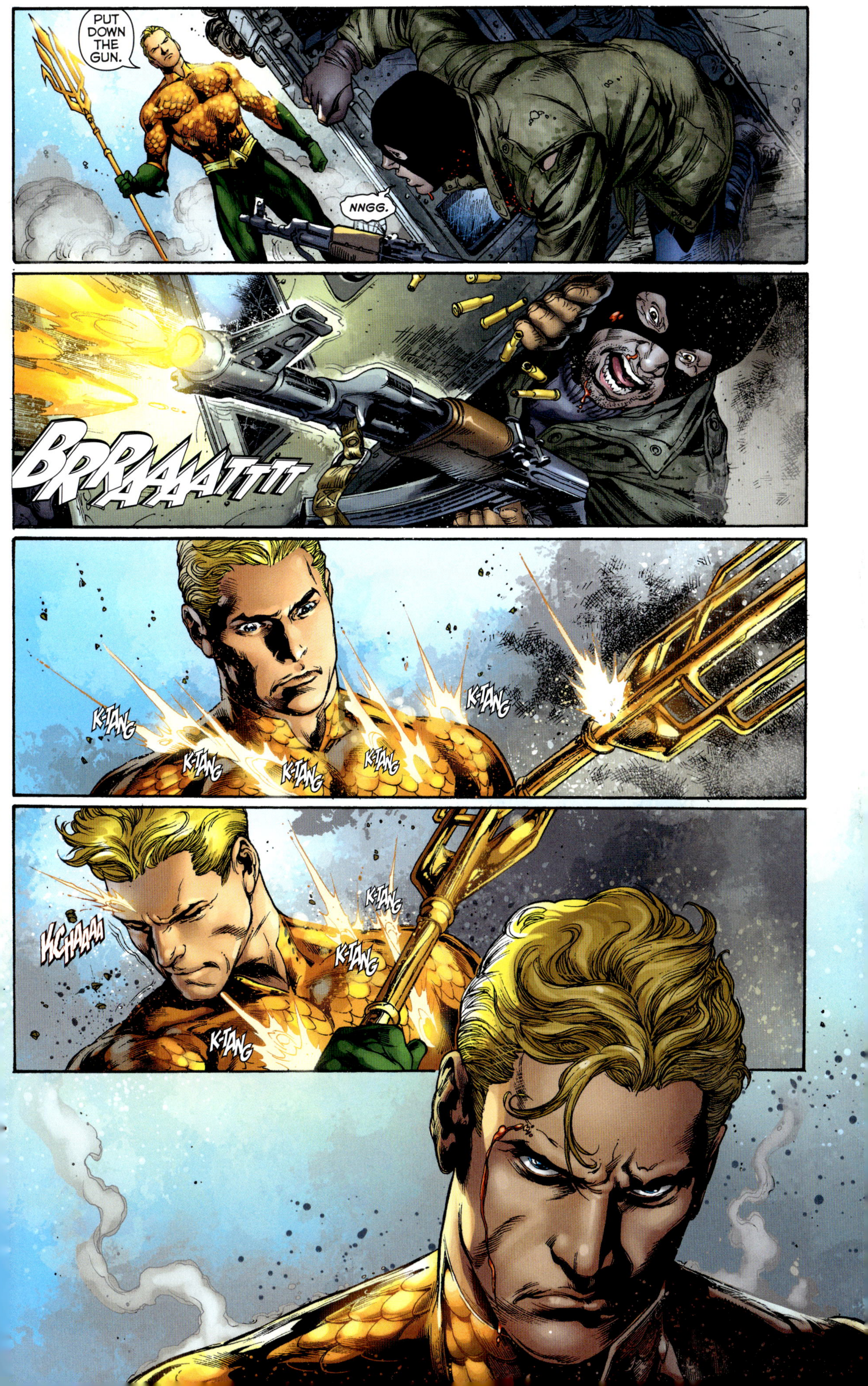
PUT DOWN THE GUN.
NNGG.
BRRAAAATTTT
K-TANG
K-TANG
K-TANG
K-TANG
K-TANG
KCHAAAA
K-TANG
K-TANG
K-TANG

KKKRRKSHH
AQUAMAN? WHAT'RE *YOU* DOING *HERE?*
I HEARD THE SIRENS FROM THE HARBOR.
YOU NEED A GLASS OF WATER OR SOMETHING?

NO.
I CAN'T BELIEVE WE JUST GOT UPSTAGED BY AQUAMAN.
THE BOYS AT THE STATION ARE NEVER GONNA LET US HEAR THE END OF THIS.

CINDY, TABLE FIVE HASN'T GOTTEN THEIR CLAMS YET.
SAM'S
SEAFOOD
I THOUGHT JOEY HAD TABLE FIVE.
YAWN I'M ON BREAK.
THOOOMM
WHAT IN THE WORLD WAS THAT?
HEY!
YOU'LL NEVER BELIEVE WHO JUST WALKED IN!
IT'S REALLY HIM, ISN'T IT?
OH, MY GOD.
MBB

AQUAMAN? HERE?! WHAT THE HELL IS HE DOING HERE? THIS IS A SEAFOOD RESTAURANT.
I FEEL SO GUILTY.
WHAT ARE WE SUPPOSED TO DO?
GO SEE WHAT HE WANTS!
AQUAMAN? I...

I'M SORRY I, UH...I MUST LOOK TERRIBLE. THIS IS MY THIRD CONSECUTIVE SHIFT.
TRYING TO PUT TWO KIDS THROUGH COLLEGE AND IT'S... OH, GOD. I'M SORRY AGAIN.
MY PROBLEMS ARE PROBABLY RIDICULOUS COMPARED TO YOURS, HUH?
NOT AT ALL. AND YOU LOOK FINE.
HE LOOKS FINE.
I'LL HAVE THE FISH AND CHIPS.
WHAT?
YOU CAN'T GET THE FISH AND CHIPS.
WHY NOT?
BECAUSE YOU TALK TO FISH.
I DON'T TALK TO FISH.

YEAH, YOU DO. AQUAMAN TALKS TO FISH. EVERYBODY KNOWS THAT.
FISH DON'T TALK. THEIR BRAINS ARE TOO PRIMITIVE TO CARRY ON A CONVERSATION.
SO WHAT DO YOU DO?
I REACH INTO THEIR MIDBRAINS AND TELEPATHICALLY PUSH THEM TO HELP ME OUT. SQUIDS, SHARKS, EELS, IT'S ALL THE SAME.
THOUGH DOLPHINS ARE ANOTHER STORY.
NICE TRIDENT.
YOU DON'T MIND IF I TAKE THIS OPPORTUNITY TO, UM, INTERVIEW YOU, DO YOU? I HAVE A BLOG.
WHAT ARE YOU DOING HERE?
ACTUALLY, I--
I'M TRYING TO HAVE LUNCH.
IN YOUR SHINY ORANGE SHIRT? LOOKING FOR ATTENTION?
I JUST GOT DONE WITH SOMETHING.
SOME AQUAMAN SOMETHING?
RIDING WHALES AND SWIMMING WITH SEA LIONS?
YES. EXACTLY THAT.
HEY, HOW DOES SOMEONE LIKE AQUAMAN PAY FOR ANYTHING IF YOU DON'T HAVE A DAY JOB?
I GET BY.

AND WHY THIS RESTAURANT? THE DECOR?
MY FATHER USED TO BRING ME HERE.
YOUR HUMAN FATHER, RIGHT? AND YOUR MOTHER WAS SUPPOSEDLY THE QUEEN OF ATLANTIS. SO THAT MAKES YOU KING NOW, DOESN'T IT?
IF ATLANTIS IS REAL.
IT IS.
YOU MIGHT BE THE ONLY ONE WHO BELIEVES THAT, Y'KNOW.
IS THAT WHERE YOUR REDHEADED MERMAID IS FROM? I HEARD SHE'S STRONGER THAN WONDER WOMAN.
PLEASE, BUDDY. I JUST CAME HERE TO HAVE LUNCH.
OKAY, OKAY! ONE LAST QUESTION!
HOW'S IT FEEL TO REALLY BE, Y'KNOW... AQUAMAN?

WHAT DO YOU MEAN?
I MEAN, I'M SURE YOU'VE HEARD ALL THE JOKES AND SEEN ALL THE SKITS FROM SATURDAY NIGHT LIVE ON YOUTUBE.
SO HOW'S IT FEEL TO BE A PUNCHLINE? HOW'S IT FEEL TO BE A LAUGHINGSTOCK?
HOW'S IT FEEL TO BE NOBODY'S FAVORITE SUPER-HERO?
SHINGG
KEEP THE CHANGE.

SEAFOOD
HEY!
WHAT AM I SUPPOSED TO DO WITH THESE?
PUT YOUR KIDS THROUGH COLLEGE.

AMNESTY BAY.
WHY ARE YOU A LIGHTHOUSE KEEPER, DAD?
YOU COULD BE THE CAPTAIN OF YOUR OWN SHIP!
I COULD.
BUT SOMEONE HAS TO STAY ON LAND TO HELP THOSE CAPTAINS, ARTHUR. SOMEONE HAS TO WATCH THE SHORES.
IT'S CALLED RESPONSIBILITY
ARTHUR?

IT'S GETTING LATE.
I KNOW.
COME TO BED.
I'VE MADE MY DECISION, MERA.
AND?

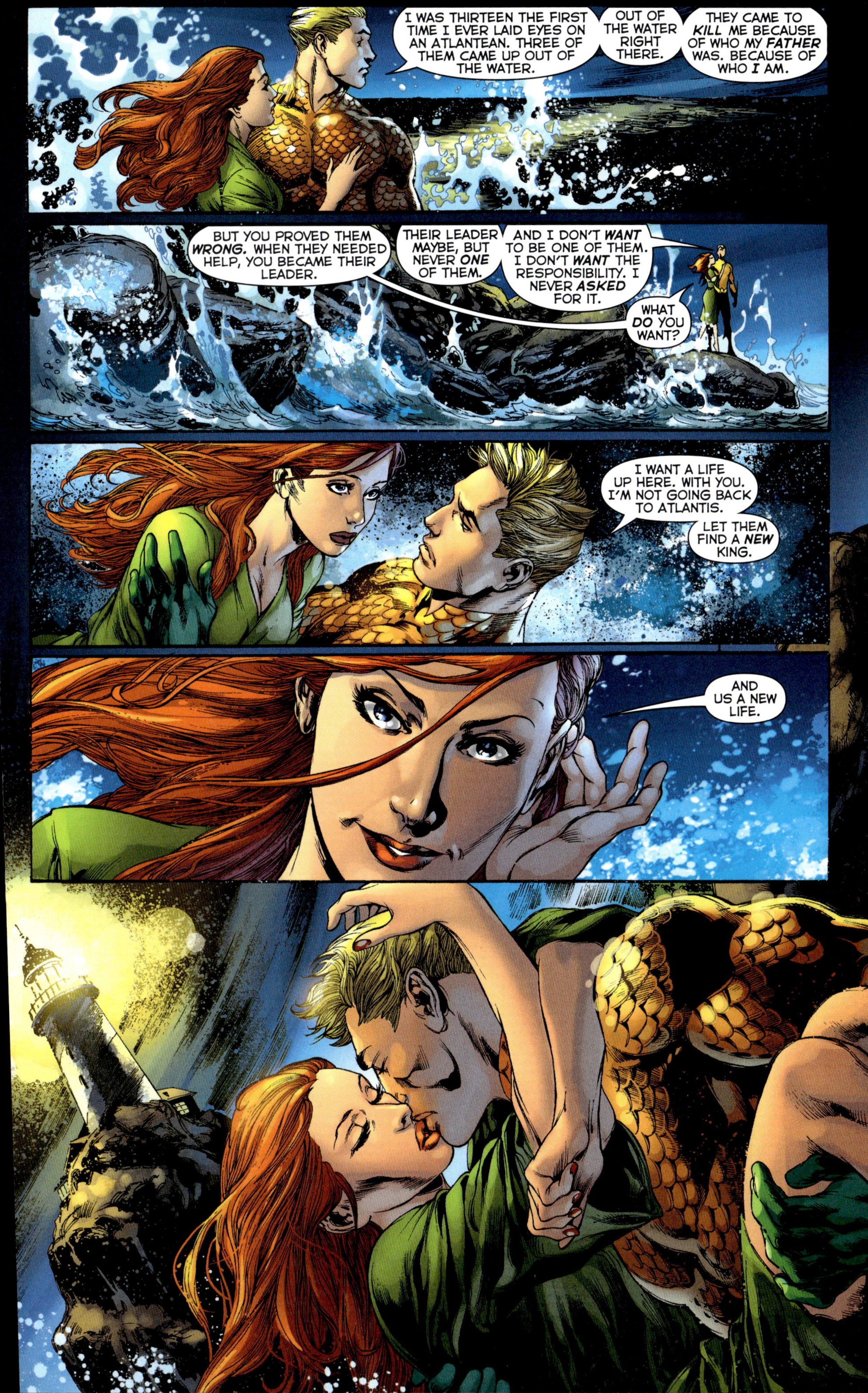
I WAS THIRTEEN THE FIRST TIME I EVER LAID EYES ON AN ATLANTEAN. THREE OF THEM CAME UP OUT OF THE WATER.
OUT OF THE WATER RIGHT THERE.
THEY CAME TO KILL ME BECAUSE OF WHO MY FATHER WAS. BECAUSE OF WHO I AM.
BUT YOU PROVED THEM WRONG. WHEN THEY NEEDED HELP, YOU BECAME THEIR LEADER.
THEIR LEADER MAYBE, BUT NEVER ONE OF THEM.
AND I DON'T WANT TO BE ONE OF THEM. I DON'T WANT THE RESPONSIBILITY. I NEVER ASKED FOR IT.
WHAT DO YOU WANT?
I WANT A LIFE UP HERE. WITH YOU. I'M NOT GOING BACK TO ATLANTIS.
LET THEM FIND A NEW KING.
AND US A NEW LIFE.

WE'VE BEEN AT IT ALL DAY AND NOT A SINGLE BITE.
SOMETHING'S UP. THESE WATERS AREN'T OVERFISHED.
MAYBE THEY CAN SMELL YOUR BOOTS.
HA. HA. H--
RRENCH
HNN.
GOT ONE, BOYS! AND IT'S A *BIG*--

AHHH!
YOU SEE HIM?
WHERE THE HELL'D HE--?

ROCK
THERE'S FOOD UP HERE.

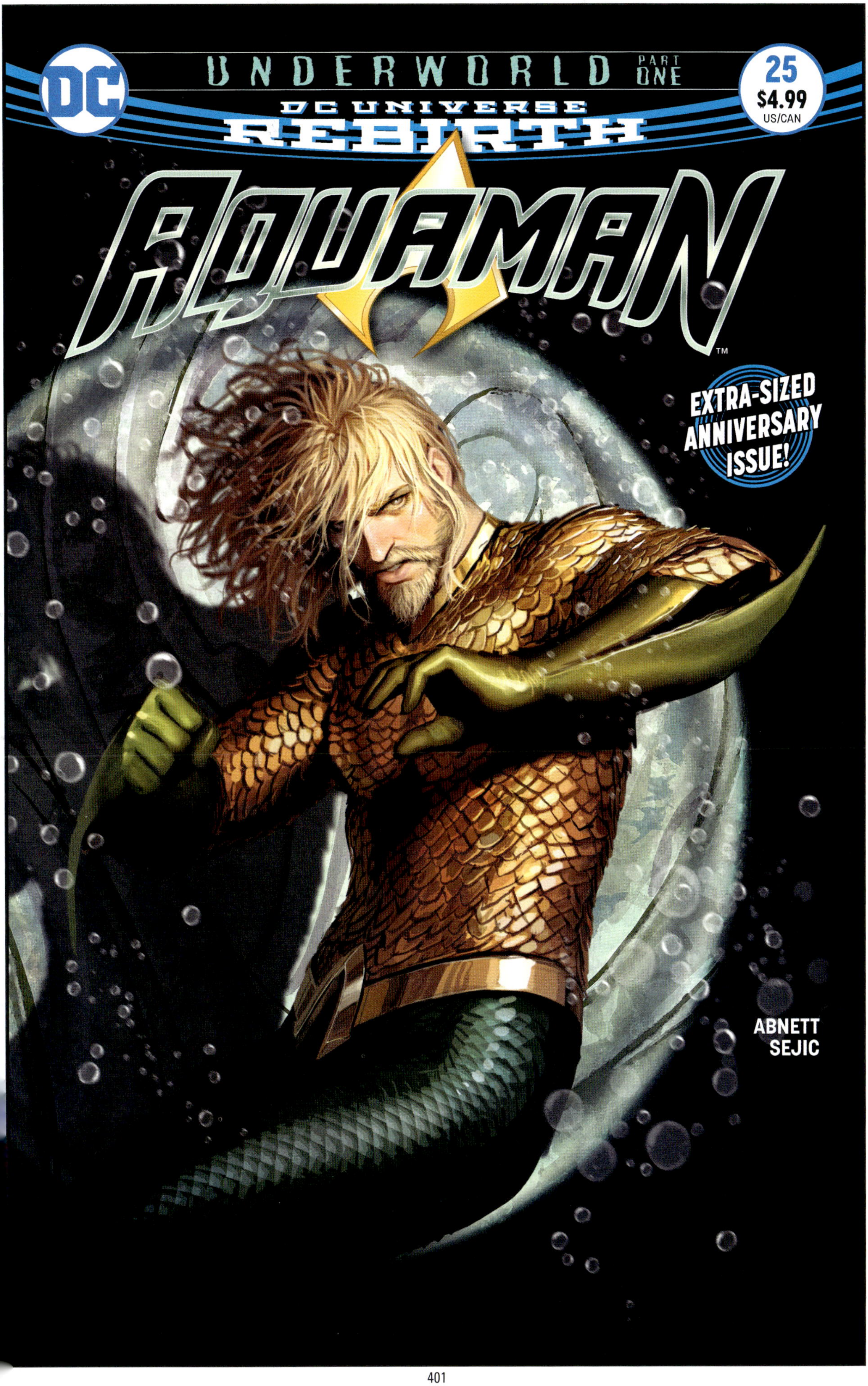
UNDERWORLD PART ONE
DC UNIVERSE REBIRTH
25
$4.99
US/CAN
AQUAMAN
EXTRA-SIZED ANNIVERSARY ISSUE!
ABNETT
SEJIC

LIVES AGAIN!
AQUAMAN STANDS ALONE!
LEGEND OF AQUAMAN
JUSTICE LEAGUE of AMERICA
METAMORPHO
AQUAMAN
SUPER FRIENDS
Adventure COMICS
AQUAMAN
Manhunter Mars Hawkman
AQUAMAN
AQUAMAN
DOOM from DIMENSION AQUA!
AQUAMAN
URBAN RENEWAL!
UNDERWORLD
DC UNIVERSE REBIRTH
AQUAMAN
DC UNIVERSE REBIRTH
AQUAMAN
AQUAMAN
Who Destroys the Sea King
The OCEAN MASTER or BLACK MANTA?
ARTHUR CURRY JUNIOR
DC COMICS
THE NEW 52!
AQUAMAN
AQUAMAN
IS THIS MY FOE?
AQUAMAN
AQUAMAN
JABBERJAW
CAPTAIN CAVEMAN
the BRAVE and the BOLD
BATMAN
AQUAMAN
The SLEEP-WALKER from the SEA!
DC COMICS
THE NEW 52!
JUSTICE LEAGUE
AQUAMAN
AQUAMAN A COWARD? IS HE REALLY IN TERROR OF... The OCEAN MASTER?
THE BEGINNING OF TOMORROW!
AQUAMAN
AQUAMAN
IN THE SHADOWY DEPTHS OF ATLANTIS, HIS LIFE WILL CHANGE FOREVER!
DC COMICS
THE NEW 52!
AQUAMAN
YEAR ONE
AQUAMAN
1995 ANNUAL
Who Destroys the Sea King
GENESIS
AQUAMAN
AQUAMAN
SWORD OF ATLANTIS
KURT BUSIEK
BUTCH GUICE
AQUAMAN
Leads his army to Battle!
AQUAMAN
YOU DIP THIS TO HER!
AND NOW... YOU DIE!!
AQUAMAN

"ARTHUR CURRY IS DEAD.
"AQUAMAN IS GONE. THE HOUSE OF ATLAN HAS TOPPLED. KING ARTHUR'S REIGN IS OVER."
Atlantis

I AM *CORUM RATH,* OF THE HOUSE OF RATH, *KING OF ATLANTIS.*
MY WORD IS LAW.
DRIFT COMMANDER *URCELL*... ELDER *LEOT*....I WANT THAT FACT MADE *CLEAR* TO *ALL* IN THE ROYAL COURT.
I WILL NOT BE *WEAK* LIKE MY PREDECESSOR. THAT HALF-BREED HAD TOO MUCH OF THE *SURFACE* IN HIS BLOOD.
ATLANTIS IS A *GREAT* NATION. IT WAS ONCE THE GREATEST AND MOST *ADVANCED* CULTURE ON THE PLANET.
AND IT WILL BE *AGAIN.*
RESTORING OUR NATION FROM THE TURMOIL THE OLD KING LEFT IT IN WAS *NEVER* GOING TO BE ACCOMPLISHED IN A DAY.
AT LEAST WE HAVE MADE A GOOD *BEGINNING,* LORD KING...
...THANKS TO THE *DILIGENCE OF COMMANDER MURK* AND THE ROYAL GUARD.

NOW, ELDER LEOT...WE MUST CLEAN HOUSE AND REBUILD.
GREAT KING, MANY CITIZENS FROM THE LOWER TRIDES HAVE VOLUNTEERED TO LABOR IN THE RESTORATION PROGRAM.
THE RECENT CONFLICT WITH THE AMERICANS HAS LEFT--
I DON'T JUST MEAN THE FABRIC OF THE CITY, LEOT.
THOSE SYMPATHETIC TO THE OLD KING MUST BE ROOTED OUT, ALONG WITH ALL THOSE WHO ARE NOT TRUE ATLANTEANS.
I HEAR TALK OF MUTATION...
A CURSE, MY LORD...
SUCH UNDESIRABLES WILL BE FOUND, LORD KING. THE DRIFT HUNTS FOR THEM SYSTEMATICALLY.
GOOD, URCELL, GOOD.
BUT SEARCH FOR ITEMS OF MAGICAL POWER TOO. MANY OF OUR NOBLE FAMILIES HAVE HEIRLOOMS THEY HAVE NOT DECLARED.
THE STRENGTH OF OUR REIGN...THE VERY SECURITY OF ATLANTIS...WILL BE FOUNDED ON THE MAGIC KEPT BY THE SILENT SCHOOL.
I WILL NOT HAVE THAT POWER DILUTED BY UNLICENSED TRINKETS.
SIR, THE NINTH TRIDE, IN PARTICULAR, IS A NEST OF UNDESIRABLES. I BELIEVE UNLAWFUL ARTIFACTS ARE COMMON IN THOSE STREETS, TOO.
I KNOW THAT DISTRICT IS ESPECIALLY DEAR TO YOUR HEART--
IT IS WHERE I WAS BORN AND BRED, LEOT. REST ASSURED, I HAVE EYES AND EARS IN THAT ZONE...

...FOR THE NINTH TRIDE OF ATLANTIS IS HOME TO ME.
The Ninth Tride
THE NINTH TRIDE IS SOCIALLY AND LITERALLY THE LOWEST QUARTER OF THE CITY-STATE.
IT STRADDLES, AND FALLS SHEER INTO, THE CARNAC ABYSS THAT SPLITS THE CITY NORTH TO SOUTH, A RELIC OF THE CATASTROPHE THAT SANK ATLANTIS.
HERE THE CITY CLINGS LIKE CORAL TO THE CLIFF WALLS OF THE TRENCH.

THE PEOPLE OF THE NINTH TRIDE REFER TO THEMSELVES AS HADALIN, THE WORD FOR THE ORGANISMS OF THE SUNLESS ZONE THAT LIVE OFF ORGANIC MATTER SINKING FROM ABOVE.
THE NAME BEGAN AS A SLUR, BUT IS NOW WORN WITH PRIDE. THE HADALIN, LIKE THEIR BOTTOM-FEEDER NAMESAKES, TOIL TO KEEP THE SEAS CLEAN.
AND NOW THEY TOIL TO REPAIR THE DAMAGE DONE DURING THE LAST ATTACK ON ATLANTIS.
I WORK TO RAISE STONE AND REBUILD. IT IS HONEST LABOR.
NO ONE TROUBLES ME. I KNOW NO ONE. I HAVE NO FRIENDS. NO ACQUAINTANCES.
NO ONE LOOKS TWICE AT ME. JUST ANOTHER ITINERANT WHO'S COME TO THE NINTH FOR WORK.
I HAD A DREAM OF ATLANTIS ONCE.
THEN I AWOKE, LOOKED UP AND FOUND THE DREAM WAS GONE.

KING CORUM RATH IS A USURPER. HE STEERS ATLANTIS INTO PARANOID ISOLATION.
OUR FUTURE IS BOUND IRREVOCABLY TO SURFACE.
KING ARTHUR KNEW THAT!
KING ARTHUR IS DEAD, VULKO.
YES. MURDERED BY THE ROYAL GUARD.
BUT RATH MUST NOT REMAIN ON THE THRONE. HE WILL TAKE US INTO A WAR THAT WILL END US.
THAT'S WHY I ASKED YOU TO COME HERE, FROM ALL PARTS OF THE CITY. I KNOW EACH OF YOU IS SYMPATHETIC TO--
ARE YOU SUGGEST-ING WE OVERTHROW HIM?
THEY'LL BEHEAD US AS TRAITORS!
WE CAN'T DO IT ALONE. WE NEED HELP FROM OUTSIDE!
NO ONE CAN LEAVE! ONLY THOSE WITH SPECIAL PERMIT FORM THE KING HIMSELF CAN PASS THROUGH THE CROWN OF THORNS!
FACE THE TRUTH, VULKO. WE ARE ALONE IN THIS.
THE NINTH HAS ALWAY BEEN A SAFE HAVEN FOR THE LOST AND NEGLECTED.

IT IS A PLACE OF REBELS AND ICONOCLASTS, A SANCTUARY FOR UNDESIRABLES.
IT HAS ALWAYS BEEN A NOTORIOUSLY LAWLESS ZONE...
...BUT SINCE THE CORONATION, ENFORCEMENT GANGS OF THE LOCAL CRIME LORDS HAVE TAKEN TO PATROLLING IT LIKE THEY OWN THE PLACE.
THEY COME LOOKING FOR THINGS TO STEAL...
YOU THERE! HADALIN! WHY DO YOU SKULK IN THE SHADOWS?
YOUR LIGHTS HURT MY EYES.
DO YOU HAVE COINS? TRINKETS OF VALUE? OLD THINGS FROM BEFORE THE SINKING?
I HAVE NOTHING.
WORTHLESS FOOL. I SHOULD JUST GUT YOU.
YOUR FACE SEEMS FAMILIAR. WHAT IS YOUR NAME?

HMM.
I DON'T LIKE THE LOOK OF YOU, HADALIN. WE DON'T LIKE TROUBLE IN THE NINTH, AND YOU LOOK LIKE A TROUBLE-MAKER TO M--
ORIN.
HEY! HARAK! WE GOT ONE!
YOU'LL KEEP, HADALIN.
THEY'VE SIGHTED SOME OTHER POOR UNFORTUNATE.
IT WASN'T ME THEY WERE LOOKING FOR. NOT THIS TIME.
THEN, WHY SHOULD THEY?

I'VE BEEN DEAD FOR WEEKS.
Amnesty Bay
MERA? YOU MUST EAT SOMETHING!
YOU DON'T EAT. YOU DON'T SLEEP. YOU DON'T EVEN SPEAK.
PLEASE...
WHAT HAPPENED TO ARTHUR WAS AWFUL. YOU WATCHED HIM DIE. I UNDERSTAND THE SCALE OF YOUR LOSS.
YOUR GRIEF.
BUT YOU MUST LET ME TAKE CARE OF YOU.
MERA? 'S ME. TULA. OUR FRIEND. FROM ATLANTIS?
PLEASE TALK TO ME.
"FOR PITY'S SAKE, NO!"

TELL KRUSH HE'LL HAVE HIS PAYMENT!
KRUSH. I'VE HEARD THAT NAME AROUND. ONE OF THE CRIME BARONS WHO NOW CONTROLS THE STREETS OF THE NINTH.
TOO LATE FOR THAT, SQUIRT. KRUSH WANTS US TO MAKE AN EXAMPLE OF YOU.
NO! PLEASE! PLEASE!
IN ANOTHER LIFE, I HAD A FRIEND. A BRAVE MAN WHO WAGED WAR ON THE CRIMINALITY OF HIS CITY.
WHAT THE--
MY FRIEND USED FEAR AND SHOCK TO KEEP THE CRIMINAL ELEMENT IN LINE.
HE NEVER SHOWED HIS FACE.
I WILL NOT SHOW MINE.
VUU VUU VUU VUU VUU
WHERE DID THIS SHOAL COME FROM?

NYAAARGH!
GAAAAH!
WHUNNCH
KKNNCHHH
HNNNN!

WHAT IN THE DEPTHS OF--!
CRRNNCH
WHO-- WHO ARE...?
WAIT, I KNOW YOU...
I HAVE HEARD THE STORIES!
YOU ARE THE GHOST OF THE DEAD KING, COME BACK TO PROTECT US!
HEY! WHAT THE DEVIL'S HAPPENING OUT HERE?
PLEASE! YOU ARE THE AQUAMAN!
COME BACK SO I CAN THANK YOU!
THE... WHAT?
"MAGIC."

MAGIC IS OUR CONCERN, GREAT KING.
YOU HAVE ENCIRCLED OUR NATION IN THE CROWN OF THORNS, A SHIELD OF DEFENSIVE SORCERY THAT HAS NOT BEEN USED FOR A THOUSAND YEARS. YOU HAVE LIBERATED OTHER INSTRUMENTS FROM THE ARSENALS OF THE SILENT SCHOOL AND SANCTIONED THEM FOR USE.
THINGS OUR ANCESTORS SHUT AWAY IN THE VAULTS FOR GOOD REASON.
ARE YOU QUESTIONING MY WISDOM, REVEREND MOTHER CETEA?
WE OF THE WIDOWHOOD MERELY OFFER OUR COUNSEL. THE WIDOWHOOD ONLY EXISTS TO SAFE-GUARD THE WELFARE OF ATLANTIS.
AND AS WAS THE CASE WITH MY PREDECESSORS, CETEA, THAT COUNSEL IS RECEIVED WITH THANKS.
YOU TOOK THE THRONE MANY WEEKS AGO, GREAT KING. IT HAS TAKEN US THIS LONG TO SECURE AN AUDIENCE WITH YOU.
THE KING'S SCHEDULE HAS BEEN BUSY, REVEREND MOTHER! IT--
PERHAPS SO, ELDER LEOT.
BUT IN THOSE WEEKS, THE KING HAS ARMED HIMSELF WITH MORE MAGIC FROM THE SILENT SCHOOL THAN ANY PREVIOUS MONARCH HAS DONE IN THEIR ENTIRE REIGN.
INCLUDING ORM.

THE DEVICES OF THE SILENT SCHOOL ARE PERFECTLY SAFE WHEN EMPLOYED WITH DUE CAUTION. ISN'T THAT SO, MAGISTER LOKE?
WITH DUE CAUTION, YES, GREAT KING. BUT--
YOU SEE? EVEN THE MASTER OF THE SILENT SCHOOL SAYS SO.
BUT TO SEAL US OFF WITH THE CROWN OF THORNS? TO EMPOWER THE CITY GUARD WITH ARCANE WEAPONS?
THE PEOPLE ARE SCARED--
THE PEOPLE ARE JOYFUL, YOU WITHERED OLD WITCH!
THEY REJOICE THAT WE HAVE AT LAST A KING OF STRENGTH AND DETERMINATION--
NOW, NOW, URCELL.
DRIFT MISTRESS URCELL APOLOGIZES, REVEREND MOTHER.
THE SURFACE IS A THREAT TO US ALL. IT ALWAYS HAS BEEN. I WILL NOT DEAL WITH THE AIR-BREATHERS, NOR WILL I ENTANGLE MYSELF IN THEIR POLITICAL GAME PLAY.
I AM SIMPLY MAKING US SAFE.
ATLANTIS HAS THE TECHNOLOGY, THE MAGIC AND THE WILL TO REMAIN SECURE AGAINST ANY AGGRESSOR.

AND I WILL RUIN ANY ENEMY THAT COMES TO OUR GATES!
OR THREATENS US FROM WITHIN.
"AND MANY UPSTANDING CITIZENS IN THE LOWER TRIDES LABOR TO SUPPORT MY INTENT."
YOU SAID WHAT HAPPENED TO HARAK AND HIS BOYS?

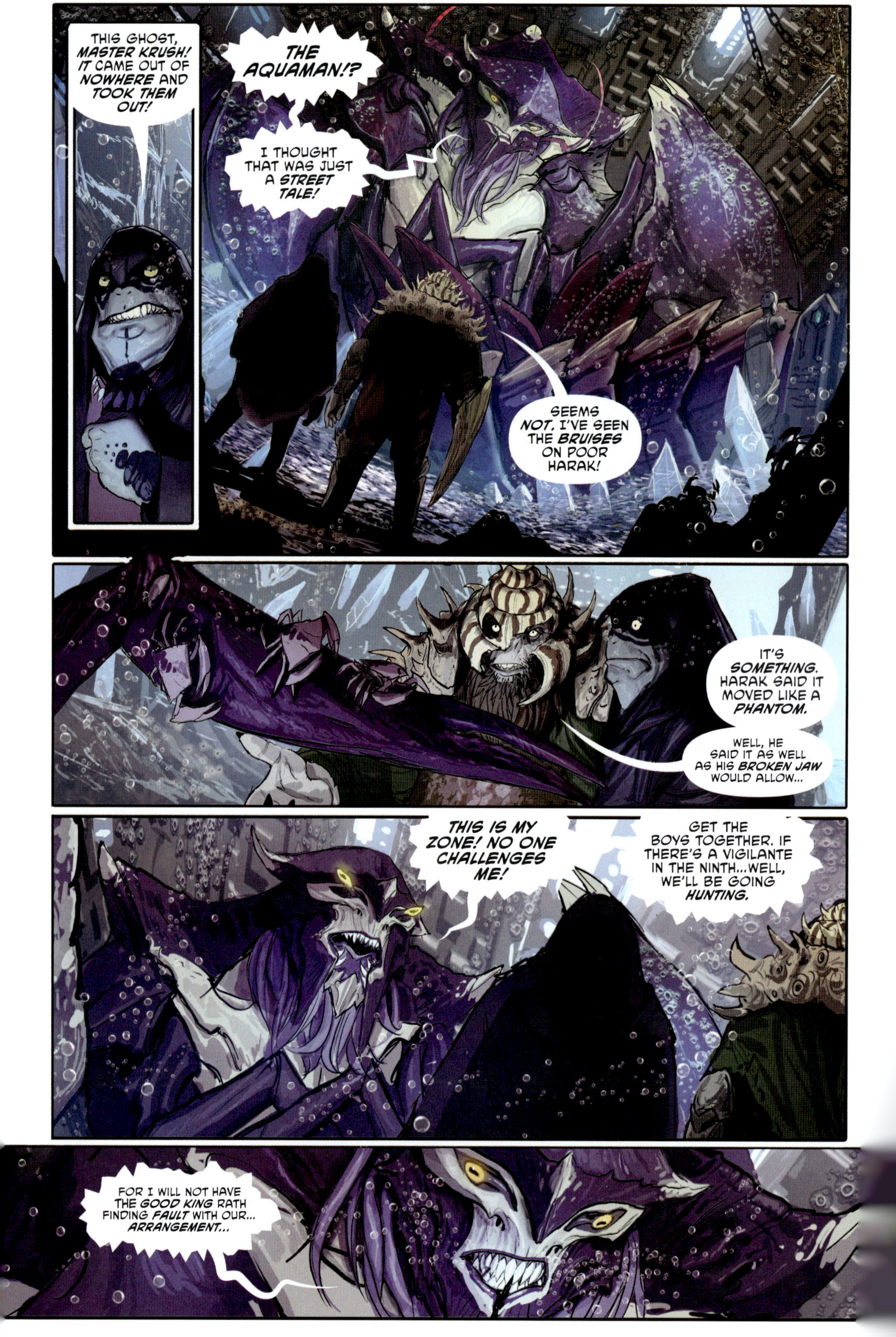
THIS GHOST, MASTER KRUSH! IT CAME OUT OF NOWHERE AND TOOK THEM OUT!
THE AQUAMAN!?
I THOUGHT THAT WAS JUST A STREET TALE!
SEEMS NOT. I'VE SEEN THE BRUISES ON POOR HARAK!
IT'S SOMETHING. HARAK SAID IT MOVED LIKE A PHANTOM.
WELL, HE SAID IT AS WELL AS HIS BROKEN JAW WOULD ALLOW...
THIS IS MY ZONE! NO ONE CHALLENGES ME!
GET THE BOYS TOGETHER. IF THERE'S A VIGILANTE IN THE NINTH...WELL, WE'LL BE GOING HUNTING.
FOR I WILL NOT HAVE THE GOOD KING RATH FINDING FAULT WITH OUR... ARRANGEMENT...

The Silent School
THMMP THMMPP-BUMP
HOW DID YOU KNOW THIS TRAPDOOR WAS EVEN HERE, VULKO?
I KNOW THE PALACE COMPOUND LIKE THE BACK OF MY HAND.
I WAS A COUNCIL ELDER BACK IN THE DAYS WH--
SHHH! SHHHHH! KEEP YOUR VOICE DOWN, VULKO!
IF THE DRIFT FINDS US HERE--
IF YOU CONJURE WITH ANY OF THIS STUFF, THEY WILL! THE SILENT SCHOOL IS ALERT TO MISUSE OF MAGICAL DEVICES!
THEY CAN DETECT THE ENERGY OF--
I KNOW. WE WILL HAVE TO ACT FAST.
AND THESE ARE THE VERY THINGS WE CAME FOR.

THE... AQUAMAN?
THERE HAVE BEEN SEVERAL INCIDENTS IN THE LAST TWO WEEKS, MY LORD. ALL DOWN IN THE NINTH.
WHY WASN'T I INFORMED?
MY DRIFT CAPTAINS THOUGHT THEY WERE JUST STORIES, SIRE. RAMBLINGS OF DRUNKEN HADALIN SCUM.
BUT THIS SO-CALLED AQUAMAN WOULD SEEM TO BE SOMETHING MORE.
A MYSTERY FORCE OF GREAT POWER.
A MOMENT, URCELL...
WELL, IT HAS BEEN A PLEASURE, REVEREND MOTHER. I LOOK FORWARD TO HEARING YOUR WISE COUNSEL AGAIN.
I...
MY LORD KING. THANK YOU FOR YOUR TIME.
YOU THINK THIS AQUAMAN IS ARTHUR, URCELL?
NO. HE'S DEAD.

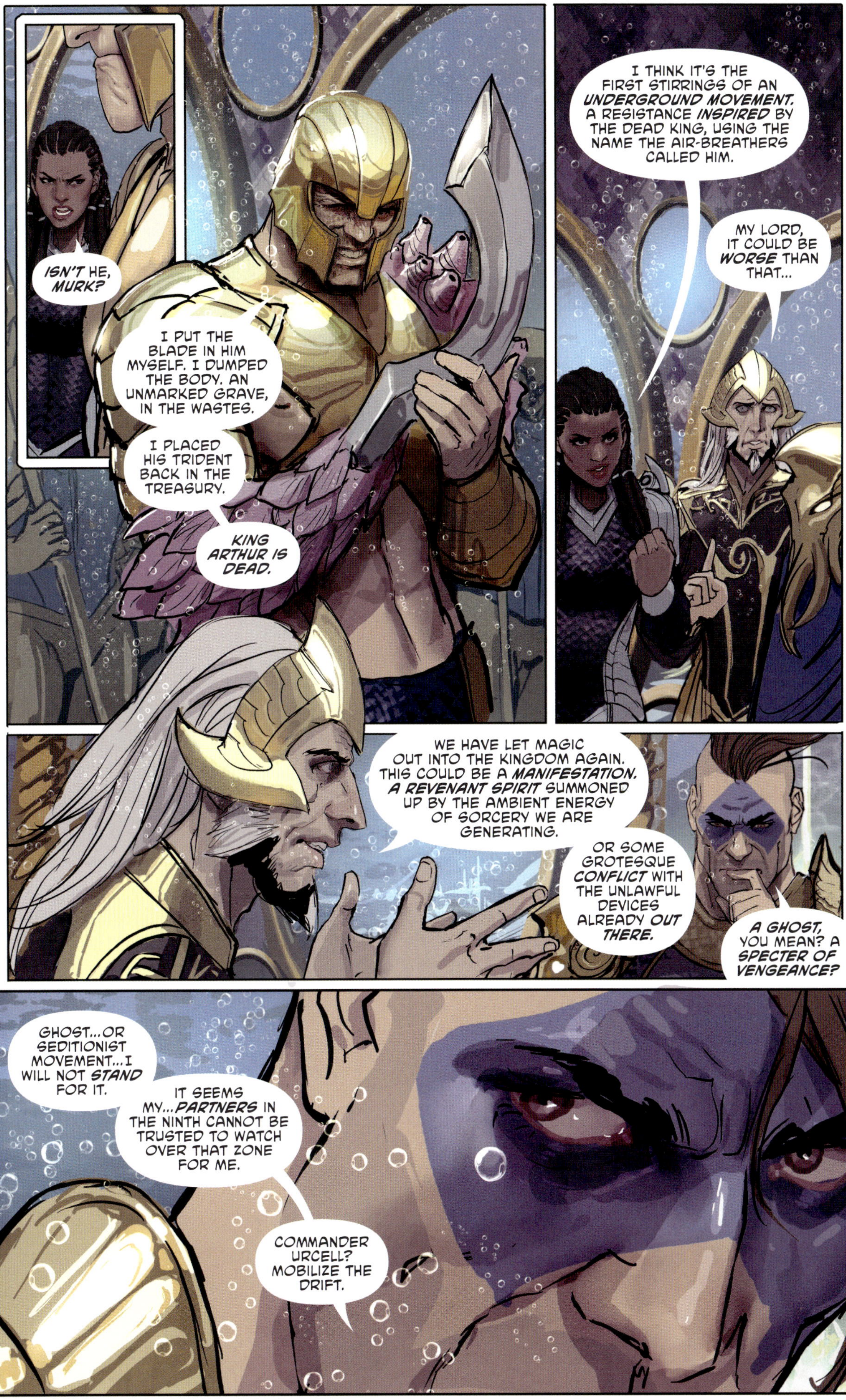

ISN'T HE, MURK?
I PUT THE BLADE IN HIM MYSELF. I DUMPED THE BODY. AN UNMARKED GRAVE, IN THE WASTES.
I PLACED HIS TRIDENT BACK IN THE TREASURY.
KING ARTHUR IS DEAD.
I THINK IT'S THE FIRST STIRRINGS OF AN UNDERGROUND MOVEMENT. A RESISTANCE INSPIRED BY THE DEAD KING, USING THE NAME THE AIR-BREATHERS CALLED HIM.
MY LORD, IT COULD BE WORSE THAN THAT...
WE HAVE LET MAGIC OUT INTO THE KINGDOM AGAIN. THIS COULD BE A MANIFESTATION. A REVENANT SPIRIT SUMMONED UP BY THE AMBIENT ENERGY OF SORCERY WE ARE GENERATING.
OR SOME GROTESQUE CONFLICT WITH THE UNLAWFUL DEVICES ALREADY OUT THERE.
A GHOST, YOU MEAN? A SPECTER OF VENGEANCE?
GHOST...OR SEDITIONIST MOVEMENT...I WILL NOT STAND FOR IT.
IT SEEMS MY...PARTNERS IN THE NINTH CANNOT BE TRUSTED TO WATCH OVER THAT ZONE FOR ME.
COMMANDER URCELL? MOBILIZE THE DRIFT.

"THE NINTH TRIDE WILL BE PURGED."
LOOK HERE! A NEST OF UNCLEAN RATS!
GET OFF HER! LEAVE US ALONE!
WE'VE DONE NOTHING--
THIS ONE DOESN'T SPEAK. WHAT ARE YOU HIDING, GIRL?
SLASH
GYAAAH!
DAMN! YOU SEE THAT?
MUTATION!
YOU KNOW THE RULES.
REJECTS OR TAINT-BLOODS ARE FORBIDDEN INSIDE THE KINGDOM.

VULKO!
FOR NEPTUNE'S SAKE! THE DRIFT IS HERE! THEY'RE ROUNDING UP PEOPLE IN THE STREETS OUTSIDE!
I JUST NEED A FEW MOMENTS...
THE DRIFT CAN GO TO HELL. THIS IS IMPORTANT. THIS COULD SAVE US ALL.
THE NINTH IS OUR HOME. WE HAVE LIVED HERE FOR GENERATIONS AND WE'RE JUST TRYING TO SURVIVE--
SHUT IT. YOU HAVE NO RIGHTS. NO VOICE.
!
THE KING SAYS IF YOUR KIND ARE FOUND, THEY MUST BE PUT DOWN.
SANCTION THEM ALL.
C-CAPTAIN--?

UGHHHKKKK!
HHHNNN!
KKKNNNNK
GAAAH!

UGHKKK!
BWMMFF
GET HIM!
I DON'T KNOW WHO YOU THINK YOU ARE, BUT YOU'VE JUST SIGNED YOUR OWN D--
UNNGH!
HOLD HIM STILL, BOYS! HOLD HIM STILL!
BIFF
GUURKK!
BFFF
GUUGHH!
KLNNNK

YOU'RE THE AQUAMAN! AREN'T YOU?
GO NOW. HIDE.
YOU CAN'T STAY HERE. MORE ARE COMING.
EVERYONE-- SCATTER! NOW!
DRIFT REINFORCE-MENTS ARE HERE!
DO LIKE YOUR FRIENDS AND GO!
CAN YOU UNDERSTAND ME?
YOU... YOU WANT TO COME WITH ME?
OH FOR GOD'S SAKE...

COME ON!
DO EXACTLY WHAT I TELL YOU.
CAN'T YOU TALK?
WHAT'S YOUR NAME?

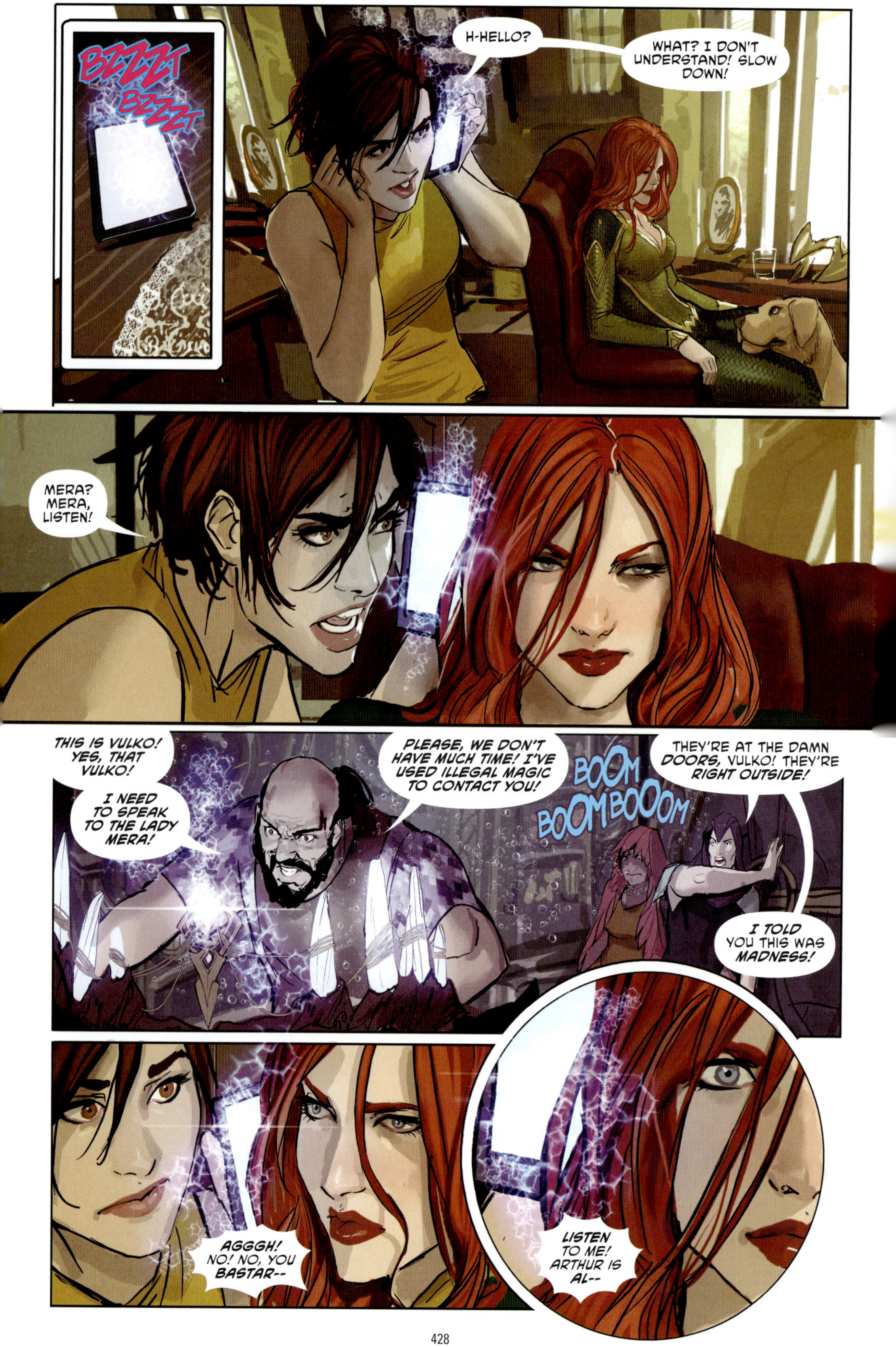
BZZZZT
BZZZZT
H-HELLO?
WHAT? I DON'T UNDERSTAND! SLOW DOWN!
MERA? MERA, LISTEN!
THIS IS VULKO! YES, THAT VULKO!
I NEED TO SPEAK TO THE LADY MERA!
PLEASE, WE DON'T HAVE MUCH TIME! I'VE USED ILLEGAL MAGIC TO CONTACT YOU!
BOOM BOOM BOOOM
THEY'RE AT THE DAMN DOORS, VULKO! THEY'RE RIGHT OUTSIDE!
I TOLD YOU THIS WAS MADNESS!
AGGGH! NO! NO, YOU BASTAR--
LISTEN TO ME! ARTHUR IS AL--

IT'S GONE DEAD.
MERA?
HE'S ALIVE.
WHO'S ALIVE?
ARF!
MERA, WHAT ARE--
GET OUT OF MY WAY, TULA.
ARTHUR IS ALIVE. AFTER ALL, HE'S ALIVE.
AND EVEN IF I HAVE TO DRAG THAT WHOLE KINGDOM TO THE SURFACE...

"...NO ONE IS GETTING BETWEEN US AGAIN."
UNDERWORLD
DAN ABNETT STORY
STJEPAN SEJIC
ART, COLOR AND COVER
STEVE WANDS
LETTERING
JOSHUA MIDDLETON
VARIANT COVER
BRIAN CUNNINGHAM
GROUP EDITOR
HARVEY RICHARDS
ASSOCIATE EDITOR
ANDY KHOURI
EDITOR
AQUAMAN
CREATED BY
PAUL NORRIS
THE END

GREEN LANTERN GREEN ARROW
JUSTICE LEAGUE of AMERICA
GREEN ARROW
MORE FUN COMICS
GREEN ARROW and BLACK CANARY Wedding Special

The Silver Age

The Brave and the Bold presents
MAR. NO. 28
JUSTICE LEAGUE of AMERICA
THE WORLD'S GREATEST HEROES TEAM UP TO BATTLE
"STARRO THE CONQUEROR!"
10¢

DEC. NO. 18
AQUAMAN
AQUAMAN AND MERA, I PRONOUNCE YOU-- MAN AND WIFE!
IT REALLY HAPPENS...THE MARRIAGE OF THE CENTURY! YOU AND THE WORLD'S GREATEST SUPER-HEROES ARE GUESTS FOR THE KINGDOM OF ATLANTIS
The WEDDING of AQUAMAN!

OCT. NO. 29
AQUAMAN
AQUAMAN! LET THE SWORDFISH ATTACK! WHAT'S WRONG? WHY DON'T YOU LET US FIGHT BACK?
AQUAMAN A COWARD? IS HE REALLY IN TERROR OF... The OCEAN MASTER?

AQUAMAN NO. 42 DEC.
"IS THIS MY FOE?"
12¢
AQUAMAN

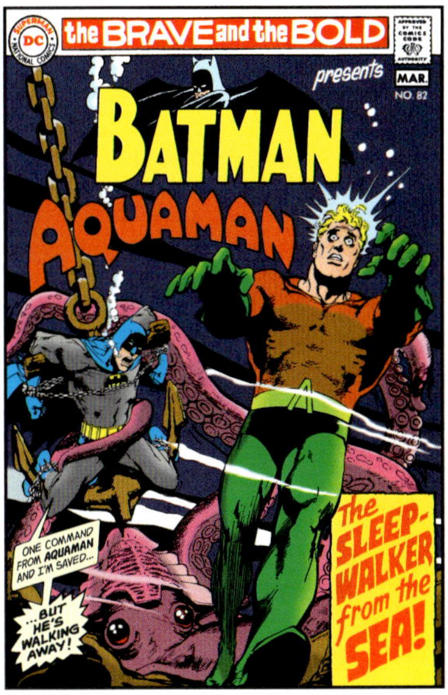
the BRAVE and the BOLD
presents
MAR. NO. 82
BATMAN
AQUAMAN
ONE COMMAND FROM AQUAMAN AND I'M SAVED...
...BUT HE'S WALKING AWAY!
The SLEEP-WALKER from the SEA!

Moments from the Silver Age: Although Aquaman debuted in the Golden Age of comics, he didn't receive his first cover appearance until 1960's *The Brave and the Bold* #28 (**Mike Sekowsky/Murphy Anderson**); Aquaman and Mera's wedding in 1964 beat Reed Richards and Sue Storm's nuptials to the punch by almost a year (**Nick Cardy**); the first (but not the last) time Arthur fights his half brother, Orm, the Ocean Master, over the right to rule (Cardy); Black Manta catches Aquaman off guard (Cardy); caught sleepwalking—er, swimming (**Neal Adams/Dick Giordano**).

ARROW
SEASON 2.5
MORE
FUN
COMICS
Detective Comics
BATMAN
MORE
FUN
COMICS
GREEN
ARROW

the BRONZE AGE

AQUAMAN
APR.
NO. 50
CITY ON THE EDGE OF NOWHERE!
EXTRA!! IN THIS ISSUE
DEADMAN LIVES AGAIN!

DC TV COMIC
SMASHING OUT OF THE TV SCREEN-- YOUR SATURDAY MORNING FAVORITES--
NO. 1
NOV.
THE
SUPER FRIENDS

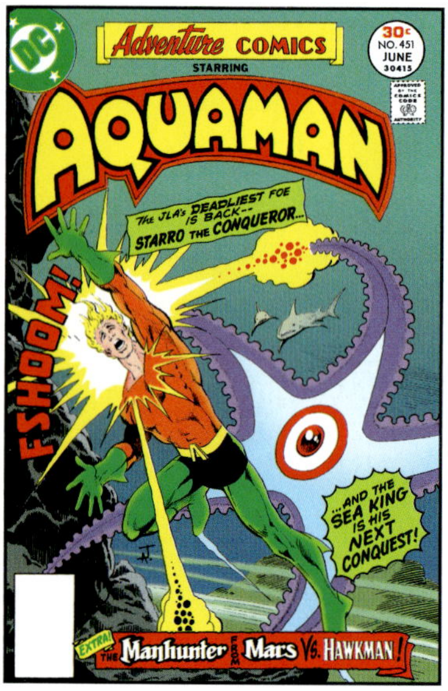
Adventure COMICS
30¢
NO. 451
JUNE
STARRING
AQUAMAN
The JLA's DEADLIEST FOE IS BACK-- STARRO THE CONQUEROR...
FSHOOM!
...AND THE SEA KING IS HIS NEXT CONQUEST!
Manhunter FROM Mars VS. HAWKMAN!

NO. 59 JAN.
35¢
AQUAMAN
NATO
ASSAULTED BY THE AUTHORITIES!
ATTACKED BY AN UNKNOWN FOE!
AMBUSHED BY THE FISHERMAN!
AQUAMAN STANDS ALONE!

GUEST STARRING: BATMAN
35¢
AQUAMAN
YOU THOUGHT BATMAN COULD SAVE YOU--
--BUT YOUR DEATH WILL BEGIN MY DOMINATION OF THE WORLD!
HE'S THE DEADLIEST MAN ALIVE-- KOBRA!

Moments from the Bronze Age: Aquaman visits a city even stranger than Atlantis (Cardy); Arthur's ability to communicate with undersea creatures comes in handy during his adventures with the Super Friends (**Ernie Chan/Vince Colletta**); Aquaman vs. Starro, round two (**Jim Aparo**); tangling with the surface world yet again (Aparo); Arthur teams up with Batman to prevent Kobra from unleashing an environmental threat (Aparo).

GREEN LANTERN
GREEN ARROW
JUSTICE LEAGUE of AMERICA
GUILTY!
GREEN ARROW
MORE FUN COMICS
GREEN ARROW and BLACK CANARY
Wedding Special

the DARK AGE

4 PART MINI-SERIES
AQUAMAN
THE SEA KING IN MORTAL COMBAT FOR THE FUTURE OF ATLANTIS— AND THE WORLD!

AQUAMAN
TIME AND TIDE
No.1 DEC 93
PART ONE OF FOUR
1 ISSUE BLOCKBUSTER!
FLASH
PETER DAVID
KIRK JARVINEN
BRAD VANCATA

PETER DAVID • MARTIN EGELAND • BRAD VANCATA
AQUAMAN
2
TO THE BONE!

YEAR ONE
AQUAMAN
1995 ANNUAL
1

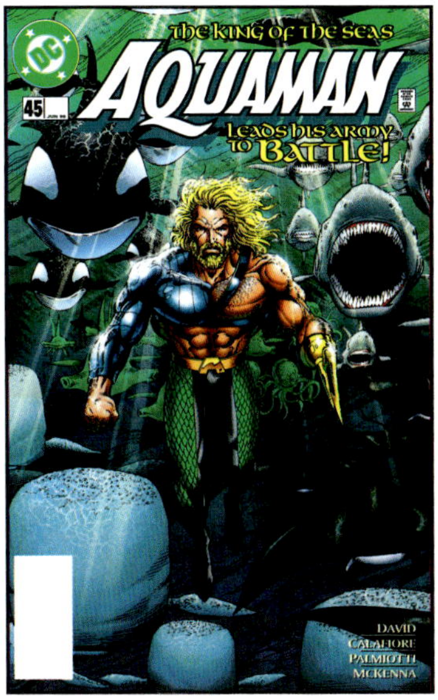
THE KING OF THE SEAS
AQUAMAN
45
LEADS HIS ARMY TO BATTLE!
DAVID
CALAFIORE
PALMIOTTI
MCKENNA

Moments from the Dark Age: Arthur gets some fancy new duds for the eighties (**Craig Hamilton**); the king finally lets his hair down (**Kirk Jarvinen**); the seeds for the live-action Aquaman's look are planted in his first new ongoing series since 1978 (**Martin Egeland/Brad Vancata**); a flashback to a clean-cut Arthur in his year one origin tale in *Aquaman Annual* #1 (Hamilton); never cross a man possessing a harpoon for an appendage and an undersea army (**Jim Calafiore**).

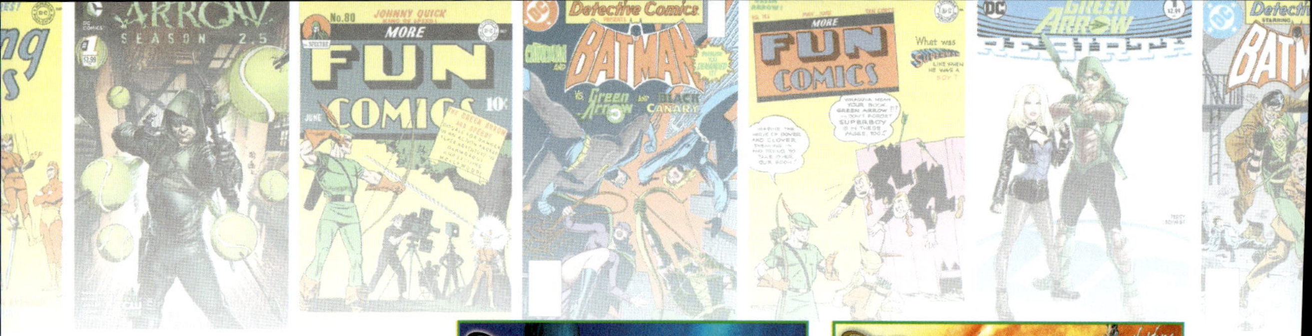
ARROW
SEASON 2.5
MORE
FUN
COMICS
Detective Comics
BATMAN
MORE
FUN
COMICS
GREEN ARROW
REBIRTH

the MODERN AGE

DC
AQUAMAN
SWORD OF ATLANTIS
NO.40
KURT BUSIEK
BUTCH GUICE
YEAR 1 LATER

DC COMICS
THE NEW 52!
4
$3.99
JUSTICE LEAGUE
GEOFF JOHNS
JIM LEE
SCOTT WILLIAMS

DC UNIVERSE
REBIRTH
DC
25
$3.99
AQUAMAN

DC
AQUAMAN
JABBERJAW
1
$4.99
ABNETT
PARKER
PELLETIER
KOLINS
HENNESSY
BONUS!
A CAPTAIN CAVEMAN TALE!

DC
JUSTICE LEAGUE 11 SNYDER • MANAPUL

Moments from the Modern Age: *Sword of Atlantis* sees a "new" Arthur inheriting the undersea throne (**Butch Guice**); the original Arthur Curry returns, suited and rebooted for The New 52 (**Jim Lee/Scott Williams**); Atlantean intrigue forces Aquaman to fake his death yet again (**Joshua Middleton**); in one of Arthur's strangest adventures yet, he teams up with a chatty shark who gets no respect (**Paul Pelletier/Andrew Hennessy**); DC celebrates the release of the *Aquaman* motion picture with a slew of variant covers (**Francesco Mattina**).

Pencil art for this book's cover by
DC Comics publisher and chief creative officer **Jim Lee**.

JIM LEE
2021

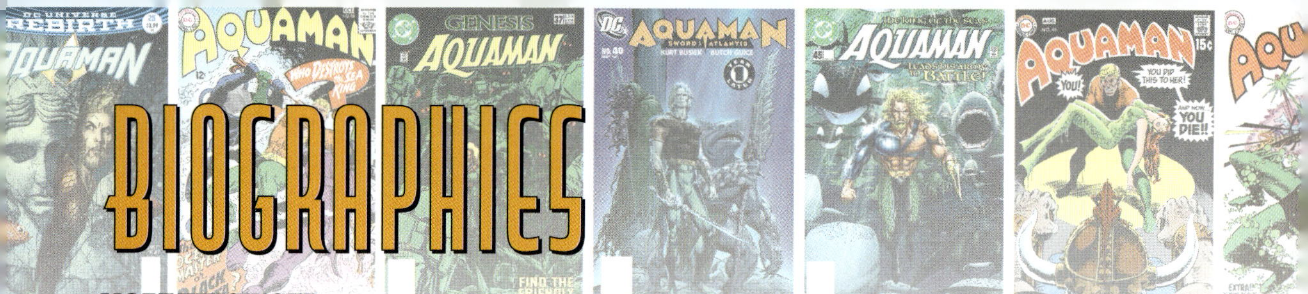
REBIRTH
AQUAMAN
AQUAMAN
GENESIS
AQUAMAN
AQUAMAN
SWORD OF ATLANTIS
AQUAMAN
AQUAMAN
YOU!
YOU DIE!!

BIOGRAPHIES

MORT WEISINGER

Born on April 25, 1915, in New York City, editor Mort Weisinger was a fan of science fiction from its earliest days and is credited with co-publishing the first science fiction fanzine. He came to work for DC Comics in 1940, where he coordinated many characters and titles. Beginning in the mid-1950s he became the sole editor of the Superman brand. Under his legendarily stern guidance, writers such as Jerry Siegel, Otto Binder, and Jim Shooter carefully wove a sprawling, imaginative mythos around the Man of Steel that is still celebrated to this day. Weisinger died on May 7, 1978.

PAUL NORRIS

Paul Leroy Norris was born in Greenville, Ohio, on April 26, 1914, and studied at Midland Lutheran College and the Dayton Art Institute. After working as a cartoonist at the *Dayton Daily News* for a number of years, he moved to New York seeking other illustration opportunities and wound up in comics.

Among his numerous credits, Norris drew the Yank and Doodle, Power Nelson, and Futureman strips for Prize Publications; *Flash Gordon* and *Secret Agent X-9* for Kings Features Syndicate; and *Tarzan of the Apes* and *Magnus, Robot Fighter* for Western Publishing Company. He is perhaps best known for co-creating Aquaman for DC Comics and for his 35-year run writing and illustrating on the science fiction-themed *Brick Bradford* newspaper strip. Norris passed away on November 5, 2007.

JOE SAMACHSON

Joe Samachson was born on October 13, 1906, in Trenton, New Jersey. He earned a doctorate in chemistry and became a biochemist, and as a writer he translated a number of scientific papers, as well as writing books on theater and ballet with his wife Dorothy. His science fiction work, written under the pseudonym William Morrison, includes two novels serialized in *Startling Stories* and several Captain Future novels written around 1942. Later that same year he began working for DC, where he wrote for such characters as Batman, Air Wave, Robotman, the Star-Spangled Kid, and the Seven Soldiers of Victory, as well as a string of science fiction stories between 1955 and 1956 for *Strange Adventures* and *Mystery in Space*. Samachson died in 1980.

OTTO BINDER

Otto Oscar Binder's résumé reads like a who's who of American folk heroes. During his 30-year comics career the veteran science fiction writer penned the comic book adventures of Superman, Doc Savage, the Shadow, Captain America, Blackhawk, and most notably Captain Marvel and his supporting cast, the majority of whose Golden Age exploits sprang from Binder's fertile imagination.

The secret of Binder's productivity was his versatility. Though a science fiction writer by nature, he scripted horror tales, Westerns, and humor with the same professionalism he lent to his superhero work, while simultaneously producing dozens of science fiction novels and short stories. Binder retired from comics in 1969; he passed away on October 13, 1974.

ROBERT BERNSTEIN

The versatile Robert Bernstein's career extended far beyond the Superman stories he penned for editor Mort Weisinger in the late 1950s and early 1960s. Born in 1919, Bernstein cut his teeth writing pulps in the early 1940s and then sold scripts to a variety of comic book publishers, including Hillman and Lev Gleason. In the 1950s he wrote war, Western, and crime tales for Atlas and E.C. before settling in at DC Comics, where he scripted features for *Superman*, *Superman's Girl Friend Lois Lane*, and *Superboy* for Weisinger as well as working on Green Arrow, Congorilla (which he retooled from the Congo Bill strip), and Aquaman. Bernstein employed several pen names, including R. Berns at Marvel in the mid-1960s, and he co-created the Archie Comics superhero the Jaguar. Outside of comics, Bernstein was a promoter of classical music concerts and community theater performances. He passed away in 1988.

JACK MILLER

A DC editor from 1964-1969, Jack Miller handled such titles as *Strange Adventures*, *The Inferior Five*, *Maniaks*, *Wonder Woman*, and various romance titles. From the 1940s through much of the 1960s he was also a prolific comics writer—particularly for DC, where he contributed to dozens of different features including Deadman, Blackhawk, Aquaman, Batman, Jimmy Olsen, and Congo Bill. Miller also wrote novels, nonfiction works, and television animation, employing over 30 different pen names in the course of his long career. He passed away in 1970.

BOB HANEY

Born in 1926, Robert G. Haney grew up in Philadelphia and received an M.A. from

AQUAMAN
AQUAMAN
AQUAMAN
AQUAMAN
IS THIS MY FOE?

Columbia University in New York City. He entered the comics field in 1948, writing war, crime, and Western stories for a wide variety of publishers, including Fawcett, Quality, Fox, Harvey, Toby, Hillman, and St. John. By 1956, however, he was working almost exclusively for DC, where he would remain until the early 1980s. In the course of his long career Haney worked on a vast number of DC titles, but he is perhaps best known for his pivotal role in the creation of Metamorpho, Eclipso, and the original Teen Titans; his long runs on *Batman and Robin*, *Suicide Squad*, *Tomahawk*, and *Mystery in Space*; and his prodigious contributions to editor Robert Kanigher's line of war comics. After a brief tenure in the late 1980s scripting episodes of the animated series *ThunderCats* and *The Comic Strip* for Rankin/Bass, Haney retired from professional writing and settled in the seaside town of San Felipe in Baja, California. He passed away on December 5, 2004.

PAUL LEVITZ
Paul Levitz has worked for DC Comics in various capacities for over 35 years, with tenures as an editor (*Adventure Comics*, *Batman*), a writer (*All Star Comics*, *Legion of Super-Heroes*), and ultimately president and publisher. As a writer, he is best known for his long association with the Legion, which began in 1974 and has continued off and on ever since—with a particularly fan-favored run published between 1982 and 1989. In 2009 Levitz stepped down from his executive role at DC to pursue writing again full-time, and he is now the author of the relaunched *Legion of Super-Heroes*.

STEVE SKEATES
A native and longtime resident of New York state, Steve Skeates began his work in comics as an assistant editor at Marvel Comics in 1965—a job he quickly abandoned in favor of writing comics as a full-time freelancer. Over the next twenty years he did work for nearly every major comics publisher, including DC, Marvel, Charlton, Tower, Warren, and Gold Key. Since leaving mainstream comics in the mid-1980s, he has worked as a reporter, bartender, and Zamboni operator, as well as publishing his comics titles, which he continues to do from his home base in Fairport, New York.

PAUL KUPPERBERG
Former DC Comics and fake-news tabloid *Weekly World News* editor Paul Kupperberg has written more than 1,400 comic book stories, from 1979's *World of Krypton* (the first comic book miniseries) to 2014's "Death of Archie" storyline for Archie Comics. In between, he scripted tales for (among others) Superman, Supergirl, the Doom Patrol, Vigilante, Checkmate, Takion, and Arion, Lord of Atlantis. He has also written books of fiction and nonfiction for readers of all ages, including 2013's GLAAD Award-nominated young adult novel *Kevin* (Grosset & Dunlap). Follow him on Facebook, Twitter, and PaulKupperberg.com.

J.M. DeMATTEIS
J.M. DeMatteis doesn't make much sense to us. One day he's writing spiritually infused titles such as *Moonshadow* and *Seekers into the Mystery*. The next day he's writing funny books like *Mister Miracle* or *Dr. Fate*. Then another day he's doing superhero work on *The Amazing Spider-Man* and *Captain America*. Still another day he's dipping into the fantasy realm with *Abadazad*. Make up your mind, Marc!

KEITH GIFFEN
Keith Giffen works *waaaay* too much, and frankly...it worries us. A true Renaissance man, Keith has provided either plotting, scripting, breakdowns, pencils, or any combination thereof for titles such as *All-Star Comics*, *Legion of Super-Heroes*, *Ragman*, *Creeper*, *Lobo*, *Suicide Squad*, *The Defenders*, *Hero Squared!*, and, um... *Ambush Bug*. Most recently he's been involved with the weekly series *52* and *Countdown to Final Crisis*, as well as *52 Aftermath: The Four Horsemen* and *Midnighter*, plus a gazillion other things. We'd name even *more* projects, but we're really worried about cutting other bios short, which would be a real bummer.

PETER DAVID
Peter David is a prolific author whose career, and continued popularity, spans nearly two decades. He has worked in every conceivable medium: Television, film, books (fiction, nonfiction, and audio), short stories, and comic books, and acquired followings in all of them.

Peter's comic book résumé includes an award-winning 12-year run on *The Incredible Hulk*, and he has also worked on such varied and popular titles as *Supergirl*, *Young Justice*, *Soulsearchers and Company*, *Aquaman*, *Spider-Man*, *Spider-Man 2099*, *X-Factor*, *Star Trek*, *Wolverine*, *The Phantom*, *Sachs & Violens*, *The Dark Tower*, and many others. He has also written comic book-related novels, such as *The Incredible Hulk: What Savage Beast*, and

REBIRTH
AQUAMAN
AQUAMAN
GENESIS
AQUAMAN
AQUAMAN
AQUAMAN
AQUAMAN
YOU!
15¢

he co-edited *The Ultimate Hulk* short story collection. Furthermore, his opinion column, "But I Digress...," ran in the industry trade newspaper the *Comics Buyer's Guide* for nearly two decades.

Peter's awards and citations include: the Haxtur Award 1996 (Spain), best comic script; OZCon 1995 award (Australia), favorite international writer; *Comics Buyer's Guide* 1995 Fan Awards, favorite writer; Wizard Fan Award winner 1993; Golden Duck Award for Young Adult Series (*Starfleet Academy*), 1994; UK Comic Art Award, 1993; Will Eisner Comic Industry Award, 1993; Julie Award, 2007; and the SDCC Inkpot, 2016. He lives in New York with his wife, Kathleen, and is the proud father of four daughters and proud grandfather of two grandsons and a granddaughter.

JEPH LOEB

Jeph Loeb is a Peabody Award-winning and two-time Emmy-nominated writer/producer. His television credits include *Daredevil*, *Jessica Jones*, *Luke Cage*, *Agents of S.H.I.E.L.D.*, and *Legion*, as well as *Lost* and *Smallville*. His career started with writing and producing the films *Teen Wolf* and *Commando*. His graphic novels *Batman: The Long Halloween* and *Superman for All Seasons* have been cited as influences on Matt Reeves's *The Batman*, Christopher Nolan's Dark Knight trilogy, *Smallville*, and *Gotham*.

WILL PFEIFER

Will Pfeifer began his writing career on *FINALS*, a well-received Vertigo miniseries he did in collaboration with Jill Thompson. Since then, his writing has appeared in numerous titles for DC Comics, including *Catwoman*, *Aquaman*, *Blood of the Demon*, *H-E-R-O*, *Captain Atom: Armageddon*, and *Wonder Woman*.

G. WILLOW WILSON

G. Willow Wilson is the writer of the acclaimed novel *The Bird King* (2019), the comic book series *Wonder Woman*, and the Hugo Award-winning *Ms. Marvel*. Her first novel, *Alif the Unseen*, won the 2013 World Fantasy Award for Best Novel; her 2010 memoir, *The Butterfly Mosque*, was a *New York Times* Notable Book. In 2015, she won the Graphic Literature Innovator prize at the PEN America Literary Awards. Her work has been translated into more than a dozen languages. She lives in Seattle.

GEOFF JOHNS

Geoff Johns is an award-winning screenwriter and producer and one of the most successful comic book writers of his time. He has written dozens of *New York Times* bestselling graphic novels, including some of the most recognized and highly acclaimed stories featuring Superman and the Justice League. He has also reinvented lesser-known characters with great commercial and critical success. Under his Mad Ghost Productions banner, Johns is currently in various stages of production on an extensive list of projects in television and film. Among other projects, he wrote and produced *Stargirl* for the DC Universe streaming service and he is writing the anticipated *Green Lantern Corps* feature film. He also produced the second installment of the *Wonder Woman* film franchise, *Wonder Woman 1984*, which he co-wrote with director Patty Jenkins. On the comic book side, he developed the commercial and critical hit *Doomsday Clock*.

DAN ABNETT

Dan Abnett graduated from Oxford University in the late 1980s, and made his Marvel Comics debut writing *The Punisher*, *Conan*, and *War Machine*. In his prolific career since then, he has been acclaimed for the DC series *Resurrection Man* and the Vertigo miniseries *The New Deadwardians*, and also for a significant run on *The Legion of Super-Heroes* that began with *Legion Lost*. At Marvel, his reimagining of *The Guardians of the Galaxy* inspired the blockbuster movies, and his stories have appeared regularly in the UK's iconic anthology magazine *2000AD* for the last two decades. In recent years his work at DC has included *The Titans*, *Aquaman*, *Mera: Queen of Atlantis*, and *The Silencer*. Beyond comics, Abnett's career as a novelist has placed him on the *New York Times* bestseller list eight times, and he has also written extensively for the games industry on such projects as *Alien: Isolation* and *Shadow of Mordor*. He lives in a haunted house in Kent, the most southeastern corner of the United Kingdom.

RAMONA FRADON

At a time when few women worked in the business, Ramona Fradon (born in 1926) entered the comics industry in the 1950s at the counsel of her husband, *New Yorker* cartoonist Dana Fradon. She honed her crisp, lighthearted style during a remarkable 10-year run illustrating the Aquaman feature in *Adventure Comics*, during which time she introduced the Sea King's sidekick, Aqualad. In the 1960s she co-created Metamorpho, the Element Man, with writer Bob Haney, and designed Metamorpho's

AQUAMAN
AQUAMAN
AQUAMAN
AQUAMAN
IS THIS MY FOE?
AQUAMAN
AQUAMAN
JABBER

freakish appearance and outlandish supporting cast. In the 1970s Fradon delighted readers with her work on a revival of cartoonist Jack Cole's Plastic Man, and she also illustrated a variety of stories in *House of Mystery* and *House of Secrets* and helped to win a new generation of DC fans with her work on the TV-tie-in title *Super Friends*. A 2006 inductee to the Will Eisner Comic Book Hall of Fame, Fradon has also drawn *The Brave and the Bold*, *Freedom Fighters*, and a fill-in issue for Marvel's *The Fantastic Four*, as well as following creator Dale Messick on her comic strip *Brenda Starr* for an impressive 15-year stint. In 2006 Fradon published a scholarly book, *The Gnostic Faustus*, based on the Faust legend, and in 2010 she contributed artwork to the satirical graphic novel *The Adventures of Unemployed Man*. She also wrote and illustrated a children's book, published in 2012, entitled *The Dinosaur That Got Tired of Being Extinct*.

NICK CARDY

Nicholas Peter Viscardi was born in 1920. He was an early recruit in the shop of the legendary Will Eisner, where, among other features, he worked on Lady Luck, one of the backups of the Spirit comic sections. During World War II, when people with Italian (or German or Japanese) names were often subject to prejudice, he took the name of Nick Cardy, and went on to work directly for Fiction House and Quality, both companies with which Eisner's shop was associated. At Quality he was an early artist on Wonder Boy and the original Quicksilver.

Cardy went on to become one of DC's top talents of the 1950s and 1960s, usually doing full art (both pencils and inks) on such characters as Congo Bill and Tomahawk. Drawing several Aquaman backup stories in *World's Finest Comics*, Cardy took over the character on a permanent basis after he received his own title. When the Teen Titans were launched as a team, Cardy became the group's regular artist throughout its original run, usually as penciller/inker, but also inking other pencillers including Irv Novick, Gil Kane, Neal Adams, George Tuska, and Art Saaf. Cardy also drew the entire run (usually solo, occasionally inking Mike Sekowsky) of DC's short-lived but fondly remembered Western hero of the 1960s, Bat Lash.

In 1971, Nick Cardy became the main cover artist for most of the DC line, and remained so for several years. He dropped out of comics shortly afterward to concentrate on advertising art, until DC editor Mark Waid tracked him down and talked him into drawing occasional covers and other work. Cardy's work was the focus of several books, including *The Art of Nick Cardy* and *Nick Cardy: The Artist at War*. He passed away on November 3, 2013.

DICK GIORDANO

A veteran of more than five decades in the comic book field, Dick Giordano began his career as an artist for Charlton Comics in 1952 and became the company's editor-in-chief in 1965, launching the short-lived but well-remembered Action Heroes line. In 1967 he moved to DC for a three-year stint as an editor and became part of a creative team that helped to change the face of comic books in the late 1960s and early 1970s. Together with writer Dennis O'Neil and penciller Neal Adams, he helped to bring Batman back to his roots as a dark, brooding "creature of the night," and to raise awareness of contemporary social issues through the adventures of Green Lantern and Green Arrow. The winner of numerous industry awards, Giordano later returned to DC and rose to the position of vice president-executive editor before "retiring" in 1993 to once again pursue a full-time freelance career as a penciller and inker. He passed away on March 27, 2010.

CURT SWAN

Curt Swan entered the art field intending to become not a cartoonist but a "slick" magazine illustrator like Norman Rockwell or J.C. Leyendecker. While serving during World War II illustrating the army newspaper, *Stars and Stripes*, Swan worked with DC writer France "Ed" Herron. On Herron's suggestion, Swan found work at DC after the war. Swan's versatile pencils, which he remembered applying first to *Boy Commandos*, soon appeared on various DC features, including Superman, Batman, the Newsboy Legion, Big Town, Mr. District Attorney, Tommy Tomorrow, and Swan's longest assignment up to that time, Superboy. His familiarity with both Superman and Batman specially suited him to draw the original Superman-Batman team-up in 1952. Swan served various stints, regular and semiregular, on almost all the Superman titles of the 1950s and 1960s and remained the near-exclusive Superman penciller throughout the 1970s and much of the 1980s. Although he "retired" in 1986, Swan continued to work for DC until his death in 1996. To generations of professionals and fans, Curt Swan's Superman will always be the definitive version.

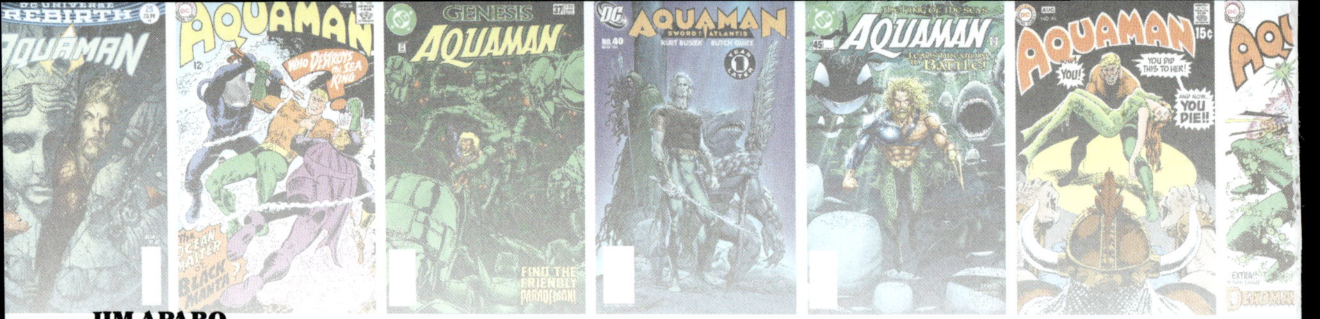
REBIRTH
AQUAMAN
AQUAMAN
GENESIS
AQUAMAN
AQUAMAN
AQUAMAN
AQUAMAN

JIM APARO

A self-taught artist, Jim Aparo first attempted to break into the industry in the early 1950s at the legendary EC Comics group. When EC rejected his work, Aparo turned to advertising art in his native Connecticut, where he specialized in illustrating newspaper fashion ads while continuing his efforts to work in comics. His dream was finally realized in 1966 when Charlton Comics editor Dick Giordano hired him to draw a humorous character called Miss Bikini Luv in *Go-Go Comics*. Sharpening his skills on such features as the Phantom, Nightshade, Wander, and Thane of Bagarth, Aparo followed Giordano to DC Comics in 1968, where he quickly gained notice for his smooth, realistic style on such titles as *Aquaman*, *The Brave and the Bold*, *The Phantom Stranger*, *The Spectre*, *The House of Mystery*, *The House of Secrets*, *Batman*, *Detective Comics*, and *Batman and the Outsiders*. An artist whose work is still considered a high-water mark for the industry, Aparo died on July 19, 2005.

MIKE GRELL

Mike Grell is a writer and artist with a uniquely cinematic style of storytelling. His creations include *The Warlord*; *Starslayer*; *Jon Sable, Freelance*; *Shaman's Tears*; *Bar Sinister*; and *Maggie the Cat*. These works, together with his successful runs on such features as *Superboy and the Legion of Super-Heroes*, *Green Lantern*, *Green Arrow*, *Batman*, *Iron Man*, *X-Men Forever*, *James Bond: Permission to Die*, the *Tarzan* Sunday comic strip, and the internationally acclaimed and Eisner Award-nominated *Green Arrow: The Longbow Hunters*, won him the comics industry's coveted Inkpot Award for Outstanding Achievement in Comic Art. In 2000, he published his first novel, *Sable*, based on his graphic novel series *Jon Sable, Freelance*, which was adapted for television by ABC in 1987. Grell has also been voted as one of *Wizard* magazine's top 10 comics writers, and he was recently named to the Wizard World's Hall of Legends and the *Overstreet Comic Book Price Guide*'s Hall of Fame.

PATRICK GLEASON

Patrick "Pat" Gleason, is a *New York Times* bestselling author, illustrator, and cover artist, best known for his writing and illustration work on *The Amazing Spider-Man*, *Superman: Rebirth*, *Batman and Robin*, *Green Lantern Corps*, *Robin: Son of Batman*, *Super Sons*, *Young Justice*, *Aquaman*, and more. Following his work on *Batman and Robin*, Gleason launched *Robin: Son of Batman*, continuing Damian Wayne's journey of redemption alongside his mother, Talia al Ghul; Nobody's daughter, Maya Ducard; and the lovable behemoth Goliath. Gleason's breakthrough Webhead and Elemental-style covers for *The Amazing Spider-Man*, *Venom*, *Carnage*, and more are published by Marvel through the PAT Shop, of which he is owner and CEO.

JOSHUA MIDDLETON

Joshua Middleton began his career as a comic book artist in 1999, and since then he has provided illustrations to every major publisher as well as branching out into animation and film design. In 2005 he began his long-running relationship with DC Comics, illustrating *Superman/Shazam!: First Thunder* before rising to prominence as a premier cover artist on a wide variety of DC titles, including recent notable runs on *Aquaman* and *Batgirl*. His exceptional artistic skills and uncommon range as an illustrator have earned him a place among the very best cover artists working in the industry today.

IVAN REIS

Ivan Reis is a Brazilian comic book artist who began his international career working for Dark Horse Comics on such titles as *Ghost*, *The Mask*, and *Xena*. For Marvel, he has worked on *Iron Man*, *Captain Marvel*, *The Thing*, *She-Hulk: The Long Night*, and *The Avengers*. For DC, his work includes *Action Comics*, *Rann-Thanagar War*, and *Green Lantern*.

STJEPAN ŠEJIĆ

Stjepan Šejić started his career in comics in 2006 as a colorist for Arcana Comics series *Kade*. From there he moved to work at Top Cow, tackling most of the company's properties for extended runs. These include *Witchblade*, *Artifacts*, *Aphrodite IX*, and *Darkness*. Since then, Šejić has created the critically acclaimed series *Death Vigil* and the bestselling *Sunstone* series of graphic novels, among other things. His recent works include art duties on DC Comics' *Aquaman* series, miscellaneous issues of *Suicide Squad*, and *Justice League Odyssey*. Alongside those projects, Šejić has created a large amount of comics covers and additional work for various publishers. He resides in the silence of Croatia's coastline enjoying the sea breeze and excessive amounts of coffee.

AQUAMAN

A

MAN

AQUAMAN

AQUAMAN

A

MAN

AQUAMAN

AQUAMAN

A

AQUAMAN

AQUAMAN

AQUAMAN

AQUAMAN

THE LEGEND OF AQUAMAN